JASON JAMES KING

THE LURE OF
FOOLS

THE AGE OF
THE INFINITE OMNIBUS

Appropriate for Teens, Intriguing to Adults

Immortal Works LLC
1505 Glenrose Drive
Salt Lake City, Utah 84104
Tel: (385) 202-0116

For Andrea King
For telling me I was a brilliant writer when I was just getting started
I miss you Grandma

INTRODUCTION

The Lure of Fools was my first published novel, and in fact I broke a cardinal rule and pitched it at a writing conference before it was even finished (don't be like me).

It was published in 2013 by Curiosity Quills Press to who I am immensely grateful for giving me my big break. Next came The Soulless Grave in 2015 and by Summer of 2017 The Age of the Infinite Trilogy concluded with The Fork of Destiny's Road.

However, from its inception, the legend of Shaelar was meant to be written as one work. Problem is, you just can't publish a 300,000 word fantasy epic as your debut novel (unless you're Terry Goodkind).

Now with several published novels, and a lot more name recognition, I feel like I can take the risk and publish The Age of the Infinite as it was meant to be. I hope you enjoy it, and please, please, please leave a review. It's what keeps authors young...and unnaturally immortal.

~Jason James King

PART ONE
THE LURE OF FOOLS

CHAPTER

1

Jove stumbled away from the blaring heat of the inferno, hot wind and stray embers stinging his back. When he was finally far enough from Almott to turn around, he did so, eyes hungrily taking in the scene before him. It was as beautiful as it was terrible. Voracious flames engulfed every house of the small village, creating a spectacular nimbus of orange that lit the night sky. Jove half giggled and half sobbed. The people of Almott had been hospitable and kind to him, despite his ragged appearance and green eyes. Never had Jove known such a charitable welcome as when he had staggered into their village half-dead from exposure. They had loved him and treated him as one of their own until they caught him trying to hide the corpse of a young woman in the loft of Shedrek's barn. That was when Almott's collective sentiment toward Jove had shifted to something approaching disdain.

He reached up and felt the bald patch on his scalp where a tuft of black hair had been ripped free. Shedrek, himself, had hauled Jove by the hair to the village square, where he was beaten and then tied to a post. Jove had tried to explain around a mouth pocketed by broken teeth and filled with blood that he hadn't meant to hurt the girl. That she had welcomed his advances and their cavorting had only turned violent when she started to feign disinterest.

Of course, it had been a lie, perhaps true only once in Jove's life – the first time he killed in the heat of passion. He had been a young man then, his violence confined to secret fantasies and only somewhat accidentally materializing into reality. *What was that girl's name again?* He couldn't remember. There had been so many. So many lovely dolls he'd played with, all of which he had broken.

Jove winced against a blast of heat released by Almott's granary falling onto Shedrek's barn. *What happened to me?* Jove wondered. The villagers had been enthusiastically decorating the ground at his feet with kindling, Old-Man-Hessop watching with his crackling torch at the ready. That was when Jove had felt it take him, *The Hunger*. He had no other name for it. A cold emptiness had swept over him, a desperately hollow feeling that concentrated first in his chest before spreading into every limb and digit. At that moment, just as Old-Man-Hessop had made to set his feet aflame, Jove lashed out with something. A translucent tendril of greenish, warped air, like a tentacle, exploded from his chest and plunged directly into the chest of Old-Man-Hessop, who convulsed and dropped to the ground writhing.

Jove had watched in astonished wonder as the old man's face drained of color and his eyes dried before falling from their sockets. He had withered away before Jove, until the man was only a prune-like husk. Immediately, Jove had felt a surge of strength, and, in one fluid motion, he broke the ropes tying him to the wooden post. The surrounding villagers had gaped, their eyes wide with frightened incredulity. As if by instinct, Jove threw up both of his arms, and multiple tendrils of warped air exploded from his chest, lashing out at them. One took Shedrek in the back. Jove recalled watching in fascination as the burly man quickly withered into what looked like a mummified corpse.

At this, the rest of the angry mob turned to flee, but Jove had not let them get five paces away before launching out another spread of tendrils, taking each of the fleeing villagers in the back. A chorus of screams kissed his ears before abruptly cutting off as the thirty or so people fell, withered, and died.

By that time, more of Almott's citizenry had been roused from sleep by the clamor. Jove had smiled as curious heads poked out of doors and windows, and then, with speed that was more than human, he launched himself at the nearest house and its unwitting spectator.

What had happened next turned out to be a new thrill for Jove, one that surpassed even the excitement of his sadistic pleasures. He smiled as he vividly recalled feasting upon every living thing in Almott. Not the flesh of his victims, but their very life force, greenish tendrils of energy siphoning away the light in their eyes and giving it to him, making him stronger. And his feast wasn't confined to people. Animals, plants, and even the very grass at his feet withered before him. By the time Jove was finished, Almott was a ghost town.

He set the fire that now immolated the town out of habit more than sadism. He had always felt a compulsive need to be thorough in disposing of evidence. In fact, he had planned to burn down Shedrek's barn once he had hidden the girl's corpse beneath piles of hay. Now, instead of hiding one corpse, Jove ended up disposing of dozens, the inferno serving as an effective crematorium.

What *had* happened to him? Who or what saved him? Not God, he was certain of that. Could it have been the devil? Jove had heard tales of demons claiming humans as their mortal vessels, but he always discounted those stories as superstitious myths to explain away mind-sickness. Jove barked a laugh. He was either mind-sick or possessed, both options equally damning.

After several minutes of thoughtfully watching Almott burn, Jove turned away and began making for the west road. He wasn't sure why he chose that direction, but something inside him urged him forward.

He paused. *What of supplies?* he thought. *I am alone and miles away from the nearest village, Almott excepted.* But he wasn't hungry, or thirsty, or sleepy. *In fact,* he thought as he began walking again, his step lighter, *I feel healthier than I have in months.* He shrugged. Just the adrenaline rush of nearly being burned alive invigorated him. But, no, he shook his head, this was different. This sense of physical wellbeing was synthetic, just as energizing as food and rest, but somehow not natural.

By dawn, Jove was more than twenty miles away from the village he destroyed and still not famished or fatigued. *Not natural,* he thought.

The road veered north, but he continued west. After walking some distance from the road, he stopped and surveyed the terrain ahead of him. An expansive forest stood a dozen or so miles in the distance. Sudden anger flared inside of Jove as he gazed upon the forest. No, it was not exactly anger, he decided, but something more akin to disgust. Why did he suddenly hate the forest? The urge to burn the tall aspens down consumed him, and his hand habitually went to his pocket for a tinderbox that was no longer there—he having used all his fire-starters to burn Almott. Unthinking, he glanced back in the direction of the town, though he had long since passed out of viewing distance.

That's when Jove saw something that gave him pause: a perfect trail of dead grass behind him, running all the way back from where he left the road. He looked down to his feet and found the grass upon which he stood dried and brown, while all around him it remained healthy and green. He took an experimental step forward and drew in a sharp breath as the patch of meadow withered before his eyes. *I've changed*, he concluded. *The power that came over me in Almott changed me.*

Jove took two more steps, both causing the grass beneath his feet to wither and die. He looked up and spotted a thicket of trees less than a hundred yards away. He trotted toward them, slowed to a stop, and laid a hand on the nearest aspen. The green leaves dressing its branches began to change colors and fall to the ground. A shower of brittle leaves trickled like raindrops until every branch was utterly naked and the tree grey with death. His hand dropped to his side, and he stared at it as though it had touched the face of God.

"I am death," Jove whispered. "I am death," he repeated, this time a little louder. He barked a harsh laugh and turned to look at the forest on the horizon. The trees within the woods were much taller than those of the thicket – taller, older, and arrogant in their upward struggle from the ground. That's when Jove realized what so offended him about the forest. All that greenery and growth represented life, and, if he were death, then naturally life would offend him. *All* life.

Jove began to laugh. He was a fool. He didn't need flint and steel to destroy the forest, he could kill the woods and everything living there simply with a touch.

He *was* death.

CHAPTER 2

Jekaran just *barely* evaded Mull's latest attempt to grab him. Although he was athletic and no stranger to wrestling, the tall and burly Mull moved deceptively quickly. Jekaran needed to dodge and shuffle to avoid being seized. If Mull caught him, he knew he would have little chance of escaping the man's bear-like arms. His only chance was to keep moving and wait for an opening to strike.

Jekaran scrubbed the back of his wrist over his forehead to wipe sweat-soaked strands of black hair out of his eyes. He stumbled as he danced away from his opponent, falling into a roll and then springing up again on Mull's left flank. That's when he finally saw his opening. Without thinking, he threw himself forward, just as Mull turned to face him, and ducked under a swing of a beefy arm before barreling into him and grabbing him around the waist. The forward momentum carried the two of them to the ground at which point Mull shouted "Not fair!" and began to cry.

Jekaran dropped next to him, his shoulders heaving as he caught his breath. He patted the larger boy's back sympathetically. "It's all right," he soothed. "You just about got me with that death grip of yours."

Mull's face changed from dejection to delight. "I'll get you next time, Jek!"

Jekaran laughed as he leapt to his feet and shot a hand down to help Mull rise. Although Mull was nineteen, three years older than Jekaran, his child-like mind remained trapped forever at an eight-year-old's capacity. And, like a child, he bounced back and forth across the continuum of emotion very quickly.

Mull dried his tears with the back of a dusty wrist. "We'll wrestle when you get back?" he asked, his tone searching for reassurance.

"Of course!" Jekaran clapped the boy-man on the back. "You know, Vestus says that we might be traveling all the way to the sea this year."

"Really?" Mull grinned.

Jekaran nodded. "And, if we do, I promise to bring something back for you."

"A shark?"

Jekaran laughed. "I don't know if I could manage that. I was thinking something more along the lines of some pretty shells."

"Well, if you see a shark, catch it!" he admonished.

"I'll give it my best." Jekaran laughed again.

"Jekaran!" an irritated voice called.

"You're in trouble," Mull warned.

Jekaran turned to see a short, young woman enter the small meadow where he and Mull had been wrestling. Her black, shoulder-length hair and large blue eyes contrasted the dirty apron covering a grey, utilitarian dress. She rushed toward them in long, purposeful strides, her hands balled into fists at her sides, a look of fury coloring her face a deep red.

"You're right, Mull. Maely never uses my full name unless she's mad at me."

Mull nodded, but said nothing.

"JEKARAN!" Maely shouted as she walked up to him, poking him in the chest with her index finger. "I have been looking *everywhere* for you two!"

Jekaran rubbed away the painful remnants of her jabbing finger. "Sorry, Mae. He found out that I was going and I had to settle him down."

Maely's expression softened. "The Thatcher's brat, Loemis, told him. He hardly slept last night after hearing about it."

"Which explains why you're in such a foul mood," Jekaran chuckled, and she punched him square in the stomach. He doubled over, half laughing, half groaning. She hit him harder than he had expected.

"What was that for?"

"*That's* for being an idiot!" She appraised him coolly before continuing, "Your uncle sent me to fetch you."

"Is it time for lunch already?"

Maely narrowed her eyes at him and put her clenched fists on her hips. "It's almost supper-time! Honestly, Jek, how do you ever get any of your chores done?"

"I wait until others get impatient and do them for me!" That earned him a kick to his left shin. "Mae!" he yelped in surprise, "that one really hurt!"

"Good!" She smirked before turning to look at Mull. "Mulladin!" she said in a tone less harsh than the one she'd used for Jekaran. "You are supposed to be mucking the cattle stalls! I've had Bess, Jora, and Leena grazing in the field for hours! Any longer and there won't be any grass left!"

"Sorry, Mae." He tucked his hands in his pockets and stared down at the ground.

Maely sighed. "It's ok." She shot Jekaran a nasty glare before turning back to pat Mull softly on the shoulder. "It isn't *your* fault!"

Jekaran decided not to push his luck by teasing Maely any further and leapt into a jog toward the trees that lay between him and the village of Genra.

As he entered the woods, he heard Maely behind him. "Look at you, Mulladin! Your clothes are all dirty!"

"Sorry."

Jekaran chuckled. Maely acted more like's Mull's mother than she did his younger sister. He supposed that was because she was all the mother he had. After all, she had been taking care of him ever since she was ten, when their mother died.

Their widowed mother had lived a chronically tragic life. She prostituted for several years before fleeing from Jeryn City and its metropolitan life in order to settle down in Genra and find peace. She instead found more tribulation and heartache. You couldn't hide many secrets in a community as small as Jekaran's village, so it was no surprise that when word of her past profession got out, the other village women began to persecute and shun her. The men of Genra were no less cruel with their lewd advances and constant harassment. The only ones in the village to befriend her family had been Jekaran and his uncle, Ezra. Jekaran remembered, as his feet pounded against the ground beneath him, how he and his uncle had been the only ones to provide aid and comfort when Maely's mother took ill with the fever and died.

Since then, Jekaran's uncle kept an eye on the two children, regularly supplying them with food and other necessities. In return, Mull would often help Jekaran with his work on the farm while Maely would launder their clothes and cook supper for them. The arrangement suited Jekaran just fine, as he didn't have any brothers or sisters of his own, and life with Ez could sometimes get dull. He was an orphan too, or he would've been, his father having abandoned his mother before he was born. His mother died shortly after his birth, and, had Jekaran's uncle not been there to adopt him, he would have ended up just like Mae and Mull.

"Jekaran!" a voice called from a short distance away.

Jekaran looked up to see a spindly man standing at the door of his log house, waving Jekaran over. His uncle was in his early fifties with gray streaks invading his unkempt, brown hair. He wore loose fitting pants and a hide vest over his scrawny, bare chest—a farmer, through and through.

"Uncle Ez," he said as he slowed to a halt. "Listen, I lost track of the hour and I'm sorry. I still have time for my most pressing chores, though."

"It's ok, Jek," his uncle said in a thoughtful tone.

He noticed a faraway look in Ez's brown eyes. "Is something wrong?"

Ez shook his head. "I need to talk to you."

"All right."

"Sit." Ez pointed at a milking stool Jekaran had left in front of the house the day before.

"Ez, I'm sorry. I meant to put that away this morning, but I forgot and ..."

"Shut up, boy," Ez said, not unkindly.

Jekaran nodded and sat on the stool. He looked up at his uncle waiting for him to say something. It was nearly a full minute before he finally turned to look at him and said, "When you left for last year's well-find, I started thinking about a lot of things."

"Like what?"

"You remind me of myself when I was your age, Jek."

"I'm probably better looking than you were."

His uncle didn't laugh. "You leave tomorrow for your second well-find, why?"

Jekaran shrugged. "For the money. You know we need it."

Ez nodded. "Perhaps. But there are many other, less dangerous, ways to earn our bread. Why choose that one?"

Jekaran shook his head, plucking a blade of grass to roll around in his fingers. *Where was this going?* "I dunno. I guess because it's a good deal more exciting than felling trees or digging ditches."

Ez nodded to himself as if confirming something. "You feel The Lure."

"The wha ..."

"Adventure is the lure of fools," Ez began reciting, "and excitement glamor to the gullible. The siren song of the world is as music to the wanderer's feet, but that dance leads only to the soul-less grave."

"Wow, old man." Jekaran's tone dripped with sarcasm. "I never knew you were a poet."

"Listen, Jekaran!" Ez snapped.

Jekaran fell silent, more from shock than to obey his uncle's command. Ez was sometimes grumpy, but he was usually an easy-going man who loved to laugh. Jekaran rarely saw him this serious. It gave him pause.

Ez ran a grizzled hand through his wild hair and sighed. "I am forbidding you from going on this well-find."

Jekaran leapt to his feet. "Ez!" he demanded. "You can't ..."

"The hell I can't," Ez barked. "You will go into town and tell Vestus to take your name off of tomorrow's roll call."

Jekaran couldn't believe what he was hearing. Like any parent, Ez set limits to what Jekaran could and could not do and punished him when Jekaran broke his uncle's rules. But the man was always fair in his punishments and although stern at times, he never acted harshly or dictatorially.

"But, the money ..."

"There are other jobs." Ez turned away, waving a hand in the air as he stepped into the house.

"Ez," Jekaran pled.

"Do as I say!"

Jekaran stood motionless for a long moment, the surprise of it all shoving conscious thought from his mind. That confusion quickly turned into anger and Jekaran kicked the milking stool so hard that it sailed ten feet; judging by the sharp pain that followed, he probably broke his big toe. He tried not to limp as he left the yard and began heading into town.

Half an hour later, Jekaran walked down Genra's one street where two giggling little boys crashed into him. Instead of an apology, they said in unison, "Hi Jek!" before running off. He barely noticed. The shock and indignation of his uncle's rash and inexplicable action had driven away his normal playful cheeriness.

How could Ez do this to him? He had given Jekaran his permission to join the expedition weeks ago. Why change his mind on the very eve of the well-find? He hadn't had a problem with him going *last* year, and he was fifteen then, a whole year under Lord Gymal's required age. Fortunately, for Jekaran, none of the team really liked Gymal, so no one would give him away and he was able to get away with it. Now Jekaran was of the proper age to go and Ez was forbidding him? It made no sense.

He grit his teeth. He had so been looking forward to seeing the city of Rasha, the western rock lands, and perhaps even the great west sea. What would he tell Mull now? Of course, the boy-man would probably be so happy Jekaran wasn't leaving, he wouldn't care about not getting a sampling of sea shells.

Maybe it had something to do with that poem Ez recited. How did it go again? *Adventure is the lure of fools?* Was he saying that Jekaran was a fool for wanting to leave the village and taste life outside of the mundane work of raising crops and tending livestock? He clenched his jaw so tightly that his teeth began to hurt. He really did hate the so-called *normal* life of their small village. His childhood dreams were of traveling the world, seeing the capital city, sailing the sea, maybe even visiting one of the two other kingdoms in Shaelar. As he grew older, he conceded that, for the most part, those dreams were probably not going to come true. But the well-find offered him a chance to taste what that life would be like.

Why take that away from me, Ez? He ground his teeth. He *would* get an answer out of the old man when he went back. It was, at least, his right to know *why* he couldn't go, wasn't it?

Jekaran looked down the street to Vestus' shop. The tall man was standing just outside his shop door on the boardwalk talking with a customer. He had begun to wave when a group of five unfamiliar men, just beyond Vestus, made him lower his arm. A potent terror abruptly struck him, begging him to turn in panicked flight, but he couldn't. His feet felt stuck to the road, paralyzed, his mind muddled. He stood, gaping like a fool. Genra often had visitors, usually caravan travelers passing through or peddlers hocking their wares. These men were neither of those.

Each was dressed in leather armor of various designs, and, underneath their traveling cloaks, Jekaran could clearly see swords hanging from sheathes at their hips. Too much time drinking and smoking engraved their faces with harsh lines.

Around him, the milling villagers hushed as they took notice of the men, and a few women spirited their little ones out of sight. These men were dangerous, and it was clear everyone sensed it.

Jekaran stepped out of their way when they passed him on the boardwalk, the foremost of their group leering at him with a humorless rictus for a smile. He stared at the man's face, unable to hold onto a thought or even frame words. The stranger was ten to fifteen years older than his cohorts as was evidenced by a streak of grey mixed with his slicked back, black hair. But not so old that he looked weak. If anything, the man gave Jekaran the impression that he was the most dangerous of the five. He looked to be in his late forties with a beardless face and a sharp nose.

The man turned his full attention on Jekaran, making him hold his breath. The man's eyes were chilling: The left iris was brown, the right iris blue. Jekaran never saw anything like it.

And I thought my green eyes were strange. He would have chuckled if he wasn't so terrified.

Although not unheard of, Jekaran was among a minority of people in Shaelar to be born with green eyes. It had branded him a novelty when he was a child and gave bullies an excuse to target him, but the people of Genra had eventually become accustomed to it. And, as odd as his green eyes were, this man's eyes were an unholy aberration in comparison, though he doubted anyone with more sense than a chicken would try to bully *this* man. They passed him, and Jekaran couldn't help but stare as the men walked away and then turned left into the blacksmith's shop. A heartbeat of silence reigned, and then the palpable fear was gone. Life in the village square unthawed as everyone resumed their business, and Jekaran shifted his gaze, looking ahead to find Vestus staring in his direction.

Vestus nodded in greeting as Jekaran jogged toward him, his eyes still fixed on the blacksmith's door.

"Who're they?" Jekaran asked.

The middle-aged grocer shook his head and said in his bass voice, "Don't know, but I don't like the idea of leaving my family behind tomorrow morning if *they're* still here."

The customer Vestus had been talking to, a short man with a thick, black beard named Hyric, chimed in. "They were asking if anyone had seen a man with a crescent-shaped tattoo on the inside of his forearm."

"What's that mean?" Jekaran shot another glance over his shoulder.

Vestus slowly shook his head, "Not sure." He looked at Jekaran and smiled. "So. Come to pick up supplies for tomorrow's trip?"

He dropped his eyes to the ground as his stomach turned. "I've come to tell you that I won't be going and that I need you to take my name off of the roll call." He had to force the words out of his mouth.

Vestus' smile faded. "Why?"

Jekaran shook his head. He wanted to blurt out "because Ez won't let me" but thought that would sound childish, and so he lied. "Ez needs me on the farm." Well, it might not be a lie. Maybe that's why his uncle forbade him, though Jekaran doubted that. No, this must be about something else.

"Can't say that I'm glad to hear that. We're already short-handed as it is." His smile returned. "You're a good lad, Jek. Family comes first."

"Yeah," he scoffed.

Vestus' eyebrow shot up, but instead of saying anything more, he returned his attention back to Hyric.

Dropping his shoulders, Jekaran turned to head back home, but slowed as he passed in front of the blacksmith's shop, trying to unobtrusively peer in the front windows to catch another glimpse of the strangers and their leader with the mismatched eyes. He saw the men standing at the front counter talking with Jerall, the village's only blacksmith. His brows furrowed as he caught the worried look on the burly man's face. He never considered Jerall, bear of a man that he was, would ever be afraid of anyone, but his obsequious head bobbing and refusal to meet the men's eyes made it obvious.

Jekaran started as the leader of the strangers turned to look straight at him. The man's knowing smile made him shiver, and he backed away from the window.

He hurried on, trying to put the men out of his mind by focusing on his indignation in a deliberate attempt to blot out his apprehension.

There, Ez, he thought, *I've done what you told me to do. Now you owe me some answers!*

CHAPTER 3

Running made Jekaran's sore toe protest each time his foot hit the ground, but he ignored it. As hard as Jekaran tried to hold onto his indignation and anger, they slipped away the more he thought about the dangerous looking strangers he had seen come into town. That made him eager to get back and tell Ez, which in turn fueled his sprint. He ran down the road, making the trip in a record twenty minutes, then dashed into his yard, frightening a group of foraging chickens into flight before slowing to a jog. He burst into the log house and looked around. No one. "Uncle?" he called out

No one answered, and, after a moment's thought, he rushed to the kitchen to look out the back window. "Ah." The door to the slaughtering shed was open. Only one reason it wouldn't be locked.

Jekaran rushed out the back door and into the small, smelly shack.

Ez looked up from behind the high wood table, holding the carcass of a rabbit by its ears and a hunting knife in the other. He cocked an eyebrow. "You're back already?"

Jekaran stopped, only nodding in response as he worked to catch his breath.

"You look as if you ran the whole way," Ez said as he went back to skinning the animal.

"There are strangers in town," he heard himself saying, his demands for an explanation now overshadowed by the news of the man with mismatched eyes.

Ez didn't look up at him. "That's not so remarkable."

"They look rough, and they're asking around for a man with a crescent moon tattoo."

He abruptly froze. "What did you say?" he asked.

Jekaran shifted his eyes from the corpse dangling with pink skin laced with crimson streaks of blood to study his uncle's face. His brows furrowed, had Ez actually gone pale? It was hard to tell in the dimness of the shed. "They're looking for someone with a tattoo shaped like a crescent." He tapped the inside of his forearm. "Right here."

Ez dropped the rabbit and put the knife down on the table with a *clink*. He drew in a sharp breath as he reached for a cloth towel hanging from a nearby grimy hook and quickly wiped the blood off his hands.

"What's wrong?" Jekaran asked.

"What did they look like?"

"They were wearing cloaks, had swords, and one man had different colored eyes."

Ez's face grew even more ashen. "Impossible," he whispered.

The last lingering bit of Jekaran's anger faded, snuffed out by a sudden feeling of unease. "Do you know him?"

Ez rested both palms on the wooden table and bowed his head.

"Ez, what's wrong?"

His uncle didn't answer. Instead, he raised his head and peered nervously out the shed's open door. Then he startled Jekaran as he abruptly pushed past him, exiting the slaughter shed and disappearing into the house. Jekaran followed him inside.

"Ez?"

He silently waved Jekaran toward the pantry where a trapdoor set in the floor. He wrenched it open and descended a ladder. Jekaran followed him into the cellar, a claustrophobic hole stuffed with wooden crates and barrels covered with cobwebs.

Ez rummaged around for a moment before locating an old chest. He knelt before it and blew the dust off of a rusty padlock. Jekaran folded his arms and tapped his foot against the dirt floor as his uncle painstakingly cycled through a ring of old keys before finding the one that matched the lock. Ez wrenched open the chest and carefully drew out a long object bundled in a dirty white cloth. He carefully unbundled it.

Jekaran's mouth fell open as he gazed upon a stunningly beautiful sword. His eyes widened as they roamed over the large, round amethyst set into the blade's silver crossbar and its tapered blade inlayed with trailing designs, *and were those tiny emeralds?* They appeared to pepper the flat of the blade and sparkle green whenever they caught a bit of the light pouring in from above.

"What *is* that?" Jekaran reached a hand out to touch it, but Ez batted it away.

"Never touch it!" he snapped.

"Where did you get it?" he asked incredulously.

After a pregnant moment, Ez finally said, "I stole it from a noble's mansion in a city you don't know the name of, over thirty years ago."

"Stole from a noble? Wait, this is a talis?" Jekaran took a second look at the sword. "Divine Mother, it's a weapon talis!" He lowered his voice conspiratorially, although he knew that no one was likely to overhear them. "You could go to prison just for having this!"

Ez nodded. "Hanged is more likely."

"What are you doing with a weapon talis, Ez?" Jekaran demanded.

He lowered the sword and looked him in the eyes. "I'm a criminal, Jek, an infamous criminal. You ever hear of the Rikujo Band?"

He nodded, still unable to look away from the weapon. "They still cause problems for travelers along the eastern highway."

Ez placed the sword on a nearby crate and then tapped on the inside of his forearm where there was a discolored patch of scarred skin. "I burned myself to hide the crescent moon tattoo, so no one would ever know what I was."

"Those men are looking for you?" He shook his head. "No," he said. "No, that's not possible. You're not a bandit."

"I am afraid it's true." Ez sighed and a bit of the tension seemed to leave his shoulders. "I left that life behind over sixteen years ago, when Anarilee died and you were born." He chuckled nervously and cast his eyes to the ground. "There I was, a hardened criminal, a man of the world as the monks of Rasheera would say, alone with a brand new baby boy and absolutely no idea how to care for him. Almost funny, if you think about it."

Ez looked up at him and must've mistaken his bewildered expression for a question, because he asked rhetorically, "Then why didn't I just abandon you?" He shook his head. "Your mother was the only one in our family who didn't disown me. She never approved of the life I had chosen, but she always treated me with love and kindness. Because of that, leaving her baby with a wet-nurse or on the steps of an orphanage just felt wrong." Ezra scoffed. "I tell you Jek, if you knew me like I was then, you would understand just how remarkable it was for me to consider anything *wrong*."

Jekaran scratched the back of his neck. "But no one leaves the Rikujo."

Ez nodded again. "Which is why I changed my name, burned off my tattoo, and became a farmer."

"Changed your name?" His mind suddenly reeled at the revelation that his uncle Ezra, the man who had selflessly raised him, was actually another person.

Ez hesitated. "Argentus."

"Argentus, The Invincible Shadow?"

Ez chuckled nervously. "Some people called me that."

"*Everyone* called him," Jekaran corrected himself, "called *you*, that. You were one of the Rikujo lords?"

Ez shook his head. "Who I once was is not important."

"Then why tell me?" Jekaran asked, his mind a mass of confusion.

"I hadn't planned to, but it seems that my sins have returned to haunt me."

"They've come to kill you for leaving the Rikujo?"

Ez glanced at the sword. "Probably."

Jekaran followed his uncle's gaze and pointed at the jeweled weapon. "They want that?"

"It is *very* valuable," he slowly said.

He guessed that, but couldn't begin to come up with a reasonable amount. Probably guessing too high, he figured. "How much is it worth?"

Ez shook his head as he stared thoughtfully at the sword. "Kingdoms and glory," he softly said, almost as if to himself.

Jekaran didn't understand. "What?"

Ez's eyes hardened. "We have to leave."

Jekaran felt his head begin to swim and he blinked, trying to make quick sense of the flood of information. If anyone else would have told him his uncle was a wanted criminal, he would have laughed and then punched them in the nose for accusing the old man. This couldn't be happening. "We can't just …"

"They'll find me and kill me," Ez said as he begun re-bundling the sword. "And anyone close to me."

"Will they leave you alone if you just give them the sword?"

Ez's eyes flashed with a dangerous look Jekaran had never seen on his uncle's face. "They must NEVER get this sword." The fierceness of his words startled Jekaran. "Especially not the man with the mismatched eyes."

"You know him, don't you?" Jekaran said. "I saw it in your face when I mentioned him."

Ez began tying twine around the bundled cloth. "His name is Kaul. He was my," Ez corrected himself, "Argentus' lieutenant. He is as wicked and dangerous as they come, a sadistic and ambitious monster with an unpredictable temper."

Jekaran took a deep breath in an effort to calm himself. His whole life felt like it was being stolen from him. "But where are we going to go?"

Ez picked up the bundled sword and ascended the ladder out of the cellar. "You are going to rejoin the well-find expedition."

"What?" Jekaran snapped as he took hold of the ladder and stared up at his uncle. "Just over an hour ago you said I was forbidden from going." He climbed the five rungs and emerged from the squared opening in the floor.

Ez helped him out before letting the trapdoor fall and slam shut. "We need to leave and the smartest way to do that is by splitting up. Besides, you'll be safer leaving with Gymal's company."

"But my name's been taken off the roll."

Ez opened a closet, rummaged through it until he found a large, animal-hide duffel bag and slid the sword into it. "They're shorthanded this year, and won't turn away any extra help."

Talking of the well-find reminded Jekaran of the explanation he intended to wrench from his uncle. Although it now seemed like such a small thing, he couldn't help but ask, "Why did you stop me from going?"

Ez sighed, keeping his back to him. "Because you feel the lure."

He groaned. "What does that even mean?"

"When I started recognizing the same thirst for adventure in you that had led me into a life of violence and crime, I had to stop you from making the same mistakes I did."

"I wouldn't join the Rikujo," Jekaran protested.

"No, boy!" He turned to face him. "You don't understand!" He closed his eyes and drew in a deep breath. "When I was young like you, I never set out intending to become an infamous crime lord." He shook his head. "Like you, I simply wanted adventure. I felt the *Lure* and was unhappy with my life as a farmer, a life I thought was dull. So, like you, I left my small town looking for what I thought would bring me excitement and pleasure."

"And did it?"

He slowly nodded. "I found plenty of both, but what I should've wanted was happiness. Excitement and pleasure are short-lived, but happiness endures." He picked up the satchel with the sword in it and looked Jekaran directly in the eyes. "I didn't want you to end up like me – an old fool with a list of haunting regrets. I want *you* to be able to live the simple life, the happy life."

Jekaran felt ashamed for being so angry with his uncle. Ez hadn't been trying to unfairly oppress him by forcing him to quit the expedition. He had only been trying to protect him. He had been doing exactly what a good parent was supposed to do, making sure that their child avoided the pitfalls they themselves had fallen into.

Ez walked out of the back room and into Jekaran's bedroom. "And now, damn me, I'm sending you straight into the very world I was trying to protect you from." He put some of Jekaran's clothing into the bag.

"This season's well-find will take you through the city of Rasha. I have an old friend who lives there, a man named Irvis. He was in the same business that I ..." again Ez corrected himself, "... that Argentus was in, and like me, he has retired. I want you to hide this talis in your things and take it to Irvis when you reach Rasha."

"Wait, I'm taking the sword?" Jekaran blurted out.

Ez nodded as he retrieved an inkwell and some paper from a trunk on the floor. He then moved to a small desk where he pulled open a drawer and rifled through it until he found a quill. He settled at the desk and began quickly scrawling on the paper. "I'm writing Irvis a letter that I want you to give to him. It will explain what's happening, and ask him to help you keep the sword safe." He finished writing the letter and handed it to Jekaran.

He looked down at it and was surprised to find a dozen unreadable symbols.

Ez must've noticed his confusion because he said, "It's in a cipher. Irvis is the only one who knows the key."

"Where are *you* going?" Jekaran folded the paper and shoved it into a trouser pocket.

"I will wait until you leave and then go to Jeryn. I have a safe-house there that I have kept over the years. Irvis knows where it is, and he will take you to meet me there."

"Are we coming back?"

Ez looked at him and ruefully shook his head. "I don't think so, Jek."

"What about Mae and Mull?" The sudden realization that he would never again see his adopted siblings stabbed his heart.

Ez sighed. "They're old enough now to take care of themselves, and I will leave Maely a note telling her that she can have our house and farm. I've also saved some money over the years, and I can leave them whatever we don't need for traveling." He shook his head. "I really am sorry, Jek. I never thought this would happen, I never thought Kaul would find me, and I certainly never wanted you to learn who I was."

With everything weighing so heavily on him, Jekaran was only able to manage a trite, "It's ok," as a reply.

"No, it's not," Ez said, and then he surprised Jekaran by pulling him into a tight embrace. "You deserve better than this."

Jekaran felt tears threatening but choked them back. He pulled away from Ez and looked his uncle in the eyes. They were not the eyes of a wicked man. Whatever his uncle had been, whoever he had been, Jekaran knew Ez had changed.

Changed for me.

"You can find Irvis by making inquiry at the Rasheeran Monastery."

"The Monastery?" Jekaran asked. "Why there?"

Ez tightened the drawstring of the duffle, just barely able to close the mouth over the sword's cloth-wrapped pommel. "I can tell you the full story another day. For now, just promise me that you will hide this well, and no matter what you do, don't touch it! Keep it wrapped in the cloth, even when you present it to Irvis."

"Why can't I touch it? Is it cursed?" Jekaran was suddenly wary of the bag.

An odd look came over his uncle's face, an expression Jekaran wasn't sure he recognized, though if he had to name it, he would've called it regret.

"You could say that." Ez put the long duffle into Jekaran's arms. "I am sorry to have to do this to you, son, but you must trust me. You will be safer leaving Genra without me." He shook his head. "Kaul would never expect me to part with the sword, and so he should ignore you, even if he finds out that you're my nephew."

"I'm more worried about you," Jekaran said honestly.

"I'm not so old that I can't take care of myself, Jek" he said. "And, at the risk of sounding like a proud fool, I can claim that I have always been a clever man." Ez grinned at him, and for some reason that made Jekaran feel as though there was at least one part of his world that wasn't falling apart.

Chapter 4

Maely stared at herself in the full-length mirror. The breeches she wore were loose enough to hide the curve of her hips, and a chest wrap covered by a baggy tunic did a decent job of flattening her breasts, although she was still young enough that there wasn't a whole lot to flatten. There was only one thing that she needed to do now. Maely looked down at the pair of shears in her right hand, hesitating as she wistfully touched her shoulder-length hair with her free hand.

Divine Mother! What am I doing? She had lost count of how many times she asked herself that question. But even as often as she had asked it, she still didn't have a real answer, at least not a rational one. Maely glanced at the sealed envelope lying on her bed. In her explanatory letter to Ez, she had listed several reasons *why* she was leaving, all of which sounded weak when she read them back to herself. Why *was* she doing this? Certainly Jekaran would return, and he didn't need *her* to keep him safe. She rolled her eyes at the thought. How had she ever thought she could protect him? She didn't even know how to fight.

So it wasn't to protect him.

The road to the western rock lands did pass through several towns and villages, and even a large city. Those places all held pitfalls of a different sort, especially for a young man. She could make sure Jekaran wasn't tempted with the poppy dens or the whorehouses, but he was never the kind to indulge in such things.

So it wasn't to anchor him.

Three months was a very long time to be away from home. Surely, Jekaran would miss his uncle. Perhaps having someone with him would help him when he became homesick. But then, Jekaran had gone on last year's well-find and hadn't said a word about yearning for home while he traveled. In fact, he sounded as though he had thoroughly enjoyed himself.

So if it wasn't to keep him company, then why?

The sound of Mulladin snoring drew her attention, and Maely peeked out from behind her dressing screen at her brother sleeping on his cot in the far corner. The sight of his peaceful face evoked a pang of guilt, and her shame for abandoning him intensified. *Ez will take care of him,* she told herself—again.

Maely let go of her hair and closed the shears. She had written to Ez that she was going to take care of Jekaran, but it was obvious he needed no one to look after him. The truth was, Maely already knew that he didn't need her to go with *him.* Then was she going for herself? Last year's well-find was the first time they had been apart since Ez had adopted Maely and her brother. It had impacted her more than she expected. She hadn't let anyone know—who was there to tell anyway— but she had cried herself to sleep the night he left, worry and insecurity gnawing at her every day thereafter.

"I'm being a stupid, silly girl," she whispered to herself. What did she think was going to happen anyway? That Jekaran see her, discover what lengths she had taken to be with him, and then—*what?*

Mulladin's snoring stopped, and she heard him turning over on his cot. A moment later, the snoring resumed. Maely closed her eyes, knowing her brother would be near-inconsolable when he found out both she and Jek had left him. She wanted to say goodbye, but to do so would ruin her opportunity to slip away. She already said goodbye anyway, after a sort. She had fixed Mulladin his favorite dinner that night and told him he could sleep in this morning. *Was that love, or guilt?* She wondered. Probably guilt, but perhaps guilt *because* she loved him and knew what she would be doing to him. *I'll be gone and he won't know it until he wakes up.* That was when she instructed him to take the letter to Ez.

Maely felt a tear rolling down her right cheek, and she wiped her eyes with the sleeve of her oversized tunic. She sniffed, composed herself, and then held the shears in front of her face. *No,* she shook her head, *this was madness.* She set the shears down on a table, gripped the bottom of her tunic and began to lift it up. She caught sight of herself in the mirror and stopped, letting the tunic fall back down.

She stared at the face looking back at her in the mirror, and that's when she realized the simple truth. She had known the *why* of her insane plan this whole time. It was just that it sounded too simplistic, too foolish, too embarrassing to admit. Oddly, that realization drove home her decision, and she whispered, "I'm going because I have to go. I just have to."

Maely turned away from her reflection and peeked again at Mulladin. *He will be fine,* she told herself. *Ez will take care of him, and maybe the separation will be good for him.* She returned to staring at her reflection in the mirror.

A long moment passed. Then, without further hesitation, she grabbed the shears, lifted them to the back of her head, and began to cut. When she was done with the back, she clipped away her bangs and then shortened the sides. She lifted her hand and tentatively ran it through what was left of her hair. She had never worn it long, but this was *very* different. *Still,* she thought, *I don't look like a boy. Jekaran will still be able to recognize me.*

Maely washed her face of makeup before smearing some soot she had collected from the hearth onto her cheeks. She rumpled her hair so that she had a cowlick, and put on a pair of Ez's old reading spectacles. Last of all, she retrieved an old tan hat, also something she stole from Ez. The short rimmed, poofy-topped hat was the keystone to make the rest of the disguise work.

Maely smiled at the boyish reflection. Women were not allowed to go on well-finds by order of Lord Gymal. He claimed the sex was too much of a distraction for the finders, and the delicacy of the women slowed down the company. *What a pig,* Maely thought. Then again, perhaps it was a veiled protection from abuses. She knew all too well what women suffered when they took to the road with a group of men. Her mother had told her. She shrugged off the moral question and straightened her hat. Now all she needed was a name.

She looked like a pre-pubescent boy of perhaps twelve, and so she needed a name that fit the persona. She mentally cycled through several boy names before finally settling on Lyam. She had known a boy named Lyam when she was little, before her mother died. Last she heard, his family stilled lived in the province, which would lend credibility to her disguise should anyone ask where Lyam was from. She nodded with satisfaction and then quietly practiced talking in a lower tone. After a few pathetic attempts, she decided her male voice was going to take some work. She should probably keep talking to a minimum. Lyam would be quiet and shy.

The first rays of the morning sun shone through her window, signaling it was time to go. She quickly grabbed her satchel and turned toward the door, and then hurried back to the dresser to stuff a ring with a piece of twine threaded around the band. It was her mother's lucky ring, credited for getting the richest, safest clients. She wasn't sure why she felt she should take it with her. Perhaps it was because she always associated it with the comfort and security her mother once provided. Just as she was about to bury it beneath her spare clothing, she paused. Somehow it didn't seem respectful to keep it at the bottom of her satchel. Maely stared at it for a moment and then pulled the twine over her head. The cold metal pressed against her skin as she tucked the ring beneath her shirt.

Her mother's lucky ring. *Hope it works for me, like it did for you, Mother. Well, maybe not exactly like it worked for you,* she corrected.

Maely stepped out from behind the dressing screen and took one last look at Mull.

My little brother, she thought.

Although he had the face of a man, his child's mind always made her think of him as a little boy.

He needs you, an accusing voice said inside her head.

Ez will take care of him, Maely told herself again, and then worried that she would lose her nerve, she pushed herself quietly out of their cabin.

Ez will take care of him.

CHAPTER

5

Gymal was a bully, a self-important, pompous ass of a man. And, like all bullies, he had an advantage that gave him the power to push others around. In his case, it wasn't physical stature, for he was a short, weaselly man, and though not yet into his forties, was already balding. No, Gymal was a well-finder, a man from a minor noble family and one of a hundred attaches to the king himself. His position was one of note to be sure, but, in reality, he held little real authority. He was just good at acting like he did.

His family long possessed several utility talises, the most valuable being their dowsing stone. Unlike most talises, the dowsing stone didn't need a charge to function. In fact, it was deliberately crafted so as to not to be able to hold a charge. This way the stone could sense the energy emitted by an Apeira well and shine more intensely the nearer it came to one. The octagon-cut amethyst stone was set in a golden medallion around Gymal's his neck, proudly displayed to remind others that he was their better.

Jekaran snorted to himself. The gaudy gold-colored medallion looked incongruous with the natural beauty of the talis' amethyst-colored stone. It couldn't have been the stone's original setting. That had likely been lost long ago, forcing Gymal's family to have the stone set in the obviously bargain-crafted medallion. Despite the noble status it could grant, talis possession alone did not make one rich, and Jekaran suspected Gymal's family was likely considered poor among the nobility of the king's court.

Staring at his dousing stone made it all but impossible for Jekaran to ignore the sword stowed in the duffle he carried on his back, and sweat began to bead the back of his neck. The need to look over his shoulder settled on him like a possession, but when he turned around, the man with the mismatched eyes wasn't there, ready to take what was left of his life.

He breathed in and out, in and out. No Rikujo, but that didn't mean he was out of danger. If Gymal found out that he had an illegal talis, that bitter little man would immediately have him arrested. Jekaran was certain of it.

Jekaran again shrugged the duffle's shoulder straps. It was something that he noticed was becoming a nervous tic. He'd have to watch that. He didn't want to draw any more of Gymal's attention than he had to.

His thoughts circled back to the last few minutes he spent in the home he'd known all of his life. He and his uncle were saying their good-byes, and Jekaran worried the talis would accidentally activate while in his bag, but Ez allayed those fears by telling him the sword had long since exhausted its Apeiron charge.

"What does it do?" he had asked, but Ez wouldn't give him a straight answer and Jekaran got the distinct impression Ez was hiding more than just what he knew about the talis.

Not Ez, Argentus, he told himself. *My uncle is The Invincible Shadow.* That was going to take some getting used to.

Even in a small village like Genra, people knew of the Rikujo. Jekaran had heard stories of the man people said couldn't be caught or defeated. *He came and went, and no man could stop him,* he had once overheard an old peddler telling Vestus. *Not Ez,* Jekaran thought again, still having not fully processed the revelation. He tried not to think of the murders Argentus was said to have committed. Had his uncle really killed men? He hoped it was only men. *Ez is not the man he was,* he told himself again. If Jekaran had ever had any doubt about his uncle's conversion to Rasheera, and the transformation that turned a ruthless crime lord into a gentle farmer, he need only think of Ez's eyes. He could now recognize sadness and regret in those eyes, but they were not the eyes of a murderer.

"Line up!" Gymal shouted in his nasally voice.

He did not dismount from his ghern, and Jekaran knew it was because of the man's inferiority complex. *Doesn't want to be shorter than any of the other men in the company*, he thought sourly, *and he likes the status symbol of the ghern*. Faster and more expensive than a bullock, the long-haired, bipedal mammals were financially out of reach of the peasant class.

Jekaran fell into line, his position ending up toward the end in between two large men with brown skin. He folded his arms behind his back to resemble the military stance he had seen soldiers take when they were being addressed by their captains.

Gymal casually rode his ghern down the line looking each man square in the face as they spoke their names. He waited for his secretary to confirm that they were on the roll before moving onto the next man until he at last came to Jekaran.

"Jekaran," Gymal drawled before Jekaran could state his name. He reined in his ghern and glowered down at him.

"Yes, Lord Gymal." He forced his tone to stay respectful. Only an hour in Gymal's presence and he was already irritated with the pompous, little man.

"I thought your name was removed from the roll." Gymal frowned.

"Must be a clerical error as I signed up weeks ago." Jekaran cast a glance down the line at Vestus, whom he hoped hadn't heard what he had just said.

"I am surprised you signed up at all," Gymal said. "After all the trouble you caused me last year.

"Trouble, my lord?" Jekaran asked, trying to keep his tone steady.

The year previous, Jekaran had retaliated against Gymal's bullying by waging a secret campaign of practical jokes on the lord. Somehow Gymal had figured out who was behind it and, although he had no proof, threatened to press charges against Jekaran. Apparently, Gymal thought his threat would've kept Jekaran away from this year's well-find. Well, he was wrong.

Gymal leaned down from his ghern and hissed, "Don't play dumb with me, peasant! I know it was you that let that salamander loose in my personal latrine! And I know you were the one who hired that male prostitute to pay me a visit in front of all of the men."

Guess he didn't figure out that I was also the one who gave his ghern diarrhea. Jekaran had fed the beast buckets of curdled milk in the middle of the night. The constant mess was bad, but the smell was worse. He tried not to smile now at the memory. Gymal wouldn't like that act of insubordination.

"Please, Lord Gymal." Jekaran worked to sound as respectful as he could. "I would never dishonor you so."

Gymal snorted skeptically. "If we weren't in need of more strong backs, I would tell you to go home, but it is what it is." Then he added in a low tone, "If I ever find proof that you had a hand in humiliating me, or if you try something like that again, I swear that you will spend no less than a year in the king's dungeons! Understand?"

Jekaran was about to reply with a veiled insult when the sword secreted in the bag on his back made him think better of it. "Yes, my lord," he finally said. It irked him that he would have to treat Gymal carefully on this trip. *At least it's only for a short time.* He only had to endure the man's presence until he reached Rasha and found Irvis.

Gymal's glare lingered on Jekaran for several long seconds before moving on to the next man, who confidently announced his name as "Tork." Next he heard Vestus state his name followed by his adult son Haulek. The roll call continued until ending with a shy, skinny boy named Lyam.

Lyam? Jekaran leaned forward. There was something familiar about that voice.

"Your name is not on the roll," Gymal accused. "And you are obviously too young. I doubt you could even lift a pickaxe."

He couldn't hear the boy's soft reply, but, whatever he said, it made Gymal stare at him for a long, awkward moment.

"Fine," Jekaran heard Gymal concede. "But don't think you will receive the same pay as the other men and don't think this will be a holiday. Since you're too young to mine, you're going to be digging latrines, carrying water, and a host of other unpleasant work."

The boy dipped his head in thanks.

Gymal turned and trotted his ghern back to face the center of the line. In his irritatingly condescending way, he asked, "Raise your hand if this is your first well-find." After a moment's hesitation, about a third of the men's hands went up. Gymal pinched the bridge of his nose and sighed. "This is a dowsing stone." He raised the amulet off of his chest by its chain. "It allows me to know when we are near an Apeira well. The king's polymaths study the land and use several means to ascertain possible excavation sites. It falls to me to locate the exact spot of the well, and you to dig it up. Understand?"

There was a collective response of agreement.

"If we are successful in finding a well, the king will pay me a finder's fee out of which I will pay each of you. The usually wage is fifty silver Aies'." Gymal made a point of looking at Jekaran before warning, "But that amount may decrease based on individual performance."

Jekaran gritted his teeth. That had been the one downside to his campaign of pranks the prior year. Although Gymal hadn't had proof to formally prosecute Jekaran for tormenting him, his suspicions had significantly impacted Jekaran's pay. In fact, last year, he had only received half of what the other men on the expedition had been paid.

Gymal's lecturing faded as Jekaran's attention turned to the road behind him. What would Mae and Mull do when they found out he and Ez left them? He knew what his uncle said about the two being old enough to care for themselves to be true, but he couldn't help feeling like he was abandoning them.

He had asked Ez if he could go to their cabin and say goodbye, but his uncle said that could put them in danger. The argument was brief, and Jekaran finally conceded the point. Another stab of grief dug into his chest. He was leaving two people whom he considered family, leaving them without any explanation.

Perhaps Ez is just being paranoid. Perhaps we can come back in a few months. He hoped so, and that thought was the only thing soothing his pain and guilt.

Movement at Jekaran's sides told him Gymal was done lecturing them. He looked to his right and saw the wheels of the supply wagons begin to turn as the driver whipped the team of bullocks into action.

"Goodbye," Jekaran whispered to the wind.

CHAPTER
6

Ezra—it had taken him years before he had started calling himself that in his own mind—dug frantically inside the old trunk. He was in the cellar again, this time going through storage and looking for a few of *Argentus'* old possessions. The trunk had not weathered the years well. Moisture warped the wood and blasted Ezra with a strong musty odor the moment he lifted the lid. If Jekaran were here and Ezra had said as much out loud, the boy probably would've made some quip about how he was just like the trunk – old and stinky. That made him chuckle, but the mirth immediately evaporated as he thought about the task he had set his nephew to.

"Damn me," he whispered. *I should've gotten rid of the sword years ago.* But his fear someone else would find it kept him from doing so. *Liar,* he chided himself. That wasn't the real reason he hadn't disposed of the talis, and he knew it. Even after all these years, being apart from it made him uneasy, though not in the same way it had when charged. He imagined that was probably a psychological side effect of the bond-breaking.

Divine Mother, please see that my boy doesn't walk the same path of sorrow I have trod. Don't let anything happen to him, and don't let it get a hold of him. Ezra's mental prayer had no sooner ended than he found what he was digging in the trunk for – a cloth bag full of jewelry.

"HA!" Ezra exulted, pulled out the bag and left the cellar.

Ezra scooted onto the kitchen floor to sit cross-legged and dumped out the contents of the bag in front of him. A ring, a bracelet, and an earring clattered against the wooden floor. Each piece of jewelry was cast of a different precious metal: the ring of gold, the bracelet of silver, and the earring of platinum. But they all had an amethyst stone set into them, a stone from an Apeira well. They were talises.

He stared at them, knowing he probably should've sold the talises years ago as leaving the Rikujo drove him into near destitution. But a farmer selling powerful talises would have certainly drawn the attention of his former friends, to say nothing of Gymal's family who governed their province. He picked up the ring first, and, although not really surprised, he was disappointed to find the talis completely drained of an Apeiron charge. The bracelet also proved to be empty of the energy that would enable its magical effects. But the earring still held a charge. Not a full charge, but enough to get a few uses out of it. Ezra smiled as he examined the small platinum spike capped by an amethyst stone. Of the three, this was the most useful.

Thank you, Rasheera, he prayed.

He lifted the earring to his ear, found the place where there was once a hole in the soft tissue, and then pressed the pin of the earring into his flesh until it pierced through his ear lobe. He gritted his teeth and sucked in a sharp breath, but a quick stinging followed by a little bit of blood was worth the power the earring would grant him. He fitted a small, metal clutch onto the pin protruding out of the back, and immediately felt a connection form between himself and the talis.

Ezra scooped up the bracelet and ring and deposited them back into the cloth bag. He then stood, groaning slightly as his joints protested. "The Invincible Shadow," he scoffed at himself, "has arthritis."

Ezra hurried into his small bedchamber and dug a leather satchel out from beneath his bed. He opened the top flap, loosed the drawstring, and shoved his bag of talises into the mouth of the satchel. Leaving the bag waiting on his bed, he went to the closet, indiscriminately grabbing clothing, and returned to stuff the pile into his satchel. He was cinching the drawstring when something on the nightstand caught his eye.

Ezra dropped the bag and walked around the foot of his bed to stare at a framed image of his sister, an image created just two years before she died. It had been a harvest celebration gift. He remembered the day he had paid an exorbitant amount for one of the visiting merchants with a color trap talis to make it. She had insisted that he have his image trapped for her as well. It was all Ezra had left of her.

No, that's not true. I have Jekaran, he thought. Jekaran, Anarilee's only son. And he just sent him into the wicked world carrying something more dangerous than a venomous snake. Ezra's eyes fell onto the second image, the one of Jekaran at fourteen. In the picture, he stood next to his nephew, who at the time was of the same height. Now Jekaran was a good two inches taller than Ezra.

It had been another harvest celebration gift, this time from Jekaran to him. Unbeknownst to Ezra, his nephew had been hiring out with Vestus for odd jobs and saving the money. It very nearly made Ezra cry when he found out.

"The Invincible Shadow crying," he scoffed again.

Ezra scooped up both framed images and was about to stuff them in his satchel when a loud sound startled him. Before he knew it, his belt knife was in his hand, and he was crouching low and peeking out of his room toward the sound. It was pounding on his door that he had heard. Again, the pounding came in a short burst, and Ezra thought he could he hear someone outside laughing. *Wait, not laughing,* he realized, *but weeping.*

Ezra stood and carefully walked to the door. As he did so, he heard the wailing louder and immediately recognized the voice. Ezra quickly unbolted the door and found Mulladin kneeling on the ground, shoulders shaking as he sobbed.

"Mulladin!" Ezra said as he sheathed his knife and crouched next to the man.

Not a man, he had to remind himself, *a child in a man's body*. "What's wrong, son?" Ezra asked in a tender voice.

"Where's Mae?" Mulladin violently shook his head and moaned as he rocked back and forth.

That's when Ezra saw a crumpled paper clutched in the boy-man's left hand. "What's this?" he asked as he reached down and gently pulled the paper out of Mulladin's clenched fist. He unfolded it to find an envelope.

Ezra stood and opened it. Inside was a note scrawled in Maely's neat, slanted handwriting. He felt a flash of pride over the girl. She had not known her letters when Ezra took to watching over them, but that was one of the first things he had set to change. And, despite his clumsy efforts to educate Maely, the girl had learned to read and write faster than Jekaran had.

Uncle Ez, the letter began, *I have left to go with Jek on the well-find. I am dressed like a boy, so don't worry, no one will know it's me. I am going to keep an eye on Jek to make sure he minds his manners and comes home safe. Please take care of my brother while I am gone. I know it's a lot to ask, but he will need someone to look after him. I am sorry that I didn't tell you, but I knew you would never have let me go if I had.*

Love,

Maely.

And then there were postscripts with instructions for what Mulladin liked to eat and other routine things the boy-man needed in order to keep him happy and calm.

"Damn it!" Ezra snarled as he crumpled the paper. The girl couldn't have picked a worse time to go chasing after Jekaran.

Maely claimed her reason for going was to keep an eye on Jek, but Ezra knew the truth. She was deeply in love with him, but his thick-witted nephew was totally oblivious to the fact. Ezra had hoped in a few years that he would've caught on, and that the two would marry, but all of those hopes evaporated the moment he heard Kaul had come looking for him.

"Come on, Mull," Ezra said as he reached down and helped the weeping man stand to his feet.

"Where's Mae?" he asked again, his words punctuated with hiccupping sobs.

He gently pulled Mulladin into the house and closed the door behind him. "She went on a trip, with Jek."

That was the wrong thing to say, for as soon as the words fell from Ezra's lips, Mulladin started to wail and shake his head again.

"Golden womb of the goddess!" Ezra swore as his patience escaped him. "Settle down, son!" he snapped, but Mulladin couldn't hear him over the weeping. Ezra closed his eyes, his shoulders drooping, knowing he couldn't leave the boy alone. He was going to have to take Mulladin with him. Ezra drew in a steadying breath. "We're going too!"

Damn that girl, she didn't leave me a choice!

"What?" Mulladin asked as he looked at Ezra through watery, blood-shot eyes.

Ezra smiled and nodded, "We're going to go on a holiday and meet up with Jek and Mae!"

A smile slowly crept onto Mullidan's face, and his sobbing morphed into laughter.

Ezra sighed. "We best be getting you packed and ready to go."

Mulladin scrubbed his eyes with the back of his hairy forearm as he nodded, still hiccupping aftershock sobs. Ezra turned away from him and took two steps toward his bedroom when he was struck by a wave of icy panic. It hit him like a physical force, and, for a few heartbeats, Ezra was paralyzed. Old reflexes resurfaced, and, just as quickly as he froze, he cleared his mind to shove the fear aside to whip around and wrestled the boy-man to the floor just as an explosion rocked the house. Shelves rattled, dishes shattered, the table knocked against the floor like it was asking someone to let it in.

Mulladin cried a frightened screech, and Ezra hissed, "Quiet!"

"ARGENTUS!" a voice called from outside the house.

Devil in hell, he's found me!

Ezra *shooshed* Mulladin one more time and coughed as smoke began to seep into the room. *He's trying to smoke me out,* he realized, *or maybe just burn the house down with me in it.*

"ARGENTUS!" Kaul called again, his voice accompanied by another house-rocking explosion. "I SAW YOU WALK INTO THAT HOUSE! COME OUT AND FACE ME YOU COWARD!"

Thick, black billows began rolling into the room, snuffing out the air and leaving it impossible to breathe. Gasping, Ezra stood and threw open the front door, towing a cough-crying Mulladin with him. He looked up to find Kaul standing a dozen meters away with four armed men. Ezra walked several paces away from the house, glancing over his shoulder to see the roof completely engulfed in flames, and stopped to finish a fit of coughing.

"Time has not been kind to you, old friend," Kaul chuckled. "You're skinny and wrinkled."

"And your eyes still don't match," Ezra coughed.

Kaul grinned and spread his arms as if he were welcoming Ezra to come and embrace him. "Argentus! It's good to see that the agrarian life hasn't dulled your wits."

Ezra noticed the ring on a finger of Kaul's right hand. It was gold with rubies encrusting the band and was capped by an amethyst stone. *I know that talis.* It was a flame ring that had belonged to another of Argentus' friends among the Rikujo lords, a Tolean woman who had once been his lover

"You're burning down my house with Arynda's ring!"

Kaul nodded. "I knew I needed more than just my dread medal to confront you, Argentus. Even at your age, that sword could make you dangerous." Kaul put on a face of mock sorrow. "Poor Arynda never did learn your trick for resisting the fear."

"You killed her," Ezra growled.

"Not at first." Kaul smiled wickedly. "I decided long ago, Argentus, that I would have everything you had and more. So, I started with her."

Although that love affair ended over twenty years ago, Kaul's cruel revelation stung. Ezra had loved Arynda. She was the only woman he had *ever* loved. "You bastard!" Ezra shouted. Besides him, Mulladin covered his ears and began to whimper.

Kaul shrugged. "I make no pretenses to be anything else. Unlike you, I accept what I am."

"So you came here to kill me and take my talis, like you did to Arynda?"

He nodded. "I am going to need it for what I have planned."

"And what is that?" Ezra scoffed.

"I'm glad you asked, because I was really hoping to tell you," he said, his voice dancing with excitement. "See, unlike you, Argentus, I have a grand vision for the destiny of the Rikujo. I want to make it much more than a prestigious thieves' guild. I'm going to make the Rikujo a real power in Shaelar. I want kingdoms and glory for myself and all who follow me."

"Ambitious." Ezra's breathing returned to a steady rhythm as he pushed away the last lingering effects of Kaul's talis. He couldn't let Kaul rile him like that again lest he lose his mental discipline and succumb to the artificial fear caused by the man's dread medal. "You're gonna first have to take control of the Rikujo before you can use its power to win any kingdoms or glory."

Kaul waved his hand dismissively. "Oh, I did that years ago."

The thought of this sadistic monster controlling an organization of hundreds of highly skilled thieves and assassins made Ezra's stomach roll. "So you killed Jaris too?"

"You should've seen him, Argentus—at the end I mean. You wouldn't have recognized him. I broke him, made the man with the reputation for having a heart of stone weep like a child." He smiled. "It was beautiful."

"You must be amassing quite the collection of talises." Ezra ground his teeth. Jaris had been a friend. The man was a conniving thief, a pathological liar, and a skilled assassin, but a friend all the same. In an odd dichotomy of character, he also possessed a strong sense of honor. That was why Ezra arranged for Jaris to become his successor when he fled his life of crime instead of the maniac standing in front of him.

Kaul lifted his left arm to display a silver bracelet wrapped around his wrist. "Quite a remarkable piece of talis craft. The shield has saved my life on several occasions." He laughed as though he were repeating a joke to a friend. "You should've seen Arynda's face when I took one of her fireballs to the face without it so much as singeing my eyebrows."

With so many weapon talises, Kaul was already a terrible threat. Gaining the sword would make him practically invincible. Ezra found himself feeling vindicated in giving it to Jek to smuggle out of the village. "And so you're here to add my sword to your collection?"

"There is no weapon talis more powerful than the legendary sword of the Invincible Shadow!" Kaul said in a mock voice of grandeur. Then his smile disappeared. "Give it to me without a fight, old friend, and I'll let you go back to your *glorious* retirement."

"We both know that's a lie, Kaul."

He shrugged. "Fine, I'm going to kill you either way, but you can mitigate your circumstances by cooperating." He frowned. "Where's the sword?"

"I don't have it," Ezra said and he quickly focused on an image in his mind—a dilapidated fisherman's shack ten miles away. He had discovered it when he had taken Jekaran fishing two summers ago, and, for some reason, the abandoned shack stuck in his memory.

"Do you think me a fool, Argentus?" Kaul snapped. "I know you have it. It may not hold a charge, but there is no way you would willingly part with it."

Another wave of fear slammed into Ezra and he had trouble keeping hold of the image of the shack while countering the artificial fear Kaul directed at him. "I may be old, Kaul, but that pathetic medal of yours still doesn't work on me!"

Kaul smiled again. "I am glad to see that at least something of your old strength remains."

Ezra looked at Kaul's entourage. "You think that they would be of any help to you if I *did* still have the sword? They'd fall before they knew what was happening!"

"WHERE IS IT?" Kaul shouted as he raised his hand again, this time directly at Ezra. Heat distortions bent the air in front of Kaul's palm and Ezra knew that he was out of time. He just hoped there was enough Apeiron left in his earring for two people.

Ezra grinned defiantly. "Rot in hell!"

The last thing Ezra saw was an explosion of fire in front of Kaul's outstretched palm and then everything around him changed in a flash of purple light. A moment later, he found himself lying on grass pock-marked with small rocks. He quickly turned his head to his right, relief washing over him as he saw Mulladin rising to all fours with a thoroughly confused look on his face. Ezra cast a glance to his left and saw the abandoned fishing shack he had fixed on in his mind. It worked! His earring brought him and Mull a distance of ten miles in the blink of an eye. He reached up and rubbed the talis. Transporting two people had cost him dearly; the earring was completely drained.

Ezra stood up and looked to the north. Jeryn, he had to make it to Jeryn. Then he could search for an Apeira well and recharge the talis. But with no supplies or money, that was going to be difficult. He would likely have to sell his displacement talis to get what they needed to make the trip. But what if Kaul came after him again? No, not *if*, but *when*. Kaul *would* come after him. He needed the earring.

That's when a thought occurred to him, one that made him sick. His options were beg or steal, and he had never been any good at begging.

Rasheera forgive me for what I am going to have to do, he prayed.

KAUL DUG through the charred wood of the collapsed house while his men looked on in confusion. He didn't answer their unspoken questions. Digging through the rubble, a little manual labor, was necessary. Some jobs just required personal attention instead of delegating the menial task to another. In this case, if any of his lieutenants discovered the sword talis and bonded with it, he shook his head. No, he wasn't going to allow that happen. Even if there was very little chance it held any Apeiron. If the sword still held a charge, Argentus probably would've attacked him.

He had been afraid of that, which is why he brought four of his best lieutenants, each a master swordsman in his own right. A little caution never hurt anyone.

"It's not here!" He stood and brushed his hands together to clean them of black soot. He had known it was a possibility, but had assumed his old master would've held onto it. *What have you done with my prize, old friend?* Anger welled up inside Kaul and he kicked a pile of rubble. Charred debris flew a dozen feet and a piece of black wood struck his first lieutenant in the back. The man yelped and turned to look at him. Kaul smiled, as though the assault had been deliberate. Causing injury to his allies ensured they remained intimidated, subservient. Uncomfortable.

Kaul glanced down. *If it's not here, maybe there are some clues to where it is.* His foot prodded the debris, pushing it in one direction and then another. Not much remained of the farce Argentus created for himself. Perhaps the fire wasn't such a good idea after all. He clenched his teeth, his jaw setting in a firm line. He took a step, prodded again, and saw a framed image buried in the soot. He bent and picked it up, wiping ash off of the soft, white canvas. It was a picture made by a color trap talis, an image of Argentus and a boy with green eyes. The same young man Kaul had seen earlier in town. From the look of the picture, it was clear Argentus and the boy were family. In fact, they looked like father and son.

"Clever bastard," Kaul said aloud. *He must've given the sword to that boy with the green eyes—his son.* He wanted to laugh at the idea of his old friend being a father. Oh, not just him fathering a child, for Argentus had spread his seed around and was sure to have a few children out in the world. Hell, Kaul probably had a dozen bastards himself given the number of women he had bedded, both willingly and not. No, the humor he found was in the idea of Argentus settling down, raising a child – of The Invincible Shadow changing diapers and speaking sweetly to calm a crying baby.

Kaul looked at his men and barked, "Back to town." The boy was sure to be gone too, but Kaul would find out where he went, and, if none of the inbred villagers of this goddess forsaken place would tell him, then he would burn the town to the ground. Apeiron cost be damned.

Chapter 7

Tending to her garden relaxed and distracted Kairah. She was particularly gifted horticulturally, even amongst the Allosians, all of whom excelled in growing things by virtue of their nature. In Kairah's garden, however, grew an array of rare flowers, some of them the last of their kind. The metallic-gold, five-petal Dawn Stars, the blue luminescent Ice Roses, and, of course, Kairah's personal favorite, the white Spirit Lily, of which she only had one.

These unique, telepathic plants were said to exist only in Allose. Because they absorbed Apeiron instead of sunlight, they were different than regular plants, having a measure of basic sentience. Consequently, they were once believed by the humans to be conduits for speaking to the spirits of their dead loved ones, which of course was ignorant superstition.

The humans, Kairah mourned, the thought spoiling her attempt at self-distraction.

Are you sad, Kairah? The white flower, which she had long ago named Aeva, asked her telepathically.

Kairah nodded as she dipped her fingers into a nearby reflecting pool.

Why? The plant asked in its characteristic child-like tone.

"The synod rejected Jenoc's latest proposal," Kairah said aloud.

That is good, Aeva said.

She withdrew her hand from the pool and sprinkled droplets of water on the stone bench where she sat. "It will not hinder his efforts. In fact, just this morning he confided in me that he has been working secretly for months, without the knowledge of the synod."

What has he been doing?

Kairah was never certain just how much Aeva could comprehend. Her limited sentience made her little more than a child in understanding. Still, Kairah had never hesitated to tell Aeva anything and never tried to dumb it down. She had a connection with the flower, one that was forged when her mother had joined Apeiron. She was a child then, not fully understanding what death was, and so found solace in speaking with the flower. At first she had believed, like the humans, that the Spirit Lily was the soul of her mother. That had been why she named it Aeva, her mother's name. As she grew older though, she had discarded such childish notions. Still, their bond held and was so strong that she could communicate with Aeva even across great distances.

"He has been visiting the human leaders, trying to turn them against each other in war. He also tried," Kairah hesitated, the very thought disturbing her greatly, "reaching for *the other magic.* Fortunately, that failed."

That is bad, Aeva said.

Did Aeva even know what the other magic was? Kairah wasn't sure anyone did. "He plans to start working more aggressively now, showing the humans how to make weapon talises."

A long moment passed before Aeva asked, *What are you going to do, Kairah?*

"Do?" she asked, surprised. "I cannot *do* anything."

Why not, Aeva asked, her flower-mind lacking the understanding to recognize just how ridiculous her question was.

"I have tried persuasion, but Jenoc will not change his mind. I suppose I could try warning the synod, but it would take weeks for me just to be granted an audience with one member of the council to say nothing of the entire synod." Kairah sighed. "This is why I am sad. I do not know what I can do. I do not wish to betray him or bring our family dishonor—" She slowly shook her head, her amethyst-colored hair falling off a bare, alabaster shoulder. "But the humans—"

What? Aeva asked.

"Apeiron desires life for all creatures, even the dangerous ones. Driving the humans to extinction would be like annihilating all the serpents in Shaelar just because many are poisonous. It feels wrong." Kairah sighed in frustration and then stood. "Even to enslave them, like Jenoc proposed to the synod this morning, feels wrong."

Then do something, Aeva gently suggested, and for just one moment her voice sounded like that of Kairah's mother. It gave her pause.

"I suppose I could warn the humans," she finally said. "But leaving Allose secretly would be difficult. And how shall I move about the human lands without drawing their attention? I do not have Jenoc's skill with the Fourth Discipline and so cannot alter my appearance."

The Fourth Discipline, or the Sensory Discipline, was one of the most difficult of the Five Disciplines to learn. It was second in complexity only to the Fifth itself, which was time. In line with Kairah's talent, and like most Allosians, she excelled in spell casting using the First Discipline: creation, as was evidenced by her talent for gardening. Kairah had some talent with the Second, the elemental discipline, and even some use of the Third, which was space. But she was entirely inept in the Fourth Discipline, the ability to influence, communicate through, or deceive the senses of others, something her brother had mastered long ago. In fact, it was only through a disproportionate amount of concentration that she could mentally reply to Aeva, which was the reason she usually answered her by speaking aloud. Fortunately, by the nature of its magic, the Spirit Lily was able to perceive her audible words in spite of having no hearing organs.

You could pass for one of them, Aeva said.

Kairah laughed, "Perhaps they would dismiss my pale skin, but I doubt that they could ignore my hair or eyes.

Use a talis, Aeva suggested.

"I do not possess an illusion pendant, they are too rare." Kairah paused. "However," she said slowly, "there is one in the college's historical treasury." Suddenly Aeva's suggestion to undermine her brother's plans didn't seem so impossible. *But no,* Kairah thought, *it would take just as much time to requisition it for study as it would to gain an audience with the synod.*

Then just take it, Aeva said.

Kairah started. She wasn't directing her thoughts at the Spirit Lily, and therefore hadn't expected a response.

"I cannot," she finally said, shaking her head. "Such a theft would get me expelled from the college."

Then you are going to let the humans die? Aeva asked, her tone honest though the question seemed manipulative.

"I—" Kairah began, but the words died in her throat. Did she really believe in the Will of Apeiron? Did she really think her brother misguided? Could she live the rest of her long life with the genocide of a species on her conscience, when she had the knowledge and power to prevent the extinction? That last question stung her. The wrongness of what her brother was attempting barreled over her every sense. Kairah hooked a lock of her long, amethyst-colored hair behind an ear. "I have no choice, do I?" she asked Aeva.

Why do you so often ask me questions for which you already know the answers? The Spirit-Lily's telepathic tone communicated a sigh.

She would do it, Kairah decided. She would steal the illusion pendant from the College of Disciplines and leave Allose to warn the humans of Jenoc's plans, no matter what the cost. It was the right thing to do.

See, Aeva said smugly.

Chapter 8

Kairah's thoughts were not on the lecture. She heard what was being said, but retained only occasional pieces, something she did deliberately in case she was called upon to answer a question. She sat on an ivory bench in the third seating tier of the stadium-like lecture hall. The light from the noon-day sun poured down through the purple, dome-shaped skylight dappling the chamber with an assortment of refracted hues.

The lecture she had opted into for the morning was one on the evolution of talis crafting. While initially it had sounded interesting, it turned out to be nothing more than a dry recitation of names, dates, and places with little in the way of the actual science behind making a talis.

But intellectual stimulation was not the reason Kairah had reserved a seat in Elder Tardun's lecture hall. No, she was here to steal the college's only illusion pendant, kept in the historical treasure room, the corridor to which opened up directly behind Elder Tardun's lectern. She eyed the arched doorway and the soft light of the hallway pouring in from beyond.

You are nervous, Aeva observed.

Of course I am nervous! Kairah mentally snapped and she felt an immediate backlash of regret. *I am sorry. It is just that I have never done anything like this before.* The flower seemed to send a wordless communication of patient understanding for which she was grateful.

It was true. Like the majority of Allosians, Kairah had no experience with crime, it being something of a rarity among their kind. Her brother once said that was because Allosians had everything they could want and possessed no motive for stealing. He also had said it was because of their enlightened and superior nature over the other races in Shaelar. While that ran counter to her understanding of the will of the Apeiron, she couldn't dispute the facts Jenoc cited.

Kairah couldn't deny that her brother was right. Humans were by far the most petty, selfish, and violent of the four races inhabiting Shaelar, as was evidenced by their near constant warring. And when they weren't at war, smaller scale violence abounded in their cities and villages. The Vorakk and the Ursaj were violent too, but most of their killing was the result of hunting animals for food or defending themselves from other predators. Oh, they killed each other too, just not nearly as often as the bloodthirsty humans.

But Kairah was not a lawless human and so, for her, criminal methods and motives were a foreign concept. In a way this gave her the advantage. For as alien as it was for Kairah to steal, she knew that her instructor and classmates were just as inexperienced in expecting and preventing crime. Thus, they would never suspect what she was about to attempt.

"It was when Sorlan of Trallister welcomed the humans to Shaelar that we entered into the age of innovation that produced most of our modern talises," she heard Elder Tardun say. "And so ends part one of our lecture. Tomorrow we will have a recitation of facts from three students selected at random after which we will begin part two."

It was over, the lecture was over. A panic thrilled Kairah as she watched the other students begin to rise from their seats. *This is it*, she thought, *now is my chance.*

She rose, carefully smoothed her lavender silk dress and began slowly descending to the lecture floor where a group of students clustered around the lectern, each waiting their turn to ask Elder Tardun questions. *They'll be the perfect distraction.* Her muscles grew rigid, her skin alive with tingling pulses, and she licked her lips with each measured step.

You are doing well, Aeva encouraged.

Kairah wasn't so sure.

As one foot followed by the other eased off the final step, she felt like her lungs would collapse. Still, she pressed herself forward to blend herself in with the other students, lingering on the far edge of the group, the corridor within eyeshot. She listened as a polite debate began between Elder Tardun and one of the students. Their voices went back and forth, but she couldn't decipher what they were each saying. Something about human aggression and Allosian execution mandates. Kairah didn't care. The timing was perfect.

She slowly rounded the lectern, easing herself closer to the corridor, and gently rotated her shoulders.

Elder Tardun called her name.

Kairah froze, heart pounding so hard she was certain it echoed throughout the entire stadium.

"Kairah," Elder Tardun repeated.

She took a deep breath to calm herself—it didn't work—and turned to face her instructor and twenty-seven of her fellow students. "Yes, Elder?" she answered, hoping her voice didn't sound as shaky as it felt.

Elder Tardun motioned at the student he had been debating. "Perhaps you know enough of your brother's research to be able to settle a question for us?"

"I know much of my brother's work," Kairah answered with forced calm.

"Then answer us this," Elder Tardun began, "are any of the three modern human kingdoms still actively hostile to the Allosians? And if so, which ones?"

Kairah could feel the stares of the other students as they fell silent in expectation of her answer. To her horror, her mind suddenly went blank. The moment stretched, and her palms grew sticky, until Aeva's voice inside her mind said.

Is the answer not, Haeshala?

"Haeshala," she said. "They are the only human nation whose mandate to kill or capture Allosians has never been rescinded."

"Haeshala," Elder Tardun repeated thoughtfully. He then turned to re-engage the student he had been debating.

Kairah sighed inwardly as all eyes returned to her instructor.

You are welcome, Aeva said.

Kairah eyed the group of students warily as she slowly stepped through the arched doorway behind the lectern. Her heart skipped a beat as she realized the first hurdle of her plan had been overcome. She looked around, making certain she was alone in the corridor and then she broke into a swift stride. Her ankle-length silk dress *swished* at her feet as she hurried toward a bend in the corridor. She turned the corner, pressed herself against the wall, and closed her eyes. *I made it, I made it.* She gulped in air and listened as the rhythm of her heart slowed. She eased her eyelids open and glanced down the hall. Empty. Good.

Again she looked down the corridor to twenty-foot double doors of white stone set in the terminal wall. Kairah rushed toward the massive entry and paused to listen. When she was satisfied that the treasury was empty, she reached for the ornate golden handle and turned it. The door on the right cracked open. The treasury wasn't locked; Kairah had guessed right about her people's criminal naiveté working both ways.

The dome-shaped Historical Treasury was similar to the college's lecture halls, but twice as large. Its walls were lined with shelves packed with cubicle glass containers or large leather-bound tomes. An ivory staircase spiraled up from the center of the room, granting access to a dozen split level balconies and the storage shelves that lined the interior walls of the chamber.

There are certainly a lot of artifacts in here, Aeva said, her mental voice thick with wonder.

"Yes," Kairah whispered. "I need the treasury's catalog or it will take the better part of the day for me to find the pendant."

She strode into the chamber, leaving the door open in case she would need to make an expeditious retreat. She descended three stairs that dipped into the concave floor of the treasury, and quickly located a fluted pedestal topped with a glass orb. Kairah touched the orb and willed the record talis to show her the location of the illusion pendant. A disembodied image of her standing in the chamber formed inside her mind and her view flew, as though she was a bird, to the third level where a large glass case mounted on the wall. Inside of the glass case was a cerulean, teardrop-shaped pendant with an amethyst shard encased inside the jewel itself. Kairah's eyes snapped open and she drew her hand back from the orb. She glanced up to the third level and, finding the very same glass case she had seen in vision, turned and began to quickly climb the ivory staircase.

As Kairah wound her way up to the third level—a height of fifty feet —she caught sight of two statues just below the staircase. They were flatted against the wall opposite the door through which she had entered. The statues were a curious piece of art – twenty-feet-tall humanoid figures that looked to be carved entirely from glass. They were faceless, but had a single amethyst sphere set where their eyes should have been. Kairah had never seen anything like them. Were they new? She didn't know for she hadn't been in the treasury since she was a child, some seventy years ago. The statues were beautiful. Quite possibly the most gorgeous work of sculpted art she had ever seen.

I did not know that they stored anything but talises in this room, she thought to Aeva.

They frighten me, Aeva replied.

That had not been the reaction Kairah expected, but her attention abruptly shifted as she reached the third level and spotted the glass case containing the illusion pendant. She stepped off the staircase and hurried past three large storage shelves. Kairah's warped reflection stared back at her as she leaned over the lid. Inside, placed decoratively on a red velvet pillow, lay a clear, tear-dropped shaped gem about the size of her thumb. Etched into the face of the jewel was the colorless image of an open eye behind which was the amethyst shard encased inside the gem.

Kairah reverently traced the glass with her fingers. *It's beautiful,* she thought. Aeva didn't respond. Instead, she felt apprehension flow from the Spirit Lily. The emotion mixed with her own feelings and caused her to quickly withdraw her hand from the glass. With renewed urgency, she quickly slid her fingers across the underside of the case and caught on two metal clasps. With her thumbs pressed against the side for counter-weight, the tips of her index fingers raised the metallic flap, startling her as it clicked against the other side of the enclosure. She paused, looking around the chamber, frightened someone might have heard her. Satis-fied she remained alone, she turned back to the jewel, carefully lifting the glass cover.

Kairah was about to reach down to take the pendant when a sound from the floor below gave her pause. It was an odd sound, one that she had never heard before, a high pitched whine rising to an almost inaudible crescendo. The closest she could compare it to was the sound of an empty talis receiving a new Apeiron charge. Without closing the case, she quickly scanned the levels below, her heart beating so fast that she thought it would explode. Her pulse began to slow as she could find no source for the noise. She dismissed it and returned her attention to the case.

Kairah quickly reached in and snatched up the illusion pendant, then gently and quietly lowered the glass cover. Wrapping the pendant's platinum chain around her hand, she rushed back toward the helical staircase, hiked up her dress a few inches, and began to descend as quickly as she could. As she reached the bottom of the stairs, a flash of purple light washed over the chamber. Kairah stopped and whipped her head around. To her shock, she found one of the glass, humanoid-shaped sculptures moving toward her. Its single amethyst eye was now glowing, sending beautiful refracted light throughout the sculpture's entire body.

Not a sculpture, Kairah realized with a stab of panic, *but a golem.* Not a golem of clay or stone, as she had read about, but a golem made from crystal, one apparently with orders to protect the inventory of the talis museum.

RUN! Aeva mentally shouted.

Kairah tore herself out of her panicked stupor and began sprinting toward the exit. The sound of the second crystal golem waking thrilled Kairah with another wave of fear and she redoubled her speed. As she barreled down the corridor leading back to the lecture hall, she unwound the pendant's delicate chain from around her hand and slipped it over her head. Immediately she felt a connection to the talis and intuitively understood how it worked.

Cloak me! She mentally shouted.

Immediately the colors of her vision muted, and her reflection vanished from the hall's shiny marble floor. She could still see herself in regular color if she looked down at her body, but, beyond her, it was as if she were looking through a foggy, color-suppressing lens.

Kairah slowed and turned back to look at the door to the talis museum. The two crystal golems stood in front of the white stone doors, their amethyst jewel-eyes intensely shining. They halted and appeared to be scanning the hallway. Relief washed over Kairah at their hesitation. *It worked.*

Kairah, Aeva said in a warning tone.

Just then the amethyst jewel-eyes of each of the crystal golems changed color from purple to red, and one of them turned to look directly at her. Immediately the second golem did likewise and the two sentries resumed their hurried march down the hallway.

Impossible! Kairah thought.

RUN! Aeva projected.

Panic impelled Kairah forward, and she broke into a desperate run, turned the corner and exploded into the lecture hall. Most of the students had vacated the stadium-like chamber, but Elder Tardun still stood behind his lectern debating the same student. Parchment on the lectern blasted into the air as she blew past, both Elder Tardun and his student starting at the ghostly cyclone. A heartbeat later Kairah heard her teacher and fellow student gasp, the sound immediately followed by the duel cadence of heavy footfalls.

"Someone has robbed the museum!" she heard Elder Tardun call.

Kairah took the stairs leading up through the benches two at a time. When she reached the top landing she risked a glance over her shoulder. What she saw accelerated her already racing heart. The two crystal golems could not fit in the narrow aisle of ascending stairs, and so they were systematically climbing the long stone benches, their weights causing the benches to crack, break, and crumble. They had fanned out, one golem climbing on each side of the stair aisle. Stone dust exploded into the air with each step they took, their cycloptic crimson eyes tingeing the dust blood red.

Kairah hurled herself through the exit and into the adjoining hall, nearly colliding with a group of curious students amassing outside the lecture hall. She made a sharp right to avoid the crowd and sprinted down the hallway. An explosion of stone mixed with frightened screams told her the crystal golems had exited the lecture hall and entered the corridor. She glanced over her shoulder and found both automatons lumbering in her direction.

How is it that they can see me? Kairah desperately thought to Aeva.

Heat, was Aeva's prompt reply.

How had she known that? Kairah wondered. *Heat,* she mentally repeated in acknowledgement. The revelation rang true, sending a thrill of relief through her. Although she was not a master of the Second Discipline, elemental manipulation, calling up a chill wind to hide her body heat would be a simple thing. She was about to begin the casting when a realization doused the flame of her hope. If she cast while cloaked, any Allosian would be able to see her expend the needed Apeiron.

All spell casting required that the caster release a proportional amount of Apeiron to make the spell work. That flared the caster's Apeiron aura, making them shine in the eyes of other casters. She need only expend a little amount for a simple elemental spell, but in a corridor filled with two dozen fellow students, it would be enough to give her away.

Kairah's panic resurged and she began to glance desperately out the tall windows lining the outer wall of the building. She couldn't hide, she couldn't cast, and, glancing over her shoulder, she saw the crystal golems gaining on her at a frightening rate. She redoubled her run and quickly turned a corner. The hall opened up into the college's antechamber. It was another domed room as big as one of the lecture halls serving as the navigational plexus of the building. In the center of the chamber was a thirty-foot-tall, multi-tiered decorative fountain.

I cannot keep this up forever, she thought in despair. Virtually all Allosians were perfect physical specimens until the day they died, but, even so, none but the trained athletes could hold a sprint long term. And Kairah knew she couldn't sprint the requisite twenty miles she would need to run in order to leave Allose. She huffed, struggling to catch her breath and ignored the burn in her legs. She couldn't stop.

Upon reaching the center of the chamber, she leapt into the basin of the fountain in order to shave some distance off of her dash toward the college's front doors. The move proved to be folly as she slipped and fell forward into the shallow water. Kairah quickly rose up on her hands and knees, sputtering and coughing as she wiped strands of soggy amethyst hair from her face. *This was it,* she despaired. *If the golems do not catch me, then everyone who saw the splash will.*

She struggled to pull herself up, slipping into the water and falling on her back with a silent *oomph.* She was about to sit up, but the water-distorted image of a crystal golem standing above the fountain made her rein in her reflex. To her surprise, the glass automaton did not reach down into the pool to pull her out. It just stood there, head moving from side to side, searching for her. As she stared, waiting, she felt a tingling in her fingers and realized the fountain's water was cold. Not ice water cold, but chilled enough for her extremities to be numbing.

Though her lungs burned, Kairah held her breath and remained as still as she could. Her intuition paid off as a moment later the crystal golem moved out of her view. When she could feel it lumbering away, Kairah launched herself out of the water, gasping desperately as she scrambled out of the fountain's wide basin. She slipped a couple of times on the marble floor of the chamber before her bare feet caught some traction. She must've still been difficult to see, because it was a full ten seconds before she heard the golems resume chasing her.

Kairah made it to the towering, arched twin portals of the college's front entrance and used the full force of her momentum to push the door open, hitting a fellow student in the face as he tried to enter. The force threw him to the side of the archway, and he covered his nose as blood began to pour from the nostrils.

"Sorry," Kairah caught herself saying aloud. *Foolish,* she scolded herself, but then realized her speaking an apology to a half-dazed student was the least of her mistakes. By now, dozens of people had witnessed the effects of her escape, even if they hadn't seen her directly, and peacekeepers would be descending on the College of Disciplines at any moment.

I have to lose them now or I will never make it out of the city, she thought.

Aqueduct, Aeva suggested.

She cast her eyes toward a public water well a hundred meters down the street. The well was a portal to the city's aqueduct, the subterranean waterway providing a quick and secret exit from the city. She would be underwater for a while, but she could hold her breath for several minutes. Behind Kairah, two crystal golems clamored through the College's front entrance. She held her breath, a single *thump* of her heart screaming in her ear, and one golem fixed his crimson jewel-eye on her.

She was out of time.

Kairah exploded into a renewed sprint toward the well and wove through people and statues, hoping to slow the golems down. She threw a look over her shoulder and smiled. The distance between her and her pursuers grew with every step. *Thirty feet, almost there.*

She was going to make it.

She winced and toppled to the ground, her side shrieking in pain. An angry welt hardened under her shirt, and, as she lowered the material, she noticed the chunk of marble resting in front of her, debris hurled through the air as the golems mowed over statues behind her. Kairah gritted her teeth and pulled herself to her feet. The pounding steps behind her were gaining, she couldn't stop now.

The well was now only twenty-five feet away.

Then twenty.

Fifteen.

Twelve.

Her lungs burned in her chest, the bruise on her side crippling, and Kairah felt lightheaded, like she couldn't take another step. She huffed, her vision struggling to focus the blur of colors before her, and then she slammed into the circular lip of the well. Without looking back, she launched herself into the dark shaft.

It took her longer than expected to hit the water and, when she did, the cold of it nearly drove the air from her lungs. Still, she held on, and, after a protracted three minutes, she surfaced in a dark tunnel. Gasping, Kairah swam over to the wall of the aqueduct and held onto a small protrusion in the otherwise smooth stone. She didn't know its function, but didn't care. For the moment she was safe.

Kairah willed the illusion pendant to drop its cloak and, after taking a moment to spell cast her wound closed, began swimming against a mild current for another twenty minutes. Eventually, she was forced to re-submerge and when she surfaced again, she found herself in a dark chamber, the echoes of her splashing telling her it was massive. *Must be some kind of underground lake,* she thought. She swam to the rocky shore and climbed out of the water. Kairah collapsed to the ground and closed her eyes. She couldn't hear anyone or anything behind her, but she doubted they gave up the chase. She just couldn't go any further.

Are you alright? Aeva asked.

The Spirit Lily's apprehension soaked through her. "Yes," Kairah said, her voice hoarse. "That did not at all go as we had planned."

Life seldom does, Aeva said. Again she sounded like Kairah's mother.

"I meant to have time to return for you." Her voice echoed through the cave, and she shuddered.

Do not worry, Kairah, Aeva said. *I will still be able to hear your thoughts so long as you do not travel too far away from Allose.*

"How far is too far?" Kairah asked as she rose to all fours and sat on her haunches.

Aeva did not answer.

After another moment of rest, Kairah stood and began working her way up a moss-covered incline until she was high above the water. She followed a constructed trail for what she guessed was a mile before light began to leak into the cavern. The tension in her shoulders eased, she was getting closer.

After another mile, Kairah emerged from a small opening into daylight. She looked toward the mountains and saw—nothing. Allose was not there. She sighed. Somewhere behind her lie the boundaries of the city's massive cloaking spell making it so that she could no longer see her home.

Kairah settled on a nearby rock and gathered her thoughts. *I did it! The first phase of the plan is complete."* The elation faded. *Now what?*

For the first time in over a decade, she was away from the Mother Shard. The distance meant she'd have to ration her Apeiron reserve until she could find another Aeose. She chuckled. *That means I am going to have to sleep,* something Kairah had not done in years. Normally, it would be a difficult thing, as she was not accustomed to it, but the excitement and exertion of escaping Allose had primed her for it.

Kairah checked the charge of the illusion pendant. Fortunately, it was still full, so she would be able to hide from danger or disguise herself when she found a human city. After about an hour of sitting, Kairah began walking across the sparse grass of the foothills until she found the lee of a small hill where she decided to spend the night. As the sun set, she tested her connection with Aeva and was glad to find it still strong. That brought her a measure of comfort, and she heard herself say "Good night, Mother" to Aeva as she drifted off.

Good night, Aeva replied, and again she sounded like Kairah's mother.

CHAPTER 9

Jenoc hoisted his blue robe higher on his waist, careful of the embroidered fringe as he toured Elder Tardun's ruined lecture hall. The chamber looked as though a ground quake had ripped it open with chunks of marble strewn everywhere and the semi-circular benches riddled with cracks and breaks, others missing altogether. He grinned; the crystal golems were an impressive piece of talis craftsmanship to be sure.

Jenoc eyed the two automatons flanking the chamber's entrance at the top of the stairs. Looking at them patiently waiting in their dormant state, Jenoc was impressed at just how nondescript they appeared.

It must have been a total surprise to Kairah when they awoke and began chasing her, he thought.

Kairah.

Jenoc was still trying to process the fact that his younger sister had been the one to rob the Historical Treasury. It certainly had been out of character for her; Kairah always being so careful to respect rules and observe traditions. The others, of course, had not yet realized who their thief was. Jenoc was only able to guess it was her when he found out what had been stolen—an illusion pendant.

This is my fault, he chided himself. Had he not confided in her this never would have happened. Still, how was Jenoc to have foreseen Kairah would resort to such drastic means? He knew how she felt about his plans, for she had tried to persuade him to abandon his work. *She never could understand.* Bound by the traditions of their mother, that Apeiron actually had a sentient will, Kairah had always seen the world differently from Jenoc, some would say more benevolently. Jenoc had long tried to persuade his sister that the world was only a thing of forces and counter-forces, of varied life forms competing for survival. A contest that had no rules except one: the strong live and the weak die. "Master Jenoc," a voice called.

Jenoc brushed strands of pale, ice-colored hair out of his face as he turned to see one of the peacekeepers approaching him. When the man was within a few paces, he stopped and bowed. "Master Jenoc, Lady Kairah."

Jenoc looked to his right where the perfect apparition he created of his sister dipped her head in deference. Jenoc smiled, the illusion he conjured to protect Kairah appeared to be working. No one could suspect her involvement if they saw her touring the aftermath of the crime scene with him.

The back of Jenoc's head throbbed, no doubt from the strain of his concentration. It was a difficult thing to produce convincingly, even for a master of the Fourth Discipline. Every moment Jenoc had to sustain the phantom was like bearing a heavy load, made all the heavier any time he had to make the illusion interact with others.

"Dear sister," Jenoc spoke quickly. "I think you should return home. I fear today's events have left you exhausted."

The apparition nodded, flashed a smile at the peacekeeper, and then retreated from the lecture hall. Jenoc willed the phantom to turn down an empty corridor until she was out of sight and then he released the spell, wavering on his bare feet from the wash of relief.

"Are you well, Master Jenoc?" the peacekeeper asked.

Jenoc massaged his closed eyes and nodded. "I too am weary from the day's events," he lied. "Thank you for your concern, Captain."

"Elder Jariel said you wished to speak with me."

"Indeed," Jenoc nodded. "I believe I can help with your apprehension of the Historical Treasury's thief."

"How is that?"

Jenoc turned to look up at the crystal golems. "I believe I can spell cast a way for those two talises to continue their pursuit, even beyond the confines of Allose, if necessary."

The peacekeeper looked surprised, "How?"

Jenoc flashed an indulgent smile. "Forgive me, Captain, but it takes my teaching an entire season here just to acquaint my students with the basics of such a spell."

The peacekeeper nodded thoughtfully.

"Suffice it to say," Jenoc went on, "I can set them to the task."

"You really believe the thief would leave Allose?" the peacekeeper asked, a touch of skepticism in his tone.

Jenoc intentionally paused for dramatic effect and then leaned in closer to the peacekeeper. "Captain," he began in a low, conspiratorial tone. "I met with the Synod earlier today, and, while I cannot say what we spoke of, I will tell you part of our discussion included rumors that someone was giving the human nation of Haeshala powerful talises."

The peacekeeper captain looked shocked. "An Allosian?"

Jenoc slowly nodded. "If that is true, then we want to take every precaution to ensure this thief is apprehended, and we cannot discount the possibility that they will leave Allose."

The peacekeeper captain looked up at the two crystal golems. "Very well. Do what you need to. Just make certain they do not cause further mayhem or destruction."

"May I then have their command word?"

The peacekeeper captain nodded curtly and whispered, "Elayse."

Jenoc nodded respectfully and watched the peacekeeper turn and walk away to rejoin a group of his subordinates. After lingering for a moment, Jenoc climbed the chamber stairs until he stood between the two motionless golems. He extended his arms outward to touch the talises simultaneously and then formed a mental connection with both of them.

Elayse, Jenoc said with his mind.

Both golems responded with a wordless acknowledgement.

Jenoc projected upon them a memory of Kairah and showed them her distinct Apeiron aura. He then curtly commanded, *Find this woman! She will be without the confines of Allose, likely making her way to one of the human cities. Split up and search to the east and west for her. She will be disguised by the illusion pendant she stole, so use all of your senses to locate her. When you apprehend her, alert me, but do NOT bring her back to Allose!*

Jenoc felt the crystal golems acknowledge his instructions.

And one more thing, Jenoc added. *Your new command word is Sirus. Forget all others.*

Both golems paused a moment before confirming they understood Jenoc was their new master.

Now go, Jenoc ordered, and the two glass-like automatons exploded into motion as suddenly as a lightning strike. They left the lecture hall, their heavy footfalls mixing with the startled expressions from students.

Jenoc lingered in the College of Disciplines for a few minutes and then purposefully made his way through the streets of Allose, heading for the large, ivory tower where he and Kairah lived. As he walked, his mind involuntarily manufactured a number of horrible things that could happen to his sister.

She does not know the humans like I do, he thought. *Her altruistic naiveté is bound to get her injured or killed.* Sending the golems to apprehend Kairah had been as much about her safety as it had been to safeguard his plans. Despite their disagreement on rightful Allosian dominance, he loved his sister. She was his only family, after all, and they shared a closeness of the kind born of shared tribulation.

Jenoc entered the ivory tower, began climbing the stairs to the fourth floor, and, in less than a minute, found himself standing in his living quarters. The large apartment was circular in shape with walls made of smooth seamless alabaster, as though the whole thing had been sculpted out of a solid piece of white marble. Several light talises woke as he walked through the apartment, casting the room in a soft, white light. Jenoc didn't tarry or relax as he usually might, but instead went straight to the atrium located in the center of their apartment. He opened the glass door and stepped out into the garden—Kairah's garden. Immediately, Jenoc was greeted by an aromatic cocktail of sweet smelling flowers. He breathed in the symphony of fragrances that Kairah had so carefully worked to produce. *Mother's Smile,* she had called it.

Jenoc followed a flagstone path as it wound through a tangle of decorative flora, emerging into a circular clearing with a shallow reflecting pool. From the center of the garden, one could be convinced that they were not inside a stone tower at all, so dense was the greenery. Yes, Kairah was superbly talented in the First Discipline—creation. Even more so than their mother had been, and she was considered great among the practitioners of botanical spell casting.

Jenoc scanned the flora before fastening his eyes on a single, white flower. It was Kairah's Spirit Lily.

"Where is Kairah?" he demanded.

The Spirit Lily did not respond.

"I know that you are still in contact with her," he warned.

Again, there was no response.

"Very well," he said as he drew closer. "If you will not tell me where Kairah is, then at least relay this message to her." Jenoc shifted to communicating solely with his thoughts to ensure the Spirit Lily understood him. *Tell Kairah I am not angry, but that I am afraid for her. The world is more dangerous than she realizes, and humans are not to be trusted. Return now and all will be as it was. Only I know she stole the illusion pendant, and if she will return, I can return it to the college without them having to know who took it.* He hesitated and the added in complete sincerity, *Please.*

Although the Spirit Lily didn't respond, Jenoc felt it acknowledge his message and was certain it was relaying it to his sister.

He lingered a moment, awaiting a possible reply from Kairah, but none came.

Very well, he thought to himself. *Perhaps this experience will open your eyes, sister. Perhaps seeing the depravity of mankind firsthand will awaken you to the truth of things. Perhaps you will come to see the need for their removal from Shaelar.*

Yes, he nodded as he left the atrium to fix a remedy for his lingering migraine. He would allow his sister to wander the world of the humans for a short while, at least until the golems found her. Maybe that was the only way she could be made to understand.

CHAPTER 10

Night had fallen on the well-finder's camp and Jekaran found himself stretching out on his bedroll somewhat earlier than usual. He yawned, tears welling in the corners of his eyes. The grueling, monotonous walking of the day only broke for brief moments when Gymal needed to relieve himself. Six or seven breaks lasting a mere five minutes hadn't done much to relieve his aching feet.

Jekaran snorted a laugh to himself as he rubbed his reddened toes. Rumor had it Gymal, although only a score of years older than Jekaran, had developed the *Old-Man's-Pissing Disease* at a young age. Contrary to its name, the malady made it difficult and painful for a man to relieve himself, resulting in more frequent and urgent trips to the latrine. Or, in this case, the trees on the side of the road. In retrospect, Jekaran supposed the number of times they halted *had* amounted to about the traditional length of a worker's noon-day break. That, combined with Gymal's expressions of discomfort, and the occasional yelp from behind a curtain of trees, more than made up for the lunch Jekaran had missed.

Uncle Ez would have a hearty laugh at Gymal's expense when Jekaran shared the story. He smiled as he rolled over to find a position comfortable enough to invite sleep, but the thought of his uncle quickly pushed away any good humor he had been feeling.

Was Ez safe? He wondered, and not for the first time.

Since leaving Genra, Jekaran's fear that the man with mismatching eyes was following him retreated into the background, as he hadn't seen any sign of pursuit. Of course, these were Rikujo elite. The very word Rikujo meant shadow, so Jekaran couldn't be sure if he would even know they were coming for him, but still the fear faded the further his company traveled.

But the concern for his uncle's safety grew. If no one was following him, did that mean they followed Ez? What if they caught up to him? Did the Invincible Shadow have any tricks left?

Jekaran grimaced. His uncle had implied as much.

He rested his hands on his palms and glanced toward the cook-fire where some men were finishing their dinner of chicken legs and over-cooked rice. The dry sawdust taste lingered on his tongue; if he wasn't so hungry, he would have tossed his plate in the fire. Definitely the worst part of the well-find, even worse than dealing with Gymal.

Jekaran smiled ruefully, and then noticed the boy, Lyam watching him from his spot around the fire. He tilted his head and narrowed his eyes just as Lyam diverted his eyes to the fire and shifted his weight on the log.

Does he know me? He had caught Lyam staring at him periodically ever since they left Genra. Something in the boy's eyes resonated as familiar with Jekaran, but, for the life of him, he couldn't decide how he knew him. He shrugged. Maybe it was just a case of natural gravitation, they *were* the youngest in a company comprised of grown men. Jekaran sat up on his elbow and locked eyes with Lyam. The boy started, stood from the rock where he sat, and hurried away from the cook-fire, leaving his half-eaten drumstick on the ground.

That was odd, Jekaran thought as he lay back down, his arms crossed behind his head. For some reason, as he drifted off to sleep, an image of Maely flashed before his mind.

"VORAKK!" The cry tore Jekaran from the world of nonsensical dreams. Urgent bell tolling followed a heartbeat later, prompting Jekaran to abruptly sit up and throw off his wool blanket. He glanced around as other men of the company jumped to their feet and drew their knives, or strung their bows. Having nothing but a hunting knife himself, Jekaran briefly entertained the idea of digging out Ez's sword, but his uncle's emphatic insistence that he not touch it, combined with the thought of giving Gymal an opportunity to have him arrested, immediately squashed the notion.

"What's going on?" he heard Gymal shout to no one in particular.

Jekaran scanned the camp until he caught a sight that set his heart beating faster. Three indistinct human-like shapes were quickly moving away from the embers of the camp cook-fire. The shapes would have been completely invisible save for the light of several low-burning lamps hanging from posts surrounding the fire pit. A man cried out in pain as one of the shapes took a swipe at him. He attacked back with an awkward swing of his hatchet, but failed to connect. The man stumbled to the ground, a long gash marring the left side of his face.

Jekaran stumbled to his feet, serrated hunting knife in his right hand as he sprinted toward the center of camp. A blur of translucent motion appeared in front of him and he swept the blade in a wide arc. The shape launched into the air at the precise moment, and Jekaran's blade missed. The *thud* of something behind him shook the ground, and Jekaran pitched forward as a violent shove sent him to his knees while his weapon slipped from his grip. He instinctively rolled to spring back up, the vision of his sparring sessions with Mull dancing in his memories. He snatched his knife from the ground and gave chase after the shape, now barely visible in the shadows of the outer camp.

The sounds of commotion and fighting faded behind him, and Jekaran thought he heard a woman call his name as he ran after his near invisible quarry. He put the oddity out of his mind as his eyes fixed on a small, jagged line of luminescent green hovering several paces in front of him. As Jekaran gained, the glowing, jagged line became clearer.

Blood.

The realization hit Jekaran like a blow to the head. *The glowing line of green must be a wound.* Jekaran immediately made the gash his point of focus, the strategic feints of the creature ineffectual as he now kept it in his sights. They were now completely clear of the camp and running through an open field toward a dark mass on the horizon Jekaran recognized as the forest's border.

If it reaches the forest, I'll lose it. The realization prompted Jekaran into a faster sprint and he began to close the distance between them. When he had closed to just four paces away, Jekaran lurched to his right, a small incline leading directly to the creature. He leapt and slammed hard into something hard and leathery. Both he and the creature crashed to the ground and rolled. As they struggled, Jekaran felt something sharp clamp down on his arm. Pain like fire burned on his skin along with a warm wetness he knew must be blood.

Jekaran groped at the ground for his knife, which he had dropped again, and settled for a rock the size of his hand. He raised it and drove it down onto the blurred shape still latched on his arm. Immediately, the teeth withdraw from his flesh, and he jerked his arm away while slamming the rock onto the monster's head. It released a guttural groan and stopped struggling. Jekaran dropped the weapon and pinned the creature on its back.

He quickly found his knife and brought the blade to the monster's scaly throat.

It was then Jekaran realized it had become fully visible. He gasped as he looked down at the creature's face.

Although shaped like a person, the thing had bronze, scaly skin and small bone-like spikes protruding along the line of its lower jaw. The same bone-like spikes ridged its brows, and its nose was little more than two tiny holes at the end of a small muzzle. Two yellow eyes with slits for pupils focused on Jekaran, and the Vorakk made a noise low in its throat that sounded to Jekaran like a cross between a hiss and growl.

"Don't move!" Jekaran growled as he pressed the blade harder against the creature's throat. Though softer than the rest of its skin, the Vorakk's throat was tough like leather, and Jekaran knew he'd have to use a disproportionate amount of force if he wanted to cut it.

"Reka, human boy, just kill!" the creature said in a guttural tone that ended like a hiss.

Jekaran faltered for a second, but then tightened his grip on the handle of his knife and demanded, "Why were you in our camp?"

"Food, aka," the creature said.

Jekaran's stomach turned. Had the three Vorakk raiders been intent on eating them? "Well, you won't be tasting human flesh tonight!"

The Vorakk made a noise Jekaran thought sounded like a scoff. "Isk, not human meat, stupid boy! Vorakk want rest of meal. Cooked bird, yes?"

Jekaran's anger cooled, replaced by surprised pity. "You wanted our leftovers?"

The sounds of shouting grew louder, evoking a shift in the Vorakk's stare. He looked beyond Jekaran and hissed again, "Aek, do not make Vorakk a slave! Just kill!"

Jekaran slowly withdrew his knife from the Vorakk's throat as he warily stood. He stepped back, cast a glance over his shoulder at his approaching fellows and then looked back at the creature on the ground. It stared at him with a clinical detachment Jekaran could only guess was the Vorakk's version of surprise.

"Go!" Jekaran snapped as he waved his hand at the empty darkness beyond.

The Vorakk slowly nodded, the now familiar blur of motion, like heat lines, stood up. Jekaran took a step back and raised the knife in warning. But the creature didn't attack. It lingered for the briefest of moments, and then the luminescent green line of the Vorakk's open wound moved away before fading altogether.

"Jek!" a concerned voice called out.

Jekaran turned to greet a group of four men led by the tall Vestus.

"You okay, Jek?" Vestus asked as he slowed out of his jog.

He nodded as he gingerly touched the bite on his arm. "It got away."

Vestus nodded. "So did the others. But Torkas wounded one of them pretty bad. I'll be surprised if it isn't already dead, what with all the glowing blood it lost."

For some reason that made him feel nauseous. *They had just wanted our leftovers.* He couldn't help but grimace.

"Sure you're okay, Jek?" Vestus asked again, his eyes falling on his bloody forearm.

"Yeah." He forced a smile. "It's not deep."

"Well, be sure to clean it out. Who knows what those lizards have been eating." Vestus cast a glance over his shoulder. "Lord Gymal will want a report from you."

Jekaran groaned.

"I know," Vestus said sympathetically. "Best to get it over with."

Jekaran nodded as he tore a strip of cloth from his tunic and tied it around the wound. As Jekaran fell in with the group, he noticed Lyam was one of the men that came to his aid, and eased next to the boy to say hello.

"Hi," the boy muttered. He wore an oversized hat, a set of old spectacles, and kept his head down so Jekaran had trouble seeing his face.

"I'm Jekaran, but everyone calls me Jek. You're Lyam, right?"

The boy only nodded.

Shy kid, Jekaran thought again. "Are you from Genra?"

The boy shook his head and replied in a barely audible, "Searsey."

"I know it. Not too far outside the white forest."

Lyam nodded again.

"I feel like I know you, Lyam. Who's your father?"

Just then Jekaran heard the nasally shout of Gymal, apparently still in a panic, call his name. "Jekaran!" the man repeated.

Jekaran sighed and cast a tacit glance at Vestus, who just smirked and shook his head. It was time for Jekaran's daily insult session. *And I thought I was going to escape being humiliated today.*

RELIEF WASHED over Maely as she watched Jekaran jog away. She took the opportunity to quickly disappear into the shadows and make for her bedroll. *That was stupid!* She scolded herself. But she couldn't have hung back while Jekaran ran down a Vorakk raider all by himself. *From now on, I'll have to take more care to avoid him as much as possible.*

Maely found her bedroll and knelt down. She removed her boots and loosened her chest wrap. She wouldn't take it off, lest someone see, but she did allow herself some comfort for sleeping purposes. She lay down and drew her wool blanket up almost over her head. The chilled air seeped through the edges of the covering and Maely shivered. Her spine tightened, but she knew it wasn't only the temperature making it hard to fall asleep. The excitement of the attack, and the unfamiliar surroundings, her decision to be here at all, she was starting to think she had made an enormous mistake.

Her brother's face eased its haunting grin into her trailing thoughts. "Ez will take care of him," she muttered to herself.

Chapter 11

Jekaran woke to a series of minor aches and pains and a tender left forearm. An involuntary groan left his lips as he slowly sat up. He flexed his shoulders back and forth, then drew in a deep breath of fresh morning air. The smell of frying meat evoked a growl from his stomach, which gave him the will to overcome the protests of his painful bruises. He quickly packed his belongings, threw the bag over a tender shoulder, and headed for the cook-fire.

After a leisurely breakfast and time spent in the latrine, Jekaran found himself trudging along the dirt highway once again. He continuously pulled on the straps of his duffle, trying to adjust them to keep the point of Ez's sword from poking him—as it was wont to do—but he never could get the positioning quite right. Growling under his breath, he thought about carrying the bag, and let it slide down his arm into a hand. Twenty minutes later, his arm complained of the weight, and he settled on minor discomfort over unnecessary exertion.

Just a few more days of travel, he reminded himself.

They were en route to Rasha, the launching point of the expedition proper. There, Gymal would give the men a day to rest and buy additional supplies, not out of any real concern for their welfare, but likely so he could visit the whorehouses and secure a fresh supply of cannabis for himself. That would give Jekaran the opportunity to slip away and find Irvis. He doubted Gymal would even care if he didn't return. *Actually, he would probably prefer that.* Jekaran scoffed at the thought.

The days and nights following passed without incident, and it was on the morning of the eighth day from when they left Genra when Rasha appeared on the horizon. The city was one of the largest in all of Aiestal, said to be home to hundreds of thousands of people. It was un-walled, situated at the base of a grassy hill on the west end of a glittering lake, and mostly circular in its design. As the miles passed, Rasha grew larger and Jekaran could soon make out the gigantic statue of a robed woman rising above the hundreds of buildings. It was the goddess, Rasheera, mother of life and creation. Her statue was at the center of Rasha, which itself was originally founded as a colony for ascetic devotees. Despite this, Jekaran knew Rasha was far from a *holy* city. Ez had explained Rasha had largely become a way station of the southwest, a haven for travelers and a rest stop on the way to the capital. Of course, the transient population attracted merchants like fetid meat-attracted flies, and so the once reclusive religious colony had grown into an urban collage of inns, bazaars, and other operations of commerce, many of dubious legitimacy.

It was evening when Gymal's company finally reached the city, the light of the sun not quite gone, but the shadows quickly lengthening. Gymal turned his ghern to face the men and announced, "You are on your own for food and lodging until tomorrow. You may purchase supplies, visit kin, or carouse, gamble and whore for all I care. Just be back here at two hours past noon tomorrow, understand?"

Jekaran heard a murmur of agreement as the men began to disperse.

"I will not wait for anyone," Gymal warned. Then he abruptly turned his ghern and trotted it into the city, his weary pack servants and secretary struggling to keep pace.

"You heard the boss," Vestus said as he clamped a big hand down on Jekaran's shoulder. "What say we court lady fortune at the dicing tables tonight? I promise I won't tell your uncle if you won't tell my wife."

Jekaran laughed. "That sounds great, but I have to first run an errand for my uncle." The lie invoked a pang of grief at the thought of Mae and Mull. Now he would part ways with Vestus and was likely never to see the man again.

"One that can't wait 'til morning?" Vestus asked, sounding crestfallen.

"I'll try to get done before it gets too late."

Vestus nodded. "Then come find us at the Wandering Willow. My cousin owns the inn and can get us a discount on rooms and food."

"What about companionship?" a rowdy voice sounded from the group of men.

Vestus turned and laughed. "No one has enough coins to buy *you* companionship, Del. You're too damned ugly!"

Jekaran laughed with the others and then affectionately gripped Vestus' bicep. "I'll catch up with you," he said, although, to him, the words sounded like *goodbye.* Vestus nodded, and Jekaran turned away.

As he did, he caught a glimpse of Lyam out of the corner of his eye. The boy had been keeping his distance, deliberately avoiding Jekaran if he read it right. But now Lyam looked poised to follow. *I can't have that,* Jekaran realized, and kept his eyes locked on the boy.

Lyam caught him staring and, as Jekaran expected, became uncomfortable and turned away. Satisfied he wouldn't have a tagalong, Jekaran slipped into the ranks of a passing merchant caravan. He wove in between the merchants and found cover behind a particularly large gentleman.

Jekaran looked back and caught Lyam looking about frantically for him.

Good, he sighed. Under normal circumstances he would've gone out of his way to befriend the boy. After all, he knew how it felt to be an outcast, and he recognized the lonely desperation in Lyam's shadowing him. But he had himself to worry about, himself and Ez.

"Sorry, kid," he whispered.

Even at dusk, Rasheera teemed with life. Streets flooded with people from all corners of Aiestal created an ambient roar like nothing Jekaran had ever heard. At first, it was almost overwhelming, but, within a half an hour, he successfully relegated it to background noise in his mind. Jekaran wove his way through the congested streets for over an hour before finding the center of the city. It was then that he got his first clear look at the gigantic statue of the goddess. It rose higher than any other building, a height Jekaran guessed was close to fifty feet. The statue was cut from white marble and depicted Rasheera dressed in a low-cut, sleeveless robe-like dress. Her hair was long and wavy, falling past her waist almost to the back of her knees, and she held her right hand aloft as if reaching for the sky itself. It was a magnificent testament to the skill of the artisans who sculpted it.

He ran his fingers through his hair and then tucked his hands into his pants pockets. Maely would have loved to see this. And Mull too. Especially him. A newly familiar sense of loneliness settled over him again, and he quickly pushed it away. *No time for that.*

Lifting his eyes skyward, he noticed the statue's amethyst eyes were glowing. He tilted his head, surprised he hadn't noticed the feature when he first beheld the sculpture. *A reflection from the setting sun, nice effect.* Curious, he searched the sky and then realized the sun was setting on the opposite side of the statue. His eyebrows furrowed, and he drew closer, craning his neck for a visual confirmation. A soft sound chimed from behind him, like a crystal bell, but he ignored it.

"Incredible," Jekaran whispered aloud.

His breath caught, for Jekaran realized then that he wasn't just looking at an impressive piece of art, but an Apeira well. The statue was a shell created to protect the crystal monolith beneath, only the eyes giving away its secret.

If the face of the goddess were at the top of the monolith, then the well was the tallest Jekaran had ever seen. Not that he had seen a lot of wells, but he had seen enough over the course of last year's well-find to know that Rasha's Apeira well was abnormally large.

It makes sense, he thought. The devotees that had built Rasha would've seen the well as a physical manifestation of Rasheera's power, and not wanting to promote dependence on anything except their goddess, they would've done something to tie her to the source that powered all of the talises in their city.

Thinking of the goddess' disciples reminded Jekaran of his urgent need to find Irvis.

After one last marvel, he crossed the city center toward a four-story stone building with fluted columns lining a covered causeway leading to its front entrance. It was the Rasheeran monastery, the place Ez had told Jekaran he would find Irvis. *Odd place for a retired Rikujo crime lord,* he thought. *Then again what better place to hide from a thieves' guild than in a holy place?*

As Jekaran passed through the aisle of columns, he saw small, milky white glass orbs hanging inconspicuously from the ceiling. As if welcoming him, the orbs began to glow until they reached a luminescent shine that lit up the entire causeway. He marveled again, never having seen so many light talises in one place. He craned his head as he walked and almost collided with one of the columns.

After that, he restricted his marveling to short glances.

Jekaran reached the double, wooden doors of the monastery. He tried to push and pull it open, but was surprised to find the door locked. He gripped a large, iron ring hanging from the front of the door at his right and banged three times. He tapped his fingers against his leg, counted to ten, and was about to knock again when he heard the shuffling of steps from behind the door. The sound grew louder and was followed by the unmistakable sounds of locks unbolting. Jekaran stepped back just as one of the double doors swung inward, revealing a tall, robed man with long wispy-white hair.

"Yes, child?" the monk asked in a fatherly tone, although it was undercut by a current of repressed irritation.

Jekaran dipped his head in respect. "I am sorry to disturb you, but I am looking for a member of your brotherhood."

"Come back tomorrow then."

The monk began to close the door, so Jekaran blurted out, "Your sanctuary turns away petitioners?"

The old man gave Jekaran a flat look. "We serve The Divine Mother's children from dawn to dusk. Even the servants of Rasheera need rest."

He started to shut the door again, but Jekaran stopped the door with his foot.

"Do I need to send for the city guard?" the monk asked.

"I am looking for a man named Irvis. I have important business with him."

A knowing look passed over the monk's face. "Ah, I see. Well, Brother Irvis isn't here right now."

"What?" Jekaran asked in surprise. "When will he return?"

"I am sure I don't know," the monk said dryly.

"Is he on a pilgrimage?"

The monk smirked. "Something like that." And then he pulled the door shut.

Jekaran stared incredulously at the monastery's doors for what felt like an eternity. Where was his uncle's friend? He sighed as he turned and began walking away. He would come back in the morning when the monastery was open and find a different monk to ask. Maybe he could get a better answer then.

Tired and frustrated, Jekaran wandered through Rasheera until long after dark. What was he supposed to do now? Every minute he carried the sword, he risked being arrested for illegal possession of a weapon talis. The possibility unnerved him. And then there was the Rikujo. What if Kaul had used a speaking stone to send word to the band that worked this city? What if they were on the lookout for him? Jekaran's anxiety heightened and he obsessively surveyed his surroundings. The alleyways, rooftops and darkened doorways stoked his fear; men could easily wait to ambush him in those shadows.

Jekaran abruptly stopped walking as he caught sight of a barefoot woman dressed in what looked like an expensive, sleeveless gown. Her long, dark hair grazed her creamy skin, and a stunningly perfect feminine shape swayed as she moved. *Divine Mother, but she's beautiful.* Absolutely the most gorgeous woman Jekaran had ever seen. Probably not much older than himself, she was a noblewoman to be sure. But what was a lady doing walking alone and barefoot on the city streets after dark? He looked around, searching for a gentleman escort, which she didn't have. *Strange.*

His gaze stopped short, though, as he spotted the gang of footpads trailing her at a distance. There were six of them, all dangerous looking men, all watching the lady intently.

Oh no, Jekaran groaned. *She doesn't even see them.*

Whatever the noblewoman's reason for being out after dark, by herself and without shoes, she was in danger. He clenched his teeth. He *had* to do something.

The sparsely occupied street met his scrutiny with a mocking silent laughter. The handful of quiet travelers paid no attention to him, the woman, or the band of men waiting for their chance. *And no guards,* his thoughts growled. Where were they when you needed them?

Jekaran swiveled his head back in the woman's direction, his muscles tightening as she turned down a darker side street. "Dammit!" He said aloud as the gang of toughs sped up to overtake her. His hands tightened into fists at his side. He couldn't let them have her, but at the same time, interfering would get the attention of Rasha's police. With an illegal weapon talis in his pack, and possibly Rikujo assassins after him, getting involved in an incident like this would draw a terrible amount of attention. He might as well jog down the streets shouting his name. And that's if he survived the encounter, which was a dubious prospect at best.

Jekaran almost convinced himself to turn away, but his conscience wouldn't allow it. And if he was completely honest with himself, it wasn't just his conscience. He had always wanted to test himself in a fight. He was fit, a hunter and a wrestler, and had long fantasized about playing the hero. Well, here was his chance.

Jekaran drew his hunting knife and sprinted across the street. He had no idea what he was going to do when he caught up to the men, but he couldn't leave the woman to her fate. Maybe he could scare off the foot-pads somehow, or maybe just his catching them would drive them away. *Or maybe they'll tear you apart,* he thought ruefully.

When Jekaran reached the side street, the scene greeting him gave him pause. The six toughs had encircled the woman, and, although they were making lewd and menacing comments, she looked completely oblivious to the fact that she was about to be raped.

"So you *can* help me secure an audience with your king?" the woman asked.

The toughs snickered and one of them said, "Of course we can. You just need to come with us."

"Where?" the woman demanded.

"There's a large wine cellar in a house not too far from here," one of the shorter footpads supplied with a suppressed giggle.

"Why there?" the woman asked.

"Because that's where the king is," a burly man wearing only a vest and trousers answered in a patronizing tone.

The woman hesitated a long moment before finally shaking her head and answering cautiously, "No, that is all right. I thank you for your generous offer, but I will not be needing your assistance." She turned to walk away but had to stop when one of the footpads refused to move out of her path.

"Please allow me to pass," the woman said in a dignified tone. That surprised Jekaran, for the woman had obviously caught on to the fact that she was in danger, yet she didn't sound afraid. In fact, her tone made Jekaran think of a queen issuing orders.

"We can't let a pretty thing like you walk around the city all alone, especially at night." The speaking tough's voice was drenched in patronizing menace. "There are dangerous men about. Lecherous creatures that might," he giggled, "take advantage."

A wave of knowing laughter passed around the circle of toughs.

"Thank you, but I will be going now," the woman said. This time Jekaran caught concern in her tone. She circumvented the footpad blocking her path, but was yanked to a halt as he grabbed her by the arm.

This is it, Jekaran realized. Suppressing his instinct for self-preservation, he leapt out of the shadows and hurled himself at the back of the tough closest to him. Jekaran crashed into him and the man pitched forward. Before he knew it, Jekaran found himself lying awkwardly on the back of the footpad, the other toughs looking down at him in a stunned stupor. Strangely, the noble woman was gone. The moment became frozen in confusion, the footpads standing, dumbfounded, staring down at him and then searching for the woman.

"Where did she...?" he heard one of the toughs trail off in confusion.

Then the moment thawed.

The burly man beneath Jekaran bucked him off and quickly scrambled to his feet. Jekaran urgently scooted backward, putting as much distance between he and the thieves as he could before rising to his feet. When he stood, he saw the six footpads were all locking angry stares onto him. Jekaran made to raise his hunting knife in warning, but froze in horror as he realized that he no longer held it. *I dropped it!* A quick scan of the ground proved ineffectual in the dark and the reality of the danger he was in settled on him with nauseating dread.

The man Jekaran had tackled, a bald, muscular man wearing a goatee, took a step toward him and growled, "You scared that girl away!"

"You certain it was me, or was it that ugly face of yours?" The words left Jekaran's mouth before he could stop them. *That was stupid,* he berated himself. *Really stupid!*

The goatee man grinned and took another step forward. "Oh, see. We were just going to beat you and take your coin, but now I think we're going to have to slit your throat."

Jekaran inched backward, trying to purchase himself as much turning distance as possible. "So you need money?" Jekaran asked in a sardonic tone. "That why you were going to take that woman? Cuz you're randy and didn't have enough coin for a night at the brothels?" he paused and eyed a stack of wooden crates on his right side. "I guess you must be tired of buggering each other."

The grin faded from the goatee man's face and he lunged at Jekaran who, at the same moment, lurched to his right. Using both his hands in an explosion of effort, Jekaran tipped the stack of wooden crates over, collapsing them between him and the gang. Without waiting to see the crates hit the ground, Jekaran turned and exploded into a sprint. He heard the man's surprised yelp as a crash echoed through the street, and then him snarling, swearing and calling for help from his men.

Jekaran reached the connecting street and darted left. He had settled on the monastery as a destination, hoping to find a place to lose them along the way. If not, then he hoped there would be enough people still in the city square to discourage the toughs from attacking him. The shouts of the men behind him echoed through the streets, and he gauged how far back they were without having to turn around. His breathless, lopsided smile grew and then faded. He managed to put enough distance between them that they would no doubt have a difficult time seeing him in the dark of the night. That would give him an opportunity to hide and not be seen.

But where?

A bridge crossed the city's main river a short distance ahead, and the sight stirred an idea in Jekaran's mind. With every ounce of will and physical strength he possessed, he doubled his speed and soon found himself crossing onto the bridge well ahead of the gang. Trusting the distance he had managed between himself and his pursuers, plus the shadows of the poorly lit street, was enough, Jekaran climbed up over the rail of the bridge, and lowered himself to hang above the river. He pumped his legs to give him momentum and then swung underneath the bridge. He landed on a small ledge of stone, his shoes struggling for a foothold on top of a patch of slick moss. Jekaran's arms flailed as he fought to gain his balance, struggling to keep from falling into the water. Frantically he searched for something to grab onto. A protuberance in the arch glared at him, and he gripped onto it, his fingers flaring in pain. A curse died in his throat as he heard voices above him.

"I saw him run this way!" one of the footpads affirmed.

"Then where did he go?" another asked skeptically

"Just go!" he heard the goatee man bark, and then the sound of fast heavy footfalls.

Jekaran breathed a sigh of relief, waited a long moment, and then began to climb up the side of the stone bridge. His head had just crested the rail when two pairs of strong arms grabbed him and roughly pulled him over the rail and onto the bridge. A blow to his gut took the wind out of him, and Jekaran found himself lying on his side, looking up at six angry faces staring down at him.

"You must think we're blind *and* stupid!" The goatee man kicked him hard in the ribs.

Jekaran gasped, sucking wind so hard that his vision began to dim. "Just stupid," he wheezed. That provoked a hard kick to his back drawing out a harsh grunt from his throat.

"You don't learn, do you?" the goatee man said with a measure of incredulity. He leaned down, hauled Jekaran to his feet, and then back-handed him so hard he spun and fell eight paces away from the group.

As he hit the ground face-first, Jekaran felt his duffle slide up to the back of his head and something fall out. A metal clatter on the cobble-stone bridge told him that Ez's sword had fallen out of the bag. Through double vision and involuntary tears, Jekaran saw the sword lying on the bridge only a few inches in front of him.

"Not going to crack wise?" he heard the goatee man deride. A round of laughter rang in the night air.

He knew that he should just keep his mouth shut, but Jekaran couldn't help himself. "Don't need to," he groaned. "Your friends have noses. They can smell you."

Surprisingly, that evoked laughter from the goatee man's fellows as Jekaran pushed himself to all fours. The muscles in his legs tightened to stand, but a shoe in the middle of his back slammed him back to the ground.

"I think we're going to have to cut out that sharp tongue of yours," the goatee man growled as he grabbed Jekaran by the hair and yanked his head back.

Having no other options, Jekaran reached toward Ez's sword and touched the handle with trembling fingers. He slid the handle into his palm and gripped it.

Then everything changed.

Time itself seemed to freeze and the clouds of panic veiling his mind cleared. Jekaran's eyes fell on the amethyst jewel embedded in the face of the sword's cross-guard and the pulsing purple light it emitted. In the same instant, he became aware of a mental tether-there was no other way he could describe it-connecting his mind to something in the sword. It was as if he was talking to a person, but without words. Knowledge flooded his brain: battle tactics, sword techniques, a dozen different possible actions he could take against the thug pressing down on his back.

And he understood it all. It was as if Jekaran was suddenly an expert fighter, swordsman, general and martial artist.

Jekaran threw his head all the way back, a loud crunch followed by a pained yell confirming he had struck the goatee man square in the nose. He rolled left, knocking the thug off him in the process. Before Jekaran knew it, he was on his feet with Ez's sword in hand.

In a roar of pain and rage, the goatee man launched himself to his feet and lunged at Jekaran with a dagger. He pivoted at the last moment, sidestepping the thrust and swinging Ez's sword down on the man's forearm. Blood splashed Jekaran's shirt as the severed arm fell to the ground amidst shocked howling. Something took control of Jekaran and his right leg shot up, connecting with the goatee man's chest and knocking him over the rail of the bridge.

A heightened sense of his surroundings alerted Jekaran to an advance by three members of the gang. As if he had trained with the sword all of his life, he whirled toward his attackers and effortlessly lopped off one of their heads. The other two had no time to react as Jekaran fluidly brought his free elbow down on the second man's face and then shoved the sword into the third man's chest. He yanked the blade out and spun, swinging the sword at the second man. Blinded by the blood and tears from his now broken nose, the defenseless tough never even saw the edge of the sword as it sunk into his shoulder and then cut all the way through. He fell to the ground in two pieces. Jekaran quickly spun to face the remaining two thugs who stood several paces away at the beginning of the stone bridge. Their eyes grew wide and their faces pale. A long, silent moment passed between them, and then the thugs turned and sprinted away.

Jekaran lowered his arm and wearily dropped the sword to the ground. As soon as it left his hand, the mental connection he felt retreated. It was still there, but it felt muted as though it was no longer at the front of his thoughts. The expert knowledge of fighting and sword-play vanished, and he suddenly had no idea how he had fought with such deadly grace. His confidence gone, Jekaran's senses were abruptly assaulted by the stench of blood and spilled viscera. He vomited and stumbled away from the corpses, collapsing to his knees near the front of the bridge.

As a farmer, he had done his fair share of slaughtering animals, but this was different. This was terrible. He retched again. Although sick at the sight of so much carnage, death he caused, he felt no guilt. No, instead he felt a thrill of accomplishment, of pride, but no remorse—as though he had done something great.

That disturbed him, and his stomach twisted again.

The clanking of armor drew his attention up to four men of the city guard rushing toward him, weapons drawn. *Great,* Jekaran thought, *now they show up.*

When the guards reached him, one hauled him to his feet and began interrogating him immediately while the other three moved onto the bridge to survey the carnage. "What happened here?"

"I was att—" Jekaran began.

"Captain!"

Jekaran turned his head and saw the guard holding Ez's sword. *This is bad,* he realized with an inward cringe.

"A weapon talis!" the guard called.

The guard looked at Jekaran, the man's eyes growing hard. "You're in a lot of trouble, son."

⸻✦⸻

TEARS STREAMED DOWN Maely's cheeks as she watched two of the four armored guards bind Jekaran in hand shackles and then march him away. She had fetched the city guard to save Jekaran, not to get him arrested. Surely *he* had not killed those thieves, but, if not Jekaran, then who? And even if he had killed them, the law was clear about a person's right to defend themselves, even unto death. What was going on?

Maely scrubbed her eyes with the back of her hand. Certainly, this was all a misunderstanding. She had to get help and she could think of only one person who could give it. *Jek's not gonna like this,* she thought as she turned away and began to sprint down the street.

She didn't know exactly where to go, but she decided to start at The Wandering Willow.

CHAPTER

12

Stripped of all his possessions and tossed into a small square cell already occupied by someone sleeping in the corner, Jekaran stared down at his clothes, still stained with splotches of blood. Not being a nobleman, he knew he would have no trial, or even the opportunity to plead his case to a tribunal. He would rot in this cell indefinitely until one of Rasha's magistrates had time to review the charges against him and declare a sentence, perhaps even death by hanging, as Ez had suggested. Not for killing the four thieves who had attacked him, but because he had been in possession of and used a weapon talis, a grievous violation of the king's law.

Under the Aiestal caste system, nobility was determined by talis possession. The richest merchant in the city would therefore be of an inferior social status to even a poor family if they lawfully owned a talis. Of course, that was a ridiculous example, for talises could be bought and sold, and a wealthy merchant would likely own several. However, weapon talises were a different story. They could only be awarded by the king and then only to high-ranking military leaders or celebrated soldiers. Illegal trafficking and unlawful possession of a weapon talis was severely punished. And Jekaran had done far worse. He had actually used a weapon talis.

Jekaran leaned his head against the cold stone of the prison wall and closed his eyes. He had heard of a man who was caught with a staff capable of emitting balls of fire. The king stripped the nobleman of everything he owned, his wife and children were sold into slavery and he was exiled from the kingdom. And that was a *nobleman!*

He trembled. Ez's claim that hanging was not outside the realm of possible punishments for a farmer caught with a weapon talis took on a new level of credibility. Jekaran opened his eyes to realize he had unconsciously been touching his throat and quickly withdrew his hand.

"Who're you?" a voice asked from behind him.

Jekaran looked over to the corner of the cell and saw a round-faced man staring blearily at him. His full face sprinkled with stubble and disheveled peppered hair seemed out of place against the clean, but worn, brown robe and tattered soft leather boots.

"A dead man," Jekaran replied morosely.

"What did you do?"

"I don't care to talk about it," Jekaran said, his voice taut.

"What's your name?" the chubby man persisted.

Jekaran's already frayed temper flared and he turned toward the chubby man and snapped, "I don't want to talk to you!"

The chubby man looked taken aback. He settled back into his corner and calmly said, "I can see you wish to be alone with your thoughts. If, however, you need counsel in this, your desperate hour, please feel free to call upon me. My name is Brother Irvis of the Rasheeran Monastery."

The words shocked Jekaran like a full-bore dive into a freezing pond. *Irvis? Ez's friend from his days in the Rikujo? It couldn't be!* This man was a monk. Then again, Ez *had* told him to look for Irvis at the monastery. Jekaran slowly turned to face the man.

"Irvis?"

"Yes, child," the monk replied as he settled back onto a pile of hay and closed his eyes.

"Do you know a man named Ezra from the village of Genra?"

Irvis opened his eyes and sat up at the mention of Jekaran's uncle. "Depends," he said with a note of very un-monk-like suspicion in his voice. "Who's asking?"

"I have a message from him," Jekaran fished in his pocket and produced a piece of paper, the one thing the guards hadn't taken from him.

Irvis took the letter, unfolded it, and squinted as he read. "Oh dear." Irvis glanced at Jekaran. "Kaul?"

Jekaran nodded his head in confirmation, and Irvis resumed deciphering the message.

"This is not good," he muttered. After another moment of reading, his head snapped up and he looked at Jekaran with new eyes. "Where's the sword?"

The question made Jekaran wince.

"Divine Mother!" Irvis gasped. "Tell me that you didn't use it!"

Jekaran grimly nodded. "Against a gang of footpads trying to kill me."

Irvis nodded slowly. "Then you really are a dead man."

"Thanks for the words of comfort," Jekaran scoffed as he turned away from Irvis. "Is that why the other monks sent you here? Because you're so good at comforting the damned?"

Irvis chuckled nervously. "They didn't send me here."

Jekaran whipped around. "You're a prisoner?"

"Technically—"

"What did you do?" Jekaran demanded.

Irvis' eyes fell to the ground, shame shading his chubby face pink. "There was a," he hesitated, "misunderstanding with myself and Lord Eckleton's wife."

"A misunderstanding?"

"Yes." Irvis raised his eyes to meet Jekaran's. "I was at his manor, tending to his sickly mother when I, by pure happenstance you understand, saw Lady Eckleton bathing in an adjoining room. Seems," he chuckled nervously, "one of the servants had left the door open just enough to allow me to see her disrobe and enter the bath. Lord Eckleton caught me watching and accused me of spying on his wife for perverse reasons."

The incredulity of Irvis' story almost made Jekaran laugh aloud. "You're a peeper!"

"I most certainly am not!" Irvis said indignantly and then seemed to shrink. "I just saw a beautiful woman and couldn't help but want to see more of her."

This time Jekaran did laugh. "A horny holy man!"

Irvis scowled. "Living a celibate life is very difficult for a man who used to bed a different maid every night. Rasheera forgive me, but I do try. Until yesterday, it had been almost three months since my last," he paused to choose his words carefully, "lapse in commitment."

Jekaran felt the death cloud over him lighten a little, and couldn't help but to continue to laugh.

Irvis' face reddened. "You know, back in his day, your uncle was a bigger womanizer than even I was!"

Seeing his indignant reaction stifled Jekaran's laughter. "I'm sorry," he cleared his throat. "I'm not laughing *at* you. It's the idea I find funny."

"Well, I am glad I was able to raise your spirits in your desperate hour." The sarcasm dripped from his every word as he turned his back to Jekaran to lay down on his pile of straw.

He's pouting! Jekaran realized, and then he began to pity the older man. "So you joined the brotherhood of the goddess to hide from the Rikujo?" He hoped the topic change would assuage Irvis' wounded pride.

Irvis rolled onto his back and stared at the ceiling. "That was part of it."

"You're a true believer?" Jekaran asked, not able to mask his surprise.

"Yes," Irvis answered simply. "I left the Rikujo just a few months after Argentus," he paused to correct himself, "I mean Ezra. I had wanted out for years, but it wasn't until your uncle left that I had the courage to leave myself. In fact, he helped me get out."

"And then you found religion?"

Irvis nodded awkwardly, his fingers laced together behind his head. "That's something of an oversimplification, but yes. I found the Divine Mother's mercy."

Like Ez

Jekaran was about to ask for details when he heard the door to the dungeon open. He scooted forward; his face pressed against the bars of his cell, cold fear reminding him of his plight while he strained to see who was coming. *They couldn't have reviewed my case already!* But what if they had? Could this be the hangman coming for him?

Footsteps brought three figures into view. One was clearly the jailer, and the two who followed were …

Oh no Jekaran groaned as he sank on his haunches. Lyam and Gymal.

The shy boy must've somehow seen what had happened on the bridge, and taken the news to Gymal.

Gymal grinned as he stopped in front of Jekaran's cell. "Well, well. It looks like you've finally been caught, Jekaran. I knew it would happen eventually. I just didn't think it would be for such a grievous offense."

"What's going to happen to me?" The pathetic fear in his voice filled him with angry embarrassment.

"That's for the magistrate to decide," Gymal said. "You could be facing the noose."

Jekaran saw Lyam shoot a shocked glance at Gymal. Apparently, the boy hadn't expected the short, nasally man to act so coolly.

Gymal continued, "However, because I am a gracious lord, I entered a plea for mercy on your behalf. I am not sure how well it was received, but your youth may earn you a degree of forbearance. I'd say the most you could hope for would be lifelong, indentured servitude. Perhaps the magistrate will even sell you to me."

Jekaran saw Lyam nervously look back and forth between him and Gymal. Had the boy actually thought Gymal would help him?

"And the sword?" He grimaced. The thought had come into his mind and left out of his mouth before he had time to consider it.

Gymal looked a bit surprised by the question. "When the magistrate here learned that you were part of my expedition, he turned it over to me so that I may present it to the king upon my return home." He paused to study Jekaran. "How *did* you come by a weapon talis, anyway?"

Jekaran wasn't about to give away his uncle's involvement. "It fell from the sky, right into my lap." He flashed his teeth in a grin of defiance.

Gymal's expression darkened. "Fine, keep your secrets. It doesn't really matter how you got it." He turned away from the cell. "I will pass through here when the expedition is finished to see if you have been spared execution. If so, I will make an offer on you, if someone hasn't already bought you. Perhaps the months of waiting will give you time to consider how fortunate you are to have me as your liege-lord." With that, he strode out of view.

Jekaran heard the dungeon door swing open and then shut as Gymal left, punctuating the finality of his condemnation. He fought the threatening tears, and looked up again, feeling eyes upon him, to find Lyam staring.

"What?" he snapped.

"I-I was just trying to help," the boy said softly.

"Yeah, well, you didn't!"

Jekaran's angry words appeared to strike Lyam as though he had physically slapped him.

"I'm sorry," the boy whimpered.

"Leave me alone."

"But ..."

"GO!" he screamed.

Tears rolled down Lyam's face and the boy broke into a shamed retreat.

The jailer curiously studied Jekaran before turning to leave the prison.

The backlash of his own cruelty struck Jekaran and he sank to the floor feeling utterly defeated. *How had this happened?* he asked himself. *It was the crazy noblewoman,* he remembered. Had she not been so foolish as to walk the streets of the city alone, and at night, he wouldn't have needed to intervene and wouldn't have needed to use the sword. No, he couldn't blame this on the woman. He *had* been sincere in his desire to rescue her, but he knew there was more to it than that. The Lure, Ez had called it, Jekaran's appetite for excitement and adventure. He knew and could not deny his uncle was right. It was the Lure that had driven him to defy fear and danger, and she had been merely an excuse. He hadn't needed to jump right in so recklessly. He likely could have found a city guard had he looked harder, or scared the toughs away by making a lot of noise and shouting for help. But something about the danger had been alluring, even intoxicating.

"You were right, Ez," he whispered. "You were right."

CHAPTER 13

Kairah cautiously approached the sobbing girl. She was sitting on the ground, back up against the alley-side wall of the Wandering Willow Inn. She wasn't dressed like the other human females Kairah had seen since entering Rasha, who all appeared to go to great lengths to accentuate their breasts and show off their hips. No, this girl was dressed to appear as non-feminine as any man Kairah had seen.

The girl started and looked up at Kairah through blood-shot eyes. She said nothing, but Kairah could sense the fear rising in her.

"Do not be afraid," Kairah said as she raised both of her hands, her open palms facing the girl. Jenoc had taught her doing so was a sign humans understood as lack of intent to harm. He also said humans had no compunctions about lying, but she was certain that didn't apply to this girl.

The girl appeared to relax. She scrubbed her eyes with the sleeve of her shirt and said, "You're the one Jek rescued. Forgive me if I don't stand, *my lady*."

Something in the girl's tone seemed wrong. *Sarcasm*, Kairah abruptly realized. The girl must resent her for the arrest of the girl's friend. Kairah tightened her lips. Well, there was some truth to that.

"I do apologize," Kairah said sincerely. "Although I was never in any real danger, I am truly grateful for his intervention on my behalf."

The girl looked up at Kairah with a strange look on her face. "They were going to rape and murder you," she said flatly.

Do not forget that you look as helpless as any other human female, Aeva said. Kairah didn't respond. She was so far away from Allose now that communicating with the Spirit Lily took a distracting amount of concentration.

"Why are you dressed like that?" Kairah asked. The question was equal parts curiosity and effort to steer the conversation away from her verbal slip.

Suddenly, the girl looked nervous. "Sorry?"

"You are not dressed like the others of this city."

"That's because I'm poor," the girl replied stiffly.

Kairah shook her head. "I was not referring to the quality of your clothing, but the style. I have observed other women dress to call attention to the fact they are female, whereas you dress to hide your figure."

The girl's eyes widened. "You know I'm a ..." she cut off and dropped her eyes to the ground.

"You are trying to hide your gender?"

"What do you want from me?" the girl snapped.

Like you, she is in disguise, Aeva observed.

"I want to help you secure your friend's release."

The girl looked at her for a long moment before finally asking, "You're a noblewoman?"

Kairah hesitated. "Yes," she said. It wasn't a lie, exactly, for she *was* descended from an Allosian Oracle, granting her family a measure of honor and prestige.

"What can *you* do?"

Kairah straightened. "I can speak to the authorities and clarify that your friend, Jek—"

"Jekaran," the girl interrupted.

Kairah nodded. "That Jekaran was simply coming to my aid. That those men meant harm and he defended me."

"That's not why he's in prison," the girl said morosely.

"He did something other than take life?" Kairah suddenly felt confused. She had been sure she had a thorough understanding of basic human jurisprudence.

The girl drew up her knees and hugged them. "He was arrested for using a weapon talis, and will either be sold into slavery or executed."

"That is a capital offense?" Kairah said before she could stop herself.

The girl stared at her with a look of confused suspicion. "Of course it is."

Kairah could feel Aeva's wordless disgust for her continued carelessness. Ignoring the Spirit Lily's disapproval, she nodded to herself and said, "Then we will need to use other means to free him."

The girl's expression grew darker. She glanced at Kairah's bare feet and said, "You are very odd, even for a noble. Are you sick in the head?"

Kairah wasn't sure how to answer that, so she didn't. "Do you wish to help me free your friend, Jekaran?"

The girl slowly nodded. "Why do you care what happens to people like us?"

People like us? It took a moment for Kairah to realize the girl was referring to their human caste system. "I wish to honor his gallantry, and I am also in need of a guide."

Now *that* was a lie. True, a guide would make it easier for her to reach the king, but Kairah had seen something in the boy—Jekaran— that marked him as a *Fated Soul.* Not many among her people understood or accepted that concept. But, being the descendant of an Oracle, Kairah had made seeing the signs of fate the focus of her early studies at the College of Disciplines. She had not yet experienced the gift of The Fifth Discipline, seeing into the future, and she knew she may *never* experience it. However, she had learned to recognize when people and, sometimes, things were destined to play a significant role in the near future.

It manifested as a slight shimmer of light that pulsed away from the person, like the ripples that flowed away from an object that disturbed a body of water. It wasn't a constant thing, displaying only in moments when the Fated Soul's choices were locking them into a pattern of events that would lead them to their destiny, and when the seer's future intertwined with the Fated Soul. She saw these ripples of light emanating from Jekaran when he attempted to rescue her, and then again when she watched him bond the sword talis. Keeping Jekaran close seemed wise.

It is the will of Apeira, she heard Aeva echoing her own belief.

"A guide to where?" the girl asked.

The question interrupted Kairah's reverie and she asked, "I am sorry?"

The girl sighed in frustration and then repeated herself in a patronizingly slow cadence. "You–said–you–needed–a-guide. A guide to where?"

"To your capital city to seek an audience with your king."

"Who *are* you?" the girl demanded.

Kairah hesitated for a moment. "My name is Kairah, and I am a messenger. I have vital information I need to deliver to your king. However, I continue to encounter unanticipated complications and, therefore, require a cultural native to guide me. Your friend won my admiration with his selfless effort to aid me at his own peril, and, as a result, I have chosen him to be that guide."

The girl stared at her for a long moment, skepticism rife on her face. Finally she said, "You can get Jek out of jail?"

"I believe so," Kairah said.

The girl replaced her spectacles, slowly nodded, and stood. "Then I'll help," she said.

JEKARAN SPENT the better part of the next day in depressed indolence. Not that there was much else he could do but lounge and sleep. Not much passed between him and Irvis. The monk appeared to have lost his desire for conversation, and so Jekaran left him alone and took to counting rats for a distraction.

He was up to twenty-four.

Although he didn't have a clock, he could tell that it was hours past noon which meant Gymal and the crew had departed the city. *With Uncle Ez's sword*, he mourned. *How had things gone so completely wrong?* One moment he was at the threshold of excitement and adventure, and the next moment, a condemned prisoner sharing a cell with a reluctant pervert.

Jekaran cast a glance at Irvis. The man sat with his back to Jekaran, shoulders slumping and white hair disheveled. He looked as pathetic as Jekaran felt. The sorry sight of the man bound to a similar situation struck a chord of empathy in Jekaran.

"How long are they going to keep you in here?" he asked.

Irvis slowly shook his head. "According to Rasha law, as long as I didn't touch my victim or have intent to touch her, I can't be charged with any kind of attack. So I don't have to worry about castration or execution – the same in my book if you ask me." He shook his head. "No, I think I'd rather be executed then have my man parts cut off."

"I'd agree," Jekaran chuckled.

Irvis continued, "Because they can't prove my motive, I'm probably looking at a couple of months for *unseemly behavior toward a lady*."

"Sounds like you're in a much better situation than me." Jekaran put his hands behind his head and lay down on his straw mat.

"There are things worse than death," Irvis said quietly.

"Like castration?" Jekaran chuckled.

"I will be expelled from the brotherhood for my transgression."

Jekaran didn't know how to respond to that. And when Irvis said no more, he let the conversation die and sought another distraction to keep his mind off his plight. The conversations of distant prisoners in the darkness of dungeon allowed him to doze into the space of half-dreaming, half-listening.

Jekaran found himself in Maely and Mull's small cottage, kneeling before the hearth, stoking the fire with an iron poker. Although his front was almost uncomfortably warm, his back was freezing. He turned away from the hypnotic fire and saw a frosted window. So, it was winter, then.

"Jek!" Maely called.

"Coming," he said, and then pulled the poker from the fire. He laid it down just in front of the hearth until it could cool enough for him to stow it away.

Jekaran stood, and turned to find Maely walking into the room. Her head was bowed down, and she held her right arm out against the wall to steady herself. Her belly was swollen with pregnancy, and there was a rigidness to her movements.

"Jek, I think it's time," she said in obvious pain.

Maely was having a baby? And he was the father?

What the hell?

The sound of the dungeon door swinging open jolted him from his nap and he sat up, fear rising with the bile in his throat. *Was it time for his hearing?* he wondered. *Did Gymal really persuade the magistrate to exempt him from execution?*

Jekaran stared at the wall outside his cell, his mind racing with a dozen different possible fates. Time stretched in expectant silence, and, oddly, no one appeared. Jekaran glanced at Irvis, who looked just as puzzled as he felt. He hadn't heard the dungeon door close, nor had he heard any guards interacting with the other prisoners. Jekaran stood and walked to the bars of his cell, straining to see through them and down the hall. It was then that he caught sight of a translucent rippling in the air, just below the ceiling, almost imperceptible in the dim lighting.

Before he could say anything, something dropped to the floor in front of his cell. Jekaran instinctually backed away as a human-like shape materialized before him. It wasn't human, Jekaran realized, it was Vorakk.

"You," Jekaran said. "What are you doing here?"

"You know him?" Irvis asked, the chubby monk had also stood and was backing away from the cell bars.

The Vorakk flashed a grin through a muzzle filled with razor sharp teeth. "Karak is here for you, human boy aka."

Jekaran's pulse began to race, and he unconsciously touched the scabbed-over bite on his arm as he scanned the floor for anything that he could use as a weapon. The Vorakk pulled a ring of keys from a small leather pouch at his side and began cycling through them until he found one that fit the cell lock.

"I'll call the guards!" Jekaran threatened.

The Vorakk ignored his threat and wrenched open the cell door. "Come, rok," it demanded.

Jekaran heard murmurs arise from the other prisoners. "What do you want?"

The Vorakk hissed in what Jekaran assumed was irritation. "Isk, not much time!"

His eyes grew wide, his jaw dropping. "Are you ... freeing ... me?"

The Vorakk cast a wary glance in the direction of the dungeon's outer door and nodded. "Aeks!" it beckoned urgently.

His mind racing, Jekaran could think of nothing else to do but comply. He began to leave the cell when Irvis caught his arm.

"Please take me with you," he pled.

"You could win a noose next to mine if we're caught," Jekaran warned. "Why risk it just to get out of a couple months of imprisonment?"

"There is nothing left for me here." A sober sadness framed his face, his grip still tight against Jekaran's arm.

Jekaran stared at the chubby monk for a long moment before nodding. As they left the cell, the other prisoners called out pleas for release, some even threatening to call the guards if refused. A menacing growl-hiss from the Vorakk effectively silenced them, and Jekaran and Irvis slipped out through the dungeon door.

Jekaran began to follow the corridor back the way he remembered being escorted in, when the Vorakk hissed, "Isk stupid human boy! Guards that way!"

"Then how do we get out?" Jekaran irritably demanded.

"Karak spend night exploring jail. Daka, find other way out."

"Your name is Karak?"

The Vorakk nodded, checked to see if a connecting hall was clear, and then hurried them on. They quickly moved down the corridor, Karak freezing and disappearing from visibility each time they approached a connecting door.

Wish I could do that, Jekaran thought.

They crept through the hall which ended at the foot of a stone stairwell and descended into a basement storage room. Light from a small window near the top of the room's ceiling filtered into a room filled with dozens of waist-high barrels and stacked, cobweb-shrouded crates.

Karak quickly led them through the maze of wooden storage containers to where he crouched over a trapdoor set in the floor, the hatch secured by an iron padlock. Again, the lizard man reached into his leather pouch and produced the stolen ring of keys.

"Just out of curiosity, did you eat the previous owner of those keys?" Irvis asked with a nervous tremor in his voice.

Karak hissed. "Isk human meat taste bad."

"So you *have* eaten people," Irvis shot Jekaran a worried look.

The lizard man didn't answer Irvis' follow-up question, but instead explained, "Karak get keys when guard goes in little room with human female aka."

A knowing grin spread across Irvis' face that Jekaran ignored.

Karak smiled as one of the keys he had tried fit into the padlock. He turned it, a pronounced *click* announcing success to the small band. The lizard man wrenched open the trapdoor, and Jekaran was assaulted by a foul stench, one that smelled like an old latrine.

"What's down there?" Jekaran asked as he pulled the collar of his tunic up to cover his nose.

"Sewer," Irvis said, the sleeve of his robe muffling his voice.

Karak nodded, "On map in guards' sleep room aka."

"You mean you haven't been down there?" Irvis asked.

"Isk if Karak go in tunnel, why it locked?" he motioned at the iron padlock lying open on the floor.

"Good point," Irvis said.

"Where does this come out, Karak?" Jekaran asked, nose still covered.

Karak shook his head. "Map just say *out* aka."

Jekaran studied the ladder that descended into the dark of the sewer. He looked up at Karak and asked, "Do you have a torch?"

Karak shook his head. "Spirits light tunnel aka."

"What?"

Karak held out his hand and a small ball of light appeared floating just above his open palm.

Irvis' eyes widened.

"He's a shaman!"

Karak nodded and the small orb of glowing white rose into the air to float by his shoulder. He turned and began climbing down the ladder.

Jekaran leaned over the trapdoor, watching as the Vorakk shaman splashed down into dark, knee-high water. He had to suppress his gag reflex as he thought about what Karak must be standing in, what Jekaran himself would have to wade through in order to escape. He gritted his teeth. The thought of a waiting noose was enough to motivate him and he descended into the sewer.

He landed in the murky water with a squelching splash. The water was cool but not cold, and Jekaran could feel clumps of human waste brushing up against his legs. Vomit swelled in his throat, and he was only able to choke it back at the last second by sheer willpower. He looked up to see Irvis peering down over the ladder, an uncertain look on his face.

"Come on!" Jekaran called.

Irvis looked over his shoulder, and Jekaran wondered if the man was reconsidering his choice to escape.

"Too late to turn back now" Jekaran called.

"I know!" Irvis snapped, and then he awkwardly turned himself to begin the climb down.

He landed in the knee-high raw sewage with vomit pouring from his lips. The acrid smell of bile mixing with human excrement took the nauseating stench to a new level of repulsiveness. Only the thought of death or being Gymal's lifelong slave kept Jekaran from turning back.

An hour of sloshing through the sewer accustomed Jekaran to the smell, and, while far from pleasant, it was no longer overpowering. Their path took them down three connecting tunnels and very soon, Jekaran completely lost his bearings. He caught up to Karak, who had taken the lead, and asked, "Where are you taking us?"

"Out ka," was all the Vorakk said.

"Right." Jekaran nodded. "But how do you know which way is out?"

The Vorakk cast Jekaran an incredulous side-long glance, an expression Jekaran thought was strikingly similar to Ez's *How could you be so stupid* look.

"Karak always knows where to go aka," the lizard man finally answered.

Great, Jekaran thought sardonically, *we're going to be lost forever in these tunnels!* He returned to his normal pace and, a moment later, Karak was again several steps in front of him.

"Vorakk possess an innate sense of direction," Irvis' muffled voiced said over Jekaran's shoulder.

He glanced back to see the chubby priest working to catch up to him, the sleeve of his robe covering his mouth and nose. It was wet, and Jekaran realized the monk must've had another bout of vomiting.

"Child, I think something is following us!" Irvis said.

Jekaran shot a glance behind them and saw only the dark tunnel. "Like one of the Rasha guards?"

Irvis shook his head. "No, child. Not a person."

"Then what?"

"I don't know," Irvis said. "I heard it sloshing behind us in the water."

"It's probably just rats."

"I hope so."

They continued, Karak abruptly turning into connecting tunnels without any warning or explanation and Irvis lagging behind occasionally emitting emetic noises. As they skulked through the dark, Jekaran lost all sense of direction and time and so retreated to his thoughts.

The contemplative state eased the smell and took him away from the frenzy of the dungeon, but only for a moment as a feeling of unease moved in like a thick fog. It was as if he wasn't alone in his mind, like someone else listened to his thoughts. *That's mad.* Jekaran shook it off and tried to think of something else, but the effort failed.

Hello? Jekaran finally asked to the mental intruder.

After a protracted moment of mental silence, and as he started to feel relieved and foolish, an answer came. It wasn't in the form of an internal voice, but a vague, formless impression communicating the basic idea of a response. Jekaran stopped walking.

Who are you? He demanded of the alien presence in his mind.

No answer came.

A scream of pure terror startled Jekaran. He whipped around to find Irvis scrambling toward him, running so desperately that he slipped and fell into the stream of sewage. He didn't even complain as he fought to his feet, although he spat foul liquid from his mouth.

"What's wrong?" Jekaran rushed to the man's side and gripped his arm, helping the man to find his footing.

"WORM!" Irvis bellowed as he yanked his arm free and pushed passed him.

"What?" Jekaran asked, but then didn't need an explanation as something snake-like exploded out of the water and into the radius of Karak's magic light. The creature's grey, wet skin looked soft and slimy, and branching out of its sides were several flailing tentacles. But the thing the struck Jekaran most about the giant worm was its mouth full of pointed, pin-like teeth.

The worm lunged at Jekaran and he was able to snap out of his shocked-paralysis just in time to kick at it. His boot connected with the underside of the worm's mouth just as it came down at him, and the creature rolled to the side bellowing an inhuman shriek of pain. He lost his footing, about to slip into the muck, when a pair of leathery hands grabbed his shoulders and arrested his fall.

Karak set him back on his feet and turned toward the worm. He threw out his right hand and hissed. Jekaran winced as a small ball of blue light emitted from the Vorakk's hand. It immediately exploded into a wind that threw the worm back into the water amidst a torrent of raining raw sewage.

"Human boy run aeks!" Karak said as he turned and began loping down the tunnel.

Jekaran didn't hesitate, but broke into a run, mindful of his footing so that he didn't slip like Irvis had. He caught up to Karak, who had just overtaken Irvis; apparently, the chubby monk had not even stopped to look back. A shriek ripped through the air and Jekaran sensed the worm pursuing behind them. The worm wouldn't be so easily dissuaded from its prey.

"Karak! Can't you burn it with a fire spell or something?" Jekaran shouted.

"Isk stupid human boy!" the Vorakk shaman replied. "Your dung makes dangerous gas. Fire burn us!"

"Then what do we do?" Jekaran shouted.

"Hold still and be silent!" Irvis cut in as he regained a measure of his wits.

Jekaran looked over to find Irvis flatting his back against the curvature of the tunnel's wall, leaving as much space as possible down the tunnel's center. Jekaran did likewise and noticed Karak copying them. They stayed like that, all of their stares nervously trained on the worm flying down the tunnel toward them. When it reached their position, it slowed and then stopped. Jekaran's heart pounded so loud, he was sure the worm would be able to hear it as it slinked by, but it didn't stop. It continued past them and then splashed back into the water, its water trail turning right into a connecting tunnel.

Oh, I hope we don't have to go that way, Jekaran thought. In unspoken consent, they all waited until the sloshing sound of the worm faded before speaking.

"Where now?" Jekaran whispered to Karak.

He stared down the tunnel and motioned for them to follow. They cautiously sloshed down the corridor, each taking controlled steps to limit the amount of noise they made. They reached a *T*, the tunnel on the right leading in the same direction the worm had gone. Karak motioned for them to turn left, and Jekaran's worry subsided.

As they turned left, he lost his footing and slipped, falling backward into the sewage. An involuntary yelp escaped his lips just as he hit the foul water. As soon as he regained control, he scrambled to his feet.

"Isk human boy stupid!" Karak hissed.

A distant shriek echoed behind them. Jekaran traded a glance with Irvis and then looked at Karak. Another shriek, this one louder, confirmed he had given away their position.

"Aeks!" Karak growled as he mimed something before breaking into a run.

Jekaran didn't know what the communication was supposed to mean, but he didn't have to. He leapt forward to follow Karak. Another, closer, shriek spurred Jekaran into a reckless sprint and he overtook both Irvis and Karak. As his burst of energy faded, Karak overtook him and Jekaran was again following the Vorakk shaman. He glanced over his shoulder and caught a view of Irvis trying to keep up. The serpent-like shape of the worm appeared as it shot out of the water only a few paces behind the lagging monk.

It's going to get him.

Jekaran slid and almost fell again as he double-backed and ran toward Irvis. He arrived just in time to throw himself between the monk and the attacking worm. Pain flared in his outer forearm as the creature sank a dozen pin-like teeth into his flesh. Adrenaline took over, and Jekaran flung his arm out wide, successfully throwing the worm off him and into the tunnel wall. It wriggled and writhed as it fell beneath the water, and then two tentacles slapped Jekaran in the side of the face, knocking him back.

Hands, this time belonging to Irvis, caught him and hauled him to his feet. Irvis' eyes widened when he saw Jekaran's bloody arm. A beat later, the worm shrieked as it exploded back out of the water. Irvis pulled Jekaran along until he was stable enough to run on his own, the splash behind them the only indication the worm continued to hunt them. Panting, they caught up with Karak, who had slowed to meet them.

"Rok," he growled as he waved to something ahead of them.

That's when Jekaran noticed a shaft of sunlight illuminating a ladder only a hundred or so paces away.

"It'll ... be ... on ... us ... before ... we can make it out!" Irvis said between breaths.

"Karak!" Jekaran said as the idea came to him. "You two get up the ladder and open that cover. I'll distract it!"

"Isk" Karak snarled. "Human boy will die!"

He shook his head. "Just go and be ready to use a fire spell!" Before the Vorakk could argue, Jekaran broke away from them and ran to the left wall of the tunnel where he began stomping and splashing as much as he could. The worm veered toward him and reared up out of the water with a shriek. Jekaran waited for it, and then threw himself to his right just as the creature closed to within inches of his face.

With lightning speed Jekaran did not anticipate, the worm changed direction and plowed into his side. He slammed into the wall, his head striking hard against the curvature of the stone. A hundred stars exploded across his vision and he suddenly wanted to vomit. The next thing Jekaran knew, he was on his back looking up through sewer water at the worm rearing to strike. He rolled to the right and scrambled out of the water with a desperate gasp. The worm flew at him, and Jekaran was only able to move to the side enough to avoid a face full of the worm's teeth.

Instead, it sank its open maw into his left shoulder and Jekaran screamed. He could feel the worm's mouth ungulate as it began to suck his blood. His vision began to darken and his thoughts slowed. Desperately realizing that he was seconds away from syncope, Jekaran acted on his first impulse, turned his head to face the worm, and bit into its slimy grey body. Immediately the creature released him and shrieked as it pulled back.

"JEKARAN!" Irvis shouted.

Jekaran spat out a chunk of bloodless worm flesh and looked over to see the monk at the top of the ladder, Karak having already exited the sewer. Jekaran scrambled into a sprint toward the ladder. He stumbled and almost fell a few times, but somehow managed to stay upright. The worm raced after him through the water. He knew he couldn't outrun the vile creature, so he jumped the last yard onto the ladder, where Karak and Irvis quickly hoisted him out.

"Fire!" Jekaran shouted.

Karak slammed the grated cover shut and then motioned with his hand. His hovering ball of white light changed into one of red fire and then shot down through the slots of the grate just as the worm ascended the shaft. A heartbeat later, a tongue of flame exploded from the sewer culvert, and Jekaran heard the worm scream in pain. The fire was no more than a brief flash, but when it went out, only silence remained.

CHAPTER 14

Jekaran had scarcely drawn a relieved breath before vomit involuntarily spewed from his mouth and nose. He wasn't sure if it was the fact that he was covered from head to toe in raw sewage, or if the worm had injected a poison into his veins. He had just enough time to catch a glimpse of his surroundings before retching again. They were in a large, metal culvert, the open end facing out over Rasha's wide river.

"Hold him still!" he heard Irvis scold.

"Reka, human boy poisoned?" he heard Karak ask as his scaly arms reached up beneath Jekaran's armpits and gripped him.

"I am trying to find out," Irvis snapped.

A tingling sensation washed over Jekaran's shoulder and extended down his arm just as sound began to fade and his vision became a tunnel of darkness, and he knew he wasn't facing just unconsciousness, but death. In that quiet moment on the threshold of oblivion, Jekaran found that he was not alone. The alien presence skulking in the back of his mind was there, this time in full force.

Who are you? Jekaran asked.

The presence did not reply although somehow he knew it heard him.

Where are you?

Jekaran's mind shifted and rolled, casting him into a vague vision-a description somehow inadequate. It was more than sight, sound, or any other of his senses. It was as if the communication cut through all of that and forced itself directly into the very core of his consciousness. He saw a road, then a group of men traveling, then a wagon, and then a large, long, wooden lockbox. It took a moment for Jekaran to put it all together, but when he did, the realization struck him.

You're the sword.

It responded with a wordless confirmation.

Light and sound overwhelmed his senses and he gasped as though he had been drowning and had just broken the surface to taste desperately needed air.

"Got him," he heard Irvis say with a weary tone of relief.

"Reka human boy live, yes?" Karak asked.

"Jekaran!" Irvis called his name. "Can you hear me, child?"

Jekaran blinked his eyes until the forms of Irvis and Karak changed from indistinct blurs to discernible shapes. It took a few more blinks for his vision to completely clear, but when it did, he quickly sat up. And that's when the pain returned. His hand reflexively shot to his shoulder where he could feel drying blood and torn flesh.

"Easy," Irvis said as he gently put a hand on Jekaran's other shoulder.

"What happened?"

"Isk stupid human boy!" Karak spat. "Worm almost kill him!"

Jekaran looked at Irvis for an explanation. The round face monk nodded and said, "Don't you know that a worm's bite is toxic?"

"Poison?" Jekaran asked.

Irvis shook his graying head. "Not exactly. Their bite spreads a fast-acting infection that can kill very quickly, usually over a course of hours."

"Then why?" Jekaran began.

Irvis cut him off. "Because you're a damned fool that got bit twice as well ate a bit of the monster's flesh!" Irvis gagged. "Disgusting!"

"But how am I alive?"

Irvis raised his right hand and turned it so Jekaran could see a silver ring with an amethyst stone strangling the man's chubby ring finger.

"A talis!" Jekaran said.

Irvis nodded. "All monks of Rasheera have some variety of healing talis. Technically it belongs to the monastery, but I guess it's mine now."

"If you healed me, then why," Jekaran reached up to gingerly touch his shoulder, "am I still wounded?"

Irvis sighed. "Because my talis' power only diagnoses and purges disease or toxins. I am, or was," he corrected himself, "little more than an initiate. Higher ranking brethren are entrusted with more powerful, more comprehensive healing talises." Irvis scowled. "And you're lucky we're so close to Rasha's well! Healing you cost twice the Apeiron of what my ring can hold on its own!"

"Thank you," Jekaran said sincerely.

Irvis' scowl faded as he slowly nodded. "We best wash off in the river." He waved at the blue river flowing placidly before them. "Else we all get sick." He shivered. "I think I swallowed some of that shi—" the monk caught himself and finished, "—filthy water!" With that, he hopped the three feet down from the culvert to the riverbank and began jogging toward the river.

Karak helped Jekaran down from the culvert. When he winced from his shoulder wound, the Vorakk shaman said, "Karak can make medicine to help fix bite aka."

"Sounds good," Jekaran said through gritted teeth. "But you help me any more than that, and we won't be even anymore."

Karak looked at him, a puzzled expression on his face. "Reka even?"

"You know," Jekaran said as he stepped carefully down the muddy bank toward the shallows of the river. "I spared your life, and you freed me from prison. We're even."

The Vorakk shaman shook his head. "Not why Karak get human boy out of prison aka."

Jekaran reached the river and waded in until the water was up to his chest. It was cold, but it felt good on his wounded arm. "Then why did you come for me?"

Karak sloshed after him. "For stop Eater aka."

Jekaran bent his knees slightly so that the cool water washed up over his shoulder. At first, it sent a shock through his whole body, but a moment later, it began to numb his flesh, which dulled the pain. "I have no idea what you're talking about."

Karak made an expression Jekaran thought was probably the Vorakk version of confusion. "Reka humans no word for this?"

Irvis abruptly surfaced from the river at Jekaran's side, startling him.

"We do," Irvis said with river water pouring out of his mouth. "What?" he said after catching Jekaran's disapproving stare. "I'm trying to clean my mouth."

"Fat monk knows Eater tak?" Karak asked.

"I know the word, shaman. But like Jekaran, I don't know what you are referring to," Irvis said, again with a patience he used when acting like a holy man. Jekaran suspected it was a trained reflex to the anger triggered by Karak's description of him as *fat monk*.

Karak glanced up to the sky, now streaked red in the wake of the setting sun. "Uska, Vorakk shaman talk to spirits. Spirits tell Vorakk priest of Eater. Vorakk priest send Karak and brothers go for find Eater, to stop."

"The priest is the leader of your people?" Irvis asked.

Karak shook his head. "Ssk only lead Vorakk shaman, no warrior no hunter."

Irvis nodded in understanding, but Jekaran was lost. "Vorakk priests are shaman mentors?"

Irvis nodded. "They find those among their people who can use magic, and then train them. It sounds like Karak's priest sent him on a quest."

"No Karak's priest aeks!" the Vorakk snapped. "Priest of Vorakk."

Irvis looked surprised. "You were sent by your High Priest?"

Karak nodded. "Ssk Karak brothers for stop Eater."

The raiders, Jekaran realized. *All three were shaman!* "Where are your brothers?" Jekaran wasn't sure if Karak had meant fellow shaman or literal kin.

His features elongated. "One die, one lost ska."

"I'm sorry," Jekaran said. "You should have just asked for our scraps."

A fire came into Karak's eyes. "Humans hate Vorakk. Hunt and Kill aeks!"

Jekaran slowly nodded. It was true enough. In the southern cities-those closest to the Vorakk desert-nobles tracked and killed the creatures as a kind of sport, their scaly skin turned into bags or scabbards. Jekaran had never thought much about it, he had believed the lizard men were little more than animals. Now, he saw just how wrong he had been. The

Vorakk were people with an organized society and culture. And they possessed some sort of magic, which is something humans lacked.

"What is this Eater?" Irvis asked.

Karak appeared to search for the right *human* words. "Uska Eater is end. End of Vorakk, end of humans, end of trees, end of birds, end of life. Humans no word for Eater?"

"Do you mean like a natural disaster?" Irvis clarified. "Like a storm or a ground quake?"

Karak shook his head, a grim look on his face. "Isk not natural. Eater evil. Spirits tell Uska, Vorakk priest say Eater born. Start in East and move closer. Spirits say Eater kill whole forest. No left, not even creepers ska."

"He means insects, child," Irvis said to Jekaran without looking at him.

Jekaran felt a flash of irritation at the monk. Ez sometimes did the same thing, talk to him like he was dumber than he was. "So what does this have to do with me?"

Karak looked away from Irvis and stared hard at Jekaran. "Uska Human boy go to Eater."

"What?"

Karak paused again before speaking. "Humans call fate. Reka human boy know fate, yes?"

Jekaran nodded.

"Uska fate like web of spider. All strings join, all strings go to middle. For Karak, Eater is middle. Human boy is string that goes to middle. Karak go with human boy aka."

"You think that I'm going to lead you to this Eater?" Jekaran shot an uncertain glance at Irvis. "Why?"

"Isk human boy green eyes." Karak's tone suggested the answer was obvious.

He caught Irvis obnoxiously leaning in to stare at his face. He pushed the monk back with a splash and said, "So what! It's unusual, but not unheard for humans to have green eyes."

"Is for Vorakk," Karak said. "Vorakk not see many humans aka. Priest say green eyes sign for follow human boy. Human boy no find Eater if in jail, so Karak get human boy out jail aka."

Jekaran stared hard at Karak. *The Vorakk must be crazy.* Karak saved him based on a superstition that he could lead him to a destiny. Jekaran shook his head. "I'm sorry, Karak. I can't go looking for this Eater of yours. I have to go to Jeryn to find my uncle. He could be in danger."

His argument faded as the sword pulled on Jekaran's mind, forcing him to look northwest into the mountains.

I am not going that way.

Irvis slapped Jekaran on the back. "Splendid! Rasheera smiles on us. With your liege lord taking the sword, it will make its way into the hands of the king. Not even Kaul would dare try to steal it from *him*." Irvis bellowed a laugh of relieved joy. "I can't wait to see Argentus again! It's been at least five years since we spoke face to face. Last time we were together we got so drunk that I couldn't tell a wench from a wagon-wheel." He timidly added, "Which led to some embarrassing confusion on my part."

Jekaran was about to remind Irvis that monks of Rasheera weren't supposed to drink when the sword pulled on his mind again. This time it made the thought of his going in any direction other than northwest feel wrong. He distantly heard Karak asking Irvis what he meant, and the monk stuttered a vague answer.

I can't come for you, Jekaran said. *I have to find my uncle.*

A wordless plea for help needled Jekaran's thoughts, pathetic and demanding all at the same time like a hungry infant's panicked wail for the next meal. Denying it stabbed Jekaran's heart with an anxious sadness followed by nausea.

But what about Ez?

An image flashed in his mind. It was of him standing between Ez and the man with mismatched eyes. Jekaran had the sword raised to a blocking position. It was as if the sword was saying to him, *together we can protect your uncle.*

"Child?" Irvis called.

Jekaran started and turned to find that he had moved a dozen feet toward the middle of the river, his feet touching the very edge of the shallows. Both the monk and the Vorakk shaman were staring at him.

"Where are you going?" Irvis asked. "Jeryn is the other direction and we don't need to swim the river to get there."

"Reka worm poison hurt human boy brain?" Karak asked.

"I have to get Ez's sword back," he announced before Irvis could reply to Karak's question.

Irvis waded toward him. "From your liege lord?"

"Stop calling him that!" Jekaran snapped. "Gymal's not my liege lord. He's just a self-important bully who happens to have a dousing stone!"

"Still ..." Irvis said uncertainly.

"Ez is counting on me to protect that talis!" He motioned to Irvis. "Counting on both of us. We are going to catch up to the well-finders, steal the sword back, and then take it to him."

"Child?" Irvis looked worried. "That talis is extraordinarily dangerous. It's best that you just forget about it."

That suggestion actually made Jekaran nauseous. He couldn't just *forget* about it. The damn thing was inside his head after all. *With it, I can protect Ez from Kaul.* That last thought had the distinct feel of a rationalization, but it no longer mattered. His path was chosen for him.

"I'm going to get the sword," he said defiantly. "I could use your help," he then added in a friendlier tone.

Irvis stared at him for a long moment before finally nodding. "Argentus would blame me if I let anything happen to you."

"Good," Jekaran said and then turned to face Karak. "I'm sorry, Karak. I *am* grateful for your getting me out of jail, but I can't go with you to find this Eater. I'm sorry."

Karak shook his head. "Isk human boy not know fate. Human boy lead Karak to Eater. Not matter where he goes."

Jekaran slowly nodded. "Well, that invisible thing you can do is sure to come in handy."

Karak flashed a sharp-toothed grin.

Jekaran turned to face the direction of the sword's psychic call. *I'm coming,* he thought. The response felt pleased, like an ethereal smile. Jekaran raised his eyebrows, and then dropped them without response. This was going to take some getting used to.

Chapter 15

Maely tried not to stare at Lady Kairah, who currently took the uncanny form of Rasha's magistrate, a sixty-year-old man with bushy white eyebrows, a balding scalp, and a hunched posture. Her voice even sounded like the old man's gravelly tone.

She must be a very high-ranking noble to possess a talis that could change her very appearance, Maely thought for the tenth time.

Kairah had secured an audience with the magistrate the previous day in order to petition for Jekaran's release. Unsurprisingly, the magistrate refused, but Kairah had explained to Maely that part of her plan was for her to get a good look at the man. Maely hadn't understood why until later when Kairah transformed from a striking beauty into a gnarled old geezer right before her eyes. Although she had needed some coaching on how to *talk* and *act* like the magistrate, had Maely not known the truth, she wouldn't have been able to tell the difference.

Their plan was for Kairah to go to the Rasha jail and order Jek's release. Maely would go with her, and if anyone asked questions, Lady Kairah, in the form of the old magistrate, would say Maely had witnessed Jek fighting off the bandits in defense of a noblewoman, and that such extenuating circumstance warranted him a full pardon. It was true enough. Maely just hoped the jailers wouldn't think to verify the order by sending a runner to the magistrate's office where they would find an identical old man hearing cases.

They entered the jail's annex as three guards dealt a deck of cards.

Kairah cleared her throat, and the men did a double take as they dropped the cards to stand at attention. One hit the table in his haste, spilling a stein of ale across the small, round table and knocking over two of the four chairs. He saluted, trying to ignore the ale pouring off the edge of furniture to splash into a puddle on the wood floor.

"M-m lord," he stammered, eyes flicking to the cards on the table. He looked passed Kairah to Maely. "Where is Captain Sauler?"

"That is not your concern," Kairah snapped in the old magistrate's gravelly voice. "I have come in person to order the release of the boy you arrested three nights ago for possession of a weapon talis."

Maely thought it sounded a little too formal, but the man was the magistrate after all. It wouldn't be unusual for him to use stiff language. The guard shot a glance at his comrades, an odd look of bewilderment suddenly passing over all of their faces. *Something's wrong,* Maely's instincts shouted.

"I'm sorry, my lord. I must have not heard you right."

"The boy you arrested three nights ago for using a weapon talis!" Kairah slowly emphasized the words in what Maely thought must've been an attempt to sound condescendingly irritated, though it came across as making the magistrate sound drunk or slow. "I want him released immediately!"

The guards shared another confused look and then their leader cleared his throat. "Did not Captain Sauler go to speak with you earlier?"

"About what?" Kairah snapped in what Maely thought was a more convincing expression of frustration.

"The boy is not here." The guard's voice quivered.

"Where is he?" she demanded.

"Escaped sir." The guard audibly gulped. "This afternoon, along with that voyeur monk."

"How?"

The guard shared another look with his peers. "Someone let them out. We think they escaped the city through the sewer system."

Maely cringed as Kairah looked at her, eyes begging for direction. "Well, thank you for your time." She grabbed Kairah by the elbow and gently turned her toward the door. "I trust you will not mention this to anyone," she said to the guards in a semi-hushed tone. "No one must know of his worsening condition."

The three guards slowly nodded, each wide-eyed as they absorbed the implied meaning of Maely's lie. "Come along, my lord. It is time for your medicine," she added as she steered Kairah out of the jail annex and led her silently into a side alley.

The noble woman returned to her true form, although her eyes still held that look of uncertain confusion.

"That could've gone badly had those guards not been so afraid of getting in trouble." Maely sighed.

"What do we do now?" Kairah asked.

"*We*," Maely sarcastically emphasized the word, "don't do anything. *I* am going to go try to find Jek."

"You will no longer help me?"

"Look, Lady Kairah." Maely rounded on the noblewoman. "I am not sure what you want with my friend, but you didn't fulfill your end of the bargain to free him; therefore, we owe you nothing!"

Kairah slowly nodded. "Your social strata are more fractured than I previously understood."

"What are you talking about?" Maely said incredulously.

"Your place in the lower caste has instilled in you an animosity and distrust toward those of higher station."

Maely wasn't certain what Kairah was saying, but it had the unmistakable sound of aristocratic condescension. "Look, I don't care how rich and powerful you might be. Your kind may have wealth, talises, and education, but you don't own us! You can't tell us what to ..." Screams and excited shouting rang from a neighboring street, immediately stifling her indignant tirade.

Both she and Kairah turned to look in the direction of the clamor. Unable to help herself, Maely cautiously moved to the mouth of the alley and peered around the corner. She gasped as she saw what looked like an enormous statue tromping down the street, its footfalls kicking up bits of cobblestone road.

"Oh no," she heard Kairah gasp. She looked up to find the noblewoman leaning out of the alley over Maely's head.

The behemoth stood twenty feet tall, glossy in a way that made it look like it were made of glass, and it held a glowing jewel set in its face like a Cyclops' eye. The living statue appeared oblivious to the panicked people, the fruit stands, and handcarts as it moved in a systematic pattern.

Like it's looking for something, Maely thought as suspicion began to germinate in her mind.

"Golden womb of the goddess," she swore. "What is that thing?" When no answer came, Maely turned to see Kairah moving quickly away from the mouth of the alley. Maely turned and jogged to catch up to her.

"I need to leave the city," Kairah said in an urgent tone.

"That thing is after you, isn't it?"

"Yes," Kairah said simply. "I do not know how he did it, but he has sent them after me."

"Who?" Maely caught Kairah by the arm.

Kairah looked down at her in surprise. "My brother. He sent that talis and probably another to apprehend me."

"*That's a* talis?"

Kairah resumed her brisk stride. "Yes, a very powerful crystal golem."

Maely overtook Kairah and rounded on her to block her path. "*Who are you?*" Maely demanded. "You have a powerful talis, but you don't act like a noble. And you don't know things that everyone else knows! Things *you* should know."

Kairah's eyes flicked to the side, but she made no reply.

"Who are you?" Maely repeated and was startled as she felt the words accompanied by a rush of force, as though they were arrows striking their mark.

Kairah's eyes widened as she opened her mouth to answer, but was cut off as screaming flooded the alley.

Maely looked passed her and felt her stomach clench. The golem stood in profile at the mouth of the alley, a mob of terrified people sprinting away from it. A group of Rasha's guards rushed out of the fleeing crowd and hurled spears at it, but they bounced off the glass skin and clattered to the ground, causing the guards to turn and join the retreating mob. The golem slowly turned its head in their direction, its glowing jewel-eye bathing the alley in purple light.

"Run!" Kairah grabbed Maely by the arm and hauled her into a sprint.

The golem exploded into a run toward them, it's pounding footfalls shaking the ground like small earthquakes. The buildings surrounding the alley trembled, chunks of stone and brick raining from their walls. The women dodged and hurdled over the debris, and Maely could feel as much as hear the statue was gaining on them.

They reached the far end of the alley and darted out into the street where Kairah paused, her eyes darting in one direction and then the other.

"Come on!" Maely snapped as she grabbed her wrist and yanked her to their right.

They had only made it two dozen feet down the block when screams erupted from the crowd behind them. Maely cast a glance over her shoulder to see the golem exit the alley, smashing through two warestables and sending their merchants screaming in retreat. It paused, searching for its target. Tripping on some street flotsam, she stumbled, her palms throbbing as they caught the impact of the ground beneath her. Kairah pulled her to her feet just in time for the massive creature's footfalls to resume.

It's spotted us. "We can't outrun that thing!" Maely shouted.

Kairah abruptly stopped running and turned to face the creature, her hands balled into tiny delicate fists.

Maely pulled on her arm. "What are you doing!"

Kairah didn't answer, but instead closed her eyes as if in concentration or prayer.

Maely felt the ground shake as the gigantic, translucent golem barreled toward them. She was just about to break away and leave Kairah to her chosen fate when she saw the golem stumble. With what appeared to be a disproportionate amount of exertion, the statue attempted to continue forward, but couldn't seem to lift its leg. Maely's eyes dropped to the cobblestone street, and she gasped. The ground, muddy and swelled with water, trapped the Golem's legs in a thick mixture of dislodged cobblestones and mud. It struggled to loosen itself, but each time it pulled one leg out with a *squelch,* its other leg sunk further into the muck. It was stuck.

Maely tore her stare from the Golem to look at Kairah. Her eyes, now open, lit with triumph. "How did…" she trailed off when Kairah turned and launched back into a sprint.

"That will not hold it for long!" she called over her shoulder.

Without looking back, Maely caught up to her. "What now?"

"I need to get out of the city," she said. "The crystal golem will depart once it realizes I am no longer here, and the wanton destruction will stop."

An idea popped into Maely's mind. "Can that thing swim?"

She shook her head. "It is not likely."

"Then we need to get to a riverboat!" Maely searched until she caught sight of one of Rasha's canals. She redoubled her run, following the water as the canal snaked to the north. Renewed screams from the crowd echoed behind them, and she knew the golem escaped Kairah's impromptu marsh and would soon be upon them.

The boat was moving at a steady pace, like it was under ore-power from an unseen galley. Maely quickly made her way to the sheer edge of the canal. The boat was too far from the canal's edge for them to jump onto it from the side, but they could jump onto its deck from one of the several high bridges which spanned the canal at regular intervals.

The next one was less than a hundred yards ahead of them.

"Come on!" Maely shouted as she grabbed Kairah's wrist.

They easily outpaced the boat, and it was less than a minute before they reached the canal bridge. As they turned left and began ascending the arch, Maely felt the ground shake and looked up to see the crystal golem closing the distance between them at a startling rate. Panic swelled her heart, beads of perspiration tickling the back of her neck.

They reached the center of the bridge as the riverboat began to pass underneath. "Come on, this side." Maely crossed to the other side with Kairah at her heels and swung a leg over the wooden rail. The bridge shook beneath them, and she nearly slipped as she brought her other leg over. She looked up to find the crystal golem tromping up the arching bridge.

"Hurry!" she snapped at Kairah and helped the woman over the rail.

The bridge shook again, drawing Maely's attention behind them. The crystal golem bounded forward and was almost to the center of the bridge. She looked down and found the riverboat's prow just emerging from beneath the shadow of the arch. She was going to have to time their jump just right, which meant waiting until the last possible second.

Kairah gasped, and Maely's head pivoted skyward to see the hulking form of the crystal golem looming over them. A quick check of the boat below showed only a few feet of visible deck. Another shake of the bridge hailed the golem's advance, and Maely knew that they were out of time.

With one last glance at the living glass statue, Maely threw an arm around Kairah's waist and jumped. Her stomach rose into her throat as they fell, but before she had time to fully contemplate the situation, she slammed hard into the deck of the ship. Kairah hit a heartbeat later— *when had she let go of the woman?*—and rolled halfway off the deck. Maely caught her just before she went over and was able to haul her back to safety.

"HEY!" a man's voice angrily shouted. "Just what in the hell do you think you're doing?"

Maely looked up to find a leather-faced man with a knobby nose rushing toward them.

"Get off my boat!" he demanded.

"Please, sir" Maely began.

The riverboat captain glanced over his shoulder to his crew and snapped at them. He's *going to throw us overboard* she realized with a stab of panic igniting hot anger.

She shot to her feet and hissed, "You are not going to touch us!" Again, that strange undercurrent of power accompanied the words, and somehow she felt as though she assailed the man.

The riverboat captain flinched and he cowed. "Y-Yes, mistress," he stammered.

Mistress?

Just then, the riverboat rocked backward, its prow suddenly rising up out of the water with a deafening crash and the cracking of splintering wood. Maely and Kairah began to slide toward the stern. As she desperately searched for something to grab onto, Maely looked up to see the crystal golem falling through the deck of the boat.

It jumped onto the boat!

She hadn't expected that.

Panicked shouts rang out as men dove overboard, some voluntarily and some involuntarily. A final loud crack signaled the boat had split into two as water rushed over the center of the ship. Without thinking, Maely gripped Kairah's wrist, hauled her to unsteady feet, and then leapt off the prow. Her spectacles and hat flew off as she fell, gasping, into the cold river water. Every nerve tingled frozen, her senses clouded by icy liquid gushing down her throat and drowning her lungs. In the black starless night, there was no difference between water and sky, and disorientation took hold as she struggled to swim toward a gulp of life sustaining air. Summer days of swimming with Jek and Mulladin in a forest lake near Genra played across the shadows of her eyelids as she sunk toward a watery grave.

CHAPTER 16

Darkness encroached upon the edges of Maely's vision, and a strange sense of oxygen-deprived euphoria began to take her. Her head felt light and, as inappropriate as she knew it was, she felt like bursting into laughter. Then the water expelled from her lungs in a rush of vomit and the relief of sweet air replaced it. Her vision cleared and she found herself lying on the stony edge of the canal, Kairah leaning over her.

"What happened?"

"The golem will be at the bottom of the river long enough for me to get away."

"I was drowning," Maely said.

Kairah flashed a smile. "I spell-casted the water to lift us out of the canal, and then drew the water from your lungs."

"You what?" Maely asked incredulously. "Just how many talises do you own?" That's when she noticed the woman's hair. It was no longer black, but a jewel-like shade of purple, and her skin appeared paler.

"Your hair," Maely gasped.

Kairah's eyes widened and she clutched at her neck, as though feeling for something.

Her necklace, Maely remembered. *She had been wearing a necklace.*

"Oh no," Kairah looked stricken. "I lost it." She jumped to her feet and ran for the cover of nearby trees where she could hide from the crowd of people amassing at the edge of the canal.

Maely scurried after Kairah, her feet struggling for traction against the wet stone. The woman kept her head down, apparently trying to hide her hair but was doing a poor job of it. Maely caught up to her, grabbing her arm and forcing her to stop.

"What are you?"

Kairah's eyes nervously darted around the street. "Someone will see me," she hissed.

Maely cast a glance over her shoulder to the crowd gathering to gawk at the wrecked boat. None of them looked back at her; all eyes were watching the crew swim to safety.

"Come on," Maely led her to stand behind a wagon stacked high with hay. "We just need to get you a cloak."

She nodded, her eyes still wide with fright.

"Wait here," she said. "There's a general store just down the street. I'll see if I can beg one for you."

Kairah nodded, and Maely quickly moved down the street through a mass of people. Scanning store fronts, her heart skipped when she located the universal bread symbol painted on a splintered marquee. General goods for sale. *Found it.*

A bell rang as she entered the shop, and a fat, middle-aged man glanced away from a dirty window. "What's going on out there?" he asked.

"A riverboat sunk," Maely said. It wasn't a lie. She just didn't tell the portly merchant a giant living statue made of glass sunk it. He wouldn't believe her anyway.

The merchant turned to stare back out of the window, unaware the spectacle was half a block upriver.

"Do you have cloaks?" Maely asked.

The merchant looked at her, apparently noticing for the first time that her clothes were soaking wet. Under the man's scrutiny, Maely reflexively reached up to pull her hat down over her brow, but stopped as she realized she had lost the hat in the chase.

"You're as sodden as milk toast," he said with a question in his voice.

"I got splashed when the riverboat smashed into the side of the canal."

"It ran afoul of the shipping lanes?"

Maely nodded and then quickly added, "It was scary." *That was too much*, she chided herself.

The merchant stared at her for a long moment before saying, "Two Aies."

TWO? Maely's temper began to rise. Even though she had lost her bag, and therefore her coin, while running from the crystal golem, she was indignant at the price the merchant was asking. A good cloak rarely cost more than one Aies, and she was sure that the man was taking advantage of her because she was a young woman. *But I don't look like a girl,* she remembered, *but I am obviously young.*

"I don't have any coin," Maely confessed, working to keep the anger from her voice.

"I don't abide beggars, and I don't have any work for you," the fat merchant pointed at the door.

"Please sir," she said in her best orphan voice, "I'm wet, and it's cold. I need something to wear while I dry my clothes."

"Go naked," the merchant said apathetically as he turned away from Maely.

So he does think I'm a boy, she decided. *Or he's a pervert.*

"Don't you have a used cloak that I could borrow for a night?"

"Borrow?" the merchant scoffed. "If I lent you a cloak, we both know that I'd never see it again. And even if you did bring it back, I'd have to drop the price because of its use."

"Please—" Maely began.

"Get out!" the merchant shouted. "Or I'll call the guard."

The offense tipped the scale and all of Maely's stress from losing Jekaran, being chased by a living statue, and nearly drowning broke her emotional control and she erupted, "I want a cloak!" For a third time Maely felt a force thrill through her chest and strike out at the shop keeper. The man stumbled back, daze curtaining his eyes.

"Yes, mistress," the shopkeeper said quietly.

Maely couldn't help but smile to herself as she left the store, the man's finest sable cloak folded and tucked beneath one arm. She had no idea why people were doing what she said, but she hoped the trend would continue. She jogged back to where she had left Kairah hiding behind the wagon.

"Here," Maely proffered the cloak.

Kairah nodded gratefully, unfolding it to swing onto her shoulders. She then pulled the hood up as far as she could and tucked a few stray strands of purple hair into it.

"Perfect," Maely said.

"Thank you, Maely," Kairah said as she examined her reflection in the window of the building behind the wagon. "How did you acquire so fine a cloak with no currency?"

Feeling smug, Maely grinned. "At first he didn't want to give it to me, but then I got mad and demanded one. After that, he was more than happy to provide me his finest cloak at no charge."

Kairah turned to face her, eyes sharp with suspicion.

"What?" Maely asked.

She glanced down at Maely's hands, then at her neck. Before Maely could ask what she was looking for, Kairah's hand shot out and grabbed the front of her over-sized tunic.

"Hey!" she snapped and was about to order Kairah to back off when the woman took hold of the leather cord around her neck and snapped it off in one fluid motion. Kairah dangled her mother's ring in front of her face, the purple-haired woman's eyes narrowing as she considered the ring.

"That's mine!" she made a swipe for the ring, but the taller Kairah lifted it out of her reach.

"This is an abomination," she said in a cold tone.

"It's my mother's lucky ring!" Maely snapped back, anger rising inside her.

"This is a compulsion talis!" she hissed.

Maely stopped reaching for the ring. "A what?"

"A compulsion talis," Kairah repeated in a more amicable, if not still a cold tone. "It impresses your will upon another's mind, and forces all but the strongest of will to obey."

Maely stared at the ring. Now it all made sense. Her mother had said she used it to get better prices and favors from her clients, and Maely had used it on the shopkeeper and probably the riverboat captain; both men having called her *mistress*.

"I didn't know," she confessed.

Kairah didn't seem to hear her. "Among my people, using such a foul thing is a most egregious offense."

"What did you just say?"

Kairah looked up at her, eyes widening with fear.

"What are you?" Maely demanded, although this time there was no undercurrent of power to her words.

Kairah remained silent.

"You act like you don't know how the real world works. You have a powerful talis or talises. Your skin is the whitest that I've ever seen, and your hair is the color of an Apeira well. I'm not stupid!"

She sighed and nodded. "Your unsolicited aid facilitating my escape from the crystal golem has earned you an explanation."

"And you talk funny, even for a noble," Maely added.

Kairah flashed an amused smile. "Your suspicions are correct. I am not human," she said in a lower tone. "I am an Allosian."

Maely stared at the woman, her mind working to digest what Kairah had just told her. "One of the fey-folk?" she excitedly asked.

Kairah shot a nervous glance out from behind the wagon, and then put a finger to her lips. "Please, not quite so loud."

"Sorry," Maely whispered. The outburst was childish, and could have garnered attention neither of them needed. "It's just, I always thought your kind were just a story."

Kairah nodded. "That is the common assumption among your race, a fallacy we have encouraged."

"What are you doing in Rasha?"

Kairah glanced over the stacked hay in the bed of the wagon at the crowd massed near the edge of the canal. Maely followed her gaze and saw a group of Rasha guards approaching the group.

She looked back at her. "Not here." She left the cover of the wagon and began walking briskly up the street.

Maely caught up to her. "You still have my ring."

Kairah nodded. "And it would be a dereliction of my duty as a student of the College of Disciplines not to take it back to Allose for destruction."

Maely's anger bubbled up and she snapped, "It's mine!"

"It is dangerous," Kairah calmly replied. "Do you realize the kind of trouble this talis could cause? I make no exaggeration when I tell you such talises have been at the root of rapes, murders, and even wars among your people."

Before Maely could retort, Kairah turned right onto a narrow side street. Maely had to work to keep pace with the taller woman's long strides.

"Where is Allose?"

Kairah shook her head beneath the hood of her cloak. "That is our most closely guarded secret."

"Why?"

Kairah glanced at her and Maely saw something in her face that looked like surprise.

"Because of you," she said in a matter-of-fact tone. Maely thought that her look must've betrayed her confusion because Kairah added, "humans" in clarification.

"You're afraid of us?" In light of all the legends of Allosians with their powerful potions, talises, and magic, the very idea they would be intimidated by puny, non-magical humans was laughable.

Kairah was silent for a long moment before answering, "You are not educated, are you?"

That remark affronted Maely's pride and again she had to stamp out the flames of rising anger. "I know my letters!" she snapped. "That's more than most farm women!"

"I meant no offense," Kairah said patiently. "I was referring to education in a specific discipline, namely history."

"I don't know much of history." Maely conceded.

"Well, suffice it to say." Kairah made another unexpected right turn, this time into a circular commons with benches and trees. "Your kind drove us into hiding by abusing the talises my people had gifted to them. The majority of Allosians have come to accept our decline as a course of the natural order, but not my brother, Jenoc."

"He's the one who sent that crystal golem after you?"

Kairah nodded. "Probably two of them."

Two? The thought terrified her.

"Jenoc believes Shaelar rightly belongs to my people and the humans must either be controlled or ..."

"Or what?" Maely probed.

"...eradicated."

"Like, killed?"

Kairah nodded.

"All of us?"

"Yes," she said sadly. "To that end, my brother is trying to incite your people to war amongst yourselves."

"War is nothing new," Maely said. "My mother said that my father died in the war with Haeshala when I was a baby."

Kairah shook her head as she wound around a tree. "You do not understand."

Maely bristled, her eyes narrowing. *She really has a talent for accidentally talking down to people.*

"Jenoc," Kairah continued, "plans to teach your people how to create weapon talises."

"What?" Maely stopped. "But we don't have magic."

Kairah stopped and turned to face her. "There are talises that allow humans to spell-cast like my kind. It is how your ancestors were able to make enough weapon talises to become a threat to us. Fortunately, for us, that secret has been lost to your people. But Jenoc plans to teach it to the military leaders of your three nations."

Maely felt her heart sink as the awful realization of what Kairah was suggesting settled on her. "He wants us to wipe each other out." Kairah looked surprised that Maely had figured it out. "What?" she snapped defiantly. "Surprised I'm not as stupid as other humans?"

The hood of Kairah's cloak shifted as she shook her head. "I do not share my brother's beliefs, Maely. I do not think humans need to be destroyed. I believe all life is sacred, and that humans have as much a right to exist as Allosians." She turned and resumed walking. "That is why I am here. I plan to warn your leaders so they will not be deceived by my brother's warmongering."

Maely resumed following her. "That's why you're trying to get to the capital," she said. "And why you wanted Jek to be your guide."

"And now I think that I will need more than just a guide. I will need a protector."

Maely scoffed. "And you still want Jek? Sure, he's athletic, but except for wrestling, he doesn't know how to fight. He's also clumsy."

"I believe your friend has bonded with a powerful ego talis."

"That sword?"

"Yes. I would guess that, like your ring, this was the first time the sword has been near an Apeira well in years, and so it began working after regaining a charge. Apparently, the sword makes its wielder into a skilled warrior. And it is of Allosian make, I could tell that even from afar. It is too elegant and subtle to be the work of ancient humans." She cast a concerned glance at her, "Forgive me, Maely, but your people as a whole lack subtlety. The weapon talises humans crafted were crude, showy, and usually resulted in an explosion of some sort."

"The point?" Maely asked through clenched teeth.

"Like I said, the sword is an ego talis. An ego talis is a talis that has been imbued with a rudimentary intelligence, and can think and communicate through a psychic link it establishes at bonding a wielder."

"It's alive?" Maely asked.

"Yes." Kairah descended a flight of stone steps into a public garden. A large tree surrounded by stone benches stood guard over the colorful array of flowers bursting around its roots.

Maely's eyes widened as she drew in a breath, there was nothing like this back home. She turned toward Kairah. "It's lovely ..." Then she stopped short. To her surprise, the Allosian woman stopped and bent to examine the flowers. After a moment, she straightened and turned to face Maely.

"The bond will endure until the talis loses all of its charge. Until then, your friend Jekaran will not be able to ignore it, and will likely feel drawn to retrieve it."

"Gymal took it with him," Maely said in a tone of realization. She looked up at Kairah. "To the western rock-lands."

"Then that is where I must go." Kairah turned and began striding toward the west.

"Wait!" Maely shouted as she rushed to catch up with the Allosian woman.

"You wish to accompany me?" Kairah asked.

Maely nodded. "I need to keep following Jek."

Kairah cocked an eyebrow. "Following? Were you not traveling with him?"

Embarrassment made Maely's face feel warm. "Yes, but," she hesitated, "he doesn't know it."

"You are in disguise, then?"

"I was."

"Why?"

"It's none of your damn business!" she snapped.

"Is Jekaran your mate?"

"No!" Maely inwardly cringed as her sharp denial surely had given her away.

Kairah eyed her. "Very well. I will question you no further on the matter."

Maely's only reply was a forced scoff. She tried to appear unruffled, but Kairah's questions had strummed chords too close to her heart. No, she was not Jek's wife. But she wanted to be, wanted it more than anything. For years, she had imagined the two of them wedding in the village square amidst dozens of friends. Then Jek would move into her small house and the two of them would borrow a plow from Ez to begin planting. With the money she had saved over the past five years, they could buy a couple of swine from Tegrall or maybe even a cow. They would have their own farm, in their own corner of the world.

She had replayed that fantasy so often that every detail was perfected, so much so that it was almost as clear as an actual memory. It was silly-girl day dreaming, but it didn't have to be. If only she could convince Jek that he needed her as much as she needed him. She had tried to tell him how she felt on several occasions, but always lost her nerve. And Jek was so thickheaded that he never read deep enough into any of her hints. All the meals made from his favorite foods, mending his clothes, tending to him when he was sick, a dozen other subtle *I-love-you's* he didn't recognize.

She fully intended to dissuade him from joining Kairah's quest. *Let someone else worry about the big problems,* she thought. The Allosian woman could find another guide. But they needed a way to get rid of that sword talis, and giving it to her seemed the perfect way to avoid a whole heap of trouble. *Maybe Gymal will agree to go with Kairah to the capital,* she thought. *He is a noble after all, and aren't magic and politics a noble's business?* And maybe the urgency of a crisis would overshadow Jek's crime.

What was more important, an illegal possession of a talis or the extinction of … all of them?

She nodded, everything seeming so clear. They could go home and start a life together. Maely just had to tell Jek how she felt and hope that he wouldn't reject her. Her jaw clenched tight. That possibility terrified her more than the idea of a talis war. A talis war might kill her, but rejection by the man she loved would destroy her.

CHAPTER 17

Kaul made certain to meet the eyes of the pair of Rasha guards he passed, smiling as menacingly as he knew how. Their faces flushed and they quickened their pace, pointedly moving to the other side of the street. Kaul chuckled to himself. This close to an Apeira well he didn't have to worry about having to budget his dread medal's Apeiron charge. It was satisfying to know everyone feared him on what they thought was an instinctual level.

Oh, how he loved to see confusion and terror in people's eyes. It made him feel powerful.

Kaul sauntered up to the jailhouse. Once he would have been afraid to go anywhere near such a place, but that had been in the days before he had earned his way into the leading ranks of the Rikujo. Back then, *he* had been the one to be afraid, *he* had been that one that was weak. How he hated that fear. It was an emotion for those who were weak, and he was *not* weak. The thought made him clench his teeth as tenuously controlled rage boiled up within his chest. It swelled like the cumulative pressure of a steam cooker, and he only knew of one way to relieve it.

I've come a long way since then, he told himself. *Now there are very few whom I fear.* And when he finally claimed Argentus' sword, there would be no one: not guard, soldier, general, or king.

Kaul climbed the three stone steps to the porch to the jailhouse and threw open the door. He smiled at the fear in the eyes of the two guards sitting at the table. They were bound and gagged, and Kaul could see the sweat rolling down their foreheads. He took a step in and that's when he saw a third guard lying on the floor in a pool of blood still leaking from his open throat.

"Lord Kaul," one of his lieutenants said as he deferentially bobbed his head. The man's name was Arkell and he was the only other person in the room.

"Lysan said you found out something," Kaul said as he carefully stepped over the blood as it oozed across the floor. "What is it?"

Arkell stepped over to one of the bound guards and ripped the gag from his mouth. "Tell him what you told me."

The trembling guard looked at Arkell and then to Kaul. "W-we arrested a boy with green eyes, almost a week ago."

"Argentus' nephew," Kaul said. He had learned from the villagers he questioned in Genra that the boy's name was Jekaran and that he was not Argentus' son, but his nephew. Kaul chuckled as he called to memory the screams and panic of those peasants as they desperately ran about, trying to escape or fight the fires he had started. He wasn't sure if the village burned down, he had to leave so quickly, but he hoped it had.

"It gets better," Arkell nodded at the guard. "Tell him what you arrested the boy for!"

"For possession and use of a weapon talis," he quickly answered.

Kaul was across the room in two steps. "What did you say?" he demanded.

The bound guard visibly paled. "H-he used a weapon talis fending off a gang of thieves."

"What sort of weapon talis?" Kaul automatically directed the full potency of his dread medal at the guard. He used the talis so often he didn't even have to think it anymore, it happened as naturally as he breathed.

The guard's eyes widened and he began to tremble violently. He made a few choking noises and then slumped off the chair and crumpled to the floor, dead. Kaul shrugged. Apparently the intensity of fear had been more than the guard's heart could take. That happened sometimes.

Kaul turned to the other guard and tore the man's gag from his mouth so hard that it jerked the guard's head forward and audibly made the man's teeth clatter. "Same question," he said, and this time he drew down the level of fear he was radiating so as to not kill the man before he had a chance to answer the question.

The guard's wide eyes vacillated between Kaul and the man's dead comrade on the floor. "S-sword," he stammered. "It was a sword!"

He bonded it! Kaul ground his teeth in frustration. He knew the possibility existed from the moment he saw the boy's image and caught onto what Argentus had done. He had just hoped his old friend wasn't going to allow his own kin to bond the talis.

Argentus' agrarian retirement hadn't gentled the man's ruthlessness as Kaul had originally assumed.

Kaul leaned in so that he was inches from the guard's face. "Where is it?"

"T-the magistrate, h-he gave it over to the boy's lord, a w-well-finder. H-he s-said he was going to take it to the k-king." The guard's teeth chattered as though he were standing naked in a midnight blizzard.

Kaul straightened and turned to Arkell. "The boy will be able to lead us to it," he then looked back at the guard. "Take me to the cell of the boy with green eyes."

The guard looked horrified. "H-he, h-he, h-he," the man stammered.

"He what?" Kaul said as he reflexively increased the potency of his fear aura.

"E-escaped," the guard choked out.

Kaul gritted his teeth. "And your magistrate let you live? Is not the penalty for allowing a prisoner to escape, death?" He focused his fear aura into a single wave, all directed at the guard with full potency.

The guard couldn't muster a response. Instead he just shook, tears streaming down his pale face. He coughed and grimaced with pain, and then his eyes rolled back as he, too, slumped to the floor, dead. Kaul seldom killed this way, for two reasons: first it wouldn't work on everyone, and second it cost a gross amount of Apeiron, nearly half of what his talis could hold. So it was that he really could only employ the method when he was in the vicinity of an Apeira well.

As Kaul watched a line of blood trickle from the man's nose he felt the pressure of his rage wane if only slightly. Like a steam cooker, Kaul needed to relieve the cumulative pressure that built up inside of him. In this case the boiling pressure was his rage, and the method of relieving it, bloodshed. And like a steam cooker, failure to vent the heat would result in an explosion. Kill here and there, and he could avoid an eruption of violence, although there were times when he enjoyed losing control.

"Find the others and then catch up to me on the west road. The well-finder will have left for the rock lands by now and the boy is certain to be following."

Arkell nodded and then left the jailhouse annex.

Kaul lingered a moment, taking in the sight of the three dead guards. He certainly was going to have to kill Argentus' nephew now. Not that he really planned otherwise. But his bonding the sword would make it necessary if Kaul wanted to wield it himself.

Killing Jekaran would also make his task more dangerous.

Although fighting Argentus while he wielded the sword would've been challenging, Kaul's old friend was nearing sixty years of age. Even the sword could only work with what it had, and Kaul knew Argentus enough to anticipate the man's tactics. The boy, however, was a different matter. His body would be energetic, resilient, strong.

And if he is newly bonded, Kaul thought, *he will be erratic and unpredictable.*

He would have to strike quickly, perhaps while the boy slept. Or perhaps he could paralyze him with fear. Either way, it was going to be a hazardous operation. Those thoughts stirred something inside of Kaul.

Was that fear that he was feeling?

"NO!" Kaul snapped aloud. He wasn't afraid. To be afraid was to be weak, and Kaul was NOT weak. Memories of a thousand beatings suddenly paraded before Kaul's mind, times when his father had turned from beating his mother to pummel him. *You're afraid!* He would scream at Kaul as he sobbed through the beatings. *Weak and afraid!*

Kaul chuckled in spite of himself. He treasured the memory of the day when he had stopped being afraid, when he had stopped being weak.

That was the day he had carved his father up like a roasted pheasant at Harvest Festival and fed the pieces to the hogs.

Kaul smiled. For all the terror and pain his father had caused him, the cruel bully of a man had taught him to be strong. Anger had turned out to be the key, the only thing that would chase away and replace the fear. He supposed that, in a way, he ought to be grateful to his father. And he *was* grateful. He showed it every time he shed blood.

Kaul left the jailhouse, laughing so loudly that he drew the attention of a dozen passersby's, but he didn't care.

He wasn't afraid.

CHAPTER 18

The rocks and wild grass scratched at Jekaran's stomach. He rolled to his side and pulled his shirt down before rolling back onto his belly. He was lying on the incline of a hill peering over the crest and down at a circle of tents a mile away. At this distance they were little more than the size of toys to Jekaran's eyes, making it difficult for him to properly assess the scene.

"You think lying on your belly is uncomfortable while spying on an enemy," Irvis began, "try it when you're watching a couple bathing and—"

"That's disgusting!" He shot him a look.

"What?" Irvis said, sounding affronted. "I'm just saying that—"

"I know what you're saying." Jekaran returned his focus back to the camp. "I just don't wanna hear it!"

"Don't act like you never get randy. At your age, I—"

Jekaran turned back and hissed, "*I* don't sneak around spying on naked women and doing goddess only knows what else!"

Irvis didn't reply.

Jekaran let his stare linger on the chubby monk to emphasize his point before turning back to survey his target: Gymal's camp.

A quiet rustling behind him, but he didn't flinch. It was only Karak. A distorted translucent shape moved up at his left and then materialized into the reptilian Vorakk shaman. "Three walk circle of camp aka."

"How far out?" Jekaran asked.

Karak hesitated a moment before asking, "Reka what human word for measure of far?"

"Measure of far?" Jekaran turned to look at the lizard-man.

Karak struggled with Aiestali, and with good reason. His native form of communication was a combination of hissing, growling, and hand signs. The concept that Vorakk had no spoken language was foreign to Jekaran, and he still had a hard time understanding it. The Vorakk did use sounds to communicate, though they were little more than syllables spoken at the beginning or end of a sentence to communicate the context of the message. This was followed by the message proper relayed through a series of sharp hand signs. *Who talks without talking?* Well, apparently the Vorakk did.

"Miles?" Jekaran heard Irvis clarify.

"Yes." Karak bobbed his head. "Half of one mile aka."

Aka, Jekaran repeated in his mind. He was learning the syllable communicated at the end of a statement connoting a simple statement of fact. As a Vorakk shaman, Karak had studied human languages and learned to vocalize words, but he hadn't been able to drop the habit of beginning and ending his sentences with Vorakk syllables. It sometimes made deciphering what the lizard-man said difficult, although Jekaran was getting used to it.

Jekaran turned back to stare at the circle of tents in the distance. It was late afternoon—almost dusk. With the sun setting behind them, Jekaran had no worries any of Gymal's security thugs would see him. But distance made seeing detail problematic. "I really wish I had Ez's looking glass with me."

"Reka need more looking?"

Jekaran looked at Karak as he twisted his scaly claw-hand palm up and produced a floating sphere, translucent like the Vorakk shaman was when he camouflaged himself. The small sphere floated over to Jekaran and hovered at eye level.

"Uska," Karak said as he mimed for Jekaran to look at the sphere.

"I see it," Jekaran said.

Karak shook his head. "No! Rok look at camp in ball."

Comprehension dawned on Jekaran, and he leaned forward to peer through the translucent sphere with one eye as though it were a telescope. He started as Gymal's camp suddenly appeared to be right in front of him. Jekaran pulled back and shot a glance at Karak, who flashed a sharp-toothed grin.

Jekaran quickly looked back through the sphere and at the magnified view of the camp. The awe of Karak's wondrous magic fled, and his heart sank as he saw armored soldiers mingling amidst the circle of tents. "Oh no."

"What is it?" Irvis asked anxiously.

Jekaran pulled back from the sphere and looked at the chubby monk. "It looks like Gymal hired a band of mercenaries."

"Why?"

Jekaran shook his head and leaned forward to peer through the sphere again. "For security. He didn't do it last year, but he was probably rattled by the raid on our camp by Karak and his friends."

Karak's only response was a grunt.

Jekaran pulled back and looked at Irvis. "So, what should we do now?"

Irvis looked confused at the question. "Why are you asking me?"

Jekaran barked an incredulous laugh. "Because you have experience with this sort of thing."

Irvis shook his head. "I've never raided a camp."

Jekaran's humor faded into rapidly rising irritation. "But, you were a member of the Rikujo."

"I wasn't a raider." Irvis spread his hands helplessly. "That was men like your uncle and Kaul."

His chest compressed as though a pile of rocks were piled on top of it as nausea swept him. "Then what *did* you do?"

Irvis suddenly looked ashamed. "I mostly counted the coin and tended to ledgers."

Irvis' answer brought all of Jekaran's stress to bear, as if all of his fear, frustration, guilt, and confusion came crashing down on his shoulders. He heard himself snap, "You were a bookkeeper? Why didn't you say so? You filthy fat pervert!" His frustration with the man had come out harsher than he had intended, and Jekaran realized he was shouting.

A scaly palm pressed against his mouth. He shoved Karak's hand away and shot him a warning look, and the Vorakk shaman answered with a hiss. "Isk!" He then motioned to the camp below. "Shouting goes far from high place to camp."

His face flushed red, embarrassment extinguishing his anger. He glanced at Irvis and felt even worse as he saw the man's pained eyes. Why had he railed on him like that? Irvis had saved his life and had come to help him in spite of the man's objections to Jekaran's plan.

"I'm sorry." He cast his eyes to a patch of ground off to Irvis' left. "I don't know why I said that."

It was a lie. Jekaran had a very good idea what was setting his teeth on edge. He cast his thoughts out to the sword locked up among Gymal's personal possessions. It responded instantly, mirroring his anxiety over their distance.

His fingers combed through his hair. The connection forged between himself and the talis was growing every time he reached out with his thoughts, and making his anxiety grow. The sword mirrored every emotion, making him far more irritable than he had let on.

"Are you well?" he heard Irvis carefully ask.

Jekaran closed his eyes, put his palm against his temple and nodded. "Just a little overwhelmed. After all, it was only a couple of weeks ago that I found out that the man who raised me was really Aiestal's most infamous bandit, and that he had a talis that could make me into a warrior."

"Reka human boy have head pain?" Karak asked, a strange note of concern in his rasping voice.

"Yeah," Jekaran said. "Ever since ..." he stopped. *Ever since I used the sword.*

"Ever since what?" he heard Irvis ask.

Jekaran shook his head, looked up at the chubby monk, and forced a smile. "I'm fine."

Irvis nodded acceptance of his excuse. He knew Jekaran was becoming obsessed with the sword.

He turned from Irvis and found Karak staring at him intently. "I'm fine," he repeated. "Really."

After an uncomfortable moment, Jekaran rose up and sat back on his haunches. "Well," he said cheerily as he clapped his hands together to brush the dust off his palms. "Looks like we're going to have to figure out how to get me past a group of armed mercenaries – a dozen people who will recognize me – and into Gymal's tent without anyone noticing."

"Oh, is that all?" he heard Irvis grumble.

"Isk stupid human boy," Karak hissed. "Karak go."

Jekaran slowly shook his head. "I thought of that. But if I'm caught, the worst that will happen is that I will be arrested." He smiled ruefully. "Again. If they find you, Karak, they'll kill you for sure."

"Daka, humans not see Karak."

Jekaran turned to look at the Vorakk shaman, who had also risen from his stomach. "I saw you and I caught you."

Karak's reptilian eyes narrowed. "That what spirits want ska."

"That may be," Jekaran agreed, not wanting to argue with Vorakk fatalism. "But this is something I need to do." He left it at that, not caring to let his two companions in on his powerful mental, physical and emotional compulsion to reunite with the sword as quickly as possible.

"Do you have any ideas?" Irvis asked hesitantly.

Another pang of guilt shoved Jekaran. Shouting at this man had been way out of line. He remained silent for a long moment before finally nodding. "I think so."

After another beat of silence, Irvis stirred, then leaned toward him. "Well, tell us, child!"

Jekaran looked at Irvis and just smiled.

CHAPTER 19

Jekaran stumbled again. He had lost count of how many times he had tripped over Irvis' robes. The chubby monk wasn't taller than he was, but his girth required larger robes, which, of course, added to the length. *Why not have them tailored to a better fit?* He shook his head, sure he didn't know. And how the monk never tripped over his own two feet …

He must draw his robes up like a lady lifts her dress to step over a puddle in the street. He snickered to himself at the mental image of Irvis wearing a dress when he tripped again, this time falling flat on his face.

"Who goes there?" a gravelly voice demanded.

Jekaran froze in the middle of rising onto all fours. His torch lay on the ground just out of arm's reach, the guttering of the grounded flame giving him only the barest glimpse of an approaching figure.

"A humble servant of Rasheera," Jekaran said as he risked sitting back onto his haunches. A beat later a white light exploded, blinding him, and he lifted his forearm to shield his eyes.

A light talis!

"You're a long way from your brothers, monk," the voice accused.

Still shielding his eyes, Jekaran grasped for his cover story, all thought made slippery by the surprise of meeting a scout for fifteen minutes earlier than he expected. *He must've been watching me from the dark.* With clouds hiding the moon, Jekaran's torch would've been as bright as a sea beacon.

"Please child"—he was proud of himself for remembering what Irvis said about calling laymen *child*—"I am brother Ulan." For some reason, Irvis had objected to Jekaran pretending to be him. "And I come on a mission of mercy."

"Child?" The mercenary scoffed. "You look young enough to be *my* child."

Jekaran bobbed his head and quickly recited what Irvis had told him to say if someone questioned his age. "I am young in body, but old in soul."

While it would be unusual for a teenage boy to be anything more than an acolyte in the brotherhood that served the Divine Mother, orphans raised by monks often ascended their ranks quicker than those who joined later in life.

The mercenary lowered his light so it no longer shined directly into Jekaran's face. *He had blinded me on purpose.* His anger flared once again.

"Are you alone?"

That was a dangerous question. What if this wasn't one of Gymal's mercenaries? What if it was a robber? The wrong answer might make Jekaran a dead man. "The servants of the goddess are never alone, child." He smiled at his clever, deliberately ambiguous answer.

The mercenary reflexively lifted his eyes to scan the surrounding area. After a moment he returned his stare to Jekaran. "Where are you going?"

Jekaran thought about answering *wherever the goddess wills it*, but decided against pressing his luck. "I was sent by my brothers to search out Lord Tyrus Gymal. He is captaining an expedition that was headed out this way."

"Why?" the guard demanded, voice suddenly turning hard.

So it is one of Gymal's men. The thought brought a measure of relief to Jekaran.

"It is a delicate matter, and the servants of the goddess are charged to keep such matters private."

"You will answer me if you wish to see Lord Gymal." The armored mercenary put his free hand on the pommel of the sword sheathed at his left hip.

Jekaran's thoughts reeled. Irvis had said threatening a holy man was considered bad manners at best, an affront to the goddess at worst. He also said, most civilized men respected the tradition, but there were plenty who did not. Especially when no one else was watching.

"You are one of Lord Gymal's men?" he asked, hoping to sound like he naively hadn't noticed the threatening gesture.

"Your business, monk!" the mercenary snapped.

Jekaran deliberately chewed his lower lip. He waited just long enough to bait the mercenary into repeating his command and then spoke just as the man was opening his mouth. "Lord Gymal asked for healing before he left Rasha, but at the time, no healers were available to minister to him. When my brothers learned he had departed, they sent me to find him and fulfill his request."

"He doesn't look sick," the mercenary said through slitted eyes.

Jekaran gave his best nervous titter before clearing his throat. "The symptoms of his particular ailment are not..." he paused, pretending to choose his words carefully. "... obvious."

"That sounds like an assassin's excuse," the mercenary said, hand now fully gripping the handle of his sword.

This time Jekaran made a show of seeing the gesture and raised his hands defensively. "No-no-no, you misunderstand. Lord Gymal suffers from a social illness."

"What are you talking about?" the mercenary demanded.

"Lues!" Jekaran said, genuine anxiety lending credibility to his pretended panic. "He visited the whorehouses and caught the lues disease from a harlot!"

For a long moment, the mercenary's face remained impassive, and then he broke into a fit of laughter.

Jekaran chuckled nervously, working to look embarrassed.

"Then I sure hope your ministrations don't involve having to touch him." The mercenary continued to bellow his deep laugh. "And are you sure it was harlot and not a bugger? Story is Gymal had one show up to answer a summons in front of his men last year. Whole camp saw it!"

Jekaran had to work to keep the smile from his face. He had hoped his prank would have endured in memory and sparked the worst kind of gossip. The fact that it had was *very* satisfying.

The mercenary leaned down, extended a hand to Jekaran, and

helped haul him to his feet, laughing to himself the entire time. "Come on, monk. I'll take you to him."

It worked.

After trudging over the rocky plains for about half an hour, and, hearing an endless confession of the mercenary's various violations of Rasheera's moral laws, Jekaran finally arrived at the well-finder's camp. It was set up as usual, a ring of tents circling an impromptu fire pit, with one exception. Gymal's tent was set closer to the center and guarded by no less than four armored soldiers.

"Piss!" Jekaran whispered under his breath.

"What was that, brother?" The guard's question interrupted a particularly tawdry confession of what the mercenary had done on his last visit to Jeryn city.

Jekaran chided himself for breaking character and then quickly danced a few steps in place. "I am sorry, child. I must relieve myself."

The mercenary chuckled and pointed to a latrine just outside the ring of tents. Jekaran hurried to the pit, enclosed on all sides, save the entrance, by a line of portable pickets. He entered and made as though he were urinating. When it came time for him to finish up, he bent slightly and checked his robe pockets for his tools: lock picks and a utility knife.

Three days ago, they had passed through a village—well, he and Irvis had, while Karak passed around the hamlet to avoid being seen—where Irvis was able to invoke his monk's right to free provisions. Fortunately, the mayor had been an observant worshipper of the goddess and had made sure they had more than enough of what they needed. Last on the list Irvis had unabashedly made was lock picks. This invoked suspicious stares from the village blacksmith, but Irvis passed it off as necessary replacements for lost keys to his wardrobe closet back in the Rasha monastery. The man was remarkably good at lying, something that struck Jekaran as incongruous to the chubby monk's round friendly face.

When Jekaran left the cover of the pickets, the mercenary walked over and resumed escorting him into the camp. He also resumed his detailed and disgusting confession as if there had been no break in their conversation. The camp was quiet; the only noises Jekaran could hear being the snoring of the men and the hushed conversation of the guards.

"This is brother Ulan," Jekaran's escort introduced him to the men guarding Gymal's tent. "He is here to tend to Lord Gymal's sickness."

"He doesn't look sick," one of the guards said as he looked Jekaran up and down.

Jekaran's escort grinned. "Burning in the nethers."

The other guards looked at each other and then broke into a round of chuckles.

"He been spending time in the bath houses?"

"Buggering the water boys I'll bet," one of the other guards scoffed.

Jekaran worked to look uncomfortable, something that wasn't hard to fake as his desperation mounted with every step he took toward the sword. "I do not know the cause. I am just here to heal him."

"I'll wake him," one of the guards said as he turned to lift the tent's entrance flap.

"No," Jekaran blurted out.

The guards looked at him, first with looks of confusion, then with growing suspicion.

"I must maintain at least the appearance of confidentiality. I fear he will suspect his *condition,*" Jekaran put a diplomatic emphasis on that word, "and all it implies is known, should one of you announce me." He inwardly cringed at the weak excuse.

A tense moment of quiet followed as all of the guards looked to Jekaran's escort for instruction. "Let the monk do it his way." The mercenary smacked Jekaran on the back—hard. "The task is unenviable as it is. We don't need to make it any more difficult for him."

They all chuckled at that.

"Lord Gymal has thickened canvas and pelts hanging from the walls, making it as dark as a cave in there. You have a light?" Jekaran's escort asked him.

Damn! He hadn't thought of that. He didn't have a light, and if Gymal woke while he was in the tent, it would all be over. Jekaran bit his lip and was about to answer when a thought entered his mind, as though the sword implanted it.

I will be your eyes in the dark.

That was enough for Jekaran. "Yes," he lied.

His escort chuckled again and slapped him on the back before lifting the bottom of the tent flap.

"Thank you," Jekaran dipped his head, working to suppress a grin, knowing he would soon hold his sword again. *My sword?* He caught himself. *When did it become my sword?*

But, then, maybe it was now.

He bobbed one more thank-you to the mercenary guard before crouching and entering the tent. The flap closed behind him, thrusting him into utter darkness. And not just darkness, he realized, but quiet, the thickened walls effectively blocking every sound of the outside world.

I'm here.

Nothing.

He was about to repeat himself, this time in an audible whisper, when the sword pushed its way into his mind so suddenly, it caused Jekaran to stumble and fall to one knee. Although his eyes remained sightless, the darkness was no longer an obstacle. Through his psychic link to the sword, he knew where everything was with absolute confidence.

Jekaran stood and ascertained his position. Gymal's bed—the man *actually* carried a four-post bed with him—was ten feet directly in front of Jekaran. Five feet to the left of the bed was a small table with the remnants of Gymal's dinner, the greasy bones of what had probably been a pheasant. Five feet to the right of the bed was a large travel trunk, on top of which lay a leather satchel and an unusually long, wooden lockbox.

That's you! Jekaran said with his mind. The sword responded with wordless confirmation.

Jekaran hurried over and knelt down at the side of the trunk. He felt along the smooth top until cold metal met his fingers. The box fitted to the sword with perfection, and Gymal must've had it custom designed for concealment of the weapon-*his* sword. That thought was accompanied by a fierce pang of jealousy that faded as quickly as it had come.

Strange, he thought.

Jekaran shook off the oddity and quickly found the box's keyhole. Drawing a thin metal pin from the inside of his robe pocket, he inserted it into the lock and held his breath.

Jekaran knew this was going to be the hard part. Because he had never picked a lock, Irvis had given him a rushed lesson on the basics. "The problem is"—the monk had said with a tone of thieving expertise that belied his round, honest face—" no two locks are the same. Even of the same design, each has its own quirks."

Great. *I don't suppose you know how to pick a lock*, Jekaran thought to the sword.

There was no response.

I'll take that for a no. He began to manipulate the pin; five minutes later, the effort snapped the pin in half. Jekaran bit off a curse and quickly drew another pin from his robe.

Although he was more careful the second time, the result was the same: a broken pick and a still-locked box. He fished in his pocket for another pin – Irvis had bought five – and froze as his fingers found a tear in the pocket lining.

A tear and no more pins.

"Damn it!" Jekaran hissed.

A snort from Gymal turned his blood cold and he froze, not even daring to draw a breath until the man's snoring returned to a steady rhythm. *I'm in trouble*, Jekaran thought. Frightened, his thoughts began to race in time with his quickening pulse. *What do I do?* He could walk away, tell the guards he had ministered to Gymal, and be twenty miles away from camp by dawn. But the thought of never again holding the sword scared him more than discovery and capture. Logic and his sense of self-preservation screamed at him to get out of the situation now, but he found himself rooted to the spot.

I can't leave it, Jekaran realized. *It won't let me.*

That should've frightened him more than anything else, he realized, but for some reason, the fact that he couldn't leave the sword seemed perfectly normal. Criticizing it would be like trying to find fault in a mother's inability to abandon her newborn infant.

Jekaran felt around in his pocket for the dagger Irvis had acquired and drew it out. At first, he tried to fit the tip of the blade into the lock, but it proved too small for the knife. He ground his teeth in frustration, some inner instinct warning him time was quickly running out. Jekaran stood and hefted the lockbox. He could carry it easily under one arm, but it was too big to hide under his robe. He chewed his lower lip, trying to keep his rising panic from overwhelming him.

In the complete dark of Gymal's tent, Jekaran groped for inspiration, but all that came to mind was taking the box and running. Sucking in a breath, he decided to do just that. With the lockbox under his left arm, Jekaran crept toward the back wall of the tent. He gently set it on the ground and then, brushing aside a thick fur pelt, stabbed his knife into the tent wall and began to cut the canvas downward. He moved at a maddeningly slow pace to minimize *rip* whispering in the darkness and listened as Gymal continued to snore evenly behind him.

So far, so good.

The loose flap fluttered inward as Jekaran's blade reached the bottom, inviting a chill wind and the sounds of camp into Gymal's tent. His heart began to pound as the loss of total quiet caused the man's snoring to become inconsistent. In a rush of adrenaline, Jekaran dropped to all fours and crawled out of the tent.

Once outside, he turned around and quickly reached in for the lockbox. But, while Jekaran was rushing to pull the box out of the tent, one of its metal hinges snagged on the torn canvas resulting in a very loud tearing sound. Gymal's snoring suddenly turned into a choke, and Jekaran heard the man begin thrashing in his bed. He stopped pulling the lockbox out of the tent and froze, waiting with breathless hope that he would hear the rhythmic snoring once again resume.

It didn't.

Light from a talis exploded out of the tent, and Jekaran saw Gymal's legs swing out over the edge of the bed and lower to touch the floor. *Please don't let him notice the tear*, Jekaran silently prayed to Rasheera.

Jekaran's heart began pounding in his ears as he watched Gymal's hairless chicken legs move closer to him. He was sure to feel the breeze blowing in through the hole in the tent wall. But just when Gymal was about to catch him, the man turned and walked back toward his bed. Jekaran mentally thanked the goddess and carefully released his pent-up breath. As soon as he saw Gymal sit down on his bed, he began to slide the lockbox the rest of the way out of the tent.

RIPPPPP!

Icy panic stabbed Jekaran square in the chest. He had forgotten that the lockbox was still snagged on the canvas wall, the tearing sound louder to him than the voice of God. Silence followed, and then Gymal's face peered out at him from inside the tent.

"Guards!" Gymal shouted in his nasally tone. "GUARDS!"

"Dammit!" Jekaran swore aloud as he scrambled to his feet, the lockbox coming loose with another loud *rip*.

Gymal's shouting soon mixed with urgent bell tolling and voices of mercenaries calling to one another. Thoughts blurred, Jekaran spun and began sprinting away from the tent as fast as he could. He passed four gherns tethered to a wooden picket, and considered stealing one to make his escape. The thought was fleeting, however, as Jekaran had never ridden a ghern and wasn't even sure how to mount one of the bipedal mammals.

Jekaran shot a look over his shoulder as the shouts grew louder, and he caught sight of no less than three armored mercenaries, with swords drawn, sprinting after him. Jekaran weaved through the outer ring of tents and was soon running on the open plain into the darkness. A thick grouping of trees, too small to be called a forest but large enough to provide a place to hide from his pursuers, lay before him. *But how far away?* Jekaran wondered. He had seen the trees through Karak's magic when surveying the area, but hadn't thought to judge the distance between the thicket and Gymal's camp. In the dark, it was next to impossible to tell, but that didn't matter. Reaching the thicket was now his only chance to lose Gymal's guards.

Jekaran settled into a steady pace, content his chosen path would carry him to freedom, when he felt the front of his robes pull tight. And then he pitched forward, sparse grass and small rocks racing up to meet him. He hit the ground face first and then involuntarily rolled down a small hill. He came to a stop amid a cloud of dust and scrambled up as quickly as he could. He had lost his hold on the lockbox in the fall, and was quickly scanning the ground around him when the sword called out to him. Immediately he knew where it was—ten feet off to his left.

Jekaran whirled, blinded by the light of two talises shining into his eyes from the top of the hill. Although he knew he was no match for trained soldiers, Jekaran's sense of self-preservation prompted him to reach inside his robes for the knife Irvis had bought for him. It wasn't there. Had he left it back in Gymal's tent, or had he dropped it in his flight?

"I heard that it was difficult to get alms from the nobility"—Jekaran recognized the voice of the mercenary who had escorted him into camp —"but this seems a little extreme, wouldn't you say, *brother Ulan*? Or is it just ... Ulan?"

A light on his periphery caught Jekaran's attention and he turned to his left just in time to see a third mercenary place a booted foot on top of the grounded lockbox. Realizing that he had no escape, Jekaran raised his hands in surrender.

It was over.

J enoc pleads with you to answer, Aeva said. *Do you wish to respond?*

Kairah hesitated for a long moment before finally shaking her head. "No," she whispered aloud at the same time she said it with her thoughts. "It would do no good."

Aeva wordlessly acknowledged Kairah's answer, and the Spirit Lily's presence faded from her mind. It was becoming more and more difficult for Kairah to communicate with Aeva the farther away from Allose she traveled—a distance nearing three hundred miles. It was somewhat disconcerting not having Aeva's presence constantly in her consciousness. It had been years since she experienced the kind of mental isolation she now felt, and it was wearing on her.

Another hardship was her being so far away from an Apeira well. Rasha had only been a few days travel away from Allose, and so she hadn't needed to go long without being able to touch a well instead of her own stored energy in order to spell-cast. Now, it had been ten days, Kairah felt *very* vulnerable. If she didn't carefully budget the Apeiron she still held, it could run out. She hadn't been in danger of running out in almost seventy years, not since she had been a child. The very thought terrified her.

Not long after taking to the road with Maely, Kairah began to realize *how* much she had taken for granted living in the shadow of the Mother Shard. She hadn't been aware of how much spell casting she did as a matter of course until she could no longer freely draw the energy. She was forced to resort to time consuming and menial ways of doing easy things, like rubbing sticks together to light a mound of tinder, sticks that had taken her almost an hour to collect. How did the humans live each day of their lives like this? How did they live without magic?

The sound of someone approaching—another frustration to actually listen with her ears or see with her eyes to perceive such things—drew her attention away from the leaf she had been idly fingering. She looked up and saw Maely jogging out of the village toward her. The girl shouldered a bulky satchel and wore a pleased smile on her face.

She must've found someone who had seen Jekaran.

Although the fine sable cloak Kairah wore concealed her amethyst-colored hair and bare alabaster shoulders, the cloak itself was of such a fine make that it still attracted too much attention. Along with what Maely considered Kairah's odd use of the human's language and regal demeanor—the girl used less flattering words to describe both of these —they both thought it best Maely go alone into the village for information and supplies.

Before leaving Rasha, they acquired some human currency by selling a small jewel Kairah had brought with her from Allose. The diamond fetched enough coin to impress Maely, but she was still disappointed that Kairah hadn't allowed her to use the compulsion ring to gain what they needed.

She still doesn't understand, Kairah had to remind herself in order to quell her anger at the girl's offensive suggestion. It was bad enough Kairah had kept a cloak acquired through such distasteful means. Had her situation not been an emergency, she never would have accepted it.

Kairah dropped her leaf and rose from her seat on the grass underneath the tall oak. Its wide branches full of leaves had been a most pleasant shelter from the sun. She turned and placed a hand on the tree's trunk and said *thank you* with her mind.

"What're you doing?" Maely asked.

Kairah turned to look at the human girl and said, "Thanking the tree."

Maely's smile faded. "For what?"

"For allowing me to enjoy its shade."

"Do you often talk to trees?"

"Yes," Kairah said.

"What do they say?" Maely asked.

Kairah could hear the scornful laugh behind the words. "Most floras do not have the intelligence to respond," she said patiently.

"Most?" Maely asked, and then she couldn't hold back the laughter.

"What did you acquire?" Kairah deliberately changed the subject.

Maely shrugged the satchel off her shoulder and put in on the ground. "I got two loaves of bread, some fruit, a wheel of cheese, some cured ham, another water skin, a bar of soap, and some cloths for washing."

"That is excessive," Kairah said.

Maely's eyes flashed, and Kairah thought she was about to experience another explosion of the girl's short temper, but the flare appeared to fade. "Well, we gotta eat," she said in a tone of justification.

Kairah nodded to herself. "Of course, I forget that."

Maely fished an apple out of the bag and took a bite. "Don't tell me that you don't eat," she said, chewing with her mouth open.

Kairah tried to swallow her disgust at the display of bad manners and shook her head. "No, we do. Just not as often as you do."

Maely paused, seemed to look Kairah up and down, and then she touched her own stomach. After that, the girl appeared to lose interest in her apple for some reason.

"Because my people channel Apeiron through our bodies, we rely more on that energy to sustain us than we do food and drink."

"So when do you eat?"

"Usually we do so as part of our rituals or celebrations, or when we are away from a well long enough to need it." Maely was about to open her mouth to ask another question, but Kairah pre-empted her. "You have news?"

Maely nodded. "The people in that village saw Jek."

"So we have confirmation that he is indeed pursuing the sword talis." Kairah let her gaze shift past the village and toward the horizon. "Did they report anything else?"

"Yeah," Maely said, "He was with a fat Rasheeran monk who had come for free supplies." She laughed. "Apparently the monk upset the villagers by taking more than they thought right and proper."

Kairah looked back at Maely. "Jekaran is keeping company with a thief?"

Maely shook her head. "No," she laughed. "Our holy men have a right to take what they need in the way of supplies. He just took too much."

Maely's expression visibly darkened. "My mother used to say some of the monks had a liberal interpretation of what maintenance they were entitled to. Hypocritical bastards!"

"Your mother?" Kairah asked, genuinely curious.

Maely appeared startled at the question, as though she had forgotten that Kairah was there. She dropped her eyes to the ground. "Yeah," she said. "She was a courtesan."

"Courtesan?" Kairah asked, a part of her recognizing the human word, but her memory failing to define it.

She looked up at her, eyes again full of fiery defiance. "We all do what we gotta do to survive. Mother was beautiful, and after father died the only way she could feed us was—"

Kairah lifted a hand to forestall the girl. "Ah, *courtesan*. A prostitute for the higher human classes."

Maely looked surprised.

"I remember the word now." Kairah smiled what she hoped was a kindly smile and said, "I pass no judgment upon you, Maely, or your mother."

Maely did not reply, but instead turned away to gaze at the horizon.

"That is how your mother came by the compulsion ring?" Kairah probed, trying to do it delicately.

Maely nodded. "She stole it from a man who"—Maely paused and turned to look at Kairah—"didn't pay her," she finished. Kairah could tell that there was more to that explanation, but decided not to press Maely any further.

After a moment of uncomfortable silence, Maely turned around, wearing a completely different expression. The girl changed emotions so rapidly Kairah had a hard time keeping up. But she was beginning to learn to match her expressions to what the human girl was likely feeling. This expression bespoke curiosity.

"You don't eat. So does that mean you don't go to the privy either?"

Kairah faltered, not certain how to answer that question. "We—" she began, but Maely cut her off.

"What about sex? Do your people do that?"

Kairah wasn't sure how to answer. In Allosian culture, such biological functions were considered private and it was the height of rudeness to discuss them in public, or with strangers. She had thought the humans had shared that custom. Apparently, she was wrong.

"All life has things in common," she said carefully.

Maely took that for a "yes" and, to Kairah's relief, didn't ask for any details of Allosian digestive or reproduction systems. She thought it safest to change the subject and so asked, "Did anyone offer an indication of how much time has elapsed since Jekaran left this village?"

Maely looked up at her and nodded. "Not more than two days ago."

"That is better than I had hoped," Kairah said.

Maely shot her a suspicious look. "What are you saying?"

Kairah shook her head, the hood of her cloak catching her hair in the motion. "Simply that we have been fortunate."

The girl didn't look like she quite believed that, and in truth, Maely *was* slowing them down with her needing to sleep and eat. Kairah had not meant to let that sentiment slip, another sign she was feeling the effects of being so far from an Apeira well. Something else was creeping in as well—*was it hunger?* It had been so long since she had felt hungry that she almost didn't recognize it, but there it was.

"What other fruit do you have in your satchel?" she hesitantly asked.

Maely just smiled, and resumed eating her apple.

THE NEXT DAY was much like the one before, hours upon hours of walking a dusty dirt road. They took the occasional break and left the road to eat or avoid being seen by groups of travelers. Now that she had become somewhat used to Kairah, Maely opened up, talking more about herself, Jekaran, her simple brother and a man named Ez. When she ran out of things to tell Kairah about, she switched to asking questions. Mostly she asked about Allosian life, physiology, and their history. But she seemed most curious about what she termed *witchcraft*.

Kairah tried to break her of the habit of calling it that, but failed —miserably.

"So you get your witchcraft—"

"—magic," Kairah corrected." That was an inadequate, generic term, but far more accurate than the girl's superstitious one.

Maely ignored her. "—from an Apeira well, like a talis does?"

"That is oversimplifying the magic behind it, but basically, you are correct."

"And the crystal wells grow up from the center of our planet, which is round and not flat," she paraphrased.

That had been a hard sell for Kairah. Eventually, she had resorted to using an apple and an ant to explain the curvature of the planet to Maely, and she sensed the girl still didn't fully accept it.

"And that power is what lets you cast spells?"

"Yes," Kairah said, but then quickly added, "But it is not something that we do instinctually. Learning to take Apeiron into yourself, hold onto it, and then use it to spell-cast requires a combination of natural talent, mental discipline, and years of training."

"So you had to be trained to be able to turn dry ground into mud, or make the water obey you, like you did back in Rasha?"

Kairah nodded under her hood. "And those effects were just part of the second of five classes of spells. We call it The Second Discipline, and it deals with manipulating the elements. It took me years to learn it, and I am only considered adequate by Allosian standards."

"How many years?"

That question gave Kairah pause. The answer would give away her age, and certainly lead to a new round of questioning. "Thirty."

Maely stopped walking and stared wide-eyed at her. "Just how old are you?"

"It is rude in my cultural to ask such a question," she said as she continued to stride forward.

Maely jogged to catch up to her and said, "I'm fourteen and a half. There, now you can tell me how old you are."

Kairah sighed. "I would be considered eighty-nine by your reckoning."

"You're almost a hundred years old?

"It is considered just beyond the age of youth among my people."

"Do you live forever?" the girl asked eagerly.

"No," Kairah said. "Our lifespans are generally three to four hundred years. And"—she faltered at the thought of her mother—"our bodies are just as fragile as yours. We can die in accidents and be killed much like humans."

Maely elapsed into silence, rewarding Kairah with almost an entire hour of not having to endure relentless conversation and questioning.

By late afternoon, the two had passed through a small forest and entered into grasslands and hill country. The setting sun in the west made it hard to see very far down the road, and so Kairah suggested that they leave the road and make camp.

Maely readily agreed. For one so thin, she certainly did have a difficult time enduring their marathon of walking. When Kairah mentioned this, she received a tirade of scathing insults and blame for the human girl's difficulty in keeping up. "If you weren't so damned tall"—she had said—"you wouldn't take such long strides, and I wouldn't be so winded."

Kairah didn't take offense. The girl was obviously anxious and found relief in expressing her angst through slander. *Are all human females like this?* Maybe Maely was suffering from hormonal imbalance due to her monthly menstrual cycle. Asking the girl that question had proved to be a poor decision resulting in another angry tirade.

They ate in silence – Maely was still offended by Kairah's questioning her menstrual hormones – and laid their bedrolls across the lumpy ground.

Kairah laid still for a moment, listening to Maely's instant heavy snoring, and then rolled on her back with a roll of her eyes. She didn't like having to sleep, and nearly forgotten how – it had been decades since she needed to rejuvenate through physical rest – but as she closed her eyes, she found the darkness restful. Traveling for over two weeks and being away from an Aeose left her feeling drained, and, now reacquainted with the habit she despised, she quietly slipped into slumber.

KAIRAH'S PERIMETER ward woke her. She crafted the spell to ignore small rodents and insects and only alert her if something the size of a dog or larger crossed the boundary. The quiet chiming, audible only to her ears, told her the intruder was large, which likely meant bandits. She prepared to touch the wind and cause a hurricane-strength gale to blast the intruder. The expenditure would bring her dangerously close to depleting her Apeiron, but it couldn't be helped.

Kairah slowly turned her head to focus her spell on a target, but there wasn't anyone there. She quickly sat up, looking around, but still didn't see anyone. Fear rose inside her as the ward continued the report of an intruder she couldn't see.

"Maely," she whispered urgently.

"What?" the girl groggily responded.

Kairah *shooshed* her, which only made Maely snap, "You be quiet! You're the one talking!"

The air in front of Kairah wavered, and something abruptly appeared out of the darkness. It was man sized and humanoid, but its scaly skin, sharp claws, and long muzzle made it clear it was no human.

"Vorakk!" Maely screamed.

At the same time, Kairah siphoned Apeiron from her core and used it to seize the air. A sudden blast of wind exploded from her outstretched hand and slammed into the surprised lizard-man, lifting him off the ground and hurling him several yards.

Kairah quickly stood and began moving toward the creature. A scream from Maely turned her back to see another figure approaching. This one was human, but portly with white hair.

"Wait!" he called as he raised his hands defensively. "I'm unarmed."

Kairah looked back at the Vorakk, who had risen and settled into a crouch, forked tongue rapidly tasting the air as it hissed angrily.

"Karak!" the man called.

The man's voice relaxed the lizard, and he stood, raising his hands to show they were empty.

"What do you want?" Maely said as she backed into Kairah.

"Reka why sorceress and human girl follow?"

"We were not following you," Kairah said in a tightly controlled voice. She had enough energy for one, maybe two more blasts of wind.

"I've seen you!" the man abruptly said.

Kairah glanced over her shoulder to see him pointing at Maely. "You came to see Jekaran when he was locked up."

"How did you," Maely began, then recognition washed over her face. "You were with Jek in that jail!"

"Karak, I don't think they were following *us*," the man called out to the Vorakk. "I think we're all looking for Jekaran."

CHAPTER 21

Jekaran was miserable. Not only was he now a prisoner of the man that he hated, but his legs ached, it was raining, the ground was muddy, and he was developing a sniffle. As painful as all of these things were, the loss of his sword somehow felt worse. He groaned softly, careful not to let the guards hear him. He wouldn't give them the satisfaction.

The sword called to him, making the pain burn inside him even more. *Didn't think that was possible.* He hadn't exactly *lost* it; he could feel it only a hundred or so feet in front of him, inside the lockbox which was buried in the back of a bullock-drawn wagon which was dragging him down the road. It had been taken from him—*again*. And there wasn't anything he could do about it.

Jekaran lifted his chained hands to wipe a strand of wet black hair from his eyes and slipped. He fell, his face buried in the road as he breathed in the mud, scrambling with his cuffed hands to stand, and slipped again. He struggled to breathe, unable to catch a breath as he skidded across the ground. *I'm going to die like this.*

A hand grabbed the neckline of his robe and lifted him to his feet. "Next time I'll let you drown in the mud, *brother Ulan*," said the mercenary that had been Jekaran's original escort, a man named *Hort*.

Jekaran coughed violently, spitting mud from his mouth. "Maybe you should have," he finally said.

Hort chuckled darkly. "Maybe," he agreed. "But I like you, monk."

"I'm not really a monk," Jekaran coughed again.

"I know that," Hort said. "But it's always how I'll remember you."

"Thanks," Jekaran said sardonically.

"You know," Hort said as he resumed walking. "If I wasn't employed by your lord, I would've gladly helped you steal whatever is in that box."

The thought of someone else claiming his sword invoked a sharp explosion of jealousy from within Jekaran and he snapped, "No!"

Hort looked surprised. "No need to get angry," he said in a mildly offended tone. "I was just saying that I don't judge you wrong for thieving. I've done a fair bit of it in my day."

Jekaran nodded sheepishly, embarrassment now capping his mountain of miseries.

"I'll make sure you get a chance to wash up at our next stop." He laughed and clapped Jekaran on the back. "Which with as often as your lord stops to piss, shouldn't be more than an hour."

Hort walked ahead to confer with one of his fellow mercenaries.

The rain poured over his face and washed away the mud. Jekaran looked down the front of his robe—Irvis' robe—and saw it caked from neck to hem. If he ever got out of this mess, he was going to owe Irvis another cloak. He reached up again to wipe the mud-soaked hair from his face.

Irvis and Karak.

Where did those two go? He didn't think either of the men would just abandon him, Irvis having ties to his family and Karak believing Jekaran was the fulfillment of some Vorakk prophecy. He wiped his eyes again with tethered hands and then cast a glance over his shoulder. The road behind wound over a brush-covered plain until it disappeared into a distant forest. He looked down at the muddy ground. The grass had gotten sparser over the course of the day's travel making the ground rockier and, consequently, muddier.

They were nearing the western rock lands where Gymal hoped to discover another Apeira well for the King.

What's he going to do with me then? Keep me chained to a picket line with all the ghern? Jekaran wondered.

It was worse than that.

After another night of camping, they reached the rock lands late the next afternoon. Gymal's dousing stone led him to a rocky monolith half jutting out of a large sandstone wall. After doing several control dousings to ascertain the best point to start digging, one of Gymal's men handed Jekaran a pickaxe and ordered him to start swinging at the rock. The task would've been difficult enough if iron manacles had not chained his hands together. With them, it was painfully exhausting. He had to learn to swing the pick high over his head to get enough momentum for an effective blow. Even when he did it right, the rock only yielded about half of the time.

Laughter erupted from Gymal and the soldiers when once Jekaran forgot himself and swung the pick up over his right shoulder, causing the chain tethering his manacles to draw taut and break his grip on the pick's handle. The tool struck him on the shoulder on its way to the ground, doing only superficial damage, but severely wounding what was left of his pride.

Blessed dusk came, and when Jekaran could no longer see his target well enough to be effective, Gymal ordered him to stop. He dropped the pickaxe, sat down on the rocky ground, and was handed a cup of water. The relief of it was the sweetest thing he ever tasted.

Until Gymal reminded him that he would spend the entire next day doing what he had just done for only three hours. The man then did something that Jekaran hadn't expected. He drew a rod from his pocket. It was clearly a talis, as the end was capped by an amethyst-colored stone. The other end of the rod had a thin point like a needle. Jekaran started as Gymal leaned down, grabbed him by the hair to shove his head forward, and pricked the back of his neck with the needle end of the talis. Jekaran yelped, but was too exhausted to make a fight of it and he hadn't needed to, for Gymal withdrew the needle as quickly as he had jabbed it into him.

He let go of Jekaran's hair and said, "Just in case you try to slip away. And you'll eat when everyone else is done, if there's any left, so don't think to beg." Then he walked away chuckling.

What was that about?

Jekaran groaned and lay down on the rocky ground—he could only lie on his side because of his manacles—and tried to ignore the enticing smell of stew wafting over to him from the cook fire.

An hour passed with Jekaran lying on the ground, muscles stiff beneath him. He had slipped into a half-sleep when the sounds of someone approaching him startled him to full wakefulness. Booted feet invaded his field of vision and he craned his stiff neck up just enough to see Vestus kneel in front of him, a dented tin bowl in the man's right hand.

"Ah, Jek," Vestus said in a tone that reminded Jekaran of how people talked at funerals. "What've you gotten yourself into?"

Jekaran groaned as he sat up. "That for me?" he asked.

Vestus nodded and handed him the bowl. Jekaran didn't wait for Vestus to offer a spoon, but tipped the bowl into his mouth and slurped the stew so quickly he started choking on it. Vestus slapped him on the back as he coughed and took the bowl from him so he wouldn't drop it.

"Careful, now," he said.

Jekaran nodded, trying not to cough and hoping Vestus didn't think his watering eyes were tears. "I'm ok," he said in a hoarse voice. He raised his tethered hands to stop Vestus from pounding on his back.

Vestus nodded. "I'm sorry it ain't warmer. Gymal hung around to make sure no one fed ya first."

Jekaran nodded his thanks as he picked up the bowl and resumed slurping his dinner.

"We heard that you were locked up in Rasha. Did they let you out?"

Jekaran shook his head, a motion that almost caused him to choke a second time as he attempted it while drinking.

Vestus looked confused. "If ya escaped, then why come after us? Why not run?"

Jekaran finished the bowl of stew and dropped the tin bowl to the ground. "Gymal has something of mine," he said. "I want it back."

"What is it?"

Jekaran stared at him for a long moment, worried that if he told him, Vestus would want the sword for himself. "It's better that you not know."

Vestus nodded thoughtfully. "You're in deep ghern muck, Jekaran. Gymal plans to see you get what he thinks you deserve."

"Hanging?"

Vestus shrugged. "He didn't get into specifics. But I'm sure it's something like that."

Jekaran nodded to himself. "Any chance you can bribe one of the mercenaries to drop the key to these?" Jekaran raised his manacled wrists and drew the chain taut for emphasis.

Vestus dropped his eyes to the ground, a look of shame coming over his face.

"He threatened you, didn't he," Jekaran said.

Vestus nodded. "He knows we're neighborly with you. He said that if any of us try to help you that our lands would be seized and our families put off the farm. I still have little ones at home, Jek. I can't—"

"Then you best not be seen talking with me," Jekaran interrupted.

Vestus nodded solemnly, rose to his feet, and picked up the tin bowl from the ground.

"I'm sorry, Jek. I really am."

"It's my own fault," Jekaran said. He hadn't needed to come after the sword, not in the truest sense. But the link didn't allow another course of action. If that were the only reason, Jekaran wouldn't feel so foolish. The truth was that the excitement of stealing the sword back from Gymal had been just as much of a lure as the sword pulling on his mind. *Adventure is the lure of fools* he heard his uncle's voice echo in the ears of his memory. "And I am a fool," he whispered to himself.

The next four days became Jekaran's own personal hell. Being chained made it difficult to sleep at night, even though he was beyond exhaustion. Vestus did his best to save a portion of each meal for him, but the man was not always successful. And even when he was, there was often not much left for Jekaran to eat. To top it all off, Gymal made a public ritual out of ridiculing him- which for some reason stung more than Jekaran's physical pains. The work itself was hard, but ironically, it became the easiest part of his suffering. The whole ordeal muddled his mind so that he had a hard time seeing beyond the moment. That made him all the more vulnerable to despair and he soon found himself in an angry melancholy. He channeled that fire into his work. At first it was to give vent to his anger, but later it became a fire that gave him energy. And so he nurtured it by chanting a mental mantra with each swing of his pickaxe.

Swing and *CLANK!*

Damn Ez for giving him the sword!

Swing and *CLANK!*

Damn the sword for pulling on his mind!

Swing and *CLANK!*

Damn Irvis and Karak for not coming to rescue him!

Swing and *CLANK!*

Damn Rasheera for ignoring his prayers!

Swing—but most of all, Jekaran would damn himself for being a fool —and *CRACK!*

The change in sound jolted him from his thoughts and Jekaran looked up to see shards of rock fall from the rock wall to reveal a soft amethyst light. His eyes focused on a smooth, translucent, crystalline surface buried beneath the rock.

He heard his pickaxe hit the ground, and, a beat later, one of his fellow excavators began shouting something. The rhythmic sound of picks striking rock had ceased all around him, replaced by excited chatter and more shouting.

He had found the Apeira well.

CHAPTER
22

"Well, I suppose this proves the gods have a sense of humor," Gymal drawled.

Jekaran flexed his brain in order to think of a biting comeback witty enough to make the entire onlooking camp laugh aloud, but nothing came. He was too exhausted, or maybe it was worse. Maybe Gymal *had* finally broken him.

"No clever cheek, Jekaran? Maybe you *have* begun to learn your place." He smirked.

Again, no retort would come. That frightened him.

"What of the reward?" one of the men called out.

Gymal smiled, not taking his eyes off Jekaran. "I did promise something to the man who first found the well, didn't I."

Jekaran didn't like the dangerous note in Gymal's tone.

"Jekaran was the first to find it, and being a man of my word, he will get the reward!" Gymal's announcement ignited angry murmuring, and one well-finder went so far as to jeer.

"Quiet!" Hort shouted and the camp fell silent.

"Well, Jekaran?" Gymal asked. "What is it that you want?"

He's baiting you, Jekaran warned himself. *He's going to turn whatever I ask for around on me.* He tried to think of everything he could ask for and how it might be turned ill. *If I ask for freedom, he could kill me, and if I ask for rest, he might have me knocked unconscious. I definitely don't want to ask for my sword or extra water.* Asking for food would also grant Gymal a wonderful array of options. Jekaran looked down at Irvis' filthy, tattered robe.

"I would like some new clothes," he said, confident there was no way Gymal could twist that into a punishment.

He was wrong.

The soldiers and some of the well-finders laughed, hooted, and catcalled as Hort shoved him out of one of Gymal's tents. He clenched his jaw, looking down at the humiliation Gymal exacted on his request. Velvet and green, Jekaran could only guess why Gymal would own the evening gown, much less have brought it on the expedition. The weaselly little lord was thoroughly enjoying this, even going so far as to tie red ribbons in Jekaran's hair and fitting him with a black choker. He reached up and twisted the thin crimson material between two fingers and dropped his hands to the side. Gymal had his eager vengeance for the pranks the year before.

At least they had needed to remove his manacles in order to dress him for the spectacle.

Jekaran stumbled to the ground, quickly deciding it best to stay down and keep his eyes shut. If hard labor and half starvation hadn't broken him before, this would almost certainly do the trick. He listened hard for Vestus' laughter and was grateful when he didn't hear it among the derisive chorus.

The laughing seemed to go on without end and Jekaran retreated inward to escape. He fixated on his psychic bond to the sword talis, instantly knowing where it was and how far away he was from it. That didn't make him feel better, but the power of the distraction took the edge off the ridicule. It worked so well, that Jekaran didn't even hear the voice whispering in his ear until it repeated itself a third time.

"Uska stupid human boy be ready," Karak hissed into his ear.

Jekaran opened his eyes and glanced toward the sound. He had expected to see a slight wavy distortion to the air marking Karak's presence in his veiled form, but there was no sign of the Vorakk shaman. He was about to chalk the voice up to intense wishful thinking when he caught movement on his right periphery. Jekaran looked to his right and found a small, marble-sized ball of light hovering just above his ear. It looked like a glow fly, but glow flies didn't shine bright enough to be seen during the day. Jekaran squinted at the sight and then gasped. There was no mistaking it – it was one of Karak's spirit orbs.

It zipped away and Jekaran half lifted a hand as if to catch it. *Be ready for what?*

A sound like rumbling thunder stilled all of the laughter and Jekaran snapped his head up in time to see Gymal, the soldiers, and all of the well-finders glancing around in confused silence. The rumbling grew louder and then the ground began to shake. Jekaran sat back on his haunches and looked around stupidly.

What was—?

A cracking sound accompanied an explosion of dust from the ground and Jekaran saw a fissure form, snaking its way across the camp and tearing open the earth. What followed was pure pandemonium as the soldiers and well-finders scattered to find safety. Jekaran struggled to stand as the ground heaved beneath his feet and tipped him into a backward fall. Hands on his back steadied him and Jekaran turned to find the boy Lyam standing at his right side, gripping his forearm. The shy boy wasn't wearing the oversized hat and spectacles that always half-hid his face.

"Mae?" Jekaran gasped. *What was she doing here?*

"Move you idiot!" She pulled on his arm and forced him to the right.

They stumbled into a run, Jekaran having to hike his dress up with his free hand in order to keep from falling. Men shouted and scrambled about as the ground continued to quake. No one cared to pay attention to Jekaran running through the camp. The quake subsided to a manageable tremor by the time they reached the outer ring of tents and the ghern picket line. The beasts bayed, bucked and strained against their bonds. A man stood near the animals, a long serrated blade held in his right hand. He was dressed in a simple white tunic and brown trousers, but the round face and white hair were unmistakable. It was Irvis.

The monk laughed when he saw Jekaran's dress and whistled as he made a show of looking Jekaran up and down. "You make a pretty little thing, don't you child?"

Jekaran shot him a glare as he tore the black choker from his neck. "Took your sweet time coming for me," he snapped.

"Your grateful sentiment is very endearing." Irvis laughed, and sawed on the rope tethering the nearest ghern until it snapped. The beast bellowed and shouldered past him, breaking into a run out of the camp.

"What are you doing?" Jekaran asked.

"Making sure we're not followed," He severed the tether of another ghern. "Don't worry. Karak has mounts waiting for us. Go on ahead. I'll be done here in a second."

"Not yet!" Jekaran pulled out of Maely's grip and began running back into the camp.

"Jekaran!" he heard her shout.

He quickly touched his bond to the sword and hurried to Gymal's tent in the center of the camp. He hesitated at the tent door and listened to see if it was occupied. The din of confused and frightened shouting made it difficult to tell, so Jekaran threw caution to the wind and lifted the canvas flap.

Empty.

The only light filtering into the tent came from the sun at his back and a small hole near the floor in the back of the tent. Jekaran hesitated a moment before the sword flooded his mind a second time with miraculous familiarity of the tent's interior, making sight unnecessary. Jekaran rushed to the side of Gymal's four-poster to the long lockbox lying next to Gymal's travel trunk.

At least the man is consistent.

"Jekaran!"

He started and glanced at the tent door to see Maely's backlit head poking into the tent.

Had she cut her hair?

He turned back, grabbed the lockbox, and then stood.

"What *are* you doing?" the girl hissed.

Jekaran moved toward the door—he would let Irvis pick the lock this time once they were safe—and gently pushed passed Maely and out of the tent.

"You're going to get us caught!" she snapped at him.

Fitting words, Jekaran realized, as he saw Gymal, Hort, and two mercenary soldiers rushing toward them.

"Come on!" He grabbed Maely's arm and pulled her from the tent.

A glance over his shoulder showed the soldiers overtaking Gymal as the short, skinny man started to flag. "Don't kill him!" he heard Gymal shout to Hort, who had already put considerable distance between himself and his lord.

The bastard probably wasn't finished tormenting me, Jekaran thought. *Why else would he order his men to spare me?*

Jekaran looked ahead to find that he and Maely were heading for a naturally formed stone arch beyond a narrow path that inclined up one side of a rocky hill. *Hill* might have been an understatement, he realized. The monstrous monolith of eroded, orange stone looked more like a miniature mountain. He was about to bank right to avoid the treacherous path, but Hort and the mercenaries were closing so quickly that they would definitely overtake them if he changed direction.

He sped up and towed Maely furiously through the archway.

"Where are we going?" she shouted.

He shook his head. The path they headed toward could frighten her more than she already was, and the incline slowed them. He glanced over his shoulder and the strain lightened. Hort and his two mercenary comrades were struggling, and the distance between them growing.

Their armor will tire them out before we run out of energy. We can outrun them!

Just when Jekaran was starting to feel smug about his projected victory, his feet tangled on the hem of his dress and he pitched forward taking Maely with him. The lockbox slipped out from underneath his arm and crashed down to the rocky ground behind him. Jekaran heard the distinct sound of splintering wood followed by the *clang* of steel.

"My sword!" he blurted out as he hit the rocky ground.

He rolled down the incline, but not in straight line and before he knew it, Jekaran was going off a rocky ledge. He dug his fingernails into the ground, which slowed his momentum enough for him to purchase a tenuous grip on the ledge, but not before his lower body had swung over, leaving Jekaran's feet dangling free while he desperately worked to keep his upper body from sliding down further.

"Jek!" he heard Maely scream from somewhere up the path.

At least she hadn't fallen off the side of the cliff. That thought made Jekaran look down, a terribly stupid mistake. His heart leapt into his throat. He was dangling more than thirty feet above a very rocky ground.

He closed his eyes and gritted his teeth, kicking his legs and throwing everything he had into to trying to pull himself up over the ledge. The effort rebounded on him, his tense muscles releasing and betraying him to exhaustion. He began to slip, a second straining effort doing nothing more than slowing his fall.

His fingers slipped against the rock, and dread filled him as he closed his eyes. He was going to fall.

In a final effort, he clawed the surface, and then felt his dress pull tight around his back and underneath his arms. He looked up and saw Hort's beefy arm pulling him up. The man strained and dragged Jekaran up over the rock ledge, the sharp rock ruthlessly scraping Jekaran's arms and legs and tearing his dress.

That's a shame, he thought. *It looks expensive.* Then he chuckled at the absurdity of the thought, or the giddy relief of his escape from death.

"What's so funny?" Hort breathlessly demanded as he unceremoniously dropped Jekaran to the ground.

Jekaran rose up on his hands and knees and shook his head. "I ruined Gymal's dress," he laughed. It was no longer a laugh of mirth, but more a bitter admission of defeat.

"That is kinda funny," Hort said. Then he kicked Jekaran soundly in the ribs.

His vision dimmed, his breath robbed from his lungs. He fell back to the ground, rolling onto his right side as he desperately gasped for air. He heard Maely shouting, the sound a distant thing as if it was nothing more than a particularly lively memory. The next sound was a scuffling followed by Maely screaming, not in fear, but in anger.

"Bastards! Get your hands off me!"

For some reason, that comforted Jekaran. He wasn't sure why, but the idea of Maely's consistency of temper even in a crisis made him feel better. Not much, but enough for his mind to clear. Or maybe that was the return of oxygen to his brain. It didn't matter. He rolled back onto his stomach and rose again to all fours, and then rocked back onto his knees. He saw Maely kicking back at the ankles of a mercenary more than three times her size as he dragged her back to the group.

"Let her go!" Jekaran shouted. "She's not a part of this!"

"She is now," he heard Hort call from behind him.

Jekaran turned and was struck with a sudden, fierce jealousy as he saw Hort lift the sword talis from the ground. The man stared at the blade, a look of surprised admiration on his face.

"So this is what you were trying steal from ol' Gymal?" The mercenary reverently touched the amethyst stone embedded in the silver crossguard and barked a short laugh. "I can't say I blame you."

"Put it down!" Jekaran heard himself scream. He had once seen an overprotective mother alienate her sister over a jealous obsession of who could hold her newborn baby. He had never understood that mindset until this moment. "I'll kill you!" he heard himself growling.

Hort looked genuinely taken aback by Jekaran's sudden ferocity. "What's this to you?" he asked. "I'll grant that it's a fine blade, and no doubt worth a great deal, but you act as if—"

Jekaran was on his feet in a flash, lunging for Hort like a wild man. Hort reflexively swung the sword at him, a swing apparently intended to lop off Jekaran's head. The mercenary cried out in surprise as the blade abruptly halted in midair, as though he had hit an invisible wall.

Jekaran stopped up short, the reality of his near death shocking his mind to clarity. *Divine Mother! What was he doing attacking a trained soldier?*

All froze in stunned paralysis. Hort was so shocked he even kept the sword raised, the blade only a hair's-breadth away from the right side of Jekaran's neck.

The distant clamor of the chaos of the camp below was the only sound piercing the air.

He can't use it against me, Jekaran realized. The sword was his and would not let anyone else use it against him. His confidence rallied and he smirked at Hort, as though he had known this all along.

Attack, he heard the sword say, actually say—in words. And so he did.

Jekaran brought up his boot and slammed the toe into Hort's codpiece. The man grunted and dropped his arm. Jekaran took the opportunity to grab Hort's wrist and forearm. *Wow, I can't even get my hands around his wrist,* Jekaran realized with a stab of panic.

Hort was big.

Hort was muscular.

Hort could destroy him.

The sudden image of him twisting Hort's beefy wrist hard to the right flashed before Jekaran's mind and he found himself doing exactly that. Hort cried out and let go of the sword. It hadn't even touched the ground before Jekaran grabbed it, so quickly that he caught it by the blade. He stared down at his hand, which should have been badly sliced, but remarkably, the blade didn't harm the soft flesh of his palm.

Jekaran quickly turned the sword around and grabbed the handle. Relief like nothing he had ever known washed over him. It was as if he had been thirsty to the point of agony and now his lips touched cool, clean, refreshing water.

He had his sword, and the world felt right again.

Chapter 23

Maely felt her eyes widen as Jek performed a standing back flip away from the large mercenary leader as though he were some kind of acrobat. The soldier shook himself out of his stunned stupor, drew his own sword, and lunged at Jek, who confidently whirled to the left just in time to dodge the swing. He then snapped up his right foot, striking the mercenary leader's wrist and the man cried out in pain, dropping his sword.

In one fluid motion, Jekaran twirled his sword so that the blade pointed down, swung his arm, and slammed the pommel into the big soldier's nose. The man's hands shot to his face and he fell to his knees, blood gushing down the front of his armor.

The soldier holding Maely abruptly released her, and drew his sword as he rushed forward. His two fellows, both of whom converged simultaneously, joined him.

Jek didn't hesitate. With practiced timing, he dropped to the ground and shot a leg out to sweep the soldier charging him. He then somersaulted forward over the sprawled mercenary and sprung to his feet just in time to parry two swinging swords at once. He threw off the two mercenary's blades and spin-kicked the soldier at his left in the face before landing and elbowing the soldier at his right across the nose. It was all incredibly heroic, save for the fact that Jekaran still wore a green velvet dress with white sequins fringing the hem.

The first soldier struck at Jek from behind, but ended up skewering one of his companions as Jek presciently sidestepped the attack. He didn't even have time to register what he'd done to his own companion when Jek struck him in the back of the head with the sword's jeweled pommel, the resounding *crack* so loud Maely had no doubt the man's skull had been broken. The mercenary crumpled forward, landing on top of the man he had impaled. The last soldier without debilitating injuries—the one Jekaran had spin-kicked in the face—didn't rise for another attack. Instead, he scrambled away like a crab, blubbering and begging that his life be spared.

Jek responded by slamming the toe of his boot hard into the fork of the man's legs with a casual brutality that frightened Maely. He then turned to face the mercenary leader. The man was still on his knees, right hand cupping his gushing nose.

"Please Brother Ulan," the soldier pled."

Brother Ulan?

"Don't kill me!"

A sudden fear rose in Maely's heart. Would Jek kill this man? He hadn't inflicted any overtly lethal injuries on the other mercenaries, but he had ruthlessly slaughtered the bandits that attacked him in Rasha. That had been awful, but justified self-defense. This was different. Killing this man now in his helpless state would be—murder.

He won't do it, Maely told herself. *That's not him.* The boy she had grown up with, the boy she loved, was not a murderer. He was mischievous, true, but his mischief never crossed into the realm of cruelty. But what if the ego talis had changed him somehow? What if he wasn't able to control himself? What if the sword had turned him into a monster?

"I like you, Hort," Maely heard Jek say just before he raised his sword to a decapitating trajectory.

The mercenary leader's eyes widened.

No, Jek, Maely thought. *Please don't.*

Jekaran's face was completely devoid of emotion and for the first time in her life, Maely couldn't read him. That frightened her. The mercenary leader began to cry and plead for his life, promising a hundred different things if he spared him. The moment stretched, and Maely began to panic. *No, Jek, no,* she silently pled. Then a thought occurred to her.

"Jekaran!" she shouted, working to keep her voice from trembling.

"Jekaran!" She saw him flinch, and that gave her courage. She began walking toward him. "Jekaran, what would Ez say if he saw you like this?" she tried to sound accusing.

Jek's expression started to flicker.

Golden womb of the goddess, was the talis controlling him? Like her ring controlled the shopkeeper?

"You know he'd disapprove. You know he'd be disappointed."

She slowly sidled up to him, lightly placed her hand on his raised arm, and said in a gentler tone, "What would Mulladin think if he saw you murder this man? He looks up to you. *I* look up to you."

That seemed to do it and Jek let her force his arm down. He then looked at her, his eyes focusing and his countenance warming with feeling. "Mae?" he asked, sounding confused.

What was that talis doing to him?

"Leave him," she said. "We need to go."

Jek cast a glance at the mercenary leader and nodded.

The large soldier's shoulders dropped, and he fell to the ground weeping like a child.

Goddess, send that we don't run across Gymal on our way out, Maely prayed. She wasn't sure she could coax Jekaran out of a murderous rage if *that* bully tried to stop them. "Come on," she said as she pulled on his arm.

The two broke into a quick jog down the mountainous path, through the natural sandstone arch, and back into camp. Kairah was still shaking the ground, albeit not as violently as before. That surprised Maely, for the Allosian woman had claimed to have very little power left, and that she would only be able to manage a few moments of—

Then Maely saw a glowing amethyst light shining out through open patches on a rock wall.

"They found the well," she said to herself.

"Actually, *I* found it," Jek said sounding disgusted for some reason.

Still staring at the soft glow—it *was* quite beautiful—Maely said, "That's how she had the strength to keep this up."

"Who?"

Maely shot a glance at him. "No one." She wasn't sure why she didn't tell Jek about Kairah. He would meet the Allosian soon enough. Maybe she was worried that her beauty would smite Jek. Hell, who wouldn't be taken aback by how thin and perfect the woman looked. And skin free of blemishes? Would Jek fall in love with her?

That's stupid, Maely chided herself.

"Jekaran!"

Jek skidded to a stop.

Oh no, Maely thought with a stab of panic. *Gymal.*

"Halt!" The short lord pointed from a hundred paces away, and the two mercenaries flanking him began to charge.

Jekaran smiled wickedly so Maely gripped his hand tighter. When had she taken a hold of his hand? "No!" she snapped. "We need to get out of here!"

Jek stared at her for a long moment, face starting to go blank again.

Divine Mother! Was he losing control again?

The sound of thundering footfalls drew Maely's attention to her left, where two Gherns galloped toward them. Irvis was riding the one in front and holding onto the reins of the second beast. He reined in before them and glowered down at Jek.

"By Rasheera's breasts!" he swore. "What do you think you are doing, child?"

Why did that man remind her of Ez?

Jekaran opened his mouth to speak, but Irvis cut him off.

"We don't have time for that now!" he snapped. "We have to go!" He proffered the reins of the second Ghern to Jek.

Jek shot an uncertain glance at the bipedal beast and said, "I've never ridden one of these."

"Stop them!" Gymal's nasally scream was closer now.

Jek shot a glance at the short lord and his mercenary entourage, now only thirty paces away. He looked at the ghern, nodded, and then put his right foot in the stirrup while grasping the pommel of the saddle with his free hand. The beast stamped and snorted and Jek pulled his foot out of the stirrup.

"Give that to me!" Irvis motioned to the sword.

Maely's anxiety increased as she saw Jek's face go blank again. It lasted only a moment before he nodded and reluctantly handed the sword to Irvis. With both hands free, he was able to climb into the saddle and then lean down to help her climb up behind him. She hugged him around the waist, probably a little too tightly.

"Stop them!" Gymal shouted from just ten paces away.

Irvis thrust the handle of the sword at Jek who took the weapon back greedily. The chubby man then snapped the reins of his beast and shouted "Ya!"

Jek copied the motion and sound, and their ghern leapt into a gallop behind Irvis' mount.

Panicked well-finders crisscrossed their path, some not even noticing them coming until the last moment when they were forced to leap out of the way.

Maely cast a look behind them and saw Gymal shouting at his mercenaries and pointing after them. *They were in for a surprise when they found out that Irvis had scattered their mounts.* She smiled to herself and tightened her grip around Jek's waist.

They left the camp behind, galloping along a sandstone wall bending north. Something moved at the corner of her vision, and she turned to see a rippling in the air like that of heat lines on a summer horizon. A beat later the lizard man appeared, running as fast as their ghern was galloping. It was so sudden that she yelped, which drew Jek's attention to the Vorakk keeping pace with them.

"Alka stupid human boy!" the Vorakk hissed loudly.

Jek actually laughed at that and shouted, "It's good to see you too, Karak!"

Karak? Did all Vorakk names end in k? She rolled her eyes. Before this one, she hadn't actually met any of the reptilian humanoids, but she had heard plenty of tales and always they had names like: Iark, or Septok, or Naltuk. *Ridiculous.*

"Where's your mount?" Jek shouted.

The lizard man grinned showing an unnerving mouth full of pointy teeth. "Karak only use ghern for food. Vorakk run fast aka."

"I can see that," Jek laughed.

Disgusting, Maely thought. *Who ate ghern?* They smelled bad and were too expensive besides.

Their flight carried them a mile from Gymal's camp, where they slowed to a halt inside of a sandstone gorge. Maely looked around, searching for Kairah. She began to ask Irvis, but the question only formed on her lips before the Allosian woman came out from behind a large boulder.

An untethered ghern obediently followed her without the woman doing anything to coax it.

Does she talk to animals too?

Kairah glanced at Maely before looking at Jek, offering a deep, pink-lipped smile.

Maely growled under her breath.

Chapter 24

Jekaran's breath caught in his throat, and, for a brief moment, he felt as though he were suffocating. The woman standing before him was without a doubt the most incredibly beautiful woman he had ever laid eyes on. Even beneath her sable cloak, Jekaran could see the perfect proportion of her body highlighted by the right amount of curves. And she was tall, but not so tall as to be mannish. She reminded him of the sculpture of the goddess carved around Rasha's Apeira well, perfect in a way only seen in works of art.

Who was she? He had seen her before, of that he was sure, but where? Then Jekaran remembered. "You were in Rasha," he blurted out.

The woman dipped her head as she drew down the hood of her cloak, revealing her hair.

It wasn't the beautiful dark color she wore when he rescued—*tried to rescue,* he corrected himself—her from the rape gang in Rasha. No, this was a color he had never seen on anyone. It was the same amethyst color of an Apeira well, and seemed to glow against her alabaster skin.

"She's a beautiful creature, isn't she," Irvis whispered. "Probably the most beautiful woman *I've* ever seen and I've seen a lot of women. A *lot* of women."

Jekaran ignored the monk's lascivious implication. "Uh, my lady." He bowed awkwardly in the saddle and was suddenly reminded that he was wearing a torn up, green velvet dress.

Ah, hell!

"My courageous protector," the woman said as she dipped her head a second time.

Jekaran thought he heard Maely mutter something, but ignored it and said, "Don't know about courageous. Foolish maybe."

The woman laughed. It was a musical sound like a cord playing on a harp, a sound Jekaran was sure he could never get tired of hearing. "You are not a fool, Jekaran."

"I look like one." Jekaran chuckled nervously and motioned at the dress he was wearing. "Could I have my lady's name?"

Maely scoffed again.

That nettled Jekaran, for he was trying to be a gentleman and polite, both things Maely often accused him of not being.

"I am Kairah of Allose."

"You're an Allosian?" Jekaran blurted out in a way that ended his awkward attempt at chivalrous formality.

"Yes."

"Then I have you to thank for *my* rescue?"

"She only caused the quake," Maely snapped.

"Only?" Jekaran scoffed as he shot her an amused glance. The girl glowered at him, and her new short hair made her look like her brother when *he* was pouting. Jekaran laughed. "Don't be like that, Mae."

"Something's wrong with him," Maely said to Kairah in a tone that reminded Jekaran of when she would tattle on him to Ez. "The sword was controlling him."

She knew about his connection to the sword? Did they all know?

Jekaran felt the sword project some kind of emotion. Was that unease? *Ridiculous*, Jekaran thought. *It's just a weapon, a magical weapon, to be sure, but nothing more.* The sword's mental communication shifted again at the thought. *That was odd.* If Jekaran didn't know better, he would have thought the sword was offended.

"He couldn't control himself when fighting the soldiers. He almost executed one on the spot, when the man was helpless and beaten." Maely said.

"Mae!" Jekaran snapped. "What's wrong with you? I was in complete control."

"Your face changed, Jek," Maely said, and now she did sound worried. "And so did your eyes."

"I—I—"

The Allosian woman strode toward him, face professional as though she were a magistrate and Jekaran at court. She reached up and touched his temple. This close he caught her scent. It made Jekaran think of spring trees and fresh water. If beautiful had a summary-smell, it would've been this.

At her touch, Jekaran felt something brush his mind. It felt similar to when the sword communicated with him, except more potent, more real. Jekaran could sense Kairah looking at his very soul, and it was both exhilarating and unnerving at the same time. Like being naked on your wedding night.

She touched his link to the sword and strummed it like strumming the string of a lute. It was an entirely novel sensation, both fascinating and uncomfortable. He could feel the sword's displeasure and had to agree with its sentiment, but, before he could protest, the experience was over.

"His link is out of balance," Kairah said as she removed her hand from his temple.

"What?" Jekaran asked.

Kairah looked at him, and, for the first time, he noticed her eyes were the same color as her hair. "You have bonded an ego talis."

"A what?"

"It's like the sword is alive," Maely added.

So it is alive! That confirmed Jekaran's suspicions but did nothing to ease his fear. Though he denied it to Maely and Kairah, and to himself, he felt the sword taking over while he had been fighting Hort and the other mercenaries. And, at the end, he *had* lost control. Had it not been for Maely's distant voice calling him back from the edge of madness, he would've killed Hort. Would've killed him and enjoyed it.

"How alive?" Jekaran said, his taut voice belying his bravado. "I mean, is it like an animal or a person?"

Kairah stared at him for a long moment before answering him. "It depends on the talis. Has it communicated to your mind in actual words or just feelings and impressions?"

Jekaran bit his lower lip.

"Jek?" he heard Maely press.

"It told me to attack the soldiers, okay!"

Kairah nodded gravely. "Only the most powerful ego talises could speak to one's mind in words. They have personalities of their own, and a will."

"A will?" Jekaran repeated. "Like, it has its own ideas and feelings?"

"Yes," Kairah said. "And bonding such a talis requires constant mental vigilance to keep its will from dominating the host's."

"Then it's evil?" Jekaran asked, sudden fear making him mentally retreat from his contact with the sword.

Kairah shook her head. "Talises are only tools, even ego talises. They will want to answer the ends of their creation. That is their driving directive. In this case, the sword's purpose is to fight and kill. It will therefore influence you to do that at every opportunity."

Jekaran looked down at the sword lying across his lap, a sudden wariness making him shut the weapon talis completely out of his mind. It was a hard thing, like plugging a hole in a fishing boat while actually on the water.

"Can you fix him?" Maely asked. "Can you separate him from the sword?"

The suggestion caused Jekaran a sudden stab of panic. He shot his head up and snapped, "No!"

"Jek!" Mae scolded.

"I can control it."

"Listen to her, child," he heard Irvis say from behind him. "That sword caused your uncle to do some terrible things. Things I know he regrets to this day."

Jekaran now understood his uncle better, understood how he might've turned into a killer. The power the sword offered was intoxicating, the drive to destroy almost overwhelming. *I can control it,* he told himself again. *I won't turn into a murderer!*

Mae looked at Kairah with the same look she displayed when she was trying to persuade Ez to side with her on a contested issue.

Kairah's expression faltered. "Such a thing is"—she hesitated—"difficult."

"I don't know much about magic, but can't you just cut the link, like a cord?"

Kairah thoughtfully shook her head. "That question does not have a simple answer, Maely."

Jekaran saw Maely's cheeks redden, a look he knew all too well. The short girl was losing control of her fiery temper. "Maybe you could dumb it down and speak slowly so we stupid humans can understand."

Kairah sighed wearily—apparently, she was already accustomed to Maely's short fuse—and said, "That is not what I mean."

"Then what *do* you mean?" she snapped.

"The more powerful an ego talis, the stronger and faster the bond forms. You must understand there is protocol for this kind of thing. Hosts usually undergo long periods of mental training before they bond their ego talis, and the process itself is best if undertaken gradually so the talis' will does not overpower the will of the new host."

Kairah stared at him.

"The extreme circumstances under which Jekaran has bonded the sword has made their connection unusually strong. The speed at which this has occurred is leading to Jekaran's being overpowered by the sword's will. Cutting the link is not something that I am certain I can do. Even if I were to attempt it, the shock could seriously harm, or even kill, him."

"It nearly drove Argentus mad," Irvis solemnly added.

"Who's Argentus?" Mae asked.

Jekaran didn't answer, but instead turned to look at Irvis. "How did he do it?"

"He allowed its charge to run out," Irvis said. "I was with him when it happened, taking care of you while your uncle went through the withdrawal."

"Are you talking about Ez?" he heard Mae ask. "He used this sword?"

Again, Jekaran ignored her question. "That sounds like an addict coming off poppies."

"It was worse."

"Isn't there anything you can do?" Mae pled.

Golden womb of the goddess, Mae must really be worried for her to be begging, Jekaran thought.

"I would need to take Jekaran to Allose. Our elders could likely break the bond safely."

"Then let's go," Mae said.

"Maely," Kairah said in a chiding tone. "You know that I need to see your king."

"I don't care about your stupid—"

"—how do I keep it from taking me over?" Jekaran interrupted.

Kairah looked at him. "I know some mental exercises I can teach you. They will help you maintain control. You will also need to make certain the sword does not lose its Apeiron charge. That would have the same effect as incorrectly severing the bond."

"But my uncle survived it."

"Barely," Irvis added. "And even then it did something to him. He was different afterward."

"You should also travel with me," Kairah said.

"No!" snapped Maely. "He's not going to help you get to Aiested!"

"Maely—" Kairah began.

"—was this part of your plan? To string us along with promises of help, given only if we served you?"

"Mae," Jekaran said.

"No!" she snapped at him. "We're going home, Jek! Home to Ez and Mull! Give the sword to her, and let's go home!"

How was he going to tell her that Genra was no longer home for him? He knew she wouldn't take it well. Mull certainly wouldn't.

Maely sniffed derisively. "I bet she's lying about the danger of breaking the bond anyway."

"I don't really wanna risk testing that," Jekaran said. He could feel the sword pressing its will against the mental barrier he had formed. He didn't need to communicate with it to know it was probably trying to dissuade him from listening to Maely. How did it hear? For that matter, how did it see?

"Aek!" Jekaran heard Karak call from above him.

He looked up to see the Vorakk shaman clinging to the rock wall of the gorge by the claws of one hand, a spirit ball floating above one of his reptilian eyes.

"Human warriors find gherns!" Karak dropped twenty feet to the ground as easily as though he were hopping off a stump. "Must go now rok!"

Jekaran nodded and Kairah rushed over to her ghern, effortlessly climbing into the beast's saddle.

"Rok," Karak hissed and then he exploded into a run.

"Jekaran!" Maely said.

"We'll argue about it later, Mae!" And with that, he snapped the reins of his ghern and they were again riding through the sandstone gorge—away from Gymal's camp.

CHAPTER 25

Jeryn was much the way Ezra remembered leaving it: noisy, crowded, and filthy. But it wasn't just the refuse in the street, or the horrid scent created from the mixture of urine, feces, rotting garbage, and goddess only knows what else. No, the city's filthiness went beyond the tangible. Jeryn's people, nobles, and governor were all corrupt to the core in a way Ezra had rarely seen in the other cities of the world. Coin would buy absolution from almost any offense, no matter how vile, and was extorted by guards as a *preventative measure,* ensuring access to their services in time of need. Failure to pay up could very well result in the guards looking the other way while you were attacked and robbed. Or worse, the guards might do those very things themselves.

Those *qualities* had made Jeryn the perfect place for the Rikujo to thrive. While not their headquarters-Rikujo didn't have a central location-Jeryn could be said to be the unofficial stronghold of the criminal syndicate.

That's what made it the perfect city for Ezra to hide out in.

Knowing Kaul, as he did, the man would assume Ezra would stay completely away from Jeryn, and so would spend his time searching for him in the many hamlets scattering the countryside.

Jeryn was also the last city in which Ezra maintained a safe house, a two-story cottage located in one of the nicer parts of the city. *Well, maybe nicer was too generous a word*, he thought. *Not as rotten works better.*

When Ezra had cut ties with his former life, he had abandoned all of his other safe houses save this one, partly for its closer proximity to Genra, and partly because he had kept this one secret from even his closest allies. He hadn't even told Irvis about it until he wrote it in the letter he sent with Jekaran.

Jekaran, he thought with a spike of worry. *Where is that boy?*

Ezra stepped away from the window and let threadbare curtains fall back to obscure his view of the street. He and Mulladin had arrived in the city two nights ago, which was almost a week later than he originally planned. For that reason, he expected Irvis and Jekaran to be waiting for him, but the cottage was just as empty as when he had left it years earlier. Well, not exactly empty. A family of raccoons had taken up residence on the second floor. They had sent Mulladin into a frightened fit, as he had been the one to discover them. They had apparently gotten in through a hole in the roof, one probably made by a thief. That would explain why his cache of weapons and Aies were missing. But the raccoons were probably to blame for his depleted food stores.

Being robbed galled Ezra, and he was so frustrated that he almost reported the crime to the captain of the city guard. When he realized the ridiculous irony of that course of action, he had burst out laughing. He could just imagine it: Argentus, the Invincible Shadow, reporting the burglary of money and things he had stolen from others. It wasn't really a crime against him as much as a well-deserved serving of poetic justice. Of course, he knew he deserved much more than just the inconvenience brought on by his house being burgled.

Guilt clutched Ezra's chest, threatening to grab his heart and drag it down into the depths of sorrow. He had long ago faced the fact that he was a wicked man destined for the deepest pit of hell, and his committing his soul to the goddess was the only hope of escaping such a fate. Part of that commitment had been a pledge to never again lie, steal, or do any man violence. But over the course of the last two weeks, Ezra had broken the first two of those three pledges. It made him sick how quickly it all returned to him, how easy it had been to remember the language of lying or the ritual of stealing.

In the last two weeks, Ezra had stolen food from the stores of an old farmer who had taken them in for the night, clothes from the drying line of a goodwife, and coin from a peddler selling a bulbous yellow fruit

Ezra didn't recognize. He had told himself it had all been necessary, but that did little to relieve the gnawing worry that he had offended the goddess and was on the road to becoming Argentus once more.

Don't be a fool, he told himself. It was the sword that turned him into a monster and his redemption hinged on his abandoning it. He could never bond with it again. That would be the line, he decided. He would lie and steal as needed, and even kill to defend the ones he loved, but he would not wield the talis that had almost cost him his very soul.

But what if you need it to defend Jekaran? A voice whispered from some dark corner of his mind. Would he not soon have the opportunity to bond it again? He fingered his earring, the displacement talis. Being near Jeryn's Apeira well had recharged it, and he could now use it at will while in the city. When Jekaran brought the sword back, it, too, would re-charge.

No! That was the one line he wouldn't, that he *couldn't,* cross. The cost was too great.

Mulladin's soft crying drifted down from the second floor. "What's wrong, son?" Ezra called up the stairs to him.

"Where's Mae?" came the congested reply.

"She'll be along soon," he said with as much nonchalance as he could muster. It, of course, was an act.

Damn me, he thought. Giving Jek the sword and sending him to Rasha made Ezra feel as though he had sent a toddler into a cave of hibernating bears. What if Kaul had sorted it out and went after Jekaran instead of him? He hadn't seen any sign of his old colleague, but that could mean a variety of things. *What if* his ruse had failed? What if Kaul had found Jekaran? What if Gymal discovered the sword and had Jekaran arrested? Or worse yet, what if his nephew had bonded the talis when it re-charged from Rasha's well?

No, he thought. *I can't let myself be paralyzed with fear.* He drummed his fingers against his leg. *But I can't wait any longer.* That would mean putting himself and Mulladin in danger of being discovered. And, it would likely mean more stealing in order to make the journey, but Ezra couldn't wait around and do nothing.

"Come on, Mull!" he shouted up the stairs. "We're going to go find Jek and Mae."

KAUL WATCHED atop a sandstone ridge as the caravan in the gorge below finally began to move. Wagons pulled by bullocks trailed two dozen men in commoner's clothes led by a ghern mounted nobleman surrounded by armored guards. It was the well-find expedition from Argentus' village, and they were leaving the rock lands.

"The men from the village were complaining their lord was planning on disbanding their expedition as soon as they are out of the rock lands. They think they will be sent home without pay," Arkell said. He had been down among the group of miners, posing as a traveling peddler in order to glean information. He had only just returned and was standing at Kaul's left, just inches from the ledge of the ridge.

Pushing him would take almost no effort, Kaul idly thought. But no, he needed Arkell and the man was loyal. Best of all, he was absolutely terrified of him, even when Kaul wasn't using his dread medal on the man.

Still, it was tempting.

"They didn't find a well?" Kaul asked, still staring down at the caravan.

"Actually they did," Arkell said. "That's why they're so upset. Their lord didn't allow any of them to excavate it."

"They're just leaving it?"

The man nodded. "Apparently, the camp was raided by some bandits, and the miners claim one of the attackers used a gaia stone to cover their escape."

Gaia stone? The talises that could cause ground quakes were as rare as they were powerful. In fact, Kaul only knew of one lord in all of Aiestal who owned one and he was cousin to the king. How could common outland bandits have come by a gaia stone?

"And what of the boy with green eyes?"

Arkell smiled. "He escaped with the bandits and took the sword with him."

Kaul looked back down at the caravan. "That lord must be going after Argentus' nephew. That's why he's disbanding their expedition. He wants the sword."

"Brilliant deduction, Lord Kaul."

The man could be so obsequious. Kaul eyed the edge of the ridge one more time, but decided against hurling him hundreds of feet to his death. "Do they have any ideas as to where the boy has gone?"

He shook his head. "No one said anything about that, but I think I saw their lord with a blood seeker."

"If what you say is true, then that weaselly little lord is going to lead us straight to the sword."

"Perfect," Arkell laughed—a *too-relaxed* laugh. Was the man losing his fear of Kaul?

That thought made the rage inside of Kaul boil up, the stress of his anger like pressured steam needing a release. Kaul abruptly threw his left arm out to strike Arkell square in the back. The man yelped as he pitched forward and then screamed as he fell. He hit his head on a stone outcropping ten feet into his fall and was blessedly silent for the remainder of his descent. Kaul drew in a deep breath, the feeling of pressure having ebbed.

After a moment, he turned and walked away from the ledge of the ridge, ignoring sputtering questions from his remaining three lieutenants, all of whom were wide-eyed and frightened.

They were afraid of him. That was good.

He would allow them to live as long as they stayed that way.

CHAPTER 26

Nightfall found Jekaran's group camping on the edge of the rock lands. The gradual return of foliage and grass to the landscape was a comforting sign to Jekaran. The ordeal was ending. If he could help it, he would never return to the rock lands as long as he lived. Jekaran puttered around the outer perimeter of their camp, searching for kindling, grateful for the freedom of movement now that he was dressed again in tunic and trousers—or "man-clothes" as Karak had called them. He planned on burning Gymal's velvet dress on the cook fire once their meal was done.

He glanced back at the camp. He knew the sword was safe, but it still unnerved him not to have it with him. Right now, the Allosian woman was studying it, a fact he sensed the sword didn't appreciate very much. The thing was like a child, Jekaran scoffed.

And I'm acting like its damned mother.

Jekaran lifted some dry sticks from the ground and added them to his armful. He figured he had enough to sustain a decent sized fire—apparently both Karak and Kairah could use their magic to light one—but this was his excuse to escape Mae, and would draw it out as long as he could. She had badgered him all afternoon about returning to Genra and leaving the sword with Kairah.

Irvis had told her some of what had happened with Ez, Kaul, and the sword, but just the skeleton, leaving Jekaran to fill in the rest. One thing

Irvis had left out was that both Ez and Jekaran could never return to Genra.

Maely seemed to have taken the news well, better than he had expected. He had thought she would explode on him, but she had only listened in patient silence.

When he was finished telling her he had to meet Ez in Jeryn, a worried look came into her eyes. Apparently, she had left Mull in Ez's care, and was hoping Jekaran's uncle had taken her brother with him.

"Knowing Ez, he probably did," he had told her, but decided to deliberately down-play the fact that a dangerous Rikujo lord hunted his uncle. He also omitted the fact that if her brother was with Ez, Kaul would kill him, too, if he caught up to them.

Ultimately, she announced she would go with him to Jeryn, which ignited another argument about what to do with the sword. Mae was adamantly against his staying with Kairah for any appreciable amount of time. She treated the Allosian woman with a wary vigilance, as if she intended him harm and it was her job to protect him.

A real Allosian, Jekaran marveled. He had heard the legends of the fey-folk and their beauty, but nothing had prepared him for actually meeting one. Focusing on that beauty was the only line of thinking that allowed him to ignore the pleading summons of the sword. *I'm going to have to learn to keep that that thing shut out*, he resolved, and not for the first time. Could Kairah really teach him to do that?

When Jekaran knew he couldn't carry any more wood—his arms were so full, he was dropping sticks with every step—he reluctantly returned to camp. He found Kairah kneeling on the ground, eyes still intent on his sword. Even in kneeling on the ground, she projected the regal grace of a noblewoman—*or a queen*. Across from her, on the opposite side of a newly dug fire pit, sat Mae, cross-legged and unabashedly glowering at her.

Jekaran walked up to the empty pit and dropped his armload of sticks into it.

Irvis walked over to the fire pit lugging a medium-sized cook pot full of water. He was angrily muttering to himself, and nearly let the metal caldron spill as he hung it from a tripod built over the pit.

"Have a tough time finding water?" Jekaran asked.

Irvis scowled at him. "It's not as easy as gathering wood."

Jekaran laughed and put his hands up defensively. "Hey, I won the cast fair and honest!"

"The creek that you said wasn't too far from here is over a half mile away. So, yes, I did have a *hard* time finding water. That's why I filled the pot with my piss!" Irvis stalked angrily away from the fire pit.

"Gross," he heard Maely say.

He chuckled and glanced at Kairah. She had looked up from the sword, a quizzical expression on her face. "We are having urine in our stew?"

He laughed. "He's just sore that I got the easier job. Come on, Brother Irvis!" He called out to the monk. "Don't be like that!"

The man made a reply as he stalked into the darkness Jekaran couldn't entirely hear, but one that sounded a lot like a very vulgar, very offensive suggestion for how Jekaran should spend his alone-time.

"*He's* a holy man of Rasheera?" Mae asked with her eyebrows high on her forehead.

"An aspiring holy man." He laughed. "He'll be ok. Just needs some time to cool his head." Jekaran cupped his hands and shouted after Irvis, "Maybe in the creek!"

The monk repeated his early admonition, this time loud enough for Jekaran to be sure of what the man was suggesting. It was at this moment that Karak returned with a brace of rabbits.

"Esk good fire sticks!"

"Thanks," Jekaran said flatly. He never could tell when the Vorakk was complimenting or mocking him.

The lizard man flashed a toothy grin as he summoned a spirit ball of fire. The marble-sized miniature sun streaked down at the fire pit and disappeared beneath the pile of sticks. A heartbeat later, a full-fledged campfire roared to life, as though it had been tended carefully for an hour.

"That's a handy trick," Mae said, apparently more to catch Jekaran's attention than to make conversation.

Jekaran pointedly avoided looking at her. "*I* never get tired of seeing it."

"Esk, better when no worm." Karak hissed a chuckle and then went to work expertly skinning and carving each rabbit up with his sharp claws, tossing the pieces into the cook pot as he went. He then knelt on one scaly knee, poking the flames with a stick.

Jekaran shot another glance at Kairah; this would make over fifty just in the last few minutes. He had determined that anything more than thirty would've been rude, but he couldn't help it. The woman was so absolutely perfect.

This time, she caught him.

She's gonna think me as big a pervert as Irvis, he thought as he quickly averted his eyes.

"This talis"—she began as she hooked a strand of amethyst hair behind her ear—"it is not what I expected."

Jekaran looked up at her, trying not to let his embarrassment at being caught staring touch his expression. "What do you mean?"

"Well"—Kairah said as she returned her focus to the sword—"it feels different."

"Felt like a sword to me," Mae said in stiff tone.

Mae, Jekaran inwardly groaned.

"I am not talking about the tactile sensation"—she said with a glance at Mae—"but the feel of its psychic communication."

"I don't understand," Jekaran said.

Kairah silently stared at him for a moment before thoughtfully dropping her eyes to the side. "It is like this talis speaks a foreign tongue."

"I heard it in Aiestali when it spoke to me."

"She's using a metaphor, you dullard," Mae snapped at him.

"Oh," Jekaran said feeling stupid. What was it about Kairah that made him so self-conscious? Sure, she was gorgeous, and he always felt a little nervous around pretty girls, but this was different. This was almost like he felt every single one of his words and actions counted. *Counted toward what?*

"So what does that mean?" Jekaran asked hesitantly. *She must think I'm some kind of back country simpleton.*

Kairah stared again at the sword and shook her head. "I am uncertain. I have never encountered something like this. It is almost as if this talis was not created by my people."

"Then humans did create it!" Mae said, sounding smug for some reason.

Kairah shook her head again. "Human talises resonate with the same tone as Allosian talises, albeit significantly more inelegant."

Out of the corner of his eyes, Jekaran saw Mae stick her tongue out at her. The Allosian woman didn't even notice.

"Who else could have created it?" he asked. He turned to look at Karak. "Do the Vorakk make talises?"

Karak snorted. "Isk Vorakk have spirits."

Jekaran expected further explanation, but apparently, that was supposed to have answered his question. "What about the Ursaj in the north?" He heard Karak hiss at his mention of the bear - people.

Kairah looked up at him, her amethyst eyes intent. "I know of no others who possess the knowledge or ability to craft talises." She picked up the sword and scrutinized some etchings on the crossguard. "I also do not recognize these symbols. They are not of the Allosian language."

"You speak a different language?" Mae asked.

"Of course," Kairah said. "All races have their own tongues, often several variations of the same tongue."

"But you speak perfect Aiestali."

Kairah flashed a small smile. "I spent some time among your people as a child."

Before Jekaran could ask any more questions Irvis returned, drawing everyone's attention by asking somewhat petulantly, "Is it ready yet?"

"I was just wondering what was stronger"—Jekaran said—"your pride or your stomach. Apparently it's your stomach."

Irvis shot him a scowl, but didn't say anything.

Kairah handed the sword back to him and he felt the talis' relief at their being reunited. *It really is like a baby,* he thought, sharing the sword's sentiment. *And I really am like its blasted mother.* Dinner came a half an hour later, although Jekaran wasn't sure there had been enough to be considered an official meal. "Those coneys had barely any meat on them," he complained.

Irvis nodded, "I suspect it would take at least five just to fill a man's stomach."

"Ten to fill yours," Jekaran laughed.

That invoked a half-hearted swat from Irvis, which he easily avoided by ducking the chubby monk's swing.

"Esk Karak told human boy that Karak should cook ghern," the Vorakk shaman said with a toothy grin.

"No, we're going to need those to go to Jeryn," Mae emphatically said.

The camp suddenly went uncomfortably quiet.

"Mae," Jekaran groaned.

"Don't 'Mae' me, Jek! You know we have to make sure my brother is with Ez!"

"Mae, I can't just leave the sword!"

"Then bring it with you!" she snapped.

"Maely, you know I require help to accomplish my task," Kairah said.

This was the second time Jekaran had heard the Allosian woman make mention of it. "What task?"

"It's not our business," Mae quickly interjected.

"Mae!" Jekaran snapped at her. Surprisingly, that quieted her.

Kairah stared at Maely for a long moment before finally turning to look him directly in the eyes. "I must journey to your capital city and meet with your king. He needs to be warned."

"Jekaran, please," he heard Maely plead quietly. He ignored her.

"Warned of what?"

Kairah hooked another stray strand of amethyst hair behind her ear as she looked east. Was that where Allose was? "My brother, Jenoc," she began, "is not like most others of our kind. He is not a pacifistic intellectual dedicated to the pursuit of knowledge for its own ends." She looked at him. "He longs to restore the greatness of my people's past, and reclaim our rightful place as rulers of all of Shaelar."

"Your people used to rule this land?"

Kairah nodded. "We were here even before the Vorakk or the Ursaj."

Was that another hiss from Karak? Did his people fear the bear-people?

"So what happened?" Jekaran asked. "Where did all of your people go?"

"Into hiding," Irvis chimed in.

"Hiding from what?" Jekaran hated it when people made him draw out information piecemeal like this.

"Us," Irvis said. "It was mankind that drove the Allosians into hiding."

Kairah looked at the chubby monk, an expression of surprised approval on her face. "You are an educated man?" she asked.

Irvis snorted, "I wouldn't go that far, but—" he seemed to abruptly remember that he was speaking to a woman of pristine physical perfection, one that he no doubt desired to impress *or see naked*. Irvis cleared his throat and continued in his practiced *holy man* tone. "Yes, my lady, I am something of a student of history."

"Why?" Jekaran deliberately cut in before Irvis had a chance to carry on further. "Why run from us?"

Kairah looked back at him. "You were trying to destroy my people. Your people declared war against us."

"But your magic and power are legendary. How could we be a threat to you?"

"Mankind breeds faster than Allosians do, and it only took a few generations for your people to vastly outnumber mine. You had also acquired talis-craft, and used the skill to create powerful weapons."

Jekaran glanced at the sword in his lap.

"We betrayed them, Jekaran," Irvis said solemnly, not in his false sanctimonious tone, but with genuine regret. "They took us in and we destroyed them."

"I don't understand."

"Humans are not natives of Shaelar, as are the Vorakk, Ursaj, or my people. Your people arrived here on ships almost eight hundred years ago."

"Where did we sail from?"

Kairah shook her head. "No one is really certain."

"Nobody asked? Nobody has since gone to look for our homeland?"

"We were refugees, Jekaran," Irvis added. "We fled our homeland and no one wanted to return."

"The surviving accounts of the humans interviewed by my people are fragmented and inconsistent." Kairah hooked another strand of her jewel-like hair behind a white ear. "However, they all seem to indicate humans of that era were fleeing their lands for the purpose of finding safety. It is assumed war or a natural disaster of some kind forced them to abandon their homes, and by the time they landed on Shaelar, half of them had succumbed to starvation and disease. Even so, your people arrived in great numbers; accounts estimate close to one million."

A million? Jekaran had a hard time wrapping his head around such a large number. Genra had a population of four hundred at most, and the most people he had ever seen in one place were in cities like Rasha, which numbered in the tens of thousands.

Kairah continued. "At the time, our people were spread all across this land. We took pity on you, and did all we could to rescue the humans from their plight. Food, clothing, and lands for settlement were provided, and so commenced your race's life in Shaelar. When it was discovered humans had no innate magical ability, our altruistic elders decided to share our knowledge of talis-craft, and we gave mankind many treasures and the means to create objects of great power."

"And we made weapons," Jekaran concluded aloud.

Kairah nodded. "We, too, created weapons for the purpose of defense, but my people were more interested in other applications of talis-crafting. Your people, however, seemed to have a natural aptitude and drive for devising various ways of causing destruction. We forcefully discouraged the practice, but humans continued their weapon-making in secret. Scarcely seventy years passed from the time humans landed on Shaelar before one human tribe attempted to conquer another, ironically for the purpose of seizing the weapon talises of their neighbors.

"War quickly spread, which only caused the humans to refine their weapon talises as well as to increase their production, which in turn rapidly compounded the crisis. At first, we tried diplomacy to quell the conflicts, but those attempts universally failed. It was only as a last resort that the Allosians took up arms to try to end your fratricidal wars."

"What happened?" Jekaran asked.

"Our military action against your people *did* stop their in-fighting, but only because it united them against us. From that time on, my people, greatly outnumbered by yours, began to lose our cities and treasures, which only grew our enemies' advantage. Eventually, it was decided that the remaining Allosians would go into hiding, with as many of our books and talises as we could preserve. And that is where we have stayed."

A solemn lull fell over them.

"I didn't know," Jekaran said.

"What did our people do when the Allosians disappeared?" he heard Mae ask.

Kairah flashed a sad smile. "You turned on each other, and another three centuries of total war followed. Forgive me for saying so, but your race seems to become intoxicated with battle the way a man loses his wits with strong drink."

"There is that side to us," Irvis somberly agreed.

"Humans hunt Vorakk too. Drive them to desert lands where many die ska," Karak added.

Though Jekaran knew he had no part in humanity's crimes against the peoples of the land, the gentle sorrow with which Kairah told the tragic story invoked a pang of guilt. "It sounds like my people have done little more than consume and destroy Shaelar."

"That is at the heart of why my brother desires your destruction." Kairah looked east again, mouth turned down in a frown as though she were concentrating on something.

"What is it that he's planning?" Irvis asked.

That snapped the Allosian woman out of her reverie, and she turned to look at them. "There were several times during the war in which the fighting reached such intensity that it appeared humans would destroy themselves. Jenoc wants to ignite another war of such destructive magnitude that, when it is over, humans will be all but wiped out."

Irvis chuckled darkly. "Your brother doesn't need to do much. The three nations are always on the brink of war."

Kairah nodded. "True. However, your social caste system of assigning authority to talis ownership has, over the centuries, resulted in hoarding and secrecy. This has in turn led to the loss of the majority of Shaelar's weapon talises, and the knowledge you once possessed of talis-craft itself."

"Divine Mother!" Irvis exhaled suddenly. "Your brother is going to re-introduce the knowledge of how to create weapon talises, isn't he?"

"Yes," Kairah said softly.

"And your people condone this?" he asked.

"My people do not know. Only I do. That is why it is vital that I reach your capital city and warn your king."

The idea of war stirred the sword's will and Jekaran could feel an eagerness spill across their link. It *wanted* him to fight, and joining Kairah in her quest would likely afford him the opportunity to do just that. He worked to shut out the talis, but wasn't entirely successful and the prospect of combat continued to appeal to him. That, compounded by the woman's unmatched physical allure, pushed him over the edge of indecision.

"I will help you," he heard himself saying.

"As will I," Irvis said, though Jekaran doubted that the man's motives were entirely pure.

"Jekaran!" Mae shouted.

He looked at her. She was standing, fists clenched into balls at her sides. Even in the dim light of the campfire, he could see her face was red with anger.

"She needs help, Mae."

"Leave the big problems to lords and kings!" she said, her voice trembling.

"This affects us all, Mae."

"Human boy must go so he can lead Karak to Eater aka," the Vorakk added.

That drew a questioning glance from Kairah, but before Jekaran could answer the Allosian woman, Maely picked up a fist-sized rock and hurled it at his head. Reflex seized his muscles, and Jekaran swung the sword up in a vertical swing just in time to strike the rock in mid-air, and cleave it in two.

"Divine Mother," he whispered as he stared at the sword. He looked up at Maely who stared wide-eyed at him. The brief subsiding of her rage caused by the wonder quickly expired, and her eyes again turned hard. She looked at each of the party in turn, and then turned and stomped off into the darkness.

CHAPTER 27

Maely found the creek Irvis had described, and fell to her knees on its soft bank. Hot tears streamed down her cheeks as quiet sobs racked her body. "Damn fool of a man," she whispered.

She doubted his decision to join Kairah had been entirely made by his head. All men were randy fools. It was if they lost all sense of logic and reason when confronted by an hour-glass figure, long legs, and large breasts. She glanced down her chest. It was no longer wrapped to conceal her femininity, but, even so, she had nowhere near the sexual capital Kairah naturally possessed. How could she compete?

Why did this have to happen? Why did Ez give him that damned sword? This wasn't how things were supposed to be. She had planned to go on the well-find with Jek and—and what? What had she been planning to do? She shook her head and scrubbed her eyes with the back of her sleeve. She had never gotten that far.

She pounded her right fist on the ground, and a soft clod of dirt and roots broke free from the bank and plopped into the creek. Why couldn't Jek understand he was *supposed* to be with her? That their entire lives had pointed to it? They were *supposed* to get married, spend their lives together. She was certain of it. This Allosian woman was an anomaly, a cruel joke of the goddess to punish and torment Maely for her mother's sins. If Jek didn't love her back, what would she do? She couldn't stay with him and Ez anymore. She'd have to make her own way in the world, like her mother.

I will never be so desperate as to sell my body, she thought. Was that part of her obsession with marrying Jekaran? So she could find security and avoid repeating her mother's mistakes?

Was it a mistake that she loved you enough to degrade herself in order to feed you?

Her inner voice asked the question, and Maely clenched her jaw. She simultaneously loved and hated her mother, both sentiments potent with equal intensity. She loved her for her gentle kindness and self-sacrifice, but hated her for what she was. *No, that wasn't it,* she realized. It wasn't the fact that her mother had been a whore that made Maely so angry with her, it was because she died and left her. Maely's mother had left her alone to care for Mull and fend for herself. If it hadn't been for Ez, she would've ended up a street urchin begging for scraps, and then, when she got older, she would've become a prostitute, just like her mother.

Was that why she was chasing Jekaran? To make sure he wouldn't leave her too. But that's exactly what he was doing, wasn't it? Her mother had married, too. It was only the combination of tragedy and misfortune that led her mother to become a courtesan.

Confusion and angst twisted Maely's stomach into knots, and she raked her fingers through the soft earth. Fat tears, like drops of rain, pattered to the ground in a hypnotic rhythm. She did love the fool boy, and she knew her pursuing him wasn't just about avoiding her mother's fate. If only she could make him see her the way he saw Kairah.

A disturbing idea entered her mind as quietly as a whisper on the breeze.

Her mother's ring.

She had used it to help Kairah escape the crystal golem, and to get her a disguise. Could she use it to turn Jek away from his course? Not to enslave him, but to make him see?

Just to get his attention?

"No!" she whispered, shaking her head and flinging tears onto the dirt in the process. She wouldn't compel Jekaran to love her. That wouldn't be real love. It would be false and she couldn't live with that.

"Mae?" Jekaran said from somewhere behind her.

She quickly scrubbed again at her eyes with the back of her sleeve, sniffing as she wiped away her tears.

"What do you want?" she said, trying to sound more angry than heartbroken.

"I didn't mean to upset you," he said sheepishly.

"You never do, you dullard!" she quipped.

She heard Jekaran step up to her right side and kneel beside her. "Why did you follow me, Mae?"

Embarrassment dispelled her anger, and she looked away, ashamed.

"Mae?" Jek softly insisted.

Now was her chance. She could tell him how she felt, and why it had compelled her to follow him. She could take the chance now while she had his attention. The setting was wrong, in her dreams it happened during a moonlit stroll, or in a beautiful garden, not the edge of a creek in the middle of nowhere because she had thrown a tantrum. But if he rejected her—

"Why do *you* think?" she heard herself say, not harshly, although she had intended it to be an angry remark.

"I really don't know," Jek said, and the worst part was that the idiot sounded sincere. He really didn't have any clue, did he?

"Someone needs to keep an eye on you."

She felt his fingers lightly touch the back of her hair. "I can't believe you cut it. I never thought you would."

Maely hiccupped a laugh. "I needed to look like a boy or else Gymal wouldn't have let me go on the well-find."

"It suits you."

The compliment thrilled through her and she looked up to meet his eyes, suddenly feeling very vulnerable. "You like it?" she asked as she lightly touched her hair.

"Yeah," Jek said as he touched it again.

Maely turned away. The dark likely would've hidden her blushing, but she wanted to make sure he didn't see it. "Thanks," she whispered.

Jekaran rocked back onto his bottom and stretched his legs out over the bank of the creek. He then leaned back, propping himself up on his bent elbows. "Sure has been a hell of few weeks, hasn't it?"

His swearing always stabbed at her, not because the words were offensive, but because she knew Ez had taught Jekaran not to swear in the presence of a lady.

She tightened lips against her teeth.

He must've taken her silence for consensus because he went on as though she had verbally agreed with him. "I've killed bandits, been thrown into prison, met a Vorakk, was bit by a giant poisonous worm, and have been in the company of an actual Allosian. I even got to see her use real magic!"

"Well, I was chased by a giant living statue made of crystal," she said.

Jek looked at her. "I'm gonna need to hear about that."

"Not now," Maely said as she drew her legs up to her chest and hugged her knees. "Jek, are you really going to go with her?"

He didn't say anything.

"What about my brother? What about Ez? He's got to be worried that you haven't made it to Jeryn yet."

"I know," he said quietly. "But the sword—"

—"We'll figure that part out without Kairah," she cut in. "You don't need to be her servant and follow her all over Shaelar."

He didn't answer. *Divine Mother, did he really want to go with her?*

After a pregnant lull, he finally said, "Adventure is the lure of fools and excitement glamor to the gullible."

Was he reciting a poem?

"The siren song of the world is as music to the wanderer's feet, but that dance leads only to the soul-less grave."

"What's that?" she asked.

Jekaran chuckled. "Something Ez told me before I left. He meant it as a warning to avoid getting entangled in dangerous situations just for the thrill of it."

"Wise words," she said. "Are you going to take his advice and go back with me?"

"You know that I can never go back to Genra," he said. "Ez plans to find a new place for us to live, somewhere the Rikujo won't find us."

"We'll"—she was about to say *I'll,* but caught herself—"go with you."

Jek smiled and put his arm around her to pull her into a half-hug. "I love you, Maely."

Those words paralyzed her and for a moment, she was struck dumb.

How she had long to hear those words from him. But the flutter in her heart quickly faded as she registered the context of Jek's statement. It wasn't the longed for, oft fantasized declaration she prayed for, just an expression of familial affection.

She had to work to restrain the new wave of tears threatening to pour out of her eyes. She leaned her head on his shoulder, and he didn't pull away.

That was something, she tried to tell herself.

"How about we go with Kairah as far Imaris? We need supplies for our trip to Jeryn, and we can help her charter a ship to take her up the coast."

"But that's going to add at least another two weeks to our journey." She wrapped her arm around his middle. "Ez is going to think something's happened to you."

"We'll send Irvis on ahead to let Ez know we're safe. He can use his monk ploy to get food in the nearby villages, and it shouldn't take him longer than a week to get there by ghern."

"Will he go?"

Jek chuckled. "He got expelled from the monastery for being a pervert and so he has nowhere *else* to go."

"He's a pervert?"

"A mostly harmless pervert." He looked at her. "Just make sure you have good cover when you change or need to use the privy."

"Gross."

Jekaran laughed. "Yeah, he can be. But he saved my life in Rasha when I was bit by that giant worm, and Ez trusts him."

She looked up at him to find him looking down at her. They were close. It would be nothing for her to move in and kiss him. She could feel a magic to the moment. *He can't be so dense that he doesn't sense it,* she thought. She just about did it, but he turned away.

The magic faded and the moment passed.

"So we have a deal?" he said. He threw a pebble into the creek with his free hand.

Disappointed, Maely broke away from him and nodded. "I guess so."

"Good!" Jekaran said as he stood up. He reached down and helped her stand. "We should get back."

Maely nodded. She berated herself for not having taken the chance to kiss him. The moment had been right, but she was afraid. A mental scenario of him pulling away and then laughing at her stopped her.

Her mother's ring abruptly came to mind. *No!* she told herself. *I won't use it. I won't force him to love me.*

He had freely chosen to go with her to Jeryn instead of with Kairah to Aiested. Surely, that meant something, didn't it?

It would have to be enough—for now.

CHAPTER 28

Kairah watched as the cook fire smoldered to red embers. It was late in the night, all the others having fallen asleep hours ago. She probably should've slept, too, in order to conserve the Apeiron within her, but sleep still felt a bit unnatural. The day before she wouldn't have had a choice, but the well in the human mining camp had restored her to an energized state.

Kairah looked at Maely sleeping on the ground on the opposite side of the fire. That girl was a strange one, but then again, all humans were strange. She hadn't expected her to oppose Jekaran's joining her. She still did not entirely understand it. Had the girl come to this mindset recently, or was that her feeling on the matter this entire time, and she had only been concealing it from her?

You are strong again, Aeva said. *I can feel it.*

"I found a well," Kairah whispered.

That is good. The Spirit Lily's voice was fainter than it had been.

I will soon be too far away to reply to you, Kairah thought. The communication was starting to take more and more effort, and she had to conserve her energy.

I know.

Is Jenoc still there? Kairah asked.

Yes, Aeva said. *Did you want me to relay a message to him?*

Kairah thought for a moment and then said, *no.*

You are troubled, why?

Kairah considered how much the flower would be able to understand and then decided to tell her anyway. *I have encountered a puzzle, a talis of unknown origin, but one crafted with the skill of my people.*

This disturbs you?

A little, Kairah said. *Instinct tells me that it is a fact of great import, but I cannot reason out why.*

"Reka fey girl not need sleep?" The quiet hiss of the Vorakk shaman startled Kairah, and she snapped her head up to find the lizard man standing above her.

"Not at the moment," she said. "What of you? Do you not need rest?"

The Vorakk shaman shook his head, "Spirits no let Karak sleep ska." He stepped to her side, tail lashing out to his right so that he could sit on the ground. "Spirits fill Karak's sleep with death ska."

"You had a nightmare?" she asked, not certain what the term spirits meant to the lizard man. While she was quite familiar with humans and their history, she hadn't taken the time to study the other races in Shaelar. Jenoc knew a lot about the Vorakk, though, and for a fleeting moment, she wished he were here to explain what Karak was referring to. *If he was here, then I would not be,* she thought to herself in ironic amusement.

"Ssk," Karak replied as he made a sharp gesture with his two right fingers. "But not fake. Real aka."

"I do not understand."

"Spirits show Karak Eater ska."

"Eater?"

Karak nodded. "Eater come. Eater kill all ska."

"And that is why you are following Jekaran?"

"Ssk," Karak said. "Spirits say human boy find Eater. Karak follow. Karak stop Eater or Karak die."

Spirits say human boy find Eater? That had the distinct ring of prophecy to it. Could the Vorakk also have Oracles? Did this shaman also see in Jekaran the signs of a *fated soul?*

"What is this Eater?" Kairah asked.

Karak looked at her, reptilian eyes intent. "Death."

That brought another round of quiet, the crickets and snoring of the man called Irvis the only sounds. The two of them sat together until the lizard man rose and disappeared into the night.

Kairah couldn't shake the feeling that something beyond her knowledge was happening, something important, something terrible. Could Jenoc be the enemy the Vorakk shaman was referring to? No, Karak sounded like he was describing something more abstract. Could it be a talis war? That certainly would tie her into whatever fate Jekaran was marching toward.

One thing was for certain. Jekaran needed to stay with her.

These questions continued to swirl in her mind for hours until the dawning sun began to touch the eastern horizon. The others' sleep had grown restless and she knew they would soon wake. Karak was nowhere to be seen, but Kairah guessed the Vorakk was not far away.

What is going on? Why did something in the world feel wrong? She decided it would be worth some energy to cast her mind out as far she could to see if there was anything to discover about Karak's *Eater.*

She could feel a significant portion of her stored Apeiron ebb away as her mind covered mile after mile in seconds; her deficiency in the fourth discipline required Kairah to use more of her energy than she otherwise might have needed to use for the spell. In a flash, she perceived the whole of the land and its inhabitants in a wide circle with her at its epicenter. There were thousands of humans, some Vorakk raiders, and even one of the Ursaj was roaming the woods to their north, but nothing she could identify as the Eater—not that she knew what she was looking for. She was about to contract her senses when she felt something different. A gasp escaped her lips.

She focused all of her attention on this one thing, a kind of psychic scrutiny, but as she did, it abruptly rebuffed her. Her eyes shot open and she gasped again. It was like the thing had slapped her in the face. *What was that?* The contact had been so startling that she found herself wet with perspiration, her chest rising and falling with hard breaths. Maybe she had just hit the limits of her psychic reach. After all, she was not very good with the Fourth Discipline.

You said inept, Aeva said.

Kairah tried to reply with a sarcastic quip, but found herself unable. It wasn't because she wanted for energy, her Apeiron storage was still nearly full. It was as if she had stared at the sun too long and momentarily blinded herself.

Kairah? The Spirit Lily anxiously called. *Are you well?*

A moment later, she regained her psychic sense. *I believe so.*

What was that thing? Aeva asked.

Kairah shook her head. "I am not certain," she answered aloud.

"What?" Maely asked as she blearily stared at her. "Who are you talking to?"

"Dawn is here," Kairah quickly said. "It is time to rise from your sleep."

"It's still dark," she complained.

"What's this?" Jekaran said in a gravelly voice.

Karak returned, carrying a deer over his shoulders. "Daka breakfast," he grinned as he threw the carcass down by the smoldering fire pit.

The sight of the dead animal made Kairah feel ill, and she was glad that she had enough energy stored to not require food. She hated seeing death. As she stared into the buck's lifeless eyes, something slipped into place inside her mind, a familiar feeling mixed with sudden understanding.

Karak asked, "Reka fey girl no like deer?" She looked up at the lizard man and found him staring at her, his reptilian eyes full of suspicion.

"I am fine." That was a lie. For in that moment of staring at the dead deer, Kairah recognized the feeling she felt when rebuffed by the alien force. It was death. She had felt death. It had been a potent feeling of lifeless rot, far stronger than a mass grave of animals, or even humans. She looked at Karak, a dread settling over her. "I think I sensed your Eater."

The lizard man's face changed, and he knelt in front of her. "Reka?" he signed something with his left claw.

Kairah shook her head. "I do not know. It happened so fast, and I was not mindful of the physical direction." She looked at the dead deer lying next to the fire pit. "However, I now understand what you mean when you say the Eater is death."

"What's this about?" Jekaran asked as he got up from his bed on the ground. "Is something wrong?"

Kairah shared a long look with Karak before finally answering, "Yes."

Jekaran hadn't been able to get any real answers from Kairah about what she had sensed. It was frustrating. Had the woman not been so strikingly gorgeous, he might've even been irritated with her.

Their breakfast had taken over an hour to prepare and another hour to cook, but a belly full of venison had been worth the wait, and they had some leftover for the road. Jekaran waited until after they all ate before breaking the news to Kairah that he could only escort her as far as the port city of Imaris before having to resume his journey to Jeryn. He hated to disappoint her, but the thought of the man with mismatched eyes killing his uncle wouldn't leave his mind. That, coupled with Maely's pleading tears from the night before, made the prospect of joining Kairah a virtual impossibility.

Irvis took his assignment to ride alone to Jeryn much better than Jekaran would've thought. He clearly regretted leaving Kairah's presence, but the thought of being reunited with Ez seemed to soften the blow. If Karak had not approved, he hadn't said so. The Vorakk shaman had said very little all morning. He was withdrawn and introspective. Clearly, he understood Kairah's cryptic remarks when no one else had.

The mid-morning suns inched closer to their peak overhead, and the time finally came to strike camp, pack up their things, and begin the day's journey. The work progressed quickly and just as they were about to mount their gherns, Irvis called Jekaran over to him. He put his arm around him and said, "Watch yourself, child. You belong to Ez, and that sort of makes us related."

"Meaning?" Jekaran asked, half irritated, half amused.

"Meaning," Irvis said seriously, "I took care of you when you were a baby, and you're likely the closest thing to a son that I'll ever have."

"From the way you brag about sowing your seed, I'd think you'd have a bastard in every town from here to Maeis Tol."

Irvis looked ashamed. "I've been known to exaggerate a little when it comes to my love life. Just be careful, child, and promise me you won't use that sword."

"I promise," Jekaran said, knowing full well it was a lie. That should've made him feel ashamed, but it didn't.

The chubby monk pulled himself up into the ghern's saddle, the beast snorting in annoyance as he did so.

"Thanks, Uncle Irvis."

That made the man grin. "I like the sound of that." He started to ride off when he paused. He turned back and waved Jekaran closer.

"What?" Jekaran asked.

He leaned down from his saddle. "Listen," Irvis said in a conspiratorial whisper. "If you bed that Allosian woman, I insist you share with me every filthy detail upon our next meeting."

"That's wrong!" Jekaran said loudly as he stepped away from Irvis' mount.

The man laughed. "I'm your uncle, aren't I?"

"That's what makes it wrong," Jekaran swatted the ghern's backside. "Get out of here you lecher!"

Irvis laughed as he galloped away from the group.

Jekaran turned and looked at the others. "Guess it's time for us to be going."

They mounted up, Maely with him, and Kairah on her own ghern, while Karak again insisted he could keep up on foot. They headed northwest toward the coastal city of Imaris, each one with uncertain dread clouding their heart.

Chapter 29

The journey progressed quicker than any Jekaran had ever undertaken before. Of course, he had never traveled by ghern before, he thought as he stretched his arm out to pat the animal's neck. He understood why the animals were so highly valued, and half wondered if *he* would ever be able to afford one. All of his mathematical and entrepreneurial mental scenarios pointed to a disheartening *no*.

He thought with a smile how much the sword would fetch on the illegal talis market. His psychic link informed him it didn't appreciate the notion.

He was beginning to get a feel for the weapon's personality. At first, he thought its mind was similar to that of a child's, but he was quickly rethinking the position. During a stretch of idle thought, he had called to mind one of Irvis' bawdy jokes. It was a filthy thing about a farmer's daughter and three strangers, but it made him laugh to himself. He was very surprised when he felt the sword mirror his amusement.

Because Maely had been uncharacteristically quiet for the first day of their trip—unless he became engrossed in conversation with Kairah, then she became obnoxious and rude, Jekaran took to testing the sword's intelligence. He tried asking it direct questions, trying to illicit a response in words, like back in Gymal's camp, but so far it had yet to do so. He asked who created it, or where it came from. Wordless impressions of sincere ignorance were his only answer.

Jekaran decided to take a different approach and asked the sword more mundane questions. What's your favorite time of day? Was it aware of color, and if so which was its favorite? The first question invoked an impression of confusion, the second surprised Jekaran, the question repeated back to him. Jekaran answered that he liked blue. The sword then replied with an impression that it liked the same color as its master. But still no words.

I'm your master? Jekaran thought in surprise.

Yes.

Weren't you the one trying to control me? he asked.

The sword didn't understand. *I serve.*

Do you remember things?

The sword answered in the affirmative.

That intrigued Jekaran. *Do you recall events before you joined with me?*

It seemed to not understand the concept of any time before the two had linked in Rasha, and that surprised him.

Odd, he thought. *Do you lose your memories when you lose your Apeiron charge, or do you start anew with every new host?*

Again, the sword seemed confused by the questions.

By the end of the second day, they reached the coast, and a small fishing village. Mae's bad temper suspended as she caught sight of the ocean extending endlessly to the west. They stopped for supplies, and, while Jekaran and Kairah bargained with the merchants, she ran to the village's single dock for an up close view of the infinite water.

With supplies secured to the gherns, Jekaran headed to the docks to retrieve Mae. He chuckled as he saw her, standing on the edge of the pier, frozen except for her cropped hair playing with the breeze. Mae seemed to age backward there, her eyes as bright and wide as a small girl.

"Isn't it beautiful?" she asked him as he walked to stand beside her.

Jekaran stared out over the blue expanse and studied the slowly churning waves and foam. "It makes me feel very small," he answered.

"Do you think this is the ocean that humans sailed on to get to here?"

Jekaran shrugged. "Maybe."

Suddenly Mae asked him, "Did you know the world was round?"

"What?"

"Round," she repeated. "Kairah told me the world was round and not flat."

Jekaran stared into the ocean as it stretched on. "I think she might've been teasing you, Mae."

That earned him an elbow to the ribs and he doubled over.

"I'm not stupid, Jekaran."

"Okay," he wheezed. "The world's round."

They stood on the dock, watching the waves rhythmically reach up onto the beach before retreating until the sun began to dip toward the horizon.

"Come on, Mae, we only have a couple of hours of daylight left, and we should probably move away from here so no one gets suspicious of Kairah. Besides, Karak is waiting for us outside of town."

Maely slowly nodded, turned from the picturesque view, and began striding back toward the center of the village. Jekaran started to follow, but stopped as something occurred to him. He leapt over the left side of the pier and landed in the squishy sand just above the tide line.

"Jek?" he heard Mae call. "What do you think you're doing?"

He scanned the beach without answering her. It took a moment, but he was able to find a shell. He leaned over and scooped it up, then jogged up the beach to meet Maely on the village-side of the pier.

He extended his hand out to show her the pink, palm-sized shell. "I promised Mull that if I got to see the ocean, I'd bring him back something." Jekaran laughed. "He wanted a shark." Maely laughed, and Jekaran was glad to avoid another elbow to the ribs.

They rode out of the small fishing village and returned to the road where the Vorakk shaman rejoined them. The four of them traveled through dusk and didn't stop to rest until twilight. After a hurried dinner of dried pork and soft bread, they went to sleep without a fire, Karak not wanting to risk attracting human attention.

Jekaran noticed the usually unflappable lizard man seemed exceptionally anxious around groups of humans. Well, Jekaran couldn't blame him. After all, *he* had tried to kill Karak upon first meeting him.

He wondered if the Vorakk got that reaction a lot, and if they had any official dealings with humans.

The third day led the party past the ruins of an ancient tower.

Although most of its top was missing, the base was nearly the entire size of Genra, which hinted the structure must've been tall, very tall. Kairah seemed particularly interested in the ruins, and they had left the road for a few hours so that she could tour and study them. It turned out the tower had been built by her people hundreds of years prior to even the arrival of the humans in Shaelar. She even claimed to know the name of the tower, something Jekaran couldn't properly pronounce and definitely did not remember.

When Jekaran asked how tall the tower had been, Kairah said it had likely reached over three thousand feet into the sky. It had taken a while for him to wrap his head around the concept, as Jekaran had never seen any building rise higher than a hundred feet, and that had been in Rasha.

Maely grew bored with the ruins and wandered off, looking for a river or lake she could bathe in. She had been complaining ever since they left the rock lands that the ghern's smell was sticking to her. It made her gag, and Jekaran took every opportunity to tease her about it, asking, "Do you smell ghern?"

She'd respond with a frosty star and often physical harm, except once when he joked she smelled so much like ghern that he should be able to ride her. For some reason, she blushed at that and fell silent.

Girls were strange.

With Maely off looking for a bath, Jekaran had a rare opportunity to be alone with Kairah, and he was going to take full advantage of it. Irvis passed through his thoughts.

Not his kind of advantage, he thought with a shudder.

Jekaran did want to get to know her, though.

Beyond the physical perfection she personified and the exotic appeal of her hair and eyes, Jekaran felt drawn to her on an emotional level. Her touching his mind had done more than just give him a diagnosis of his bond with the sword. The contact had been an intimate thing, and Jekaran hadn't been able to forget the feeling of taking in the entirety of her being all at once. He felt a profound closeness to her since then and wanted to know if their mental contact had the same effect on her.

He found her examining some etchings on a weathered and half-crumbled wall. "What do they say?" he asked, instantly worried that she would be annoyed at his interrupting her.

She looked away from the wall and directly into his eyes. She always did that, he realized, whenever she talked to him. Did it mean something?

"It is a poem meant to commemorate an event in history I am unfamiliar with." She turned back to study the etchings.

"Can you read it to me?" *What are you, Jekaran, a child demanding a story?* he scolded himself.

Kairah glanced at him and flashed a smile that made his chest tighten. "It is about two lovers from opposing kingdoms."

"Allosians had different kingdoms? I thought your people were united."

"We were not always as mature as we are now. In fact, once we were not so different from you humans in our struggles against each other for power."

For some reason, her use of the term *you humans* stung.

She continued. "The poem may lose some of its meaning in translation, but this is what it says:

> *"Two worlds, but one heart,*
> *opposites that are one.*
> *Can fire love ice?*
> *Can the dark love the dawn?*
> *So were the two lovers,*
> *a prince and princess opposed.*
> *Yet in the secret midnight of a garden,*
> *their love could freely flow.*
> *Yet the universe is balance,*
> *and fate would have her due.*
> *Their love would bring destruction,*
> *and end the worlds each knew."*

"That doesn't sound like a happy ending," Jekaran said.

"It is not a fiction. It is true, and truth can sometimes be cruel." She turned to face him. She was as tall as he was, but it only added to her beauty. "You must come with me to the capital."

Why was she asking him this? Was there anything more to it than just needing help for her quest? Oh, how he longed to go. "Kairah, I want to. I really do, but—"

"—you will come with me," Kairah said with an authority that surprised Jekaran. It wasn't a demand, but more as though she were stating a simple fact. Something she knew simply would be.

"Jekaran!" Maely appeared as if out of nowhere. "We need to get moving. I need a bath, and there isn't any water larger than a puddle in these parts."

Jekaran stared into Kairah's eyes as long as he could and was encouraged when she stared back. It was like waking from a deep comfortable sleep when Maely towed him away.

It was on the fourth day of travel that they caught their first sight of Imaris. The city began on flat ground, but sloped downward toward the sea. It was walled on all sides, save the west, where its ship docks were located. Even being several miles away, Jekaran could see the tall masts of sailing ships rising high into the sky.

In late afternoon, they entered the city gates. The coastal city was so much more than he ever dreamed, and Jekaran stared wide-eyed at the sailing ships the size of buildings, captivated by their masses. Mae cleared her throat behind him, breaking into his wonderment, and he realized his jaw hung open like an invitation for flying things. He snapped it shut, tightening his jaw. He knew he was a farm boy, but he didn't want to look like one.

"Golden womb of the goddess, Jek!" swore Maely.

"What?" He turned to find her glaring daggers at him.

"You're not doing it!"

Jekaran was supposed to be counting backward from one thousand by increments of three. He had lost track of where he was somewhere after seven seventy-eight and stopped.

The counting was one of Kairah's *exercises*, the Allosian woman claimed it developed one's ability to hold focus. "That was the very first thing those who bore ego talises learned," she had told him. "Holding focus was like lifting something heavy," she had said. "And just as repeatedly lifting heavy objects worked muscles and built up strength, so counting worked the mind and increased one's ability to focus."

"I'm sorry, Mae." It came out sounding petulant.

"You need to take this seriously!" she scolded.

"I am." Jekaran waved at the large sea vessels. "I've just never seen real ships like these. Did you see the mast on that one?" He pointed to a particularly large ship. "It's gotta be a hundred feet tall. Divine Mother, but I'd love to sail on one of those."

"And where would you go?" she asked flatly.

"Anywhere!" Jekaran spread his arms.

"Maely is correct," Kairah said. She was walking a few paces in front of them with the hood drawn up again to avoid stares from passing sailors.

Well, they were staring anyway at her perfect figure. Jekaran just didn't want any of the men to realize she wasn't human.

"You are in danger of losing yourself again until you discipline your mind."

"See!" Maely taunted.

Out of reflex, Jekaran was about to appeal to Karak to support his point, but then remembered the Vorakk shaman wasn't with them. He had opted to stay outside of Imaris until dark.

While, he said, some Vorakk walked openly among men, he had never done so, and wasn't about to start.

Apparently, a relative of his—Jekaran couldn't remember if had been an uncle or a cousin—had lived a long happy life, until meeting his end the first time he entered a human city. Consequently, the plan was to send for him once they found suitable lodgings at which time he would veil himself and sneak into the city.

Money was not an issue with Kairah, for no sooner had she asked what to look for in their lodging then Maely began to list the luxuries and characteristics she expected Kairah to pay for. Brass bathtubs with hot water, absolutely no dancing girls or waitresses with low-cut blouses, a common room that served pudding, and finally, beds stuffed with feathers instead of straw.

Jekaran rolled his eyes at the haughty demands, and the search took a little longer than it might otherwise have, but eventually they found an inn that Maely approved of.

The Rose's Thorn was the finest establishment Jekaran had ever dared to enter. The common room was almost as large as a dancing hall and had no less than three different minstrels taking requests from an enthusiastic crowd. The drapes looked woven from expensive silks, and all of the bustling serving girls wore clean and neat uniforms. Jekaran hadn't objected to Maely's choice because—well, she would be angry—and he knew Kairah would blend better in a more expensive inn. They paid for two rooms, one for Kairah and Maely, and the other for Jekaran and Karak.

It wasn't long after sunset when something the size of a bug began to pester Jekaran as he dozed in one of his room's plush armchairs. He was about to swat at it and then realized Karak sent a spirit ball to find him. Through it, he told Karak how to find their inn, and which room he was staying in. Kairah had left Jekaran with enough money to order ham for himself and a large, meaty drumstick which he had waiting for Karak.

The lizard man startled Jekaran when he came in through the window, an outside climb of over twenty feet. He gladly tore into the drumstick, stripping the flesh from the bone and even breaking the bone to suck out the marrow. After the meal, Karak curled up next to the hearth where Jekaran had built a small fire. The sight of the Vorakk shaman sleeping made Jekaran think of a giant reptilian dog. He laughed at the thought, stripped to the waist, kicked off his boots, and climbed into bed.

After life on the road for a month, sleeping in a bed felt wonderful. *Maybe Mae had been right to demand the feather-stuffed mattresses,* was his last thought before sleep took him.

Chapter 30

The steaming bath water was perfect. Not so hot that it scalded Maely, but hot enough that it took her a moment to adjust to the temperature. She sat back and closed her eyes, savoring the deliciousness as the water relaxed her muscles and washed away a month's worth of dirt and grime. Even breathing in the steam felt good.

"You're sure you don't want me to have the serving girls fill the other tub?" Maely asked with her eyes still closed. "Who knows when you'll get another chance for a bath?"

"I am clean," Kairah said dispassionately.

"Baths aren't just for cleansing the body," Maely said as she sank down. "They're also for cleansing the soul."

"My soul is clean," Kairah said in the same tone.

Maely opened her eyes and looked through an open door at the Allosian woman sitting on the bed in the next room. She was brushing her hair, not that it ever needed brushing. For some reason it always looked smooth, full, and never out of place. Maely hated that about her, among other things. Why did Rasheera bestow such perfection on the woman? Were all Allosians as beautiful as Kairah?

"Kairah" Maely began.

"Yes?"

"What happens if you run out of Apeiron?" The question had been born in Maely's mind hours ago when they first arrived in Imaris. Kairah had been expecting the city to be built around an Apeira well like most other human cities, but, to her dismay, it didn't have one. While she had said she would be fine, Maely had caught a bit of worry in the woman's voice.

She smiled to herself. Although Kairah always carefully controlled her emotions, the time Maely was spending with her taught her how to recognize the subtle changes in the woman's tone for anger, sadness, or fear.

"It has never happened to me," Kairah answered.

"That's not what I asked."

Kairah sighed. "I am beginning to think that, even by human standards, your manners are poor."

"You're lucky I'm feeling so good right now, otherwise I'd give you a tongue lashing you wouldn't ever forget."

Kairah remained silent.

"Well?"

Kairah stood from the bed and walked into the bath chamber. Surprised, Maely slid down and crossed her arms over her breasts. "Hey!"

She arched an eyebrow and then turned to the side so that she wasn't looking at Maely. "Allosians draw their power from Apeiron, much the same way talises do. The difference is that while talises only use Apeiron to power their spells, we use Apeiron to sustain our bodies."

Maely rose up a bit and uncrossed herself. "I thought you said that you can live off of food and sleep, like humans."

Kairah nodded. "We can and we do. But we always have some Apeiron within us, even if it is but a small amount."

"Can you lose that?"

"Yes," she answered. "If I took my spell-casting too far, or spent too much time away from a well, my store of energy could deplete to nothing."

"Then what?"

Kairah hesitated for a long moment before finally saying, "Then I would die."

"Die?" Maely abruptly sat forward, water sloshing against the side of the brass tub. "For good?"

She turned back toward her. "That is what death is, is it not? The end of life?"

Maely slid down again to cover herself, but didn't let that rile her. "How do you know when you're running low?"

"How do you know when you are weary?" Kairah walked to a vanity in the corner of the bath chamber and began to examine the various soaps and perfumes.

"You don't seem tired," she said, turning in the tub to follow Kairah's movements.

"It is an inner weariness," she sighed again. "Hard to explain to one who has not experienced it themselves."

"Can you take energy from talises? If you're running out, I mean."

"Such a thing is not possible." Kairah shook her head while examining a bottle of White Rose perfume. Extremely expensive, but the best Maely had ever smelled. She had ordered it as part of her effort to deliberately spend as much of Kairah's coin as she could. She knew it was spiteful and childish, but she didn't care.

"Apeiron can only exist in its pure form inside the crystalline formations you call wells."

"You call them something different?" Maely asked.

Kairah nodded. "Aeose. It means heart of life. Every talis has a shard harvested from an Aeose, which allows it to draw from an Apeira well, the size and quality of the cut affecting how much that shard can hold. Talises are crafted to use the same spells repeatedly and they draw their energy from the shard in order to do so. The energy is poured directly into the spell, at which point it is expended."

"But you draw from wells too. Do you have a shard inside you?"

"After a manner of speaking," Kairah said as she unstopped the glass vile of White Rose and sniffed at it. "Allosian blood contains an uncountable number of tiny Aeose shards. This allows us to draw on an Aeose and hold a charge until we expend it." She re-stopped the vile and set it back down on the vanity.

Maely opened her mouth to ask another question, but Kairah cut her off. "Why did you persuade Jekaran not to help me?"

That soured her mood in spite of the bath. "Because he's only a sixteen-year-old farmer!" she snapped. "He's never been to the capital and he doesn't know how to fight!"

"You saw firsthand that, with his sword talis, Jekaran is more than a match for even the fiercest warriors."

"But using it isn't good for him." Maely felt her cheeks redden and not from the hot bath water. "You said so yourself."

Kairah shook her head. "No. I said it would be dangerous if he did not learn to restrain himself. I could help him achieve some degree of control over the talis."

Maely didn't know how to answer, so she retorted, "Why do *you* want his help?"

"I have already explained my reasons to you—twice."

"I-I," Maely stammered.

Kairah turned to look at her again. "I assure you, Maely, I am not competing against you for Jekaran's affections."

Maely was dumbstruck. *How did she know?* "That's not why," she quickly denied. "Jek's like my brother."

"Then why do you not wish him to travel with me?"

Damn you! She felt like a cornered animal. "It's just not right." The excuse sounded weak, even to her ears.

Kairah sighed and left the room.

That night Maely lay awake, unable to sleep, despite the thoroughly relaxing bath. She had refused to speak another word to Kairah, so that the Allosian woman would have a perfect understanding of just how angry she was.

How dare she speak to me as if I'm a love-struck child!

Never mind Kairah was almost a century old, or that she was exactly right.

Maely turned her head on her pillow to check on the Allosian woman. Her eyes were shut, and her breathing steady, but Maely had no other indication if she was really sleeping. When it was just the two of them traveling, Kairah always had a difficult time finding sleep, claiming she wasn't *used* to it.

How can someone not be used to sleep? Maely scoffed. Still, she had waited an extra hour just to be sure.

Satisfied, Maely slipped out of bed and quietly made her way over to the wall by the room's door. Hanging on a peg was Kairah's sable cloak. Maely shot a furtive glance back at her while she found the cloak's outer pockets. After a thorough search, she checked the inside of the fur cloak. It had four small pockets, a selling point the shopkeeper had continued to remind Maely of when she had taken it from him. When under her power, the man had seemed almost desperate to please her.

Maely checked inside the first pocket, then the second pocket, and then she *found it!* She pulled out her mother's ring and hurried back to her bed.

None too soon, because she heard Kairah ask, "What are you doing up?"

"Privy," Maely breathed out quickly, then rolled over in her bed so her back was to her.

I have it back! She exulted. *Not to use it on Jekaran*, she told herself, *but because it's all I have left of my mother.*

The lie didn't alleviate any of Maely's guilt. She knew why she wanted the ring, and it stung, but she buried the guilt within more self-deceptions.

The next morning, she was wakened by stern knocking on their chamber door. She looked over to find Kairah lifting her head from the pillow.

We both overslept, she realized. *I guess that means she's not so perfect after all.*

"Hey!" Jekaran called. "We got to get to the docks early if we want to find anything nicer than a fishing boat."

Maely jumped out of bed, remembering at the last moment she still had her mother's ring clenched in her fist. She hid her hand beneath a set of new clothes the servants had brought to her the night before and ran into the bath chamber where she slammed the door closed.

She heard Kairah let Jekaran into the room. She didn't like to leave the two of them alone, but it couldn't be helped. She placed her mother's ring on the vanity and lifted her shift over her head to pull on a fresh set of underclothes. She stuffed herself into a corset, and then a knee length, sky blue sundress. Settling onto the toilet, she pulled stockings up her legs and slipped into some new lady's boots. A choker wrapped around her neck, and then she began to tie a ribbon in her hair.

She stopped and looked at the ribbon, realizing buying it had been a waste as she no longer had hair long enough to wear it.

Oh well, she shrugged and tossed the ribbon onto the floor; it was Kairah's money, not hers anyway.

When finished, she slipped the ring into a pocket and examined herself in the mirror. She had planned to apply face paint, but she would have to let that go because of the time. She turned, looking at her back in the mirror before turning back and smiling at her reflection in approval.

She had made certain to pick clothes that would make her look decidedly feminine again.

Now to see if Jek would notice.

She opened the door and unobtrusively stepped out of the bath chamber. Jekaran was casually shouldering their supply pack and talking to Kairah with that fool look in his eyes again, the one that meant he had fallen under the spell of her beauty.

Maely pointedly cleared her throat and they both turned to look at her.

Jekaran raised his eyebrows. "Tired of looking like a boy, huh?"

Not exactly what she had hoped he would say, but at least he noticed.

Idiot boy!

"Let's get going," she said as she grabbed Kairah's cloak from off of the wall and tossed it to her.

Well, more *tossed at* than *tossed to*. Of course, the Allosian woman gracefully caught it. *Too bad*, she thought.

"Has Karak already left?" Maely asked.

"Just before dawn," Jekaran said. "He'll be waiting for us a mile or so out of the city."

The three of them stepped out of the room and Jekaran stepped aside for Kairah to take the lead. She dipped her head deferentially and walked out. Maely was about to do the same when Jekaran stepped right in front of her and moved to walk at Kairah's side.

Maely clenched her teeth as she surreptitiously felt in her pocket for her mother's ring. She had half a mind to put it on and command Kairah to mess herself in front of Jekaran. See how beautiful he would think she was when she reeked like a latrine.

She didn't do it of course, but the fact that she could made her smile.

JEKARAN INHALED INDULGENTLY. The smell of the sea combined with the call of gulls, and the gentle morning breeze was glorious. "I think I was born to be a sailor!"

Maely snorted.

That nettled him. "You don't think I could do it?" he asked sharply.

"*I think*," Mae said, "that any man who longs to spend months at a time alone with other men at sea is the same kind of man who likes to wear his mother's lace and face paint."

He couldn't help but laugh. "I'd never thought of it that way."

Mae's expression softened and she turned her face to hide a reluctant smile from him.

They were walking the docks now, making their way toward a large ship called the *Queen's Honor*.

Did Aiestal even have a queen? Jekaran wondered. He guessed it was just a name to make people think it was vessel for lords and ladies. That's what drew Jekaran to it when he had checked the daily roster, and so far it appeared to live up to its name. The ship looked cleaner and better cared for than many of the other vessels.

Traveling by sea wasn't the only way to reach Aiested, but it was the fastest, and likely the safest. While piracy was always a danger, it was much less likely that your ship would be boarded than you would be waylaid while traveling the roads.

He idly wondered if his uncle had ever been a pirate. Did the Rikujo attack ships? The thought brought his worries for Ez's, and now Mull's, safety back to the forefront of his thoughts. *I hope Irvis has found them. I hope they're ok.*

Jekaran, the sword suddenly said to his mind. *Danger!*

He froze, hand immediately going to the bag on his back. It had actually spoken to him again, this time calling him by name. That was something it never had done before.

"Jek," he heard Maely scold. "Stop gawking at those ships!"

He was about to call for both women to stop so he could tell them what had just happened when a familiar, nasally voice made his heart sink.

"Thought you could escape by sea, did you?" Gymal said from behind him.

Jekaran whipped around to see the short, balding man emerge from a crowd of sailors. Five armored soldiers, one of which was Hort., flanked him.

"Jekaran!" He heard Mae shout.

"You look surprised to see me, Jekaran." Gymal smirked.

A sudden urge to draw the sword from his pack assailed Jekaran, but he beat it back with a mental countdown starting from one thousand and decrementing by three's just as Kairah had instructed.

"How did you find me?" he said as he took a step back, surreptitiously waving a hand for Maely and Kairah to do the same.

Gymal held up a small rod with a needle sticking out of the top and a round amethyst capping its bottom. Jekaran's hand shot to the back of his neck where Gymal had pricked him with the talis. *Just in case you slip away,* he remembered Gymal saying to him.

"This is a Blood Seeker." Gymal stared at the rod in his hand. "Once it tastes your blood, it will allow its bearer to track you anywhere in the world. Up until now, I've only used it to find escaped ghern, but I am told it was *made* for tracking people. I'd say it works rather well, wouldn't you?"

"I don't want any trouble," Jekaran said as he shot a glance at Hort. The man grinned, and for the first time Jekaran noticed the mercenary's nose was crooked in a way it hadn't been before. *Did I do that?*

"Jek," he heard Mae squeak.

He turned to look at her. She was looking at something beyond Gymal and his soldiers. Jekaran followed her gaze and inwardly cringed when he realized she was looking at armored soldiers, at least twenty of them, quickly pushing through the crowd as they made their way toward him.

Apparently Gymal had noticed what Jekaran was looking at, because he smiled and said, "After hearing what you did to my men when you escaped, I decided to take some extra precautions. So, I enlisted the aid of the Imarin city guard."

Jekaran's fear slowly began evolving into anger.

Fight, the sword told him.

"Nine hundred sixty-seven, nine hundred sixty-four," Jekaran found himself whispering.

"Jekaran." Mae anxiously grabbed his elbow.

"Nine hundred sixty-one," he said a bit louder.

"Jekaran," Kairah said warningly, "Remember, *you,* not it, are in control."

"Nine hundred fifty-eight," he raised his voice louder.

Gymal's smile slowly faded "What is this you are saying?"

"Nine hundred fifty-five," Jekaran shouted.

Gymal nervously backed away, "Take them!"

"NINE HUNDRED FIFTY-TWO!" he screamed and drew the sword from over his shoulder in one quick motion.

He was just about to leap forward into an attack when an explosion erupted from behind Gymal's men. Screams broke out as people on the docks started scrambling away from the flames. A second explosion erupted, throwing armored bodies into the air and scattering the Imarin city guard, a few of which had been set on fire and were running to dive into the ocean. More screams and chaos followed and the wooden boardwalk of the docks themselves were now aflame. Sailors and dock workers were running about and shouting "fire!" and calling for help.

That's when a wave of cold, primal fear stabbed Jekaran in the chest, so strong he stumbled backward, a furious thumping in his chest rising to pound his eardrums. Sweat ran down the small of his back as he trembled, and it felt as though he couldn't inhale enough air. All Jekaran wanted to do was fall to the ground and curl into a ball.

He did fall to the ground, but didn't curl up. Instead, he went down on one knee, as though he were bowing before royalty, his body and mind were paralyzed with fear and panic.

Somewhere in a world far away, he heard Maely scream. Jekaran managed to force his head up and that's when he saw a figure walking straight out of the flames in front of him, as though the man were a demon from hell itself. It was the man with the mismatched eyes—Kaul.

How did he know to follow me? Did he torture it out of Ez? Was Ez dead? Those thoughts only served to augment the panic Jekaran already felt, and it was all he could do to keep from retching.

Kaul grinned as he raised an open hand, the palm aimed at Jekaran.

An eruption of fire burst from Kaul's hand and roared toward his face; he could feel the heat radiated by the fireball intensify as it flew at him.

Time slowed down and Jekaran felt himself launching from the ground. Independent of his own power to physically command his body, Jekaran's right arm whipped the sword up in a sharp, vertical motion.

Heat seared Jekaran's face as the fireball exploded only a foot in front of him. He was hurled backward to the ground by the force of the blast, and felt his head strike cobblestone. He quickly opened his eyes and his face felt as it did when he took too much sun in the fields. Had the fireball hit him in the face? *No*, he realized. *If it had, my face would be charred.*

Then what had happened?

He looked to the sword that he still clutched in his hand. While unmarred, the blade was smoldering. *Divine Mother! I caught the fireball on my sword.*

Jekaran quickly rose to find Kaul striding toward him. The man's grin was gone, replaced by a look of rage as hot as the fire he threw.

Jekaran was about to leap at him when the cold fear again gripped him by the heart, a vice-like pressure holding him in place. Kaul raised his hand and launched another ball of fire at him. It flew five feet before slamming into an invisible wall and exploding.

Abruptly, the intense fear was gone and Jekaran could breathe freely again. He looked to his right where he found Kairah standing, a look of prayerful concentration on her face.

She was spell-casting to shield them from Kaul's attack.

"I am sorry, Jekaran. That man's fear aura caught me off guard," she said in a distracted tone.

"Fear aura?" Kaul was using a talis to make him afraid? It made sense. That had been what he had felt the first time he saw the man back in Genra, except this was much more potent.

"I am countering it," she said as they both backed away.

"We have to run!" Mae said as she yanked on Jekaran's left arm.

FIGHT the sword urged.

Another fireball crashed into Kairah's invisible shield.

"No!" Jekaran hissed as he twirled the sword in his hand and made to sprint toward Kaul. "I'm going to kill him!" His voice was far more eager than he expected. *I'm in control,* he told himself.

"No!" Kairah snapped.

Jekaran looked at her. "I can take him!"

"But I do not have unlimited energy in this place," Kairah said while keeping her eyes forward, her brow creased from mental exertion. "These spells are taking a lot of my Apeiron and I sense this man is unusually formidable."

Jekaran looked back at Kaul and gritted his teeth as he fought back the waves of temptation the sword was continually throwing at him. That's when he saw Hort and three mercenaries charge Kaul from behind. How had they overcome Kaul's fear magic? *Perhaps it had something to do with their training as soldiers,* he thought. *Could I learn to do that?*

To Jekaran's horror, Kaul did not fall to Hort's attack. He didn't even flinch when the big mercenary brought his sword down on his shoulder. There had been a flash of purple light and Hort's sword bounced back as though the man had struck a rock. Hort stumbled backward, his face the very picture of shock.

"Divine Mother!" Jekaran heard Maely swear.

Just as the first of Hort's men made to strike, Kaul spun to his left and backhanded the soldier. The man cried out as he crashed to the ground, his cheek bearing a severe burn. The next soldier swung, and although his blade caught Kaul on the arm, a manifestation of crackling purple light hovering an inch above Kaul's skin prevented it from making contact. The man's eyes widened and Jekaran saw Kaul shoulder into him as he rammed his right fist into the man's chest plate. There was an explosion, and the soldier was thrown back into the man behind him. When he landed, Jekaran could see that his breastplate bore a blackened scorch mark.

FIGHT, the sword insisted again, but Jekaran's fear had gotten the better of him. Not magical fear, but sobering, self-preserving fright. This man had a talis that shielded him from harm. Jekaran wouldn't even be able to touch him.

"Come on!" he shouted as he turned and shoved Maely into a run.

Kairah hesitated a moment before ceasing her spell-casting and turning to run with them.

"Where are we going?" Maely demanded as they barreled down an alley spanning between a merchant's warehouse and a dockside pub.

"We have to get out of the city before they raise the alarm and shut the gates," he said around a gulp of air.

Jekaran heard another explosion and more screaming behind them.

Fight him, the sword insisted.

How the hell am I supposed to fight someone who can paralyze me with fear, throw fire, and can't be hurt?

The sword did not reply.

Jekaran turned a corner onto a connecting street and intentionally barreled into a stagnant crowd of curious locals staring at the smoke billowing into the sky above the docks. There were surprised shouts and angry murmurs as Jekaran shoved people out of their way.

There was another explosion and then more screaming, this time closer. Jekaran didn't look back. Instead, he made for an open shop. The storekeeper yelled something at them as they knocked goods off his store shelves, but Jekaran ignored him as he led the two women through the store and behind the counter. They ran into a store room and then out the shop's back door.

A five foot, stone wall stood before them. Jekaran helped Kairah and Maely over in turn before he climbed up. But before he could make it over, the roof of the shop behind them exploded into flames. Jekaran shook off another impulse to fight Kaul and leapt down from the wall to rejoin Kairah and Maely on the other side where they resumed their desperate run.

CHAPTER 31

K aul ground his teeth as he looked over the crowd of people fleeing from him in every direction. This was going *all* wrong. He had trapped the boy and should've charred his head to a blackened skull, but the sword protected him. And then there was that woman with the talis, shielding against magical attacks. *That would be useful if I could get my hands on it,* he thought. *I bet it was she that also used the gaia stone back in the rock lands.* He would need to kill the woman and take her talises, but first he had to get the sword.

Kaul shoved the short, bald lord forward. "Which way did he go?"

The little man shook so bad he could hardly walk, and was that piss dripping from the leg of his trousers?

Pathetic!

"Th-th-that way," he stammered as he pointed at a nondescript general goods store.

Kaul raised his hand and launched a fireball at the building's roof. "That should draw him out!"

He needed to end this quickly. Fighting and killing those soldiers had already expended half of the Apeiron charge in his flame talis, almost as much with his dread medal, and a quarter of the power of his shield bracelet. Perhaps he should've brought the others to help him, but he couldn't risk anyone else bonding the sword once the boy was dead.

"H-he's moving away," the little lord said. "He's not in the shop anymore."

He must've escaped out the back, Kaul clenched his teeth. "Where?" he roared.

The little lord pointed past the shop and up the hill to the center of Imaris. "City square."

"Run!" Kaul shoved the little man forward almost making him stumble to the ground and the two broke into an uphill sprint.

SUDDEN BELL TOLLING began resounding throughout the city and Jekaran swore under his breath. *How had they gotten word around so quickly? They shouldn't have had time for that!* Panicked screams and desperate shouting pierced the air, but not from behind them. The alarms weren't because of the fire on the docks, he realized.

"Divine Mother!" he gasped.

Screaming people scattered in every direction as a hulking form turned into the square. The behemoth was as tall as most of the city's buildings, glossy in a way that made it look like it was made of glass, and had a glowing jewel set in its face like a Cyclops' eye.

"Jenoc, no," he heard Kairah breathe.

"Jekaran!" Maely screamed as she pulled on his free arm.

As though Maely's screaming had been the only sound in all of Shae-lar, the Crystal Golem stopped and turned to look directly at them.

"Run!" Kairah shouted, and the three of them turned and began doubling back.

You can fight it, the sword urged.

That's what you said about Kaul, and he nearly roasted my head off. Still, as insane as the sword's suggestions were, they tempted him.

Jekaran began to countdown from one thousand by three's again. "Nine ninety-seven—"

They ran down Imaris' center street, a cacophony of screams, shouts, and breakage trailing them. Jekaran couldn't help but cast a glance over his shoulder, and he saw the crystal golem tear through a passing wagon in an explosion of wood, scattered goods, and ghern blood. It crushed the street carts, animals, and people who were not able to clear out of its way in time. The ground shook as it gained.

"Use magic!" Mae shouted at Kairah.

Kairah looked hesitant, but then nodded and adopted the look of concentration she displayed when shielding them from Kaul's fireballs. A moment later, a thick spike of rock exploded up from the ground in a spray of dislodged cobblestones and dirt clods. The rock monolith shot up directly in front of the charging golem who collided with it, breaking the rock into pieces as it fell forward. The ground shook as the golem crashed to the ground.

Jekaran took the opportunity to shepherd Kairah and Maely down a smaller side street and then into a narrow alley. He glanced over his shoulder and glimpsed the golem rise to all fours. Its translucent head turned so that its amethyst jewel-eye focused directly on him. Jekaran turned back to look at Kairah and his question of how to fight the golem died in his throat. The Allosian woman's already pale face was even paler, and stray strands of amethyst hair fell down her face as she leaned against the wall of the alley.

"Kairah?" he asked.

She straightened and made a dismissive wave with her hand. "I am well, Jekaran. Worry not."

Maely screamed and Jekaran looked up to see the crystal golem trying to squeeze into the alley amidst a storm of mortar dust and dislodged bricks. Jekaran towed Kairah by the hand around a corner and onto another wide street. "Mae, you said it couldn't swim."

"The docks!" she said in comprehension.

Jekaran nodded. "If we can lure it to the edge, Kairah can use her magic to knock it into the sea."

An explosion of stone followed by screams behind them caused Jekaran to reflexively glance back. The crystal golem had torn through the buildings making up the alley and emerged onto the street, dust marring its pristine glossy skin. Jekaran redoubled his run, Kairah in tow and Maely running beside him.

"What about Kaul?" Mae asked.

Jekaran shook his head. "I'm pretty sure we lost him."

The words no sooner fell from his lips than a wave of fear struck him, knocking him to the ground. He looked to his left and saw Kaul striding toward him from a connecting street, followed by a disheveled looking

Gymal. The short, balding lord was flagging as he worked to keep up with Kaul. That's when Jekaran saw what Gymal was holding.

The blood seeker! That bastard is leading Kaul to me!

Jekaran was fairly certain Gymal wouldn't have opted to help a Rikujo crime lord by choice, but the fact he was doing it at all ignited a fierce anger inside of him. Remarkably, the emotion provided Jekaran with a buffer that tempered Kaul's fear aura, and he was able to stand.

Fight, the sword insisted.

"Jek!" Mae screamed as she tugged on his left arm.

Why was she not feeling the effects of the fear aura? Perhaps Kaul was directing it all at him. Was that even possible? They resumed their run, and Jekaran noticed Kairah had started to flag. Jekaran's anger faded, and he began to feel an overwhelming despair. How were they going to get out of this? They couldn't deal with both the threat of the golem and Kaul.

Fight, the sword pushed with a new urgency in its mental tone.

Jekaran's jaw set. The sword was right. If they were to have any chance of getting out of Imaris alive, he *had* to fight. He slowed and turned to face Kaul, who had stopped a good distance down the street. Catching sight of a hulking monster made of crystal gave the crime lord pause. Jekaran twirled his sword and raised it to a blocking position.

He was going to fight. And that pleased the sword.

"Jek!" Mae screamed. "What are you doing?"

"Go, Mae! Get Kairah to the docks, and lure that thing into the ocean. I have to fight Kaul."

"No!" Maely snapped as she clutched at his arm. Her tone was not angry, but frightened.

"The same technique for controlling your link to the sword will help shield you from that man's fear aura," Kairah said in a weak voice. "His shield talis will drain each time you strike him. Exhaust its charge and he will be vulnerable."

"So it comes down to which man's Apeiron charge will outlast the others'," Jekaran said as he mentally gauged how much energy his sword held. It was nearly full. *Good,* he thought. *Now if I can just avoid being paralyzed by fear and burned to a crisp, I might have a chance.* He began to move forward.

"No!" Mae shouted. "He'll kill you!"

"Go!" he shouted back and then broke free of her grip and launched into a run toward Kaul. He didn't look back, but he was sure that Kairah had to drag Maely away.

Maely watched as Jekaran charged down the connecting street toward Kaul. She had just about used her ring to make him stay with her, but he had broken away before she had the chance to fish it out of her dress pocket.

"Come!" Kairah said as she grabbed Maely's hand and began to run.

She resisted, making sliding half steps as Kairah dragged her along. "I can help him!" she shouted. "I can use my mother's ring!"

"You would likely be killed before you even got close enough to use it."

"You don't know that!"

"Maely, I need ..." The Allosian woman suddenly stumbled to one knee.

She's lost too much Apeiron, Maely realized. *She's dangerously weak.*

The ground shook as the crystal golem drew closer, now only fifty paces away.

Maely helped Kairah stand, and the woman shot her a glance that said everything. She needed Maely's help.

"Dammit!" Maely swore. "Come on!"

She helped Kairah resume their run downhill. *Protect him!* She pleaded to Rasheera as she resumed running downhill. *Please!*

"If he dies, I'm blaming you!" she half-sobbed. When had she started crying? Had Kairah seen her tears? She hoped not.

"We will submerge the golem as we did in Rasha and then return to help Jekaran," Kairah responded in an even tone. Had she even heard Maely?

"Can he win?" The words came out sounding like a plea.

"He has a very powerful talis," Kairah replied.

That wasn't really an answer.

Stronger shaking of the ground made Maely cast a glance over her shoulder. The crystal golem was loping downhill at an even faster pace than before and was quickly closing the distance between them. It suddenly became clear they would not be able to outrun it. She searched around the street for another alley to slip into, but paused when she saw something.

On the other side of the street was a medium-sized, wooden push-cart, spilling assorted vegetables onto the ground. Maely guessed it had been abandoned when the owner caught sight of the glass behemoth crashing down the street. She veered to the left and grabbed the cart, turning it so that its rear was facing downhill, spilling a few heads of cabbage onto the ground with the other vegetables.

"What are you doing?" Kairah demanded as she glanced back at the golem that was now only twenty paces away.

"Get in!" she said as she tipped the pushcart so that the front touched the ground.

Realizing what she intended, Kairah climbed in.

The ground shook as the crystal golem drew even closer. Maely raised it, balancing it on two wheels. With a strain, she pushed it into motion, running with it to help it gain momentum. Gravity caught the cart and it began to accelerate. When it began to get away from Maely, she leaped up and fell head first into the cart's wooden bed. Her weight made it pick up even more speed as it bounced over the cobblestones.

As their race downhill became wilder, Maely began to wonder if she hadn't made a mistake and poked her head out, screaming as she saw the golem almost upon them. Panicked, she threw her back against the front of the cart and the shift in weight pushed it forward. To her relief, the cart accelerated even faster, and they began outpacing the loping golem. Before long, they purchased an appreciable lead as they hurled down the cobblestoned slope.

Then she realized she hadn't thought of how to safely stop the cart, and her breath caught again.

The street became crowded with people who hadn't seen the golem coming yet, and Maely shouted for them to move out of the way. Most heeded her warning and quickly moved out of their path, but one man didn't see them coming and the cart clipped him on the left side, spinning him like a top. He fell out of the cart's path and landed on his behind.

"Sorry," Maely shouted at the bewildered man.

"Maely," Kairah said. The woman was crammed into the cart's front left corner, her eyes wide with fright. It almost made Maely laugh.

"We are nearing the bottom of this slope," Kairah said with obvious forced calm.

Maely looked at the street ahead and saw that they were fast approaching the back wall of one of the dockside warehouses. "Magic!" Maely screamed.

Kairah hesitated, but then nodded and began to concentrate. Maely lurched forward as the cart's wheels locked. It abruptly pitched forward and flipped, spilling them onto the street as it skidded away, crashing into the outer wall of the warehouse where it exploded into several pieces.

That wasn't exactly what she had expected Kairah to do, and she turned to chide the woman for it, but paused.

Kairah lay on the ground with her eyes closed. Maely picked herself up, ignoring the intense burning from a thousand scrapes on her legs and arms, and ran to kneel over the Allosian woman.

"Kairah!" she shouted as she patted the woman's cheek.

She slowly opened her eyes and Maely helped her sit up. "Are you ok?" she asked.

Kairah looked at her, and Maely could see in her face that she was nearing total exhaustion. *What happens if you run out of Apeiron?* The question echoed in Maely's memory. *I would die,* Kairah had said.

"Come on," Maely said as she helped Kairah stand. "We're almost there."

CHAPTER 32

K aul watched as the gigantic moving statue made of glass lopped downhill after the girl and the woman in the expensive cloak. What *was* that gigantic creature? It couldn't be a talis, could it? Kaul had seen the amethyst stone on the glass monster's head, but could a talis be made to come alive? Maybe, once he finished this, he could find out. Possessing a talis like that would indeed make him powerful. Who wouldn't fear him if Kaul commanded a titan such as that? The prospect evoked a lust that almost rivaled his desire for Argentus' sword.

Kaul smiled as Argentus' nephew barreled straight toward him. He had chased the boy all over Aiestal, and now was rewarded by his quarry coming, instead, to him. He heard the pathetic little lord at his right trying to creep away and idly thought about rewarding the man's nauseating cowardice with a blast of fire, but no. He already depleted the flame ring's charge to an uncomfortably low level. Unless he took the sword now, he would have to withdraw and strike again another day.

The thought of retreat made his rage intensify. He *would* kill Argentus' nephew, Jekaran, and claim the sword as his own. Then he would find Argentus and take his old friend's head.

When the boy was twenty paces away, Kaul focused the full intensity of his dread medal on him. He smiled as Argentus' nephew stumbled to a halt and then fell to his knees. Perhaps he would get lucky and the stress of the terror would kill him. It wasn't likely, as the boy was young and strong, but he could always hope. Kaul grinned at Jekaran as he began to prowl toward him.

JEKARAN COULDN'T UNCLENCH his teeth, let alone raise his head to see the man with mismatched eyes approach, but he knew he was coming for him. *Kairah said I could fight the fear the same way I control the sword,* he thought. He began counting down from one thousand by three's. The fear made concentration all but impossible, and he had to keep restarting the countdown. He tried three times, never making it below nine hundred and eighty-two before having to start over.

He could now see Kaul's boots as the man stalked toward him. *Anger,* he remembered. *That's how I did it before.* Jekaran worked furiously to focus on something that would upset him. He tried thinking of the mocking jeers he suffered when the villagers of Genra had only considered him a freak with green eyes, but that didn't work. He tried to think of when Maely laughed at him for his awkward attempts to woo the mayor's beautiful, and much older, daughter. But that only made him worry after her. He thought of Gymal betraying him to Kaul and that stirred something within him, but his knowing that the cowardly lord was compelled to do so out of self-preservation doused that spark.

It was hopeless. He was going to die.

Kaul's hand cupped his chin and forced his head up. Jekaran stared at the man's eyes – one blue, one brown. "Do you know who I am?"

Jekaran couldn't have unclenched his jaw to answer if he had wanted to.

Kaul's sadistic smile told Jekaran the man knew this. *So why ask me a question? To brag,* he realized. *He's gloating over defeating me. Well, it wasn't much of a fight, anyway.* He hadn't even had the fortitude to strike once at the man.

Give me control, the sword abruptly said.

What? That's exactly what Kairah had told him *not* to do.

"My name is Kaul. Your uncle Ezra knows me," he chuckled.

Ez! Jekaran's despair deepened. Had Kaul killed his uncle? Had he killed Mull?

"Your uncle is a very clever man, sending you away with the sword like that, but I'm smarter. I figured it out. So I let him think I was chasing him, when, in fact, I was chasing you."

He's alive! That gave Jekaran the tiniest bit of relief.

Kaul's smile widened. "But, after I take the sword, I am going to hunt him down and kill him with his own weapon. Then *I* will be the Invincible Shadow!"

Jekaran, the sword called him by name, *turn your will over to me.*

I can't!

Kaul let go of his chin and straightened. Jekaran's frozen muscles kept his neck propping his head up to look at the man. Kaul raised his right hand at Jekaran and lifted it so the palm was inches from his face.

This is the end, he realized. Oddly, the thought brought him a bit of comfort. Not enough to counter the fear, but he did feel a sense of relief that his ordeal would soon be over. Jekaran closed his eyes.

Your will, the sword pled.

Jekaran remembered when he had been fighting the bandits and how he had been completely engrossed in the sword's power. It was as if he hadn't needed to do anything but let the sword guide him. There had been no forethought, no fear, just clarity and death to his enemies. It had been much the same when he had fought Hort's men in the rock lands, as though his mind was shoved to the side to make room for something else.

He hadn't allowed that state of altered consciousness to take him ever since Maely had called him out of it. Kairah's warnings that the sword could dominate him had scared him into keeping his mental distance from the talis, but now, facing death, he knew that didn't matter anymore.

So Jekaran lowered the barriers of resistance in his mind and let the sword have his will.

Kaul took a three-foot step back from Argentus' nephew. Although his shield bracelet would protect him from the heat of the blast, he didn't want to waste any more of that talis' charge as he may need it to help him escape the city. He set his rage free of its already loose constraints and willed an explosion of fire to erupt from his palm, strong enough to take the boy's head off at the neck. It raced from Kaul's hand and struck in a flash of flame and a wave of heat he could feel even through his shield. Kaul smiled and took a step toward the clearing smoke.

Then he froze.

Argentus' nephew was standing, his smoldering sword raised to cover his face. The blast had singed him, as was evidenced by a patch of missing hair at his right temple, but he was otherwise unharmed.

Kaul felt the emotion he thought he had banished long ago. That loathed familiar feeling stabbed at his heart at seeing the boy's cold, green eyes.

Kaul was afraid.

He instinctively refocused his dread medal on the boy, pouring as much Apeiron into the effort as he could.

Jekaran didn't react. He didn't even flinch.

Kaul raised his hand and launched another fireball, but it came too late as the boy leapt into the air, spinning as he performed an aerial somersault. He crashed down on Kaul with the edge of his sword, and Kaul flew backward in a flash of crackling purple light. The shield had protected him, but the blow took an alarming amount of his bracelet's Apeiron charge.

Kaul rolled to his right just as Jekaran struck at him again, this time leaping to land where he had only a heartbeat ago been lying on the ground. The boy's sword bit into the cobblestone street as easily as though it were a heated iron and the street were melting snow. Kaul leapt to his feet and managed to throw another fireball, which Jekaran batted out of the air with prescient timing. He began to back away, desperately wishing he had brought his men. Arkell was the best swordsman of the group, but Kaul had shoved him off a cliff. That now proved to have been a poor decision.

I don't need him! Kaul snarled. He drew his sword and sought the one thing that could counter his fear—rage.

He willed a small amount of Apeiron from his ring to wrap his blade with an aura of fire. The effect was more theatrics than it was to enhance his weapon, and he had often used the trick to intimidate his foes, but

Argentus' nephew looked as though he didn't even notice. He let that anger him further as he rushed forward to strike.

Kaul whipped his blade in a horizontal cut, but was rebuffed as Jekaran snapped his sword up in time to block. He immediately pivoted and swung in from the other side in a downward slice. Jekaran voided the swing, and Kaul sliced opened air, the fire from his sword fluttering like a torch in the wind. He recovered quickly, spinning and channeling his momentum into a desperate thrust.

When Jekaran knocked his sword aside, he abruptly dropped it and emitted a blast of fire. The feint worked, and Jekaran didn't have the time or space to block the blast. It struck him in the left shoulder and knocked him back, spinning him to the ground. Kaul hurled another fireball, this time striking him in the back. The sword clattered to the ground. He rushed up, found the sword three feet out of the boy's reach, and picked it up. The boy still lay motionless.

Kaul's fear evaporated as his eyes hungrily roved over the blade, glittering with emerald sparkles, and the large amethyst stone set like a keystone in the silver crossguard.

The sword was his!

A full-toothed grin spread wide across his face. He had beaten Argentus.

With this sword, there would be no one Kaul would have to fear; people would fear him, *all people*. He stepped next to the boy, looming over his grounded form, and kicked him hard where the burn flared by the second fireball. The boy didn't react. Was he dead? Had Kaul killed him? *Best to be sure,* he thought.

He leveled the point of the sword at the back of Jekaran's neck, touched it with the edge. He then raised the sword and brought it down in a furious decapitating slice.

The sword stopped less than an inch from the boy's neck. The shock of the abrupt recoil had barely subsided when Jekaran rolled over and kicked Kaul straight in the kneecap. He cried out as he dropped the sword and stumbled back, keeping his feet only by the full exertion of his will. He looked up and found the boy standing with the sword already in hand. Had it even touched the ground?

Kaul lunged to his left and scooped up his sword by its handle, having just enough time to bring it up to block Jekaran's slash. He limped backward, bringing his sword up again to block the follow-up strike. Kaul continued to limp backward, working with all of his might to parry Jekaran's increasingly ferocious attacks.

Clang, Kaul knocked the sword to the left.

His father was throwing him repeatedly against the garden wall for having snuck a strip of salted pork from the pantry.

Clang, Kaul shoved the thrusting blade to the right.

He was huddled on the ground, his father kicking repeatedly at his ribs, the sharp pain in his side telling him that at least one was broken, probably more.

Clang, Kaul barely managed to parry a rising cut.

His father held his small feet inches off the ground, strangling him for trying to restrain the pummeling his sobbing mother had received.

Argentus' nephew brought the sword up sharply and swung in a downward slice. Kaul brought his sword up, the two of them so close he would have to catch it just above the hilt. The swords struck each other, but this time Kaul did not rebuff the attack. Instead, Jekaran's sword sheared through his, leaving the remaining inch of blade above the hilt glowing a cherry red. The sword struck Kaul at the same time that he heard his severed blade *clang* against the ground. His shield manifested, protecting him from being eviscerated. The follow-up swing came as a horizontal cut, the blade catching as Kaul's shield crackled just three inches from the left side of his neck. However, it did not stop the blade.

As if time had slowed, Kaul saw the blade of Argentus' sword slowly pushing through the crackling purple barrier protecting his neck. He willed all of the bracelet's Apeiron into the shield, but it didn't slow the blade. As if tearing free from something, the sword broke through the shield and bit into his neck. In this, the last of his living moments, Kaul felt absolutely no anger. The only emotion he could feel was fear.

JEKARAN WATCHED from some place in the back of his mind as his sword pushed through the barrier of crackling, purple energy guarding Kaul's neck. The blade slowed for a moment, and then like the last autumn leaf desperately clinging to the branch abruptly torn away by the winter wind, the sword broke through the shield and took Kaul's head off in a blur.

The emerald shards peppering the blade lit up like tiny stars, and he could feel something rushing into the amethyst stone set in the sword's crossguard. The sword's Apeiron charge—which had decreased by a quarter since the start of his fight with Kaul—suddenly refilled, as though Jekaran had been near an Apeira well. Instinctually he had known there was more than enough to charge his sword, and the excess energy began flowing into him. This hadn't happened when he had killed the bandits in Rasha, no, this was new, and it was frightening.

Panicked, Jekaran tried to wrest control of his body back from the sword but it resisted him. He tried again, but the sword held on. One side effect of his surrendering his will to the sword had been that he could not feel the pain of his wounds or the fatigue of his muscles. In spite of this numbing, Jekaran was still aware of those sensations; they floated at the borders of his consciousness, and he knew that when the sword did return control to him, if it did, that he would experience them in full force. As the energy flowed from the sword into him, he felt his weariness vanish and the pains of his throbbing burns begin to dull. What was happening to him? There was also another feeling, this one not muted by the sword's bond—exquisite satisfaction. It was as if Jekaran were eating a harvest night feast after having worked in the fields all day without having had so much as a scrap of bread.

The sensation abruptly ceased, and Jekaran felt himself walk a short distance to the left where he stopped and looked at Kaul's severed head. The mismatched eyes, one blue and one brown, stared glassily at the sky, and there was an expression of unmistakable terror frozen on the man's pallid face.

"Jekaran?" a nasally voice hesitantly called.

Jekaran felt his head snap up and turn to the right. There he saw Gymal, fine clothes disheveled and his nose leaking blood. He stood next to Hort who, in spite of a serious and painful looking burn on his right cheek, held his sword at the ready, free arm stretched out protectively in front of Gymal. A feeling of eagerness surged from the sword at seeing Gymal, and Jekaran knew it wanted to attack him.

No! Jekaran clawed at the bond in an effort to regain control of his body. The sword rebuffed him with greater ease than before. Was it somehow stronger now? Jekaran felt his body take a step toward Gymal.

Kairah! he mentally shouted at the sword. *We have to save Kairah!*

The sword paused. Saving Kairah meant fighting the crystal golem. The thought swayed the sword, and Jekaran felt his body turn and sprint down the hill.

CHAPTER 33

Kairah could not remember ever feeling so weak. It wasn't physical fatigue, though if she didn't reach a well soon it would become that. No, her weakness was a dangerously low level of Apeiron as reported to her senses in the form of a feeling of vulnerability at her center. Her core, which was usually warm and solid, felt cold and shaky.

She closed her eyes. *I am in trouble.* But she knew the Spirit Lily couldn't hear her. She was too far, and too weak, to communicate with Aeva now. If she had stopped spell-casting after creating that spike of stone, she would be fine, she was sure of it. The spell to stop their runaway cart weakened her to this state.

Kairah turned to look at Maely running at her side, and the lines of worry wrinkling her young forehead. For one so given to emotional volatility, the girl's underlying sense of personal empathy seemed to be a constant—although she tried to hide it.

"Are you—" Maely began.

"I am fine," Kairah cut her off.

They reached the docks, where several of the ships were a mass of milling activity making her think of a disturbed anthill. The human shipmasters had caught sight of the golem, which was now turning onto the street that ran parallel to the docks. Several ships were casting off, some so recklessly fast that they dropped their gangplanks, and some-times those walking on them, into the water. The Queen's Honor was one of those, although it had not yet cast off.

Kairah glanced over her shoulder to see the golem loping toward them. Jekaran had been right to suggest this course of action. If they lured the creature onto one of the piers, it certainly would not be able to support its weight, and would crash into the sea. This close to the shelf the living statue could climb back onto land, but not before they had ample time to escape.

Until it finds me again, she thought.

"Where's Jek?" Maely's voice shook.

Kairah didn't answer. She couldn't. If Jekaran tried to fight the man with the three powerful talises, then it was very possible that he was dead. That stabbed at Kairah's heart more than she expected. Had she been growing fond of the boy— of a human? She was fond of Maely in the same way that a child was fond of its pet, but the feelings that Jekaran's possible death invoked were somehow different, more like the grief for a lost equal—or a friend.

"This way," Kairah said to Maely, grabbing the girl by the wrist and towing her toward the pier. They reached the pier where the Queen's Honor was moored and leapt onto the wooden walkway leading to the ship's gangplank. They ran several yards, and then Kairah stopped and turned to watch the golem. It drew close, but stopped before setting foot onto the pier.

It knows what we are attempting!

"Why is it stopping?" Maely asked, her voice edging on hysteria.

Kairah didn't know much about the talis, she hadn't even been aware of their existence until they began to chase her. But what she felt from them did not indicate sentience like Jekaran's sword. Certainly, they would have some basic reasoning skills, but the hulking creature's hesitation appeared more like a display of conscious thought.

Sister, Jenoc's voice inside her head startled her. So, he was *personally* controlling the crystal golem.

Sister, Jenoc repeated. *This is over. Come with me and no more humans will be harmed.*

Until you cause them to go to war with one another, she replied. Jenoc was using the golem as a kind of telepathic relay, making her spell-casting to communicate with him easy, and therefore costing her virtually no Apeiron.

They will destroy themselves eventually. I am simply expediting the inevitable. Jenoc couldn't hide the cold hate from his voice, despite his effort to pretend he followed a logical course of action.

Kairah knew what festered inside of him. *We are not their gods, Jenoc!* Kairah did nothing to veil her anger.

Are we not? Jenoc thought. *Did we not give them lives when they were about to die? Did we not give them shelter, food, and talises?*

That does not give us the right to decide their fate!

I will not be denied this, Sister. It has become the very reason for my existence!

"Kairah?" Maely asked, her tone sounding confused. "What's happening?"

What would our mother and father think of what you are doing? She had asked him that before, but Jenoc had never given her an answer.

They are gone! Jenoc sent in a heated reply, and she could feel that the barriers of strict restraint that contained his rage were weakening, just as she had always known they one day would. One could sooner contain a hurricane in a wooden box than keep such hate pent up for so long.

Their essence remains, you know this. Nothing that is of Apeira can truly be destroyed.

Obsolete tradition and desperate superstition, Sister! That is all your belief is. It is how you have learned to cope with their loss.

And vengeance is a better way?

No reply.

I was there too, Jenoc. I saw it happen the same as you did. Yet, I do not degrade myself by wallowing in grief and hate.

Finally, Jenoc spoke, and Kairah could sense that he regained his self-possession. *Come home, Sister.*

I will not let you do this, Jenoc!

Please, Kairah. Your strength is nearly gone. It would be unwise for you to cast in such a state.

You leave me little choice, Kairah said.

Please, Sister. See rea—

"Jek!" Maely screamed.

Kairah looked to her right and found Jekaran sprinting toward the golem, sword aloft. Jenoc turned his avatar just as Jekaran leapt an inhuman ten feet into the air, sword swinging down at the golem's shoulder. The blade tore through its hard, transparent shell, shearing its arm off. Kairah sensed Jenoc's surprise.

Jekaran landed in a ready crouch, sword held horizontally out to his side. The golem turned to face Jekaran, and the purple light of Apeiron leaked like blood from its assaulted shoulder before it evaporated.

Kairah's eyes grew wide. The crystal golem's severed arm liquefied into a shimmering pool flowing of its own accord across the ground and back to the golem. His foot absorbed it, the fluid flowing out from its injured shoulder to shape a new arm. She gasped as it opened and closed its hand, testing the new appendage.

Jekaran leapt at it again, but the golem swung its new arm and swatted him out of the air. Maely screamed as Jekaran flew twenty feet, striking hard against the ground and rolling. He rose, blood running down the side of his head, his free arm bent at an unnatural angle. She saw his shoulders rise and fall, rise and fall, and then he charged the golem a third time.

Does he not feel the pain of his injuries? Kairah wondered. And that's when she saw his eyes, cold and blank, like the glassy stare of a corpse. *The sword is dominating the bond,* she realized with a stab of horror. That would mean Jekaran had lost control of his body, and the sword was dictating his movements. If that were so, the sword likely felt no pain and would fight until Jekaran's body was ruined or he was killed.

Kairah had to do something or Jekaran was going to die.

Jekaran ducked under the golem's next swing, spun to the creature's left and sheared through its tree-trunk-sized leg in one smooth motion. It fell to one knee in a crash that shook the street and Jekaran jumped, raised his sword, and plunged it deep into the crystal golem's back. The crystal golem quickly absorbed and reformed its leg and then spun to reach behind and grab Jekaran. As it did, the sword was wrenched free from its back, and it flung Jekaran to the ground. Again, he held onto his sword and leapt to his feet without showing any sign of pain at his physical damage.

Kairah quickly assessed the situation and mentally listed her options. The only way to knock Jenoc's avatar into the water was with winds several times greater than those in a hurricane. Kairah was certain she could not manage that with the low level of Apeiron she had remaining. However, the golem was close enough to the pier for Kairah to strike at it with seawater.

Drawing on what energy she had left, Kairah cast a spell from the Second Discipline and raised twin pillars of salt water. They twisted and writhed as they raised high into the air. Once tall enough to reach Jenoc's golem, Kairah threw the water forward, both columns pouring down on the titan's back. Then, while the golem was in the midst of the deluge, Kairah froze the water into a solid block of ice, enveloping the golem to the neck and rendering it immobile.

"Break the jewel in its head!" she shouted at Jekaran. Could he hear her? Would the sword, which was controlling Jekaran's body, comprehend her?

Those cold green eyes glanced at her, and then up at the amethyst jewel in the golem's head. The talis forced Jekaran forward and he ran at the golem, leapt high into the air, and brought the sword down on the golem's face in a stroke that nearly cleaved its head in two. An explosion of purple light shortly blinded Kairah, but when it subsided, she saw Jekaran backing away from the golem as it exploded into a rain of glass-like shards. She released the spell that held the ice in place, and it immediately returned to liquid, splashing to the ground and washing most of the glass shards into the sea.

Maely's shouting sounded miles away as Kairah's vision began to darken. The last thing she saw as darkness took her sight was the frothing seawater rushing up to meet her.

Jekaran tried to scream, but his mouth would not move. He clawed with all of his desperate fear at the bond in attempt to wrest it from the sword, but the sword refused. He was trapped in his own mind, helpless, as Kairah slumped to her right and fell off the pier.

She would drown, and there was nothing he could do to save her.

That thought, the thought of his never being able to see her beautiful face again, or hear her musical laugh, or breathe the intoxicating scent of her natural perfume, awoke something inside him. It was fierce, and powerful, and it focused his will.

Those feelings that had been swirling around in his consciousness for days coalesced into something tangible. At first, he thought it just youthful lust, but his conversations with Kairah had been more stimulating than physical attraction. Her naïve innocence and her gentle determination to save a people who had all but destroyed her own won his admiration. Each morning he awoke thinking of her, and each night her face was the last thing he saw in his mind before sleep took him. Was this love? The question badgered him. He wasn't sure he knew how to tell.

Whatever it was, the emotion was so powerful that he could feel his will surge, rising up to snatch the bond away from the sword. It retreated to the back of his mind, making Jekaran think of a dog that had been kicked for disobedience slinking away with its tail between its legs. He could feel the sword's confusion, and almost felt guilty.

As control of his body returned to Jekaran, sharp pain in his arm and head twisted his insides. The sensations numbed by the sword came rushing in, and he felt as though he was standing on a riverbed, facing the full aquatic fury of a breaking dam. Jekaran fell to his knees, dropping the sword as he vomited.

There was something wrong with his vision and thoughts that were clear a moment before abruptly became muddled. *Kairah* was the only thought that made any sense to him anymore. She was drowning and he had to save her.

Then sound and light abandoned him.

MAELY DIDN'T THINK, she just reacted. She dove off the pier, nearly losing her breath as cold sea water assaulted her. The saltiness stung her eyes as she swam down toward the dark shape ahead that was slowly sinking.

She pushed forward, gripped Kairah around the waist and began the difficult ascent to the surface. She had done this before. Three summers back when she, Jek, and Mull were spending a leisurely day at a lake, only a few miles outside of Genra. In an over-ambitious attempt to impress Jek, Mull had climbed a rocky outcropping that reached out over the lake. The height had to have been at least fifty feet, and, before Maely knew what her brother was doing, Mull leapt from his perch.

He had dived wrong, and he hit the water belly first with a loud *slap.* The impact had knocked the wind from his lungs, and he had thrashed about, panicked. Maely had leapt into the water and brought him back to shore. She saved his life that day, and thanked Rasheera that swimming had been one of her favorite pastimes.

Mulladin, I hope you're ok, she thought as she broke the surface of the water and took a desperate breath.

She swam to a ladder that ascended onto the pier, and with all the strength she had, Maely climbed up and pulled Kairah onto the wooden planks of the dock.

She's not breathing!

She turned the woman onto her side and began pounding on her back.

Nothing.

Maely paused to place a hand on the top of Kairah's chest, feeling for a heartbeat. It was there, but it was alarmingly weak.

She jumped as Kairah suddenly vomited water, and then began to cough, the spasm lasting an eternity before she began to breathe normally.

"Jek!" Maely called. Where was he? When she looked up, she felt a new wave of panic.

Jekaran was lying on the ground, unconscious, his head bleeding. She glanced down at Kairah to make sure she was still breathing. Nodding at the rise and fall of Kairah's chest, she scrambled to her feet and raced to Jekaran. She fell to her knees at his side.

She checked his pulse as Ez had taught them, the tension escaping her shoulders when she felt it strong.

He wasn't dying, just badly hurt.

The sound of metal scraping across stone behind her, and Maely looked up to see Gymal picking up the sword.

"This is indeed a very powerful talis," Gymal said as he ran his hands over the tiny emerald shards embedded in the blade. "With it, your peasant friend was able to take the head of that wild man with the flame talis."

Then Kaul was dead, Maely realized. *Jekaran had killed him.*

"That belongs to Jekaran!" she shouted at the lord.

He looked at her, and, although his mouth and chin were covered in dried blood, he managed a condescending smile. "This belongs to the king, little girl." He looked adoringly at the sword. "My reward for delivering this to him will surely be great, perhaps even a dukedom."

Maely stood up, balled her fists, and took a step toward the man, realizing she was almost as tall he was. Maely was about to unleash a torrent of hot angry words peppered with the most vile curses that she knew, but Gymal turned away from her, his attention distracted.

Gymal's bodyguard, the soldier Jekaran called Hort, knelt down and checked Jekaran's pulse.

Why did he care if Jek died?

"Divine Mother!" Gymal's gasp made Maely turn back to look at him. The short, balding lord was crouching next to Kairah, his hand gently holding a lock of her soggy, amethyst hair.

No! Maely thought with a stab of panic.

Gymal stood and turned to Maely. "She's an Allosian?"

Maely thought about denying it, but doing so seemed foolish. It was too late. Gymal knew. "Her name is Kairah," Maely said. "She's badly hurt and needs an Apeira well or she'll die."

Gymal looked again at Kairah and nodded. His face was oddly devoid of its usual smug expression. In fact, Maely thought, he almost looked concerned. Gymal leaned over and scooped up Kairah to carry her over his shoulder. For a man so short and so skinny, he was surprisingly strong.

"I will take her to Aiested," Gymal said. "The well there is said to radiate Apeiron to such a distance that it can power talises on ships five miles out to sea."

"She has an urgent message for the king," she blurted out. Could Kairah be enough to distract Gymal from pursuing Jek? He already had the sword, and, if Maely could somehow appear to be helping the weaselly little lord, perhaps he would go and leave them alone.

Her conscience rebuked her for being so ready to abandon Kairah, but Maely ignored it. All that mattered was saving Jekaran's life and getting away. Let the lords and kings worry about magic and wars. In a way, wasn't this what Kairah had wanted? And by letting Gymal take her, wasn't she helping Kairah accomplish her mission?

"One of her people is trying to start a new talis war between the three nations." Maely eagerly volunteered. "She is trying to stop that from happening."

Gymal nodded gravely. Although the man looked the picture of sober fear, Maely suspected his thoughts centered on rewards he received for delivering an Allosian, and vital intelligence, to the king on top of a powerful weapon talis.

Self-serving bastard, she thought, then her gut smacked her conscience. *Are you not doing the very same thing?* Maely smothered the screaming voice in her head.

Her need was greater—*it was!*

Gymal appeared to really look at her for the first time. "Go back to your village, little girl. Consider it your reward for being so helpful."

Yes! Maely inwardly exulted. *He's letting us go!*

"Bring the boy," Gymal called to Hort.

Panic filled Maely's breast as Gymal's words registered. "No!" she shouted. "You can't take him from me!"

Gymal ignored her and began walking toward the Queen's Honor. Had he been planning all along to sail to the capital once he caught Jek? Hort hefted Jekaran from the ground, slung him over a shoulder, and began to follow Gymal.

"No!" Maely cried out again. "You can't!"

She tried to stop Hort, but the man shoved her aside so hard she fell to the ground. Her mother's ring. *Use the ring.*

She had the power to make them leave Jekaran alone.

She quickly reached into her dress pocket and froze. A gaping tear ran across the pocket, and she looked down to see the flesh of her fingers poking out beneath tattered cloth. *The push cart.* She never thought to check, in all the panic, if the ring was safe. Tears filled her eyes as Maely's heart sank. She watched as Hort carried Jekaran up the gangplank of the ship, and the crew pulled it in as they readied to disembark.

Maely thought she heard her conscience laughing at her, and she broke into uncontrollable sobs.

CHAPTER
34

Jenoc's view of his sister abruptly vanished, and the psychic link tethering him to the golem snapped back as a taut rope severed. He heaved a sigh as he pressed two fingers to his right temple. In spite of being a master of the Fourth Discipline, Sensory, the effort of controlling the golem personally and communicating through it, had greatly taxed him. Although he had only been watching through the golem's eye for a few minutes as it had chased and nearly apprehended Kairah, the effort ignited another fierce migraine.

He was getting those a lot lately.

Jenoc added his left hand to the effort of massaging his temples as he sagged back into his plush chair. He had spell-crafted psychic links, like trip wires, to both crystal golems so that he would know the very moment they had found his sister, and it had worked. They had been like ever-present, nagging lights in the back of his mind, aggravating his migraines.

It had been one of those links that had alerted him less than a half an hour ago of the automaton's find. But he didn't have that to worry about any longer. The light disappeared when the boy shattered the golem's Aeose.

And, strangely, the light in his mind representing the other crystal golem had gone dark a few days earlier.

The one that I sent to the east.

That would only happen if the talis had either lost its charge or been destroyed. And since the humans did not possess the means to destroy such a powerful talis on their own, Jenoc assumed—odd as it was—that it had somehow lost its Apeiron charge.

I will have to send someone to retrieve it. He sighed again. It almost didn't matter. Sending it after his sister was no longer an option.

Kairah proved more resourceful than Jenoc would've guessed, even going so far as to employ that human boy with the green eyes to provide martial protection. He had possessed a weapon talis, a very powerful one the likes of which Jenoc had not before seen. Even with such a formidable protector, Kairah had to realize just how out of her element she was.

Jenoc sincerely hoped it was only a matter of time before she gave up her quest and returned home.

After several minutes, the throbbing pain behind Jenoc's eyes eased and he was able to stand. He made his way over to a crystalline desk where a small, disc-shaped talis rested flat on the glass desktop. Jenoc touched the disc, and a translucent three-dimensional map materialized in the air before him. The floating image depicted a map of Shaelar, specifically the kingdom of Aiestal, the very country Kairah had fled to.

It hadn't originally been Jenoc's first target. He had been planning on going to Haeshala first, they being the most war-like humans in all of Shaelar. As such, they would be less suspicious of his offer, their violent hubris blinding them to all else. And once Haeshala launched an attack on its neighbors, Jenoc would have an easier time convincing the other two human nations, Aiestal and Maeis Tol, to go to war.

That was going to have to change now. As unlikely as it was to happen, should Kairah actually manage to warn Aiestal's king of his plan, it could unravel everything. He rubbed his temples again, although they no longer hurt.

He would have to go to Aiestal first. He had, of course, been to all three nations many times in different disguises in order to prime their rulers to accept his offer, but now it was time to begin his efforts in earnest.

Now it was time to give the humans the tools they would need to destroy each other.

Jenoc touched the floating image and it zoomed in until it showed a larger view of an enormous city. It was Aiested, the capital city of Aiestal. Jenoc estimated a populace of over a million humans inhabiting the ruins of the ancient Allosian city, Taris.

He scoffed as he wondered just how many of the vermin even knew their city was stolen from his people. Taris had been great in its day, built around an Apeiron well second only in size to the Mother Shard. Its fall to the human conquerors had signaled that the Allosians had lost the war; it was the turning point that led his people to retreat into hiding. They had taken as many of their books and talises as possible before fleeing Taris, the grand Aeose falling into the hands of those who were wholly unworthy of it.

Anger began to stir inside Jenoc, but he quickly tamped it down. *No, he reminded himself, this is not personal.* He was a junior master of the college, and because of his talent and achievement, everyone knew he would, one day, be appointed to the Synod, perhaps even becoming Speaker. Professionals like him did not allow emotion to factor into their decisions. His plan for the humans was necessary in order to prevent the end of Allosian civilization, nothing more than a doctor killing an infection to preserve the life of his patient.

This is not personal.

Still, there were those who already believed Jenoc was acting out of personal prejudice. Elder Harad had all but accused him of it when he presented his arguments to the Synod. The anger stirred again, a hungry thing that demanded Jenoc feed it with his memories. One memory in particular suddenly surfaced in his mind, a still image of his mother's lifeless body lying naked and broken on the dirt floor of a log cabin. He squinted his eyes shut against another threatening migraine. Another image came unbidden to the forefront of his thoughts, and he saw his father's headless corpse bent over, kneeling in a prostrate position, as though he were praying.

Jenoc had been young, not quite a man, when his parents were killed. Slaughtered not by highwaymen or soldiers, but by a mob of human villagers, whipped into a frenzy because they had discovered they had been deceived.

Jenoc lost control of his anger and abruptly stood, hands gripping his crystalline desk and flipping the entire thing over, dumping the map talis onto the floor where it shattered into a dozen pieces.

Even before the desk and talis completely shattered, Jenoc rallied his emotional discipline to force back his rage. After a moment of carefully controlled breathing, he felt control return. Shame quickly followed, renewing the intensity of his throbbing migraine. Right hand pinching the bridge of his nose, Jenoc stumbled back to his lounge chair and collapsed.

It took the better part of an hour for the headache to pass.

When had they started coming so frequently? he wondered. Worry sparked as a possibility occurred to him. The headaches had started increasing about the same time he attempted to open a doorway to "the other magic." He scolded himself for using the folklore name for it, but he really didn't know what else to call it.

The experiment proved to be a failure, but could his attempt have damaged him somehow? Spells going awry and causing damage were not unheard of, but usually the negative effects were obvious and instantaneous. *No*, he shook off the worry *it is the increased stress, nothing more.* He had never heard of damage occurring as a lingering effect, like a brain injury, and, besides, he had been fretting over Kairah's departure. And the task that weighed upon him would naturally evoke some physiological reaction.

He waited a few more minutes, and then rose from his chair to make his way toward his bedchamber. He strode through the door and tossed open an ivory wardrobe closet and began collecting articles of clothing and other necessaries.

In the process of counting out Aiestal currency, Jenoc noticed something glittering in the back of his closet. He reached for it and withdrew a small geode not much larger than the coins he had been counting. Although pretty, geodes weren't particularly valuable except as *charms* sold to ignorant peasants by unscrupulous merchants. This particular geode had cost half an Aiestal, which was about five times its real worth.

Kairah had bought it for him at a human's harvest festival when they had been children, a memory Jenoc realized he had not revisited for quite some time—perhaps in decades. Their first year living in the village of Taratra, only a year before he and Kairah would be orphaned.

Jenoc stared at the geode for a long moment before carefully slipping it into the pocket of his traveling cloak. He wasn't sure why, it seemed foolish and sentimental, but somehow appropriate.

Jenoc's thoughts drifted afar while he mechanically went about preparing for his journey. Although his mind touched a few more times on the scene of his parent's murder, he didn't have any further difficulty keeping his emotions in check. As he left, he gravitated toward Kairah's garden and ended up in front of the Spirit Lily.

Is she still safe?

She is too far away for me to touch her mind, the Spirit Lily replied.

Jenoc refused to call the thing Aeva like Kairah did. It was a childish notion for Kairah to believe the lily was connected to their dead mother, and he was disappointed she referred to the flower by a name. *Why did you insist on keeping her location secret from me?*

Because Kairah did not wish you to find her.

And had I not cared that my sister treasures you? Had I threatened to destroy you? Would you have told me then?

No, the Spirit Lily responded without hesitation.

Jenoc hadn't been expecting that. *Is not survival your paramount instinct?*

It is, the Spirit Lily responded.

Then why would you be willing to risk yourself for her? Jenoc asked, genuinely curious.

Because I love her, the flower plainly replied.

That was odd, Jenoc thought. He knew Spirit Lilies had a measure of intelligence, and an affinity for their caretakers was not uncommon, but this felt more complex—more Allosian. He dismissed the oddity and said with his thoughts, *I also love her.*

The flower said nothing.

Slipping his hand into his cloak pocket to feel the geode, Jenoc said, *When you can communicate with her again, please tell her I said so.*

I will.

Jenoc nodded to himself, slipped his hand out of his cloak pocket, and left for Aiestal.

CHAPTER 35

The pressure on Ezra's stomach had increased and was affecting his breathing. "Dammit boy!" he snapped over his shoulder. "Do you have to hold on so tightly?"

"Sorry." Mull sheepishly loosened his grip around Ezra's waist.

Ezra inhaled deeply to catch his breath and said, "It's ok, Mull. I'm sorry."

He scolded himself for taking such a tone with the boy-man. Doing so often resulted in Mulladin bursting into tears. But keeping an even tone with him had become increasingly difficult as his worry for Jekaran festered.

They were riding cross-country on a well-trained, tan-furred ghern that had probably belonged to an animal trainer. Ezra had stolen it two days ago when they left Rasha. This ghern was a decided improvement over the one he had stolen from Jeryn. That beast had been foul-tempered, obstinate, and stinky. *If Jekaran were here, he would say that it was a perfect match for me.* The thought twisted his already strained heartstrings, which he imagined were so taut they could be strummed like a harp.

Damn me for a fool, he thought, his new mantra for whenever his worry began to get the better of him. What had he been thinking sending Jekaran on the road with that cursed sword-talis? He had thought himself cunning for doing so, but now he just felt stupid. He had been a prideful fool, and it very well could have cost him his nephew's life.

What would he do if Jekaran were dead? Anarilee, *her soul rest with the peace of the righteous,* would be disappointed in him. He had disappointed his sister far too many times in life, and had sworn he would never do so again when he decided to raise Jekaran. Now he had failed. His hubris, which he thought had died with Argentus, had led his nephew to his death.

You don't know that, his own voice of logic soothed.

Don't I?

The people he had paid for information confirmed Kaul had been in Rasha around the same time Jekaran would've been there. In fact, the maniac murdered three guardsmen. *Well, at least Jekaran found Irvis,* he told himself. Of course there wasn't any way he could really know that, but the absence of his friend and the reports of Kaul's quick departure said as much. *Rasheera, please protect him,* he prayed for what was sure to be the one thousandth time.

Ezra fingered his earring, the displacement talis, as he stared at the endless grassland ahead. He wished he could use it to teleport from city to city, but the talis wasn't good for long distance travel. Doing so would cost far more Apeiron than the talis could hold. It wouldn't be a problem if there were Apeira wells spaced at regular intervals along his course of travel, but of course that was ridiculous. Such a thing was not to be found in all of Shaelar, though it would be wonderfully useful. No, his earring was no good for extended travel. Ezra imagined it was crafted for the purpose of escape or advantage on the battlefield.

Besides, he had two people to worry about, which cost twice the Apeiron.

He shot a glance over his shoulder at Mull. He couldn't see his face as the boy-man had buried it in Ezra's back. At first, he had enjoyed the novelty of riding ghern-back, but Mull's excitement for the adventure of it long since abated. Now he was afraid of the speed at which they were traveling, and well he should be. It was precarious, at best, to ride a ghern so hard off-road. It had been a minor miracle that they hadn't broken the beast's leg, or their own necks.

Thank Rasheera for that small mercy.

Something in the distance caught Ezra's attention. It was a shape on the horizon, one that appeared to be moving toward him. A few moments later, he recognized it as a rider. Someone appeared to be in as big a hurry as he was, else why would they risk galloping across country? Ezra entertained the idea of changing course to avoid the rider, but his sense of urgency to find Jek prevailed, and he decided there was no time to be cautious.

Another worry settled in on Ezra. What if the rider was Kaul? His right hand fell to the handle of a sword he had stolen in Jeryn, a fine blade made of perfectly balanced steel. The effort of finding such a weapon had cost him some valuable time, but he learned long ago that one thing a man should never bargain for was the price of a weapon. Well, he hadn't exactly bargained for it.

The rider drew closer and he could now see that it was not Kaul. *Not unless Kaul had ballooned and started balding —IRVIS!*

Ezra reined his ghern in so that the beast drew up short. It was panting hard, and Ezra knew that if he continued to press it so fiercely that it would be dead soon. Apparently, Irvis had spotted him as well, for the man galloped straight toward him.

"Argentus!" Irvis called. He was waving a red cloth above his head to catch Ezra's attention. It was an odd thing to do, but then again that *was* his friend.

"Irvis!" Ezra called as the man closed. His ghern looked to be in a similar state as Ezra's, although that may have more to do with carrying Irvis' weight than the speed at which it was running.

Irvis drew rein and stopped less than a dozen paces away. Ezra trotted his ghern over to the man and gripped his forearm in an affectionate salute.

"Argentus," Irvis panted as though he had been the one running and not his ghern.

"My friend." Ezra forced a smile. "Where's my nephew?"

"I left him on the road to Imaris."

"Praise the goddess!" Ezra almost shouted, and relief like cool water washed away his fear. "Is he with a girl?"

Irvis nodded. "Maely."

Mull made a loud noise pregnant with the same sweet relief Ezra was himself feeling.

He couldn't stop smiling. "I thought Kaul had found him."

"He's not chasing you?" Irvis asked, his tone sounding confused.

Ezra shook his head. "He somehow puzzled out what I had done, but that doesn't matter right now. All that matters is that my boy is alive!" Irvis' concerned expression killed his relief and his chest tightened again. "Irvis?"—he asked carefully—"What's wrong?"

"Argentus," Irvis said soberly. "Jekaran has bonded the sword."

Ezra's heart sank.

In a way, it would have been better if Jekaran had died.

CHAPTER 36

J ove shook with ecstasy as he wrung the last bit of life from the creature. It was something the likes of which he had never seen, truly a thing of wonder. A gigantic, living statue made of crystal. Well, it *had* been a living statue.

He had encountered it while moving west across the Ulakel plain. At least, that's where he thought he had been—Jove hadn't seen a map in years. Instead, he had lived his last few years drifting from village to village, leaving abruptly whenever suspicions began to turn the people against him. He laughed to himself, thinking of what he would have done then if he had the power he wielded now, the power of death itself.

He *was* death.

When Jove had first encountered the crystal statue, it had completely ignored him. In fact, it would've smashed him if Jove hadn't quickly moved out of its way. At first, he wasn't sure that he could devour something so large, and, truly, it had taken him days to do so, but as soon as he lashed out with one of his tendrils, he knew the crystal man was his.

More delightfully surprising than eating it—that's how Jove now thought of this strange thing that he could do—was the potent life the crystal man had contained. Siphoning it had been pure joy, more thrilling than anything he had ever done to his dolls. Trees and animals and even people couldn't compare to the potent, pristine succulence of the life inside the crystal man. He would need to find more.

Jove stood and looked down at the sharp crystal shards, the only remnants of the living statue. As soon as he had begun to eat it, cracks had spider-webbed all across its glass skin; it finally shattered halfway through the feeding.

That's when Jove had accidentally cut himself, when he had been foraging through the shards. It had been a cut across his wrist, and at first Jove worried that it might bleed him out. But nothing happened, not a single drop of blood leaked from his veins.

Remembering the wonder of that moment, Jove pressed again on the bloodless cut. I can no longer feel pain, he realized with a thrill of excitement, and he felt like doing a jig across the remaining shards. Discomfort from the Hunger was his only concern now, an emptiness at his core, afflicting him until he filled it with the lives of other creatures.

He had been surprised when he discovered that each form of life had its own flavor—all delicious—but they differed in degrees of sating his Hunger. Plants and trees would hold him over for a while, and animals were a wonderful appetizer, but people, they tasted the best. Well, he had thought that up until he had feasted upon the life that animated the crystal man. *That* satisfied him in a way nothing else had.

Where could he find more of that delectable, potent life? Everything else paled in comparison to it. He wanted it. He needed more. It was addicting, and Jove knew that he was not a man capable of defying addiction. He giggled to himself, giddy with the full, satisfied warmth within his core. But his giddiness faded as he returned to the question of where to find more like the crystal man. That's when something caught his eye, a shimmer of purple amidst the transparent shards. Jove walked over to it, ignoring the sharp crystal shards tearing the flesh of his feet.

He reached down to pick it up, an amethyst stone fitting in his upraised palm. He squinted in hard concentration, then smiled. The jewel had been the crystal man's eye.

He laughed as he put the jewel up to his face, pretending it was *his* eye. It was a piece of an Apeira well, something found only in talises. Oddly, the amethyst color had dulled and looked to Jove as though it was changing color. Green, the stone was slowly turning green—like his eyes. What did that mean?

Jove shook his head. He didn't know much of talis craft, but he did know the things drew their power from the Apeira wells cities were usually built around. *So that means the crystal man was a talis,* he marveled. He had never seen a talis so large and so complex. That's when he made the connection. The life inside the crystal man was Apeiron. Jove had been feasting on Apeiron, and it was wonderful!

He giggled with delight.

He just needed to find an Apeira well. How much could he draw from one of those! After all, they were said to contain an infinite supply.

The thought excited him. There were plenty of wells in Shaelar, plenty of places for him to find the maddeningly addicting life—plenty of places for him to feed. *There would be people too,* he mused, wonderful appetizers that he would drain on his way to the well.

Jove sucked the last bit of life—*no Apeiron*—from the shattered crystal man. Then he turned and continued walking over the plain, the grass dying with his every step.

He stopped, noticing the circumference around his steps had increased. It now killed in a radius of at least five feet, with Jove at the center of his circle of death.

Interesting development, he giggled. Apparently the more life he consumed, the more death he could cause. He was a god now, an angel of chaos.

He *was* death.

Jove looked to the horizon. Already the Hunger had begun to return. That was another change, for usually he could go hours in between major feedings. After he drained that forest, he had actually gone a whole day without the Hunger rising inside him.

Yes, Jove would need to find an Apeira well, and soon. And for that, he would need to find a city, a large city. He giggled again as he fantasized about just how many people he could devour at once, especially now that his power had grown.

How much would it grow?

How much could he eat?

He wasn't sure, but he was going to find out.

PART TWO
THE SOULLESS GRAVE

CHAPTER 37

J ove trundled down the hill toward the outpost. It was a plain thing, tents surrounded by a palisade wall hewn from the lumber of a nearby forest. Maybe someone inside the soldier's camp could tell him where the nearest Apeira well was located. It would be in a large city, of course, but Jove still didn't know where he was or which direction he should go.

The Hunger churned inside of him, hollowing him out from the center of his chest until his entire body trembled under the stress of his need. He licked his dry, cracked lips. It had only been a couple of days since he fed on the crystal man, and he had made sure to keep up a steady diet of convenient flora and fauna. He'd even happened upon a young hunter, but none of that satisfied him—not any more. Not since he'd fed on that pure, succulent Apeiron. Now he craved it with a hot lust stronger than anything he had ever felt for his dolls.

He was twenty feet away from the palisade wall when someone called out at him. Jove stopped and looked around until he found who was shouting. It was a guard standing on the platform of a wooden watchtower rising from within the camp to loom over the wooden pickets of the palisade wall.

"WHO GOES THERE?" the guard repeated impatiently.

Jove had to work to hide his smile, confining it to a mere twitching at the corner of his mouth. He had rehearsed what he would say, and was ready with an answer. "A humble traveler waylaid on the road some miles back and stripped of all my belongings. I only seek a place to rest, and food."

He almost sniggered at that last part, but Jove restrained his laughter. When he was a lad, a troupe of acrobats, actors, and singers had traveled through his village. They were treated to food and supplies by the mayor in exchange for a single performance to which Jove's parents had taken him. Since then, Jove had been enamored with the arts, and for the better part of his boyhood years diligently practiced in the hopes that one day he, too, could become a trouper. Those dreams had long since rusted as the compulsions of his dark side consumed him. Still, all those years of practicing proved useful whenever Jove needed to lie about his crimes, or put on a false face of harmlessness in order to lure a victim away from safety. He was a good actor, as good as any trouper.

"This is a military encampment, traveler," the guard called down, "Not a Rasheeran monastery." The guard paused, and his tone softened. "I can allow you in to root through the leftovers of this morning's mess if you're not too proud for it."

Jove had to work in order to keep his grateful smile from becoming a victorious grin. "You are too kind."

The guard half turned to call down at someone inside the palisade but paused and turned back to stare down at him. "What's wrong with you?" he demanded, sympathetic tone all but gone. "You look sick."

Jove frowned. "I am famished is all," he said.

The soldier leaned over the rail of his watchtower platform for a better look. After a moment, he shook his head. "No, it's more than that. You look like you have plague."

Jove frowned. His acting skills may be excellent, but a bard couldn't put on a true performance without a costume, and he had nothing with which to hide his pallid face and mange-like scalp. He'd discovered that if he went too long without feeding, his hair fell out, and sores appeared all over his body.

It'd been over a day since he ate the young hunter, and his siphoning Apeiron had somehow accelerated his metabolism. He needed to feed more and more frequently; the memory of that sweet, potent Apeiron haunted his every waking moment.

Jove almost reached out to feed on the guard, but restrained himself with the reminder he needed directions. "Please…" Jove began.

"No!" the guard snapped. "I can't let you in."

Jove ground his teeth. "Then could you at least give me directions to the nearest city, one with an Apeira well."

The guard laughed incredulously. "You're joking."

Jove gritted his teeth. "No, I'm not."

"Why would a vagrant like you need a well? You can't own any talises."

It was all Jove could do from lashing out with his power. "Please."

The guard pointed to his left. "That way, but it's over a hundred miles. And the way you look, I doubt you have enough days left to get anywhere near it."

A hundred miles? The travel time would be too long to go without another large feeding and Jove was desperately hungry. No, that would not do.

Jove shot out a translucent, greenish tendril. It took the guard in the face, and he fell to his knees on the platform, screaming and clutching the sides of his head. His screams cut off as he quickly withered into a dry husk. A surge of strength rushed into Jove closing several of his wounds.

Shouting, followed by the blowing of a horn set the encampment ablaze with the sounds of stampeding soldiers in their clanking armor. Three more soldiers ascended to the watchtower platform, one man falling to a knee to examine his mummified comrade and the other two spotting Jove.

"Divine Mother, what is this?" Jove heard the soldier examining the corpse swear.

"WHO GOES–" one of the soldiers began to call down to Jove, but didn't get the words out before Jove whipped another translucent tentacle up and caught the man in the stomach.

The other two soldiers reacted immediately, one stringing a bow and readying an arrow while the other leapt to his feet. Jove heard a twang, and then something buried itself into his shoulder. The impact made him stagger back a step, but didn't hurt at all. He looked to his left shoulder where he found a fletched shaft sprouting from his flesh.

No blood.

Jove cackled as he threw his arms forward, and unleashed two more tentacles of warped air. The soldier with the bow attempted to dodge, but in so doing fell from the platform onto a sharp point of one of the palisades where he impaled himself. The other soldier, now cradling another lifeless husk of one of his comrades, shouted down to someone.

"HE HAS A TALIS!" Those were the last words the man ever spoke.

Horns blew again, followed by the creaking of wood. Jove looked to his left, down the line of tall pickets to where a wooden gate swung open. Twenty soldiers poured out, located him, and then charged. Jove just shook his head. He let them close to within fifteen feet before whipping several tendrils into existence, and striking out. He walked calmly among the dying men as they writhed on the ground, withering to old skeletons in a matter of seconds.

Jove rounded the open gate just in time to see three lines of pike men quickly forming up. They lowered their halberds and charged. The orderliness of their advance impressed Jove, and so he made sure to eat them in a similar manner, line by advancing line until they all lay at his feet. He could feel their life fill the hollow void in his chest, relieving his hunger but not satisfying him.

No, as delicious as people were, they were nothing compared to drinking in the pure, potent, Apeiron. Jove salivated. He needed more of that sweet, life. Is that what Apeiron was? Just a purer form of the essence that gave all things life? Jove barked a laugh. It made a sort of sense. If he was death, then he consumed life.

Something struck him in the chest, knocking him back a pace. He had smelled the burning before he saw the charred cloth of his dirty tunic. Jove looked up just in time to see a ball of fire streak toward him. He caught it on his arm, the flesh of his forearm blackened and smolder-ing. Yet, even this caused him no pain, though the smell was horrid-familiar, but disgusting. How did people eat cooked flesh? Jove never did like eating meat. Funny, that. He giggled at the irony.

"Come no further!" a voice commanded. It belonged to a woman wearing form fitting armor. Her hair was shorn like a man's, and she held an amethyst-capped, red-gold scepter in her left hand and a sword in her right. She was lovely in an exotic sort of way, the sight of her invoking the predatory lust that was so familiar to Jove.

"You are a very lovely doll, aren't you?" Jove licked his lips as he inched closer.

The woman raised her scepter to launch another fireball but not before Jove whipped out a tentacle and struck the scepter. Jove convulsed with a jolt of unexpected pleasure as his tendril of warped air drained the Apeiron from the woman's talis.

YES!

Jove exulted as the sweet energy closed his wounds, regrew his hair, and gave him strength. But it was over all too soon. He opened his eyes to find the soldier-woman looking at him, aghast.

"What are you?" she breathed out.

Jove grinned, the action causing pooled drool to spill out of the corner of his mouth. He stepped toward her and she dropped the scepter to grip her sword with both hands. With the practiced speed of a professional fighter, the woman launched forward, raising her sword for a horizontal cut. Out of reflex, Jove raised his left arm to block the swing, fully expecting to lose the appendage. To his utter surprise–he considered it remarkable that he could still be surprised by anything–the air around his arm warped with the same translucent, green energy that made up his feeding tendrils. The woman's sword swept across his arm, but didn't bite into his flesh or sever his arm. Instead, the blade broke in two, the spinning point slicing Jove's cheek as it sailed over his shoulder.

The sudden loss of weight unbalanced the woman, and she stumbled, falling into her swing, her armor clanking as she crashed to the ground. Jove stared at his arm in wonder, watching the warped air evaporate. That had happened automatically, without any effort on his part.

He looked down at the woman soldier kneeling on the ground. She was staring at her broken sword. That's when Jove saw the rust cankering the jagged metal where the blade had broken from the hilt. It looked as if the metal was left in the rain for a dozen years. He shook his head. He'd seen the blade before the woman struck out, it had been pristine, new even.

Jove grinned. Apparently, he could not only drain living creatures of life, but he could also break down the natural elements of the world. He was more than death. He was decay incarnate.

The woman snapped out of her shock, dropped the blade, and leapt to her feet. Gone was the fierce bravado of a warrior, replaced by the watery eyes and uncontrollable trembling of a little girl. Jove took a step toward her, his grin so wide it felt like it was going to tear the corners of his mouth.

"Please," the woman sobbed.

They always did that at some point; begged for their life. He laughed aloud.

The woman backed into a wall of stacked, wooden crates. She sobbed, desperately looking to her right and then her left for a path of escape, but Jove was too close to her now. She screamed as he moved to within an inch of her face. They always did that too, screamed. But he liked it when they screamed.

"Shh," Jove said softly as he traced the woman's cheek with his fingers.

As with anything else he touched, the woman began to wither. Her skin wrinkled, her eyes shriveled, and before Jove could kiss her, she was nothing more than a skeleton wrapped in a thin layer of dried flesh.

He batted the woman away with his hand, a spray of ash exploding from the desiccated corpse as it fell to the ground. So, there was a drawback to his new power. He would no longer be able to enjoy the thrills he had become accustomed to. Well, no matter. The feeling of taking the very life of another creature was more than enough to compensate. And drinking pure Apeiron magnified that a hundred-fold.

Jove licked his lips as he turned to stare off in the direction the guard had indicated he could find a city with an Apeira well. A hundred miles? He stroked his chin. How long would it take to walk that? He looked around and almost unconsciously shot out a tendril to catch a soldier trying to sneak past him. The infusion of life rushed over him, and he smiled.

It wouldn't take long if he didn't stop to eat. He didn't have to stop to eat, he realized. He could just feed on everything as he marched toward the Apeira well. That would keep him fully energized, and hold him over until he could again taste that maddeningly addicting Apeiron. Jove giggled and turned to leave, wishing he had time to set the outpost on fire.

CHAPTER 38

J ekaran...

Jekaran...

Wake up, Jekaran...

Jekaran opened his eyes, shadows and a blur of brown resolving into a ceiling made of splintered wood. Then the pain overwhelmed him. His senses reported it from almost every inch of his battered body: sharp stabs, hot burns, and dull aches all combining together in a horrible symphony of suffering. He groaned, two pains in particular winning the bid for his immediate attention. One was in his left arm; a dull throbbing that shot sharp bolts of pain-lightning each time he tried to move. The other was a steady pounding from the back of his head that was so acute it made him feel like vomiting.

Jekaran tried to focus on his surroundings, but turning his head or moving at all proved to be too difficult. Where am I?

We are on a ship, someone answered him.

Jekaran snapped his head up and instantly regretted it. He fell back down onto his pallet, pain blinding him and making him dry-heave. He would've retched if he had anything in his stomach, but it was empty as was made evident by its near constant rumbling. Although he hadn't seen much in the split second he tried to sit up, he had seen enough to know that there was no one in the room with him.

Not a room, a cell. He had seen the black-lacquered metal bars.

It is called a brig, the voice in his head repeated.

That's when Jekaran recognized it. It was the sword, and it was talking to him in full sentences.

Where are you? Jekaran asked reflexively.

Locked in the captain's quarters.

Since when did you start talking? Jekaran raised his right hand and began to gingerly massage his closed eyelids.

I am not talking, the sword replied.

You know what I mean!

While you have been unconscious, I have been examining your memories, learning much of you and your language.

That disturbed Jekaran. How long have I been out? He asked.

Since just before we left Imaris–two days, I believe.

That's when it all came back to him, a torrent of memories flooding into his brain: being ambushed by Gymal, running from the giant crystal golem, fighting Kaul and...

"Kairah!" Jekaran called out. The pain in his head flared at the movement of his jaw and vibration of his voice. When last he had seen the Allosian woman, she had fallen off the pier and was drowning in the sea.

She is on this vessel.

Jekaran gritted his teeth until the pounding in his head returned to a lesser throbbing. Is she alive?

Yes, the sword said, but weak.

"What happened?" Jekaran asked aloud, as much to himself as to the sword.

Another voice answered him this time–a human voice. "You damn near got yourself killed, brother Ulan. That's what happened."

The voice belonged to Hort.

"I figured out that much," he said. "And it's Jekaran, not Ulan."

Hort chuckled. "I think I'll stick to calling you Brother Ulan."

"Well, it would be stupid for me to argue with a trained soldier."

Hort laughed. "Which one of us is a trained soldier? I watched you duel that man with the flame ring. Damnedest thing I ever saw."

Jekaran actually heard himself chuckling, which also hurt his head. "I had a bit of help."

"The sword talis," Hort said. "Now I know why it was so important to you. A lot of men would kill for a treasure like that."

A worrisome thought occurred to him. "Is that why you're here? To kill for the sword?"

Jekaran started as Hort bellowed a laugh. "By Rasheera's breasts, no! I'm old enough to know trouble when I see it. Something tells me it wouldn't be worth it."

Was it worth it? He had thrilled with the power the sword bestowed upon him, and actually enjoyed the feeling of destroying his enemies. But was it worth never being alone with his thoughts? Was it worth the mortal danger it attracted? Was it worth losing control of his own body? Was it worth losing his very soul?

But that dance leads only to the soul-less grave, Ez's phantom voice suddenly echoed the last line of that blasted poem.

The idea of death ignited a renewed worry for Kairah and Jekaran blurted out, "The Allosian woman!"

"Don't worry she's alive, just unconscious," Hort said. "We're all on a ship sailing to Aiested. Your little girlfriend said the fey woman needed an Apeira well, or she would die. But don't worry, we'll be docking at the capitol by tonight, and Aiested's well is said to be so large that it radiates Apeira five miles out to sea. So she should start getting the help she needs before long. Your little girlfriend also told us that the fey woman has an important warning to deliver to the king. Something about one of her kind trying to start a new talis war."

Hort's report that Kairah would soon be receiving an infusion of Apeiron loosened the knot in his chest. "And Maely? Is she on board?"

"That your little girlfriend's name?" Hort asked. "Gymal let her go. She's a spitfire, ain't she?"

"Yeah," Jekaran massaged his right temple.

"You're welcome, by the way," Hort said.

"For what?"

"Who do you think tended your wounds?"

That's when Jekaran noticed that his left arm was stuffed into a sling, and his head was wrapped tightly in bandages.

"I was a field medic when I was about your age, and a damned good one too. I even considered joining your brethren so that I could become a healer."

"I'm not–" Jekaran began.

"I know, I know, you're not a real monk." Hort chuckled.

"I'm sorry, but I can't really picture you selflessly ministering to the sick."

"It's true."

Jekaran heard the creaking of floorboards and rustling of chain mail as Hort stood up. When next he spoke, he was closer, probably right outside Jekaran's cell.

"I didn't join the king's army by choice, you know. Like many young men, I was conscripted. I had scarcely a week of training when a sword was shoved into my hands, and I was ordered to kill, so you can imagine how shocked I was when I saw all of that violence. I seemed to take it harder than my fellow soldiers did. It made me want to do something about it, and becoming a healer seemed the best way to do that."

"So, why didn't you?"

"Not sure."

Jekaran heard the shrug in Hort's voice.

"Guess I just got used to the killing."

"I don't know how you could." Jekaran gagged as he remembered the reeking viscera of the bandits in Rasha strewn about on the cobblestones of the bridge. That had been the first time he had used the sword, and although he had been defending himself, the carnage he'd wrought still haunted him.

"You'd be surprised," Hort said.

"So why bother fixing me up? Isn't that a bit like washing a chicken on its way to the chopping block?"

Hort chuckled. "Maybe. But I like you, Ulan. You remind me of someone I used to know."

"And who's that?" Jekaran asked, but he didn't get an answer. The sound of a wooden door banging open reverberated painfully through his head, followed by a familiar nasal voice.

"He's awake?" Gymal called to Hort.

"You have a signal talis," Jekaran accused Hort in a low voice.

"Yes, Lord Gymal," Hort called back and then shifted to a whisper. "He wanted to know the moment you regained consciousness. He is still my employer after all," he added in a tone that was both defensive and apologetic.

The swishing of cloth and creaking floorboards told Jekaran Gymal was approaching. "I wasn't certain you would wake up at all."

"Disappointed?"

Gymal sighed. "Why do you insist on making every one of our dealings confrontational?"

"Why do you insist on being an ass?" Jekaran knew it was childish, but he didn't care. He wasn't in the mood to deal with the weaselly little lord.

"You peasants are all the same," Gymal snapped. "You think the nobility is always looking down on you. Well, we do, but not in the way you think. We look down on you the way a parent looks down on its child. You have no idea what I do to protect and prosper the lowborn under my care. The burden of making sure my children survive and behave is heavier than you'll ever know."

"Well aren't you the suffering hero?" Jekaran made sure the words were dripping with sarcasm.

Gymal sighed again. "That sword talis has only added to your insufferable arrogance." He paused, and then said, "Speaking of which, how did you come by that talis? I know you wouldn't have the coin to purchase it on the black market. Such a powerful talis would be worth a small fortune. That makes me think that someone gave it to you. Someone in your village."

Jekaran's bravado evaporated. Ez!

He had just saved his uncle from the Rikujo and wasn't about to give him up as a target for the law. He had to think of a lie—and quick. Something that would sound possible, and throw Gymal off the line of thinking he was pursuing. A line of thinking that would fast lead the man to the truth. Gymal may be a horrible person, but he wasn't stupid. Jekaran needed to remember that.

"Kairah!" he suddenly blurted out.

"The Alloslan woman?"

"Yes," Jekaran said. "She said she needed a guide to the capitol and someone to protect her. I met her in Rasha, and that's where she hired me and gave me the sword."

Gymal was silent for a long time before finally saying, "That sounds surprisingly plausible. Though I am certain you are not being completely honest with me."

"Guess you'll just have to take my word for it, unless you have an oath collar." That was stupid, Jekaran berated himself. What if Gymal did have an oath collar?

"No," Gymal drawled, and his tone sounded thoughtful. "Those are quite expensive."

Jekaran's sudden worry faded.

"But the king is certain to have one."

Damn it! "What's going to happen to me?" Jekaran rasped, and he was angry at how frightened he sounded.

"If what you say about the Allosian woman giving you the sword is true, then you will likely not be facing execution. Beyond that, I don't know."

Give your will to me, and I will free us.

Jekaran flashbacked to feeling his body move outside of his control while he was a prisoner in his own mind. "No!" he snapped.

"No, what?" The man's tone sounded confused.

I will never let you have control again! He projected to the sword. *You nearly got me killed!*

But, I destroyed your enemies. The sword said.

Jekaran could feel its hurt confusion. "Nine hundred ninety-seven. Nine hundred ninety-four..." he whispered, slipping back into Kairah's trick for keeping control of his bond with the sword.

"You said his brain was not damaged," Gymal accused Hort.

"I believe I said," Hort coolly responded, "that it was likely not damaged."

"Keep watching him and signal me if he lapses back into a coma!"

Why did Gymal care if he was hurt? Why did the man care if he even lived?

"Yes, my lord."

Gymal walked away, the slamming door jolting Jekaran's head once more.

Chapter 39

Tyrus Gymal, baron of Saldren and junior heir to the house of Myadra, shut the door to the brig behind him, perhaps a little harder than he had intended. Seeing Jekaran battered and still half-dazed had shaken him, and he offered a prayer to Rasheera for the boy's complete recovery.

He ground his teeth in frustration as he climbed a narrow set of stairs that were really no more than warped wooden rungs of a slanted ladder. The boy was making his job difficult. First with that business in Rasha–he had paid the magistrate an obscene bribe in order to keep Jekaran from being hanged–and again when they were in the western rock lands. Then there was the catastrophe in Imaris. Tyrus had been certain Jekaran was going to be killed by that fire-flinging madman, and it had only been the boy's miraculous swordplay that saved him. And saved me.

Oh, Kybon. It should be you doing this, not me.

After ascending three narrow staircases, he emerged onto the deck of the ship. He had to squint as his eyes adjusted to the new morning's sunlight. Tyrus made his way past a pair of hung-over sailors grumbling about something. The cool ocean breeze was refreshing, and for the first time in years, Tyrus' nose was clear. He breathed in deeply, relishing his unobstructed nasal passages. As he rounded the cabin that led below deck, he caught sight of something tall in the distance. It had to be tall for him to see it this far from shore, but then again the Apeira well was said to be the largest in all of Shaelar.

"Aiested," he whispered. They were almost there. If I can see the well, does that mean we're close enough to drink in its energy? Tyrus looked down at his chest where he hung his dousing stone. To his disappointment, the medallion-set amethyst was still dark.

Tyrus strode toward the stern of the ship where the captain's quarters of the Queen's Honor was situated. Tyrus snorted. Giving an old galleon a fresh coat of paint, and dressing its crew in uniformed livery did not make it a luxury liner; though the price Tyrus had paid made him feel like he had booked passage on one. He ascended the four steps to the door of the captain's quarters, fished in the right pocket of his robe for the key, and then unlocked and entered the cabin.

The interior was wood paneling decorated by hand-drawn maps adorning the walls. The only furniture not bolted to the floor was a few chairs, none of which were very comfortable to sit in. Tyrus pocketed the key and walked to a cabinet hanging on the wall to his right. He opened it, snatched a glass decanter filled with amber liquid, and took a long pull right from the bottle.

Haeshalan brandy was a rare find and technically illegal in Aiested. Tyrus would be sure to remind the captain of that should he take issue with his involuntary sharing of it. Tyrus put the bottle back and closed the cabinet.

He surveyed the small cabin while enjoying the warmth that bloomed in his chest. It had cost him an additional fifty silver Aies to rent the quarters from the captain. Normally guest quarters suited him just fine–Tyrus never had been one to indulge in comfort for its own sake–but he needed a secure place to stow the sword–and her.

He looked through an open door at his right to the room's sleeping quarters. Lying on a feather-stuffed mattress was the most beautiful woman he had ever seen. With skin as pale as ivory and hair impossibly the same color as translucent amethyst stone, the woman was an Allosian. An actual Allosian; one of the fey folk of legend!

Tyrus walked to stand just outside the doorway to the sleeping room. The Allosian woman– Kairah, Jekaran had named her–slept peacefully. He was embarrassed that she still wore her damp dress; it made the silk cling to her skin in several immodest ways, but he didn't have any maid-servants about to tend to the woman. And he wouldn't even think of being so crass as to change her clothing himself. Tyrus became conscious of staring at Kairah's form and quickly turned away, cheeks feeling hot and not from the brandy.

He walked away from the sleeping room and sat down in one of the hard wooden chairs. Yes, he had definitely over-paid for the comfort of using the captain's quarters. Perhaps that justified his polishing off that bottle of Haeshalan brandy. Tyrus made to stand but stopped as his eyes fell on the pommel of the weapon-talis sticking out from underneath his bags.

He slid off the chair to kneel next to it, and carefully drew the sword out. It was a very strange piece of talis-craft, like nothing he had ever seen before. An oval-shaped amethyst was set in the middle of the cross-guard and the tapered blade was dotted with tiny emeralds.

This is connected to Jekaran somehow. He had learned that the moment he had tried to use the talis. Tyrus supposed that made sense. While he had never seen a weapon talis that bonded its wielder, he knew of other kinds of talises that did similar things; the blood seeker that he had used to track Jekaran to Imaris for example. That posed a singular problem. If he was to present it to the king, then the connection would need to be broken. With the blood seeker, it was a simple matter of feeding it a new blood sample. Perhaps the sword worked like that? Perhaps Jekaran could willingly pass the bond to another. Tyrus didn't even want to think about what it would mean if Jekaran couldn't give it up.

Oh, Kybon. He shook his head. Why hadn't his cousin been content to marry the viscount's daughter? Life would've been so much easier and their family's status elevated had he just done his duty. Tyrus had never had any problem attending to his duties. But then again, he hadn't ever had those kinds of opportunities, he being a hopeless case when it came to attracting women.

"I'm in love with her, Ty," his cousin had affirmed. "High society will never offer me the kind of joy that I feel by just staring into her eyes."

It had all been nauseatingly romantic, but then again Tyrus' cousin had always been led more by his heart than his brain. Tyrus smiled wanly at the memory of embarrassingly bad love sonnets his cousin had tried to compose.

"Your eyes are like really blue and deep water," he whispered with a chuckle.

Between the two of them, Tyrus had been the scholar, excelling as a student as much as Kybon excelled as an athlete. In the end, Kybon had prevailed upon him to write to the peasant girl in his name. They had been as different as night and day; Kybon tall, handsome, and attracted to adventure, and Tyrus short, homely, and completely apathetic to the world outside his books. Yet they had been close, more like brothers than cousins.

The boy is just like him, down to that insufferable arrogance and a tendency to act without forethought. The only difference was the color of his eyes–green. No one in their line had green eyes, at least as far back as Tyrus had followed the genealogy.

Light–soft, purple, and dim–began to emanate from his chest. The dousing stone was beginning to glow. He looked up from his position on the floor, through the doorway at the sleeping Allosian woman. She would be receiving a trickle of Apeiron now. How much did she need to heal? How long before she would wake?

Tyrus stood, and shook out the pins and needles in his right leg as he hobbled toward the sleeping chamber. Again, he stopped just outside the room. For some reason it felt inappropriate for him to move any closer to her. And it wasn't just for the sake of propriety. Tyrus didn't want to admit it to himself, but he was afraid of the fey woman. He needed her to wake for the sake of the message that she bore, but he had seen some of what she could do. She was powerful in a way that wasn't....well, wasn't human.

She stirred, and Tyrus held his breath in anticipation of her waking, but she remained unconscious. However, he could see some life coming back into her already pale face. She moaned softly, causing him to take a wary step backward. Tyrus could see movement underneath her closed eyelids. That hadn't happened before. The only sign of life she had displayed was slow, shallow breathing. Now it appeared that she was dreaming. Was that a good sign? Tyrus decided that it was.

Kairah stood on a beach she didn't recognize. Gentle wind fluttered the fabric of her dress and tickled her eyes with strands of her loose hair. She brushed it out of her face and looked behind her. An endless, rolling sea softly churned and frothed. She turned back and took a step forward. The wet sand molded to her bare feet as she moved away from the tide line and up a sandy incline.

How had she come to be here? The last thing she remembered was Jekaran destroying the crystal golem. *I slipped into unconsciousness.* She worked through the memory. *And fell into the sea.* Could that be how she had ended up on this beach? She looked around again, but nothing was familiar and she couldn't see any signs of civilization anywhere on the coast.

Kairah gasped as she crested the sandy hill and froze. The sight before her was awesome in its terribleness. Hundreds of miles of barren rock lay before her beneath a sky of roiling black clouds. It was a scene of emptiness and death the likes of which she had never before seen.

"Where am I?" she whispered aloud, but the eerie quiet of this place made Kairah feel like she was shouting.

She took a tentative step off the soft sand and onto the black rock ground. Intuitively, she knew that nothing lived here, not a single blade of grass, scurrying insect, or tiny microbe. The land was truly dead in every sense of the word. Kairah took two more steps, the bare ground scraping the soft tissue of her feet. She ignored it as best she could and continued to make her way across the ground.

Mountains rose in the distance, black things devoid of any greenery. Nor were their peaks capped by snow like they ought to have been. They didn't resemble any of the mountains with which Kairah was familiar, and she had a superior knowledge of Shaelar's topography. A flash of green lightning washed over the dead landscape, quickly followed by an angry clap of thunder. *Green lightning?* She reflexively reached out for Aeva but stopped. The distance between the two of them would be too great for communication. She was alone here.

Kairah stopped walking and surveyed the black land. Another flash of emerald lightning lit up the sky and revealed something else in the distance. She strained her eyes at the horizon, but it wasn't until a third flash of lightning streaked across the sky that she was able to see it–a city.

It looked to be a large city; its buildings made of white stone set in architecture not unlike those of Allose.

The sight of something familiar rallied Kairah's courage, and she quickly moved off in the direction of the city. All of her senses continued to report a total absence of life, but she wanted to see the city to know for herself. It wasn't impossible someone dwelt in that city although she should be able to sense it. But then again, her core felt unusually cold and vulnerable, meaning that her Apeiron was very nearly exhausted. That could impact her ability to sense other life even from a sizable population if the distance was great enough.

Kairah lifted the fringe of her dress and began jogging. The black rock landscape cut her feet, and soon her footprints were wet with blood, but she ignored it. Something beyond her sight drove her toward the distant city, and it seemed to Kairah that she ran upon the very threads of fate.

She had to get to that city. There she would find something, something she had long searched for. Answers, the city held answers. She wasn't sure how she knew this, she just did; the same way one knows an abstract fact in a dream. She just knew.

Chapter 40

Stoic, Prince Raelen Lesta Taris stood at parade-rest next to his father's throne as he watched the men of the court file in. As was typical, the group of lords and generals were lost in a milieu of conversation that blended together into a dull roar–like a waterfall, Raelen thought. He glanced to the side and out one of the throne room's tall, narrow windows.

It had been weeks since his father had allowed him to take a trip into the northern woods, and the stress of palace life was making Raelen itch for another hunting trip. He had to call it that in order to convince his father to allow him outside of Aiested. It just wouldn't do for the king to have his firstborn son–the crown prince of the realm–taking trips into the forest solely as a kindness to his Ursaj servant, Gryyth.

Raelen glanced to the back of the room where an eight-foot-tall figure stood. He was covered from head to foot in smooth, white fur with a charcoal grey muzzle and azure eyes. The bear-man wore a fine tunic over his fur and a small spike through his ear. The earring was gold capped by an amethyst jewel–a slave awl. A talis connected to a companion ring worn by the king allowed Raelen's father to dominate the bear-man along with several others.

That had never sat quite right with Raelen when he was a child, and only became worse as he grew older. It was when he had actually started to talk to, not command, but to talk to Gryyth that Raelen began to understand that the Ursaj was not a willing servant. No, the bear-man was a slave.

"But slaving is illegal," he remembered his eleven-year-old self protesting to his father.

"That law is for men, not animals," his father had replied. "And Ursaj are fierce animals!"

The king had gone on to warn Raelen that if Gryyth were free of his slave talis, he wouldn't hesitate to claw Raelen into raw meat and he devour him. Raelen recalled having stayed away from Gryyth for several days because of his father's graphic description of what the Ursaj would do to him if it had the chance.

That fear became progressively more ridiculous each time the boy Raelen had looked into Gryyth's bright blue eyes. They were not the eyes of a ferocious monster, hunger making it eagerly strain against its restraints in hopes of breaking free in an explosion of blood and violence. No, those eyes were kind, and every bit as human as Raelen's own eyes.

It was then that Raelen had begun to notice a quiet sadness in his Ursaj servant. It was always so with the white bear-man, except when Raelen could take him into the forest to run, hunt, and climb trees. That seemed to provide Gryyth with some relief, and so Raelen took as many hunting trips as his father would allow.

As his official protector, Gryyth had been continually in the prince's presence as long as Raelen could remember. He loved the bear-man's booming voice as it told him the lore of his people, and he often slept in those huge furry arms when he was small. No, if there was a monster in the palace, it wasn't Gryyth. Raelen turned to his left where his father sat straight-backed upon his ivory throne.

King Raeleth Joran Taris the eighteenth was the very picture of kingly dignity. His handsome face was square-ish in shape, with a black beard that lined a jaw that looked cut from stone. His nose was slightly angular, and his brow beetled, but not in a way that subtracted from his good looks. But it was Raelen's father's eyes most people noted; stern, cold things that could shake even a hard man with their penetrating stare. Yes, Raelen's father appeared every bit the image of the gallant-looking statues that lined both sides of the throne room. And he acted the part superbly well.

Diction, formality, and strict emotional control were the King's most notable qualities, attributes he expected mirrored to perfection in his children. Failure to adhere to the King's impossibly high standards resulted in severe corporeal consequences when Raelen and his siblings were children, and more subtle punishments as they grew older. His older sister, Saranna, had served as his father's greatest warning example in that regard.

Prone to fits of rebellious defiance, Saranna had no fear of calling into question their father's strict and sometimes contradictory expectations. The king mostly abided Saranna's fits, as he was wont to call them, chalking them up to her monthly bout of feminine insanity. Not that they would ever go unpunished, but the punishments were not physical, not after Saranna began to become a woman.

No, it was against Raelen's father's code to strike a woman, although he had no such compunctions about striking his sons. Instead, he would publically humiliate Raelen's sister, preferably in front of her suitors. Once, the king even went so far as to have Saranna's diary stolen from her quarters, a particularly delicate passage copied, and then distributed amongst the nobility. Saranna had been so angry and embarrassed, she'd sequestered herself in her quarters for nearly two months.

The final offense that had won Saranna the full measure of their father's wrath, and taught the other children just how far the king would go in the severity of his punishments, came when she exploded at him before the court. Raelen didn't doubt the spectacle had been planned by his sister, for it had come on a day when the king was addressing a full assembly of his advisers among the military and nobility. And since such assemblies only occurred once every three months, Raelen knew Saranna had at least been thinking about it if not actively planning it.

He couldn't remember what the actual conflict had been about. No, all he remembered was the deep scarlet his father's face had flushed as Saranna aired their dirty laundry for all to see. His sister had all but accused their father of causing their mother's untimely death by his habit of fathering bastard children with a variety of mistresses. Saranna had even gone so far as to hint that not all of the king's extra marital affairs had been with women.

The consequences had been quicker than Raelen anticipated. Two days following the incident, Saranna had been married off to a duke four times her age, one who lived at the furthest edge of the kingdom. It all happened so fast that Raelen hadn't even had a chance to say goodbye.

He awoke one morning to find Saranna's room emptied, a cool, business-like announcement made by their father at the breakfast table the only word on the matter. It was less than a year later Raelen received the news Saranna had committed suicide by throwing herself off an eighth-story balcony. Even that had not been enough to turn Raelen against his father, loyal son that he was. No. It was the way the king took the news that did that.

There were no tears, no anguished words of regret, not even a formal retreat into private to mourn with the rest of the family. The king, Raelen's father, had taken the news with the same emotion he would at being told what he was to be served for supper.

It was then Raelen had started to hate his father.

Raelen's younger brothers dealt with Saranna's loss in different ways, but the eventual result had been the same. They all left the palace to live elsewhere, leaving Raelen alone with their father–a man Raelen despised, but at the same time was forced to respect. He had thought about leaving too; perhaps captaining a sailing expedition to find the legendary old land, but he couldn't. He was the crown prince of Aiestal. He had a duty to his family and their people. And so Raelen suffered in quiet, Gryyth his only confidant on the matter.

"Come to order!" the chamberlain sounded over the milieu of talking. The order didn't have to be repeated as the group of officials fell immediately and obediently silent. The mere presence of Raelen's father had that effect on people.

"His royal highness, King Raeleth Joran Taris the eighteenth, has summoned you to this council to answer the new threat posed by the nation of Haeshala."

That announcement inspired a new round of conversation, which promptly miscarried when the king cleared his throat. Raelen, of course, knew of the matter. His father had counseled–well, more like informed–him about it days ago.

That was an odd intimacy the two of them shared; a trust Raelen had never seen his father place in any of his other children. He had always assumed it was because he was the crown prince and future king of the realm, and needed to be included in such matters in case of an unexpected succession crisis. That caused Raelen a pang of guilt.

There were times, when his grieving over Saranna had been so overpowering, he had wished for an unexpected succession crisis. Upon first hearing of his sister's suicide, he'd actually flirted with the idea of being the cause of such a crisis. But no, Raelen was not a murderer no matter how angry he was with his father. Gryyth's continual schooling in the Ursaj's Seiro, or path of righteousness, had ground that sense of honor into him.

"Cubs are to do no violence to their sires, or to the memory of their ancestors," the bear-man had reminded Raelen when, in a moment of rage, he had given voice to his murderous fantasies.

"Welcome back Navarch Pariel," the chamberlain said as he motioned to someone in the crowd.

A tall, stoic man stepped forward and bowed to the king. His head was shorn after the military fashion, and he was dressed in a full suit of gleaming silver armor. He wore no sword; such was not allowed in the presence of the king. Upon his tabard was two swords embroidered crossed over an Apeira well, the family crest of Raelen's house.

Raelen had known Pariel for all of his young life–eighteen short years–and even trained with the man on occasion. Other than that, he did not know him well. He seemed to Raelen an unremarkable fixture in his father's court.

That was until last year when he won some notoriety for finding an ancient Allosian airship, a complex piece of talis craft that could actually fly. Pariel reported finding the ancient treasure while on a routine Ursaj acquisition patrol in the northern forest.

Although damaged, it wasn't inoperable, and the king's polymaths were able to fix most of the damage and return it to working order. Raelen himself had named it–White Hawk.

Raelen's father had promoted Pariel as a reward, making him the chief pilot of the airship and Aiestal's only Sky Navarch. As they only had one airship, the title was mostly honorary. Since then, the king had entrusted Pariel with progressively more important missions, the latest being a reconnaissance trip to spy on the neighboring kingdom of Haeshala.

"I bring word from the east," Pariel said with a smooth articulation that belied his gruff appearance.

"Speak," the king ordered formally.

"Prince Isara's armies are raiding our border towns. Your citizens are retreating further into the kingdom, and their reports are most troubling."

"How so?" Raelen's father asked.

Pariel continued, "The villagers claim they saw no armies, but fires descended from the sky, setting their homes ablaze. The flames were well beyond their capacity to quench, and so they retreated."

"Weapon talises," Raelen thought aloud and then cringed when his father shot him a reproving glare. Not even the crown prince could speak in court without the king's permission.

"That was my conclusion as well, my prince," Pariel said with a nod to Raelen.

"Prelude to an invasion or just an intimidation tactic?" the king asked Pariel.

"I believe it to be both, Highness," Pariel said. "I surmise that Prince Isara is testing us, goading us to respond in kind so that he can evaluate the number and power of our own weapon talises."

"Then the goddess has delivered us in our time of need!" another voice rang throughout the chamber. It was accompanied by an audible gasp at the offense to decorum.

A man among the king's soldiers and advisors stepped forward. He quickly went down to one knee before the throne, head bowed so low it was difficult for Raelen to hear his next words.

"I speak out of turn, but I am certain you will forgive the impropriety, Highness, when you hear what I have to say."

The man was Loeadon, one of the king's polymaths. He was tall and thin, with long black hair that fell nearly to his waist. He wore the traditional grey robes worn by scholars of the kingdom, and had three ring talises that he called attention to with exaggerated hand movements.

Loeadon was younger than his fellow polymaths were–appearing to be in his early forties–and was the newest member of their cadre. But by virtue of his unusual brilliance and impressive knowledge of talis-craft, he had risen to the rank of spokesman in less than two years. He was also an insufferable sycophant.

"I should hope so, Loeadon," the king said.

Loeadon bobbed a bow before raising his head. Without breaking his gaze, he stood and waved for one of the other polymaths to bring something forward. A fat man in grey robes waddled up carrying an ancient-looking tome he handed over to Loeadon.

"This book was in the hold of the ship Navarch Pariel discovered last year." Loeadon handed the tome to the chamberlain who, after a brief inspection, passed it onto the king. Raelen's father opened the tome and flipped through its pages. Although the book had to be ancient, the pages looked to be in pristine condition. No fading, or tears, and they were as malleable as though they were newly bound.

It's an Allosian bound book.

"Yes," the king said thoughtfully, "I remember inspecting this. The writing is in the language of the Allosians." King Raeleth looked up at Loeadon. "Have you finished translating it?"

Loeadon nodded eagerly. "It is a work detailing the process for creating talises."

The king closed the book and handed it back to his chamberlain. "No doubt a scholar's find of unparalleled worth, but not of much practical use without the ability to spell-cast. I am disappointed, Loeadon. This was not something urgent enough to justify a breach in the protocol of my court. I am afraid that as punishment, I will have to bar you from my presence for a term of–"

"–this was found with it," Loeadon interrupted, something that was followed by another collection of scandalized gasps. The polymath produced an object from within his robes–a circlet. It was made of what looked like ivory, and featured a large, circular cut amethyst in the center.

"What is it?" Raelen's father asked, his curiosity having suspended any anger at being disrespected in front of the entire court; something that could very well have earned Loeadon a one-way trip to the gallows.

Brave man. Raelen began to see Loeadon in a new light. *Or else that talis he's holding is something remarkable.* It turned out to be the latter.

"This is a talis that allows a human—" he spoke the word as though he were not "—to spell-cast like one of the fey folk."

That produced an explosion of indistinguishable chatter. Raelen turned to study the king's face for a sign of what the man was thinking. It was something of a guessing game Raelen had developed early on in his childhood in order to gauge his father's moods, and know just how much he could get away with. His father hadn't known they were playing, but even so, he had proved a challenging opponent. Even after a decade, Raelen could only guess correctly one out of every three times.

This time he guessed that his father's awe at Loeadon's revelation had snuffed out the king's mounting displeasure. Raelen was also certain his father was entertaining a thousand possibilities of what the circlet and the book could mean for Aiestal; an unending production of new weapon talises, and even a fleet of airships. Loeadon had gambled with his life, but it appeared the gamble had paid off.

His father's look changed–lowering brow, tightening jaw, and eyes that stared straight ahead as if into the future. That meant that the gross disregard for the solemnity of his court was again stirring his irritation. He cleared his throat and again the room immediately fell silent.

"I do not recall seeing it when we found The White Hawk." The king reached out and Loeadon handed the circlet to him directly, bypassing an aggravated looking chamberlain.

"Nor does it appear in the ledgers of the original cataloging."

The king looked up at him. "How is this?"

Loeadon bobbed another obsequious half-bow. "As I said, a gift from the goddess in our time of need."

"Or one of your men simply overlooked it."

The smile faded from Loeadon's face, and he quickly bobbed his head in acceptance. Raelen inwardly chuckled. It had been an admirable attempt.

"Navarch Pariel." Raelen's father turned to look on the armored soldier. The man had a perfectly professional blank soldier's look on his face.

He is also a hard one to read. Perhaps he had found a new player for his secret game.

"How long before Isara commits to a true offensive?"

"Impossible to say," Pariel replied. "A year perhaps? Sooner if we do nothing to strike back now."

The king nodded to himself as if he were confirming a thought. He then turned again to Loeadon. The man's self-satisfied expression was gone, replaced by one of nervous uncertainty. "Loeadon, how long would it take to puzzle out how to create a plague box?"

A plague box? Those were horrific weapon talises credited in the histories with inflicting immeasurable death and sorrow. Not a terribly effective weapon as their range was limited, and human immune systems apparently adapted quickly to the sickness, but they were nasty things.

Loeadon's eyes darted to the tome still held by the chamberlain, and then at Pariel. "Such a work of talis-craft would be very complex. We were planning on starting with something a little simpler, like a flame ring or a shield amulet."

"Can you do it?" the king asked evenly, with the subtle undercurrent of an ultimatum.

Loeadon hesitated and then bobbed his head. "I believe so."

"How long will it take?" the king demanded.

Again Loeadon looked like he was standing on the very edge of a cliff, looking down at a thousand foot drop. "Perhaps six months."

"You have four weeks," the king said. "I want to be ready to strike at the heart of Haeshala should Isara respond with a full-scale assault."

Loeadon's face drained of color. "Yes, Highness," The polymath bowed.

The king leaned forward in his throne and stared at another soldier in the group. This one was much older than Pariel, with long, white hair and a polished chest plate that likely hadn't seen battle in twenty years. The man was Osarr Rakahnas, Aiestal's supreme military commander.

"Polemarch," the king addressed Rakahnas.

"Yes, Highness." The old soldier straightened and adopted the blank look Pariel had been showing.

"Isara's insult cannot go unanswered. I want you to order three banners of infantry, two squads of knights, and our flame casters to march to the Haeshala border."

"Secure the border? Of course, Your Highness. I will begin–"

"No, Osarr," the king cut in. "I want you to lay waste to all Haeshalan towns along the border, and make certain each town is burned so that nothing remains save a smoldering ruin. We will pay Haeshala back in kind."

"Yes, Highness," Rakahnas replied.

"And Osarr," the king added, "leave only one witness, a man able to carry the tidings to Isara."

Isara let our people retreat! Raelen clenched his teeth to stop himself from blurting out the thought. He caught Gryyth's eyes, and the bear-man bowed his head as if to say "this was not Seiro."

The settlements on the border would likely be made up of merchants and farmers–and their wives and children. And Raelen's father would slaughter them all. In spite of this, Raelen knew that his father, hard hearted though he was, was not a cruel man. His order to kill the people of the Haeshalan border towns was likely not to satisfy a sadistic need for blood.

No, it would be simple calculation. His father didn't see the people as anything more than capital. In the king's eyes, it was simple: Isara stole from him, and so he would seize re-payment–with interest.

Raelen fought back the sick feeling rising into his throat. The etiquette of his father's court would certainly be flouted if he were to vomit in front of the assembly just seconds after the king gave a distasteful order. He mentally chanted one of Gryyth's meditation mantras.

> *I am a clear brook flowing among the trees.*
> *I am a meadow of clover in summer.*
> *I am the moon silently watching the night.*

It had the effect of driving back his nausea, but not his anger.

Raelen clenched his teeth and trained his gaze on Loeadon. He stared hard at the polymath and was surprised at what looked like a slight smirk on the man's otherwise ashen face.

CHAPTER

41

Ezra studied the charred boards of the Imarin docks. He was trying to sift through the rumors and piece together what really had happened here two days ago, but needed to be careful asking direct questions. Else he'd draw the attention of the city guard, who were all still on high alert.

Some of the people said the excitement and destruction were the work of a man possessed with a demon and that he could throw fire and was untouchable. Others spoke of a gigantic glass statue that moved as though it were alive, tearing up the streets and wreaking havoc. The story of the demon was clearly an exaggerated description of Kaul, but the giant?

Ridiculous. Just the tale-telling of drunk sailors and bored goodwives.

"Maybe that's where the goodwives heard the tale," Irvis said with a wink when Ezra had voiced the thought earlier. "Maybe they weren't such good wives." The comment was laughably incongruous with the chubby man's new set of monk robes. Why did he insist on procuring new ones? He'd left the order, hadn't he?

No, Kaul was definitely here, and if the gossip of the guards was true, he was dead. That rumor really troubled Ezra; there was only one weapon that could've slain Kaul while that madman possessed so many powerful talises.

The sword.

Jekaran could only have survived a duel with Kaul if he'd fought with the sword. Irvis had already told Ezra how Jekaran came to bond the sword, and how he had used it to escape Gymal's well-finder camp, but if his nephew had used it again... How many times did Ezra use the weapon before it began to take over?

It was the third time.

Ezra–no, Argentus–had been competing for a thousand gold Aies in an illegal dueling tournament. After going undefeated for several matches, he was challenged by a renowned sword master so skilled, the only way he'd been able to defeat him was by giving the sword what it demanded–his will.

Doing so had turned him into an eagerly efficient killer, and he ended up not only spilling the blood of his opponent, but of all the man's allies, and then the other contestants in the arena. And the killing hadn't stopped there.

No! He shoved the memory back down. Not right now. He hadn't dared revisit the details of what had happened that night. Even remembering as far as he just had made him want to vomit. Although he recoiled from the locked memory, something seemed to urge him to remember.

He'd always thought it was Rasheera's spirit trying to help him face what he'd done, and sometimes it actually did feel like there was someone whispering to his mind. He shook his head as if the rattling of his brain would realign his thoughts.

"Argentus?" Irvis asked.

Ezra looked up at his old friend, his cheeks feeling flushed. He quickly looked back at the ground to hide his embarrassment. "He was here."

"Kaul?" Irvis asked. "Well, we knew that."

"No," Ezra said softly, "My nephew."

Irvis' meaty hand rested on his shoulder. "Don't be so hard on yourself, Argentus."

"I gave it to him," Ezra growled. "I gave him that cursed thing! And now it's going to turn him into a monster–like me."

"You were hardly a monster, old friend," Irvis said.

Ezra whirled on him. "What about that night at the arena?" The harshness of Ezra's voice made Mulladin start to blubber nervously.

"Argentus– "

"How can you say I am not a monster?"

Ezra sank to the cobblestones and gripped the sides of his head with his hands. Now Mulladin was crying.

"Hush," Irvis gently chided the boy-man. "Argentus," he carefully began, "you are not that man anymore."

"Aren't I? I've lied and stolen, things I promised Rasheera I'd never do again."

"This time is different. This time it was for a good cause, not selfish greed."

"I gave it to him, Irvis. That's my real crime. I thought I was so damned clever Kaul would be fooled. Now Jekaran is bonded to that thing, and it will consume him the way it consumed me."

"Jekaran has an advantage that you didn't have, Argentus."

"Oh yeah?" Ezra spat sarcastically. "And what's that?"

"Someone who loves him so much he would put aside even his oaths to The Divine Mother to chase that fool boy all over Shaelar in order to rescue him."

"My love is tainted, Irvis," Ezra said softly.

"What are you talking about?"

Ezra looked up from the ground. "The sword left something behind in my mind. I'm not sure what it is, but it calls to me, now more than ever."

"You mean it left its mark upon your mind and soul."

"No," Ezra snapped. "I'm not talking metaphorically. There's something hidden inside my mind, something real. Like the sword left a part of itself behind. I think it may be like a man burying a treasure so he can come back to it someday. The sword put something in my brain when our bond was broken, in case I ever re-bonded it. So it would remember me."

"You've never mentioned this to me before." Irvis sounded worried.

"That's because even thinking about it terrifies me." He looked back down at the ground. "I feel like this whole business has awoken whatever it is that the sword left buried in my brain. I'm tempted to take it back, Irvis. What if that's the true reason I'm chasing Jekaran all over the kingdom? What if it's so I can take it back from him?"

Irvis knelt in front of him. "Listen to me, Argentus. No one knows more about temptation than I do—you know that. So trust me when I tell you that it is not the fact that we are tempted that taints us. It is only if we heed that temptation.

"The sword was a part of you for years. It was in your head, and even controlled your body. So of course it will tempt you to return to it, and it probably always will. But do you remember what you told me the night you broke the bond?"

Ezra didn't say anything.

"Do you remember?" Irvis repeated.

Ezra nodded. "My sister."

"Yes," Irvis grabbed Ezra's shoulders and squeezed. "Your love for Anarilee is what gave you the strength to break the bond. It's what protected your sanity and made it possible for you to recover."

Ezra slowly nodded.

"Your love for Jekaran gives you the same reservoir of strength to draw from, perhaps even more so because you raised him. You are doing this because you love your nephew, not because you lust for the power of the sword. And when the time comes, it will be Jekaran's love for you that will give him the strength to break the bond."

That actually comforted Ezra, and a giddy sense of relief overcome a good portion of his self-doubt. He nodded appreciatively.

"Come on," Irvis said as he stood and reached down to help Ezra to stand.

"Sometimes I really do think you belong in those robes," Ezra said as he brushed the dirt from the back of his trouser. He looked at his chubby friend and grinned. "What you said about my focusing on my sister for strength was damn-near insightful."

Irvis grinned back. "Well, women have always brought out the best in you. They bring something out in me too, but it's not on the inside."

"I take it back," Ezra said flatly.

Irvis just laughed.

"Mae!" Mulladin suddenly blurted out, and not in his usual forlorn tone. This time he sounded happy.

Ezra turned to look at the man-boy, and found him pointing eagerly at something. Ezra followed Mulladin's finger to a piece of new canvas nailed to the open door of a shop a few paces off to their right. On the canvas was the color-trapped image of a girl in a sundress leaning down over someone on the ground, the spinning wheel of an overturned cart a blur in the background.

The girl's hair was shorter than Maely's had been, but it was definitely her. That's when Ezra saw the real focus of the image, the woman on the ground. She had pale skin and hair the same color as an Apeira well.

"Allosian," Ezra gasped.

"Yes," Irvis confirmed, "that's definitely Kairah of Allose, but that picture doesn't do her justice. She's gorgeous, Argentus. The most perfect specimen of womanhood that I have ever laid eyes on."

"Did she know you were laying your eyes on her?" Ezra scoffed.

Irvis didn't make a reply.

Ezra had to sidestep a surly looking sailor to get to the image, and when he did, he tore it off the door. A few passerby's shot him disapproving looks, but he didn't care. He quickly read the words scrawled underneath the image:

By order of Imarin Guard Captain, Iskar Eraenas, two hundred silver Aies for information leading to the location of the fey woman, and an additional hundred for the apprehension of the girl.

"That was not up a full day before it was rescinded," a gravelly voice said from Ezra's left. He looked up to find a bald, old man with a milky right eye shuffling over to him. His good eye was fixed on Ezra and the man spat something foul onto the street as he came to a stop.

"Why?" Ezra asked.

"The fey girl was taken into the custody of some out of town noble who sailed away with her to the capitol."

"And the young woman?" Ezra's pulse quickened as hope surged inside his chest. Perhaps Maely and Jekaran were still in Imaris, hiding out or maybe detained by the city guard. If that were the case, Ezra would easily be able to rescue them by using his displacement talis. He fingered the amethyst-capped earring piercing his left ear lobe.

"Gone," the old man said. "Guards even saw her leaving through the north gate but didn't do a damn thing to stop her. Word is they were whipped by Captain Eraenas himself for it. So you see, that's why that paper ain't worth a load of ghern shi–"

"Was she alone?"

"What?"

"Was she alone?" Ezra repeated in a louder tone.

The old man scowled. "I ain't deaf!"

"Sorry," Ezra said. "But do you know if there was a boy with her?"

The old man shook his head. "I only heard them talk about the girl in that picture."

Ezra nodded. "Thank you."

He turned to Irvis and was about to say something when the old man made a deliberate throat-clearing noise. Ezra looked back at him.

"Something else?" Ezra asked working to suppress his rising annoyance.

The old man narrowed his eyes. "In these parts it's customary to offer a gratuity when someone provides useful information."

Ezra rolled his eyes, fished in his pocket, and flicked a coin at the old beggar. The man caught it with surprising dexterity and then flashed a near toothless smile before shuffling off.

"Where is that boy?" Ezra hissed through clenched teeth.

"Your girl has obsessively chased Jekaran for hundreds of miles. I doubt she would leave him here and run off on her own." Irvis leaned in closer to look at the image Ezra still held stretched between his hands.

Ezra nodded. "Which means Jekaran was taken on that ship with the Allosian woman."

"That old beggar said it was sailing to Aiested," Irvis added.

Ezra gritted his teeth. "That's where Maely's headed! And that's where we need to go!"

"Argentus," Irvis began in a delicate tone, "if Jekaran was captured with the sword, and is being taken to Aiested–"

"I know what it means, Irvis!" Ezra snapped. "Which is why we have to get there as fast as possible."

"But they have two days on us. That ship will be docking by now."

Ezra nodded slowly. "Do we know who the Rikujo boss of this city is?"

"You're joking, right?" Irvis said. "The Rikujo will kill us if we go back to them. Deserters are to be executed without exception! Your law, remember?"

"I know," Ezra said. "But they are the only ones who can get us access to a slipgate."

Irvis grabbed his bicep and hissed, "Argentus, this is madness! Even if they don't kill us, do you really want to get involved with them again?"

Ezra threw off Irvis' grip and moved in close so that he was mere inches from his friend's chubby face. "If we don't get to Jekaran soon," he said through gritted teeth, "the crown will hang him for using that sword–if not for the crime, then so the king can bond it." Ezra stepped back and dropped his eyes to the image in his hands. "I can't let that happen, Irvis. I promised Anarilee I would take care of him, and if that means dying or even selling what's left of my soul, I will do it."

Irvis stared at him for a long moment before smiling wanly. "Well, we left the Rikujo together, so we might as well go back to face judgment together."

Ezra felt a sudden surge of affection for Irvis. "Thank you," he choked out.

Irvis smiled again. "With the power vacuum created by Kaul's death, his lieutenants will be fighting for control. If you returned and proclaimed Jekaran the slayer of Kaul and your rightful heir, they just might help us."

"You want me to make them think my nephew has taken over the Rikujo?"

Irvis shrugged. "He does have the sword of the Invincible Shadow, which kind of does make him your heir."

Ezra nodded thoughtfully, "It could work."

"Last I knew a woman named Graelle was in charge here. We probably can find her at Racheta's Pleasure House."

Ezra scoffed. "How convenient for you."

Irvis shook his head. "Not anymore. I've given my life to The Divine Mother. I have to remain pure."

"Well, there's no time for that anyway," Ezra said. Then he rolled up the image of Maely with the Allosian woman and was about to stow it in his satchel when Irvis touched his hand.

"Can I keep that?"

Ezra cocked an eyebrow.

"Not to look at Maely," Irvis quickly supplied.

"Given your life to The Divine Mother, huh?" Ezra handed the image over to the monk.

"That doesn't mean I can't appreciate the beauty of Rasheera's creations," Irvis said defensively.

"You mean appreciate the Allosian woman's cleavage?"

Irvis tucked the rolled picture into a robe pocket. "Well Rasheera did create her."

Ezra chuckled. The fact that he had a plan helped to rein in his gnawing worry. I'm sorry, Rasheera, he prayed. I know I promised never to go back, but Jekaran's my boy. He was probably selling his soul by returning to the Rikujo, but if it saved his nephew, then Ezra decided the bargain was in his favor.

MAELY CAST another glance over her shoulder. Imaris was gone now, replaced by a dirt road that twisted behind a seemingly endless curtain of tall pine trees. She was glad to be away from that city. It had been pleasant enough, as exotic as she imagined a port city to be. But Imaris was where everything had gone wrong. Imaris was where she had lost Jekaran.

Shouldn't have let him talk me into taking Kairah there, she thought, and not for the first time. Had she put up more of a fight, Jekaran surely would've given in and they would be in Jeryn with Mull and Uncle Ez right now. And she wouldn't be clinging to the neck of a stinking ghern trying to keep a nearly invisible Vorakk shaman in her line of sight.

Where is he? She ground her teeth. Looking back had made Maely lose sight of him again. Although they were following a road, the lizard man had occasionally turned off to take shortcuts through the trees. What if she had lost him? Would this road lead her to Aiested?

"Karak?" she called out.

No answer.

Maely reined in the ghern and it slowed to a stop.

"Karak?" she repeated, and this time her echoing voice carried a hint of rising panic.

Something heavy struck the ground at her right and Maely screamed. The ghern shuffled sideways as Karak materialized from thin air.

"Golden womb of the goddess, Karak!" Maely snapped as she pressed a hand to her breast as if that could slow her pounding heart.

"Reka, Karak scare?" he asked in his unique accent of guttural hissing.

"Where did you go?" Maely hotly demanded.

Karak pointed skyward. "Top of tree, aka."

Of course. She could feel her cheeks heat with embarrassment. He was scouting out the road ahead, something he had done a few times before. "Well it wouldn't hurt you to warn me before you run off the road to climb a tree!" she scolded. "I have a hard enough time keeping track of you as it is."

"Ska," Karak replied with a dip of his scaly head.

"Well?"

"Reka?"

"Did you see anything?" Maely snapped.

Karak flashed a toothy grin. "Esk, birds."

"You know what I mean!" Maely huffed.

"Karak see big human city, aka."

The news abruptly washed away Maely's irritation. "The capitol?"

Karak nodded.

"How far away are we?"

That question appeared to trouble the Vorakk and he hesitated before answering, "Reka, days?"

Maely sighed. She supposed that the magic Karak used to extend his vision must make gauging distance difficult. Either that or communicating the answer was hard for the lizard man, whose native language wasn't anything more than growls and hisses.

She shot another glance back over her shoulder in the direction of Imaris. They had been on the road for two days, and as best as Maely could figure, had come about seventy or so miles. That was the one good thing about riding the stinky and hairy ghern–the only good thing. And remarkably, Karak was able to keep pace on foot, whether by magic or by some innate Vorakk trait, she didn't know.

Maely touched her thumb to her ring finger and brushed the underside of a metal band. Since nearly losing her mother's ring in Imaris, she had taken to wearing it in order to keep it safe. It had also come in handy in dealing with the Imarin city guard, who were still on high alert and questioning everyone who left the city. They wouldn't have let her leave had she not commanded them to.

If only I'd had it when Gymal took Jek. She choked back threatening tears. It had fallen out of a tear in her pocket, just before Jekaran clashed with the crystal golem. Of course, she hadn't known that until she reached for it to stop Gymal from kidnapping him.

Maely had watched through stinging tears as Gymal's ship sailed out of the Imarin harbor, her heart breaking on the fact that only a short time before, she could've saved Jekaran. She stayed like that for a long time, until the ship was well on its way and a mob of guards and officials swarmed the docks.

The ringing alarm bells and urgent shouts of the crowd sounded far away as Maely wandered back to the bottom of the steep hill that was Imaris' main thoroughfare. There she found the wreckage of the wooden cart she and Kairah had used to outpace the crystal golem. In the chaotic aftermath of Kaul's attack and the crystal golem's rampage, nobody had paid any attention to the small silver ring lying half-concealed underneath the broken spokes of a wooden wheel.

Almost robotically, Maely leaned down and picked up the ring. She was about to slip it back into her pocket, but caught herself, and slipped it on her finger instead. With the compulsion talis full of Apeiron, she could use it to ward off anyone who might try to take it. She was so upset at the time she had wanted someone to try to take it, but no one did. In fact, she hadn't needed to use it at all until the guards stopped her at what was left of the city gate.

It had taken Maely the rest of the morning to find Karak. He had hidden their gherns and gone to investigate the chaos in Imaris. She knew he'd be back, so Maely just sat on the ground next to her grazing ghern, staring at nothing, her tears having run dry. When Karak finally returned, she told him what happened. The lizard man had listened intently, asking few questions but seeming to understand her every word.

She thought reciting the story of her fresh tragedy would've brought more heartache and tears, but by then numbness had settled over her. It wasn't until dark that she could feel enough to cry again, and she did cry, late into the night.

It wasn't so much the loss of Jekaran that made her weep, as it was the fact this all could've been avoided had she followed her instincts and not let him go with Kairah. She ground her teeth. That Allosian witch!

Whether by use of magic or the more mundane spell of her figure, she had lured Jek into this. True, she also helped to save his life, but Maely didn't want to give Kairah any positive credit. And according to Jekaran, it'd been trying to save Kairah from a rape gang that led to his bonding the sword, which led to his imprisonment, which eventually branched out into every other trouble that afflicted them. Anyone with even the tiniest brain could see that this mess was all Kairah's fault.

"Reka, girl hear?"

Maely snapped her eyes up from her ring to find Karak staring at her intently. "What?"

The Vorakk shaman hissed, "Isk no time! Uska, find stupid human boy!"

Maely's embarrassment quickly turned to anger. "Well, if you would tell me before you leave the road to scout, I wouldn't have to stop to find you!"

"Ssk," Karak hissed as he signed something. Then he leapt into a jog, his form blurring into a translucent haze.

Maely was learning some of what Karak's native words meant. "Ssk," if she heard it right, meant that he agreed. Of course, she could've mistaken that syllable for "isk," in which case the lizard man would've been expressing disgust. Either way, he had a point. They needed to hurry to the capitol in order to rescue Jekaran before Gymal had him hanged.

Maely brushed the underside of her mother's ring with her thumb. And to get him away from Kairah.

Chapter 42

Jekaran abruptly woke to a very strange sensation in his head. It was not unlike the pins and needles he knew when his leg would fall asleep after sitting on the floor for too long–except, this was much more intense and jolted him in equally timed waves of force. He squinted his eyes and gasped through clenched teeth as the feeling ceased in his head and shot like lightning down to his arm, then to his back, and then to his legs. When Jekaran opened his eyes, his vision was clear, and his head no longer throbbed. He turned, without any pain, and saw a woman standing over him. She was middle-aged, wore a plain grey dress, and had some kind of jewelry that wrapped her head and rested on her brow.

A healing talis. The woman was a healer.

"Thank you," Jekaran breathed out as he experimentally lifted his left arm. To his delight, it was no longer broken.

"Well, it looks like you can show manners, when you choose to."

Jekaran sat up to find Gymal standing at the foot of his pallet. "That can't have been cheap." Jekaran glanced at the woman in the grey dress. "Why throw away Aies on a condemned man?"

Gymal shook his head. "I assure you, it was strictly a matter of convenience. We're disembarking, and I needed you able to walk." Gymal snapped his fingers and Jekaran felt hands grab him underneath his armpits. He turned to see Hort lifting him to his feet. The man grimaced apologetically as he produced a pair of black irons.

"Either you can put them on or he will," Gymal said sternly.

Jekaran nodded, slipped the shackles onto his wrists, and locked them into place. He looked at Hort, who quickly checked the cuffs to make sure they were locked, after which he shot a nod at Gymal.

I can free us, the sword pleaded. Our link has grown strong. Physical contact is no longer necessary for me to give you power.

Go to hell, Jekaran projected. I'm not letting you use me like a puppet, not again!

The sword responded again with hurt confusion but didn't say anything more.

"Where's Kairah?" Jekaran demanded.

Gymal walked over to the door leading out of the brig. "She will be accompanying us."

"Then she's awake?"

Gymal hesitated before finally answering with a curt, "No."

A cold, nauseating pit formed in Jekaran's stomach. What did that mean? If they were docked in Aiested, shouldn't the city's well have healed her? Why hadn't she awakened? Was her condition more serious than he'd been led to believe?

They left the brig and ascended to the deck in silence. Jekaran half expected to be blinded by a sun he had not seen in three days, and so was surprised to find that it was night. Not late in the evening, perhaps only an hour or two after sunset. They lingered on the deck while Gymal settled his bill with the captain of the Queen's Honor, after which Hort left, returning later with an unconscious Kairah held in his arms. Jekaran's heart twisted as he looked at the Allosian woman's amethyst hair hanging down and gently fluttering from a quiet night's breeze.

He took a step toward her but stopped as Gymal gripped his shoulder. "We're not going to have any trouble, are we?"

Jekaran looked down at the weaselly little lord for a confused moment before it occurred to him what Gymal was talking about. The sword. Hort was also carrying Jekaran's sword. He looked at the big mercenary and didn't need the power of his psychic link to discern where the man carried it. There was a bundled object peeking out from a satchel strapped to Hort's back.

"No," Jekaran finally said, and he felt the sword's deep disappointment.

"Good," Gymal drawled.

They marched off the ship, taking the gangplank single file. When Jekaran set foot on the wooden boards of the pier, he got his first real look at Aiested. He gasped as he looked up at a glowing Apeira well that easily could've been a thousand feet tall.

The well's gentle purple aura reflected on thousands of white buildings that looked carved of ivory in an architecture that was as artful as it was functional. Rounded arches, flowing trailing designs, and spires rising higher than any building he'd seen rose all over a city lit with thousands of points of light. The abundance of light talises made the massive city look like a starry night sky. It was beautiful in a way that reminded Jekaran of Kairah, artful, glorious, perfect.

"It's something, isn't it?" Gymal said in a tone that wasn't as nasally as it usually sounded. "I never get tired of seeing it, especially at night."

Why was the man talking so casually to him? Was it some sort of a new mind game? Or was the scene of Aiested at night so breathtaking that it could overcome even Gymal's disdain for him? Jekaran didn't answer the man. Instead, he stared anxiously at Kairah, whom Hort was now carrying several feet off to his right.

They wound their way away from the docks and toward a white coach lashed to a team of six gherns where a driver in blue livery met them. "Lord Tyrus Gymal?" the man asked, and his tone carried the hint of an accent that Jekaran couldn't place.

"Yes," Gymal answered.

The driver bowed low and then opened the carriage door. Gymal motioned for Hort to enter first, and the man carried Kairah into the coach as effortlessly as though he were holding a small child.

"Where can I take you, my lord?" the coachman asked.

"The palace," Gymal curtly replied. "And be quick about it."

"As you wish, my lord," the coachman bobbed his head.

He's afraid, Jekaran heard the sword whisper. *He doesn't want us this close together.*

"Shut up!" Jekaran snapped, and then froze as he realized he had replied out loud.

Gymal shot a glance at him. The man didn't say anything, but he didn't have to. Jekaran could see the expression on his face; curiosity mixed with pity. He must think my brain addled. He would have to be extra careful to avoid any more verbal slips lest he give Gymal more moral justification to have him executed. Put down like a sick ghern with a broken leg.

Gymal's stare lingered on him for a long uncomfortable moment before he finally grabbed Jekaran by the chain that tethered his hands together and forcefully guided him up into the coach. He fell down on a plush seat opposite Hort, who had set Kairah up next to him so that her head rested against a window. He was about to ask after the Allosian woman when Gymal stepped up into the coach, and sat next to Jekaran. He quickly produced a slender, ivory wand with a ball at the point and a handle capped by amethyst stone.

"This is a stun baton. As the name implies it delivers a shock that can incapacitate someone twice the size as my associate." Gymal casually waved the baton at Hort. "It is very nearly classed as a weapon talis save for the fact that it is non-lethal and primarily used to wrangle oxen. If I even suspect you of trying to reach for that sword, I will strike you down and watch you convulse and drool as you piss yourself. Understand?"

If I was in control, it would have no effect on you, the sword said. Jekaran ignored it and said to Gymal, "So why didn't you use that on Kaul? Or were you counting on his killing me?"

Gymal pinched the bridge of his nose with his free hand. "I assure you, I would have had I owned it at the time. I just acquired it from the captain of the Queens' Honor, and not for a petty price." He lowered his hand, opened his eyes, and stared at Jekaran. "Dealing with you has cost me a great deal of money."

"That's not going to keep me up at night," he retorted.

Gymal turned to a small, horizontal window set in the front coach wall and rapped three short knocks. Jekaran heard the driver shout something and the carriage lurched into motion. "The ride to the palace is lengthy," Gymal said. "From here on out, you are not to speak unless spoken to. Understand?"

Jekaran silently nodded. He wouldn't give Gymal any excuse to strike him with the stun baton. Apparently, Gymal had been thinking the same thing, for he grinned knowingly and said, "Smart boy."

This is going to be a long ride. He let his gaze settle on Kairah. Seeing her beauty was the only thing that could comfort him now, and even that comfort was mixed with worry for her safety. He watched her eyes dance underneath closed eyelids. That sign of life, small as it was, alleviated a little of his anxiety for her.

KAIRAH CAUTIOUSLY MADE her way down the vacant street. The city, for it was large enough to support a population of thousands, was eerily empty. The tall white buildings were full of cracks and haphazardly missing chunks of stone. The smoothly paved streets were blemished with broken up patches, and there ought to have been green overgrowth somewhere, but there was no life here. No people, no plants, no pests.

Nothing.

Kairah stepped carefully over a bundle of dried sticks lying fallen in the street. No, not sticks, but bones. It was a human skeleton. Kairah knelt down to examine it, hoping to sense some decomposition, but there was none. It was as if this place and everything in it were in a state of frozen death.

She rose, scanning the street and immediately spotting more bones, some in complete skeletons, but most just scattered appendages, a skull here, a femur there, a broken rib cage lying on its side. Kairah moved toward one of the dilapidated buildings. She shoved open a broken door, and stepped inside.

She was greeted with a truly horrific sight. Skulls were the first thing she noticed, dozens of skulls littered across the floor like trash. There were other bones too, so many that the entire floor looked to be made of them. The building had been some kind of inn or tavern, filled with people.

What had happened to them? It was hard to tell if they had gathered at the tavern in a search for shelter, or if the bones were representative of the establishment's usual crowd. But no, there were small skulls here–

lots of them. There had been as many children in this place as adults, certainly not the normal nightly drinking crowd.

Kairah stayed in the building until she could bear the sight no longer. So much death. She took to the street again, exploring the empty city, looking in vain for any sign of life no matter how tiny. A particularly bright flash of emerald lightning lit up the whole city, and that's when Kairah saw it; an Apeira well at the center of the city.

But the crystal obelisk in the distance wasn't rising proud and tall as it should. No, this well had toppled over onto its side, crushing in the roof of a neighboring building. The sight came as a surprise to Kairah; she had not sensed any Apeiron radiating from it. A dead well? Was such a thing even possible? Apeira was the essence of life. How could something that was a source of life itself die?

The very idea frightened Kairah, and she lifted the fringe of her dress and exploded into a panicked sprint toward the center of the city–toward the dead well.

CHAPTER 43

Raelen ducked Gryyth's backhanded swing. The Ursaj bear-man was quick for a creature of his size. Raelen spun to his right and attempted the same swing at Gryyth. The creature moved in a blur of white fur, twisted around to Raelen's back, and gripped the prince in a powerful hold. Raelen struggled to breathe, strained his muscles, and broke free. He dropped to the ground, rolled forward, and sprung back up to find Gryyth bearing down on him in a ferocious charge.

"Your Highness," a voice called out.

In an astonishing display of agility, Gryyth stopped short, effectively ending his charge only a foot before it was due to crash into Raelen.

"You lose, cub," Gryyth rumbled softly.

Raelen grinned. "We are interrupted. That makes this match a draw."

The white bear dipped his charcoal muzzle deferentially. "As you say, my prince."

Raelen laughed as he looked up into Gryyth's light blue eyes. The only time the Ursaj would treat him as an equal was when they sparred. Other than that, he was the picture of obsequious obedience.

Raelen untapped the transference band encircling the bicep of his right upper arm and his hands–covered in white fur with sharp claws for nails–returned to normal as he walked over to a stool to grab a towel. He wiped his face, and then dabbed at the muscles of his naked torso. "What is it, Hausen?"

The young messenger woman was clearly uncomfortable addressing

Raelen while he was only partially clothed as was evidenced by her inability to meet his eyes. "My prince, his majesty bid me send this missive to you as he was engaged with his war council and could not be bothered with it." The woman held up a paper scroll sealed with red wax. "It is from Lord Tyrus Gymal of one of the southern provinces. He claims that he has an urgent matter to present to the king."

Raelen sighed and cast a glance over his shoulder to Gryyth. "You may now refer to me as Aiestal's' royal secretary."

Gryyth didn't laugh. It took a lot to make the Ursaj emote anything, laughter most of all. But that didn't stop Raelen from trying at every opportunity. He turned back and took the scroll from the young messenger woman. Noticing her embarrassment, Raelen draped the towel over his shoulders so that it hung down over his chest. It didn't appear to help matters. Raelen chuckled to himself as he broke the wax seal and unrolled the scroll. He lifted part of the towel and began to scrub the blonde hair on the side of his head. His mind half wandered as he scanned the slanted, tightly scrawled script. Then he froze, re-read the previous line, and looked up at Hausen.

"Summon my personal guard!"

The young woman bobbed a bow and then fled.

Raelen turned to look at Gryyth. The Ursaj said nothing, but his blue eyes were full of intense curiosity.

"Lord Gymal has brought us an Allosian."

Raelen didn't have time for his usual post-spar bath, so he used a bucket of warm soapy water and a cloth to wash himself before drying and donning his plate armor and white tabard over a plain tunic and breeches. He knew he was the object of quiet ridicule for his choice to shun the lavish fashions prized by the aristocracy in favor of the soldier's garb, but Raelen had always thought the velvet doublets, colorful hose, and elaborate–poufy–hats to be ridiculous in both design and function. That was one virtue his father had passed onto him; probably the only virtue the man possessed.

Raelen emerged from his quarters to find a contingent of ten soldiers wearing full, plate armor waiting for him. Only the captain had his visor up, making the others look like statues so perfectly still were they standing.

"Prince Taris," the captain saluted fist to heart.

"Captain." Raelen nodded his acknowledgement of the salute. He waited for Gryyth to emerge from the quarters before falling into step behind him. "We have not had dealings with the Allosians since long before I was born," Raelen said quietly to Gryyth. "What could this mean?"

"I am sure I do not know, my prince," Gryyth rumbled.

Raelen shot a look up at the bear-man and smirked. "I'm surprised, Gryyth. A fly cannot land upon a scrap of moldy bread without your seeing an omen in it."

Gryyth snorted. "Do not take my ignorance to mean that I think this occurrence to not be momentous."

Raelen wanted to ask if the Ursaj had ever had dealings with the fey-folk, but couldn't bring himself to do it; any time he mentioned Gryyth's people, a little of the light left the bear-man's eyes. When I am king, I will free your people. He had sworn as much to Gryyth when he was just starting to become a man, when he truly began to understand that one day he would succeed his father. Gryyth had only responded with a patronizing, very good, my prince. As much as he knew Gryyth loved him, the Ursaj's mistrust of human nature ran deep–and justifiably so.

For hundreds of years, humans captured and enslaved the bear-people, forcing them to retreat deeper into the northern woods for safety. Despite their large stature, strength, and ferocity in battle, the Ursaj shied away from confrontation more often than not. Gryyth said it was not Seiro to fight when one did not need to. This was, of course, a demonstrative indictment of human kind's love of violence and war. How did we get to be this way? Is it just in our nature to try to dominate or destroy everything around us? Well, he wasn't a philosopher, and therefore unqualified to answer that question. But he would show Gryyth that humans could choose to be noble. He would free all of Aiestal's captive Ursaj when he became king, political consequences be damned.

It took the better part of an hour for Raelen and his entourage to reach one of the palace's huge receiving rooms. The royal palace was gigantic; going between places required an inordinate amount of travel time. Raelen heard that when the Allosians built Aiestal, they had put in place talises that made travel instantaneous, thereby putting no restraints on the size of their architecture. Slipgates, the talises were called. Extremely rare, so much so even the crown only owned two, one of which was damaged and unusable. Oh well, if we didn't have to walk everywhere, we'd all probably be fat and lazy.

"My prince," a voice called, snapping Raelen out of his reverie.

He stopped up short, causing an interruption in the hypnotic marching cadence of his armored guards. Pariel approached from a connecting corridor. The tall, bald captain jogged over to him and bobbed his head in a perfunctory show of deference.

"Word came that you had summoned your personal guard. Is everything all right?"

Raelen gritted his teeth in irritation. Father must still be having me watched! It didn't come as a surprise, Raelen's father trusted no one, but he had thought his continued loyalty even in the face of Saranna's suicide would've proven his devotion to the king.

"There is no danger," Raelen said. "But your presence would be welcome as we meet with one of the kingdom's provincial governors. He brings strange tidings."

Pariel saluted and fell into step just behind Raelen as they resumed their march. He turned down another long corridor before passing through a set of tall double doors into a room large enough to host hundreds of people. The high, vaulted ceiling made their every step reverberate with an echo that emphasized the large size of the room.

Raelen made his way over to a wooden, high-backed chair set on a velvet-draped, portable dais. He stepped up onto the platform, Gryyth taking a position just behind the dais, and to the right of Raelen's chair. The contingent of armored guards lined up, half their number on each side of the dais. Pariel was the only one who stepped up onto the velvet-covered platform where he fell into parade rest next to Raelen's chair. Raelen waited until everyone was in place before sitting.

Raelen addressed a servant kneeling in front of the dais. "You may bring Lord Gymal in to speak with me."

"Yes, my prince," the servant quickly said before rising to rush out of the receiving room.

He returned a moment later intoning in a loud voice, "Lord Tyrus Gymal of the Elridge province.

"You may approach, Lord Gymal," Raelen said somewhat less formally.

The short, balding man was dressed in clean, but faded robes of green fabric. A dousing stone hung around his neck, and he called to someone in the corridor to enter. A moment later, a youth only a few years younger than Raelen himself, stepped into the room. His hair was black, his eyes were green, and he wore the drab tunic and breeches common to the peasantry. For some reason the boy's hands were shackled in front of him.

A big man next entered the room, clearly a soldier as was evident by his muscled arms, and scarred face. He carried an unconscious woman, her hair hanging loosely over his left forearm.

Purple hair

It was the Allosian!

Raelen heard several gasps from the men of his guard. He shot a sidelong glance at Pariel and was impressed to find the man unshaken. Gymal scurried forward, the size of the room making it take an uncomfortably long time for him to reach the dais where he prostrated himself before Raelen. He rolled his eyes. He hated it when people did that, especially when a short bow from the waist was all etiquette required of them.

"Rise," Raelen curtly said before the boy or the soldier would try to mimic their lord.

"Your Highness," Gymal began, "I thank you for your magnanimous generosity in condescending to–"

Raelen cut him off. "Your letter gave me the impression that this Allosian would be alive."

Gymal bobbed his head while trying to keep his eyes on the floor. He *certainly doesn't have much experience addressing royalty. The man was almost comically overdoing it. A minor country lord, then?*

"She is alive, Your Highness."

Wait, does he even know that I am not father?

"Prince Taris will do, Lord Gymal," Raelen said.

The short balding lord looked up sharply.

He really hadn't noticed.

"The king–"

"–is busy," Raelen cut in. "But rest assured, anything you need to say to him, you can say to me. Now, the Allosian, what is the matter with her?"

Gymal hesitated a long moment before finally stammering, "C-coma, my prince. Apparently, she spell-cast beyond her strength and sleeps while her body heals."

"How did this happen?" Raelen asked.

"Forgive me, my prince, but that is at the heart of the tale I have to tell you."

Raelen waved Gymal on. "Then please, by all means tell me what happened."

JEKARAN KEPT his eyes on the floor while he listened to Gymal explain the events in Imaris that led Kairah to exhaustion, and his capture. The man could never be a storyteller as his simple recitation of facts lacked for the slightest bit of style and color.

That man is a threat, the sword whispered in his mind.

Jekaran cast a quick glance up at the bald captain standing to the prince's right and mentally scoffed. Of all of them, you think he is most dangerous. I'd say that bear creature is the one we have to watch out for. He immediately regretted saying that as he could feel his words elicit a rising hope in the sword. No, he reaffirmed. I'm never letting you take control again. Disappointment emanated from the sword, but it was not the hurt defeat Jekaran usually sensed when he denied it. Wonderful! It thinks I'm wavering.

Jekaran unconsciously shot another glance at the bald captain who this time met his eyes. For some reason that look disturbed him. Those eyes were full of incongruous knowing. He looked away but could feel the man's stare linger on him.

"And that is how we have come to be here," Gymal finished.

"And this boy?"

Jekaran looked up to see the prince pointing at him.

"Why is he in chains?"

"He-he broke the law, my prince," Gymal replied, uncertainty making his voice tremble.

"You said the Allosian woman gave him the sword talis in order to make of him her protector, a role he filled effectively it seems. If that is true, then he is no criminal."

When had Gymal told the prince that? *Well, I guess that means he believed my lie. That was something, wasn't it? Maybe Jekaran wouldn't be facing the noose after all.*

No one can kill us, the sword said with an air of proud menace.

Shut up!

"Release him," the prince commanded.

Gymal quickly produced a key from his robe pocket and grabbed the left metal cuff of the shackles. He inserted the key, turned it, and the painful pressure on Jekaran's wrist abated. Gymal repeated the process on his right cuff, and relief washed over Jekaran as he massaged his now naked wrists.

Jekaran deliberately met Gymal's eyes, planning to give the man a gloating smirk when he paused. Gymal didn't have the frustrated anger in his face that Jekaran had expected. No, his face drooped with relief? Why would the weaselly little lord be relieved that Jekaran wasn't going to be punished for defying him? *Gymal hated him, didn't he?*

"Lord Gymal, you mentioned the Allosian woman had an urgent message for my father?"

Gymal turned back to look up at the prince. "Yes, Prince Taris."

"Tell me of this," the prince ordered.

Jekaran decided he liked seeing Gymal being ordered about.

"My understanding is that she bore the crown a warning."

"A warning of what?" the prince asked.

"Her brother," Jekaran cut in before Gymal had a chance to answer, "is trying to start a new talis war."

There was an audible–gratifying–gasp from Gymal that told Jekaran he had broken some stupid rule of court etiquette.

Prince Taris stared at Jekaran for a long moment, before finally asking him directly, "The Allosians seek a war with Aiestal?"

"No," Jekaran said, and then he quickly added, "Your Highness." He may hold disdain for the upper classes, but he wasn't about to put the noose back around his neck through intentional rudeness, not when he had just slipped out of it. "Her brother is trying to cause the human kingdoms of Shaelar to go to war with each other. He is going to teach them how to make weapon talises so that they–we," he corrected himself, "will destroy each other."

"Teach us how to make weapon talises?" For some reason, the prince sounded as though he had just made some kind of mental connection. "How is he doing this? Does he have humans serving him?"

Jekaran shook his head. "That Allosian woman–Kairah–said her brother was acting alone."

"And does their magic let them disguise themselves?" that question surprised Jekaran.

"Yes, my prince." The prince adopted a faraway look–his eyes unfocusing as he muttered something that Jekaran could barely hear. Who was Loeadon?

"Pariel!" the prince barked. The bald soldier at the prince's right turned to face his liege. "Run ahead to my father. Tell him I am coming with urgent tidings. If his chamberlain tries to deny you, tell him that it is a matter of life and death."

"Yes, my prince," Pariel bowed his head and saluted fist to heart. He stepped off the dais where he shot him one last look before breaking into a run toward a chamber exit.

What was that about?

He is dangerous, the sword repeated. We should kill him quickly. Give me your will and we–

Go to hell, Jekaran thought, but this time the condemnation lacked its usual heat. Divine Mother, was he actually tempted?

He shook his head and snapped, "No!" His cheeks heated as all eyes turned to stare at him, so he dropped his gaze to the ground to avoid seeing the scrutiny, but caught a worried glance from Gymal first. Was the man afraid of him?

He should be, the sword said in a disturbingly human-like tone, one that held a distinct note of cold anger.

Rasheera, shelter my soul, Jekaran prayed.

CHAPTER 44

Raelen's father would be furious when Raelen interrupted his council. Especially when he had expected Raelen to attend to the matter of Lord Gymal's message himself. But this couldn't wait. It really was a matter of life and death, and if Raelen got some satisfaction by discomfiting his father, so much the better. He smiled to himself. It was un-princely and petty, but Raelen loved to nettle the king whenever he had the opportunity. Every subtle rebellion he could manage was a tribute to Saranna, Raelen's way of striking back at their father for driving his sister to suicide.

It took them almost another hour to reach the throne room, and the boy with green eyes made a few odd outbursts along the way, as though he were arguing with someone who wasn't there. Mind sickness. He'd seen others like that, children of his father's nobles who would cry out obscenities during formal functions as though they were possessed with demons. One constantly cried and cut himself, and another would not talk or react in any way to those around her. And the worst part was the healers could nothing to cure them.

There were talises aplenty that could mend the body, but for some reason no talis worked to heal the mind. Perhaps that was because the mind was a part of the soul? Raelen didn't know. He just wished he had something that would've cured Saranna's melancholy. Maybe then, she wouldn't have killed herself. Maybe then, he would still have someone to confide in. He glanced at Gryyth. Well, someone human.

Raelen entered the hall feeding into the throne room where he was met by Pariel. The man looked ashamed, and Raelen immediately knew why. "You were denied entry?"

Pariel nodded sharply. "My apologies, Prince Taris."

Raelen gritted his teeth and pushed past the bald soldier. He shot warning glances at the guards posted outside the throne room, and so they did nothing to bar his way. Raelen threw open the twin doors and proudly entered the throne room trailing his guards, Lord Gymal, the boy, and the mercenary carrying the fey woman. He locked eyes with his father and could see the storm of anger begin to brew behind the king's mask of calm. It didn't last long however, as gasps from the assembly drew all eyes to the unconscious Allosian. Raelen made certain to find Loeadon so that he could scrutinize the man's reaction at seeing the girl.

"What is this breach of decorum?" the chamberlain demanded. "His majesty expected you to be able to handle this matter on your own!"

Raelen ignored him and spoke directly to his father. "This," he waved to the woman, "is an Allosian."

That evoked a new round of gasps and whisperings.

"She has risked her life to come here in order to warn us of a plot contrived by her brother. A plot to incite the nations of Shaelar to war with one another."

The chamberlain opened his mouth to say something else, but Raelen didn't give him the opportunity. "Her brother intends to restore to humans the lost art of talis-craft in the hope that we will make weapon talises and annihilate one another in a new talis war."

More gasps.

"Shall I go on, Father?" Raelen said in barely restrained impudence. "Or shall we proceed with this discussion in private?"

The storm was back behind his father's eyes. He stared at Raelen for a long moment before finally turning to the chamberlain and saying, "Clear the room of all but my top advisors."

The chamberlain nodded and began ordering the removal of most members of the assembly. Loeadon was one of Raelen's father's top advisors and therefore would be allowed to stay. He let his burning stare linger on the tall man with the long dark hair. Could he be the fey woman's brother in disguise? He couldn't think of a better suspect. The man had risen to power quickly, seemingly coming out of nowhere. His knowledge of talises was second to none, and he had miraculously produced the circlet that would allow him to use the Allosian tome to start crafting talises. It had to be him.

But Raelen needed proof. Even the prince of Aiestal couldn't call a man to face justice without sufficient proof. For some reason his father was passionate about that. The king styled himself a man of the law, and crime and punishment seemed to be the only thing Raelen's father did care about.

Saranna

Raelen made certain Pariel was not evicted and when the room was emptied of most of Aiestal's high lords and military officials, Raelen relayed the full story of the catastrophe in Imaris to his father as Lord Gymal had told it. The king listened stoically, eyes flitting between Raelen and the Allosian. When he was finished, Raelen's father remained silent for almost a full minute before finally asking. "Do we know specifics of how this Allosian's brother intends to bring about his plan?

Raelen looked at Gymal who–in a display of shameless cowardice– quickly turned to Jekaran. The youth looked startled as though he had not been paying attention.

He hesitated a moment before finally answering, "No."

Raelen nodded approval at the boy in an attempt to set his mind at ease, for he looked like a frightened mouse cornered by a dozen hungry cats. Raelen was sure the boy had no knowledge of courtly etiquette, and probably thought speaking out as he did to be punishable by death. Well, in some cases it was.

Saranna

The king leaned back in his throne. "Well, we will have to wait until she wakes in order to interrogate her."

Raelen thought he caught a flash of anger in the green eyes of Gymal's peasant but wasn't sure. For some reason his instincts told him he didn't want the boy to get angry, which was odd considering that he didn't look like much of a threat–not without his sword talis, anyway. Still, the uneasiness that told him the boy was dangerous persisted. And besides, from what Gymal had explained, the Allosian woman was their ally in this.

"Father," Raelen began, and he caught a disapproving frown curl his father's lips. "Your Majesty," he corrected himself. "This Allosian woman risked her life to bring us this warning, against the will of not only her people, but of her own blood. I implore you to not regard her as a captive or an enemy."

"She is dangerous, my king," a voice at Raelen's left cut in, a voice that belonged to Loeadon. "Allosians are powerful spell-casters. It is by Rasheera's blessing that she comes to us incapacitated, and I pray that you keep her in such a state as long as possible. At least until we have mastered the use of the spell-casting talis."

Raelen shot the dark robed man as baleful a look as he could manage. Could the Allosian woman identify her brother if he was in disguise? If that were the case, it would make sense Loeadon would want her to remain unconscious.

"We need to know what she knows," Raelen snapped at Loeadon. He turned back to face his father. "That is, if we are to have any hope of foiling this plot. Is it not clear that her brother has been at work here? Have we not acquired, somewhat miraculously I would add, new and powerful talises in this past year?" He shot Loeadon another look, but the man didn't appear to catch Raelen's implication. "We need her on our side!"

The king nodded thoughtfully. "Your judgment in this thing is sound, Raelen."

Was that a compliment? Raelen was so stunned he almost missed a scowl from Loeadon. The look vanished as quickly as it had come, and Loeadon bobbed his assent.

Something else surprised Raelen; a feeling of elation at having been commended by his father. He quickly tamped it down. He thought himself long since passed the point of craving his father's approval, but there it was, and it felt good. Saranna! He reminded himself. He drove Saranna to death!

"Chamberlain," the king said to the robed man standing at his left, "Have the woman taken to one of our guest quarters and attended to by the palace physicians. Also see that the maid servants clean her up and dress her in some clean clothing."

"Yes, my king," the chamberlain said as he stepped down from the throne dais, and began snapping orders at some of Raelen's bodyguards.

The prince's men were loyal, so loyal he had to nod his approval of the chamberlain's orders before they would leave his side. He watched as one of his men took the Allosian woman from Gymal's bodyguard and carried her toward one of the room's many side exits.

"Now," his father began, "let me see this sword talis that you've spoken of."

Raelen watched as Lord Gymal ordered his man to produce the weapon. The short little lord took it, unbundled it, and presented it to the king handle first. Raelen saw the boy–Jekaran–look away, as though he couldn't bear to watch. His pained look made Raelen think of a man watching a former lover wed another man.

"Yes," the king said as he studied the emerald-peppered blade, "this is a fine weapon." He looked at Gymal and asked, "What does it do?"

"It makes one into a fierce warrior, my king," Gymal said with his eyes on the floor.

Raelen watched his father test the balance of the blade. He startled him when he stood and took a swipe at the air. "Definitely Allosian make," the king muttered. "But the talis isn't responding to me. Why?"

Gymal hesitated a moment before finally saying, "I do not know, My King."

"Loeadon," the king called."

"Yes, King Taris," the man bobbed another bow as he took a step toward the throne.

Raelen watched his father proffer the sword to the tall, robed polymath. "Make it your priority to study this talis. I wish to know how it operates as soon as possible." Loeadon took the sword and stepped back, examining the talis with a professional look as he ran one finger along the flat of the blade.

"As for you, Lord Gymal," the king said. "You shall be rewarded for your service to the crown with a public commendation and a feast held tomorrow night in your honor. Until then you shall be my guest, and lodge here in the palace."

"Th-thank you, King Taris," the man stammered.

"Raelen, please escort Lord Gymal to one of the suites on the upper level."

"And what of this boy?" Raelen was surprised to hear Lord Gymal ask.

The king pointed at one of Raelen's personal guards. He knew the man would obey this command without needing leave from him. "Take the boy to the dungeons."

"For what crime?" Raelen blurted out.

The storm behind the king's eyes was back. Whatever capital of approval he had gained with his father was just squandered. "Did he not wield a weapon talis?"

"But it was at the behest of the Allosian woman," Raelen countered.

"And that is why I will not execute him," the king said.

"But he was only complying with the request of the fey woman to protect and defend her."

"Our laws are not subject to Allosian trifling!" Raelen's father snapped. "This peasant committed a crime, and therefore he must be punished!"

Raelen's guard was already escorting the boy towards a side exit. "But surely Father– "

"I will hear no more of this!" the king had actually raised his voice.

That was the warning that he'd gone too far, so Raelen fell silent and nodded acceptance of his father's will. He turned to watch the boy being taken from the throne room. He was shaking his head and muttering, but it wasn't at Raelen's guard. Poor lunatic. Raelen glanced at Lord Gymal's face. The man had turned pale and looked on the edge of vomiting. That was odd. Hadn't he brought the boy to them in chains? Why was he surprised to see him committed to prison? Why did he care for that matter? Raelen didn't know, but at the moment he could sympathize with Lord Gymal. His father's condemnation of a naïve farm boy for getting pulled into magic and politics made Raelen feel just as ill.

Not Seiro.

Jenoc watched the boy—Jekaran—be taken from the room. Once the boy was gone, he slowly breathed out the tension that had been building in his head—another headache? He had been certain the boy was going to tap the sword and strike back, but he hadn't. Why hadn't he? Curious though it was, Jenoc inwardly smiled at the remarkable stroke of good fortune. For if the child had wanted, he could've thrown the king's court into chaos, and Jenoc would've likely been forced to spell-cast in order to stop him. He needed King Taris alive and would've been forced to protect him. It very well could've ruined his plans. A stroke of good fortune, indeed.

Of course, had the king decided to imprison Kairah, Jenoc would've slain every human in the throne room, the secrecy of his plans be damned. He would never allow this human vermin do to her what they had done to his mother.

At least for now Kairah was safe. But why did she still slumber? Jenoc could feel the Apeiron flowing into her, and knew that whatever injury she'd suffered to her body had been healed. It worried him. Still, Kairah was alive, and according to his senses, healthy. Having her here in the palace would make it easy for him to watch over her. However, it would be a problem when she finally did wake. She would be able to see his Apeiron aura as he cast from the Fourth Discipline to disguise himself; she would be able to unmask him.

That only means I need to work quickly. He could do it before she awoke. And then, once things were in motion, not even Kairah could stop the war. It would come. He would ensure that it came.

Chapter 45

Jekaran stumbled and fell to his knees. Before he could even turn back to reward the guard with a scathing remark, he heard the barred door swing shut with the pained screaming of rusty hinges. It thudded against the lock bar with a dull clang. The guard was already a dozen paces down the dungeon aisle when Jekaran scrambled to his feet and called out, "Thank you," the words dripping with sarcasm. The only response he received was the angry complaints and mocking of the unseen occupants of neighboring cells.

Jekaran sank back down to his knees, hands sliding down the black iron bars. This cell was more like a cave than the one in Rasha. It was little more than a deep alcove carved into the stone with a swinging barred door covering an arched opening. There was also no hay or even a piss bucket. Prisoner comfort was definitely not a concern of the jailer here.

Great, I can compare prison cells. He sighed and let go of the bars. Well at least he wouldn't have to worry about execution. Still, the prospect of freedom dangling so close to his reach, only to be pulled away like a lure on a fishing line was heart wrenching. Even if the king let me go, I wouldn't be free. Not while I'm bonded to you!

The sword didn't reply, but Jekaran could feel its hurt confusion. For some reason that infuriated him. Don't pretend this is my fault he mentally shouted.

It is.

Jekaran clenched his jaw and only remembered at the last minute not to speak to the sword out loud. *Really? And how's that?*

If you would only let me take control of our bond, I could free us both. We wouldn't have to remain here.

I'll sprout chicken's wings and a pig's tail before I let that happen again!

I don't understand why you will not let me fight for you, the sword said.

Jekaran exasperation in its psychic tone. Why did that remind him of Maely? *Because last time you got the hell beat out of me!*

The sword hesitated and Jekaran could feel another emotion emanating from it–embarrassment? The sword was embarrassed? Its emotions certainly had grown complex very quickly. To Jekaran, the sword no longer seemed a child. It was as if it were aging, growing, and maturing–all at an alarmingly fast rate.

I didn't know the limitations of your physical form, the sword finally said. *I apologize.*

Apologize? That gave Jekaran pause.

I have a better understanding of your capabilities now, the sword offered.

So you want me to just let you possess me again? Jekaran scoffed.

I did not possess you.

"Then what would you call it?" Jekaran forgot himself and cringed when he heard his shout echo.

"Who're you talkin to, boy?" one of the other prisoners called from a few cells down.

"Damned lunatic," one of the other prisoners grumbled. "Should put your kind down, like a rabid dog. Not lock ya up in here! You best not keep us up tonight with you're carrying on!"

"Sorry," Jekaran called. "I won't," he added weakly.

Our bond, the sword said patiently, as though it were talking down to him–now it did sound like Maely–*allows me to take control when you are incapacitated or are otherwise unable to defend yourself. Your enemy had paralyzed you with fear, and the only way to prevent your death was for me to take control. You did not understand this, and so I* resisted your attempts to reassert your domination of the bond until the threats to your safety had been destroyed.

You are the threat to my safety! When that fight was over I was burned, broken, and dazed from a knock to my head.

I did try to heal you, the sword said.

Jekaran froze. The sword was talking about the strange thing that happened when Jekaran beheaded Kaul. Then the sword had done something it never had before; drained the life from Kaul's dying body and given it to him. The result had been the closing of Jekaran's cuts, the smoothing of his charred flesh, and a wave of fresh energy invigorating him. Knowing where the power came from made him sick.

You are a strange human, the sword said. Your fellows glory in the ability to destroy and take from their enemies, but it causes you disgust and guilt.

Was my uncle the same as me? Or was he like my fellows'? The question had been weighing on Jekaran's mind ever since leaving Genra. He'd told himself it didn't matter; Ez had changed. But the truth was, the more he understood the sword and what it made him want to do, the more he wondered just how much of a monster Argentus had been.

All I know about your uncle is what you know about him.

Why don't you remember being bonded to him?

The sword projected something that reminded Jekaran of shrugging. My first memories are of waking in Rasha and fighting those bandits with you.

Suddenly it made sense. Losing an Apeiron charge is death for you, isn't it?

As it is for you.

Jekaran scoffed. I'm not a talis. The resultant echo reminded him to keep his conversation and all of its related expressions inside his head. Humans don't have Apeiron charges.

Yes, you do.

That's when it hit him. The sword could drain Kaul's life because it ate Apeiron, which meant that Apeiron and life must be one and the same.

Now you understand.

"No, I don't!" Jekaran said aloud.

"Shut up!" The shout echoed from one of the other prisoners.

He ignored it. "Those emerald chips in your blade lit up when you drained Kaul's life. I've never seen another talis with those. They look like shards of an Apeira well, but they're green. What are they?"

You don't know a word for it, so therefore I don't know a word for it.

"Then show me!"

The sword projected an idea directly into his mind. It took a moment for the concept to take shape, but when it did, the closest name Jekaran could give it was corruption. No, not corruption, he decided, but decay?

Both words are inaccurate, but they do come close to describing the concept.

"I still don't get it," Jekaran said.

You have the same inside you.

He froze, his blood chilling and his mouth suddenly feeling dry. *What did you say?*

I said nothing, the sword reminded him.

You know what I mean!

You have the same corruption and decay in your blood. It is why I was able to transfer Apeiron into you and heal your wounds.

I ate Apeiron?

Karak's words struck his memory like a lightning bolt: "Uska human boy go to Eater."

"Divine Mother," Jekaran gasped. Panic thrilled through him, and he shut off his mental contact with the sword so completely, that he almost couldn't feel their bond. He frantically scooted into the front corner of the cell, so he was pressed up against the bars. He drew his legs up and hugged himself as if for warmth, though it wasn't cold. He could feel himself trembling, and he shut his eyes so tight that it hurt.

He didn't know exactly what the connection between Karak's words and the sword's description of what it did to Kaul was, but it felt significant. *You have the same corruption and decay in your blood,* the sword had said. Jekaran had eaten Apeiron, had eaten Kaul's life force. Karak had called the monster he was hunting, "The Eater," and had said Jekaran would lead him to it. Was that because he was also an "Eater" of Apeiron? An Eater of life?

That possibility terrified him.

KAIRAH STOOD FROZEN, the sight of the dead Apeira well paralyzed her and brutally twisted her heart strings. Another flash of emerald lightning lit the night sky revealing hundreds of bones strewn about the city square. The base of the well ascended from the ground like normal, but about ten feet up the shaft broke, and the rest of the obelisk lay at an angle with its top resting inside the attic of a crumbling building. But the worst part about the sight was the color of the Apeira well. It was not the soft purple that made the crystalline growth look like a giant amethyst. No, the well was green, making it look like a giant, uncut emerald.

Kairah shook herself out of her stunned stupor and climbed three steps to a cement dais that had been poured in a circle around the base of the well. She slowly approached the well until she was close enough to see her fractured reflection in its glass-like surface. Even close up she could not feel anything radiating from it. She timidly reached out to touch it. Pain seared her finger and she yelped, pulling back her arm and stepping away from the well. Her foot landed on a skull and she lost her balance, falling backward to the ground.

The impact expelled the wind from her lungs and she lay heaving on a bed of scattered bones until she could catch her breath. When she did, Kairah rolled onto her side and rose to her knees. She quickly examined her finger to find that it was not blackened or burnt.

But the burning had not been one of heat. It was as if Kairah had touched a chunk of cardice. A breeze pressed against Kairah. But no, it couldn't be a breeze, for the air in this place was abnormally still. And it wasn't her physical senses that reported this new sensation to her; it was her core.

She could feel a power coursing all around her, flowing toward the dead well. It was like the force of a radiating Apeira well, but in reverse. As if the well were sucking in energy instead of emitting it.

"Impossible," Kairah whispered. For some reason the eerie quiet of this place made her want to be as discreet as she could, as though she were trying to avoid alerting some unseen predator.

She slowly stood, unconsciously brushing human ash from her

dress. Could this energy be "the other magic?" It made sense. It felt like Apeiron, but opposite. But what was it?

Moriora, a voice like Aeva's whispered to her mind.

A clap of deafening thunder startled her, setting her heart to race, and Kairah knew that she'd caught the attention of the unseen predator.

"I'm not going to hold your hand!" Ezra snapped at Irvis. They stood just outside the door to Racheta's Pleasure House in one of the lowbrow parts of Imaris.

"I'd poke out my eyes, but I'm going to need them later!" Irvis huffed indignantly. The man had tied a blindfold around his face and was just finishing up knotting it at the back of his head. "Please Argentus." His tone changed to pathetic. "For the sake of my immortal soul."

"Damnation, man!" Ezra spat as he reached over and gripped Irvis by the forearm.

"Wait! What of the boy? I'd hate to know that I had a hand in corrupting his sweet, innocent mind."

Ezra looked over at Mulladin, who was smiling as he carefully stroked a giggling woman's hair. She was clearly a prostitute and had congregated around him with three of her busty associates.

"Too late," Ezra chuckled before calling, "Mulladin!" The boy looked back at Ezra and obediently dropped his hand and turned away. The women jeered at Ezra, but he ignored them.

Ezra looked up at a wooden sign swinging on a pole that jutted out ten feet above the building' entrance. He took a deep breath. This could only go one of two ways, either Graelle would accept his story about Jekaran succeeding him as head of the Rikujo or she would have Ezra executed on the spot as a deserting traitor.

He used his trick for defending against psychic attacks to calm himself. Then he stood up a little straighter and tried to remember how Argentus used to arrogantly saunter into places like this, expecting every woman in the inn to fight for his business. It disturbed him how easily it came back to him.

Rasheera forgive me, he silently pleaded, and then threw open the doors. The brazen action stilled a room full of scantily clad girls flirting with men as they lounged or drank. They all turned to stare at the door, some looking startled, but all looking irritated.

"I love the smell of all that perfume," Irvis whispered, although amid the awkward silence it all but sounded like he was shouting. Ezra ignored his friend and did his best to stare down any challenging gazes. Then, to Ezra's utter surprise, all of the girls and their prospective patrons nonchalantly returned to flirting and drinking. They didn't recognize him.

For some reason that stung. *Makes sense. Most of these women were children when I left the Rikujo.* That thought made any small temptation to ogle the girls vanish.

"What's happening, Argentus?" Irvis whispered.

Before he could reply, one of the women broke from speaking to a man at the bar and moved to greet them. She was older than the other girls, perhaps forty, and the dress she wore was a little too tight, and not in an enticing way.

She eyed Ezra up and down and then said in a throaty voice, "Finally, a mature man. I tire of the usual boys we get." She smiled a ruby-lipped smile. "They're all so inexperienced. Too much in a hurry, if you know how I mean." She chuckled knowingly as she moved in closer to Ezra.

"What does she look like?" Irvis urgently whispered.

"We're not here for that," Ezra said as much to Irvis as to the woman. "I'm looking for someone."

The woman reached up with chubby arms and laced her fingers around the back of Ezra's head so that she was pressed up against him. "Well, I'd say you found someone."

Ezra looked down into her face and said, "Graelle."

The woman's entire face changed at Ezra's flat mention of the name and she abruptly let go of him. She took a step back and said in a tone that was not the least bit seductive, "Oh, you're one of them." She turned and hollered at one of the younger girls who was currently sitting in the lap of another man and playing with his moustache, "Mistiana, go tell mother that one of her cousins is her to see her."

"I'm with a client," Mistiana replied in a tone of barely strained respect.

"Not yet you aren't!" The chubby woman snapped. "Now go!"

Mistiana huffed and rolled her eyes as she stood and walked away, a hand going to her shoulder each time her quarter sleeve slipped down, which was almost with every step. The chubby woman turned back to face Ezra. "My name is Varin." She paused to leer at him again and smiled as she asked, "Mother is very busy. Are you sure you don't want to make the most of your time while you wait?"

"Perhaps we–" Irvis began.

Ezra cut him off. "We're sure."

"How about when you're finished with business you and– "

"Quite sure," Ezra repeated in a polite but firm tone.

Varin shrugged and said, "Suit yourself," before finding another target and moving off to introduce herself with the same overbearing lasciviousness she had used on Ezra.

"This is killing me, Argentus!" Irvis hissed.

"Then take off the damned blindfold!" Ezra snapped.

"I can't!" Irvis said. It almost sounded as if he were about to cry.

Divine Mother! "Do you want to be celibate or not?"

"Want?" Irvis asked, but before he could answer, another voice caught his attention.

"Well by Rasheera's breasts! Argentus!"

Ezra looked over to see a squat, stern-looking woman standing behind the bar. She had a round face, was chubbier than Varin, and wore her hair in an iron-grey bun. In an odd juxtaposition with the setting and its other players, her dress was overly modest, long and made of plain wool with sleeves that covered her arms to the wrists, and a high neck that precluded the possibility of showing any cleavage.

Ezra caught the woman shoot a glance down at his hip where he once had carried the sword. He'd worried about how one of his old subordinates would react to seeing him without it. Would they still fear him?

"Graelle," Ezra replied. "You are still as enticing as any of these younger girls."

Graelle snorted. "And I thought he was the blind one!" She waved at Irvis. "Don't bother trying to flatter me, Argentus. You were never good at it, anyway."

Ezra smiled what he hoped to be a charming smile.

Graelle glanced around the room, looking as if she had only just noticed it was full of staring people. "Why don't we move this reunion somewhere more private." She waved for them to follow her as she disappeared through the door behind the bar.

"Is she really as gorgeous as the young girls?" Irvis asked as they walked around the far corner of the bar and then slipped behind it. Before Ezra could answer, Irvis tripped on a crate and stumbled into him.

Laughing came from the group of men and whores, and even Mulladin was chuckling. "Take that off!" Ezra hissed as he swiped for the blindfold. Irvis resisted at first, but then let him remove it. Ezra made sure to pull it off extra hard and was satisfied when Irvis exclaimed, "Divine Mother, that hurt!"

"Come on!" he demanded before leaving the laughing crowd of the common room behind.

Both Irvis and Mulladin quickly followed him down the hall to a room where Graelle sat behind a wooden table. This was it. If she were going to capture or kill Ezra, it would happen now. He took a deep breath, remembering when others used to fear being in his presence. He caught himself wishing that were still the case and then ground his teeth. I am not that man, anymore, he told himself. I am Jek's uncle.

"Well I didn't know I'd hired you on as a trio of traveling jesters," Graelle quipped.

"We had a– "

"I thought he was blind." Graelle waved at Irvis.

He turned to see Irvis standing frozen in the doorway, mouth hanging open like a country fool seeing an Apeira well for the first time. Mulladin made sharp, frustrated noises as he pushed passed him.

Ezra turned back to Graelle ready to make a snide remark about his friend when Irvis spoke first. "Not blind, my lady, although if today

Rasheera took my sight I would be satisfied that I had seen the most of beauty this world has to offer after beholding thy face."

Ezra stared at the chubby monk, and now it was his turn to gape.

"What's wrong with him?" Graelle demanded.

Ezra turned back to Graelle and flashed an apologetic smile. "He is– "

"Smitten!" Irvis almost shouted as he took a quick step toward Graelle.

She was out of her chair in a flash, her right hand suddenly holding some kind of rod-shaped talis. She had been just about to use it–Ezra was certain–when Irvis dropped to one knee before her. Graelle's angry look fell away replaced by wide eyes and a furrowed brow.

"My name is Irvis," the man said still with that absurd poetic cadence. "You may smite me if you wish, but know that even death will not stop my heart from beating for you."

Graelle didn't say anything. She looked up at Ezra with utter confusion in her blue eyes. That shook him out of his surprise, and Ezra shot an arm down and seized Irvis by the scruff of his robes. He pulled the portly man to his feet with an effort, and then slapped him hard across the face.

Irvis stared at him with wide eyes for a long moment before finally raising a hand to his reddened cheek. "What was that for?"

"Whatever your game is, it isn't working!" Ezra hissed.

"Game?" Irvis repeated incredulously.

"Stop making an ass of yourself and let me do the talking!"

"If Kaul hadn't been killed right here in Imaris just two days ago, I'd have both of you in chains by now!" Graelle loudly interrupted. Then her gaze settled on Ezra. "But you would know that, wouldn't you, Argentus?"

Ezra shot Irvis one last warning glare before focusing his full attention on Graelle, who appeared to relax a bit. She made her weapon talis disappear with as deft a hand as a stage magician and then pointed at chairs placed opposite her desk. "Sit," she ordered.

Ezra pulled one of the chairs over to him and sat. Then he motioned for Irvis and Mull to do the same. Graelle tapped a small, crystal rock that was lying on her desk as a paperweight. It was smooth, making it look like a glass pebble, and there was a small shard of amethyst embedded in the center–a speaking stone.

"Varin, bring me wine and four glasses."

"Yes, mother," the disembodied voice replied in such a clear tone Ezra could actually hear the repressed irritation in the other woman's tone.

A moment later Varin walked in with a bottle and four pewter mugs. She set them down on the table, deliberately putting her ample cleavage in his line of sight. She winked at Ezra, but he ignored it. He quickly shot a glance at Irvis, fully expecting the man to be shamelessly gawking, but he wasn't. Incredibly, the chubby monk appeared oblivious to Varin's attempts to entice them. In fact, his eyes were locked on Graelle's face?

Before Ezra could ask Irvis what was wrong with him, Graelle said, "I apologize for the quality of the wine. We've been watering it down lately to cut costs."

"And adding passion root to increase business," Varin chuckled wickedly.

Ezra hesitated as he was about to pick up his mug for Graelle to fill.

"It's not in this!" Graelle snapped and she looked up at Varin while filling his mug. "Don't you have work to be about?"

Varin sighed theatrically and let her fingertips gently trace Ezra's left cheek as she walked away.

"And close the door!" Graelle called, to which Varin responded by slamming the door. "That girl," Graelle said apologetically. "I'd fire her, but my older clients seem to favor her for some reason."

Ezra expected a comment from Irvis as to why that might be, but the man said nothing.

Graelle raised her mug to him, and then proceeded to throw it back and drain its contents. She took a deep breath when she was done, and unabashedly wiped her mouth on her long sleeve. Ezra took the cue and drank some of his own wine, albeit a bit more reservedly.

"So, you're back," Graelle said. "Just like that? One would think you had something to do with Kaul's untimely demise."

"He was killed by my nephew."

Graelle nodded. "Well, I have to say that I'm not sorry Kaul is dead. The man was unhinged. My girls dreaded it anytime he came to collect guild tithes in person because he'd usually want some free services. He was a cruel bastard that one. You coming back might bring stability, something the Rikujo hasn't had for a few years. That is if they don't kill you."

"I am not coming out of retirement, Graelle," Ezra said carefully. "I am here to ensure that my nephew, Jekaran, is accepted by the other Rikujo bosses as my successor."

Graelle snorted. "Well, my watchers tell me that your successor was captured by some minor lord who sailed away to goddess-only-knows where."

"Aiested," Ezra said simply.

Graelle was about to pour wine into the other two mugs when she stopped. That evoked a displeased noise from Mulladin, who was looking on and licking his lips in anticipation of a drink.

"He's being taken to the king?"

Ezra nodded and took another drink.

Graelle finished pouring the wine, and Mulladin snatched his mug off the table so fast that half of his drink slopped onto the floor in the process. "Then this isn't just a visit to announce your taking back the guild. You're here for my help."

Ezra nodded. "I need your slipgate to get to Aiested, and a handful of your enforcers to help me mount a rescue."

Graelle stared at him for a long moment before finally sighing. "I can't."

"Not even to help free the new lord of the Rikujo, your liege?" Ezra added in a menacing tone.

"You don't intimidate me anymore, Argentus, not without that sword," Graelle said in a steely tone. "In fact, it's at my forbearance that you live. You know what the law says about deserters."

"Of course I do," Ezra fired back. "I wrote it!"

"Then you of all people know that I should've put a bolt through your brain the moment you walked into my house!"

Ezra inhaled deeply to calm himself before continuing. "Jekaran killed Kaul. That gives him the right of succession. That is also in the law."

"It's not that easy anymore, Argentus. Kaul made a real mess of things. He was so obsessed with finding you that he mostly neglected running the Rikujo. While all the other bosses outwardly supported him, we all secretly hated him for his erratic behavior, cruelty, and liberties with our resources. We were of one mind in this.

"But now that he's gone, everyone will be scrambling atop each other to seize control. They're not going to let the uninitiated nephew of a traitor lead, especially when they blame Kaul's rise to power largely on the opportunity you gave him by leaving us."

"How is Kaul's takeover my fault?" Ezra shouted incredulously.

"Don't play stupid with me, Argentus! While the invincible shadow was leading us, Kaul was checked. The day you disappeared you effectively unchained that rabid dog."

Ezra wilted. He'd known Kaul's seizing the Rikujo in his absence had been a real possibility, but always tried to deny that it would happen.

"And even if the other bosses did recognize your nephew, how long do you think it would be before one of them assassinated him?"

"He has my sword," Ezra said, and his voice was quiet.

Graelle arched an eyebrow. "Well, even so, it's too late. I sent word to the others the moment I learned of Kaul's death. They've already planned a meeting to choose an interim head while they sort out where the right of succession really belongs."

"When are they meeting?"

"Tomorrow night." Graelle stared at him for a long moment, a startled look on her face. "You really didn't know, did you," she finally said. "And I thought your showing up was deliberately timed. You're not really trying to win my support for your nephew before the Rikujo meet in council, are you? This isn't about clever political maneuvering, is it?"

Defeated, Ezra dropped his head and with it all pretense of his former self; though he hadn't really succeeded in capturing The Invincible Shadow's arrogant charm–Graelle's challenging him was evidence enough of that. For some reason, not being able to portray his former self comforted him. "I lied about my nephew. He has no intention of ruling the Rikujo."

"Then why– "

"I needed help to save him," Ezra cut in. "The king will have him executed for being caught wielding a weapon talis." He looked up at

Graelle, meeting her eyes. Not sure why he was so honest with her. She was, after all, a Rikujo crime boss. Not the safest or most trustworthy of confidants. But somehow, telling her the truth felt like the right thing to do.

"Jekaran accidentally bonded my old sword. He's a good and honest boy, not a hardened criminal like us. He didn't even know who I really was until a few weeks ago when Kaul found me. I left the Rikujo to raise him when my sister died and he's become like a son to me."

Graelle's face was ashen and she looked as shocked as though Ezra had just proven to her that she was really the goddess Rasheera in human form. "You've really changed," she whispered, more to herself than to him.

Ezra smiled wanly. "I'm a farmer now, Graelle."

After a long, uncomfortable moment, Graelle finally spoke. "The most I can do to help is pretend that our meeting never took place. You can leave and I won't say anything to the other bosses." Her grim look and solemn tone made him think of a midwife telling a woman her child was born dead.

"Please, Graelle, let me use your slipgate."

"I don't have one!" she snapped. "Neither do I have any enforcers, so don't even bother begging for those." She sighed. "I told you Kaul was abusing our resources. He had the gate moved to another city."

"And your enforcers?"

Graelle shook her head. "Kaul took them too. He said that if my girls couldn't defend themselves when things got out of hand, then they deserved whatever they got. He also said that if a man was paying for the girl, he had the right to beat her."

"So the meeting is here in Imaris?"

Graelle shook her head. "No, Erassa."

Ezra furrowed his brow, feeling confused. "That's over fifty miles away. How are you going to..." he trailed off when Graelle shook the bracelet on her right hand. It was in the shape of a thick gold chain with an amethyst stone embedded in the center on top where the chain met. Ezra laughed. "Jaris said he never was able to get his hands on that. He said that he aborted sneaking into Lord Grenlan's keep because they'd been discovered."

Graelle smirked. "Well, it sounds like Jaris lied to you."

Ezra barked a laugh. "That old bastard."

"What is it?" Irvis asked, his voice shaking for some reason.

"A shift bracelet; the most powerful portable displacement talis," Ezra answered. "Very rare."

"And don't even think of asking to use it. It wouldn't get you to Aiested, anyway. Too far, especially for all three of you. In fact, I'm going to have to take a ship to sail back here just to keep it charged."

"But Erassa will have a slipgate," Ezra said.

Graelle stared at him, an incredulous look on her face. "My bracelet won't take four that far."

"I'd only need you to take three." Ezra thumbed his earring. "This is full and should be able to manage the distance for one."

Graelle shot him another incredulous look. "Argentus," she said emphatically, "they will kill you!"

"Not if we convince them that I'm the envoy of my nephew, the slayer of Kaul and the new Invincible Shadow!"

"Please, that story didn't work on me and I–" Graelle's eyes widened. "We? No, no, no, no, no," she said shaking her head. "If you want to get yourself killed that's one thing, but I'm not going to risk my neck for you! If I support you and you fail, the best that I could hope for would be to lose my territory and my girls."

"Please, Graelle. I can't rescue my nephew without the resources of the Rikujo, and I can't get access to those resources without your support! I've been away too long. I've forgotten how to act like a crime lord. I can only sell this lie if I have your coaching and support."

"You haven't even offered to pay for my help! I'm not some celibate old Handmaiden of Rasheera doling out penance for the poor!"

"I will pay you."

"What could you possibly offer that would be worth me putting my life on the line?""

"The Rikujo," Ezra answered simply.

Graelle eyed him suspiciously. "How?"

"You help me convince the other bosses that my nephew is their rightful leader, and I will make certain you are appointed his successor when I disappear again."

Graelle snorted. "Because that worked so well last time."

Ezra ignored the jibe and said, "Think about it. You wouldn't have to pander to anyone else or pay guild tithes. You could set up in whatever territory you wished, and most of all," Ezra paused for effect, "you would be able to protect your girls."

That last part was pure inspiration, it appearing to strike Graelle in the heart. She furrowed her brow, dropping her eyes to the side as she considered his offer. A beat later she met his eyes again and nodded.

"Fine, I'll help you. But if this doesn't work, I will put a bolt through your brain! Understand, Argentus?"

He smiled. "Actually, it's Ezra now."

Graelle's steely stare bore into him. "Not if you want to convince the other bosses you're still a ruthless crime lord."

"I'm Irvis!" Ezra's chubby friend blurted out.

What was wrong with him? Why was he acting so odd?

Graelle didn't even spare Irvis a look. Instead, she rose to her feet. "We're going to have to get you a set of decent clothes. If I remember, the Invincible Shadow always did favor Tolean green." Graelle walked to a painting on the wall, a scandalous thing depicting an image that would make even a jaded sailor blush. She removed the painting and set it on the floor. It had not been just a profane decoration to arouse potential clients, but a way to conceal a square metal safe embedded in the wall.

Ezra glanced at Irvis to see if his friend's attention would shift to the obscene painting, but it didn't. The chubby monk's eyes were still fixed on Graelle. Divine Mother, he sighed. This would have to happen now.

The safe had no keyhole or opening mechanism of any kind. The only thing Ezra could see on its smooth, metallic face was a square cut amethyst. "You're going to need proof that Kaul is really dead." Graelle leaned in close to the safe and said, "Open." Ezra's eyes widened as the metal of the safe transformed into a translucent liquid.

He caught a smile at the edge of Graelle's mouth. She reached her hand through the liquid metal, grabbed something, and then pulled it back. "Close," she said once her hand was free, and the safe's liquid face solidified into solid metal again.

"That's quite a talis," he said.

"So is this." Graelle tossed something at him, activating Ezra's reflexes so that he caught the object before it could hit him in the face. He was about to snap at Graelle for her deliberately harmful aim when recognized what he was holding–a small metal disc cast in the shape of a skull. It had two amethyst stones set into the skull's eyes, and a cord looped through a small bracket on its top. It was a medallion, a talis. Kaul's dread medal.

"How..."

"One of my girls saw the duel between Kaul and your nephew, that's how I first heard about it. She was close and so was able to snatch that up before the Imarin city guard got to the body."

Ezra looked up from the dread medal and Graelle narrowed her eyes at him. She jabbed the air with a finger. "And don't bother trying to use it on me. I made sure to learn how to resist its influence the moment that maniac took over the Rikujo. Taught it to my girls too, for all the good that it did. Their real fear of Kaul was enough for them to..." she trailed off, her brow knitting down and her mouth turning into a frown.

"What about Arynda's ring or Jaris' shield br–"

"No." Graelle shook her head. "My girl barely got away with this before the guard showed up."

Ezra looked back down at the fear talis and nodded his head. "Well, this should be evidence enough to convince them."

"Oh, I didn't give it to you to use as evidence," Graelle said with a new smile. "You're going to use its magic to make them believe you!"

"The other Rikujo lords will have learned the same trick."

"Maybe," Graelle said. "Though I doubt all of them have the mental fortitude for it. Even the ones that do will be put off guard by it."

Thank you, Rasheera, Ezra silently prayed. This obvious intervention of the goddess could mean only one thing; She had accepted his offering.

CHAPTER 47

Maely hugged herself and rubbed her shoulders for warmth. It was noticeably colder this far north, something she hadn't expected or prepared for. She'd tried to start a fire the way Ez had taught them, but all she was ever able to produce from rubbing sticks together was a blister on her hand. Out of exasperation, she'd even tried to use her mother's ring to command the fire to start, but, of course, that did nothing.

Where is Karak? She ground her teeth, which were already chattering. The Lizard man had disappeared just before dusk, presumably to go hunt for their dinner. He could've told me where he was going, Maely huffed aloud. But her trembling made it come out sounding more like she was crying, which she was not! She hadn't done that since Imaris.

Maely looked up to the sky above the tree line. She could see Aiested's giant Apeira well reaching into the sky. It made the city look deceptively close, but they still had over a day's worth of travel to go. Maely clenched her teeth together to stop their chattering, which it did, but only at the cost of making her jaw ache.

Damn you, Jekaran! She used the anger to work through the pain in her jaw and keep her teeth clamped together. If it weren't for him, the two of them would be in Jeryn by now, with Mulladin and Ez—where it was warm. Thinking of Jekaran made her anger fade, worry quickly taking its place. The last time she'd seen him, Jekaran was grievously wounded, and being taken from her by that insufferable nobleman, Gymal.

Was he ok? Had Gymal the decency to hire a physician to attend him? Or was that pompous, scrawny, ugly goblin of a man just going to have him executed? *He's in trouble, and I'm just sitting around here, waiting for my dinner!* She was hungry and tired–how did one get tired from riding all day, anyway?–and were it not for the cold, probably would've drifted off to sleep by now. But that worry, it was just as cold as the air. It wouldn't let her sleep either.

What if I get to Aiested too late? Hot tears spilled down her cheeks, the wetness making the chill bite harder into her face. She had the power to save Jek. Her mother's ring would let her walk right into the palace and up to the king himself and demand Jek's release. An abomination, Kairah had called her talis. Perhaps in the wrong hands. But Maely didn't care about kingdoms or glory, or even money–well, a little bit about money. All she really cared about was getting Jekaran away from all of this trouble. Away from the sword, and away Kairah.

She was on her feet before she fully realized what she was doing. No, she couldn't wait around for dinner or sleep. She had to go to Jekaran now. He needed her, and she could save him! Rescuing him at such risk to herself was bound to open his eyes. Then he would have to see that they were meant to be together–wouldn't he?

Maely gathered her things and untied her ghern. It looked up at her as though it were irritated that she'd interrupted its grazing. "No argument," Maely snapped at the animal, and it snorted as if it had understood her.

Maely laughed, but it wasn't a mirthful sound. It was a ragged thing, exhaled involuntarily as she was teetered on the edge of hysteria. She wiped her cold, wet cheeks, and climbed into the ghern's saddle where she wrapped herself in a blanket. It was only going to get colder as she rode into the night wind. They were close enough now she could find her own way to the capitol by simply heading towards the giant Apeira well. Perhaps she could even reach Aiested by morning.

However, only a couple hours into her lone flight her ghern began to flag. At first, it was just breathing hard, but gradually its pace slowed until it was moving along at little more than a trot. And no amount of shouting at it or snapping its reins would make the beast run any faster. Finally it stopped, breathing so hard it sounded like it had just come up for air after a long dive.

"Go!" she snapped the reins, but the animal did not respond.

Tears leaked down her cheeks again, making them feel raw in the chill night air. It was not supposed to be this way! She needed to get to Jekaran. She had the power to save him! That thought gave her pause, and she brushed the band of her mother's ring with her thumb. Did it only work on humans?

"Go!" Maely shouted at the ghern, this time commanding it with her ring. She felt the familiar power carry her words to her target and the ghern froze. A heartbeat later it leapt back into a run. Maely smiled to herself. She did have the power to save Jekaran, and no one or nothing could stand in her way.

RAELEN FOUND himself unable to sleep. So, just as he always did when battling insomnia, he stood on the balcony outside his quarters and watched the city. He was bare-chested, and the cool sea air felt good on his skin. It was well into the night now, so the streets were mostly quiet and empty.

The few souls who walked the streets of Aiested at night were mostly street folk and criminals. He chuckled at himself at making that distinction, for the two were often the same thing. Not always, though.

Raelen had been using a looking stone to magnify the images below, and had taken particular interest in a young woman cradling a bundle and trailed by two small children. He'd first caught sight of them when they'd been leaving one of the market streets, probably where they'd been loitering for most of the day to beg. Now they trundled down one of Aiested's arterial streets. Raelen had an idea of where they were headed, and his heart sank when his guess was confirmed.

The vice district, it was called. It was the area of the city replete with opiate dens, gambling houses, and whores. Probably the mother hadn't been able to beg enough scraps or coin to feed her children, and so was looking to make up her losses by selling her body.

Who would care for the children while she let herself be raped? It sickened him, and when he saw the woman give the bundle to the taller of the two smaller forms, and walk into an alley with a skinny, bald, man in rags, he had to turn away.

How could anyone with the power to change these people's lives do nothing but stand as an idle witness? Well, Raelen didn't really have that power, not yet. Oh, he had money and influence, but those would only let him do so much. Certainly, he could and had done things to alleviate this kind of suffering–only symptoms–but without the crown, he couldn't do much to permanently cure the illness. That would take the authority to set policy and exact action and money from the nobility.

Only his father could do that, and the man cared little for the wretched lives of his peasants. As was evidenced earlier in his decision to slaughter Isara's villagers, a decision not made from a passionate desire to avenge the deaths of his people, but one wrought in cool calculation. As though he was playing one of his map and stone piece war games.

Earlier that evening, before his father closed their war council, Raelen had pled with him to call back the army he'd sent to the border. If the Allosian woman's brother truly were trying to ignite a new talis war between the human nations, should they really be so quick to commit to military action? For the second time that day, Raelen's father surprised him, this time by sending a messenger to halt the advance of the force he'd deployed to the border–though the king hadn't recalled them. They would stay camped fifty miles east of Aiested, ready should the command to attack Haeshala be re-issued.

"Sound reasoning, my son," the King had complimented Raelen again.

He'd even called him "my son," in public. As confusing as the change in his father's behavior had been, Raelen's emotional reaction to the compliment had been even more confusing. It had made him swell with satisfaction, feeling proud, and he'd been seized with a sudden inclination toward loyalty to his father. Worse still, Raelen had wanted to say and do more to please the king in hopes of receiving more fatherly praise. It disturbed him, and only thinking of Saranna hurling herself from a castle tower reminded Raelen of just how much he hated his father.

"He's back," Gryyth growled.

Raelen nodded without turning and said, "Let him in."

A moment later another voice spoke. "I am sorry to have awakened you, my prince, but his highness' orders explicitly stated to–"

"Report at once no matter how late the hour. Yes, and I wasn't sleeping. And don't refer to me in the third person. It's irritating." Raelen turned from the cityscape and found Navarch Pariel standing just inside the door to his quarters, the blank look Raelen associated with professional soldiers on his face.

"Of course, my prince." Pariel nodded.

Raelen stepped inside, passed Pariel, and fetched a silken night robe hanging by a gold hook from his wall. He noticed Pariel steal a glance at the sinuous gold band encircling his right bicep just before he slipped into his robe.

Raelen stopped and looked down at the talis. Aside from its amethyst well-shard, the band was encrusted with a melee of four smaller jewels. They were diamonds, but two of the four were clouded with a murky reddish-brown that contrasted poorly against the clear stones.

"It is a transference band," Raelen said. A startled flinch betrayed Pariel's cool professionalism. He hadn't known I'd caught him looking. Well, that was understandable. It was the height of rudeness in Aiestali culture to ask after a person's talises, especially when that person held a higher social station.

Raelen flashed what he hoped was reassuring smile. "It's supposed to be the only one still in existence–although I can't guess how anybody can make that claim with full surety. It drinks in the blood of an animal and grants the wearer one physical attribute possessed by that beast." Raelen slipped the robe on and began to tie the front closed at his waist.

Pariel's eyes flicked to Gryyth. The towering Ursaj was standing quietly by the wall.

"Yes," Raelen said. "I used two drops of Gryyth's blood, one for each attribute that I wanted to borrow from him. I tried for the full four, but the other two gems don't work for some reason. I think it was damaged in the last talis war."

"Impressive, my prince. You honor me by showing– "

"I am not my father, Pariel." Raelen walked over to a corner in his room where a table was set with some chairs for dining. He sat and rubbed his eyes. "I do not hold as strictly to decorum as he does. So please, stop acting so verbally circumspect."

"Of course, your highness."

Raelen sighed. "In private you may omit the royal honorifics. Sire or my lord will do just fine."

Pariel sharply nodded, apparently hesitant to try a lesser title. "I've watched the chamber where your father placed the Allosian woman as you commanded."

"Did Loeadon go there?"

Pariel shook his head. "No, Sire," he said. "And I made sure that I was not noticed by any of the other polymaths, or even the guards."

Raelen sighed and kneaded his right eye with the heel of his palm. "Damn. I was sure he would want to check on her."

"Sire?"

Raelen stopped rubbing his eyes and looked up into Pariel's face. "I have great respect for you, Navarch Pariel." He held up his hand to forestall the man from praising his magnanimity. The soldier closed his mouth abruptly, embarrassment coloring his cheeks red. "You have proven yourself loyal to my family. I trust you. That is why I need your help."

"Of course, Sire. You need only command me."

Raelen smiled wanly. "I am afraid that this cannot be an official command, Pariel."

"I don't understand."

"I suspect that Loeadon is the Allosian woman's brother in disguise, working at cross purposes against the crown in his plot to ignite a talis war." He waited for a surprised reaction from Pariel but only received a cool nod.

"I see," the soldier said.

Damn but that man is hard to read. "I have no proof, however, and as you know, Loeadon holds a station on par with the Polemarch, and the High Lords. I cannot accuse him outright."

"Why not confide this to your father?" Pariel asked.

Raelen barked a harsh laugh. "He has never been one of my confidantes. And you know he worships kingdom law. I would be censured for not following proper legal methods of presenting a formal accusation against one of the high nobility, which would only make it harder to convince him."

"I understand," Pariel said. "What is it you wish me to do then?"

"Have you been issued new orders, yet?"

"No. All that is on hold because of last night's developments."

Raelen nodded to himself. "Praise Rasheera for that small blessing." He stood. "Navarch, I need you to watch Loeadon as much as possible, especially around the Allosian woman's quarters. I need to know what he's up to in order to make a case against him."

Pariel saluted. "Of course, my prince."

Raelen placed a friendly hand on the man's shoulder. "Pariel, do not agree until you understand the risks."

Pariel looked confused. "Agree?"

"I told you I cannot command you in this thing. If you are caught, I won't be able to protect you. Do you understand this?"

Pariel gave another curt, soldier's nod. "You may not wish to command me, but your request is every bit as binding to me as though you had, for the sake of my honor."

Raelen smiled. "You are a good man, Pariel. One day, when I am king, you will play a key role in my rule."

Pariel saluted again, and then turned and strode from Raelen's quarters. After Gryyth had closed the door, Raelen exhaled and slumped his shoulders.

"You should sleep, my prince," Gryyth rumbled.

Raelen shook his head as he walked back out onto the balcony. He lifted the looking stone he'd left on the rail and brought it up to his eye, searching to find the peasant woman and her children he'd spied on earlier.

He found them. They were huddled against the outside wall of the same tavern. The woman was cradling her baby and rocking back and forth. Raelen willed the looking talis to show him a closer view. The woman's face was bloody, and she was barely keeping the front of her torn tunic from exposing her breasts. Her client had clearly beaten her, perhaps to avoid paying, or more likely because the man had been a sadist.

"How can I sleep in my comfortable bed, Gryyth, when women and children freeze in the street? How can I eat my delicate foods when babies cry out for milk that their mother is not healthy enough to give? How can I sleep knowing an enemy lurks within my own house, trying to destroy my people?"

Gryyth's warm, furry hand gently clamped down on his shoulder. "You know Seiro, cub. And when you become king, you will teach Seiro to your kind."

And suddenly Raelen felt like a boy again; vulnerable and afraid. So he did what he always did when he felt this way. He sought reassurance from Gryyth in the one way he knew how. "Tell me the story of Jarrsh and the king of dragons?"

Gryyth rumbled a soft laugh. "You have not asked that of me in years."

"I know," Raelen said. "It's one of my favorites, and I could use the distraction."

"If you promise to sleep after the telling," Gryyth said.

Raelen laughed. "You haven't made that bargain with me in years."

"It seemed appropriate."

"Well?" Raelen asked.

"Well?" Gryyth repeated.

"Fine," Raelen said. "We have a bargain."

Gryyth rumbled a low chuckle. "Jarrsh was little more than a cub when he left his den to seek adventure," Gryyth began, and for a time, Raelen was comforted.

Chapter 48

Maely tripped over a loose stone hiding half buried in the dirt of the road. She stumbled forward and skinned her knees as she crashed to the ground. Divine Mother, she was tired! She didn't immediately rise, her intense fatigue tempting her to just lie down and sleep. But no, she couldn't. Not when she was this close. She looked up at the Apeira well reaching into the sky, its top hidden by clouds. It cast them in an eerie purple light, making false dawn look more like a sunset.

She was close enough to see Aiested now. It was so large that when she'd first seen it, she'd thought she had been much closer than she was. That was hours ago, just before her ghern collapsed from exhaustion and died. She grimaced. Apparently using her mother's ring to compel the beast to keep running after it showed signs of fatigue had killed it. And the death must've been a horrendous one. Running beyond exhaustion, forced to keep going until your body literally couldn't run any more. Well, she might feel something like that at the moment.

She staggered to her feet and resumed her unsteady gait. Jekaran's life hung in the balance, and Maely would be damned if she was going to let exhaustion stop her from saving him, especially when she had the power to do so. She just wished she could command her fatigue away, but the ring didn't work like that. It didn't stave off sleep and hunger, or control the elements like Kairah's magic could. That'd be handy right about now.

For all that she envied about the perfect Allosian woman, she'd never thought to want Kairah's magic. That made her laugh at herself, though it came out weak from her parched throat and aching lungs.

Maely's thoughts were a muddled blur of unarticulated emotions as she slowly passed one mile after another. Dawn had come in full force by the time she reached the capitol city. The sight of it shocked her back into lucidity and she temporarily forget her overwhelming physical fatigue.

For all she'd seen from afar, the city was even more magnificent up close. Un-walled, Aiested was circular in shape and made up of thousands of white buildings, all surrounding an enormous palace built around the base of Aiested's even larger Apeira well. In fact, it looked to Maely as though the purple crystal obelisk rose up directly from the palace.

The sounds around her awakened Maely from her half-conscious stupor. How had she not been aware of the people bustling toward and away from the city—there were so many. Most walked, but a good number pulled handcarts or rode in ghern-drawn wagons.

From their manner of dress, Maely at first thought they were all nobility. Their clothes were clean, brightly colored, and in good repair. But after observing the carts full of produce or the men carrying packs full of assorted wares, she realized that she was walking among the peasantry, or perhaps minor merchants. Even the lowborn of the city appeared to be living more comfortably than their counterparts in the surrounding cities and villages. For some reason that made Maely bitter.

She collected her wits and made her way into the city with renewed physical energy. However, after walking for two more hours, she began to grasp the sheer enormity of Aiested. The palace loomed forever in front of her, but it could take a day's walk to reach it, and the brief burst of energy she'd received upon arriving was expended. Her mind was becoming muddled again, and the sounds around her faded in and out in tandem with the fuzzing of her vision.

Without consciously deciding it, Maely walked into one of the dozen inns lining the right side of the street. In some part of her mind, it made sense that so many inns would be grouped this close together on the outskirts of the city. Smells of hot food mixed with pipe smoke struck her like a physical force upon walking through an arched doorway. The ivory walls of the common room were not as pristinely white as the building's exterior, and Maely attributed that to the cloud of tobacco pooling near the ceiling.

She approached a tall, skinny woman at the counter and had to repeat herself when the woman shot her a quizzical look. "I need a room."

"I'll say you do, child. Do you have coin?"

Maely fished in her pockets and brought out two iron pennies, which she dropped on the counter. The woman scowled at the coins and scoffed. "That's not even enough for a drink." She made a shewing motion with her hands. "We don't abide beggars here."

Those words combined with the woman's casual dismissal penetrated the shell of Maely's emotional detachment and her rage exploded. "Give me a room, bitch!" she screamed. The familiar feeling of command the ring transmitted shot out from her chest and struck the woman so forcefully that she actually stumbled backward.

"Of course, mistress," the woman exhaled sharply. "We have our largest and most lavish room available. And would you like a bath and some food brought to you?"

"Yes," Maely sneered. "I want every amenity you offer."

"Yes, mistress." The tall woman bobbed her head and began shouting orders with such urgency, that Maely might've thought the building on fire.

Maely smiled to herself and some part of her decided this was how life for her should be.

Hours later Maely awoke with a startled splash. Her bath had been so wonderfully comfortable that she'd fallen asleep. She hugged herself as the cooled water made her shiver. How long had she slept? She cast a glance out the window and found the sun hanging low in the sky making it late afternoon.

Maely swore as she stood out of the water, more cold air assaulting every bit of her naked flesh. She nearly slipped on the marble floor as she scrambled to a soft cream-colored robe hanging on the chamber wall. She quickly wrapped herself in the robe and stumbled through an arched doorway into a gigantic bedchamber.

It was opulent with its colorful silks, soft pillows, and a bed that was the size of her entire cottage–well that was probably an exaggeration, but it looked that big. On the bed folded neatly in a pile was a brand new dress of deep velvet green. She'd demanded the most expensive outfit the innkeeper had, and was a bit disappointed with the gown–it not having as much lace as she envisioned. She shrugged out of the robe and began to quickly dress. She had to hurry if she was going to get to the palace. She didn't have any idea how much time Jekaran had left, but it couldn't be much.

That is if he isn't already dead, an accusing voice whispered. She swore again, deciding she would never forgive herself if her oversleeping in the tub cost Jek his life, but she didn't think that was the case. She finished dressing, threw on a fine, black, hooded cape brought with her dress, and snatched a cold piece of chicken from the plate on an end table.

Maely threw open the door, flew down the stairs, and into the common room. She froze on the last stair when she caught sight of two men in white tabard-covered armor. One of the serving girls was talking with them. She glanced at Maely and started pointing and shouting. Apparently, the charitable behavior of the inn's hostess was so out of place the serving girl had summoned the city guard. Probably thinks I was threatening her mistress.

One of the guards moved to block the door to the street while the other put a hand on the pommel of a sword hanging from his belt and moved toward her. "Hold right there, miss," he said.

"I don't have time for this," Maely snarled and she began walking toward the door.

The armored guard rushed forward and caught her by her left arm.

"Let go of me!" Maely hissed, and the familiar undercurrent of power launched her words at the guard.

His face changed and he let go of Maely. "S-sorry," he stammered. The guard blocking the door shot his companion a surprised glance and then reached for his sword.

"Get on the ground," Maely commanded. The guard jerked, dropped his sword, and fell to his knees, all the while begging Maely's pardon.

Maely stepped to the door and then hesitated. She looked back at the serving girl who'd implicated her to the guards. The woman began to back away, her eyes wild with fright and Maely thought she caught her breathe out, "talis!"

"Strip!" Maely commanded.

The woman started nodding vigorously, dropped her tray full of food, and then began to unbutton her blouse. Maely smirked as she left the inn, listening to a group of men raucously cheering on the serving girl. That'll teach her, she thought as she walked into the street and up to a waiting coach.

"I want to go to the palace," Maely said to the driver.

"I am sorry, my lady," the older man said. "I've already accepted payment to take–"

"Take me to the palace!" Maely commanded.

The driver leapt down from his seat and rushed to open the carriage door. Maely saw a middle-aged woman sitting inside the carriage knitting to pass the time. She looked up and began to say, "It's about time, Agnell..."

"Out!" The coachman bellowed.

"But I've already paid," the woman protested.

"Get out now," Maely hissed.

The woman reacted to the compulsion and climbed out of the carriage so fast she left her knitting and lady's bag on the seat. Maely climbed into the coach and sat down where the woman had been sitting. She tossed the half-finished knitting project–it looked like it was going to be a doily–out into the street just before the coachman closed the door. Then she rifled through the woman's bag and was rewarded with three gold Aies. She pocketed the money and sat back as the carriage lurched forward.

The ride to the palace took quite a bit longer than Maely expected, and by the time they arrived, the sun was dipping below the horizon. A long line of carriages was parked in front of the gates to the palace grounds, so Maely had the coachman let her out and drive away. She didn't need to worry about escape plans or stealth. She didn't need to worry about fighting or hiding. She would walk right into the palace and demand Jekaran's release, and she would be obeyed. Even by the king himself.

A quick magic-loaded command to the guards at the gate and Maely strolled in without stopping. Each time she was questioned or halted she would use her compulsion ring, and before long, she was inside the palace itself. It was much larger inside than she'd expected, and decided that she would need an escort to help her find Jek. She smiled as she watched a lone figure approaching her. *He will do.*

JENOC SAW the source of the psychic clamor that had disturbed his talis-crafting. It was a young human girl dressed in finery she was obviously unaccustomed to wearing. *Then she has a compulsion talis.* For a brief moment, Jenoc worried that perhaps one of his people had come for him. It was considered a great evil–not to mention terribly difficult–to spell-cast compulsion, but he could imagine an Allosian peacekeeper resorting to such a tactic to avoid an altercation with humans.

His people could be such cowards. Of course, had it been one of his people, they would've known such a spell would make so much psychic noise that Jenoc would be apprised of their coming long before they reached him. In fact, he had started hearing the booming pulses of compulsion earlier in the day from across the city. At first, it merely piqued his curiosity, but when it started to occur closer and closer to the palace, he became worried.

But this was no threat. This was a human girl with some form of compulsion talis. Probably a ring as that was the shape they most often took. He smiled to himself as the girl started to approach him.

Why did she look familiar? Then the memory slid into place. He had seen the girl before, in Imaris while he chased Kairah in the person of the crystal golem. She was the child his sister had traveled with. She was the friend of the boy with the sword. Perhaps there was something to Kairah's assertion that Apeiron had a sentient will, for this girl crossing his path seemed nothing less than an act of providence.

She walked up to him. "Where is the dungeon?"

A wave of power pulsed from the girl as she spoke. He gritted his teeth, and his head began to throb. This was indeed a powerful talis, for it required every particle of Jenoc's will to resist. That alarmed him.

While he never learned to master compulsion–no one at the College of Disciplines would dare teach it–he had puzzled out the spell in order to learn to counter it. Oddly, it drew its potency from the strength of the emotion the caster used when projecting it. Naturally, emotional control was the key to resisting it. But Jenoc was having a terrible fight of it. He'd suffered a besetting weakness in his spell-casting lately, accompanied by horrible migraines.

"This way, mistress," he breathed out.

The girl nodded, and Jenoc led her down a connecting corridor. They had walked for almost twenty minutes before he found a place he was reasonably sure no one would be–one of the palace's twenty-seven assembly rooms. He shut the door behind them and stood to bar the girl's exit. She looked around the circular room and then spun on him. "Why have you brought me here?"

The force of her compulsion made Jenoc shudder, and he nearly lost the concentration that maintained his illusory disguise. "What is your name, girl?" he asked.

The girl's face flushed red and she shouted, "Take me to the dungeons!"

That time Jenoc lost his concentration. He could feel his disguise evaporate, and his other spell-castings shatter like glass. Fortunately, the compulsion didn't take him, but it frightened him just how powerful this girl was with the talis.

Jenoc saw her eyes widen and he capitalized on the girl's confused hesitation to promptly backhand her across the face. She spun and fell to the floor with a pathetic half-choked scream. He moved quickly, kneeling and turning her over. There, on her hand, glittered a ring with an Aeose shard in it.

Jenoc nearly pulled her finger off as he took the ring from her hand. She cried out in an attempt to form commanding words, but Jenoc was too fast. He examined the ring. It was old, perhaps one of the original compulsion talises. That explained its potential for potency.

He looked down at the girl. Her wide eyes streamed frightened tears, and her nose was gushing blood. "You're Kairah's brother," she sobbed.

Jenoc extended his empty hand to trace his fingers tenderly across the girl's wet cheek. She flinched at his touch and he abruptly pushed her face so her head turned, and her cheek smashed against the marble floor. Jenoc attacked the girl's mind. To her credit, she resisted at first, but it took scarcely a heartbeat for Jenoc to break through her mental wall and take hold of her consciousness.

A cloud of images, sound, emotion, and sensations floated before Jenoc's mind–all his for the taking. He drilled into her memories with the intimate brutality of a rapist, ignoring her horror and humiliation as he breathed in everything about her. It didn't take long, for she was only fourteen years of age, an infant by Allosian reckoning.

Maely, her name is Maely. Jenoc churned over her recent memories, focusing on what she knew about Kairah. *That is interesting. This girl hated his sister. Hated her and blamed her for taking the boy, Jekaran, away from her. She was obsessed with the boy and saw Kairah as a rival for his affections. I can use this.*

Jenoc withdrew himself from her mind at the same time he pulled back his hand.

Maely exhaled sharply and began to sob.

"Do you know how compulsion magic works, child?" Jenoc asked in a calm voice.

The girl laid her head back on the floor and wept.

Jenoc shook his head. "Of course you do not. How to explain it to you?" Jenoc looked again at the ring. "The talis emits a pulse of power whenever the caster issues a command. That energy actually strikes the target before they even hear the words. However, it is so quick most cannot notice the discrepancy in timing. The spell puts the target's mind into a high state of suggestibility and if the target does not know how to resist the psychic assault, his will is overpowered, and his greatest priority becomes pleasing the one who issued the command. This does not last, however.

"As I said earlier, the talis casts this spell in pulses. It is like throwing a stone into a pond to create ripples in the surface. The ripples eventually stop as the surface of the water becomes smooth again. If you want more ripples, you need to throw another stone into the pond. Like that, a compulsion spell will eventually fade, and the target will regain the use of their will. The time this takes depends upon the mental fortitude of the target, but sooner or later, you will lose your thrall.

"To maintain a hold on someone's mind, you need to continue to issue commands, keep throwing stones into the pond so that the ripples do not stop as it were." Jenoc stood and stared down at the girl, drinking in the sight of her weeping. Causing this human vermin pain was oddly satisfying.

A primal part of him wanted to lift her from the ground and snap her neck. He tamped the feeling down, surprised at how easily it had risen. Why was it so hard to control his anger lately? Another headache started to throb behind his eyes, but he ignored the pain.

"It may interest you to know that your efforts in aiding Kairah have succeeded. Her message was delivered to your king, and as a direct result, Aiestal's armies were halted on their way to attack Haeshala. While this will not destroy my work, I cannot deny that it is a setback. To compound the problem, because of the prince's suspicions, I cannot remain near the king, and consequently will not be able to remedy the situation through compulsion given the need to continually spell-cast in order to keep him enthralled—as I just explained."

"Why are you telling me this?" the girl hiccupped between sobs.

"Maely," he said gently. "I have seen your mind and I know that you wish nothing more than to leave this city with your beloved Jekaran. You are unusually capable with this compulsion ring. I can get you into the court where you will be able to remain near the king as one of his servants."

Jenoc bent down and extended his empty hand to the girl. "If you help me compel the king to resume his military action against Haeshala, I will see that your beloved is freed. The two of you can then go home to Genra, and Kairah and the sword will be out of your life forever. Furthermore, I will allow you to keep this ring. You've tasted its power. You know that with it you can have whatever your heart desires—money, land..." he paused for dramatic effect, "Jekaran."

Her hyperventilating abating, the girl eyed his hand suspiciously. "You want me to help you start a war that will wipe out humans?"

Jenoc smiled. "It will take years for that to happen, probably decades. That may not be a long time to one of my kind, but for you it is more than enough time to live a long, happy life with the man you love."

The girl stared down at the floor. Her internal struggle didn't last long, however, for she reached up and clasped Jenoc's hand. "Okay," was all she said.

GRAELLE STARED at her warped reflection in the translucent glass sphere set on her desk–a speaking stone. She looked up at the mirror hanging on the wall to her left. The face that looked back at her always seemed a strange one, as though it wasn't really hers. She touched her double chin and jutted out her jaw to make it disappear. She used to be slim and pretty with lustrous black hair. Now she looked more an orphanage matron than the madam of the most successful brothel in the kingdom. She chuckled at that, but the laugh died when she turned to look back at the speaking stone.

Why was she hesitating? The answer came easily; it was because of what she'd seen in Argentus' eyes. It was a look of primal fear, the kind that said Argentus–no, Ezra–was willing to do whatever it took to protect someone.

He really had changed. He wasn't the same arrogant bully she'd known years ago. His scheme to recapture the Rikujo leadership wasn't about wealth or power. He was actually trying to save his nephew. He loved him.

Graelle remembered a time when she'd seen the same thing in the mirror. That was a lifetime ago, before she'd learned the cruel lesson that only one thing mattered in this world, and that was your own survival.

Survival.

Graelle had always been good at surviving. And at first, it hadn't been a selfish thing. She, like Ezra, had been willing to do whatever it took to save those she cared about. That's what drove her into prostitution in the first place. Her widowed mother had died of fever when Graelle was just thirteen, leaving her to care for three younger siblings, the youngest only two years of age.

From then on, her life had been one continuous crisis. She was worn, used up, and broken. The physical damage she'd done to her body in selling herself multiple times a day always made her ill in some fashion.

Once she'd caught a sniffle from a client that spread to her siblings. It hadn't gone that bad for Graelle, her nine-year-old brother, Ressel or eleven-year-old sister Faela, but it had ended up snuffing out the life of baby sister, Vyl.

Only a few months after that, Ressel never returned from his daily stint of begging on the streets. Although she'd looked and looked, she never found him. Faela left a few years later to join the Rasheera nunnery, and when Graelle refused to do likewise, Faela had turned her back on her. That'd left Graelle alone and without a friend in all of Shaelar.

She fared better as she got older, finally taken in by a Rikujo guild lord who, while not kind, was not exceptionally cruel. Eventually he'd fallen in love with her, and as lover to one of the leaders of the syndicate, she'd been given privilege and eventually was trusted to manage his operation.

Graelle, of course, hadn't loved the man back– she wasn't sure she could ever love a man. But she pretended as best she could, all in the name of survival. That arrangement ended the night she'd slit her lover's throat while he lie in a drunken stupor. She'd talked herself into it after the bastard had raped and beaten one of his whores because he'd caught the young girl skimming client's pay.

The other Rikujo lords hadn't found out about Graelle's treachery until six months later. But the brothel had flourished so much under her unsupervised management, they left her in charge, and even gave Graelle her lover's former place on the shadow council. Her bloody rise to power both pleased and ate at her, and so she told herself that she'd only did what she had to do to protect the women who worked for her.

That was part of it. But if Graelle truly had wanted to better their lives, she would've turned the brothel into a factory, and the whores into seamstresses. She hadn't. She'd continued the operation, improving conditions for the girls, but also working them more in order to increase revenue.

In the end, she would always use the same excuse to soothe her aching conscience; she'd done what she did to survive. And that's why she was going to do this now. It was broken thinking, but she was a broken person, and it was a broken world.

She reached for the stone but startled as motion from the open doorway drew her attention. She snapped her hand back. "Who's there?" she demanded. She let her hand hang down, twisted it slightly, and her concussion rod slipped from inside her sleeve into her hand. But before she could raise it and take aim at the doorway, a head poked out from behind the side of the doorframe.

It was Ezra's chubby monk friend, Irvis.

"I thought you said you couldn't abide the–how did you put it?–'carnal vortex that was my den of iniquity?' What are you doing back here? We're not scheduled to meet until tonight, and you said that would be at a regular inn."

Irvis stepped into full view. His eyes darted back and forth, and he unconsciously brushed a hand over the top of his balding head. "I-I…" he stammered.

Graelle slid her concussion rod back into her sleeve. "What? Did your loins get the better of you? Don't be so embarrassed. You're not the first 'holy man' I've seen come in here." She sat back down. "I'll call Varin in. She's the only one awake at this hour. But don't expect a discount!"

The chubby monk worked his jaw, opening his mouth to speak, and then closing it again before saying a word.

"What? Not interested in Varin? Well, I can call someone younger, but it's going to be double the price, and you'll need to wait an hour for her to bathe and–"

Irvis turned and fled. Graelle shook her head. Well, it wasn't the first time she'd seen that either–a customer losing their nerve. It happened more often in those who professed self-righteousness and moral superiority.

An odd lot those were. Husbands, fathers, lords, and even some ladies. They all looked mortified when they came into her pleasure house, but that didn't stop them from seeking their thrills. It was almost if someone were forcing them to come here.

He'll be back. Which meant Graelle had to hurry. She reached out and touched the speaking stone. There was one thing a person had to learn in order to become a true survivor, and that was how to ignore the accusations of conscience.

CHAPTER 49

Jekaran swept the scythe low, swinging it back and forth to sheer down the tall brown stalks of barley in his path. Their crop hadn't been nearly as large as the previous year, and Ez was already talking about having to let the soil lie fallow for a season. They'd done it before, so it wasn't a catastrophe, but it had been a year of very lean meals. The next season they were rewarded with increased production, so Jekaran knew it was a sound strategy.

He moved forward, swinging his scythe with much less energy than he'd started out with. He was by no means unaccustomed to the work, but six hours was enough to drain him. He paused, wiping his head and looking up at the sun. It hung low in the sky. That would mean it was about time for supper.

Jekaran dropped the scythe and began to backtrack, scooping up the fallen stalks of barley, binding them with twine and piling them in his wooden handcart. When he finished, he retrieved his scythe, laid it across the small cart's bed, and began pulling his load back toward the house. Every labored step was a cruel reminder of just how exhausted he was, but it wasn't the satisfying weariness that comes after a long, hard day's work. This weariness felt more like the product of emotional strain and sleep deprivation, which was odd.

Upon leaving the field, Jekaran spied Mulladin jogging toward him. Jekaran grinned, removed his hat with his right hand, and waved it high above his head. "Mull!" he called.

Mulladin saw him, changed course to intercept, and ran up to him.

"Please tell me Maely's cooking tonight," Jekaran laughed. "I've had just about enough of Ez's rabbit stew. Divine Mother, but I don't think that old man knows how to cook anything else."

Mulladin surveyed the field, and then stared down at Jekaran's cart full of barely. "You come to this place often."

"Mulladin?" Something was wrong with the big man-boy; his body language, the inflection in his tone, and the way he looked at the barley as though he'd never seen it before.

"No," Mulladin shook his head. "I am not him."

Jekaran's insides twisted. "What's happening?"

"You're dreaming," Mulladin said.

Then it slid into place. He was asleep; with his mental defenses lowered, the sword had taken the opportunity to reach into his mind.

"Why are you in my dreams?" Jekaran asked. He willed himself to wake, but something blocked him.

"That won't work," Mulladin said.

"You're keeping me here?"

Mulladin nodded. "You have shut me out when awake, and we need to communicate."

Jekaran turned away and began stalking back into the field, away from Mulladin. "I don't want to talk to you!" he snapped.

Mulladin followed. "Please, Jekaran. Do not shut me out."

"Why?" Jekaran sneered. "Are you lonely?"

"Sarcasm?" Mulladin said. "Yes, you are being sarcastic."

Jekaran stopped, threw up his hands, and spun to face Mulladin, or rather the sword's apparition of Mulladin. "Get out of my mind!"

"You are in danger."

"I've been in danger ever since I bonded you!" he shouted.

"The threat I speak of is specific."

Jekaran stopped and spun on Mulladin. "Why should I listen to you? You've only ever tried to get me killed or possess me!"

"It is my purpose–"

"to destroy my enemies, I know! And I would welcome that if you weren't insistent on being the one to decide who is or is not a threat to me!"

Mulladin looked hurt, an expression that almost made him look like the real Mulladin. "I seek only to protect and serve you."

"Well, you need to work on the serving part! Because you're terrible at it!"

"Jekaran, please listen. Your life is in danger," the sword went on.

"No!" Jekaran shouted. "You listen! I never wanted this. I never wanted you! You turned my uncle into a monster, and now you're trying to do the same to me!" Jekaran shook his head. "No, I am already a monster, and it's your fault!"

"Jekaran," a voice seemed to thunder from above, one that did not belong to the sword.

Jekaran raised his gaze to the sky and abruptly found himself blinking open his eyes. He was tucked away into a corner of his cell, a stained and threadbare blanket pulled up over his front. He shifted, and looked out through the bars to find Gymal standing there.

The short, balding lord was dressed in unusually fancy clothing, his dousing stone hanging conspicuously down over a white silk shirt and purple doublet. He gripped a bar of the cell door in each hand, face pressed against the bars as he called in a loud whisper, "Jekaran!"

"I'm awake," Jekaran growled. And while he wouldn't admit it to Gymal, not in a million years, he was glad the man had come to wake him. He felt the sword at the edge of his consciousness trying to pry its way back into his mind, but he seized on his potent fear to rebuff it. "What do you want?"

Gymal leaned back from the bars and dropped his eyes to the floor. Why did the man look nervous? "Are you being treated well?"

What? "I'm in prison—what the hell kind of question is that?"

Gymal nodded to himself. "What I mean to ask is, are they abusing you in anyway?"

Jekaran actually barked a laugh. "Aside from forcing me to eat slop that wouldn't be fit for pigs, or making me sleep on the cold stone floor with this worn rag for my only blanket? Yeah, I'm being treated like a king."

Gymal frowned. "I'm just trying to– "

"What?" Jekaran stood, dropping his ratty blanket to the floor.

"What're you trying to do? Gloat over besting me? Well congratulations, my lord, you've destroyed your fiercest rival–a teenage peasant!"

To Jekaran's surprise, Gymal didn't rise to the occasion. He just nodded, his face sorrowful. What was he playing at?

"You know, you look almost just like him."

Jekaran hadn't expected that. "Who?"

"Your father," Gymal said, and then met his eyes.

This time the little lord caught him completely off guard, and he couldn't find his voice to make any sort of coherent reply.

"Yes," Gymal nodded with a satisfied smile. "I knew him."

"How?" Jekaran finally managed.

Gymal dropped his eyes back to the floor. He opened his mouth two or three times, but couldn't bring himself to say anything. Finally he looked up. "I will see to it that you are given a nicer blanket and better food." Then the little lord turned and scurried away.

Jekaran gripped the cell bars, one in each hand and shouted, "Wait! Who was my father?"

The only reply that came was the slamming of the outer dungeon door.

TYRUS WAS A COWARD. He'd come down to the dungeon on his way to the dinner with king with the intention of telling the boy the truth, but he hadn't been able to bring himself to do it. Why? It wasn't as if he were confessing his secrets, just Kybon's.

That day came back to him unbidden, and he could see himself sitting in the library, working to devour a stack of tomes. He'd been in the middle of reading Tarsali's treatise on the Allosian influence found in western art–the title of that book would be forever burned into his memory–when hushed whispering drew his attention to the reception table.

There, the robed librarian was pointing a messenger in Tyrus' direction. The lad nodded and hurried across the room toward him. Tyrus tried to return to his studies, but a cold pit in his stomach made it just a pretense as he waited for the page to reach his table. At the time he'd wondered why he was suddenly anxious. Perhaps Rasheera was trying to warn him, for when he got the letter, he immediately knew.

It wasn't a detailed note, the message simply reading;

Lord Tyrus Gymal,

Your cousin, Baron Kybon Myadra, is dead. Your father requests you cease your university studies and return immediately.

My condolences,

Headmaster Aylen

Of course, Tyrus had obeyed and sought the first carriage that would take him the two day's journey back to the Saldren province and his home. He hadn't wept, not until weeks after the funeral. His cousin was poisoned, and though no other noble house claimed responsibility, the ritual suicide of a recent addition to the cooking staff had more than confirmed it. Kybon had been assassinated, and the worst part was, Tyrus thought he knew who had been responsible.

The Viscount's daughter.

Kybon had confided that he'd lain with her shortly after their engagement was announced, which made it all the more hurtful when he'd broken it off with her to be with a peasant woman. This was not common knowledge, of course. But somehow the Viscount or his daughter had discovered it, and her honor demanded nothing less than Kybon's death. For in Aiestali high society, Kybon's act had made the Viscount's daughter into something of a whore.

Passionate idiot! Tyrus clenched his teeth as he traversed a wide ivory colored corridor. His beloved cousin had never been able to resist a woman's charms. His athletic build and outgoing personality made it easy for Kybon to become a womanizer, and the Viscount's daughter was not the first naïve virgin he'd deflowered–just the most powerful.

But it was different with Jekaran's mother, Anarliee. Kybon didn't talk about her like his other women. There was no lurid detailed account that made Tyrus' face heat, or boasting as there had been with Kybon's other conquests. No, Tyrus' cousin was thoroughly smitten with a girl from Genra and began to talk of marriage and children as though he wanted such things.

Tyrus was sure he was the only person who knew the girl's identity, else the Viscount's daughter surely would've slain her. He guessed her knowledge only went as far as the kind of woman Kybon had left her for. It was for this reason Tyrus could never tell anyone of Anarilee or Jekaran. He had needed to stay away from the woman herself, too. That grieved him, for she certainly must've thought Kybon had abandoned her. His grief was made worse when he learned of Jekaran's birth and Anarilee's death.

That's why he had watched over the boy. That's why he'd come to Genra each year to recruit for the well-finds. That's why he'd had to distance himself from the boy by making him hate him. Though, well and truly, Jekaran had grown to be genuinely infuriating over the years. It wasn't because of a foreseen last wish of his cousin Tyrus watched over the boy. He doubted that Kybon ever thought he'd die. He watched because it was the only thing Tyrus could do to honor him.

Vengeance, of course, was out of the question. Bringing such a scandal to light would ruin his house. Having the Viscount or his daughter assassinated had been tempting, but Tyrus didn't have the heart for violence, and had never been good at political intrigue. So, in the end, he'd just watched over Jekaran, intervening in his life anonymously when the boy and his uncle were desperate for work, money, or food.

Now he'd made a mess of everything. *I'm sorry Kybon.* Well, at the very least Jekaran would be safe in the king's dungeon. And he'd bribe the guards to give Jekaran special treatment and protection. He could even set up in Aiested, representing his house in the king's court. Then *maybe in a few years I can gain enough political capital to petition the king to pardon the boy.* It wasn't much of a possibility, but it would have to do for now.

Tyrus was escorted into the mammoth chamber the king used for dining with guests. He gasped at seeing the enormous amethyst column rising from the center of the floor, and ascending a hundred feet before disappearing into the ceiling.

It's Aiested's well. At first glance, it looked as though the well had grown through the center of the palace, but that couldn't be right. Apeira wells still rose from beneath the ground but never in an area already populated with people. Therefore, it had to be the reverse. The palace had been built around the well.

"Remarkable, isn't it?" a deep voice boomed throughout the vast chamber.

Tyrus looked down from the ceiling to find a long table several meters to the right of the Apeira well's base–or rather the place where it rose from the floor. The king stood, along with the prince at his right hand, and a number of other high nobles and favored servants.

"It is said to be the largest well in all of Shaelar." The king craned his head to view the glowing amethyst obelisk. "Well, largest human-controlled well," the king amended. Then he looked down at Tyrus and motioned him forward.

Tyrus bobbed a quick, sloppy bow, and then strode as quickly as was proper over to the table. Given the size of the room, the walk took an inordinate amount of time, making Tyrus acutely aware of the eyes on him. The king and his guests all stood silently, awaiting his arrival to the table. Tyrus could not remember a more uncomfortable moment. He prayed fervently to Rasheera that he wouldn't trip, or commit some other unthinkable etiquettal atrocity.

He breathed a soft sigh of relief when he reached the table with his dignity intact. The king nodded at him, and then sat. The rest of his guests. waited until the king was comfortable before seating themselves. Tyrus quickly followed suit, sitting in an empty chair at the right of the king.

"Tonight you sit at the place of honor, Lord Tyrus Gymal," The king said.

Tyrus bobbed another quick bow before sputtering, "Thank you, my king."

A host of servers appeared, as if out of nowhere, making Tyrus almost suspect they were using talis craft. He flushed upon realizing their quick appearance had been facilitated by a culinary staging around the side of the mammoth Apeira well and not translocation.

"What will be your pleasure, Lord Gymal?" the king asked.

Tyrus was suddenly surrounded by silver tray bearing servers, all crowding in on him with presented dishes. The smells of hot food mixed, making Tyrus' mouth water in spite of his nervousness. There was honey-glazed ham, smoked pheasant, garnished cattle steaks, skewers of various meats, and an assortment of side dishes Tyrus' didn't have time to enumerate or identify.

"The ham," Tyrus choked out.

"You have excellent taste, Lord Gymal," the king said without a smile.

He clapped twice and one of the servers began to set Tyrus' meal before him while the other servers spread out, offering options to each of the other dinner guests. Tyrus eased a bit as the attention of the others shifted away from him, and for a time he was almost enjoying himself. The ham was better than anything he'd ever partaken from his family's table, and no matter how much he ate, there was always more.

The prince made small talk with a few of the generals, but mostly everyone's attention stayed fixed on their meals. Being in the presence of the king appeared to be a stressful experience for all involved, even the prince. When he could eat no more, the servants whisked away his plate and replaced it with a dish filled with yellow custard. Tyrus tentatively tasted the dessert and squeezed his eyes shut with an indulgent sigh. He'd never tasted anything so glorious. He was going to have to eat all of it and more, his inevitable indigestion be damned.

Glutton's remorse had only just begun to settle on Tyrus when the king spoke his name. "Yes, your highness?"

"I see that you enjoyed the Tolean pudding."

Several suppressed snickers alerted Tyrus that something was wrong. He quickly felt at the corners of his mouth where he found it rimmed with custard. He hurriedly dabbed at it with his napkin, catching his red face in a warped reflection from a spoon.

"Would you like another brought?"

"No, your highness," Tyrus quickly sputtered. "Thank you, but no."

"Suit yourself," the king said, and Tyrus silently praised Rasheera that the man turned his attention to a pale man with long black hair seated further down the table.

"Loeadon," the king said to the sallow looking fellow, "you sent word that there has been a breakthrough with the sword talis Lord Gymal brought to us?"

Loeadon nodded gracefully, finishing a mouthful of food behind his napkin before finally answering, "Yes, my king."

"Then please, share your news here so that Lord Gymal may also hear it."

"Very well." Loeadon looked at Tyrus, cleared his throat, and said, "After careful testing, and analysis, I have been able to puzzle out just how the sword works. Something that would've been nearly impossible if it weren't for the Allosian tome or the spell-casting talis we've recently found. In fact, it was because of a delving spell that– "

"Yes, yes, Loeadon," the king interrupted. "We all know you are brilliant. Why don't you get to what I wish to know."

"What is its exact function?" Loeadon asked. "Well, it binds itself to a host and grants that person significantly increased strength and reflexes. It is also spell-cast with recorded knowledge of a sword master's level of skill as well as expert battle tactics. I have to say that next to the spell-casting circlet we found, this is the most remarkable specimen of talis-craft that I have ever seen."

"How do you break the bond so that another can use it?" the king asked.

"Well, that is simple. The sword must lose its Apeiron charge–"

"That isn't going to happen while it's in Aiested," the prince chimed in.

Tyrus thought he caught Loeadon scowl at the prince, but the expression was gone so quickly he might've imagined it.

"Or," Loeadon continued, "the boy must die."

No!

The king released a weary sigh. "I was afraid of something like this."

"Father," the prince began, "you said– "

"I know what I said, Raelen," he cut in. Then he drew in another sigh and pinched the bridge of his nose. "But it seems that I spoke too soon. This is no longer a matter of crime and punishment, but an issue of safety."

Tyrus couldn't think, and his heart pounded so loudly that it made it difficult for him to hear.

"Have the boy executed tomorrow after morning court. Do it in his cell, with no fanfare." The king looked at Loeadon. "And make it quick and as painless as possible."

Loeadon bobbed his head, and Tyrus caught a slight smile of satisfaction on the man's face.

"Have the sword brought to me before he is put down."

That made Loeadon's smile falter. Tyrus would've found that odd if his mind hadn't been racing, and his every effort of will was being exercised to keep himself from looking upset.

"I don't want to risk someone else bonding it by accident."

"As you wish, sire." Loeadon bobbed his head again.

Tyrus didn't fully hear what was said after that–something about a plague box, whatever that was. He was too busy trying not to vomit.

He had brought Kybon's son to Aiested and it was his fault Jekaran was going to die. From the moment he made the decision to sail away from Imaris, he'd known this to be a danger, but had been naively confident he could intercede on Jekaran's behalf and at the very least buy his life with coin.

Not now. No amount of money could change a royal decree. But I didn't have any other choice! His duty to king and country demanded he bring the sword talis and the Allosian woman here and present them to the king. Not doing so could have destroyed his entire house if it became known. And it wasn't as if he could've covered up the chaos Jekaran had caused in Imaris.

At that point Tyrus did throw up, all over the floor, to the gasps of the other dinner guests. But what would've mortified him only a few moments earlier, seemed only a trifling concern now.

He'd as good as killed his cousin's son–Kybon's son.

JOVE SALIVATED as he stared up at the towering Apeira well in the distance. It was larger than any he'd ever seen before, illuminating the city beneath it with a purple light as bright as the moon on a cloudless night. It was so bright, he doubted the city ever slept. That would mean people roaming the streets, even though it was late.

Appetizers. Jove giggled.

Although he'd left a trail of withered grass, dead animals and trees, and the occasional human corpse, his Hunger was gnawing at him.

Oddly, drinking the crystal man's life had only made him thirstier for the pristine, unadulterated essence he'd come to realize was Apeiron itself. Everything he consumed since worked to take the edge off of his need, but didn't satisfy. It didn't even come close.

Four translucent greenish tendrils sprouted from him, two from his chest and two from his back, waving like stalks of corn in the summer breeze above his head. He fed so much over the course of his journey it'd been easier to leave them manifested, than to continually call them from within.

That's where they came from, he'd realized. Inside his chest, where his heart once was. That could be the only explanation for why he no longer bled–his heart was gone, replaced by a bottomless void. Nothing pumped whatever blood was left in his veins, and so naturally, he wouldn't bleed.

Not many of his station in life–uneducated peasants–knew as much as he did about the human body. And his education hadn't come from books or old corpses. No, he'd learned from experience, from experimentation. He barked a laugh. He likely knew more about the inner workings of the human body than any scholar did. That made him proud.

One of his floating tendrils snapped a swooping owl out of the air, absorbing all of its life force before its dried husk crashed to the ground in an explosion of mummified dust. A wave of delicious pleasure pulsed into him, but it was gone all too quickly, like a flash of lightning in the sky. It was enough, however, to refresh him and give him a burst of energy. That was what sustained him now, the life energy of the things he consumed. What would happen if he stopped eating? Would he die?

He didn't know, but denying the Hunger was an excruciatingly painful thing. Also, his physical body seemed to wear away and grow older when he didn't eat. His hair would fall out, his skin would begin to blacken, almost like a decaying corpse. Well, he wouldn't have to worry about that once he reached that Apeira well. There was more life in it than he could ever consume. He would feed forever. The very idea gave him chills, the kind he used to feel when he was choosing a new doll to play with.

CHAPTER

50

In a wash of purple light, the wood-paneled walls of Racheta's Pleasure House disappeared and a sudden cold breeze shocked Ezra's skin. When the light faded, he found himself staring at a dirty, brick wall. He quickly scanned his surroundings and discovered that he, Graelle, and Mulladin had materialized in a narrow alley spanning between two multi-story buildings.

"Where's your fat friend?" Graelle asked.

Ezra looked about a second time. He'd given Irvis his earring so he himself could travel with Graelle. And since his earring only had enough power to transport one this far from Imaris, they had to take Mulladin with them and hope to meet up with Irvis.

"If he didn't know the exact location, he could be anywhere."

"He said he'd been here before. He even recognized the color trap I showed him of this alley."

"He might have told you that just to save face," Ezra said. He adjusted the hose he wore in a vain attempt to relieve the discomfort it caused by pulling at his inner thigh. They were part of an expensive outfit consisting of a blue, silken tunic underneath a fine white doublet and a velvet cloak of deep green.

Not even Mulladin had been able to escape being fitted with an uncomfortable costume. Ezra spared a quick glance at the boy-man who was unintelligibly muttering to himself while unabashedly scratching his starched servant's livery in several inappropriate places.

"Why would he do that?" Graelle asked. The mistress of Racheta's Pleasure House had traded her modest gray dress for a low-cut gown of lustrous silver. It clung to her, giving even Graelle's full-figure a feminine shape. She'd also let her hair down and colored it black.

The change in her outfit had made Irvis' odd behavior worse. Instead of stammering, or making out of place comments, the chubby monk had fallen completely silent, only nodding with wild eyes anytime Graelle spoke to him.

Unbelievable. His lecherous friend–the man with an obsession for spying on young, attractive, delicate women–was thoroughly enamored with the uncouth, overweight, and middle-aged Graelle.

"Pride," Ezra finally answered.

"Well, we can't wait for him. The meeting starts within the hour." She turned and strode out of the alley and onto an empty cobblestone street.

"Come on, Mulladin," Ezra sighed, and the two followed Graelle out of the alley.

Their destination was not a seedy warehouse, or an abandoned building as many assumed such meetings of the underworld took place. No, they were headed to a large manor house in the wealthier part of Erassa. Ezra glanced up at the Apeira well that loomed over the buildings at the center of the city. Its soft glow tinged the street with an eerie purple light. It was too late in the night to summon a carriage, so the three of them were forced to hike a mile uphill until they came to the Apeira well-centric town square.

Surprisingly, the only one to have trouble making the journey was Mulladin, who was sucking air and sweating by the time they stopped at the top of the hill. Incongruously, Graelle hadn't even broken a sweat. For a woman of her size, she was in remarkably good physical condition. Ezra glanced back down the hill. The light from the Apeira well made visibility good; he searched the street below for Irvis, but there was no sign of his friend. It's just as well. Irvis probably wouldn't have made it up the hill anyway.

Ezra tried not to notice as the dread medal warmed against his chest while it drank in a fresh charge of Apeiron. It was an odd talis, unlike any other he'd ever used. Instead of waiting dormant until he mentally invoked its power, the dread medal had to be restrained when he didn't want it broadcasting an aura of fear, which was just as mentally taxing as resisting the power of the talis when he'd been on the receiving end. How had Kaul done it?

He didn't. Not unless he was away from an Apeira well. The man enjoyed having people fear him, so he would've been using the full power of the talis whenever possible.

They stopped in front of a large manor house with a stone wall enclosing the perimeter. A single, armored guard stood at a gap in the wall bridged by a black iron gate. One guard? Then it hit him. The guard was just for show, part of a Rikujo front.

If anyone actually dared to break into the manor, they would be in for a truly awful surprise. Chances were most of the petty criminals in the city–burglars and thieves–knew what this place was, or at the very least had an idea. That would be more effective than a full contingent of soldiers wandering the grounds would.

Graelle made some sort of quick gesture in the air with her right hand–the signs had changed since his day–to which the guard responded with his own gesture. He nodded at Graelle, and then shot a look at Ezra. As practiced, he flashed the appropriate sign to which the guard responded again with his own sign of acceptance.

The guard stepped aside and opened the gate. Apparently, Mulladin wasn't a problem. Servants were accepted without question. At first that seemed odd, for in his day anyone that wanted access to a Rikujo hideout had to display the proper signs, servant or not. But Graelle explained that Jaris had abolished the practice, deciding he would hold the Rikujo lords personally responsible for all the acts of their servants. That put the onus for choosing trustworthy servants squarely on the members of the syndicate. When Ezra questioned if such a policy really worked, Graelle answered, "It did after Jorial got his throat slit for the petty thieving of a coachman he'd hired."

After passing through the gate, they entered an enormous courtyard decorated with a variety of flowers as well as bushes sculpted into various shapes: life-sized animals, letters, and statuesque people. Ezra heard Mulladin giggle as they passed a tall, phallus-shaped hedge. But the centerpiece of the courtyard was a multi-tiered fountain ascending over twenty feet into the air.

The manor house itself was no less impressive, reaching up five stories, and capped by a domed roof constructed entirely of glass. The thick, fluted columns supporting a covering to the causeway leading up to the entrance made Ezra think of palaces he'd seen in the exotic eastern countries–some even smaller than this building.

Servants dressed in uniformed livery, who averted their eyes as they opened a set of wide and tall double doors, greeted them at the front entrance. It was the subtleties of the environment and the behavior of the servants that clued him in that Saijen Trous his host must be. Saijen Trous was a man from Maes Tol, and Toleans were known for their emphasis on magnanimous politeness, even when dealing with enemies.

Arynda. The Tolean woman had been Argentus' lover once, and for that fact alone had died when Kaul rose to jealously claim all that once belonged to Argentus. That was how Kaul had gotten the flame ring, something Ezra wished Graelle's servant had recovered instead of the dread medal. Not because Ezra needed it to fight–although he couldn't deny that it would be handy–but because of Arynda. Surprisingly, after almost two decades, their parting still stung. The pain was made all the worse by the knowledge it had been their affair that motivated Kaul to rape and murder her.

They were led into the foyer of the manor house; a dome-shaped chamber with a skylight set in the vaulted ceiling that let in the purple glow of the city's Apeira well. The inner circumference of the room was cylindrical in shape, each story of the manor wrapping around the sides and leaving all of the floors open to the foyer and skylight.

"Put your hood up," Graelle hissed. It brought him out of his reverie with a start, and he nearly lost his mental restraint on the dread medal. He cast her an irritated look as he obeyed the order and drew up his hood. It nearly came too late as a tall man descending the grand staircase suddenly called down to them.

"Mistress Graelle!" he said in a lightly accented tone.

Arynda

"Master Trous," Graelle responded with a smooth curtsy.

The man was dressed in a fine, white silken shirt covered with a vest of deep blue. He wore no hose, as was the Aiestali fashion, but a pair of loose, black trousers tucked into calf-high black boots. He descended the stairs with arms held open and gathered Graelle into a friendly embrace. They traded kisses on the cheeks and Trous pulled back, keeping hands on Graelle's upper arms as he looked at her.

"You are still the picture of beauty, lasa."

Lasa, Ezra remembered Arynda calling him that. It was a Tolean term of endearment close friends used with one another

Graelle chuckled nervously, "You flatter me Master Trous."

"Nonsense!" he laughed loudly. Then he turned to look at Ezra. He let Graelle go, and that's when Ezra caught sight of the five rings he wore on his right hand–talises. There was one flame ring, a restoration band, a brute ring, and two others he couldn't identify. This man was powerful in means and formidability.

"Lasa, who is your guest?"

"My bodyguard," Graelle quickly said. "Since Kaul took away my enforcers, I had to hire one for protection for myself and my girls."

Trous stared at Ezra for a long uncomfortable moment before curtly nodding. He turned back to Graelle and smiled. "Forgive me for saying so, lasa, but he doesn't look very intimidating."

"He's all I could afford," Graelle quickly added.

"Yes, well." Trous cast another glance at Ezra. "If it were up to me, I'd make sure you had all the enforcers you needed."

Clever. Trous' hosting the meeting of the Rikujo lords was obviously strategic. As host, he'd be under decorous obligation to greet each attendee personally, giving him ample opportunity to campaign and solicit support. He's going to be a problem.

"You are the last to arrive, lasa. Everyone else is waiting in the dining hall." He chivalrously extended a hand to Graelle. "If you care to follow me?"

Graelle took his hand–and was she blushing? Ezra rolled his eyes. Her succumbing to Trous' charm reminded him of Irvis. The man was dog-ass stupid when it came to facing an attractive member of the opposite sex. Perhaps the two of them would make a fair match. Where was Irvis, anyway?

Trous led them up the stairs to the second floor and through two double doors into a large room with a vaulted ceiling. A cacophony of mixed chatter greeted his ears as they entered the dining chamber. Over two dozen men and women dressed in finery and displaying an eclectic variety of talises lined both sides of the large table. They were eating, drinking, laughing, and chatting amiably.

It'd be every bit the joyous celebration it appeared to be if it weren't for the reality that any one of the guests wouldn't hesitate to plant a knife in the back of their fellows if it suited their purposes. Ezra was in a nest of vipers; a room full of dangerous people he had to convince to follow him. If he failed, he would die. Worse yet, if he failed Jekaran would die.

Jekaran

The thought of saving his nephew ignited Ezra's courage. He took a deep breath, set his jaw, and released his restraint of the dread medal. A cold rush of invisible power exploded from him, expanding out in all directions. Graelle gasped and Mulladin began to whine. Trous spun around and the entire room fell silent, all eyes fixing on him. Good. He'd needed to catch them off guard if this was going to work.

I will be Argentus again. For Jekaran.

"Since when did an assembling of the dreaded shadow council become a frivolous revelry?" he asked loudly. A few of the men and women flinched as though he'd physically struck them. "I see now that many of you have grown fat off your spoils. You are swine content to eat slop and wallow in filth all day, ignorant of your impending butchering."

"Who are you?" Trous asked. He appeared to have gotten a hold of himself, though Ezra could see a mental struggle behind his eyes.

Ezra slowly drew down his hood and the room sucked in one collective gasp. He heard repeated whispers of, "Argentus," and "The Invincible Shadow and "he has Kaul's talis!"

"Yes," he said. "It is I." He cringed inwardly at that last part. Too dramatic.

Ezra caught Trous' eyes flicking down to his side, no doubt checking for his sword. When he didn't see it, the man's face appeared to relax a bit. "Argentus," the man exhaled. "You're supposed to be—"

"Dead?" Ezra cut in.

Trous cleared his throat self-consciously. "I was going to say, retired."

"But you'd hoped I was dead." Ezra made sure to let his stare linger on the man. How did Kaul make this damned thing focus on one person at a time?

He turned to face the room full of staring Rikujo lords. "I know it's what you wanted, even when I was with you." The men and women started shooting tacit glances at each other. He recognized some of them: Curly-haired Jaggatt, a man with an opium distribution ring outside of Rasha. Stern-faced Adlere, the boss of a smuggling operation run out of the southern port city of Lyamar. Voluptuous red-lipped Shydal, incongruously the leader of a group of elite warriors, body-guards, or assassins depending on the customer's needs. And there were others, but about half of the dinner guests were unfamiliar to him.

Ezra took a step forward.

"What is it that you want, Argentus?" Trous asked, his eyes still twitching from the effort of resisting the fear aura.

"I am concerned over the disgustingly incompetent handling of my legacy!"

"Then you mean to take back control of the Rikujo?" The question came from a woman Ezra didn't recognize. She was younger than the other lords and dressed in elaborate finery with face painted like that of a noble woman.

She's not afraid of me. It made sense. Someone young and attractive like her would've had to learn how to resist the dread medal if she were to keep herself safe around Kaul. Well as safe as anyone could be around the violent maniac. Also, and probably more likely, was the possibility that she didn't fear him because she'd never seen him fight with the sword.

"No," Ezra's voice echoed throughout the hall. "I intend to continue my well-earned retirement. I am here as the envoy of the only man with the true right of succession."

"And who might that be?" Trous' polite demeanor was gone, his voice now frosted with cool contempt.

"A man named Jekaran. He is my nephew and heir. The one who slew Kaul with my own sword. The new Invincible Shadow!"

The frightened silence in the room melted and the group of Rikujo lords broke into a clamor of overlapping conversation. Ezra could only discern bits of what was being said, but the theme of all the conversations was disbelief, resentment, and anger.

Trous held up a hand and the men and women trailed off into silence.

He's already stepped in to fill the void of leadership, Ezra gritted his teeth. That would make this far more difficult than he anticipated.

"Forgive me for saying so, Argentus, but if this is true, then why did he not come himself? Why send you, alone and defenseless?"

That's a subtle threat if I've ever heard one. He shot a glance at Graelle. Why was she so quiet? He could really use her support right now.

"My nephew has gone on to Aiested to prepare for a heist grander than anything the Rikujo has ever pulled. A job that will require all of our talent and resources." Ezra paused for dramatic effect. "He is going to rob the king."

Gasps and stunned outbursts exploded from the table of men and women. Ezra smiled to himself. He'd been hoping for a reaction like this. The fear, surprise, and theatrics were all intended to put the crime lords off their guard, make them gullible. Robbing the king was a folly not even he would've attempted in the heyday of his power. Not even a talis as powerful as the sword would lead him to take such a risk. But a young man, newly inheriting a powerful army of criminals and wielding a talis that made him virtually invincible might. That was the brashness of youth, after all.

Trous' slow, deliberate clapping echoed throughout the dining hall, silencing the other Rikujo lords. "Very good," he laughed pleasantly. "Wonderful performance!" He sounded genuinely pleased. "I wondered how you were going to handle that one."

"Take care, Trous!" Ezra snarled as best he could though his insides were freezing with fear. He tried to focus the dread medal's broadcasting, but failed again. "You do not want to offend the man who wields the sword of the Invincible Shadow!"

"Perhaps," Trous replied. "But I doubt he wields it any longer."

"What're you talking about?" Ezra snapped. "He'll kill you Trous!" Ezra turned to look at the other Rikujo lords. "He took the head of Kaul and he will take the head of any who oppose his right of succession!"

"Argentus' nephew did slay Kaul with the sword of the Invincible

Shadow, this is true. But just a short time later he was captured by a nobleman and spirited away to Aiested–as a prisoner."

Ezra's mouth went dry. He tried to speak, but nothing would come.

"He will be hanged and the sword will become the property of King Taris. Therefore we do not need to concern ourselves with offending him."

"How can you be certain?" Adlere shouted out. "If you're guessing and you prove wrong..."

"I am not guessing," Trous said. He kept smiling and didn't look away from Ezra.

"How–" Ezra began, and then he knew. He turned to look at Graelle. "You contacted him with your speaking stone before we left." It wasn't an angry accusation, but a plain statement of fact. "You sold us out."

"I tried to warn you, Argentus. But you wouldn't listen." Graelle couldn't hold his gaze.

"They'll kill my nephew, Graelle."

She shook her head. "I told you, Ezra. I'm not some celibate old Handmaiden of Rasheera doling out penance for the poor. I have my own affairs to look to. My own interests to protect. I'm a survivor, and supporting Trous is the best way for me to survive."

Trous stepped forward, shot a hand out, and snatched the dread medal from Ezra's chest. In one fluid motion, he pulled it off, snapping the leather thong across the back of Ezra's neck in the motion. It should sting but at that moment Ezra was completely numb.

Trous leaned in close. "I really should thank you."

"Why is that?" Ezra said, and his voice sounded hollow to his own ears.

"Your appearance has given me a chance to kill you myself, in front of the others. I can't think of a better way to prove in their minds that I have the right to lead them."

"Then get it over with!"

Trous didn't respond to that. Instead, the man turned to face the other Rikujo lords. "Before you stands the man who founded our glorious company!"

Jeers and curses rang throughout the dining hall.

Trous raised a hand. "No, no, no! Argentus is to be honored!"

Confusion as much as Trous' authority calmed the crowd back to silence.

"Decency demands he be given a chance to reclaim his place as our leader." Trous turned to look back at Ezra. "He and I shall duel without talis craft, and the winner shall be the undisputed head of the Rikujo. The loser, of course, will be dead." Trous shot Ezra a knowing smirk.

It was as much an act as Ezra's performance had been. There was no way he could best Trous, a man ten years younger and in better physical condition than he probably had ever been–and Trous knew it. This was just a way for the man to solidify his hold on the Rikujo.

Ezra turned to look at Graelle, but she wouldn't meet his eyes. He should be angry with her, but how could he blame her? She had warned him, hadn't she? She had offered to let him go free. No, this wasn't Graelle's fault. This was his. Damn me for a fool, he thought as the cheering of the other Rikujo lords overwhelmed him.

CHAPTER 51

Kairah sensed the alien consciousness focus its attention on her. *Where are you?* she called out to the predator with her mind.

Her only answer was a clap of thunder so close and loud that it made her jump.

I am Kairah of Allose, she projected, working hard to hide her apprehension.

An image unfolded in her mind; a picture of a nude woman floating lifeless, submerged in a purple ocean the entirety of which was encased in a spherical crystal rock. The rock looked to be made of the same crystalline substance as an Apeira well, except that woven just beneath its amethyst surface were veins of green that pulsed with a soft emerald light. The image faded.

I do not understand, Kairah sent.

The invisible predator didn't respond in words, but instead impressed an idea upon her that seemed to say *this is what I am.*

Unlike Aeva or the sword, this mind didn't feel like it was broadcasting from a single physical location. No, this felt as though it were flowing through the air all around her, like a psychic wind. That was how she sensed Apeiron when it radiated from a well. *This has to be the other magic—Moriora.*

Cautiously, Kairah reached out to tap the unseen energy. Immediately her mind was racked with blinding pain. It was similar to a migraine in how it clenched the head and pulsed with waves of agony, but that was where the similarity ended. The intensity of it was like nothing she'd ever felt before. The bitter tang of bile burned Kairah's throat as she retched. She was aware of collapsing to her knees, but the pain made focusing on anything else impossible, and she struggled to form any coherent thought, to say nothing of trying to spell-cast.

Two powers warred within her; one warm like sunlight, the other freezing like a bitter icy wind. Kairah heard herself screaming, and desperately tried to expel the Moriora from her body. She'd only tasted it, but that had been enough to open the door, and now it was trying to force its way in and take the place of her stored Apeiron. Panic made it even harder to think. It was like she'd stepped into a bog and was being sucked under, the filthy mud filling her nose and mouth as she gasped for breath.

Draw from the mother shard, a voice said. Was that Aeva's voice? It had the same cadence but was weighted with a depth not possessed by the Spirit Lily.

I am too far away, she cried. Trying to draw Apeiron in her present state would be like trying to draw breath when the mud of the bog was already filling her lungs. Her panic reached a crescendo.

Space has no meaning here, the voice replied with a feeling of perfect calm. Now, reach out to the mother shard and be filled.

Feeling the last bit of her Apeiron being consumed, Kairah threw her consciousness at the mother shard–the Aeose that powered Allose itself. Hot energy flowed into her. At first, it only fed the darkness, but the more she breathed in, the more it expelled the mud from her lungs. Soon the Apeiron was driving the Moriora back, overwhelming it until it had no choice but to retreat from her soul. Kairah gasped aloud, staring down at half of a skull on the blackened ground.

The pain faded, slowly at first, but finally disappearing altogether save for a tiny headache behind her eyes. She inhaled deeply, tears involuntarily rolling down her cheeks and splattering the dark rock.

Her stomach knotted as she recognized the feeling of the power that had nearly obliterated her. She'd felt it before when scrying for Karak's Eater. But as that had been a taste, this was a potent full dose and she could only think of one word to describe it–death.

MAELY WALKED past the room where Kairah lay unconscious. Jenoc had showed her where it was when he'd brought her with him to replace the guards. Guilt attempted to prick Maely's heart, but she shoved it away. She didn't have to worry about Kairah anymore–not that she ever had, she told herself. She hated the Allosian woman, and it was probably better than Kairah deserved to be rescued by her brother.

Jenoc.

To the same degree that Kairah infuriated her, the woman's brother terrified her–maybe even more so. He had a beautiful face, a masculine version of Kairah's features, but then all Allosians were said to be beautiful. In an incongruity that was frightening, his voice had been gentle, almost tender while he'd been smashing her face into the marble floor, and he'd been equally brutal while invading her mind. But Maely didn't need a psychic link to Jenoc to feel the cold rage he radiated. It was almost a palpable thing, and she'd been sure he'd been going to kill her.

That's why it had stunned her when the man returned her ring, and offered to help her free Jek. Of course, she was required to help him in return–or else he would kill her and Jek too. He hadn't made any pretenses otherwise. In fact, he'd explained how he could sense her use the compulsion ring–which is how he found her in the first place–and if he sensed her anywhere near the dungeons, he'd go there and kill Jek first before coming to slay her. He must've known she'd been weighing whether or not she could beat him down to the dungeon for he demonstrated his power to disappear and instantaneously re-appear in another place by way of spell-casting.

Maely turned a corner, nearly tripping on her servant's dress. Damn thing's too long! Her petite frame made finding clothing that would fit difficult. Back home in Genra she'd made all of her own dresses. Older women with fuller figures didn't have that problem. She growled audibly, startling a pageboy who was crossing her in the hall. He pointedly looked away from Maely as he quickened his pace.

"Manners," she whispered to herself. "Servants have manners." They didn't scowl, or swear or growl. She berated herself for forgetting that so easily. I can't make slips like that or someone will know.

Jenoc had arranged for her to attend the king tonight in his sleeping quarters, standing by to wait on him should he desire food or drink, or anything else. She ground her teeth at that. Her mother had told her what kind of men kings and princes were; outwardly benevolent and noble, but as vulgar and randy in private as any drunken sailor.

Well she wouldn't give him the chance to touch her. As soon as they were alone, she'd use her ring on him and–and command him to start a talis war, the guilty part of her groaned. She shoved it back. That wasn't her problem. Kairah wasn't her problem. All she needed to worry about was rescuing Jek and getting the hell out of this place. Let everyone else worry about the end of the world.

Two guards took note of her as she approached the king's quarters. Jenoc had made sure she was introduced to all the servants on this floor so she wouldn't have to use her ring to gain access. Apparently trying to maintain too many compulsions at once was overwhelming for even the strongest minds, to say nothing of frightened teenage girls.

The guard on the right smiled at Maely before cracking the door and peeking in through the small open slit. He then nodded at her and opened the door wider so she could slip in. Maely did so, nearly tripping again on her too-long dress. She caught herself just before breathing out a curse and quickly made her way to a woman silently hovering over a tray on a small round table.

The king's quarters were not so much a bedchamber as they were an apartment. Doors on each wall told her this was some kind of antechamber, and this place had multiple rooms. So perhaps she wasn't expected to stand next to the king's bed ready to empty his chamber pot as she'd imagined.

Maely curtsied to the other servant and the woman spared her only a cursory glance before whispering, "You're late."

A very vulgar expletive nearly escaped Maely's lips, but she managed to tamp down her temper and bob her head in practiced humility. "I'm sorry."

The woman sighed and shook her head. She pointed to the teakettle and cups on a silver tray she'd been fussing over. "His Majesty likes a spot of tea before he retires for the night. But we never know when that will be because of his busy schedule. So to be sure the tea stays warm, you will need to dump it every hour and make a fresh pot. Understand?"

Maely nodded though she wanted to comment that this wasted an awful lot of water, and tea. Didn't the king have a warming stone?

"Now, I just made this, so you will not have to dump it for an hour."

Maely nodded, biting off her criticism with a "Yes, ma'am."

The servant woman gave her a satisfied nod and then added, "You are to remain in this room. Only go into the other rooms if the king calls you."

Maely nodded again, the temptation to compel the woman to stop telling her what to do and leave almost overtaking her, but she controlled herself. While she was sure she could get away with it, Jenoc had ordered her to only use the ring on the king, and she wasn't about to risk the Allosian man's wrath.

The serving woman gave several other irritating orders Maely only half heard, and then left. Maely waited to make sure the woman wasn't going to come back before she moved to the center of the room. The other doors were closed, and so she went to each in turn and quietly opened them just enough to see into the rooms beyond. The king wasn't in any of them. He must still be about business elsewhere in the palace, so Maely retreated back to the corner table and brazenly took a sip from one of the king's tea cups. It was delicious tea! Spiced with cinnamon. Cinnamon was Maely's favorite, and a rare commodity back in Genra.

I'll be able to have cinnamon whenever I want. Jek and I can have an entire pantry filled with all of the expensive spices! She had the power to make virtually anyone do what she wished. She would never need to farm again, or worry about money. The world was hers, and she would share it with Jekaran. The ring was her road to a better life with the man she loved.

But what if he didn't love her back?

Then I'll make him love me! The fierce thought came unbidden, almost as if it were from someone else, but Maely knew it was hers. Would she use the ring on Jekaran? The idea disturbed her, but not as much the fact that she had already decided she would do it. I won't need to. He loves me already; he just doesn't realize it. This time her mantra didn't entirely dispel her guilt.

Voices echoing from the hallway made Maely jump, and she quickly put the cup of tea she'd been sipping from down on the tray. Too quickly apparently, as it tipped over and spilled cinnamon tea all over. She quickly searched the table for something to soak up the brown liquid, and nearly knocked the entire tray to the floor. Just then the door swung open and a tall man with broad shoulders, a short trimmed gray beard, and a golden circlet swept into the room.

The king. Jenoc had inserted his image directly into her mind as she had never actually seen him.

"Why not call the army back?" another voice echoed from the hallway outside.

Maely looked at the doors just in time to see another man enter the room. He too was tall, but where the king was dressed in a robe and cape, this man was wearing armor. His hair was long and golden, curling just behind the ears and at the base of his neck, and his eyes were the bluest Maely had ever seen.

This must be the prince.

Another figure entered the room, and he was so tall he had to stoop under the archway just to enter. He was completely covered in white fur and wore a tabard like the other soldiers, but she couldn't see any armor underneath it. But it was his face that startled Maely the most. It definitely wasn't a human face, not with that long charcoal muzzle, black nose, and white fangs.

The creature glanced at Maely, and she was suddenly aware that she'd been staring. She quickly dropped her eyes to the silver tray on the table, and busied herself mopping up the rest of the tea with a cloth napkin.

"I have already told you, Raelen. I will not let the Allosian warmonger bully us."

Although Maely knew she was witnessing an argument, the king's voice did not sound angry.

"With the army so close to the border, he could use his magic to pose as any one of us and order an attack that we may not be able to halt in time." The prince, on the other hand, spoke with great passion. "I just think it unwise to leave him this advantage."

"Are you questioning my wisdom, Raelen?"

Raelen That was the prince's name. Maely stole a glance at the man, and couldn't deny that he was the very picture of what everyone said royalty was supposed to be. How old was he? His beardless, youthful face suggested he wasn't all that much older than Jekaran.

"Of course not, father."

"Then there is nothing more to discuss!"

"Father, I believe I know who the Allosian infiltrator is masquerading as!"

The king scoffed. "Puzzled it out all on your own have you?"

"No," Raelen said quickly, and Maely thought she caught a hint of indignation in his tone. "I have had some of my servants shadow the suspect ever since the Allosian woman's arrival."

"And who do you believe this 'suspect' to be?"

"Loeadon," Raelen said.

Loeadon?

"You have evidence?" The king's tone no longer sounded sardonic, as if he were actually considering the possibility.

The prince hesitated before answering. "Not as yet, but his behavior has been suspicious of late."

The king sighed. "You know the law, Raelen. You cannot bring an accusation against a member of the court without evidence."

"But you can execute a peasant boy for no reason?"

Maely looked up at that. No–She had to stop herself from lashing out with her ring. Was she already too late? Had Jenoc lied to her?

"No reason?" the king repeated dangerously. "He committed a capital offense!"

"You already sentenced him for that. You know full well that his execution on the morrow is not for the justice of the crown, but so you can take his sword!"

Tomorrow! She could still stop this, make the king rescind the order.

"You speak so nobly of honoring the law, but you're a hypocrite!" Raelen snarled. "You are no different from the politicking nobles of the court. Power is what you honor, not law!"

Maely watched through her eyelashes as the king strode right up to his son, so close that their faces almost touched. "Do not push me, Raelen!" the king hissed.

"Or what? You'll marry me off to some rich old crone?"

That was oddly specific. What was the prince referring to?

Smack

Maely flinched and just about spilled the entire kettle of cinnamon tea. The king had slapped his son. The prince's pet bear growled, and the king looked up at it. He cocked an eyebrow at that, but said nothing as he returned his attention back to Raelen, who was now holding his cheek and staring stupidly at his father.

"Do you think you are the only one who grieves for Saranna?" the king said through clenched teeth.

Who's Saranna?

"You know nothing of what it means to rule or understand the burden I carry! You are a child holding to a fantasy that kings are wise and benevolent servants of the realm. If you want to someday wear this crown," the king sharply gestured at his gold circlet, "then you need to grow up and learn what it really means to rule, what it means to make the hard decisions!

"Your fanciful idea of a people's king will bring down upon you all the vultures of the court. You would not hold the throne two days if I were to pass it to you now. Traitors and assassins are all about us, Raelen, looking for anything and anyone they could use to pull us down. We cannot afford to show any weakness even if it means we have to stomp on our conscience, or hurt those we love!"

The king stared at his son for a long moment before turning away. "When you can demonstrate to me that you understand this, then I will heed your counsel. Until then, you are suspended from the court and banished from my presence!"

Maely dropped her eyes back to the silver tray. She heard the swishing of the king's cape followed by the slamming of a heavy door. She glanced up to see Raelen standing in the middle of the room next to his bear, looking defeated. She hurriedly went back to cleaning up the mess she'd made. She almost felt sorry for the prince.

"Let me help you with that," the prince said. Maely snapped her head up to find him taking his own red and gold silk handkerchief out of a pocket.

"No, it's going to smell like cinnamon!" Maely blurted out. Why had she said that?

Raelen flashed a wan smile as he dabbed at the brown liquid. "I have others."

Maely met his eyes, and found herself speechless. The prince was probably the single most beautiful man she'd ever met. Not in the way Jenoc had been pretty, but a rugged, manly splendor.

"I apologize that you had to witness that," he said.

Apologize? To a servant? Who was this man? Maely was tempted to believe he was actually sincere.

"There we are," he said. He left his soaked handkerchief on the table and then turned toward the door.

Maely couldn't summon her voice even to thank him as she watched the prince and his pet bear leave the room. She'd assumed he had been helping her because he wanted to take advantage. But no, the prince had been genuinely polite.

Nobility.

Did such a thing really exist among the rich and powerful? She hadn't thought so. Maely had always believed that empathy came from a life of living with those who suffered together. Could a prince really care? The king seemed to think so as he accused Raelen of it.

They are going to kill Jek. That re-focused her, and she thumbed the underside of her mother's ring. She had a job to do. Jek's life depended on it now more than ever.

She let the thought of the king ordering Jek's execution fuel the fire of her anger as she strode toward the room he'd disappeared into and flung the door open. The king was sitting behind a desk, writing on a parchment with a quill.

He snapped his head up. "I did not summon you!"

"No," Maely said defiantly. "You didn't."

The king narrowed his eyes. "Who are you?" he demanded.

"Your mistress!" Maely said with an explosion of power.

Chapter 52

R aelen fumed as he stalked down the corridor.

I am a clear brook flowing among the trees.
I am a meadow of clover in summer.
I am the moon silently watching the night.

His father was a proud fool. How could he not see that Loeadon was this Allosian man in disguise? It was so obvious. He'd been an exceptionally gifted talis appraiser, arriving on the scene during one of the polymaths' rare recruiting campaigns. He'd scaled the ladder of advancement very quickly, outstripping all of his peers and endearing himself to the head of their cadre, whose suspicious death ushered Loeadon into the chief position of spokesman he now held. All of this had happened in the short space of two years–something unprecedented in the history of the kingdom so far as Raelen knew. Father hadn't seemed to think too much of that.

Raelen touched his cheek where the king had struck him. It didn't hurt anymore, not physically. The lingering sting was in his heart. He'd just begun to win the man's respect and now he'd ruined it all by losing control and bringing up Saranna. He remembered his father's surprising admission; "Do you think you are the only who grieves for Saranna?"

Did his father grieve? Did he even care? He hadn't shown it in any way Raelen could recognize, and he'd become something of an expert in reading his father although he still didn't know what the man was thinking half the time.

He turned a corner and was pleased to find Navarch Pariel striding toward him. He stopped and waited for the soldier to intercept him and offer a crisp salute before asking, "You have news?"

Pariel nodded. "Yes, your highness." And then the man pinched the bridge of his nose and squinted his eyes shut.

Divine Mother, but he must be tired. I've been running him ragged. When was the last time he slept? "Tell me your news," Raelen ordered.

Pariel opened his eyes and nodded. Then in a hushed voice he said, "I broke into the polymath's laboratory as ordered."

"What did you find?" Raelen asked eagerly.

"Loeadon has constructed a plague box, as the king commanded, but the talis does not look to be functional."

Raelen nodded. "He is having trouble puzzling out how to finish it?"

Pariel shook his head. "That was also my thinking, at first."

"What do you mean?"

"Rasheera smiles on us, my prince. For I was sifting through Loeadon's books and papers when the man himself entered the room. I had just enough time to secrete myself within a closet where I heard him conversing with someone by way of a speaking stone.

"I heard him addressing another polymath, speaking much of the sword talis, and how important it was that it not be in your father's possession at the time of the boy's execution which he is planning tomorrow after morning court."

"He wants it for himself," Raelen realized.

Pariel nodded. "And thus, it appears he has been neglecting the construction of the plague box in favor of plotting to take the sword."

Raelen shook his head. "But why? Would not finishing the plague box better further his purposes? Using such a thing on a rival country would be all that was needed to start a war."

Pariel smiled. "Had not my prince expertly frustrated his efforts by convincing his father to halt our attack on Haeshala."

Raelen nodded thoughtfully. "He's improvising. He plans to take the sword for himself, which would give him the power to challenge my father in battle, kill him, and take the throne. Then he could order the attack to resume without any opposition."

"That was my conclusion as well."

"But why would an Allosian need a talis to defeat a human?" Raelen glanced at Gryyth. "Does not his spell-casting ability give him enough power to do that?"

"Perhaps if the king held the power of the sword, it would be too much for the Allosian to best," Pariel offered. "According to Loeadon, it is one of the most powerful talises he's ever seen."

"But Loeadon is the Allosian. Can we really trust what he says?"

Pariel shook his head. "A valid concern, my prince. However, his plotting to steal the sword would imply that he is telling the truth."

Raelen sighed. "Were you able to record what you heard?" he asked hopefully.

Pariel shook his head. "I am sorry, my prince. I did not have the echo chime you'd provided me. Please forgive my foolish oversight."

Raelen waved away Pariel's apology. "Nonsense." He glanced at Gryyth and saw in the bear-man's eyes a reflection of his own thoughts. "We need to stop the boy's execution."

"Mustn't we go now to warn the king?" Pariel said.

Raelen shook his head. "No, I've been banished from his presence." Pariel waited for an explanation, but Raelen didn't give him one. "What about an oath collar?"

Pariel nodded thoughtfully. "If we could somehow get one onto Loeadon's neck, then he'd have to reveal himself. But," he hesitated and then carefully said, "The prince does know that those can be beaten. The Allosian's magic would–"

"Not one of the four originals forged by his own people."

Pariel's eyes widened. "Your father owns such an artifact?"

Raelen nodded. "He keeps it in the vault. If we can get it tonight, then I can confront Loeadon in morning court, challenge him to prove his innocence by donning the collar and swearing to the truth of his identity."

Pariel nodded. "That is a sound plan, my prince. But you said the king will not see you, and only he has the key to the vault."

Raelen smiled. "I am going to steal it."

Pariel's face visibly paled. "You cannot. It is death for anyone to steal from the king, even you, my prince. To say nothing of defying his banishing you."

Raelen chuckled. "My father may be a hard man, but I doubt he would execute his heir to the throne. Not out of any familial affection, mind you, but because it would be for him a great inconvenience." Would his father execute him? Before his father admitted to grieving for Saranna he would've been more concerned, but now... Maybe his father had a heart after all.

"Perhaps, but it could cause a world of political trouble if the other nobility think you and your father are at odds." Pariel shook his head. "No, my prince. I cannot let you risk this." He looked straight into Raelen's eyes. "I will do it."

Raelen studied Pariel for a long moment. The man was truly loyal, of the rare breed of noblemen who should make up the royal court. Raelen would have him as his general when he became king. He'd even raise the man's house to high nobility status. He smiled and placed a hand on Pariel's right shoulder.

"Very well. Go, fetch the key and bring it to my apartments. It is in my father's study in a locked desk drawer. The lock is not a talis, so you shouldn't have a problem circumventing it." Raelen glanced through a window at the dark night sky. "He was still up when he expelled me, but he should soon retire. Servants go in and out of the antechamber at all hours, so you should have little trouble getting in."

Pariel crisply saluted, turned on his heel, and began striding away from him.

"Rasheera's blessings be upon you, Navarch Pariel," Raelen called.

The man halted, offered one more heartfelt salute, and then disappeared around a corner.

"We need more men like him in this kingdom," Raelen said to Gryyth.

He was surprised when the bear-man growled, "I don't trust him."

"You don't trust any humans," Raelen scoffed.

"I trust you, cub," Gryyth rumbled softly.

Raelen smiled.

"LEAVE ME ALONE!" Jekaran screamed.

Angry jeering from his fellow inmates brought him back to the moment, and Jekaran realized he'd been talking to the sword aloud–again.

"Keep your damned mouth shut, you brain-addled lunatic!" one of the bigger men shouted.

"I'm trying to sleep, you bugger-lovin' man-whore!" another inmate snapped.

Jekaran tuned out the subsequent threats and angry shouting. This wasn't the first time he'd drawn the ire of his fellow prisoners by forgetting himself and speaking to the sword, especially since it had begun urgently pestering him to lower his mental wall.

Truth be told, Jekaran was trying to sleep just as ardently as any of his fellow prisoners. It was the sword keeping him awake, and by extension the other occupants of the dungeon. But he couldn't very well tell them that. It would reinforce their belief that he was a mad.

He might not be insane, but he was a monster. How else could he explain what he'd done back in Imaris? He had absorbed the life-force of Kaul and used it to heal his own wounds and strengthen himself. He had eaten Kaul's soul. He was an Eater, like the creature Karak was hunting. No wonder the Vorakk shaman's spirits told him Jekaran would lead him to the Eater–it was him.

Cold nausea soured his stomach, and a sob escaped his throat. He drew his threadbare blanket tighter over his shoulders and leaned his head against the cold stone wall. Maybe it would've been better if the king had ordered him hanged. He'd started to drift, trying to keep the sword from breaking into his thoughts as his defenses slowly lowered. The only time it could get to him was when he was unconscious, the only time it could break into his mind.

"Brother Ulan."

Jekaran's eyes snapped open as he awoke with a start. He'd dropped off, but had no idea when or for how long, although his body told him it hadn't been nearly long enough. Blessedly it'd been a black sleep without dreams and without the sword breaking into his mind. He looked up to find Hort staring at him through the bars of his cell. The man wore a lopsided grin that only made his crooked nose look even more comical.

"Go away, I'm tired," Jekaran said as he closed his eyes again.

That's when he heard the unmistakable metallic sound of a key being inserted into a lock. He opened his eyes again, just in time to see Hort pull the cell door open. "What are you..." he trailed off when Hort put a finger to his lips and winked. The man obviously hadn't done much winking; the motion looked forced and awkward–and a little disturbing.

"I am here to escort you to see the king," Hort said aloud in a terribly obvious attempt at pageantry.

Jekaran was on his feet and following Hort out of the cell and down the aisle in half a heartbeat. Fortunately, most of the other prisoners were still sleeping, but the ones who weren't made sure to glower at him as he passed their cells. When they left the dungeon proper, Jekaran saw the two guards lying on the floor, their hands and feet bound. Hort just smiled and produced a slender, ivory wand with a ball at the point and a handle capped by an amethyst stone. Jekaran recognized the talis as Gymal's stun baton. He must've stolen it from the short, balding lord.

"Why are you doing this?" Jekaran asked. "Not that I'm ungrateful."

Hort chuckled as he tossed the ring of dungeon keys onto one of the guards' chest. The man jerked upon impact but stayed unconscious. "I told you, Ulan. You remind me of someone I used to know."

"Who?" Jekaran asked as they left the dungeon annex.

Hort surveyed the hallway before turning back to look at him. "My son. He died when he was about your age. Fever took him." He shook his head. "I'd just opened my first apothecary, and was setting myself up as a village healer. But when I wasn't able to heal my own son...well let's just say that business venture failed."

"I'm sorry," Jekaran said, and he was surprised to find he meant it.

"He was a lot like you, ya know. Stubborn little bastard, but sharp as a sword. Got himself into all kinds of trouble, but was usually able to get himself out. Either that or I had to."

The big mercenary began moving quickly down the white hallway and Jekaran followed. They turned down a connecting corridor and Jekaran could feel the floor incline as though they were walking uphill.

"But don't think just because I like you that I'd risk my neck without compensation. I'm being paid to do this."

"By who?" Jekaran asked.

Hort snorted and looked back at him. "You're a smart kid Ulan, but you have a blind spot. Who do you figure sent me?"

"Gymal?"

Hort gave one curt nod. "Apparently, the king was going to have you executed at dawn so he could take that cursed sword of yours."

So that was what the sword had been trying to so urgently warn him about. *You are in danger* it'd told him in his dreams. Jekaran just figured it was trying to convince him to allow it to take over so they could escape. He hadn't thought the warning was specific. How had it known?

Hort continued on in a hushed tone, "He paid me to help you get out of the palace, and escape the city. Then we go our separate ways, and we never see each other, or Gymal again."

"Why?"

"Don't really know. All I can tell you is that he ain't your enemy. Never was."

Jekaran was thunderstruck. Gymal was the one responsible for his rescue? "I don't understand."

They turned another corner and Hort slowed to make sure the corridor was clear before they entered it. "Well, I didn't ask about his motives."

Was he really going to escape? He'd already resigned himself to his fate, one he might actually deserve for being the aberration that he knew he was. Maybe his condition wasn't permanent. Maybe he could be cured. He'd ask Kairah–Kairah!

Jekaran stopped abruptly, making Hort turn and stop. "Where's Kairah?"

"Somewhere on one of the upper floors in one of the king's guest apartments. From what Lord Gymal said, it sounds like she's still unconscious."

"I can't leave without her!"

Hort shook his head. "She's being guarded around the clock by the king's soldiers. There ain't no way you'd be able to get to her."

"I have to try!"

Hort sighed. "Lord Gymal said you'd do this."

Before Jekaran could protest further, Hort rammed the stun baton into his chest. A painful shock rocked his body, and then everything went dark. When he blinked open his eyes, he found himself slung face-down over Hort's shoulder. He tried to speak, but his mouth wouldn't move.

No! He screamed inside his head as he flipped himself forward, landed on his feet, and whirled around to face a very surprised Hort.

"How?" Hort began but was cut off as Jekaran rushed forward and slammed a fist into the big man's gut with far more force than he should've been able to muster.

Hort doubled over, and Jekaran found himself tearing the stun baton out of the man's hand. Hort looked up, wheezing, just as Jekaran struck him in the side of his thick neck with the talis. Hort convulsed, his eyes rolled back, and he slumped to his side.

Stop! Jekaran mentally screamed, but the sword didn't reply.

The moment he'd been knocked unconscious, the sword had taken the opportunity to seize control of his body. He tried to wrest it back, but the sword just brushed his mind aside. It was not going to let go.

They were running now, running up the incline and toward one of the palace's unbelievably tall arched doors. Jekaran saw himself push through the doors and enter into a room with two marble ramps; one descending and the other ascending. He took the path leading up and immediately knew where they were going. Rasheera protect anyone who gets in my way.

CHAPTER 53

Ezra sat in a plush, velvet chair set opposite a full-length mirror. He was locked in one of Trous's second floor guest chambers, two Rikujo enforcers standing guard on the other side of a locked bedroom door. Mulladin paced to his right, muttering in agitation and raking fingers through his brown hair. Ezra wanted to snap at the boy-man and order him to be still, but he didn't have the heart. When it became apparent he was facing his death, Ezra had pled with Trous to let Mulladin go.

The Rikujo guild lord had smiled wanly and said, "I am afraid I cannot. Witnesses and all that. You understand, don't you Argentus?"

It made Ezra sick. Not only had his hubris condemned Jekaran, but now innocent Mulladin was going to die—die because of him. He stared at himself in the mirror, noticing for the first time just how weary his eyes looked. An old Rasheeran proverb said that through a man's eyes you could glimpse his soul. Well that made sense then, for his soul had been battered, and abused, worn out from a lifetime of submitting to selfishness and violence.

His thoughts automatically turned back to that first time he'd fought a duel in front of spectators. That had been the first time the sword usurped his will resulting in an orgy of blood and indiscriminate killing. A faint echo of the sword's consciousness, the piece of itself that it had left behind, urged him to examine the memory, to dig further into that night. No!

Tap-Tap-Tap

Ezra's head shot up and he glanced around the room.

Tap-Tap-Tap

There it was again. Ezra turned to the window and saw Irvis gently tapping on the glass. The chubby man was clinging to the frame of the window, feet perched on an apparently short ledge. The wind was blowing his hair, and his eyes were wide as they kept glancing down at his feet. Ezra shot up out of his chair and went to the window. He tried to unlatch it, but found the window nailed shut.

"Argentus!" Irvis' muffled voice came through the glass.

Ezra lifted his hand, grabbed his own ear lobe, and mouthed "use the earring," not daring to even whisper for fear of alerting the guards. Irvis shook his head at the suggestion. Had he lost the displacement talis?

Ezra quickly glanced around the room, looking for anything he could use to pry the window open. His eyes fell on the iron poker set near the cold hearth. He ran over, snatched the poker, and went back to the window. He couldn't entirely tell, but it looked like Irvis' face had gone white.

"Stop looking down!" he mouthed, which, of course, caused Irvis to look down. intensifying the man's trembling.

"Divine Mother!" Ezra said with an eye roll. Then he went to work trying to quietly jimmy the window open by forcing the edge of the poker in between the sill and the pane, but his best efforts only splintered the wood.

"Mulladin!" Ezra hissed as loud as he could.

The boy-man had stopped pacing and now stared wide-eyed at the window. He raised an arm and pointed. "Irvis," he said.

Ezra cringed and put a finger to his lips. He froze as the handle of the door shook. "You locked it?" he heard one of the guards accuse. He couldn't make out the other guard's muffled reply, but the first scoffed at it and said, "Gimme the key!"

The sound of the key being inserted into the lock made Ezra throw himself away from the window and towards the hearth. He skidded to his knees on a patch of smooth tile just as the door swung open. He gritted his teeth as he realized he hadn't motioned Irvis away from the window, but he dared not look back.

"What're you doing?" the first guard–a burly bald man–demanded.

Ezra realized with a stab of panic that he was still holding the iron poker. His mind raced and he blurted out, "I'm cold."

The second guard–a shorter muscled man–scoffed. "Is this skinny old man really The Invincible Shadow?"

The first guard chuckled and strode over to Irvis. "Lord Trous did say we were to give him whatever comforts he desired." With a motion of his hand, one that exposed a loose bracelet, the blackened logs in the hearth ignited. The resultant blast of heat made Ezra wince.

"There!" The guard said. "But Rasheera help you if you try to set the room on fire! This kindle bracelet can put flames out just as easily as it can light them. Understand?"

Ezra nodded quickly, praying with every beat of his heart that the guards wouldn't look up at the window, or that Irvis had had the good sense to sidle back the way he'd come. The two guards shared a smirk, and then left the room.

Ezra heard the key slip into the lock, but it stopped abruptly when he heard the bald guard snap, "Leave it unlocked!"

There was a muffled reply that sounded like a challenge.

"Because it tips 'em off when we peek in on 'em! Gives 'em time to hide any mischief."

The next muffle had the deflated ring of forced acquiescence, and then Ezra heard the key withdraw. Damnation! He gritted his teeth. How was he supposed pry open the window without making noise or having time to hide what he was doing should the guards hear him.

He stood and quickly went to the window, but Irvis was gone. Rasheera send he didn't fall to his death. "You old fool!" Ezra whispered as leaned against the glass, looking for any sign of his friend. And why hadn't he used the displacement talis Ezra had given him. Inside the city, the well would give the earring unlimited Apeiron.

He sighed. Wherever Irvis had gone, Ezra couldn't do any more at the moment to help him. He chuckled. Irvis even needed Ezra's help to rescue him. Fool man! He was the best friend Ezra ever had, and he hoped Irvis wouldn't try again, for his own sake. Get out of here, my friend. Save yourself.

GRAELLE SAT on the corner of a gigantic bed in the room Trous had given her–a room on the same floor where he'd locked up Argentus. It was a ridiculously spacious chamber with soft chairs, silk hangings, a massive bed, and its very own fireplace. She shook her head. Trous had promised Graelle luxury like this for all of her girls, and enforcers to protect them.

She sighed. She finally had what she'd been working for these past few years, but instead of relief and satisfaction, Graelle felt only felt emptiness. She'd given up Argentus' life as payment for Trous' favor. She'd expected the shame to dissipate once she was away from Argentus, once she no longer had to look at his knowing, disappointed face, but it wouldn't go away. She'd as good as killed the man herself.

Before now, she'd only killed once in her life, and that had been to escape her lover and take over The Racheta Pleasure house. She started to repeat her mantra of survival that was the salve to her gnawing guilt, but the memory of Argentus' pathetic plea that she help save his beloved nephew stopped her.

She tried to remind herself of all the atrocities attributed to The Invincible Shadow, and how he deserved what Trous would do to him, but it failed to stoke the anger she needed to drive out the guilt. No, Argentus was dead. This man, Ezra, was a good man. An innocent man. And she had killed him. It made her want to vomit.

She looked at the clock standing in the corner of the room. Trous would soon have his "duel" and Ezra would die. No, she shook her head. She was not going to go watch the spectacle. She'd retire early and try to sleep through it. It was the cowardly way, but then, she was a coward, so it fit. Graelle was broken, and that's what broken people did–break others.

Graelle started as the windows to her room suddenly flew open. She jumped up and produced her concussion rod from within a long sleeve. She automatically raised it, preparing to blast her intruder back out the window. That's when she saw him lying prostrate on the floor beneath the window amidst a tangle of purple curtains–Irvis.

"Golden womb of the goddess!" she snapped. "How did you climb up here?"

Irvis smiled sheepishly. "I've had some experience with this sort of thing."

"Burglary?"

He hesitated before saying, "Something like that."

"What do you want?"

Irvis looked up at her, the hair on the side of his head windblown. "I need your help!"

Graelle lowered her rod but didn't put it away. Was she going to have to use it on this man? "Fool!" she spat. "Do you realize that by coming here, you've made your life forfeit?"

Irvis rose to his knees and extricated himself from the curtains. "We have to rescue Argentus!"

"Idiot!" Graelle hissed. "I'm the one who turned him over to Trous!" Why had she just confessed that?

"I know," Irvis said as he stood and began straightening his monk's robe.

"You do?" Graelle raised her weapon talis again. "How?"

"Well, I didn't know until hearing you admit it, but I've suspected all along."

Immediately Graelle made the connection. "That's why you weren't with us when we teleported into the city."

Irvis nodded. "I wasn't far from you, though. I followed at a distance, and when I learned whose mansion this was, I knew Argentus was in danger."

"You know Trous?"

Irvis nodded. "I dealt with all of the Rikujo lords when I was book-keeper—a great deal more than Argentus did. Because I wasn't intimidating or a political rival like him, they didn't bother to make any pretenses when dealing with me. It gave me the opportunity to observe their real characters. So I knew that in spite of his reputation for chivalry, Trous is one of the worst ruthless, back-stabbing bastards in all of Shaelar. That paired with the sincere warning you gave us—well, let's just say I'm good at reading people."

"If you knew what I was doing, then why didn't you tell Argentus?"

"Like I said, I wasn't certain. And..." The chubby monk looked at the ground. "I think I'm in love with you."

"What?"

"It's true!" Irvis looked up and took a quick step forward. "I love you!"

"This is a trick!" Graelle trained the concussion rod so that it targeted the monk's chest.

"You won't hurt me, Graelle," Irvis said confidently and then took another step.

"You don't think so?" Graelle aimed the rod at the open window behind Irvis and released a bolt of invisible force. The air rippled and the glass exploded out into the night.

Irvis jumped, and his eyes widened, but the determination in his face remained.

"Next time it'll be your head!"

"No, I don't think so, my lady." He took another step forward. "You don't have it in you. I watched you through the window, sitting on the edge of your bed–"

"You were watching me?" Graelle wasn't sure what to think of that.

Irvis continued talking as though she hadn't said anything. "Your face betrays the shame you feel."

He couldn't have known that just by watching her. Does he have a mind reading talis? "You don't know me!" Graelle sobbed, and she was shocked to feel tears spilling down her cheeks.

Irvis flashed a gentle smile. "But I do."

"Get back!" She raised her concussion rod so that it was aimed at Irvis' head. "I've killed before!" Graelle struggled to summon her steel, but it wouldn't come. There was something about that round face smiling at her that had broken through her defenses.

"I believe it." Irvis stepped up to her and gently pushed her arm down. "But that's not who you are."

"How do you know?"

"Because," he said slowly and now he was standing so close that she could feel his breath, "from the moment I first laid eyes on you, I knew you were like me–broken."

He must have a psychic talis!

Then, before she could say anything else, Irvis bent down and kissed her. The concussion rod clattered to the floor and to Graelle's utter surprise, she found herself kissing him back.

EZRA HAD RETREATED from the window and pulled his plush armchair over to the hearth fire. Though he wasn't really cold, the heat was somehow comforting. Mulladin must've felt the same way because he'd sat on the floor next to Ezra's chair, and was staring at the dancing flames as though he were hypnotized.

One of Trous' lieutenants had just checked in on them, warning Ezra to prepare for their duel, which would start within the hour. He ran his fingers through his wispy, unruly hair. He wasn't afraid, not anymore. Instead, he was overwhelmed with a crushing sorrow. He shouldn't be surprised it would end this way. In fact, he was beginning to think it a fitting punishment for him, one full of irony and poetic justice.

"Adventure is the lure of fools, and excitement glamour to the gullible," he said softly and on his periphery he saw Mulladin look up at him. "The siren song of the world is as music to the wanderer's feet."

Images of that night when he'd wantonly killed dozens of people surfaced in his mind, and he pushed them back down. There was something to those memories, something wrong. Of course there was something wrong, the whole event was a horrendous blot on his soul, but that explanation seemed insufficient. It was almost as if there was something buried beneath those memories, something Ezra recognized, but desperately worked to ignore.

"But that dance leads only to the soul-less grave," he finished quietly.

"I like that poem," Mulladin declared.

"That's not all of it," Ezra admitted. "I told that first part to Jekaran, to warn him against looking for excitement and thrills. I didn't tell him how it ends." He looked at Mulladin, who was staring expectantly at him. "You want to hear it?"

Mulladin nodded his head vigorously.

"Okay," Ezra chuckled in spite of himself. "But closely resemble they one another, both heroes and fools at first, and it's only at the fork of destiny's road that the truth will at last emerge. For while the fool always looks to his own regard, the hero for others is aware. And will suffer and die when called upon, even for strangers in his care."

"It's good," Mulladin said.

Ezra shook his head. "I wish I would've told that part of .it to him. I was just so afraid he was like me–a fool. But after hearing Irvis tell me what happened in Rasha, and the well-finder's camp, I couldn't have been more wrong. He's only used my sword to try to protect the ones he loves. He's resisted its destructive pull. Jekaran is not a fool. He's a hero."

Boom!

Mulladin cried out and Ezra shot up from his chair. "The hell?"

He listened but couldn't hear the guards. He crept toward the door, the hair on his arms standing up as he felt the familiar crackle in the air that always accompanied the blast of a weapon talis. The door flew open, making Ezra leap back and grab for the iron poker laying on the marble in front of the hearth. The metal was uncomfortably warm, but Ezra didn't care. He gripped it tight and brought it up ready to–

"Irvis?" He lowered the poker.

"Come on!" The chubby monk beckoned urgently for him to follow.

That's when Ezra saw the two guards sprawled on the floor in the hall. One's face was toward the door, and he could see blood gushing from the man's nose, his eyes staring sightlessly at him. He motioned to Mulladin–who'd taken to hiding behind the plush armchair–and the two rushed out of the room. That's when Ezra saw her.

"Graelle!" She was looking down the hall, her mysterious rod talis in her right hand. She whirled around and Ezra raised his poker. "Irvis! She's a traitor!"

To his surprise, Irvis snapped at him. "Put that down!" He forced Ezra's wrist down, and the two men locked eyes. "She knows where the slipgate is!"

Ezra shook off his surprise and pulled away. He looked at Irvis' earlobe where he found his old displacement earring. He dropped the poker, grabbed Irvis' wrist with his right hand and Mulladin's with his left. "Tell us!" he shouted at Graelle.

"It won't work, Argentus," Irvis said irritably. "Trous has some kind of warding talis that blocks translocation inside his estate."

"Damn!" Ezra growled.

"We need to go!" Graelle snapped at them, but Ezra noticed there was something different in her eyes. The defiant hardness he'd seen in her when she betrayed him was gone.

"Come on! She'll take us to the slipgate!" Irvis said.

"But you said the warding–"

"Most warding talises grant the bearer the ability to permit exceptions," Irvis replied. "Trous would have to exempt the slipgate if he was going to use it! But we won't know for certain if we never make it there!"

Ezra nodded, still wary of Graelle. I don't really have any other options. He towed Mulladin forward. Not if I am to have any chance of rescuing Jekaran. Rasheera had granted him this mercy, and he would gladly take it.

They jogged around a corner in the hall and Ezra froze when he saw Trous' lieutenant and four armed guards approaching them. He was about to turn to run back, thinking perhaps they could escape through a window when Graelle raised her rod and another loud boom rocked the hall. Ezra watched in astonishment as an invisible wave rippled in the air, streaking from the end of Graelle's rod and hurling their enemies back as though they'd been struck by the colossal fist of a god.

Two of the guards disappeared through the plaster of the wall, while the other two and Trous' lieutenant flew a dozen feet to land hard on the stone floor. Ezra heard the unmistakable sound of a skull cracking, which was confirmed when a pool of blood quickly formed beneath the head of one of the fallen guards.

Trous' lieutenant tried to rise, hand instinctually going to his belt for something, but Graelle released another concussion blast at him, and his head snapped back with a sickening crack! He fell onto his back and didn't try to rise again.

One guard lived, but he was groaning as he squirmed on the floor. Ezra went out of his way to plant the hard toe of his boot in the man's groin as they passed; partly to ensure he stayed down, and partly because it gave him some satisfaction.

"Others will have heard that!" Graelle huffed as they ran down the corridor. Those words had no sooner puffed out of her than angry shouts echoed from downstairs.

Graelle quickly led them to a servant's stairwell, and Ezra nearly fell down the stairs as they flew to the first floor. He was about to exit the stairwell when Graelle hissed at him, "The basement!"

Ezra paused to stare at her stupidly. "What?"

"The slipgate is in the basement!" She repeated.

Ezra nodded and the four of them resumed their descent until they reached the bottom of the staircase where they threw open the door and began running down a narrow corridor with rooms lining both sides of the hall. Some had doors, and others were little more than open archways that let Ezra see into the stores. This is where Trous would likely keep his contraband while arranging for shipping contracts. Sure enough, Ezra soon saw an entire room filled with burlap sacks marked with a slang term for poppy seeds.

They reached the end of the basement hallway and were blocked by a locked set of double doors. Graelle raised her talis–a concussion rod Ezra had decided–and blasted the doors into chunks of sharp wood. They exploded into the room, a long splintered piece burying itself in another Rikujo enforcer's head. He fell, and a cursory sweep of the large room showed Ezra that the man had been the sole guard on duty.

That's when Ezra saw it, a gazebo-like structure built over a raised circular dais on the floor, it's domed top capped by an amethyst sphere–a slipgate. He ran over to the talis, leapt upon the rune engraved dais, and quickly found the small plinth he'd been looking for. A map of Shaelar etched into the white stone was overlaid with glowing lines connecting the continent's different cities. Only one of the luminescent paths stretched between Erassa and Aiested. The receiving slipgate would certainly be in the possession of the crown, inside the palace itself. That had been why Ezra had wanted a contingent of Rikujo enforcers. Now he was going to have to rely on Graelle's concussion rod to deal with any soldiers the king might have guarding Aiested's gate. Ezra swept his hand to the right side of the console and froze. An empty, oval-shaped depression on the plinth's smooth surface made his stomach turn.

"Check the guard for the access key!" he barked. He looked up to find Irvis already kneeling over the dead guard. He quickly searched the man's belt pouch and then met Ezra's eyes and shook his head.

"It has to be here!" Ezra hopped off the dais and made for a row of shelving on the room's east wall.

He'd only made it a half a dozen steps when a wave of fear slammed into him. At the same time the floor suddenly became slick and he lost his footing. He fell hard on his left shoulder, a sickening crunch and a stabbing fire reporting that he'd broken it. He looked down and found himself lying on a patch of ice.

"Now you don't think that I would just leave my gate open, did you?" Trous said in his friendly Tolean accent. "If someone at the palace discovered that the broken slipgate the king keeps in storage actually works, and was linked to mine, they'd send an entire battalion of soldiers to wipe us out."

The room shook as a concussion blast fired from Graelle's talis. The sound was followed by a loud slap and Graelle cried out. "Come now, lasa. Was that really necessary?"

Ezra tried to roll over to see what was happening, but the pain in his shoulder proved to be too much. He heard Irvis shout, followed by a choking noise.

"And who is this, lasa? Your boyfriend?"

"Let him go, Trous!" Ezra growled.

To his relief the choking noises stopped, replaced by Irvis's urgent gasps. Pain flared and Ezra cried out as he was roughly lifted from the ground, and then hoisted into the air by the scruff of his shirt. "You really have lost your edge, Argentus."

His vision darkened and all sound faded as the pain from his broken shoulder overwhelmed him. Then, just as he was on the edge of syncope, his pain disappeared and he found himself standing on his own power and facing Trous.

The man smiled at him, deliberately wiggling a finger upon which he wore a gold ring set with an amethyst stone. "A restoration band. It's more valuable than any other talis I own, even this rare frost ring." He wiggled another finger, this one with a sapphire studded silver band.

Ezra glanced behind Trous and found Irvis kneeling next to Graelle, her nose leaking blood, and Mulladin curled up on the floor sobbing, a wicked bruise forming on the side of his face.

"Now, Argentus," Trous said pleasantly. "If you will please come with me. It is time for our duel."

CHAPTER 54

They were greeted by shouts and jeers when Trous and his enforcers paraded them into the mansion's dining hall. Gone were the feasting tables, a circular dais no more than a foot tall having replaced them. Ezra winced as spittle slapped his cheek and began to ooze toward his chin. Mulladin was making sharp, panicked shouts as the on-looking Rikujo lords and their subordinates threw trash at the boy-man.

Irvis appeared to be shielding Graelle from similar treatment, and actually got struck in the head by an empty bottle for his trouble. But he appeared to pay little attention to the blood that began to run down the side of his head.

The mass of spectators–there had to be a hundred people–exploded with renewed enthusiasm when Trous stepped up onto the dais. He smiled and stretched his arms out expansively to encourage the cheering. He let this go on for a full minute before finally motioning for quiet. The clamor of the crowd tapered off as Trous began to speak.

"Did I not promise you entertainment?" The crowd erupted again, and Trous bellowed a laugh. "And now, I deliver on that promise!" he shouted as he pointed at Ezra.

One of Trous' burly enforcers shoved Ezra forward so hard that he nearly tripped instead of climbing up onto the dais. Ezra shot a worried glance at Irvis, who had taken to comforting a sobbing Mulladin by letting the big man cringe under his outstretched arm.

"Here is Argentus, The Invincible Shadow!" Trous pulled Ezra into a sort of half-hug as though they were the closest of friends.

The crowd jeered and shouted angry obscenities at him, but it all sounded faraway to Ezra. He'd retreated inside himself and was focusing all of his thoughts on his nephew. *I'm sorry, son.*

"Do not deride this man!" Trous scolded the audience who reacted with confused half-hearted shouts. "He was once our leader and deserves the ceremony due the passing of his mantle to a worthy successor!"

Trous stepped away from Ezra and over to one of his waiting servants. The man handed Trous a cloth bag, which he preceded to fill by slipping his rings from his fingers. "This is to be a fair duel. No talis-craft of any kind." Finally, Trous slipped off Kaul's dread medal, deposited it in the bag and cinched it shut. He then hung the bag around his neck. Most talises required contact with skin, at least initially, to function. This was Trous' way of removing talis-craft from the fight without actually giving up his talises. The man was polite, but not stupid.

Trous' servant next handed him a gleaming rapier with a closed hand guard. It was an elegant weapon, quick and sharp, like the man himself. Ezra recognized the blade because he had gifted it to Trous almost twenty years ago. Its make was fine and its value the highest a weapon could fetch without being a talis. *At least my blood will be spilt in style,* his sarcastic inner voice said from wherever it had been hiding. It almost made him chuckle–almost.

The crowd cheered as Trous raised his weapon high over his head. Ezra started as something was pushed into his hand. It was a short sword, not unlike his old one. That was probably deliberate on Trous' part, as it would help to solidify in the minds of the other Rikujo lords who it was Trous was dueling. The man really was an adept manipulator and by Ezra's old outlook probably would've made a worthy successor.

Trous turned and gracefully brought his rapier up so that the flat of its narrow blade kissed his forehead. It was a gentlemen's salute indicating the start of a duel. Ezra had never really held much with showy, Tolean chivalry, but mimicked the motion anyway. Then, before he'd had a chance to call to mind any of his old swordplay, Trous was across the dais and whipping his thin blade through the air.

Ezra had barely enough time to parry the blow, and the crowd roared with delight as he stumbled back. Trous grinned at him, letting Ezra regain his balance before assaulting him again, this time with a series of quick swipes punctuated by sharp thrusts. Only pure survival instinct allowed Ezra to parry the attacks, and only just barely. He would've allowed himself a little pride at having retained sharp reflexes if he hadn't known that Trous was merely toying with him.

The barrage continued, driving Ezra back until he actually fell off the dais. Trous relented, watching with one raised eyebrow as the jeering crowd roughly placed Ezra's sword back into his hand and angrily shoved him back up onto the dais. Trous deliberately turned his back on Ezra as he walked back to the opposite side of the circular platform. Trous was baiting him, but Ezra wasn't likely to get an opening like this on his own, so he struck, swinging his sword down in a diagonal arc.

With blurring speed, Trous whirled around, parried the blow, and then moved in to land a booted kick on Ezra's thigh. He cried out as he fell back, nearly dropping his sword a second time. This time Trous didn't let him recover, but instead moved in so fast that he had the point of his rapier pressed against Ezra's jugular in less than a heartbeat. The crowd roared with delight and called for Trous to dispatch him.

"I am sorry to say this, Argentus, but you've disappointed me. And I wasn't expecting all that much."

A memory forced itself into Ezra's mind. It was a blurred panorama of that day of his shame. The day when he'd slaughtered not only his opponent, but dozens of spectators after losing his will to the sword. It was never a welcomed memory, but this time it seemed particularly repugnant. As if his past was reaching forward to mock him and make certain he didn't miss the irony of his death like this. It made him angry.

Without thinking, Ezra whipped his blade up to knock aside the point of Trous' rapier. He felt a sharp sting at his throat followed by warmth and he knew that he'd cut his neck, but it was a shallow thing. Trous cried out as Ezra launched himself at the man, crashing into him and forcing Trous to stumble backward.

Ezra locked eyes with him just before he slammed his forehead into

Trous' nose. He heard a sickening crunch and then blood poured down the Tolean man's face. Trous roared as he shoved Ezra away and retreated back a pace, free hand cupping his gushing nose. Ezra regained his balance and smirked as insolently as he knew how.

"So you have some fight left in you after all," Trous said in a nasal tone. Then he smiled and removed his hand.

Ezra's own smile faded as he caught sight of Trous' nose. It was bloody, but no longer gushing blood. Neither was it swollen as it should've been. It was as if Ezra hadn't even struck the man. He's somehow still connected to his restoration ring! He's cheating! As if beating Trous in a fair duel wasn't unlikely enough, now it would be impossible. Ezra wasn't sure why that surprised him. The man was a backstabbing thief.

Trous came at him with increased aggression, and Ezra suffered three painful, but superficial slashes to his forearm, shoulder, and cheek respectively. Trous was continually moving to the sides, intentionally keeping Ezra away from the edge of the dais. He was looking to end this.

The roaring crowd caught his attention reminding him again of the day he'd slaughtered dozens of people in a dueling arena not unlike this. The echo of the sword's mind beckoned to him again, promising him something if he would delve into the memory of his shame, but he couldn't. What'd he'd done had been too hideous. To this day, the horror of it could still wake him in the night shaking and sweating.

Hot pain in Ezra's thigh made his eyes tear up, and the crowd's roar drowned out his own scream as he fell onto his side, his sword clattering to the wood a few feet away. He looked down to the locus point of the pain and found blood already seeping through his trousers. A shadow loomed above, and he looked up to find Trous smiling down at him. He saluted Ezra with his bloody rapier and whipped the blade to his side in preparation for the killing stroke.

"Ez!" a familiar voice bellowed.

Ezra saw Mulladin climb up on the dais and launch himself at Trous. The man was so stunned he was taken down without even trying to move. Ezra watched as Mulladin and Trous rolled across the dais, Trous losing his rapier, and the bigger Mulladin coming to rest on top of him. Ezra quickly found his sword, sat up, and tried to stand. The pain knocked him down the first two times, but the third attempt succeeded, and he rose, pressing all of his weight on his uninjured side.

Mulladin was holding Trous down using a wrestling move Ezra had seen Jekaran teach him, and Trous' nose was gushing blood from a blow the boy-man hand landed while they'd rolled. The crowd jeered as Mulladin held fast. By this time, Trous had overcome his surprise and was straining against the hold. No, he was straining to reach something. He followed Trous' outstretched hand to where the fingers were touching a small brown pouch–his talises.

Ezra took a step toward the bag but nearly fell from the pain in his thigh. He pushed through the agony to take another step, but it was too late. Trous's fingers were inside the bag. A flash of lightning followed by a thunderclap rocked the room, and Mulladin was abruptly thrown off of Trous and into the watching crowd.

The memory Ezra had been repressing pushed its way back into his mind, and this time he didn't have the focus to push it out. In an instant, he found himself in another time and place. People screamed as he whirled through wooden bleachers, slashing throats or lopping off heads. A child of no more than six stared up at him, frozen in place with fear. His accusing brown eyes seemed not to blink as Ezra cut him down. Who would've brought their child to a blood match? Goddess damn that little boy's parents! He'd cried out inside his mind.

The killing continued until the ground was covered in blood and the arena entirely devoid of living creatures. That's when the sword let go. Ezra remembered falling to his knees and vomiting in between sobs. He remembered the sword wondering what was wrong with him, and he mentally screaming at the talis to leave his mind. Of course, it couldn't. He remembered staying like that for an indeterminable amount of time until Irvis hesitantly touched him on the shoulder. Even his best friend was frightened of him. That sword had made him into a monster.

Ezra blinked away tears, though from the pain in his thigh or in his heart he couldn't say. Trous was on his feet again, brushing himself off and casually walking over to retrieve his rapier. A calm came over Ezra, and he finally understood. He'd used the memory of that awful day to compartmentalize what the sword left inside his mind so long ago. He'd wanted nothing further to do with the weapon, and having a piece of it still inside his brain threatened to break him. So, on that day when he'd broken the bond, he'd hidden the fragment of the sword's mind in a corner behind those terrible memories, because he knew he'd never let his mind go there.

Truly he was no longer linked to it. That curse had passed to Jekaran. But the sword had left something else behind aside from a piece of its consciousness–power! It had left a portion of its power inside him. As Ezra watched Trous approach, he knew there was only one way he was going to be able to win this duel. And he had to win it. Jekaran needed him, and Mulladin had sacrificed for him. He couldn't lose. So Ezra allowed the memories of that terrible day so long ago, when he'd killed so many innocent people to return in full. Then he tapped that piece of itself the sword had left in his mind.

Trous whipped his rapier up and thrust. The crowd sucked in a collective gasp as Ezra casually knocked aside the attack. Trous himself looked confused, but quickly stepped back, to the side, and sliced at Ezra's neck.

Clang!

This time he caught Trous's blade mid swing and knocked it down, all without even having to move. He turned his head to the side to see Trous' face pale. Ezra smiled and then launched a flurry of swings at the Tolean man. The pain in his thigh throbbed, but no longer hindered his movement, and he struck at his enemy with the lithe grace of an expert swordsman. It was all Trous could do to stave Ezra off, his entire effort now devoted to parrying Ezra's blows.

The crowd remained utterly silent as the two men dueled. Trous was fully invested now, and landing superficial wounds every now and again–the man really was quite skilled. After a particularly intense exchange of swordplay, the two broke apart.

Sweat poured down Trous's brown face and he panted, "You are using a talis!"

Ezra shook his head. "Not this time." Well, it was technically true.

Trous narrowed his eyes. "You lie! You have broken the rules!"

Ezra almost laughed aloud at that. Hadn't the man broken them first? Yes, in fact, he was still breaking them. Ezra had seen several of his landed cuts heal instantaneously meaning Trous was still using his restoration ring. He needed to part the man from his healing talis, or else he would succumb to blood loss long before Trous would tire. But where? Where was the man keeping the ring? It had to be somewhere it could touch his skin.

Trous had retrieved his talises after attacking Mulladin, but they were again in the bag hanging from his neck. Ezra looked at the man's free hand and found only a white depressions on his skin where he usually wore the rings. He hadn't been able to heal when Mulladin was beating him, a voice seemed to whisper. Ezra's eyes fell to Trous's closed hand guard. The ring had to be there, somehow fixed to the inside of the guard. When had the man done that? Ezra hadn't been paying attention when he brought him to the duel. It must've been then.

Trous attacked, and Ezra's enhanced reflexes forced his arm up in time to knock away the thrust. Without thinking, Ezra whirled, slammed an elbow in the side of Trous head, spun to the man's other side and lopped off his sword arm with a long downward slice. Blood sprayed and Trous screamed as he grabbed the stump terminating just below his elbow. Ezra didn't wait to see if Trous could heal himself, but rammed his sword through the man's heart. They locked eyes for a moment, and then Trous' exhaled his last breath.

Ezra collapsed backward to the ground, letting go of his sword so as to not bring Trous' corpse down onto him. Without a connection to the actual sword, the power it left behind was finite, and Ezra had used it up. Through his blurred vision, he could see the crowd of Rikujo lords and their enforcers rushing to leave the room. They were afraid of him again. They must think he somehow still had access to the power of the sword. That was good. But it wouldn't help him if he died right now.

Ezra reached for Trous' rapier and slid it over to the wooden floor. He looked underneath the hand guard and found the restoration ring threaded through the very handle so that it held fast. Ezra touched the ring, and immediately its healing power flow into him. He didn't have much experience using healing talises, and Irvis had told him that they actually required medical knowledge and skill to use to their full effect. But the receding pain told Ezra that he was doing something right, so he continued to focus his attention on the wound in his thigh until it was gone.

"Argentus!" Irvis called.

Ezra sat up and found the chubby monk kneeling with Graelle over a body on the floor. Mulladin! Ezra leapt up and rushed down from the dais. He brought Trous' rapier with him as he had not had time to remove the ring from the handle. When he reached the three, he found Mulladin lying on his back, the front of his tunic blackened and burned.

"No," Ezra exhaled.

"He's alive," Irvis said. "But he took a bolt of lightning to the chest."

Ezra shoved the rapier handle first at Irvis. There was a moment of confusion on his chubby face that quickly resolved to understanding when he saw the restoration ring under the hand guard. He reached for the rapier with one hand and placed his other on the boy-man's burnt chest.

"This is bad, Argentus. I'm not sure I can save him."

Ezra nodded his understanding, and Irvis immediately went to work. He watched in tense silence as the monk shut his eyes in concentration and whispered a prayer. Graelle held Mulladin's head in her lap, gently caressing the boy-man's cheek and whispering what sounded like comforting words. Mulladin's eyes fluttered, and he groaned and cried. The time stretched on, and Ezra fervently prayed to the goddess that they could save Mulladin. He saved my life, and possibly Jekaran's. Spare and heal him, please Divine Mother of Creation!

Finally Irvis sighed and removed his hand from Mulladin's chest. Ezra could see through the tear in his tunic that the burn was gone, but he knew that a lightning strike could do serious internal damage. He met Irvis' eyes.

"I mended what I could. This ring is powerful, and I don't have the discipline to control the healing flows as well as I should. So a great deal went everywhere, while only about half went to the places I was trying to heal. It's in Rasheera's hands now."

Ezra nodded.

"How did you fight like that, Argentus?" Irvis asked.

Ezra sighed. He really didn't want to talk about it, not now, but he owed his friend at least a brief explanation. "Remember how I told you that the sword left something behind in my mind?"

Irvis' eyes widened.

Ezra shook his head and waved dismissively at him. "No, it's gone now."

Irvis slowly nodded, and opened his mouth to ask something but was cut off by Graelle.

"He's waking!"

Ezra turned to look down at Mulladin. The boy-man's eyes fluttered opened and then darted up at Graelle, then to Irvis, before settling on Ezra. He smiled down at Mulladin. "You saved my life, son."

Mulladin closed his eyes and sucked in a breath. "That was sort of the idea."

Ezra froze. Something was wrong. "What did you say?"

Mulladin opened his eyes and sat up. "I said, that was the idea. You were getting your sorry ass beaten so badly that I had to do something."

The voice belonged to Mulladin, but Ezra had never heard the simpleton speak like this. He shot a glance at Irvis and found the man's eyes wide with shock. He looked down at the restoration talis. "It healed him–completely."

"What?" Mulladin said as he glanced between Ezra and Irvis. "Of course it healed me. How else would I survive a lightning bolt to the chest? I want that talis by the way–the lightning one."

"Listen to yourself, son," Ezra said.

"Ez, what are… " Mulladin's eyes widened and for a long moment he stared silently at Ezra. "I'm different," he finally said in a tone of wonder. "I've changed."

Ezra grinned. "You have the mind of a man, now."

"Praise Rasheera twice over and a third time for luck," Irvis gushed.

"So all he needed to be normal was a healing talis?" Ezra asked Irvis.

Mulladin's expression darkened. "Normal?"

Ezra ignored that. "If I had known, I would've taken him to the Rasha monks years ago."

"No, Argentus," Irvis said. "I think this is more than a regular restoration ring."

"What're you talking about?"

"We need to be moving," Graelle said urgently. She was no longer kneeling on the floor but standing and nervously watching the chamber doors. "When their shock wears off, we're going to be in danger again."

Ezra shook his head. "No." He stood and stepped back up on the dais where he leaned over Trous' lifeless corpse and snatched the cloth bag that was hanging at the Tolean man's chest. It was soaked with blood, but Ezra paid that no heed as he opened the pouch and removed Kaul's dread medal.

He looked down at his three companions. "No more running."

CHAPTER 55

The hour was late, and Raelen was tired, but there was no way he could relax enough to sleep, despite Gryyth's insistence, not while he awaited Pariel's return from the treasury. It'd been over two hours since he'd sent the man to retrieve the oath collar, at great peril to his life. Pariel had volunteered, of course, but Raelen still felt as though he'd sent the loyal soldier to his death.

A knock on the door startled Raelen out of his brooding. He shot Gryyth an anxious glance before striding to the door and throwing it open. It wasn't Pariel, but Raelen's pagegirl, Hausen. Apparently, his answering the knock so suddenly and in person had surprised the young woman, and she gaped up at him stupidly.

"What?" Raelen asked tersely. He knew he'd feel guilty later for being rude to the girl, but right now his anxiety was making him cross.

The girl appeared to remember herself and hastily curtsied. "A message from the king, my prince."

Why was his father still awake? Had Pariel gotten caught trying to steal the vault key? Raelen forced down his rising panic. "Speak."

Hausen kept her eyes on the floor and began in a rush, "Be it known to all lords and ladies of his majesty's royal court," she slowed as she regained possession of herself, "that Aiested hath declared war on Haeshala, and as we speak our noble warriors are marching to engage the forces of Prince Isara in glorious battle."

"What?" Raelen choked out. Hausen began to repeat the memorized message but he cut her off. "Who gave you this message and when?"

"The chamberlain," she answered in a confused tone. "Not but an hour ago."

Raelen shot Gryyth a glance. The Ursaj made no response, but Raelen could guess that his thoughts mirrored his own. They had to act now!

Raelen looked back down at Hausen. "Did my father give you this message personally?"

The page girl shook her head. "No, my prince. I was summoned with other pages to receive instruction from the chamberlain. I haven't been in the presence of the king for days."

That alarmed, Raelen. Had Loeadon killed his father and replaced him? Or had he sent word in his father's name? He turned to Gryyth, "We have to find my father!"

The Ursaj bear-man grunted his agreement and went to the wall to fetch Raelen's armor.

"I heard the chamberlain issuing messages to the other pages, ordering them to rouse the generals for a war council. I am uncertain why I wasn't instructed to invite you, my prince. I assumed that you'd be receiving that word separately or– "

"War room!" A sudden warm appreciation for Hausen's loyalty to him made Raelen quickly kiss her on the head. The girl turned red as he stepped around her and rushed out of the room.

Gryyth was at his side as he ran down the hall. "Your armor, cub?"

Raelen smirked. "You're all the armor, I need.

"Not very comforting," Gryyth rumbled.

Raelen patted his bicep where he wore his transference band. "I meant this."

"Physical prowess may not be enough against a foe that can wield Apeiron."

"Then let's hope Seiro makes up the difference." Out of the corner of his eye, he saw Gryyth nod approvingly.

They ran down the hall, startling a group of chatting maidservants as they turned a corner. One actually screamed, but Raelen paid them little heed as they kept running for the war room. He considered taking a detour to the treasury to find Pariel and get the oath collar, but the urgency of what was happening made him discard that plan. If Loeadon was controlling or impersonating his father, it would come to battle no matter what he did. So trying to force the polymath to put on the collar and confess wasn't likely to work. He did pray to Rasheera that Pariel hadn't been caught, or killed. That would certainly not be Seiro, and he'd be forced to bear that guilt for the remainder of his days.

Even at a full sprint, it took them close to half an hour to reach the war room. Two armored guards crossed their spears before the closed set of double doors. "I'm sorry, my prince," one of them said. "We have specific instructions not to admit you."

Before Raelen could reply, Gryyth roared and lunged forward. The guards instinctively leapt out of the way as the eight-foot-tall, white-furred juggernaut crashed through the doors, throwing them both open. A room full of startled dignitaries stared up at them, faces pale. They were standing around a circular table, above which hovered a three dimensional, translucent map of Shaelar. Raelen moved into the room and stood a step in front of Gryyth.

"Raelen!" The king actually shouted. "You dare!"

Raelen ignored his father and quickly locked onto a dark haired, sallow-faced man standing two persons to the right of the king. "It's over, Loeadon!" He raised his hand to point at the polymath. "I know your secret!"

Loeadon frowned. "And what is it that you think you know, boy?"

Raelen saw his father shoot the polymath a startled glance. The man's tone was insolent, and no one but the king dared to refer to Raelen as "boy."

"I know that you are Aiested's enemy!"

Loeadon smirked and then threw his hand forward. A thunderclap shook the room, and Raelen saw a shaft of blue lightning lash out through the ghostly map toward him. He was shoved out of the way by Gryyth, who took the bolt of lightning for him. The Ursaj roared in pain as he was hurled back into the wall.

Raelen cried out as he saw his protector crumple to the ground, fur on his stomach blackened and smoking. He leapt to his feet and quickly found Loeadon. The black-robed man held his right arm out to the side, a whip-like bolt of lightning arcing and crackling as it bent toward the floor. It wasn't whip-like, it was a whip; a whip made entirely of lightning. The other dignitaries in the room scattered away from Loeadon, Osarr Rakahnas having put himself in front of the king.

The polemarch drew his long sword and gripped the handle with both hands. It was a talis, a firebrand. A sword that burned as much as it cut. Rakahnas' blade ignited and was instantly wreathed in flames. He watched as the old general attacked Loeadon, the aura of fire burning his blade throwing out a wave of heat as he swung it.

There was another thunderclap as Loeadon snapped his lightning whip up at Rakahnas. It curled around the man's sword, and Rakahnas cried out and frozen mid swing. The polemarch began to convulse as the lightning whip crackled and arced violently. After a moment of this, the old man crumpled to the ground, his eyes having burst and his sizzling corpse smoking.

Raelen tapped his transference band and immediately his hands changed, enlarging and becoming a perfect copy of Gryyth's clawed paws. He launched himself into the air, flipping over the table and landing with a swing at Loeadon's head. The polymath ducked the swing and snapped his lightning whip up in reprisal. Years of training with Gryyth in the martial arts the Ursaj held sacred activated, and he dropped to the ground just in time to avoid a face full of crackling lightning.

Loeadon dismissed the lightning whip, backed away, and then waved both hands out as though he were doing a swan dive. A blast of hurricane strength wind slammed into Raelen, actually lifting him from the floor and hurling him into a bookshelf set against the wall. Wood splintered, and cracked, and dozens of thick, leather-bound books rained down on his head and shoulders.

When the deluge of books stopped, he looked up to find Loeadon moving toward his father, the polymath's hands now wreathed in flames that did not appear to harm him. The king raised a sword, not his own, but the one that belonged to the farm boy brought in by Lord Gymal. It wouldn't be much use to his father while still bonded to the boy.

He struggled up, preparing to charge Loeadon again. That's when he saw a serving girl standing in the corner of the room, eyes fixed on Raelen's father. He recognized her. It was the girl he'd helped clean up spilt tea just a few hours earlier. Why had she not fled the room? Even the high lords and some of the military commanders had done that. Raelen shook off the distraction and charged forward.

MAELY BACKED into a corner and pressed herself against a stone column that jutted out from the wall. What was happening? What was she supposed to do? Jenoc never told her how long she had to remain with the king. She'd made him order the army to resume their advance, and then forced the king to have his servants gather all of the communication talises in the palace and toss them into the ocean, so the order to advance on Haeshala couldn't be rescinded. Would that be enough? Could she run now? Would Jenoc kill her if she did?

"Why this treachery, Loeadon?" The king demanded as his dark robed wizard slowly approached him, his hands literally on fire.

Loeadon chuckled. "I need that sword, Highness."

"Why?" the king demanded.

"You made a terrible mistake in allowing me to examine it. I have discerned its potential and come to believe that it is likely the most powerful weapon in all of Shaelar. With it, I shall be invincible."

Maely saw the king scowl. "You seek my throne!"

"Of course I do!" Loeadon scoffed loudly. "It has been my purpose from the first day I entered your service."

Maely started as a blurred shape crashed into Loeadon. The wizard cried out, and a wave of heat washed over her as one of his flaming hands flared. The prince–why did he have the hands of a bear?–yelped as he stumbled away from Loeadon, his shoulder blackened and smoldering.

The king made to move forward to join the fight, but Maely whispered, "No, you stay near me. Protect me!"

The king jerked to a stop, and began to back toward the wall, Jek's sword raised protectively in front of him. She was probably not in much danger; if it came to it, she could use her ring, but the chaos in the room caused by a talis battle made her nervous. She wished she could just sneak away, find Jekaran, and get the hell out of here.

The heat from Loeadon's burning hands was abruptly gone, replaced by a cold wind as the man caused a sheet of ice to frost the stones of the floor beneath the prince's boots. He slipped mid-charge, and Loeadon used the moment to fire a shard of ice from his outstretched palm. The thick icicle buried its sharp point into the prince's already burnt shoulder, and he screamed. It looked as if he were losing this fight.

Maely glanced to her right where the prince's white bear lay on the floor. He was sitting up now, straining to rise. Maely winced at the sight of his blackened stomach and the blood trickling down the side of his muzzle. How badly had he been hurt by the lightning? Was he dying? Maely shrieked as the bear suddenly launched himself forward and barreled into Loeadon.

The wizard was slammed into the wall with such force Maely was sure he'd been killed. A sudden explosion of stone told her otherwise as the bear was thrown backward into the room's large, circular table. With a shattering noise like glass, the floating ghostlike map of Shaelar flickered and then disappeared.

Loeadon stepped out of a cloud of dust, no longer looking smug. His hair was hanging down over his eyes, blood trickled from his nose, and he was clenching the bicep of his left arm, which hung lifeless at his side. The bear stood, but Loeadon pointed at him and a cold wind washed over the room. Ice formed over the bear's feet, but it didn't stop there. It grew over the bear's legs, and then up to its thighs. The bear struggled and roared, but the ice kept creeping up his body. Loeadon was going to encase him in a block of ice.

Maely looked to where the prince lay on the ground. He was trying to yank the shard of ice out of his burnt shoulder, but the pain made him falter.

Perhaps now was the time for her to intervene, but to do so she'd have to give up control of the king. She'd discovered–to her disappointment–that she could only control one person at a time with her compulsion talis. The king would still remain enthralled, but it would quickly begin to fade without her maintaining her focus on him.

Something blurred on her right periphery. She instinctively turned. "Jek!" she shouted. But he didn't look at her.

His arrival did have the effect of stopping Loeadon, just as he was growing ice up the bear-man's neck. He stopped and hurled a bolt of lightning at Jekaran, who dodged it as though he knew it where coming before Loeadon even struck. Maely expected Jek to charge Loeadon, but instead he ran toward her. Had he somehow come to know of her plight? Had he escaped and come to rescue her?

He passed by without even noticing her, and approached the king. The man glanced at Maely as if expecting instruction, but she had no time to give any. In a blur of motion, Jekaran stepped inside the king's defenses, smashed an elbow into the underside of his jaw, and then reached forward and broke his sword arm backward.

Maely heard the sword clatter to the stone floor just as Jekaran stepped to the side of the king, reached up to cup his chin with his right hand, and the back of his head with the other. He roughly jerked the king's head to the side and Maely heard his neck snap. That's when she realized what was happening. The sword had taken control again as it had in Imaris.

"Jekaran!" she called, but he didn't even look at her.

He picked up the sword and swung it just in time to knock a missile of ice to the side. He batted two more away as he made for the open doorway. Where was he going? Maely glanced at the dead king, and then ran after Jek.

Loeadon didn't even see it coming when Raelen shoved the spike-like shard of ice into his side. The polymath cried out and Raelen's forward moment carried them both to the floor. He didn't give the man a chance to cast another spell, but brutally struck him in the face, his claw raking across Loeadon's eyes and nose. The man's head struck the stone and something fell off of his head and clattered to the floor.

"It's over Allosian!" Raelen actually growled.

Loeadon grimaced with pain, panting loudly and trying to clutch at his left eye, which looked to have been destroyed by Raelen's claw.

"Show your true nature!"

"W-what are you t-talking about?" he whimpered.

Raelen heard a cracking sound and looked to his left just in time to see Gryyth break out of his icy shell. The Ursaj looked injured but was able to stand on his own power. Raelen looked back down at Loeadon, who was now sobbing like a girl.

"Enough deception!" Raelen shook him.

"I-I'm not him," Loeadon sobbed.

Raelen froze. He looked at the floor just behind Loeadon's bleeding head and saw an ivory circlet with an amethyst jewel in its center lying upside down. It was the casting crown; the talis that let a human wield magic like an Allosian.

"No," Raelen breathed out. Loeadon was a usurper and an enemy, but he wasn't the Allosian. The irony of the coincidence would've been laughable had not the very existence of mankind been at stake.

A cold paw lightly touched his uninjured shoulder. "Cub." Raelen looked up at Gryyth. The bear-man was holding his slave's awl in his palm. That could mean only one thing.

Raelen scanned the room and quickly found the fallen form of the king a dozen feet away. He leapt up, knowing full well Gryyth would keep Loeadon pinned, but kicked the circlet away from the man just to be safe. After a few quick steps, he found himself kneeling next to the king. His eyes were open, staring fixedly at nothing, and he wasn't breathing.

He was dead.

Raelen was surprised to find himself weeping uncontrollably. He laid his head on his father's motionless chest and sobbed like a child. Although at times he had wished for this, in Raelen's heart he'd loved his father. That's why all the criticism, all the cruel treatment, and betrayals had stung him.

If he'd truly hated his father, he might've rejoiced that the throne was his. But no, King Raeleth Joran Taris the eighteenth was dead. And the worst part, the cruelest part, was that Raelen was just beginning to understand the man. Perhaps in time it would've led to the kind of father-son relationship he'd always hoped for. Now that opportunity was lost.

"Did he do this?" Raelen growled as he shot a baleful glare at Loeadon writhing on the ground.

Gryyth had his massive paw around Loeadon's throat, making it hard for the man to breathe, but not strangling him. "It was the boy from Genra," he rumbled.

Jekaran

"I will make him pay for this!" Raelen snarled.

He rose and took two steps toward the door but stopped when Gryyth rumbled, "Cub."

"I know it's not Seiro!" Raelen snapped. "And I don't care!"

"No," Gryyth said, rising to stand. "You are king, now. Aiested comes first. It is a king's Seiro."

Raelen stood there seething, breathing in and out, and trying to stifle his sobbing. He began mentally chanting Gryyth's meditation mantra,

> *I am a clear brook flowing among the trees.*
> *I am a meadow of clover in summer.*
> *I am the moon silently watching the night.*

"You are right," he finally conceded. "I will let the guards hunt him down." Raelen took a step toward Gryyth. "We need to find a speaking stone and order the army to return."

Gryyth nodded and casually put a foot on Loeadon's chest. The man croaked out a cry of pain. "Perhaps he can do it with that talis."

Raelen looked at the ivory circlet on the floor and then at Loeadon. He strode over and stood above the defeated polymath. "Can you spell-cast to send a message? And do not lie!"

Gryyth increased the pressure of his foot and Raelen heard one of the man's ribs crack.

"No," Loeadon croaked out. "I only know a few castings."

Raelen sighed. It was probably safer not to allow the man to use the talis anyway. He likely knew a spell-casting for healing himself, or perhaps he'd attack them somehow.

"We need to find the Allosian infiltrator." Raelen gingerly touched his injured shoulder. It had started to feel numb, which probably meant the burn was serious. "We need to get the oath collar, and begin testing the members of my father's court." He looked up at Gryyth, suddenly remembering. "We need to find Pariel!"

Chapter 56

Maely sprinted down the corridor, her slippers sliding on the smooth floor as she turned a corner. She spotted Jekaran running down the far end of the wide ivory hallway.

"Jek!" she screamed, but he didn't even flinch.

He was about to pass out of sight again so Maely threw a wave of compulsion at him. "Jekaran, stop!"

His abrupt stop caused him to stumble and fall to one knee. Maely was relieved. She had worried that the sword would somehow protect him from the magic of her mother's ring. She ran down the corridor until she was five paces away from him. He turned and looked at her, and she saw Jekaran's green eyes–bright and clear. They were no longer clouded by the battle trance of the sword.

"Mae?" he asked, sounding confused.

Maely flung herself down at him and wrapped him in a tight embrace.

"How did you do that?"

"What?" she sobbed.

"You broke the sword's hold over my body."

Maely shook her head, it rubbing against Jekaran's chest. "It doesn't matter," she sniffed.

"What are you doing here?"

Maely sobbed a nervous laugh. "I came for you, stupid!"

"But–"

"I'll explain everything later. Right now we have to go." Maely stood and then helped Jekaran to stand.

Warm relief continued to wash over her as she stared at Jekaran's dirty, pale face and ragged clothes. He hadn't been treated well during his time here that was for certain.

"I know a way out," she said as she took his hand in hers and began towing him down the corridor.

"Wait!" Jekaran stopped her. "Are you here alone?"

That irritated her. "Does it matter? I saved you!"

Jekaran shook his head. "We need to find Kairah!"

Maely angrily wrenched her hand free of his. "No!"

"Mae, we don't have time to arg–"

She moved up to him, reached up behind his head to bend it down, and pressed her lips against his. It wasn't quite the romantic revelation she'd always envisioned, but it was time he knew what she had already come to know; she loved him and they were meant to be together. She pulled back, breaking their kiss and staring up into his stunned face.

"Mae..." Jek trailed off. "I..."

"Idiot!" she snapped. "You really didn't know, did you?"

She moved in to kiss him again, but he gently stopped her. "Mae..." he said again.

"What?" she asked.

"I love you," he said.

She smiled involuntarily and said, "And I've always loved–."

"But not like that," he finished.

Maely's smile fell away and the giddy flutter in her stomach was smothered by a cold nausea. "What?" she asked in a trembling voice.

Jekaran cast a furtive glance down the corridor. "We can talk about this after we get out of here."

"No!" Maely snapped as tears pooled in her vision. One escaped and rolled down her cheek. "We're supposed to get married!"

Jekaran shook his head and said, "It's not like that for me. I'm sorry, Mae." His look of pity made her want to die right there.

"But, I came for you," she squeaked out in a half-whisper.

"Mae, please..."

His placating tone enraged her. "It's Kairah! Isn't it?" Tears were now spilling down her cheeks like a waterfall. "You want her instead of me!" She reached out and slapped his chest.

"Mae..." Jekaran said and he reached out to gather her into another hug.

"No!" Maely shouted as she pulled away. She balled her fists and felt herself trembling. "This isn't how it's supposed to happen."

Jenoc's words suddenly echoed in Maely's mind. I will allow you to keep this ring. You've tasted its power. You know that with it you can have whatever your heart desires—money, land...Jekaran.

"No," Maely said as she shook her head. "No, you do love me. You do love me!" The wave of power exploded from her chest with a strength she'd never before managed.

Jekaran stumbled back, the psychic force so strong it actually caused him to drop the sword. He stared at her, eyes wide and mouth agape. Then a smile crept onto his face and he moved toward her. He didn't say anything but took her in his arms and kissed her passionately. Maely's heart thrilled and she kissed him back as fiercely as she knew how. Although it only lasted a moment, it seemed to Maely as though the kiss had gone on for hours. This is what she'd wanted. This is what she'd longed for. To be loved by the man who she loved. To be held, protected, and cared for.

She pulled away and sucked in a deep breath. Jekaran's smile faltered and he moved in for another kiss, but Maely stopped him. She giggled, "I do need to breathe." Jekaran chuckled nervously, and Maely knew he shared her giddiness.

She took his hand in hers and began towing him back the way they'd run. "Come on, we need to get you out of here," she said. "After killing the king, I'm sure they'll be sending guards to take you."

"Yes, mistress," he said.

Maely froze, causing Jekaran to bump into her. She slowly turned to look at him and her heart dropped. The look on his face was utterly adoring, even worshipful, but it wasn't Jekaran's look. Gone was the twinkle of mischief in his eyes or the look of practical goodness she'd so often studied when he wasn't looking. This wasn't him.

She let go of his hand. This wasn't right. At first she'd told herself using the compulsion ring on Jek would only draw out the romantic feelings he must already have for her. That it would be nothing more than a psychic slap to the face to wake him up to the truth. But this was different. The look in his eyes was the same look he got when the sword took over. This wasn't Jekaran.

Tears spilled down her cheeks again. Perhaps they had never stopped falling, as she'd been ecstatic a moment earlier, but now they were bitter. He didn't love her the way she loved him, and not even her mother's ring would let her change that. She suddenly felt dirty. How was she different from the men who'd raped her mother? They had paid her for her love, true, but it was still forced. The price she was paying for Jekaran's love was Jekaran himself.

"Mistress?" Jekaran asked, his tone very concerned. "What's wrong?"

Maely shook her head and began to back away. "Don't call me that," she sobbed.

Jekaran reached out for her, but she turned and began to run. "Don't follow me!" she shouted as she turned out of the corridor.

JEKARAN WATCHED Maely disappear around a corner. *I love her, I love her, I love her...*The thought continued to whirl around in his mind so loud that it drowned out all others.

Jekaran a voice called from far away.

He turned to look behind him at the sword that lay on the ground. *It was important,* something seemed to whisper, *it was valuable.* He walked toward it, heart wrenching at letting Maely go, but unable to follow her because of her command. He bent down and grabbed the sword by the handle, and then he awoke. The circling thought of loving Maely and needing to do whatever she asked of him evaporated.

"What the hell?" He raised his free hand to the side of his head.

I broke the spell over your mind, the sword said.

"What spell?"

The compulsion spell she put upon you. It shouldn't have affected you like that, but she caught me by surprise.

Jekaran gently touched his lips as he stared off in the direction Maely had fled. "She kissed me," he said. "I tried to tell her I didn't love her like that, but then I wanted her more than– "

It was a powerful spell-casting, the sword said. But that doesn't matter right now because you are in danger. Give me control.

"Like hell I will," Jekaran scoffed.

. It is my function to protect you.

"By stealing my body?" he snapped.

You were unconscious and in danger.

"And when I woke up, you still wouldn't let go. No, I'm not letting you do that again."

Voices echoed from a connecting corridor and Jekaran tensed.

Guards, the sword said. They come to kill you.

Just then a dozen soldiers in armor flooded into the corridor.

But why are they hunting me? Then Jekaran remembered. "Right, the king," he said ruefully.

"There he is!" one of the guards shouted and then pointed at him.

Give me control, the sword repeated.

"Go to hell," Jekaran said.

He turned to run in the other direction, but stopped up short when another contingent of soldiers burst into the hallway.

Give me control!

"And let you slaughter every single one of them?"

The sword projected confusion. They intend to kill you.

"They're just following orders. I'm the one who killed their king!" I'm the real monster, a voice inside him accused, and he couldn't refute it.

He was going to have you executed. The sword rebutted, which did ease Jekaran's guilt–a bit.

"We need to get to Kairah," Jekaran quickly decided. "Help me like you did in Rasha, without taking over."

That way is less effective. We are more powerful when I am in total control of your movements.

Jekaran heard the snapping of a trigger and whipped the sword up just in time to deflect a crossbow bolt only feet before it would've struck him in the face.

See, the sword said. I could've dodged that entirely.

"Cocky, aren't you?" Jekaran scoffed.

The soldiers ahead and behind closed, more of them raising crossbows and taking aim. Jekaran cast a glance over his shoulder in the direction Maely had fled.

"I'm sorry, Mae," he whispered.

She wouldn't want him anyway, not if she knew what he really was–an Eater. His only hope now was that Kairah could somehow fix him, or knew how to. If she couldn't, well, then he might very well have to die.

The soldiers before and behind him charged.

Chapter 57

Jove trudged uphill toward the Apeira well. He was disappointed there were not more people walking the streets of this city. He'd assumed from the massive well's constant light the people wouldn't follow a traditional day and night sleep schedule. The streets weren't empty, of course; it just wasn't how Jove imagined it.

A woman screamed upon seeing him with his floating tendrils of warped green air waving in the air above him. She attempted to dart off the main thoroughfare, but Jove struck her without slowing or stopping. Refreshing and delicious energy pulsed into him, but it wasn't enough to slake his appetite. Never again would the lives of men or animals be enough. Not now that he'd tasted Apeiron.

He licked his lips as he focused on the looming spire of glowing purple crystal. He could actually smell the Apeiron radiating from the well. Not with his nose, of course, but that was the only way he could describe it.

It made him hungry.

Dawn was not far off as was evidenced by the sky lightening on the horizon. Years of habit made Jove apprehensive about walking so openly in such a large city, but he shook off the impulse to retreat to the shadows. His days of skulking in the dark, and hiding in corners were over. Now he could gratify his passions as much as he liked, and never have to fear arrest or execution.

No prison could hold him. Nothing could kill him. For how would one kill death itself? He giggled as he caught sight of a coach parked a little further up the street. If he could restrain himself from eating the coachman long enough, he could ride to the Apeira well and be feasting much sooner than if he continued walking.

He walked up to the front of the carriage and found the coachman snoring as he leaned his head back against the front of the cab. He was a portly fellow, about ten years past middle age. He had a high forehead, but Jove couldn't tell if that was due to balding or because of the tri-corner hat he wore.

"Hello, friend," Jove said.

The man choked on his snoring as he started and sat forward.

"Need transit, my good–" The man cut off when he looked at Jove, and his eyes flicked to the floating tendrils that were waving above Jove's head.

"Divine Mother!" he cried and reached for the reins controlling his team of six bridled ghern.

Jove shot out one of his tendrils and drained the life from the ghern at the front of the team. It bleated as it shriveled into a dead husk. That had the desired effect, and the coachman froze.

"Pl-please don't kill me," he began to sob. "I have a wife and eight little ones to feed."

"Feed?" Jove repeated and laughed. Appropriate. "I'm not going to hurt you," he said using his best trouper's voice. "I only want a ride."

"Where?" the coachman asked, his eyes continually darting to Jove's translucent green tendrils.

Jove pointed up hill to the Apeira well, and actually had to wipe the drool from his mouth before saying in a throaty voice, "There."

"You are the counter force to Apeiron," Kairah shouted at the sky. "Ape-iron is life and you are death. Is it not so?"

She felt the alien mind agree.

"Did you do this?" She motioned at the ruined city, shattered Apeira well, and the countless scattered bones. "Did you lay waste to this place?"

To her complete surprise, the mind seemed to answer No.

"Then who destroyed this place?" she demanded.

This thing was the shadow to the light of life, the antithesis of growth and everything that made up the core of Allosian purpose. In retrospect, its reality didn't surprise her. Jenoc had told her the universe was balance and order. So, that meant if there was a power that created and grew life, then there must be a counter power that withered and destroyed it. Still, natural it be, it disgusted her.

"Who did this?" she demanded of the dark clouds above her.

You did, the force seemed to reply.

"What?" She hadn't expected that. "Tell me what you mean!"

The force did not answer.

"Answer me!" Kairah shouted.

The thunder rumbled, but there came no response.

That's when Kairah heard something else. It came first as indistinct sound but grew louder and louder. It was her body, she somehow knew. It was beginning to wake. Although muted, she could hear the ambience of the room in which she lay, smell the newly laundered bedding, and feel...

"What is that?" she cried out.

There was something wrong back where her body lay. Something very wrong. It had the same feeling as the Moriora, but somehow differ-ent–mixed. It wasn't omnipresent like this power. No, this was focused to a single location, intersecting her reality through the space of a single living creature. It made her want to retch again. It was an aberration, a violation of natural law so hideous that she could scarcely comprehend it. And whatever it was, it was coming.

The thunder rumbled, and the alien mind answered with an actual word–Vessel.

RIDING in a coach was very pleasant, Jove decided. He'd never ridden in one before, the closest thing to it he'd ever rode in was a wagon. But the two didn't really compare, not with the coach's enclosed cab and plush seats. He wouldn't be picking splinters out of his backside when this ride was over, that was for certain.

Thud!

Something landed on the top of the cab, rocking the whole carriage. He heard a startled cry from the driver, and peered out the window next to his seat to see what was going on. The portly driver was rolling to a stop on the side of the cobblestone rode. He's leapt off the driver's seat! Well, he's a fool if he thinks I can't still—

Jove was jolted away from the window as the carriage abruptly lurched right. He was thrown into the opposite wall of the cab as the coach tipped. He looked out the window against which his face was pressed and saw the ground speeding up to meet him. Then the carriage crashed to its side.

Jove hit his head several times as he was tossed about inside the rolling coach. When it finally came to rest, he found himself lying on his back on shards of glass while looking up at the open door. Jove growled as he struggled up, and climbed out the side door that was now like a top hatch. The effort was difficult as his leg stubbornly refused to work properly.

When he finally hoisted himself out of the carriage, he whipped a tendril in the direction of the ghern team intending to syphon the energy his body would need to rebuild his leg. He bit off a curse when he saw the five bipedal animals racing down the street away from the carriage, completely untethered.

Despite his broken leg, Jove managed to climb down from the over turned carriage. One of its back wheels continued to spin slowly as he rounded the vehicle. Where was that driver? The man had obviously leapt from the carriage to escape being eaten, causing the resultant accident. Well, Jove wasn't going to let him get away. That man would pay for Jove's broken leg with his life–literally–as he would use the man's essence to heal himself.

Something struck Jove in the back of the head, and he whirled around to see who would dare throw a stone at him. But there wasn't anyone in sight. He looked up at the roofs of the buildings behind him, but he still couldn't see anyone. Another stone struck him in the side of the head, this one flying from the opposite direction. Jove growled as he spun in that direction. Again, no one.

"Who's there?" Jove demanded.

He heard a faint whistling sound punctuated by something striking him in the neck. It didn't hurt of course, none of the attacks did. It was just terribly rude, and Jove couldn't abide rudeness. He felt at his throat and found a needle sticking out, fletched at the end with the feathers of a small bird. He yanked it free and smelled the tip. He knew that smell. Destra root. A paralytic he'd often used to incapacitate his dolls when they became unruly.

Jove tossed the dart away and began to laugh loudly until he couldn't control himself. He stumbled back against the overturned carriage, doubled over with high-pitched laughing.

"Fool!" he was able to manage in between sucking breath. "Poison can't touch me. I have no blood!"

He wiped tears from his eyes as his wild laughing began to abate. That's when he saw it, a faint rippling in the air not but ten paces to his right. He lashed out at it with all of his tendrils but found nothing except for a small cat crouched behind a rain barrel. It was enough to mend his leg to the point that he could put weight on it, and he was able to let go of the carriage and stand on his own.

He began to creep around the coach, scrutinizing the night to watch for that rippling in the air. He'd never heard of a talis that could make one invisible, but it could be nothing else.

"I've played this game before," he said in a singsong voice. "And I must say that I'm rather good at it. I will find you."

By this time, several of the town's nocturnal inhabitants had begun to appear on the street. They came from all directions, no doubt drawn by the sound of the crash. Jove smiled and then lashed out at the closest spectator. It was a young man holding a woodcutter's axe. Strength pulsed into Jove as the man's life ebbed away. At seeing this, the other investigators began to cry out and scatter.

Jove breathed in the night air and tested his leg. It was completely whole.

"Show yourself, he called to his invisible assailant. Or I will do that to every man, woman, and child on this street." He would do it anyway, but his enemy didn't need to know that.

Flickering on his left periphery made him turn his head. The air in front of him distorted, waved, and shimmered leaving a man-sized creature standing in the dark. It was reptilian, with scaly skin that looked grey in the night.

"Vorakk!" Jove laughed with delight. "I've never seen a real one before!"

The lizard man didn't answer. Instead, he made a sound that sounded like a mixture between a hiss and a growl, waved his hand, and turned it so that it looked like he was going to show Jove something he'd been clutching. A bluish-white ball of crackling light appeared hovering above its upraised palm.

"What is that?" Jove asked, his tone full of childlike wonder.

The Vorakk smiled a toothy grin, and then threw his hand forward. Jove was blinded by a flash of brilliant light accompanied by a deafening thunderclap. Something struck him in the chest, where his heart used to be. It threw him back and he found himself staring up at the night sky, chest smoldering.

He barked a laugh that quickly became a string of uncontrollable cackling as he struggled to his feet. The Vorakk still stood facing him, its brave smile gone. Apparently, that was supposed to have done Jove in. He wiped a lock of dirty black hair out of his vision and slowly took a step toward the lizard man.

It hissed something and summoned another floating ball of light, this one looking to be made of fire. He pointed at Jove and the little ball flew forward becoming a wall of flames. Jove pulled his power back to him so that it enveloped him like a translucent green cloak. When the wave of fire struck him, it immediately dissipated, and Jove was the stronger for it.

Now the Vorakk's expression had changed from determined to uncertain. It summoned another ball of light, this one a frosty blue. But before it could spell-cast, Jove struck out with one of his tendrils and consumed it. Eating the magic wasn't a pleasant experience like eating Apeiron. No, this burned him and refused to breakdown and add to his strength. In fact, it was painful. Jove ejected the ball of light from his chest as though he were spitting out a bite of spoiled fruit, and it vanished.

"What was that?" he choked out.

"Spirit eck," the Vorakk said, its smile now returned.

"It's disgusting!" Jove said.

The words had scarcely left his mouth when the lizard man charged, swinging its right claw down to rake Jove across the face. It didn't hurt, but the sensation of the numb flesh of his cheek being parted by sharp claws was disconcerting. The Vorakk hissed and drew back, cradling the claw he'd struck with, a look of utter shock on its lizard face. Jove glanced at the hand and saw that it had withered and was breaking apart into a cloud of ash drifting away on the night wind.

He grinned at the Vorakk and wondered what it was going to taste like. The creature cowered back and clutched its stump, a glowing green liquid spilling from its wound. Then, before Jove had a chance to manifest one of his tendrils, the Vorakk vanished, a trail of luminescent blood leading away from him.

Jove was about to follow, but he was so close to the Apeira well he could taste the energy it was radiating. He turned and began moving up the street and toward the palace, toward his prize.

CHAPTER

58

Raelen didn't slow or stop for the monk's ministrations. The scrawny little man huffed, and muttered in frustration, but never overtly complained. Raelen toyed with the idea of breaking into a jog, just to urge the monk to move faster, but one did not treat the goddess' servants that way–even when they deserved it. Tingling, and then feeling rushed back into his shoulder causing him to flinch from the pain as the puncture wound from Loeadon's shard of ice knitted closed.

He ground his teeth. That treacherous snake may not have directly caused his father's death, but he was as much to blame as was the boy, Jekaran. It still galled Raelen that he couldn't join in the hunt for farm boy. But now that he'd had a few moments to overcome his rage, he knew it was for the best. He still didn't quite know what to make of his sudden feelings of love and grief for his father. If someone had told him he'd feel this way a week prior, he would've laughed at the notion. But there it was.

He still wasn't sure he could forgive the man for what he'd done to Saranna, or their mother, but he would make sure the king was laid to rest with all the honor due a ruler of Aiestal. Despite all of his father's faults, and their dysfunctional relationship, he did love the man. After all, he was Raelen's father.

Raelen and his entourage–Gryyth, the Rasheeran monk, one of the ranking generals, and two dozen members of his honor guard–rounded a corner into a hallway that ended with a smooth metal door, one with no visible seams or handles. It wasn't really a door. It was the portion of the massive vault talis that hadn't been walled away by the ivory palace architecture.

As they neared the vault, Raelen touched an object that was hanging around his neck by a leather thong. It was star-shaped with an amethyst jewel in its center–the vault key. He'd fetched it from his father's study, hoping to find Pariel in the process, but there had been no sign of the man. The key was still there, so he hadn't yet gone to the vault, so where was he? Had he been caught sneaking into the king's apartment? Raelen wanted to keep looking for his loyal Navarch, but he needed the oath collar in order to find out which member of his father's court was the Allosian warmonger in disguise.

"Open," Raelen commanded.

The smooth surface of the door appeared to liquefy, and then pull back like a silver curtain. The liquid metal disappeared into the door's frame, revealing a room to rival the size of the palace's largest audience chamber; one that could easily accommodate twenty thousand spectators. Glass shelves arranged in narrow aisles ran the length of the room, most apparently empty. This had been one of the fabled talis stores of the Allosians once, before the city was conquered by Raelen's ancestors.

The fey peoples had made off with half their hoard before the palace fell, and most of what was left was awarded to supporters who would become the progenitors of Aiestal's nobility leaving a mere pittance in comparison. Still, what remained was probably the most valuable collection of rare and powerful talises in all of Shaelar.

Raelen led his entourage into the vault, and then turned to the captain of his honor guard. "Inquire at the catalog talis." He motioned at a globe on a plinth a dozen feet to his right. "And locate the oath collar talis."

Traggert saluted and moved off.

Raelen watched as the man went about his work. He was startled when the scrawny little monk said, "You are now healed, your highness."

Raelen had forgotten he was there. He supposed the man was used to that on account of his small stature. "Yes, thank you, Brother Yimin."

The monk made a perfunctory bow before turning to leave.

"Brother Yimin," Raelen called.

The monk audibly sighed, slumped his shoulders, and turned back. "Yes, highness?"

"After you heal my Ursaj, see to it that Master Loeadon is healed. You'll find him being escorted to the dungeon."

The monk's eyebrows drew up and his forlorn expression vanished. "Sire?"

"I want him in perfect health when I execute him."

The monk nodded sharply, and Raelen thought the man was hiding a smile, but he couldn't be certain. Raelen turned and walked toward one of the vault's tall glass shelves. When he reached it, he produced the casting crown from within his torn shirt and placed it on the shelf at eye level.

A ring of soft glowing light appeared on the shelf beneath the crown, indicating it was being cataloged by the talis that inventoried the contents of the vault. It was a remarkable piece of Allosian craftsmanship, unique to the palace as far as Raelen knew. It was also the largest talis he knew of, the hundreds of feet of glass shelving actually a part of the catalog talis itself.

Raelen sighed, beginning a mental list of which nobles to test first. He ground his teeth. He'd been so certain Loeadon was the Allosian. All signs pointed to it: the man's sudden rise to power, his secretive behavior, his conspiracy to take the sword talis from his father. How could Raelen have been so wrong, and who then really was the traitor?

Another idea struck him: what if the Allosian wasn't masquerading as a nobleman? What if he was passing himself off as a servant? But that didn't make any sense. While pretending to be a servant would be advantageous for spying, the Allosian would need authority to shape the decisions of the king and others. He'd have to be someone important enough to be included in councils, but not a person people knew well, else they become suspicious. He supposed that's why the Allosian hadn't replaced his father in person. Looking like someone was completely different from speaking and acting like them. Raelen would've known if his father had been replaced, and the Allosian would need to be free to come and go at will. Again, that had fit Loeadon so perfectly.

"My prince!" Traggert called and Raelen didn't like the note of alarm in the man's voice. Something was wrong.

He scanned the crystalline shelves and found the general jogging out of an aisle near the far wall. He was joined by two members of the honor guard emerging from neighboring aisles. Raelen didn't wait for the man to reach him, but strode forward to meet him.

"What's wrong?" Raelen snapped.

"It's gone, your highness."

"What?"

"The oath collar. The catalog said it was removed, and so we ran to check. Sure enough, it is gone."

"But how? The vault key was still in my father's drawer and nothing was disturbed." Raelen shot a glance at the catalog talis and sprinted toward the crystal orb hovering over the plinth. It touched his mind before he even came to a stop.

How may I assist you? It asked telepathically.

"Tell me who last inquired of the location of the oath collar!" he said, not bothering to respond mentally.

Sorias Traggert.

"No!" Raelen shouted. "Before him."

Jenoc of Allose.

There was another who fit all of Raelen's criteria for the imposter. Another man no one knew well, and who had enough clout to be included in important councils. A man so loyal that he'd had Raelen's complete trust. A man who'd fueled Raelen's suspicions of Loeadon. A man Raelen had ordered to steal his father's vault key so they could retrieve the oath collar–someone who couldn't risk being unveiled by that talis.

"Divine Mother," Raelen exhaled. "It's Pariel!"

JENOC HEFTED THE MEDIUM SIZED, black-lacquered wood box onto a shelf in the cargo hold of the Ivory Eagle, next to a parcel that contained the oath collar. He couldn't very well leave such an important artifact behind, it being one of the original pieces of Allosian talis craft. Not like this plague box. It was an ugly thing, made of all the wrong materials and utilitarian in its design.

Not like the talises his people were famed for producing. They had been as much works of art as they had been talis-craft. But the plague box would serve its purpose. Perhaps if he'd had more opportunity and time he might have been able to at least engrave a stylish design on the box, but he'd only been able to work on the talis by sneaking into Loeadon's laboratory. Sometimes that gave him hours, other times it gave him minutes. He had to be very careful, for if someone caught Navarch Pariel working spell-castings, he would be exposed.

Skulking about the human sorcerer's chamber had delivered Jenoc another remarkable boon of good fortune, the opportunity to overhear Loeadon plotting against the king. That had been perfect as the prince was already suspicious of the man, and Loeadon's secretive behavior naturally perpetuated those suspicions. Jenoc hadn't needed to do much to focus the prince on Loeadon. Fate had done it for him. If Apeiron did have a will and guided them, as Kairah claimed, did this not mean that it was aiding Jenoc? Was this not another sign his cause was just?

Even with all of his setbacks; the arrival of his sister and the delivering of her warning, the human girl with the compulsion ring unmasking him, and finally the prince's plan to use the oath collar to detect him, his goals were about to be realized. Now all he needed to do was give the humans one final nudge, and the talis war would begin.

He smiled at the plague box. Although ugly, its function was something of an achievement for Jenoc. He'd never crafted one before but was still able to improve upon the design he found in the instructional tome. Most plague boxes could only cause disease in a small radius, perhaps up to a mile. Jenoc's would emit the sickness for ten. He'd also been able to craft in a particularly vicious clause that would make the box afflict only children under five years of age. The disease would be painful too. A high fever followed by sharp stomach cramps, uncontrollable dysentery, bleeding from major orifices–all concluding with slow and painful suffocation.

Nothing enraged a creature like watching its offspring suffer and die by the deliberate actions of another. And the humans of Haeshala would know who took away their little ones. That had been why Jenoc painted two swords crossed over an Apeira well on the box's face–the symbol of the king's house, and the crest of Aiestal. The humans of Haeshala would know where the box came from, and they would be so drunk with grief and fury they'd commit their entire force to avenging their children. How convenient that an Aiestali army was already marching toward their country.

Pain exploded in Jenoc's head, and he stumbled, very nearly falling to the deck of the airship. He froze, keeping himself upright by leaning on the wall as he clenched his eyes shut and sucked in deep, ragged breaths. His headache was a continual thing now, rising and falling in intensity. He pressed two fingers against his temple until the blinding lights in his vision faded and the sharp agony was replaced by a lesser, though constant pain.

If his only affliction was the headache, Jenoc wouldn't be concerned. But there was another symptom that worsened in tandem with his ever-increasing migraines; a weakening of his ability to hold Apeiron and spell-cast. That had caused him to nearly drop his illusory disguise on several occasions, and severely limit his access to the Four Disciplines.

Weeks ago, he'd been able to hold over a dozen separate spells simultaneously across multiple Disciplines. Now it was all he could do to maintain his disguise, and a few sensory enhancements. He hadn't even been able to translocate the plague box up to the airship. He'd had to carry it to the top of the east turret himself. Jenoc had only been able to teleport in and out of the talis vault by dropping his likeness of Navarch Pariel, something that was, unfortunately, witnessed by a palace maid. Soon they would find her badly beaten body. He had to hurry.

Jenoc winced as he attempted to move. Something was wrong with him; there was no denying that now. And he could no longer explain away the fact it had started after he had experimented with the other magic. Well, he would have plenty of time to worry about that when he returned to Allose. He'd have to rely on the human's love for conflict to draw in the third nation of Shaelar–Maes Tol. It would happen, he was certain of it, though he might've been able to bring it about sooner had he the strength to go there himself, but he'd just have to be patient.

Jenoc inhaled deeply, letting go of the wall now that the throbbing in his head had decreased again to a manageable level. There was but one more thing for him to do before flying out of Aiestal. He had to rescue Kairah.

Chapter 59

Tyrus swept down the hallway, shooting glances over his shoulder, around any alcove, or into connecting halls. He couldn't be seen doing this, but he hadn't been able to stop himself from keeping vigil in one of the palace towers, deliberately overlooking the courtyard's south exit. That was where Hort was supposed to have snuck Jekaran out over an hour ago.

Clearly something had gone wrong, but Tyrus wasn't content to wait for news from the guards or goddess forbid, the king. He needed to know now! Perhaps there would even still be time to salvage his plan. He was a fool for worrying about being spotted on his way to the dungeons. If Hort were arrested, he was certain the mercenary man wouldn't hesitate to implicate him as designing the jailbreak. It was likely over for Tyrus and his house. Oddly, those dark fears were overshadowed by his worry for Jekaran's safety.

The Rasheeran monks taught that if a person was virtuous enough, they could win a chance to rescue a soul from eternal damnation. Kybon had been a womanizer, and Tyrus had always strived to be orthodox in his obedience to the will of the Divine Mother. So, he had always planned on using the boon promised the faithful to get Kybon out of where he certainly had ended up. Tyrus had always been the one to get Kybon out of trouble, and now he was doing the same for his cousin's son.

If I get caught and executed, then I'm leaving your soul in hell, cousin!

He hurried down the slanting path–the palace had no stairs–and eventually descended to the floor upon which the king had built his dungeon. Tyrus froze when he entered the hall feeding into the dungeon proper. There, sprawled out on the floor, was Hort. He quickly scanned the hallway but found no sign of Jekaran or guards. What had happened?

He ran over to Hort and strained as he lifted the mercenary from the floor, and set him against the wall in a sitting position. The man moaned softly as he cracked open an eyelid. "Lord Gymal?"

Hort put a hand to the side of his head and groaned.

"Mercenary!" Tyrus shook the big man. "What happened?"

"He attacked me! Put me out with that stunning talis of yours." Hort looked down at his pants. "Ah, hell. I pissed myself!"

Tyrus shook the man again. "Where is Jekaran?"

Hort started to shake his head, but stopped sharply with a grimace. "That damned thing leaves a headache worse than a night of soaking up over-proofed Haeshalan whisky!"

"Jekaran!" Tyrus shouted.

Hort winced at the sound but didn't complain. "He started putting up a fuss about rescuing that Allosian woman, and so like you said to do, I stunned him. He went down and was out, so I slung him over my shoulder. Next thing I know, he's awake and attacking me. He got the stun baton away from me and rammed it into my neck."

"He's going after her." Tyrus stood and began searching for his stun talis. It lay on the floor against the opposite wall. He strode over and scooped it up, then looked at Hort, who was slowly rising. "Come on!"

"What?" Hort said as he squinted and massaged both of his temples.

"Your job's not finished!"

"He's out of control. I think that sword talis is controlling him again."

That made Tyrus nauseous. "Well, we have to try!"

"Try what?" Hort was standing up straight now.

"To get him away from this place," Tyrus said. He turned and began striding up the inclining corridor, but stopped as Hort grabbed his arm.

"If he's under that damned sword's spell, he won't hesitate to kill us if we try to grab him. I know, I've fought him, and if it weren't for his little girlfriend, the buzzards would be feasting on my eyeballs right now. And what makes you think that he hasn't already been discovered by a guard? Going after the boy could mean a death sentence for both of us."

Tyrus jerked his arm out of Hort's grip. "I have to save him!"

"Why?" Hort shot back.

"Because he's my kin!" Tyrus shouted. "Now are you going to obey me or are you breaking our contract?"

Hort sighed. "I'll help you get him out. Damn me for a fool, but I'll do it." The big man flashed a smile. "I like him, and I'd hate to see him cut down before he has a chance...to become a man."

Tyrus noticed a catch in Hort's voice when he spoke those last words. Odd that. He acknowledged the mercenary's compliance with a curt nod, and the two began jogging up the inclining hallway toward the upper levels of the palace.

JEKARAN SLICED through the chest plate of the guard trying to spear him. He'd intentionally restrained the force of his swing so that his blade only cut through the armor, and perhaps a little into the man's skin. Holding back to avoid lethal force nearly cost him a bolt to the head, but the sword's magic quickened his reflexes and he leaned back just in time to see the fletched metal shaft pass in front of his eyes.

This isn't working, the sword grumbled.

"Sure it is!" he replied.

We are slower this way.

Another bolt flew at Jekaran and he batted it out of the air with a clang! It had come within a foot of his neck. The sword was right. His reactions weren't as fast, or his senses as sharp as they were while he was the one in control.

More soldiers flooded into the hall, mixing in with the guards Jekaran had been fighting. That likely brought the count of foes close to a hundred. His energy, strength, and skill were all amazing–he'd felled over a dozen soldiers already, all while dodging crossbow bolts, and spear thrusts. But sheer numbers were bound to overwhelm him if he didn't do something to access more of the sword's power.

He parried a sword swing, kicked the attacking man in his chest, knocking him backward into the mass of approaching soldiers. The force of Jekaran's kick had been such that the man took half a dozen of his fellows down with him as he crashed to the floor.

Give me control of our bond!

"Not gonna happen!" Jekaran said aloud.

He ducked a sword swing from a soldier behind him before coming up and slamming the pommel of the sword against the back of the man's helmet. It dented in and the man fell forward, stumbling to all fours in an insensible stupor.

What if we attempted a fusing?

"A what?" Jekaran kicked the man in his ribs and he collapsed to the floor.

A fusing. It is when we merge our consciousness' together so that we in essence become one being.

"So why haven't you suggested this before?" Jekaran whirled and simultaneously parried the swords of two attackers.

Our bond wasn't strong enough–it still might not be. And it is dangerous.

"Since when has that stopped you before?" Jekaran scoffed.

He felt the sword's exasperation, but it didn't comment on the jibe. We could become fused together permanently.

There was a fate worse than death. "But I would be able to use my body?"

We would both be one, so yes. But we could both cease to exist as we are now if something goes wrong.

That made Jekaran feel sick and he was about to reject the idea when a sharp sting drilled into his side. He gasped and looked down to see the fletching of an arrow protruding from his ribs. It hadn't gone deep, but Divine Mother did it hurt!

"Okay," Jekaran puffed out as he leaped out of the way of two more shots. "Do it!"

The world blurred–sound, sight, touch, smell, all of his senses immediately changing. Some heightened, some muted. His thoughts changed too, his mind expanding in a dozen different directions while contracting in others. It was like falling asleep, but instead of blackness, Jekaran's vision became tinged with green, as though he were looking through an emerald—only clearer. Each of his thoughts echoed with the sound of two voices, first far apart and discordant, then sounding closer together until there was only one voice, and Jekaran's mind was swallowed up in an ocean of greater consciousness.

⟢⟡⟣

KAIRAH AWOKE.

She sat up in the bed, glancing about. All was dark, and so she spell-cast a globe of light that floated to the ceiling and illuminated the entire chamber. It was lavish by human standards; paintings, tapestries, and shelves filled with books adorned the walls. The floor was covered in embroidered carpets and there was something familiar about the rooms smooth ivory walls, and domed ceiling.

"I am in Taris." Aiested, the humans called it now.

She looked at herself, surprised to find that she was clad only in a white silken shift.

Kairah! Aeva called, and the Spirit Lily's voice sounded on the edge of panic.

This close to an Aeose as powerful as the one in Taris–Aiested–distance wouldn't hinder Kairah's use of the Fourth Discipline. She could hear Aeva's thoughts clearly and would be able to respond with next to no effort. I am well, she sent back.

I was very worried, Aeva said, and Kairah could feel the Spirit Lily's relief.

Kairah swung her legs over the side of the bed, placed her feet on the cool carpet, and stood. Her shift fell to just above her knees as she took a step toward a shelf with a mirror mounted above a water basin. She dipped her hands into the cold water, and then sprinkled some on her face.

You've seen something, haven't you.

Kairah froze as the vision of the dead land, the innumerable bones, and the green lightning returned to her in a torrent. And that's when she felt it—the abomination from her vision. Vessel Moriora had called it. She nearly retched as she perceived its location. It was drawing closer. She had to do something!

The doors to her room swung inward startling her. Kairah looked up from the water basin and turned to see a man standing in the doorway. He was tall with a shorn head, and was dressed in armor over which he wore a white tabard. A human military man? Had they been watching for when she awoke?

"I must see your king," Kairah said as she strode toward him.

The man smirked, and that's when Kairah saw the faint purple glow surrounding him—an Apeiron aura.

"Hello sister," he said as he stepped in and closed the doors behind him. "I am glad to see you fully recovered."

"Jenoc!"

He frowned at seeing her state of undress. "The humans did not dare touch you, did they?"

Kairah shook her head. "Not like that."

"I did what I could to keep you safe, but I was not able to watch over you at all times." He moved to a cherry wood wardrobe closet set against the wall. "Time is short, and we must leave here." He threw open the doors and began to carefully examine the clothing within.

Kairah walked toward him. "What have you done?"

Jenoc withdrew a gown of deep blue from the closet, inspected it, and then turned and proffered it to Kairah. "What I came to do."

The talis war. "You have succeeded, then?"

"For the most part." Jenoc made her take the dress, and then turned around so his back was facing her. "And right now the palace is a mass of fighting and confusion, the perfect time for us to slip away."

"What is happening?"

"Your champion is loose."

"Jekaran?"

"Yes," Jenoc said. "He is wreaking havoc with that sword talis of his. Did you give that to him? I know you stole the illusion pendant, but I did not think you had taken anything else."

Kairah gripped the dress in one hand and let most of it fall to the floor. "Jenoc, you must stop this. Undo whatever it is that you have done!"

"I will not," Jenoc snapped. "I cannot," he added less harshly.

Kairah walked toward him, his back still facing her. "Please. You do not know what is at stake."

Jenoc sighed. "I tire of arguing this point. We need to return to Allose."

"No, you do not understand," Kairah lightly touched his arm. "There is something coming. Something terrible. Can you not sense it?"

Jenoc raised a hand to his right temple. "No," he said. "Something is wrong. I struggle with spell-casting, and I have blinding migraines. It has progressed to the point that it is taking all of my strength just to maintain this disguise." He turned around to look at Kairah, and she caught the pain in his eyes. "And it is more than just my abilities."

He looked away. "Inflicting harm and authoring destruction excites me. At first, I thought it just the satisfaction of revenge, but it is more than that. I crave seeing and causing death."

Those last words struck Kairah, and she made the connection. "You attempted to channel the other magic, did you not?"

He sighed. "Harnessing it and using it to destroy the humans was my original plan, yes. The records do not contain much about it, but after years of searching, I pieced together the ritual for calling it." He looked to the side and his eyes grew distant. "I failed in my attempt to wield it, and now I fear that it has scarred me."

"I need to know exactly how you did this thing," Kairah said.

Jenoc's eyes refocused and he looked at her. "I do not recommend you try it. It was an excruciatingly painful experience that nearly destroyed me."

That made Kairah think of the suffocating power that forced its way into her blood, trying to devour her Apeiron store. Her mind focused on the dark thing that even now was steadily approaching and she was forced to choke down bile.

"A monstrosity approaches, and we need to stop it! I believe it may be a byproduct of your efforts to use Moriora.

"What?"

"The other magic."

"How would such a thing be possible?" Jenoc said.

"I do not know," Kairah replied. "That is why I need you to explain to me what you did to call it."

Kairah started as the chamber doors banged open.

RAELEN SAW Navarch Pariel standing with the Allosian woman, and his stomach soured. He'd been hoping he was wrong about the man as he had been wrong about Loeadon. But the scene before him was proof enough.

"Jenoc of Allose," Raelen called. "You are under arrest for crimes against the crown. Reveal yourself now, and surrender!"

Pariel smirked. "Puzzled it out after all, eh my prince?" And then Pariel was gone, replaced by a man equal in height, but with long ice-blue hair, eyes the color of an Apeiron well, and features Saranna would've marked as gorgeous. His armor and tabard did not vanish, but Raelen did notice a ring on the man's finger that hadn't been there before.

"Where is Navarch Pariel?" Raelen demanded.

"Who can say?" Jenoc raised his eyebrows in mock innocence. "He could be anywhere now. Likely in more than one place."

Raelen seethed. "You murdered him, then?"

Jenoc's smirk returned. "Murdered implies equality. It would be like you saying the cooks murdered the swine you had for dinner. No, I slaughtered him like the animal he was, and left him in the north forest for the other animals to devour." The Allosian's smile disappeared, and his amethyst eyes hardened. "You are all animals!"

"Jenoc, no!" The Allosian woman screamed.

A shockwave exploded from Jenoc, flinging Raelen and his guards back into the hall. Raelen flew so far that he crashed into the wall opposite the chamber's entrance. Bursts of light exploded across his vision, and the next thing he knew, Gryyth was lifting him from the floor.

He quickly stood, vision still blurred as he watched the Allosian man tow his sister down the corridor. "Come on!" It came out part groan and part growl. He tapped his transference band, hands becoming bear-like and his strength increasing tenfold.

Raelen leapt into a run, Gryyth soon at his side. They left the other guards behind, most of whom hadn't fully recovered from the blast—none would be able to keep pace with him anyway. It was just him and Gryyth against the man who had deceived him; an Allosian who could spell-cast beyond anything Loeadon had managed. This was reckless, dangerous, and his father would add un-princely, but Raelen wasn't about to let the bastard escape.

CHAPTER 60

Maely leaned her head against the window's cool glass as she stared down from the spire. The light talises of milling servants and guards in the courtyard below looked like distant stars for how high up she was. A hundred feet? Maybe more? Maely had ascended the towering white turret after running away from Jekaran. She'd heard soldiers rushing to apprehend him, and was worried, but he could handle himself in a fight. Well, as long as he had his magic sword. Besides, it didn't matter anymore. Nothing did.

She stepped back and pushed open the window, a gust of early morning wind ruffling her hair and making her wince. The window was taller than she was, starting at the base of the stone floor and reaching a dozen feet up to the arched top. The single pane of thick glass and smooth hinges were no doubt another tribute to Allosian architecture as she'd never seen a window designed quite like this one. She sobbed a laugh. Since when had she become an expert on such things? She'd only seen three big cities, this being the third.

She scrubbed her eyes on the back of her sleeve. Was she really thinking of jumping? Or was this just more dramatic self-pity? "Why not?" she whispered to herself. What had she left to live for? Mulladin? Ezra could take care of him if he was even still alive. The people of Genra had never treated her well, and so there wasn't a point in returning there. All she'd had for years was Jekaran and her plans for them to be together, and now she didn't even have that.

No. I have this. Maely unclenched her fist and studied her mother's ring, held atop her palm. Her mother must've not known how the talis worked, or perhaps she'd never even realized it was a talis. The amethyst shard was small enough to make the ring look ordinary. Even so, her mother had made the association. When she wore her ring, she could get wealthier, more respectable men.

Maely snorted. "Respectable men?" How could that even apply? Was there even such a thing as a respectable man? She'd thought she'd found one in Jekaran, but he was driven by sex as much as any of her mother's clients. That was the reason he'd chosen Kairah over Maely wasn't it? Because of the woman's impossibly perfect physical appeal.

Well, at least with the ring Maely wouldn't have to resort to her mother's profession in order to survive. She could take whatever she wanted from whomever she wanted. That made her sick to her stomach, and she again clenched the ring tightly in her fist, in part so she didn't have to look at it.

After seeing the dead, puppet-like look in Jekaran's eyes, she was beginning to understand why Kairah had been so disgusted by it. Imagine if men like the ones who paid her mother had such a talis? They wouldn't need to pay for sex, they could just make any woman that caught their eye submit to them.

Hell, she was a woman and she'd used the ring to compel that waitress to strip in front of a room full of lecherous men! How much better was she than the kind of men she despised? She'd even forced Jekaran to love her, and to kiss her! Was that any different? She was no better than a rapist. She idly wondered if the spell had worn off of him by now, and cringed at what he must think of her for casting it on him.

He'll hate me.

Even thee very possibility weighed heavy on Maely's heart, and she started to breathe rapidly as though she were unable to get enough air. She'd thought that Jekaran not loving her was beyond terrible, but the idea of him hating her suffocated Maely. She quickly removed her slippers and placed a bare foot up onto the window's six-inch sill. She braced her hands against the wall on either side of the window and stepped up so that both feet rested on the ledge and all ten of her toes hung over empty air.

She looked down from the dizzying height. Was she really going to do this?

No, she wasn't.

Maely stepped backward, stumbling and falling onto her side. Her mother's ring flew out of her hand and rang as it hit and then rolled across the marble floor. She watched it spin and then come to rest ten paces away from her. She didn't get up, didn't move to recover it. Instead, she lay her head on the floor and sobbed.

How long she stayed like that, she wasn't sure. It felt like hours, but it could've only been a few minutes. Finally, she stood, walked over to where her mother's ring had come to rest and scooped it up. Maely wasn't sure what she was going to do now, or where she would go, but she knew she'd need the ring to, at the very least, defend herself.

Distant shouting made her start, and she reflexively slipped the ring onto her finger. The shouting grew louder and so she backed into a corner, hiding herself as best she could in the shadows. A flash of light came from the ramp that led up into the tower, followed by the sound of breaking stone. What was...?

A man with ice-blue hair and pale skin towed a woman into the room. She was dressed only in a white shift and had long amethyst colored hair. "Kairah," Maely whispered.

Kairah was resisting Jenoc, but the Allosian man didn't even seem to notice. He was fixated on the ramp below at which he flung two balls of crackling red fire.

"Watch out!" a voice shouted from below.

"Jenoc, please listen!" Kairah begged.

Jenoc glanced at a ramp leading to the roof of the tower and released one more ball of fire before pulling Kairah up and toward the roof. There was a woosh as a column of fire licked up into the room, and a wave of heat washed over Maely.

She looked up at the ramp leading to the roof. Jenoc had Kairah. Jenoc was exposed. Someone was chasing him. What would he do to Kairah? Maely knew the man was her brother, but he wasn't like other Allosians–he'd gone mad. Would he harm Kairah? Would he kill her? Maely touched her ring. She could stop him. She could save Kairah.

Why? What do I owe her? She took Jekaran away from me!

Of course, had Jekaran ever really been hers?

I hate her!

But she had done nothing to Maely personally. In fact, she'd been trying to save Maely's people who'd hunted Kairah's race almost to extinction.

Jek cares for her.

If Maely really did love Jekaran, would that love be contingent on whether he loved her back?

I do love him.

And if what she felt truly was love, wouldn't she want Jekaran to be happy, even if it meant saving Kairah for him?

Maely broke into a run, her bare feet giving her extra traction as she raced up the inclining ramp. She threw open the hatch set in the ceiling at the top and froze. Jenoc might be waiting with another fireball for someone to climb onto the roof. I'm an idiot! She made to duck back down, but nothing happened. No fireball. She cautiously peeked over the lip of the hatch and saw a flat circular roof, the white stone cast purple under the light of Aiested's looming Apeira Well.

"Golden womb of the Goddess!" Maely swore as her eyes fell on something at the center of the roof.

It was a large white thing that vaguely resembled a boat. But instead of a flat deck on top of a rounded bottom, it had something on top of it, enclosing the deck. It looked like a smooth ivory shell. The strange thing also had what looked like fins of a fish on the sides, and one on the top near its rear. Amethyst gems lined the underside of the craft, and a plank of wood led up to an open door on the side, just next to one of its fins.- Jenoc was dragging Kairah toward the craft, and she was resisting him, making their progress painstakingly slow.

Wind blasted Maely as she climbed onto the roof. "Jenoc stop!" She shouted, wrapping her words in a wave of compulsion.

Jenoc halted so abruptly he stumbled. Both of the Allosians looked back at Maely, and Kairah gave her a grateful nod as she broke free of her brother's grip. She drew back, facing Jenoc as her long purple hair whipped furiously in the wind, one strap of her shift falling down her shoulder.

"It is over, Jenoc." Kairah said.

Maely walked to stand at Kairah's side.

Jenoc glowered at her with so much intensity Maely took a step backward. Then he closed his eyes and his face took on a serene expression.

"Maely, get back!" Kairah shouted, but it was too late.

Jenoc broke free of her compulsion and lunged forward. He grabbed Maely before she had a chance to issue another command, drew her in, and clamped a hand around her throat. Kairah tried to pull Jenoc's hand away, but he shoved her so hard she fell to the ground. Then he met Maely's eyes, and his mouth twisted into a smirk as he squeezed. She panicked, hands gripping Jenoc's arm, nails digging into his white flesh, but he just kept squeezing. She couldn't breathe. Everything around her was darkening, and the roaring of the gale muted.

Then the pressure was gone and Maely found herself on her knees coughing violently. She looked up and saw Jenoc fallen to one knee a dozen feet away, a muscled man naked from the waist standing between her and Kairah's brother. The man's biceps were bulging and his forearms were completely covered in white fur. Another figure moved past her and stopped at the side of the man. Maely recognized the creature. It was the prince's bear-man bodyguard. Which makes that man Prince Raelen!

Raelen tensed as he met Jenoc's hard, hateful eyes. "Surrender now, Jenoc of Allose!"

A thunderclap made Raelen wince, and his eyes flicked to the sky. Roiling black clouds appeared, swirling unnaturally as they spread, blocking out the first rays of the dawning sun. He met Jenoc's eyes again, and the man smirked and slowly began to rise.

"I'm warning you!" Raelen called over the whipping wind. "I will kill you if I must."

That made Jenoc smile in full and a sudden dread dampened Raelen's confidence. He had started to believe fighting the Allosian spellcaster was little different than when they'd battle Loeadon. He had a feeling he was about to learn just how wrong he'd been.

The wind picked up as the dark clouds descended closer. The light of a new morning was gone now, their only illumination the purple glow emanating from Aiested's well.

"Jenoc, stop!" The Allosian woman's scream was nearly drowned out by the roaring wind. And then shafts of lightning fell.

The light was blinding and the thunder deafening, but Raelen's enhanced reflexes let him leap out of the way as a sharp bolt struck the ground where he'd been standing, leaving a blackened scar on the cracked stone. The force of the next one threw Raelen to the ground and he rolled just as a third hot, white shaft struck for him. He was deaf now, and his vision blurred by bright green after images.

Disoriented, he tried to stand, fully expecting to be struck down by the wrath of the storm. He looked up, wincing through the dust screen gale and was able to make out two shapes battling. Gryyth had managed to reach Jenoc, and was swiping sharp claws at him. Jenoc's agility was both impressive and surprising, he ducking the swings of the Ursaj warrior with seeming prescience. Finally, Gryyth succeeded in seizing upon Jenoc and lifting him up in a bone-crunching hug.

Incredibly, Jenoc burst into flames and Gryyth immediately dropped him, howling silently as he fell backward, arms and chest fur charred and smoking. Raelen lunged forward, his deafness making the entire scene surreal. He'd closed to within a meter of Jenoc's fiery form when he slammed into something solid. It dazed him for a moment, and when he finally regained his wits, he found himself trapped inside a faintly translucent bubble. He battered at the barrier, growing lightheaded as the air thinned.

Jenoc, no longer wreathed in flames, stared at him from just outside the barrier. The smile was gone, replaced by a frightening mask of cold rage. He turned away from Raelen and approached Gryyth, who was only now struggling to stand. Raelen's pounding lost its power, and he began to choke as the oxygen ran out.

Jenoc kicked Gryyth in the chest where the Ursaj had been burned the worst, and Raelen's protector opened his maw in a silent bellow of pain before falling back to his knees. The bear-man collapsed on the ground, smoke rising from his fur. Raelen couldn't even choke now, suffocation having paralyzed his lungs. His thoughts became disjointed, and blackness closed in from his periphery.

Then air flooded back into Raelen's lungs, and he gasped, sucking at it desperately. His hearing had also returned, and the translucent sphere around him shattered with the sound of glass before disappearing altogether. Immediately the wind died down, the black clouds swirling above dissipated, and the gentle light of a new dawn lit the white stone of the tower. Raelen coughed and choked, rolling onto his side as he regained his breath.

⋯⟶⦙⟵⋯

MAELY TOUCHED HER RIGHT EAR. She'd been deafened by the thunder but could suddenly hear again. Had Kairah healed her?

"No more, Jenoc!" Kairah shouted as she strode toward her brother, and although dressed only in a short shift, she had the poise and presence of a queen.

Jenoc looked shocked, and then his brow drew down and his amethyst eyes hardened. "Are you going to fight me, Sister?"

"If I must," she said.

"You would side with these humans?" he spat. "Even after what they did to our family?"

Kairah stopped a short distance in front of Jenoc. "It was not these humans, Jenoc."

"That does not matter!" he shouted back. "They are all the same! Parasites that leech off the land and everything in it. They destroyed our civilization and stole our treasures! They must be removed!" Then the Allosian man faltered, head bowing and both of his hands flying up to grip each side of his head.

"You are sick, Jenoc," Kairah said in a softer tone. "Moriora has injured you."

"No," Jenoc snarled, his eyes still shut tight against whatever was tearing at him.

Maely inched closer, thumbing her ring and preparing to call out another command in order to give Kairah a chance to strike. Sure, she has no problem with compulsion when it helps her! Would the woman attack her brother? The Allosian woman had waited so long to intervene. Was that because she didn't want to hurt him? Or was it because she was afraid of him? No, she couldn't count on Kairah. She would need to take care of Jenoc herself.

The pain afflicting Jenoc appeared to subside, and he let go of his head and straightened. His breathing was labored, but smoothing with each breath. "It is time for you to choose whose side you are on, Kairah."

Kairah shook her head. "Jenoc, please listen. Something is here, an aberration that we need to–

"Choose!"

Jenoc's enraged scream made Maely flinch. She looked at Kairah's face and found the woman looking as shocked at the outburst as Maely was. Time to act!

Summoning all of her courage, anger, and whatever other strong emotion brewed within her, Maely opened her mouth to command Jenoc to leap off the roof, but her voice caught in her throat as Jenoc's eyes flicked to her. Before Maely knew it, a hurricane strength blast of wind crashed into her, lifting her up and hurling her back.

"Maely!" The wind made Kairah's scream sound unusually distant as Maely arced over the low wall and into empty space.

As she came down, she grabbed the first thing she could; a small, decorative outcropping made of smooth white stone. The hard landing shocked her arms and it was only by wild primal fear that she held on. Yet her hold was tenuous, and she kicked wildly over open air as she strained to pull herself up. She looked down to see a long stretch of stone passing vertically through a wisp of lazily floating clouds. How had she ever thought this tower was only a hundred feet tall? From this vantage during the day, it was clearly much, much taller, more like a thousand feet.

Her heart pounded and she couldn't breathe as her fingers slipped. She looked up, just as the prince appeared over the stone wall and reached down with a bear-like claw to grab one of her wrists. The timing was divine, for the prince's grip took hold at the same moment Maely completely lost hers.

"It's okay, girl. I have you."

He hauled her up and over the edge, holding her in an embrace as she trembled involuntarily.

⚘

Kairah clenched her jaw as tears threatened. She hadn't been fast enough to counter Jenoc's spell and save Maely. That would pain Jekaran. Why did the idea of Jekaran suffering hurt her as well? She unleashed two spells simultaneously, a flare spell to distract Jenoc, and a paralysis net to trap him; both failed.

Jenoc laughed at her. "You are so very predictable, Sister."

Kairah lashed out with a whip of air, but Jenoc easily deflected it. Even in his weakened state, her brother was still the better spell-caster. She transmuted the stone beneath his feet into a sticky sludge, but Jenoc solidified it before he could sink. She tried to trap him inside a force shell, but he shattered it. Finally, she launched twin streams of blue fire at him. Kairah hadn't wanted to wound her brother, but she knew she had to stop him–she could heal him afterwards.

Jenoc frowned and made to block the spell with a shield of air, but spasmed as another migraine caused him to falter. The half-cast wind spell knocked aside both fire blasts, but not enough and one scorched the right side of Jenoc's handsome face. He cried out and fell to the ground. His hand reflexively went to the burn on his face causing him to scream a second time.

Kairah ran to him, preparing to cast a sleep spell to fully incapacitate her brother. She leaned over Jenoc, and placed a hand on his back both for comfort and to maximize the effect of her spell. Immediately she was hurled back by a shockwave, crashing down on the flat white stone so hard that it forced the air from her lungs. Jenoc stood, face blackened and charred around his right eye, which had been burned completely out of its socket.

He stalked over to Kairah, grabbed a fistful of her long amethyst hair, and hauled her to her feet. She tried to tell him she would heal him, but all she could do was suck air. Jenoc drew her in so that she had a good look at the horrible burn that marred his perfect white face.

"You have made your choice!" Jenoc snarled through clenched teeth. Then he let go and shoved her back to the roof.

Kairah lay on the stone watching him ascend the plank and enter the wind rider. "Brother," she finally coughed out.

He stopped just inside the craft's hatch, keeping his back to her, but turning his head to call over his shoulder. "I am not your brother, and you are not my sister. You are as dead to me as father and mother." Then he disappeared inside the ship, and the hatch closed.

For some reason those words hurt Kairah more than his attack on her. Her tears leaked onto the white stone roof as she watched the wind rider rise into the sky and then shoot away like an arrow.

"Jenoc," she sobbed. *He is right.* That was not the gentle, deep-thinking, kind boy who'd obsessively watched over and protected her. Whether changed by Moriora or his own poisonous hatred, Kairah couldn't say, but one thing was certain; he was no longer her brother. That realization dumped upon her shoulders such an enormous weight of grief that it threatened to crush her.

Courage, a voice said. *The Vessel comes.* Was that Aeva or Kairah's mother?

Kairah stood, determination pushing back her sorrow. Of course, it wasn't gone, just shoved aside until the time when she could appropriately grieve. She strode for the square hatch that led back down into the palace. As she descended from the roof, she saw a visibly trembling Maely cradled protectively in the arms of Prince Raelen. They were sitting on the roof against the battlements, both staring at her.

Kairah was relieved that Maely had survived, but she didn't say anything to the girl or the prince. Instead she left the roof and strode quickly down the tower's ramp. Only she knew the Vessel had come, and only she was able to stop it.

Chapter 61

Jekaran was himself, but not himself. He was free to use his body, but not exclusively. Something else guided his physical form, responding instantaneously to his will in a process faster than even the speed of thought. The sword was with him, but it also was him and he was it. They were one; achieving such a supreme state of martial grace and awesome destructive power that no one could stand before him.

They were invincible.

The being Jekaran had become sheered through two swords at once before whirling in between their stunned bearers. He cracked the skull of one with the pommel of the sword, grabbed the other from behind and impaled him through the back, and then turned the man about to use him as a human shield to catch three bolts at once. Blood flowed like a crimson stream, puddles of it pooling and connecting all over the marble floor of the hallway.

The part of him that was Jekaran hated killing these men, but the fact they were trying to kill him eased his conscience. Also, they stood between him and rescuing Kairah. He could feel the Allosian woman through his new senses, divine her location in the palace, and most important, discern that she was in danger.

A mountain of a man dressed in full plate armor charged him, raising a mace the size of a caber. Fused, Jekaran exploded into a full sprint directly toward the knight. The charging mass of metal brought his mace down just as the two collided.

The man audibly gasped when the skull-splitting momentum of his falling mace abruptly halted, the flanged head stopped by the blade of Jekaran's sword. Jekaran–or the sword, he couldn't tell–met the knight's gaze with a wicked grin, threw off the mace, and then swung low, sheering off an armored leg just above the knee. The armored man screamed as he fell sideways. Jekaran charged, passing on the side of the falling knight and spinning as he swept his blade through the man's neck. The knight's helmeted head clanged against the marble floor, followed a beat later by his decapitated corpse.

There were only a handful of soldiers in his way now, and upon seeing what he'd done to their champion, they fled before him. Had the sword been in control, he would've given chase, but fused as they were, Jekaran's respect for life tempered the sword's lust for destruction, and he let them go.

He glanced behind him and wasn't surprised to find dozens of slain guards littering the long corridor. How many had they killed? It didn't matter. All that mattered was reaching Kairah. He broke into a run, turning into a connecting corridor and followed the pulsing light in his mind—a beacon representing Kairah and her location in the palace. She was moving now, descending from the roof quickly.

EzRA'S IDEA of blitzing the palace and rescuing Jekaran in a lightning strike raid had fallen flat on its face. Not because he didn't have the manpower, or the weapons he needed, but because the building was just so damned big! They'd arrived nearly an hour ago, but wasted much of that time trying to orient themselves, which was just a nicer way of saying that they'd gotten lost. Fortunately, they had just found a silver, bell-shaped, wall fixture–a guide talis. It had given them the layout of the palace, and they now headed down toward the dungeons.

He glanced behind him. Fifty Rikujo enforcers dressed in black leather jerkins and bearing a variety of weapon talises trailed him. They were his again. It hadn't taken much convincing for the other Rikujo lords to submit, not after what they saw him do to Trous. Never mind the fact his display of supernatural strength and swordsmanship had been something of a fluke. They saw him fight as though he still held the power of the sword, and that was enough to quell them.

To his right strode Irvis and Graelle–were they still holding hands?–and Mulladin on his left. The former simpleton bore an expression of grim determination, something that looked completely out of place on his face. He wore a ring on his finger, Trous's lightning talis, claimed by Mulladin as it had been the weapon that nearly killed him. Something that led to his mind being healed from whatever it was that retarded his mental development.

Graelle jumped as a wailing sound shattered their stealthy silence. An alarm talis. Could the palace guard know they were here? Had accessing the guide talis given them away? Ezra tensed, waiting for soldiers to assault them at any moment.

None came.

Now that he considered it, they hadn't encountered a single guard since leaving the storage room that held the palace's supposedly 'broken' slipgate. Shouldn't they have at the very least seen one patrol? Then again, the Allosian designed building was so huge it seemed they could wander for days without encountering anyone. Still, something about the lack of security bothered Ezra. "I don't think that alarm's because of us."

Irvis shot him a glance, the chubby monk's eyebrows raising. "Who else could it be for..." Irvis trailed off. "Divine Mother! He's loose."

"What're you going on about?" Graelle demanded.

Ezra looked at the woman. "I think Jekaran might be on a rampage. The sword has the power to take control of its bearer's body if it perceives a threat. It would explain why this place is so empty. All the guards and soldiers are probably trying to contend with him."

"He'll slaughter them," Irvis said.

"For a while," Ezra said. "But there are thousands of troops here. Eventually they will overwhelm him by sheer force of numbers." He broke into a run and the others followed, Irvis breathing hard as he worked to keep up.

They descended to a lower floor by way of a gently declining ramp–

apparently, the palace had no stairs–and ran straight into Lord Gymal. He froze at seeing Ezra and his strike force. The beefy man with the little lord drew his sword and stretched out his free arm in front of Gymal.

Mulladin extended a hand to cast lightning, but Ezra grabbed his wrist. "No," he said to the man. Mulladin shot Ezra a dark look. Something of the boy's grim adult personality worried Ezra, but perhaps that was just because of the contrast with his former child-like self.

"Gymal," Ezra said. "What's happening?"

Gymal eyed Ezra's fifty black clad soldiers before answering. "Your nephew," he drawled. "He's out of control."

"It's as I feared," Ezra said. Then he noticed what Gymal was holding. "Is that a stun baton?"

Gymal half hid the talis behind his back.

"Are you planning to use that to capture Jekaran? Why?"

Gymal didn't answer.

"Let me shock the truth out of him, Ez!" Mulladin asked, an eager smile on his face.

Ezra raised a hand to signal Mulladin to back down. "What's in this for you?" He asked Gymal. This man was an opportunistic sycophant–Ezra's concept of pretty much all nobles–who was likely trying to curry favor with the king by apprehending Jekaran. Either that or he feared it would reflect badly on him if Jek got away.

Gymal's eyes darted from Ezra to Mulladin, to the fifty Rikujo enforcers and back to Ezra again. "I'm trying to help him escape!"

Ezra hadn't expected that. "Why?"

"The king was going to have him executed, in spite of his escorting that Allosian woman here to deliver her warning." Gymal sighed. "I couldn't allow that."

Ezra was speechless.

"Oh don't act so surprised, peasant!" Gymal snapped. "Even nobleman can have consciences."

"Not the ones I know," Irvis added.

Gymal shot the chubby monk a baleful glare.

"Do you know where he is?" Ezra asked.

Gymal looked back at Ezra and then nodded. "Just follow the chaos."

He motioned to a ramp leading down to a lower floor, and Ezra noticed for the first time two lifeless corpses slowly rolling down the ramp.

"How about we follow you," Ezra made sure his tone emphasized that this was not a request.

Gymal didn't refuse. After all, how could he? His one mercenary would be no match for fifty trained soldiers, all with weapon talises. But Ezra suspected fear wasn't what was driving Gymal to cooperate. As baffling as it was, the man seemed earnest in his desire to help Jekaran. It was strange. Ezra wasn't going to reject such a fortuitous happening. Another sign of Rasheera's aid.

Gymal led them down two floors, and then into the corridor that might itself have been a ballroom for how spacious it was. Even in the heat of this crisis, Ezra couldn't help but admire the mystical nature of Allosian architecture. There were no seams, breaks, or other signs of construction anywhere in the smooth ivory walls and marble floors. Trailing designs etched into the stone flowed in an unbroken pattern that stretched as far as he could see down the corridor. This palace or any other Allosian building, was as much a work of art as it was a functional edifice.

A mass of soldiers swarming the intersection of a connecting hallway interrupted Ezra's appreciating Allosian craftsmanship. Their backs were turned to him, all of the soldiers focused on something he couldn't see, but he knew what it was. He broke into a run toward the mass of excited guards.

Something shot up from the midst of the soldiers, a figure twisting gracefully as he arced ten feet in the air and then landed behind the attacking soldiers.

Jekaran.

He whirled, lopping the heads off three soldiers at once before the press of guards even had a chance to turn. The boy was clearly under the influence of the sword as evidenced by his supernatural speed and fighting skill.

"Jekaran!" Ezra shouted.

He didn't appear to hear him, or else he didn't care. Ezra remembered being taken captive by the sword's will, and how it rendered him entirely impotent, powerless to literally lift a finger. He felt that way now.

Soldiers dropped left and right as they dutifully, but foolishly attacked Jekaran. What was driving them so hard? Even royal arms men would retreat when facing a clearly superior foe. As if in answer to his question, Ezra heard one of the soldiers shout the accusation, "King killer!"

Oh no. Ezra's stomach clenched. That complicated things. If Jekaran had indeed killed the king of Aiestal, they were not only going to have to escape Aiested, but the entire kingdom. They'd have to go to Maes Tol or Haeshala. Even then, they would likely be sought after and hunted.

First we have to escape this palace. He drew in a deep breath and strode forward.

"Hey!" Gymal snapped after Ezra tore the stun baton out of his hand.

Ezra didn't even look at the short, balding lord as he slipped the talis into his pocket. Instead, he continued forward, his focus on his nephew. When he was ten paces away, just outside the ring of soldiers who were attacking Jek, he stopped and shouted, "Jekaran!"

No response, just more death. Jekaran slammed the blade of the sword into a man's armored forehead before using the buried sword to leverage a vault over the soldier. The blade tore free in an explosion of blood, brain, and bone as Jekaran landed behind the unfortunate man. Without even pausing for breath, he swung the sword down in front of himself, cleaving a soldier from crown to crotch in an unreal explosion of blood and viscera.

"Jekaran!" Ezra screamed.

Jekaran jerked as if struck on the back of the head. He broke off from attacking the soldiers and turned to look at Ezra. Two more sword-wielding men in armor attacked him, but Jekaran dispatched them easily, without looking away from Ezra. The remaining handful of soldiers fell back, and for a moment, the violence halted.

"Jekaran?" Ezra asked. "Do you recognize me, son?"

Jekaran stared at Ezra, his green eyes curious. He looked as if he were trying to remember something. "Ez," he said flatly.

Ezra smiled, placing a hand in his pocket and gripping the stun baton. "Yes, it's me." He slowly began to walk toward his nephew. "It's time to go, Jekaran."

"Go?"

"Yes," Ezra said as he took a few more steps toward him. "Will you come with me, son? Come home?"

Jekaran shook his head. "Have to save Kairah."

"Now!" one of the soldiers called, and four of them surrounded Jekaran, all preparing to charge as one.

"Wait!" Ezra shouted, pulling the stun baton out of his pocket.

The members of Ezra's Rikujo assault force surged forward, and the hall immediately exploded into a maelstrom of flashing lights and elemental clamor. Forks of lightning nearly blinded Ezra, and the heat of fire talises made him wince.

A boom resounded through the hallway, one that sounded like the noise Graelle's concussion rod made when it discharged. Through it all, he could see Jekaran battling soldiers. He'd felled the four who'd attacked him, but more had charged forward to take their places. But now they had to divide their attention between attacking Jekaran and defending against a horde of Rikujo enforcers throwing lightning and fire.

The large corridor was in a state of pure pandemonium.

With no care for his safety, Ezra pushed through the melee that now surrounded him. One attacker came too close, and he was forced to shock the man with Gymal's stun baton. The soldier dropped, eyes twitching upward and body convulsing. Just a few paces in front of Ezra Jekaran fought, deftly sheering through weapons, armor, and skin. Jekaran's back was facing Ezra, and so he lunged forward, aiming for a spot between the boy's shoulder blades.

In a blur of impossibly fast motion, Jekaran spun around and shoved his sword into Ezra's chest. He gasped, cold steel shocking his broken skin as the tip of the blade push out of his back. His whole body shuddered as he looked down at the sword sprouting from his chest. The tiny emerald shards embedded in the blade exploded to life, casting shifting green light on both him and Jekaran. He looked up, meeting his nephew's green eyes. They bore a detached look in them, the boy's face expressionless.

Then Ezra heard something he hadn't heard since just after Anarilee died. It was like thunder, but not an actual audible noise. It was a psychic shockwave that exploded out from Jekaran, invisible and probably unnoticed to all but he and his nephew.

Jekaran's brows shot up, and his mouth fell open. His eyes softened, and Ezra saw again in Jek's face the familiar countenance of the sweet boy he'd raised. The mental and emotional shock of stabbing his uncle had somehow severed Jek's psychic link to the sword. Not just snapped him out of the battle trance but severed it completely. Ezra smiled and he felt blood trickle from the side of his mouth. This wasn't exactly how he'd intended to save Jekaran from the sword, but if his death would do it, then so be it.

Well, I did tell Rasheera I would pay any price to save Jekaran, even if that price were my life.

Apparently the goddess had taken him at his word and exacted that very cost.

As the light around him faded, Ezra couldn't help but laugh, though it came out more like a ragged, shuddering cough. He had not failed Anarilee after all. He had not failed Jekaran. He had come against all odds across Shaelar to rescue his nephew–his son. He had sought redemption, and he had found it.

Jekaran was free.

JEKARAN'S MIND ripped in half. Sight and sound became a mixture of indecipherable stimuli and he fell backward. Try as he might, he couldn't form ordered thoughts. He didn't even remember his name. The only thing he could focus on was horrifying shock that quickly resolved into a deep, twisting pain in his heart. He let go of that sensation and let himself be swept away in a torrent of slippery ideas and fractured memories.

CHAPTER
62

Screaming! Oh how Jove loved the sound of screaming, particularly when those screams came from women. It stirred dark passions within him and made him hungry. He laughed aloud as he whipped a translucent green tendril at an attacking guard. The tentacle plunged into the man's chest like a ghostly sword, draining away his life. Two more guards attacked Jove from his left flank, and he devoured them without even turning to look in their direction. That display was enough to discourage other attackers, and the palace hall became a frenzied scene of fleeing maids, butlers, guards, and nobles.

He could chase after them, squeeze the nectar of life from each and every soul, but that would amount to little more than a distraction. He wouldn't really enjoy feasting on humans, not when he could have all the Apeiron he could eat. Drool spilled out of the corner of his mouth and rolled down his chin. He could taste the Apeiron radiating from the massive well. He needed that delicious, delectable pristine life. Every moment he was without it was excruciating torture. He needed to...

A woman stood at the top of stairs at the end of the foyer. She was tall with a perfectly proportioned figure. He giggled as he noticed that she was dressed only in a shift, her unusual height making it barely reach past her thighs.

Scandalous.

And what was this? Purple hair? Jove had never seen hair that color before. And no, it wasn't just purple, it was jewel-like. Glittering, like–like an Apeiron well. He barked a laugh, striding forward, forgetting the mob of fleeing people about him and focusing entirely on the most beautiful doll he'd ever seen.

As he reached the bottom of the grand staircase, the woman called down to him. "You will come no further, Vessel of Moriora!"

What was she talking about? Jove stopped, staring up at the woman as a burning lust consumed him. Oh, how he wanted to touch that perfect body, touch every inch and then break it.

"You are a very, very pretty doll," he said in a low, throaty voice.

"I am an Allosian," she said. "A child of Apeiron, your opposite. And I am here to destroy you."

Feisty. Jove always liked the ones who fought him. It made the conquest so much more satisfying.

He began to climb the stairs, his lustful stare never wavering from the woman. The marble steps in front of him exploded, and he raised an arm to protect his face. He could feel several cuts on his arm and face from the shrapnel as he stumbled down three steps. When the dust cleared, Jove looked up at the woman and grinned. Did she think that could stop him? He resumed his steady climb. A white-hot shaft of lightning crashed down on him. He could feel his insides burn, and his eardrums popped as the electricity shot from his back and out of his chest, but there wasn't any pain.

Jove found himself prostrate at the bottom of the staircase. His tendrils, seemingly acting of their own accord, shot out of his back and struck at a group of on-looking soldiers. As he drank in their essences his internal organs repaired themselves, the burns on his skin smoothed over, sound returned as his eardrums reformed, and the cuts on his arm closed.

He arose, laughing. It turned into a wild cackle when he saw the surprised look on the woman's face. "Silly doll! You can't kill me. I'm a god!"

He began to climb the steps again and she launched a fireball down at him. As before, when attacked by that soldier doll with the sword, his tendrils coalesced around him forming a kind of shield. The ball of orange fire vanished upon coming in contact with the warped, green air encasing him.

The woman's eyes widened and she began to back away. Now was the time to pounce. Still invigorated by the life he'd just drank in, Jove launched himself up in an arc sailing over the rest of the staircase and landing lithely at the top of the stairs. The woman backed away looking frantic, but Jove manifested a tentacle which exploded from his chest and caught her in the breast. She froze, and Jove began to drink.

What's this?

This woman tasted different. Her life force wasn't stagnant like the energy of other living things. It tasted pure and potent; just like Apeiron. Jove walked up to her, standing intimately close. He grabbed the woman by her amethyst hair and forced her to kiss him. She tried to pull away, but he was strongest while feeding, stronger than any normal person. When he drew back, he was surprised to find that she hadn't withered. And what was this? Her life force didn't ebb away. It kept flowing. Was she drawing directly on the Apeira well? How was that even possible?

Jove grinned as an idea blossomed in his mind. This meant that he could enjoy her in the same way he'd enjoyed his other dolls, perhaps forever if he restrained himself from killing her. He moved in for another forced kiss when he was abruptly pulled backward by something.

He hit the stairs and rolled down four steps before coming to a stop. He looked up at the woman and found her kneeling on the floor, head bowed, shoulders rising and falling as she heaved.

Who had dared interrupt him? Jove growled as he stood, looking down at the base of the stairs where a one-handed lizard man flashed a sharped-tooth grin at him. The Vorakk who'd attacked me in the coach.

This time the reptilian creature was accompanied by six small glowing spheres hovering just above his shoulders. The lizard man pointed, and all six balls of light flew at Jove. He manifested his strange shield, but it had no effect on them. They struck him as hard as though they were physical objects, knocking him back against the marble steps.

Those damned glowing lights! He couldn't eat them, and they could strike him. They were going to be a problem. He needed to kill the Vorakk quickly. Instead of standing again, Jove whipped a dozen tendrils into existence, all exploding out of his back. They struck at the lizard man who began to dodge them by ducking, jumping, and running. One of Jove's tendrils came close, but a ball of light flew in front of it, and took the strike instead of the Vorakk.

Again, Jove tasted that bitter, unbreakable essence. What was it and why couldn't he eat it? He let go of the floating light and sat up, sending more tentacles of warped air at the lizard man. The creature appeared to be slowing. It's getting tired. Even so, Jove was having an unusually difficult time catching him. Was he using some sort of Vorakk sorcery? That had to be it, for he was moving faster than Jove had ever seen anyone move.

He finally succeeded in scoring the lizard man on the ribs. The tendril didn't sink into it, but the Vorakk's scales turned white, and it fell to the ground. Jove barked a laugh.

He glanced up the staircase and found his purple-headed doll retreating through an arched doorway. She was getting away! None of his dolls had ever gotten away! He cast a wary glance at the lizard man and found that the creature had vanished with his invisibility trick.

To hell with him. Then he leapt up to the top of the stairs and followed the purple-haired woman into the next chamber. He stopped abruptly as he was greeted by a sight that made him tear up. At first it looked like a massive wall made of one huge Apeira shard, but then Jove realized what he was looking at. It was the base of Aiested's titanic well. Its glowing light illuminated the massive chamber, and he looked up to the vaulted ceiling and found that the Apeira well rose through it. The entire palace was actually built around the well.

Jove moved forward like a man possessed. He could taste that maddeningly delicious energy. A fireball struck him in the side, making him stumble. He glanced to his right to find his purple-haired doll standing fifty paces away. She threw another fireball at him, but he struck out with one of his tendrils and extinguished it midflight.

He grinned at the woman and was about to take a step toward her, but hesitated. This was a terribly difficult dilemma. Begin his feast on an inexhaustible supply of Apeiron, or gratify his more mundane passions by attacking the purple-haired woman. The logical thing would be to have the woman first, and then syphon the well, but his longing for more Apeiron prevailed, and he turned away from his doll. He'd find her again later.

He strode forward licking his lips obscenely. This was it. This is what he'd crossed Shaelar to find. The ultimate in pleasure was before him. As soon as he was close enough, Jove shot one thick translucent green tentacle from his chest and plunged it into the Apeira well.

Euphoria like nothing he'd ever known swept him away. He shuddered, moaning softly as a torrent of energy flooded into him. He could feel the well now, feel its depth. It went all the way down into the heart of the planet, connecting it to a churning mass of power so vast Jove felt as though he were contemplating the depths of the ocean itself.

He called several more of his tendrils into existence and thrust them all at the glowing amethyst. More Apeiron flowed into him, and he began to laugh from the sheer joy of it. He continued walking toward the well, and upon reaching it, pressed his whole body against its crystalline surface. The amount of life he was drinking multiplied exponentially. Now he was standing in the ocean, drinking it as it flowed over him. It was supreme ecstasy.

Raelen helped Gryyth to stand. The Ursaj roared as the pain of his scorched front made him stumble. "Perhaps you ought to stay here, and I'll bring Brother Yimin up."

Gryyth nodded, his eyes shut as he breathed slow and deep. Raelen glanced at the servant girl–Maely was her name. She was sitting on the roof's surface, arms wrapped around her legs and her cheek resting on her knees.

Who was she? Not an actual palace servant, of that Raelen was certain. He was about to ask her when the Apeira well rising behind them dimmed. It actually had gone dark for a heartbeat. It flickered again, making the purple light of the roof shift, and reminding Raelen of a sputtering candle.

"That's not possible," he said.

Maely looked up at him. Her eyes were red, and she looked beyond exhausted. Poor girl.

Raelen stared at the Apeira well for a long moment and gasped as cracks begin to spider web across its surface.

"Something's wrong."

What happened next chilled Raelen to the core. The purple-crystal monolith began to sway back and forth and since the palace was deliberately built around the well, it rocked the building. Fine cracks snaked their way across the roof's surface, and Raelen lurched forward as the tower swayed.

"We need to get back down into the palace," he said.

They were met on their way down the tower by Raelen's honor guard who'd finally managed to catch up to him. The captain blustered a dozen self-deprecating apologies upon seeing him, but Raelen dismissed his concerns with a casual wave. It wasn't the soldier's fault they couldn't keep pace with him when he was tapping Gryyth's strength and speed.

"What's happening, captain? Why is the palace shaking?"

The captain shook his helmeted head. "I don't know, my prince. But everyone is in an uproar. People are shouting things about the end of the world, and saying that Rasheera's judgment has come upon us."

A particularly violent tremor made the chandeliers' above sway. One even dropped a light talis, which shattered on the floor off to Raelen's right. "Captain, sound the call. We are evacuating the palace."

CHAPTER 63

The hall shook. Graelle snapped her head back, craning her neck to stare at the ceiling. The ornate, glass chandeliers were swaying. Not a gentle back and forth either, but a full pendulum-like swing. She looked down at Irvis, who was cradling Ezra's lifeless body, and sobbing. She gently tapped him on the shoulder.

"Irvis," she said.

He looked up at her and scrubbed the sleeve of his robe across his nose. "I couldn't heal him."

Graelle shot a glance at the mass of Rikujo enforcers all round them. They were staring at the ceiling too, all looking nervous. "Something's wrong." As soon as the words left her lips, the entire corridor lurched. Several of the enforcers cried out in surprise as they stumbled, some bracing themselves against the wall to keep from falling. Graelle herself nearly fell on her rump, but Irvis quickly stood and caught her.

A clang drew her attention to the floor. Ezra's body had rolled, the shifting of the ground so violent it had caused the sword to dislodge from his chest. Jekaran sat, frozen with green eyes staring blankly. The tilting hallway moved him physically, but he didn't so much as flinch.

"Look!" Mulladin shouted.

Graelle glanced to the wall and saw cracks forming. Dust fell from the ceiling, and the floor lurched again. "We have to go!" She said to Irvis.

He nodded and bent down to pick up Ezra, but she laid a hand on his arm to stop him. "Leave him," she said gently.

Irvis stared at her for a long moment before nodding.

Then the lights went out.

TYRUS GRABBED Hort's beefy forearm to steady himself. *What in the holy name of the goddess is happening?* Everything was shaking, and now the talises lining the corridor and hanging from the chandelier had gone dark, as if they'd lost their charge. Fortunately, a connecting corridor must've faced the outer palace wall because he could see light in the distance. That corridor would have windows.

Once his eyes adjusted, he saw Jekaran sitting on the ground only a dozen paces away. Apparently, Hort had seen the same, for the big mercenary was already moving toward the boy.

"Get him!" he said, anyway.

As they fumbled their way in the dark, pushing through Ezra's soldiers–how had the man gotten Rikujo thieves to help him?–Tyrus's foot caught something metal. He would've tripped had he not been holding fast to Hort. The object rang as his foot caused it to slide away. *Jekaran's sword talis?*

Fortunately, it felt like Tyrus had tripped on the cross guard and not the sharp blade. The way the boy was able to tear through armor and bodies, Tyrus didn't doubt the thing would've taken his toes off.

He was about to order Hort to stop so he could retrieve it, but another dark shape beat him to it. "Halt!" Tyrus shouted, but the figure had already vanished into the darkness. Well, it didn't matter now, at least not as much as rescuing Kybon's son.

They reached him, and Hort leaned down and scooped up the lean teenager. He immediately began moving toward the distant light of the connecting corridor.

"Where's Jek?" a voice shouted.

Tyrus just about didn't answer, but his conscience made him call back, "I have him! We're heading out!"

Hort stumbled only once as they groped along the wall, and Tyrus didn't want to consider what it might've been that tripped the big man. The floor was already wet and sticky, and he had kicked aside a severed head by accident. At least that's what it'd felt like. Had Jekaran really killed so many soldiers? If the king discovered he'd helped the boy escape, the noose next to Jekaran's would be his. But was the king even alive? He'd heard the soldiers shouting accusations at Jekaran as they fought, disturbing accusations.

That doesn't matter right now, he told himself, pushing the panic down.

They moved more quickly as the hallway began to lighten, and Tyrus felt a wash of relief when they turned the corner into a corridor lined on one side with tall windows. The grey light of a newborn dawn filtered in through the glass, revealing a wide marble floor that was clean of corpses and blood. Tyrus tried to ignore the squishing his boots made as he moved into the light, and refused to look down lest he see bloody footprints. That might make him vomit–again.

"Hey!" someone shouted.

Tyrus glanced back to see Jekaran's simple friend pointing at him with a ringed finger. Was it a talis? Who would give a simpleton a talis? Especially a weapon talis. Nothing happened, however, and the big youth looked confused.

"I'm trying to help him escape!" Tyrus snapped.

A Rasheeran monk standing behind and to the side of the simpleton furrowed his brow as he stared at him. "Why?" he asked. "Why would..."

The room tilted hard to the side toward the tall, ornate palace windows. One of Ezra's Rikujo thugs actually exploded through a pane of glass, screaming as he fell. Tyrus himself slammed into the outer wall. The glass panes of the other windows exploded and shattered as a large rent in the outer wall opened up above them.

"Divine Mother!" Tyrus breathed out.

The black-clad Rikujo soldiers broke into a panicked flight in all directions. Some disappeared into the darkness behind them; others slid and stumbled as they ran on ahead. Apparently, with Ezra dead, they no longer felt any loyalty to Jekaran. Nor did they obey the monk and his chubby woman friend when they called after them.

The quake subsided, and Tyrus was able to regain his footing. Blood trickled from his nose, and he wiped it with the sleeve of his robe. He'd hit the wall face first and from the pain of it likely broke his nose.

"We need to get out of here!" he snapped at the chubby monk. He winced as the movement hurt his nose, and his voice came out more nasally than usual. Yes, definitely broken.

The monk shared a look with his woman friend, and she nodded. Tyrus looked to Hort, who still held Jekaran's limp form in his arms. The boy looked as though he were dead, but his eyes were open, and he was clearly blinking and breathing. *Rasheera send he is not like this forever.*

"Come on!" Tyrus said as he took the lead. "I believe this floor connects to the palace lobby."

KAIRAH FELL TO HER KNEES. The creature, The Vessel, was syphoning not only from the Apeira well, but from every Aeose around him, including the ones in her blood. Drawing directly from the well somehow augmented his power, turning him into a vortex that sucked in all Apeiron. Kairah strained in resistance, and it was all she could do to hold onto the Apeiron inside of her

This is what happened to the land in my vision. Taris or Aiested, would soon become a city of bones with blackened ground scrubbed of all life. On top of that, Jenoc had succeeded in setting the stage for another talis war. The humans were doomed. Perhaps all life on Shaelar was doomed. She had failed.

Kairah! Aeva called. *You need to get up! Leave that place!*

"I cannot," she whispered. "I do not have the strength."

Her grip on her Apeiron store slipped, and she gasped as she felt a quarter of her energy immediately drain away. Flexing her will, she was able to staunch the bleeding and instinctively reached out to tap the well to replace the energy.

Nothing happened.

The creature was drinking in all of the well's Apeiron. She looked up at the crystal monolith. It was shaking, causing the ceiling that surrounded it at the top to crack and rain dust and stone. Kairah could also see large cracks forming in the well itself, around which the amethyst colored crystal was slowly changing color–darkening to an emerald green. Like the broken well in my vision.

"Fey girl get up, rok!"

Karak materialized in front of her. He was breathing hard, hand cradling his right side. He extended his other arm toward her and Kairah was surprised to see that it ended in a burnt stump. The Vorakk shaman had lost his hand. She reached up and gripped his stump, using it as leverage to stand. She braced herself to lose more Apeiron, but that didn't happen. Why?

Dozens of small glowing orbs swirled around her. Occasionally one would be pulled away, as if sucked toward the creature feeding on the well, but then it would come flying back as if spit out.

"What are they?" she gasped.

The lizard man flashed a toothy smile, though it looked strained. "Spirits, aka."

Spirits? That's right, Karak had said that before. But what exactly were they and how were they shielding Kairah from the all-consuming leech that was Moriora's vessel?

Kairah followed Karak as he ran toward the chamber's exit. Fortunately, the creature didn't try to stop them. Just as she was about to leave the room, Kairah glanced back to get one last look at the monster. He was little more than a dark shape in a swirling storm of purple light now, but she thought she could hear wild laughter. And she didn't just hear it with her ears. It somehow also resonated with her psychic senses. What did that mean?

"We go, rok!" Karak hissed.

Kairah turned away and joined the lizard man in a sprint out of the chamber.

"Kairah!" a familiar voice called out.

Kairah slowed and glanced to her right where she found the human named Irvis jogging toward her, and he was not alone. A plump woman, a young male, a short nobleman, and a muscular soldier carrying–Jekaran!

"Stupid human boy dead aka?" Karak asked.

Was he dead? He didn't move, and his eyes were glassy like those of a corpse. But he was blinking, and if Kairah looked close enough, she could see that he was breathing. Relief swept away her mounting dread.

The idea of Jekaran dying had threatened to break something inside of her. That was confusing. She respected all life, and mourned for its destruction, especially the destruction of intelligent creatures, but this feeling was different. Why was she more concerned for his life than that of other humans? "Is he hurt?" she asked.

Irvis glanced at Jekaran and shook his head. "Something is wrong to be sure, but it's an injury to the mind." Tears leaked from the chubby monk's eyes which Kairah just noticed were red. "He killed his uncle."

Before Kairah could process that, the room shook, and a large piece of stone ceiling crashed down on the staircase below.

"We need to go!" The short, balding man shouted.

Kairah nodded, and they all raced down the stairs. Irvis tripped, but was caught by the plump woman who steadied him before giving him quick a peck on the cheek. They left the staircase just in time to avoid another chunk of ceiling.

It crashed through the marble stairs and sent up a cloud of dust and debris. The thick pillars of ivory colored stone cracked and shook, and one fell across their path like some enormous stone tree. Karak helped Kairah up onto the fallen pillar and over, and then did the same for the rest of the company.

They continued running, through a large courtyard and past the palace wall. Kairah looked back at the Apeira well rising out of the top of the palace. It no longer glowed purple, and shards sloughed off and fell into the palace below. Kairah had been taught in the College of Disciplines that while you could chip pieces away from an Aeose to create talises, they would regenerate what was taken and so were virtually indestructible. That, apparently, was a falsehood. This well was dying, and something told Kairah that if she couldn't find some way to stop the monster leeching off it, more would follow.

RAELEN, Gryyth, the girl Maely, and a mixed group of two dozen soldiers and palace servants slowed to a halt. The hall ahead was clogged with chunks of stone, many of them too large for Raelen to move even with his enhanced strength–which he no longer had. His transference band, though still full of Apeiron had suddenly stopped functioning. Something had drained away its charge, and so his strength was now no greater than that of any other soldier. Gryyth might be able to clear away enough of the rubble for them to pass, but with serious burns covering his chest, arms, and neck, he was in no condition to try.

"Back!" Raelen ordered.

The group turned to double back when the hall lurched and a green shard of crystal, the size of a house, crashed through the ceiling creating a crystalline wall that cut off their retreat.

`"No!" Maely cried out.

"What now, cub?" Gryyth panted.

Raelen looked about feeling helpless. They were trapped, entombed alive, though that state would change soon enough. There were windows lining the outer wall of the corridor, but they were still on the upper levels of the palace, hundreds of feet from the ground. Raelen moved to one of the windows. Its stained glass panes were gone, leaving behind only tiny shards poking out from a gnarled metal frame. He looked down. They were on the east side of the palace, the window overlooking the royal gardens and the aqueduct!

It ran underneath the gardens opening at the top to act as a decorative pond. A wall enclosed the garden to keep children and animals from falling into the water, its placid surface concealing a surprising depth and deadly undertow. Raelen glanced back at Gryyth. The bear-man's blue eyes told Raelen that he'd guessed his thought. He looked back down at the pond. From this height, it would be tricky, but he could manage it. What other choice do we have?

"We're going to have to jump."

The servants in the group broke into frightened protests. To their credit, Raelen's soldiers remained stoic and grim. They understood.

"It's our only chance now," Raelen shouted over the chatter. They fell silent and he made sure to stare into as many of their faces as he could. "We jump, or we die." He turned, stepped up onto the window sill and drew in a deep breath. "I'll go first. If I make it, then follow me."

"But your highness..." one of his men protested.

"We can't let you..." another began.

Raelen didn't give them time to stop him. He let go of the frame and launched himself into empty space. The wind whipping his face stole his breath and stung his eyes producing cold tears. His stomach lurched and the roaring of air in his ears felt like it would deafen him. Then he was under water desperately working to swim back up to the surface.

The undertow caught him, and he was pulled down into the dark pipe that was the aqueduct. He was vaguely aware of more splashdowns, but couldn't see who it was that had followed him. Raelen's lungs burned, and he clenched his jaw in an effort to keep his traitorous reflexes from forcing open his mouth to gasp for breath.

He fought his lungs, lack of oxygen making panic overrule his thinking. He sucked in for a breath but instead inhaled cold water. Raelen's mind became muddled, and he tried to cough but that only let more water in. He was drowning.

Someone grabbed him around the middle and began towing him quickly in a direction that might've been up, he wasn't sure. A heartbeat later, he felt cold air sting his face, and he vomited. Water spewed from his nose and mouth as he exploded into a fit of uncontrollable coughing. He was blinded by a combination of cold water and choking spasms. He felt a hand patting his back.

Gryyth? No, the hand was too small.

Finally his coughing subsided and he found himself lying on his stomach on wet stone. The girl, Maely, was kneeling next to him. Her short hair was sticking to her face and her servant's dress was completely soaked.

"Thank you," he coughed out.

She just nodded. "I'm a good swimmer."

A growling moan off to Raelen's left drew his attention, and he found a sodden Gryyth lying on his back, eyes squinted shut as he weathered a wave of pain. The jump and swim would surely have magnified the sting of his burns.

They were on the lip of the aqueduct as it opened into a canal that ran into the city. Other soldiers and servants were climbing out of the water, but not as many as had been with Raelen. How many had not survived the jump? How many had refused to jump at all?

"Look!" one of the servants shouted.

Raelen followed his gaze and his stomach clenched. The Apeira well was cracking and shedding fragments. And then in one surreal moment, the well shattered, exploding into a thousand pieces and raining sharp shards down onto the palace below. Stone exploded in all directions as the ancient Allosian edifice fell beneath the barrage of crystal chunks. The ground shook and a dark wave of dust raced out from the crumbling palace and blinded Raelen as it exploded over them. An incongruous moment of silent stillness followed. Then, gradually, screams and shouts began piercing the air, rising from all corners of Aiested. That's when the chaos began.

JOVE WAS DEAD. But he was also not dead. He floated formless amidst an unending storm of purple clouds. No, not clouds, Apeiron. It surrounded him in every direction, stretching on into infinity.

What had happened to him? The last thing he remembered was drinking deeply from the well and everything around him. The sheer amount of energy he drank was torrential and at times it threatened to choke him. But whenever that happened, Jove simply opened himself more to accommodate the ever-increasing flow.

That pattern had escalated until Jove felt himself drawn into the Apeira well. His body had disintegrated, just blowing away and his new self, his consciousness, had dove into the crystalline monolith. Down and down he'd flown, feeling as though he were lightning striking from the sky. Then he'd splashed down into that vast ocean of life that he'd sensed churning at the center of the planet.

Jove tried to look at himself, but his hands were gone, as were his legs feet and body. His being was dark green energy, a spherical shape that looked like his translucent feeding tendrils. He was surprised to find that, even without a body, he felt hungry for Apeiron. He made to manifest a tentacle, but instead his whole self pulled in the energy around him. He broke it down inside of his core, like chewing, but his hunger didn't go away.

He absorbed more Apeiron, and it tasted as sweet as ever, but it still wasn't satisfying him. Was this some sort of cruel joke? Was he in hell? Doomed to eat and eat forever without ever feeling full? He ate more, and then more still, but the cold emptiness at his core remained. It was maddening.

Jove screamed, or at least that's how he thought of it, and the swirling clouds of purple around him shuddered as he sucked them in. Finally, he felt some relief, though it had taken more Apeiron than he'd ever eaten before to do it.

He perceived the world around him, looking in all directions at once and somehow he understood that the Apeiron flowed from somewhere. It had a source that perpetually produced more. Jove decided he would find that source of life. He would consume all of the Apeiron inside the planet, and then the fountain itself. And then, if that didn't satisfy him, he'd eat the world. He would eat everything.

PART THREE
THE FORK OF DESTINY'S ROAD

CHAPTER 64

Jove swam in an endless ocean of purple Apeiron. It was delicious. It was succulent. It was sweet. It was also not enough.

His core ached with the Hunger, the pain refusing to abate no matter how much energy he sucked in. It was maddening, and the only relief he found was in that small moment of tasting the nectar of life as it passed into him. But it came with no satisfaction. He'd eaten too much back in Aiested, and now even this unlimited supply proved insufficient.

Rock islands of all sizes floated above and beneath him in the vast purple ocean, the only physical things that existed in this place. Was he in hell? He'd died, hadn't he? Or at least left his body. He looked at himself, not with eyes, but with unobstructed consciousness. He didn't even look human anymore; his form only a ball of black, pulsating darkness.

I should've taken that doll with the purple hair before drinking the well.

She'd been so beautiful with her white skin and perfect figure. Now Jove didn't have a body, and so the chance to enjoy the doll with the purple hair, or any other woman, was gone forever. He unleashed a tortured scream. The sound didn't echo but instead produced visible ripples that exploded out from him in all directions, making the purple light swirling about him quiver.

Jove stopped screaming and floated through the glowing ocean. He wept without tears, translucent tendrils of murky green wrapping around his dark sphere form as though he were hugging himself for warmth. He stayed huddled like that until the frustration within rose again to overflowing and he screamed another agonizing cry.

The strange purple world around him trembled, and Jove sucked in Apeiron with angry abandon. Surprisingly, the Hunger gave way, if only slightly. Encouraged, Jove sucked in more Apeiron, and then more still. He kept on guzzling the surrounding power, unable to stop.

Green electricity crackled around Jove, and he shot shafts of emerald lightning out into the surrounding purple ocean. They were angrier, more forceful versions of his feeding tendrils and absorbed entire wells of Apeiron with each strike. Jove didn't stop to further consider the change, but instead poured his rage into the lightning, increasing its frequency and ferocity. Blinding green bolts flashed all about him, and small patches of blackness began appearing in the vast purple nebula.

MAELY STARTED as a thick shaft of green lightning struck the building on her right. It tore through the structure, hurling pieces of wood and stone into the sky. A deafening thunderclap exploded half a second later, drowning out the screams of the panicked mob. She forced herself to look at the sky at what used to be Aiested's towering Apeira well—now a jagged emerald shard that rose only to half its former height. Roiling clouds of blackness spiraled around it, spreading outward like ripples in a pond.

The birthing dawn was obscured by a darkness that rapidly encompassed the entire city; flashes of green lightning high in the clouds providing the only light. To make matters worse, no one had any light talises. Well, they had them, but they were drained of their Apeiron charge. All the talises found among the crowd were empty, as though the power within them had been used up. Even Maely's compulsion ring had lost its charge. What was happening?

The thunder faded, and the screams and shouts of the fleeing masses again rang throughout the streets. "You have to stay calm!" Prince Raelen Taris shouted as a group of people surged forward.

They paid little heed to their prince as they shoved past him, and the press became so fierce Maely worried they'd be trampled. A sudden, fierce roar from the prince's bear-man bodyguard made the mob pause long enough for Raelen's guards to wrangle them back into an orderly retreat.

Raelen nodded his gratitude to Gryyth, who now hunched over, cradling his badly burned chest– the result of being burned by Jenoc's spell-casting.

The citizens of Aiested continued to move quickly through the streets, having to be reined in each time a bolt of green lightning struck somewhere nearby.

"Where are we going?" Maely shouted up at Raelen.

The prince didn't answer.

"I said, where are we going?!" Maely shouted again.

He paused to look down at her. The intense stare of his blue eyes made Maely feel naked, as though he could see into her soul. *Does he know what I am? Can he see that I've done something unforgivable?*

"The North Woods," Raelen finally answered. Then he turned and resumed barking orders and managing the crowd.

Maely was a monster for what she'd done to Jek. Forcing him to love her wasn't any different from what men had done to her mother, and she was half convinced the prince could discern her crime simply by looking into her eyes. And how many people had died as a result of her selfishly aiding Jenoc? How many more would die in the coming talis war, a war she helped start? Maely wanted to cry, but tears wouldn't come—she was too exhausted for tears.

Again, she glanced over her shoulder at the broken Apeira well. Had Jekaran gotten out before the palace fell? What if he was dead? She'd abandoned him, hadn't she? If he was crushed to death under all that white stone, wouldn't that be her fault too? Hadn't she come here to save him?

She thumbed the underside of her mother's ring. She could lie to herself all she wanted, but in the end, she'd come to Aiested only under the pretense of rescuing Jek. Not rescue. *No, I came here to enslave him.* It'd been in her heart since even before Jenoc captured her. She'd been so desperate for Jekaran to love her, she'd long ago decided she would do anything to make him stay with her. It wasn't something she was proud of. Ez would be disgusted by her selfishness; hell, she was disgusted by her selfishness.

The thought of Ezra made her think of Mulladin. Where was her brother? Was he okay? Was he angry with her for abandoning him, too? A pattern was forming in the mirror of Maely's self-reflection, and the image looking back at her was ugly. Selfish. Maely was selfish. Her leaving Genra to follow Jek hadn't ever been about looking out for him, or keeping him safe. She choked out a laugh at the absurd thought. No, what she'd done, all she'd done had been for herself, for her own supposed happiness. This came not as a revelation, for Maely had known it all along. She'd buried that truth under rationalizations and excuses, but in the end it all came down to one thing: Maely had used compulsion to force Jekaran to love her. The memory of his adoring, vacant green eyes was too much, and she collapsed to her knees.

The jostling crowd threatened to trample her. Well, let it. It was better than she deserved. Just then a strong hand gripped her right bicep, and lifted her so that she had no choice but to stand.

"Just a little farther," Prince Raelen said. "You can make it. We just need to go a little farther."

Maely wanted to tell the prince to leave her, to let her die with the city, but the words wouldn't come. She was so ashamed she couldn't speak. She couldn't even meet his eyes. She started as her feet abruptly left the ground, and she looked up to find that Raelen had lifted her to carry in his arms.

"No..."

"Don't worry." The prince flashed her a smile. "You're light enough."

She wanted to protest, but sleep was already taking her. Was she really starting to drift? *How could anyone sleep while surrounded by hell without and tormented by hell within?* Those were her last thoughts as the world faded.

JENOC STRODE through the streets of the capital city of Haeshala–Isadara. His step was quick with purpose, his strides sure. It was night, and he wore a dark cloak with the hood pulled up to hide his Allosian hair and burnt face. That burn stung terribly, and the loss of his eye made it difficult to see. But even those pains paled in comparison to the endless throbbing that pulsed in his head. It'd grown constant now, no longer coming in waves, but one continuous beat that kept getting louder. To add shame to his suffering, he no longer had the strength to maintain an illusion spell-casting, which was the reason for the cloak. He had been able to translocate himself through the city wall, but had to dismiss all other spell-castings so as to focus his entire mind on the Third Discipline–Space.

During the flight from Taris, Jenoc finally accepted the possibility that he might be dying. Even so, he remained resolute, having long since passed the point of no return. Not pain in his head, nor loss of sight, or even the betrayal of his sister would stop him from doing what he'd come to Isadara to do. Thinking of his purpose made the pack on his back feel a little heavier. The thing in his satchel wasn't particularly large, which made it confusing as to why it was pressing down so hard on his shoulders. Nor was it big enough to be evoking the labored breaths that now came from his mouth. Was he getting physically weaker?

Jenoc clenched his good eye shut and gritted his teeth. He needed to focus on his task. He had an important mission to accomplish. He couldn't stop to rest, and there would be plenty of time later–if he survived–for him to grieve the loss of Kairah. He wondered at what his sister would be doing now that he'd abandoned her, and started to worry for her safety before crushing the thought with a flare of anger.

"I have no sister," he hissed between labored breaths.

Kairah had died the moment she'd sided with the humans, a fact that stung worse than his burned face. A lost eye and charred flesh could be repaired by Apeiron, but the wound Kairah dealt to his soul, that could never be healed.

How could she choose the humans over her own people, over her own family?

Jenoc's growl startled an old beggar who'd been approaching him. He glanced at the man quickly hobbling away, and something primal rose inside him. He wanted to chase after the beggar, catch him by the collar of his dirty tunic, and pummel his face until it became an unrecognizable pulp.

Those random flares of anger and violence used to frighten him, but now he welcomed them and lusted to lose control. That'd happened earlier when he'd been in Taris. A serving woman had seen him drop his illusory disguise so that he could translocate himself into the palace's vault. Killing her, of course, had never been the issue. It was the fierce fit of violence that made the case remarkable. He'd enjoyed beating the middle-aged woman into unconsciousness and relished the popping sound her neck made when he'd twisted her head completely around.

Worry came when the rage faded. Jenoc, though always angry, wasn't usually prone to such explosions of violence. He didn't think any Allosian was capable of what he'd done to the servant woman. The other magic, no, Moriora, as Kairah named it–*where did she learn its name?*–had indeed injured him. There was no other explanation for his headaches, difficulty spell-casting, and newly-developed sadistic impulses. It was somehow changing him into a monster.

After nearly two excruciating hours of walking the streets of the Haeshalen capital, Jenoc finally reached his destination; a tall crystalline obelisk that glowed with violet light. It wasn't built into the palace as the well at Taris had been. No, Isadara was a true human city, not an Allosian treasure infested by vermin like Aiested.

Isadara could best be described as utilitarian in design. Squat, square-ish buildings arranged in austere rows nested into ever larger blocks. Even the citadel at the center of the city lacked the stylish architecture Jenoc had seen in other human palaces. It was blocky and black, without any windows on the first three of its stories. It fit what Jenoc knew of Haeshalen culture. These humans in particular were the most war-like in Shaelar. They looked like other humans save for their unusual green eyes, a trait that virtually all the Haeshalen people exhibited. Whereas in Aiestal and Maes Tol, green eyes branded one an oddity or an outcast, here they were the proud mark of royal heritage.

Jenoc repressed his scholarly inclinations and focused on the ring of stone that surrounded the base of Isadara's Apeira well. A single guard, clad in black armor, with a conical open-faced helmet stood protecting it, a post that was obviously the perpetuation of tradition and not necessity. No one would harm an Apeira well, not even an invading army. They were virtually indestructible, and too precious to the human's economy and everyday life to even risk losing. The guard spotted Jenoc and lazily brought his spear up in a sloppy warding gesture.

"Talis filling is over. Come back tomorrow."

Jenoc focused through the pain of his migraine and cast a paralysis net on the guard. His eyes widened as he went as stiff as an old corpse and tipped over. Jenoc made certain the man's eyes remained open, and even cast a spell from the Second Discipline–Elemental–onto his eyes so they remained moist. He wanted this man to witness what he was doing.

Jenoc slid the pack from his shoulder and placed it on the stone ring at the well's base. He then reached in and produced a square cube so large it required both hands to hold. It was the plague box he'd crafted while hiding in the king's court as Navarch Pariel. He set the box down so the crest of Aiestal, faced the paralyzed guard and then touched its top. He willed the plague box to begin radiating its disease aura, and then locked the talis with a command word so no one would be able to deactivate it.

He smiled as he imagined children all throughout the city waking with violent coughs and high fevers. It wouldn't take long for the magical disease to begin its work. By this time tomorrow night, thousands of little bodies would fill street carts carrying them to a mass pyre. The man on the ground would report what he'd seen; a cloaked stranger depositing a talis emblazoned with the unmistakable symbol of their enemy nation. The Haeshalan talis scholars would soon identify it as the source of their loss, and they would marshal for war. With the Aiestali army already on the march, Jenoc estimated that the first battle of the new talis war would begin before the week was out.

He chuckled, kicked the paralyzed soldier in the ribs, and walked away. He was casual about it, not wanting to attract the attention of the few late-night wanderers still milling about. He'd only gotten a mile away when the first motherly shriek rang out.

That was quick. Perhaps the dead child had already been sickly.

The agony in the woman's tone was like sweet music to Jenoc, and he couldn't help but grin. More yelling, and howls of grief followed. He stood still in the street, relishing the sounds of the suffering he'd caused.

Then something sharp rammed itself into his brain, or at least that's what it felt like. Jenoc gasped and crumpled to the ground. Pain drilled into his head, like twin daggers stabbing into the back of his eye sockets. He choked out a scream, and then his sight left him. He was blind, rolling on the paved streets clutching his head, and gritting his teeth so hard that one of them actually cracked. His first thought was that somehow the plague box was affecting him, but that was impossible. He'd made no error in defining the talis's targets–children under five. No, this was his injury, the damage he'd done to himself by calling and channeling Moriora.

Sound faded in Jenoc's ears, and blackness swallowed him whole.

CHAPTER 65

Kairah stared at the crystal spire on the distant horizon. She couldn't really see it anymore, only when flashes of lightning illuminated the dark clouds swirling about it. Green lightning, like she'd seen in her vision of the dead land. Is that what it was, an oracular vision? Or was it just a dream? She didn't have much experience with dreaming, as Allosians seldom slept, but she was increasingly certain that what she'd seen was real. Did that make her an oracle now? Could she invoke other visions? She needed information, needed it desperately. Could she use her inherited gift to find out what was going on or more importantly, how to stop it?

She shook her head. Oracles could only see what fate showed them, not see what they wanted to see. Or so she'd been told. Kairah had woefully neglected studying prophecy in favor of improving her already considerable talent with the First Discipline–Creation. Perhaps she ought to have accepted an apprenticeship with Allose's premier oracle, Shivara. If she ever made it back to Allose, Kairah would have to call on the reclusive woman.

Warm cloth enfolded her shoulders. She looked up to see the human, Irvis, naked from the waist and placing his brown cloak upon her like a shawl. That was surprising. She'd thought that the man with the overactive reproductive instinct would not have been concerned for her modesty.

"Thank you," she said.

Irvis nodded wordlessly, and then walked away. His eyes were red, and some mucus dribbled from one of his nostrils.

He grieves for the loss of his friend, Aeva said.

Kairah couldn't send Aeva her agreement. She was too far from Allose, and only retained half of her Apeiron. Additionally, she didn't dare spell-cast this close to Aiested for fear of the creature that had smashed the well. The same creature had also drained every talis in the city, and for several miles out. In fact, it was only just before they'd stopped to rest in this clearing that she'd felt the suction-like force of the Apeiron vortex relent. Karak's strange magic had shielded her from the worst of the draining, but even then she slowly lost Apeiron so long as they were in or near the city.

A bolt of green lightning flashed in the distance, followed a moment later by thunder. *This is what happened to the land in my vision.* Had that been the future of Shaelar she'd seen? No, the shape of the land and the stars were different. Could it be she was seeing the land from which humans had originated? That made a kind of sense. History was mostly quiet on the reason humans had fled their home country, and if what Kairah saw was the result of what was happening now, she understood why they'd abandoned everything to sail into the unknown. But if she couldn't stop that same fate from befalling this land, where would her people go? Where would the Vorakk, the Ursaj, or even the humans escape to? And what was to stop this from happening again?

"I asked you a question, Allosian!"

Kairah turned to see a large man with wavy black hair stalking toward her. His face was contorted with anger, and he threw off Irvis's gentle attempt to grab his arm.

"Mulladin," Irvis pled.

"I am sorry," Kairah said. "I did not hear your question."

The husky man, who was really just a youth himself, stopped a few paces in front of where she sat. "Where's Maely?"

Kairah glanced back at Aiested, and then turned again to look up at the young man. "The last time I saw her she was on top of one of the palace towers."

"And you just left her there?" he shouted.

"Mulladin!" Irvis snapped.

Mulladin? So this was Maely's brother. Kairah had thought the girl had said he suffered from a diminished capacity, but the young man standing above her didn't fit that description. Kairah didn't take his anger personally. Humans were passionate creatures with a limited ability to think rationally or control their emotions. His rage wasn't meant for Kairah. He was just worried about his sister.

"She was in the company of the prince and his Ursaj bodyguard the last time I saw her."

"She could be dead!" Mulladin waved angrily at the ruined city.

Kairah nodded. "She may be. I have already attempted to scry the ruins of the palace, but all I can see is darkness. Something blocks my vision. I am sorry."

Mulladin reached down and grabbed Kairah's arm and lifted her into a standing position. He moved in close, and hissed through gritted teeth, "You left her to die."

Kairah pulled her arm free, but didn't step away. Grieving or not, this man did not intimidate her, though he had started to irritate her. "I had no foreknowledge of what was about to happen. She was safe when I left her, and I was needed elsewhere."

Mulladin's eyes flicked to something over Kairah's shoulder, and he turned and stalked away. Kairah nodded her thanks to Karak who stood just behind her, quietly hissing.

"Fey girl well, reka?"

Kairah nodded and then glanced at Karak's left wrist, a blackened stump where his claw should've been. She then looked at his ribs where he was pressing his remaining hand against a patch of white scales. They reminded Kairah of a shed snakeskin.

She turned to face him. "But you are not well."

Karak rasped a syllable and raised his stump to sign something, but stopped when he realized what he was doing. He looked at his stump and rasped a chuckle, "Ek."

"Let me heal your side," Kairah said. She moved Karak's remaining hand away and gently placed her hand over his white scales. She expected him to wince or hiss, but apparently, the contact didn't hurt him.

"Does this not pain you?"

"No feel, aka."

The flesh was dead, then? It made sense. Karak had been fighting the Moriora Vessel, an incarnation of the power of death itself. She would have to grow new flesh from the surrounding healthy tissue. Kairah was still hesitant to cast so close to Aiested and without a nearby functioning well, but she was good at healing. That was from the First Discipline, Creation or Growth, and she was a master of growing things.

Kairah cast a healing, but nothing happened. She tried again, expending more of her Apeiron store this time, but the wound resisted her. Right at the end, just before she had to give up, something started to happen, but the result was disproportionately small. She looked up at Karak, who had a concerned look on his reptile face.

"Reka?"

Kairah drew back her hand and shook her head. "Something's wrong. That wound is resisting my ministrations."

"A cursed wound?" Irvis asked.

Kairah glanced at the chubby monk and nodded. "I suppose that description fits."

"Is she always this condescending?" The woman seated next to Irvis glared at Kairah.

"Hush, dear," Irvis said with a pat of her hand. It was resting on his knee. "You can't heal it?"

"Not without a well."

Irvis fingered a pouch hanging from a cord around his neck. With his robe gone, it hung exposed in the middle of his man-breasts. "How did Karak gain that injury?"

Kairah shared a look with the lizard man.

"Eater," Karak said.

Irvis gasped. "You found it?"

"It is what destroyed Aiested," Kairah said.

"Divine Mother!" Irvis raised his left hand to his mouth.

"What happened to Jekaran?" Kairah looked at the human boy. He was sitting against a tree, eyes unfocused and face blank.

Irvis began to cry again. "Argentus tried to stun him with a talis while he was enthralled by the sword and..." His voice caught.

"He ran Ez through!" Mulladin called harshly from several feet away. He was standing aloof, arms folded as he leaned against an Aspen.

Irvis nodded as he wiped his eyes. "It did something to Jekaran's mind."

Kairah walked over and knelt in front of Jekaran.

"He was trying to save you," a short, balding man sitting on a rock five paces away said. His tone was sharp and accusing.

For some reason, Lord Gymal's words cut Kairah. "I..."

"He fought over a hundred soldiers on his own." Gymal's burly mercenary said as he walked up to stand over Jekaran. Was he protecting him?

"All to rescue you from us wicked humans," Gymal snarled.

Jekaran had been trying to rescue her? It seemed that the only time he let the sword have control over his body was when he was fighting to save her. No, she realized. Even before he'd bonded the sword, he'd been her protector. In Rasha, when those human criminals tried to assault her, Jekaran had run to her defense although outnumbered, and bearing no real weapon. That stirred her feelings, making her growing affinity for the human boy rise to the surface.

She reached out and tenderly caressed his cheek. He didn't react to the contact—not even a flinch. As far as humans went, he was handsome, his stage of physical development not too far behind Kairah's own; although she was eighty years his senior. Kairah used the contact to delve into his mind. She gasped and pulled her hand away.

"What is it?" Gymal snapped.

Kairah shot a look at Irvis. "Tell me again exactly what happened. Omit no detail no matter how seemingly insignificant."

Irvis repeated the story of Jekaran's killing his uncle, breaking into sobs when Kairah pressed him for details. It felt to Kairah as though she were torturing the chubby human, but she needed to know.

After Irvis finished, Mulladin stalked over and demanded, "What's wrong with him?"

"Where is the sword talis?" Kairah asked, ignoring Mulladin.

Irvis shook his head. "Probably in the ruins of the palace."

Kairah returned to studying Jekaran's blank face. *He should never have come to my rescue.* Although she knew by her oracular gift that their fates were intertwined, Kairah felt real sorrow for Jekaran. Not pity, as she felt for other humans, but true, empathetic heartache. She had brought him to this fate, one worse than death. And he had willingly come. Like his *running into danger to rescue me in Rasha.*

"What's wrong with him?" Gymal asked in a tone bordering on hysteria. That was strange. Wasn't he Jekaran's enemy?

"His mind has been shattered."

"That's what your Allosian magic was able to discern?" Mulladin snapped. "We knew that already, woman."

"No," Kairah said. "It has literally shattered, broken into compartmentalized pieces."

"How does a mind shatter?" Gymal asked. "It's not like it's made of glass."

Kairah sighed. "That is the best analogy I can think of at the moment."

"Then put it back together." Mulladin ordered.

She shook her head. "I have never attempted a healing of a mind so severely fractured." Actually, Kairah hadn't ever attempted a healing of the mind at all. Such a thing was possible of course, and she had read about it in her studies. But the mind was part of the soul, and Apeiron didn't effect it the same way that it effected flesh and bone.

"I need a well."

Irvis stroked his chin. "The closest one is to the east, in Galadar."

"Across the sodden lands?" Gymal shot to his feet. "Without a boat, we'll have to go all the way around the Ridalia marsh. That's three weeks travel even by ghern. Who knows how long it will take on foot. And we don't have any supplies!"

"Can't we translocate there?" Graelle interjected. "Our talises may be drained, but can't she do it?"

"Fey girl weak from fight Eater, ska."

How did he know that? She was definitely going to have to learn more about Vorakk magic.

"What about your spirits?" Irvis asked. "Can they transport us?"

"Isk," Karak hissed and signed something with his remaining claw.

"There is a closer well," Kairah said.

Irvis crinkled his bushy eyebrows. "There aren't any well-cities besides Galadar for two hundred miles or more."

"We can take Jekaran to Allose." The words came out before Kairah had fully considered them.

Silence.

"What will happen to you if you bring a group of human outsiders into the secret city of your people?" Irvis softly asked.

Kairah stared at Jekaran's blank face. Irvis had just given her an opportunity to take back her suggestion, and she should. There was something much bigger than she, Jekaran or any of them going on. The world itself was in danger. But her heart twisted at the thought of abandoning the young man who'd sacrificed so much to protect her. It was where she was going anyway, to warn the synod about Moriora and its Vessel, but she hadn't considered before now bringing any of them with her.

Kairah sighed. "After the war, my people wanted nothing to do with humans. They are not overtly hostile like my brother, but they will get angry if I bring Jekaran there. They will publically censure me at best and exile me at worst."

"Allose is supposed to be built around the largest Apeira well in the world. Is there any chance you could bring Jekaran into range, outside your city, and heal him there?" Irvis asked.

Kairah hooked a strand of her glittering hair behind her ear. "Perhaps. But in truth, I am uncertain how to heal him, and will likely need the wisdom of our libraries, if not the actual aid of other Allosians."

"Will they even let you into the city with him—with us?" Graelle shot a nervous glance at Irvis.

Kairah looked at the corpulent woman, and her jaw tightened. "If they wish to hear my news. They will certainly have sensed the destruction of the well in Aiested, and will be wondering what happened there. If they bar me entrance, then I shall not tell them what I know."

"Then it's settled," Gymal said with a nod.

"No, it's not!" Mulladin snapped.

Karak moved closer to Kairah and she caught him hissing quietly.

"I need to find Maely."

"Son, you need to—"

"Don't talk down to me, Irvis! I'm not dim anymore." Mulladin let an angry stare linger on the chubby human. Then he appeared to deflate and tears started rolling down his cheeks. "Ez is dead. Jekaran might as well be. My sister is all I have left. I can't lose her too."

Tears fell from Irvis's face. "I know."

Mulladin nodded, scrubbed his forearm across his eyes, and strode away.

"Mulladin..." Graelle began, but Irvis silenced her with a pat on her knee.

"Let him go."

As Kairah watched Mulladin go, the unmistakable sign of a fated soul rippled in the air around him. She'd seen it before with Jekaran, which was the driving force behind staying close to him. This was different, however. She didn't feel as though the sign were prompting her to do anything. She wondered if she should stop Maely's brother, but that felt wrong. Whatever he was fated to do, it didn't immediately involve her. Even if the sign had meant she needed to follow Mulladin, she wasn't sure she would have. Again, she looked down into Jekaran's empty, green eyes. If it weren't for his blinking and breathing, the glassy stare could make someone mistake him for a corpse. She caressed his cheek one more time. For reasons she didn't fully understand, Kairah was willing to risk the wrath of her people, perhaps even permanent exile, to save this human boy.

"Fey girl's tribe kill Karak, reka?" Kairah looked up at the Vorakk shaman.

Kairah shook her head. "You are coming then?"

"Ssk," Karak said with a sharp gesture. "Need healing to more fight Eater, aka."

"Have you any idea how to kill it?"

"Ska." He signed something and looked away. *Was that shame?*

"But we have to try, do we not?" Of any in the group, she had the most in common with the Vorakk shaman.

Karak looked up, met her eyes, and then flashed a sharp-toothed grin. "Daka."

Surprisingly, Karak's smile comforted her. *That was odd.* Their situation remained dire, she didn't know what to do to stop the monster that had impossibly destroyed an Aoese, and Jekaran might be forever lost. But she and the Vorakk shared the same purpose and, it appeared, they were both committed to seeing it done.

CHAPTER 66

Raelen looked back at Aiested. Green lightning danced around the emerald shard that had once been Aiested's Apeira well. Could this be the wroth of the goddess for mankind's long history of cruelty and decadence? Was her judgment truly upon them? Well, he couldn't blame her. The run and mill of humanity disgusted him. The world was a cruel, dark, miserable place, made that way by his kind. Rape, slavery, murder, and theft were all too common among his people. Where was the nobility of man he'd read about in the histories? Where was the heroism? Perhaps those writings had never been true.

He looked at Gryyth. The white Ursaj walked hunched over, folding in on himself as he led them into the north woods. He'd been badly burned on his chest, neck, arms, and legs while fighting the Allosian wizard. Pariel—no, Jenoc—was trying to rid the world of the very same decadence Raelen himself wanted to abate. Only the Allosian man saw fit to accomplish that goal by wiping out all of humanity. Was this dark storm and the destruction of the Apeira well his doing? What if he was serving the goddess in this thing? What if mankind deserved to be destroyed? Raelen found himself staring at the column of refugees trudging along behind him. Most walked, still dressed in their night clothes. Some had brought carts, or rode gherns. There were even some fools trying to maneuver their wagons through the thick woods.

"Are you well, cub?"

Raelen snapped his head back to Gryyth. The bear-man was boring into him with his bright blue eyes. Although grievously wounded, and free of the slave talis, the Ursaj continued to worry over him. It made Raelen want to sob. He stopped walking and lay Maely down upon the soft forest floor. One of his honor guards called for the company to halt. Raelen was about to countermand the order for the sake of urgency, but then decided that everyone could use a moment to rest.

"Cub?" Gryyth rumbled.

Raelen fell to the ground, sitting next to Maely's sleeping form. He ground his teeth in an effort to staunch his threatening tears. His father would've scolded him for even approaching such a pathetic display of emotion. His eyes burned, and a tear spilled down his left cheek. With his adrenaline gone, the weight and import of all that was happening crashed down upon him. It made him slump his shoulders as though it were a physical burden.

"I'm afraid," he said only loud enough for Gryyth to hear.

Gryyth groaned as he gingerly sat down next to Raelen. It made him feel guilty for causing his friend and protector more pain. "There is no shame in feeling fear."

"Aiested has fallen, my father's dead, a new talis war is starting, and I am now responsible for thousands of refugees, and we are alone in the wild with no food or supplies." Raelen motioned toward Aiested and the broken Apeira well surrounded by black clouds. "And the world is ending."

Gryyth chuckled, a sound which quickly became another groan of pain. Raelen glanced at Gryyth's blackened chest and neck. "I fail to see the humor in all of this."

"Laughing," the Ursaj grimaced, "when all seems lost, is a form of bravery."

"Or insanity," Raelen scoffed.

"You are king, now, cub. You must be brave."

"You said there was no shame in being afraid."

"Fear is like the rain. It falls upon all of us. In this there is no shame." The Ursaj sucked in a sharp breath. "But it is also as a fork in the road. Now you must choose Seiro. You must choose to be brave."

"But what am I supposed to do?" Raelen leaned forward and bowed his head. He wanted to curl in on himself, shrink down beneath the crushing weight on his shoulders. With his face turned toward the ground, the tears flowed freely. "This all happened so suddenly. I don't feel prepared to deal with it. Father was right. I am not ready to be king."

Gryyth's huge paw touched Raelen between the shoulder blades. "Your sire was wrong."

Raelen had never heard Gryyth so openly criticize his master–or rather former master. Perhaps his being free from the obeisance awl had loosened his tongue.

He continued. "Your sire believed that your compassion and nobility were weaknesses. Like most of your kind, he did not understand Seiro. He desired you to change these things about yourself. But the very essence of what it means to lead is love. Anyone can rule, can make people do what they wish through force. A true leader inspires others to follow him, by his compassion and caring. Then people choose to follow him."

Raelen scrubbed his eyes with the back of his wrist. "Seiro."

"Seiro," Gryyth agreed.

It hadn't been specific advice about how to handle their crisis, but somehow Gryyth's wisdom had rallied Raelen's courage. Gryyth could always do that. Raelen smiled at the bear-man and gently touched his furry shoulder. He then stood and surveyed the crowd. To his relief, none of them had been paying any attention to him and would, therefore, have not seen him weeping.

Again, Raelen looked back up at what was left of Aiested's Apeira well, and then turned to stare at the eastern horizon. Mind cleared by his emotional outburst and Gryyth's counsel, he'd gained a grasp on their situation and an idea struck him.

"Your people live in these woods?"

"Somewhere," Gryyth rumbled.

Raelen looked down at him. "You don't know where?"

"We don't live in cities, cub. Not like you do."

Why hadn't Raelen known that?

Gryyth continued, "We live in dens, in small groups–mostly families. And we wander about much."

Did Gryyth have a family? Was he captured as a cub, or when he was older? Raelen had never thought to ask.

"Do the Ursaj ever gather as one? To make laws or worship?"

Gryyth hesitated before answering, "On occasion, but this is a thing we do not speak of to humans."

"Not even me?"

Gryyth looked uncertain. "I trust you, cub. But most of your kind do not know Seiro. They would use the knowledge to capture or kill us."

"Please."

Gryyth growled and it turned into a groan. Then he bowed his head as though defeated. "There is a place in these woods, sacred to the Ursaj—The Sky Temple. We assemble there when called."

"How are you called? Do you have a talis?"

Gryyth shook his large head. "It is a thing of the Mother."

Raelen wasn't sure what that meant. "How far away is this place?"

"Not close. But also, not terribly far."

"Could you make it there?"

Gryyth chuckled and motioned to his burns with one paw. "Not without your help, cub. But just you. Not any of your guards."

That was going to be a problem.

Raelen looked back to watch his refugees as they milled about, looking for food in their hastily packed gear. Some didn't even bother to do more than curl up on the ground or lean against trunks of trees to sleep or comfort their children.

"If you can call them, will they help us?"

Gryyth's blue eyes bore into him for a whole minute before he finally answered, "I am not the one who should call the others, and even if I do it, the Ursaj see all humans as enemies. It will be a hardship just to persuade them you didn't force me to aid you, and it is death for the unworthy to enter our sacred meeting place."

Raelen turned around and looked down at Gryyth. "What about Rygarr and the Hunter?"

Gryyth looked uncertain.

"Three days the hunter tracked Rygarr, intent on slaying her though she had done him no hurt," Raelen began quoting the Ursaj fable. "While watching from her hiding place, she saw the hunter spring his own trap and spear himself through the leg. He was helpless, alone, and bleeding. He would surely die of his wounds if not by the fang and claw of predators larger than himself."

Gryyth took over the recitation. "So Rygarr went to him, and freed him from the trap that had been meant for her. Then she carried him to a clear and clean river, where she tended to his wound and cared for him nine days. Then, when the hunter was well enough, Rygarr carried him out of the forest and back to his village."

"It is Siero for your people to aid mine," Raelen said.

Gryyth nodded sharply. "Perhaps, cub. But do not forget the ending of that story."

And when the people of the village saw Rygarr approaching with the hunter in her arms, they panicked, and heeding not the protests of the hunter, they took Rygarr and slew her.

"We are a broken people, now. We pose no threat to the Ursaj. As my first act as king, I will officially decree that all Ursaj held in slavery are to be freed, and your people hunted no more."

Gryyth chuckled. "You are clever, cub. I will take you to The Sky Temple and call the others to help your people."

"I can't go with you, Gryyth."

Gryyth growled. "What is this foolishness, cub?"

Raelen shook his head and knelt before him. "I am going to ride east to find Aiestal's armies and order them to stop their march on Haeshala. If I ride hard, I think I can get to them before the fighting starts, and perhaps we can yet prevent this war."

Gryyth paused for a moment before finally nodding. "You have truly learned Seiro, cub."

Raelen smiled. "You are too injured to make this journey on your own, my friend. You will have to trust one of my guards."

"No," Gryyth growled.

"Gryyth, please."

"Your guards do not know Seiro. They are men of blood and killing."

Raelen's chest tightened. Seiro demanded that he leave his people to try and prevent Jenoc's talis war. But he also had a duty to these people, his people. And what of Gryyth? If the Ursaj went alone in his current state, he would likely die.

A twig breaking drew Raelen's attention to the side where Maely watched him. She was in the process of drawing her legs up to her chest, but froze when Raelen looked at her. How long had she been awake? As if injected into his mind by the goddess herself, another idea came to him.

"You have heard what we've been saying?"

Maely nodded wordlessly, her eyes wide.

Raelen turned back to Gryyth. "What of this child? According to Seiro, her age makes her innocent. Your people would not see her as a threat."

Gryyth looked at Maely. "She is hardly a child."

"But not yet a woman."

"I'm fifteen!" Maely snapped. Then her eyes widened and she added, "Um... my prince."

Raelen knelt in front of Maely. "I don't know how you're involved in all of this, but I watched you challenge the Allosian wizard when we fought him on the tower. You have strength and courage."

"You ride to stop him?"

Raelen nodded.

"Please take me with you. I have a score to settle with him."

A score to settle?

The young lady unconsciously touched a ring she wore on her right hand. It looked like a talis, but without the purple glow of an Apeiron shard, he wasn't sure. He wanted to know what her part in all of this was, but there was no time to spare.

Raelen glanced at Gryyth and then leaned in closer to Maely so that their faces were mere inches apart. "He is my friend and protector. He practically raised me from the time I was a child. You see those burns upon his chest?"

Maely nodded.

"They will soon become infected, if they aren't already. I've seen burns half that serious cause fever and death. He needs care, and right now the only chance for that is to get him to his people. I need someone I can trust."

"You don't even know me," Maely said with a harshness Raelen didn't expect. "I'm not trustworthy."

Raelen smiled as he gently wiped a tear from Maely's cheek. "You are right. I don't know you. But my heart tells me that you have a noble soul."

"Your heart is wrong." Maely caught herself again. "Um... Your Highness."

Raelen shook his head. "I know what I'm about in this. I've been searching men's hearts for nobility all my life."

"Well, maybe that's your problem," she said with small smirk.

"What?"

"You've been looking in men's hearts."

Raelen bellowed a laugh, and it made Maely jump. He seldom laughed so boisterously, certainly never in front of his father. It felt good, as though he were expelling months of heartache. There had only been one other person who could make him forget himself this way–Saranna.

Maely chuckled uncertainly. Raelen stood, reached down, and helped the girl to her feet. "Will you do this thing for me?"

She looked at Gryyth for a long moment and then met Raelen's gaze.

By the breath of the goddess, there're steel in those eyes.

Maely nodded.

"Thank you." Raelen bent over and kissed her on the cheek. This seemed to surprise her almost as much as Raelen's sudden laughter had.

He had his honor guard find and seize one of the refugee's gherns, left Gryyth and Maely with some final instructions, and was riding east within the hour. It wasn't long before he'd left the woods and found Aiestad's royal road–a cobbled thoroughfare that extended from the capital city for twenty miles. Thunder booming behind Raelen prompted him to glance back at the city.

Flashes of green amidst the inky clouds showed him the jagged top of the broken Apeira well. It was both awesome and terrifying. It really did look as though the end of the world was upon them. Raelen responded in the only way that seemed right.

He laughed.

CHAPTER 67

Mulladin couldn't remember being dim. Well, that wasn't exactly true. He could remember events, sights, and sounds, and how he felt, but those memories were viewed through the lens of his current level of mental capacity.

I sure did cry a lot.

He was crying now. Not weeping or sobbing, but his cheeks were wet from quiet tears. Ez was dead. Jekaran was broken. He likely could never return home. His whole world had changed in a single day. The loss of his dearest friends overshadowed the blessing of his transformation.

And perhaps Maely, too.

The thought stabbed his already aching heart. What would he do if his sister were dead? Who would take care of him? He scoffed at that. It seemed to be an instinctive echo from his old life. He could take care of himself now. His lightning ring–when charged again–could let him defend himself, and would fetch a small fortune on the black market. But the practical necessities of life weren't all that Maely had provided him.

Though a few years younger, Maely had stepped in to fill the role of Mulladin's nurturer when his mother died. Maely had been the one to quiet his fears in the dead of night, to tend him when he was ill, or to discipline him when he misbehaved. Ez had also done those things on occasion, and Mulladin knew the man looked out for them, but it was Maely who had really cared for him. Well, now it was his turn to care for her. He'd find her, bind up her wounds, and carry her away from this place. Or, if the unthinkable had happened, he'd bury her. Dead or alive, he had to find his sister.

He tried not to flinch whenever a bolt of emerald lightning flashed from within the black clouds swirling about the broken Apeira well. Those seemed to be increasing in frequency, the trailing thunder sounding as though it were having a difficult time keeping up, and they were coming in bursts of three or four. The dark sky seemed a macroscopic expression of the roiling turmoil inside him.

After hours of backtracking, Mulladin found himself again inside the capital city. The streets were no longer clogged with frightened mobs of fleeing people, though to say they were empty would not be correct either. There were some stragglers frantically hefting packs, pulling handcarts, and carrying children away from their homes, but most of the street's occupants looked to be looting. Even the plunderers seemed reluctant to stay here any longer than they had to as was evidenced by their frequent, wide-eyed glances up at the broken Apeira well that rose from the center of the city.

These same people, looters and retreating peasants alike, shot confused glances at Mulladin as he jogged through the streets toward the palace ruins. Who would be fool enough to be running so eagerly to the darkness?

Maybe I still am dim.

As he ran, the true state of his exhaustion gradually asserted itself. So it was with welcome relief that he found a ghern tied to a corral outside of an inn. The beast must've somehow been left behind when the people of Aiested made their frantic evacuation. Incongruously, the animal seemed completely unconcerned that the world was ending. It bleated lazily at Mulladin when he unhitched it from its post, and didn't appear to care when he climbed into its saddle.

He nearly fell off when he prompted the bipedal animal into a trot. Fortunately, riding across Shaelar with Ez had taught him how to ride a ghern, but driving it–that was another matter altogether. It took frustratingly too long for him to make the creature go where he wanted it to go, and longer still to get it to stop when he tried to rein it in. He wasn't sure if it was his inexperience, or the beast's temperament, but in the end, he'd been forced to abandon the creature and resume his jogging.

Two more hours passed before Mulladin found himself standing before the ruins of the palace. It was as dark as night this close to the broken Apeira well on account of the roiling clouds that swirled around the jagged crystal spire above. Only the sunlight behind him made it possible to see anything; that and the flashes of green lightning from within the clouds.

There were no looters here, despite the famed wealth of the king's talis vault. No one would be foolish enough to venture this far into the unnatural darkness–well, no one but him. He moved into the courtyard, a once green field with colorful gardens now a barren wasteland devoid of all flora. Chunks of white stone punctuated the landscape in every direction, and jagged shards of green crystal stuck out from where they'd dug themselves into the ground.

Mulladin wound his way around the mammoth debris, some pieces larger than two-story buildings, and finally found himself standing before the ruined doors of the palace. He had to climb over the severed head of an enormous statue to gain access. As soon as Mulladin stepped inside, he was paralyzed by the sight that lay before him. The entire colonnade that fed into the palace proper was covered in broken white stone and gigantic Apeira well shards. From this point on, the way was impassable.

Rage boiled up inside Mulladin and he threw himself at the nearest piece of stone. He slammed into it with enough force to expel the wind from his lungs, and stumbled backward sucking air. As soon as his breath returned, he reached down for a fist-sized chunk of stone and lobbed it at the mountain of impassable debris. He repeated this futile action twice more before falling to his knees and screaming until his throat hurt. Then he fell forward onto all fours and heaved, shoulders rising and falling. He squeezed his eyes shut, and the heat of fresh tears stung his eyelids as they leaked down his cheeks.

His sister was surely dead, for no one could've survived being buried by so much stone. And even if by some miracle they had, there was absolutely no way for anyone to find or extract them. First Ez, then Jek, and now Mae. They were all gone. Mulladin was alone.

It occurred to him that the fear of being abandoned had carried over from his old life as a simpleton with its potency undiminished by the mental maturing. He remembered the panic he'd experience whenever he was away from Maely too long. He remembered not being able to believe Ez or Jek when they assured him Maely was coming back. He remembered the sweeping relief upon seeing her again. She'd always scolded him for "being a baby" but it'd always been with a smile. Now she really wasn't coming back.

He didn't know how long he stayed like that, but the sun had noticeably lowered in the distance when he rose again. He walked away from the ruined palace, and the surreal darkness caused by the cloud cover, and wandered aimlessly. The sun continued to set in the west, and by the time dusk was upon the city, Mulladin found himself at the docks. Not many ships remained, and the ones that did were full of looters hastily loading their booty.

He recognized some of those thieves as members of the Rikujo; enforcers who had come to Aiested with Ez to rescue Jek. He was about to change directions before they noticed him staring, but something drew his attention.

One of the black-clad figures stood on the deck of a ship at the top of a gangplank. She was directing others who were carrying bulging sacks that Mulladin was sure weren't full of grain. The Rikujo enforcer was alluring in her tight, black leathers, and her olive-toned face framed by twin black ringlets was exotic. But what really caught Mulladin's eye was something she wore on her curvaceous hip–a sword. It wasn't sheathed, but slid through the inside of her leather belt. The weapon had a tapered blade and a large, round amethyst set in the center of the cross guard–Jek's sword talis. Mulladin had only seen it once, when Jek was slaughtering king's guards with it. But the blade was of such magnificent craftsmanship that Mulladin would recognize it until his dying day.

"Hey!" Mulladin shouted. He raised his arm and pointed with the finger upon which he wore his lightning ring.

Nothing happened.

It was drained. He knew that, but in the heat of his rage he'd momentarily forgotten that vitally important fact. The group of enforcers froze, and their leader actually jumped. They turned as one to stare at

Mulladin. Then they laughed. Their leader's black ponytail swung back and forth as she shook her head and returned to directing the labor of the others.

Mulladin knew that the sensible thing would've been to slink away and then see if he could somehow stowaway on the ship, or follow it in a smaller boat, but he was too angry. Not so much because these Rikujo traitors had abandoned Ez and Jek, not even because they'd been looting the city or because they stole the sword. Mulladin was angry at them for laughing at him. That was another thing that carried over from his being dim. Frustration, hurt, and anger at being called names by the other children, and many of the adults in his village. He'd never been able to properly express those emotions—until now.

Mulladin picked up a loose wooden plank he found lying against an empty barrel. It was broken and splintered at one end. Mulladin smiled a wicked smile, gripped the good end in both of his hands, raised it high over his head, and exploded into a run toward the group of Rikujo thugs. They'd barely turned around when he swung the plank down on the head of the closest enforcer. The man dropped without even so much as a groan. He followed up the attack with a horizontal swing, catching the jagged edges of splintered wood on the face of another enforcer and tearing open his cheek. That man cried out as he spun and fell off the dock, a splash following a beat later.

The Rikujo woman was barking orders and shouting at him now. The other thugs dropped their bags of loot, drew various melee weapons, and dashed down the gangplank. Mulladin dropped the plank, and leaned down to snatch a knife from the belt sheath of his first victim. Then he charged his oncoming assailants. He caught the group of Rikujo thugs while they were rushing down the gangplank single file and crashed into the first, shoving the man over the side. He fell, striking his head on the dock just before he plunged into the sea. Mulladin held the knife upside down so that he could swipe at his target with the blade as though he were swinging punches. He laid open the throat of the next thug, dropping the man to his knees just as Mulladin began his back swing. The next man was ready for him, however, and brought a sword breaker up just in time to catch the swing. That threw Mulladin off balance, and he nearly fell from the gangplank, but his rage seemed to give him the power to defy even gravity itself.

He threw himself forward before he could fall, grabbing the man's wrist and forced the hand with the sword breaker down. This did two things: it let Mulladin regain his footing, and it gave him the chance to stab the man in the right side of his neck. Blood sprayed Mulladin as he wrenched the knife free, and then shoved the gurgling thug off the gangplank. The way was clear now, and he locked eyes with the Rikujo woman as he stepped over the only enforcer still lying on the inclined bridging the dock and the ship.

She was no longer smiling. Her eyes were hard, and she cautiously backed away. Her lithe build lent her a grace that Mulladin couldn't help but appreciate. It reminded him of a cat. He stepped up onto the deck of the ship, knife now held point up. The woman drew Jek's sword, though she held it awkwardly like it weighed more than she expected. Mulladin thought that odd. When Jek had wielded it, he swung it as though it weighed next to nothing. Being a talis, it would've been drained like his lightning ring. Did that mean the sword's magic made it lighter?

"That belongs to my friend," Mulladin growled.

"You were with Argentus," the woman said with the faintest hint of a Tolean accent. "You were the man playing a simpleton. That was very clever."

"How's that?" Mulladin took a careful step toward her.

"It made the others think you were not a threat, and so we ignored you." She smiled. "The stratagem made it possible for you to interfere in the duel and save Argentus from Trous."

Mulladin flashed a toothy grin. Let her think what she would, especially if it made him look smarter than he was. "That face of yours is too pretty to cut up. So how's about you give me my friend's sword, and I'll let you swim away from here?"

"How's about," she mimicked his speech, "you try and take it from me?"

Mulladin charged. The Rikujo woman raised the sword, but the weight of it made her motion too slow. He crashed into her, and the momentum carried the both of them down to the deck of the ship. The sword clanged to the ground less than a meter off to Mulladin's right. He rolled off the woman and scrambled toward the sword. Her weight pressed down on his back. She hooked an arm around his throat, pulling him backward as she cut off his airflow. Mulladin thought of his stolen knife, but only realized then that he no longer had it. He hoped she didn't either.

"That sword is mine by right," the woman hissed into his ear.

He opened his mouth to make a sardonic reply, but only choking sounds came out. As his head began to swim, he summoned his rage and threw himself backward. The woman cried out as something–he hoped her head–struck the deck with a deep thud. The strangulation abruptly stopped, and Mulladin sucked air as desperately as he knew how. He rolled to the side, and rose onto his hands and knees and crawled toward the sword. He'd just gotten one hand around its handle when the wind rushed out of his lungs.

The woman had leapt on him again, this time coming down on his back with her full weight. Had she jumped? Sucking air for the second time in under a minute, Mulladin held tight to the sword. The woman's small, tan hand gripped the wired handle just above his as she commenced striking him in the back of the head with her free hand. Stars exploded across Mulladin's vision.

"Let go, you big dumb ox!" The woman interwove the words so they were audible in between blows.

A sharp crack of thunder made them both freeze and look back at the broken well at the center of the capital city. A second clap of thunder sounded, this one even louder and deeper. All fell deadly quiet, and then a hissing sound enveloped them. It reminded Mulladin of rushing air, although he didn't feel the slightest breeze. Just then the tiny emeralds peppering the blade of Jek's sword lit up, casting a green glow on both he and the Rikujo woman. They shared a look, and then by unspoken consent, resumed struggling for possession of the blade.

Their struggle was short-lived, however, as snapping wood made them pause a second time. All around them the deck of the ship was turning pale; as though the varnished wood had dried beneath the sun for a thousand days. Mulladin's blood chilled when he caught sight of one of the enforcers he'd left sprawled on the dock. The man's flesh was gone, leaving behind only a pile of bleached bones held together by his black leathers.

He looked back at the dark-haired woman. Her tan face had paled, and she was also looking about with wide eyes. Still, they both held to the handle of Jek's sword, the glow of the emerald shards shining brighter. Dust rose from the deck of the ship. No, not dust. The wood was wearing away before his very eyes, decaying and breaking down.

The entire ship groaned and creaked. Then, with a dozen overlapping snapping sounds, the hull broke apart and the deck split. They both held onto the sword, even as they fell through the ship toward the dark water. Mullidan gulped down a mouth of air just before he submerged. The cold, salty ocean tried to steal away his air, but he held his mouth shut tight. He opened his eyes and found the green light of the sword's emerald shards illuminating the face of his enemy.

Incredibly, they both held onto the sword. The Rikujo woman met his eyes and their furious struggle resumed. Mulladin sank and his lungs started to burn, but something inside him told him not to let go of Jek's sword, and so he gripped the handle of the sword even tighter. He kicked frantically, trying to propel himself toward the surface, but the weight of the sword and his struggle with the Rikujo woman continued to pull him down.

The emeralds on Jek's sword faded, and everything went dark. Instinctually, Mulladin kicked out with his right leg, connecting with the woman, probably in her stomach he thought. A gurgled grunt validated his guess. Mulladin wrenched the sword out of her grasp and furiously swam up. He broke the surface at the same time he inhaled and got a breath that was as much water as it was air. He coughed, sputtered, slipped beneath the waves a couple more times before his feet touched ground. How had he gotten to the surface so quickly? He must've been at least twenty feet under water when he broke free of the Rikujo woman.

His uncontrollable fit of coughing and retching continued as he slogged out of the ocean. He steadied himself against one of the wooden pylons and cut himself on a jutting piece of splintered wood. The pain made him inhale sharply, which led to another round of coughing. After a seeming eternity, Mulladin was breathing normally again, albeit very quickly. He collapsed to the ground, and that was when he noticed where he was. He sat directly beneath the remnants of the dock where the Rikujo ship had been moored.

He looked down at the ground and found black rock littered with fish skeletons and then back up at the ruined dock. Hadn't the water risen much higher than this? He could've sworn it was only five feet below him when he ran onto the boardwalk and attacked that first Rikujo enforcer. But no, the water level had clearly diminished by at least ten feet. Had that been how he'd reached the surface so quickly? Perhaps it had something to do with that strange wind that tore the deck of the ship apart. He thought of the skeleton on the dock that was, just a few moments ago, a fleshy corpse. Why hadn't Mulladin withered like the rest of his surroundings?

Mulladin glanced again at Jek's sword. The emeralds peppering the blade remained dark. Had the sword protected him somehow? Not just him, he realized, but that Rikujo wench, too. He looked about, but didn't see any sign of her. Of course, it was dark enough now that she might've been ten feet into the lapping water, and he wouldn't know it. Well, he wasn't going to wait around to find out. He had to find Jek and bring the sword back to him. Perhaps that would help heal him? Admittedly, he didn't know. But he was sure of one thing. He needed to get out of Aiested in case that withering wind came again. He slid the sword into his belt and climbed the rocky shelf back up to the docks.

CHAPTER 68

Another deafening clap of thunder split the sky and thrummed through Maely's chest. The sheer ferocity of it made her want to fall to the ground and cover her head. She forced herself to look back at Aiested, still visible even though she and Gryyth had left the refugee camp that morning. How many miles had they gone? Maely couldn't be sure. The Ursaj's severe burns made walking with him a slow thing. Flashes of green lightning exploded from within the black cloud cover, increasing in frequency until it looked like the broken Apeira well was surrounded in green fire.

Gryyth groaned in pain. Maely shot a look at him, worried that the bear-man was succumbing to his burns, but the Ursaj's blue eyes bespoke more than physical pain.

"Gryyth?" Maely stopped and let the massive beast put his arm around her for support.

It was a laughable thing to do, for Maely weighed a fraction of what the creature weighed, and she was unable to stop Gryyth from slumping to the ground.

"What's wrong?" Maely asked, her anxiety quickly rising toward panic. What would she do if Gryyth passed out? She damn well couldn't carry the bear, and she had no idea where he was taking her.

"The Mother," Gryyth growled.

Maely was about to ask him what he meant when the forest all about them started moving. She looked up to find the tall pines swaying in a breeze that wasn't there, and they were withering. Not in the process of dying, but withering right before her eyes. Pine needles that had just moments before been dark green were changing color, turning an orange-brown and falling off branches in sheets, deluging the ground in sharp and brittle drops of needle rain. The branches of the trees creaked, and some began to snap off and crash to the forest floor.

Now Maely was panicking.

"Come on," she said to Gryyth as she tugged on his right paw. "Get up!"

Gryyth looked up at her in surprise, as though seeing her for the first time. He nodded, and groaned as he stood. Maely gave up her efforts to be gentle and towed Gryyth into a run. He panted heavily, groaning from the pain of his burns. A backward glance heightened her panic. The decay was following them; trees, grass, and bushes dying as though an invisible predator moved up the slope after them. Instinct told Maely that if this thing overtook her, she too would also wither away. So she ran faster, pulling Gryyth with all of her might. They scrambled up a hill using a game trail and had just about crested the top when Gryyth fell to the ground.

"Dammit!" Maely tugged frantically on the Ursaj's furry arm.

The wave of decay flowed toward them, naked branches snapping, and even entire trees breaking from their stumps and falling over. Grass and shrubbery died before her eyes, and even the ground changed from healthy brown dirt to black sand. A bird that took to the air too late froze and fell from flight, its tiny body a featherless husk when it crashed.

"Get up!"

Gryyth tried, but shuddered and fell back to the ground.

Maely thumbed the underside of her mother's ring, and opened her mouth to command Gryyth to rise, but remembered the compulsion talis had no charge. The wave of death ran up the hill, eager to overtake them.

"Gryyth!" Maely screamed.

It was close now, so close Maely could see a warping to the air where the wave touched the ground. It was translucent green, faint and nearly invisible in the light, but shown whenever it flowed over a shaded spot of the forest floor. Maely yanked so hard on Gryyth's arm that he bellowed.

The sound was so sudden and loud that she nearly dropped his hand and ran.

The wave of energy neared the top of the hill, now, and Maely squeezed her eyes shut preparing for death. *I'm sorry for leaving you, Mull.*

She waited, heart pounding loudly in her chest, but death didn't come. She opened her eyes, expecting to be surrounded by translucent green wind, but she wasn't. The dirt beneath her knees remained soft, damp, and brown. She looked down the hill and found the warping air pulling back. It had risen almost to the top of the hill, as was evidenced by the black sand that stopped only a meter away from where they'd fallen. But the decay was pulling back now, like the retreating tide of the ocean.

"Praise the goddess," Maely whispered the prayer as the pounding in her chest began to slow. "What the hell was that?"

When she received no response, she looked at Gryyth. The Ursaj's eyes were shut, and his breathing came in ragged gasps. Maely reached out and felt the top of his muzzle, just behind his black nose. It was hot. She made a closer examination of a patch of charred flesh. Angry red skin surrounded the black, and yellow pus oozed from jagged cracks. As Raelen predicted, Gryyth's burns had become infected, and he had developed a fever.

Tears spilled down Maely's cheeks and she rested her forehead against the Ursaj's fury shoulder. His fur was softer than she'd realized which was comforting. He was going to die, and she was lost in the wild without any supplies. Oh, they'd gathered what they could from the refugees, there had even been an apothecary who'd had some poppy oil to help dull Gryyth's pain, but none of it was enough to—the refugees!

Maely lifted her head and stared back through the forest, through skeletal trees rooted in charcoal-black sand. She could see the husk of some mid-sized animal, but it was too emaciated to recognize its species. A sick feeling rose in her stomach as she realized the refugees were back behind all that dead forest; surely all dead themselves. How many people had that been? Maely heard one of Raelen's soldiers' claim it was in the thousands. And what of Raelen? Had the prince made it far away enough from Aiested to escape whatever this was? She choked back vomit.

Rustling from ahead caught Maely's attention and she bit off a scream as something large and brown approached her. It ran on all fours, but stood as it neared them. It was a bear–no bears didn't wear breechcloths and shoulder satchels. The creature was another Ursaj. It closed to six paces before stopping, big brown eyes staring at Gryyth before turning its large head to look at Maely.

"Human," it growled. It took a wary step forward, but froze and looked past her. It said something in a language that sounded like little more than blowing and teeth clacking.

For a long time, it just stared into the dead forest. Finally, Maely's impatience won out against her fear, and she shouted, "He's hurt!"

The brown Ursaj huffed, and looked down at Maely, and then at Gryyth. It rumbled something unintelligible and then stooped down to examine the white bear-man.

"Can you help him?" Maely asked, and she had to choke off a sob.

The Ursaj lifted its head and met her eyes. Maely did as best she could to return the stare, but could feel herself trembling. Finally, the brown Ursaj gave a sharp nod, gently rolled Gryyth onto his back, and then proceeded to lift him from the ground. To Maely's astonishment, the brown bear-man appeared to have little trouble carrying Gryyth, though he wasn't much larger than him.

The brown Ursaj carried Gryyth back in the direction it had come, which–to Maely's relief–was the opposite direction of Aiested and the dead forest. She took a step to follow and then froze. What was she supposed to do? What if the Ursaj saw her following as unwelcome or offensive? Would it kill her? She looked behind her at the dead trees. What choice did she have? Would the wave of death return? If so, how long before it came back, and would it stop next time?

The brown Ursaj made a kind of sound that was a mix of a moan and a bark. Maely looked back and found it waiting for her. Relieved, she jogged toward him, and the brown Ursaj resumed walking.

They traveled until it was dark, Maely losing all sense of direction as she could no longer see Aiested's broken well through the dark canopy. She made certain to stay close to the brown bear-man so as to not get lost. She even attempted to talk to it, though all her questions were met with short grunts or loud huffs. These things were as difficult to understand as Karak. Well, that wasn't completely true. Karak could speak more human words than the brown Ursaj. In fact, all this creature could say was "human." After her fifth attempt at communication, Maely gave up.

It was cold this far into the north forest, and Maely soon found herself shivering uncontrollably, and her breath misted out in front of her. She'd been cold on her journey from Imaris to Aiested, but that seemed a trifling chill compared to this freezing death. Just when she began to lose feeling in her feet, she caught sight of a soft glow through the trees ahead. She hugged herself, rubbing her shoulders as they drew close to it. The light was pouring out of a large cave, its mouth easily the size of a house.

Her Ursaj guide made another bark-moan and nodded toward the cave, and then entered. Maely was hesitant to follow, but quickly decided that the cold was more likely to kill her at this point than bear teeth or claws, and so hurried inside. What she found surprised her. It wasn't the barren rock cavern she'd been anticipating. No, the inside of the cave was every bit as comfortable as any cottage she'd been in. Deer pelts blanketed the floor making a sort of mismatched carpet, glowing paper lanterns hung from wood trusses that bridged the top of the cave, and artfully rendered glyphs were painted on the rock walls.

A cauldron hung from a tripod over a fire pit near the center of the room, the smoke drifting up and out of the cavern through a hole in the ceiling that didn't look to be natural, as though it were carved out of the rock for the very purpose of ventilation. If she didn't know better, this cave could've been the winter shelter of a fur trapper.

"What is a human girl doing alone in my forest with an injured Ursaj warrior?" The voice echoed from the dark that was the back of the cave, and Maely bit off a scream at the sudden breach of quiet.

A small black bear walked into the light. It had streaks of gray in its fur, and was wearing a tunic made of animal hide. Its eyes were milky white, and it walked with one hand feeling along the cave wall. Was it blind? How then did it know what was happening? Apparently, Maely's silence begged the question and the black Ursaj tapped its nose with one sharp claw.

"I caught the scent as soon as you stepped into my den." This Ursaj was much more articulate than even Gryyth, and its higher pitched voice marked it as female.

"I-I..." Maely stammered.

The brown Ursaj grunted and said something in a guttural language to which the black she-bear responded by pointing at a large fur sprawled out near the fire pit. The brown bear-man laid Gryyth gently down on his back.

The she-bear sniffed the air. "Burns."

"He has a fever," Maely said.

The she-bear nodded as she felt her way along the cave. The brown Ursaj quickly moved to her side and she grabbed his arm as he led her over to Gryyth. She bent over and sniffed at Gryyth's blackened chest. Maely started as the she-bear snapped her head up and fixed her milky white eyes on her.

For someone who's blind, she sure does act like she can see me.

"These burns reek of sorcery," the she-bear growled. "From one of your foul talises, no doubt. What did you do to him?"

Maely's icy fear melted as her temper rose. "Me?"

"Your people," the she-bear said as she returned her attention to Gryyth's burns.

Maely balled her fist. "We didn't do this to him."

The she-bear scoffed. "An accident then? Fools can't even handle your own evil tools."

"He was burned fighting an Allosian!" Maely shouted.

The she-bear stared at Maely with sightless eyes for a long moment before finally asking, "What's your name, girl?"

"Maely!" she answered hotly. It made her sound childish and she inwardly cringed.

"And his name?"

"Gryyth."

The she-bear nodded. "Maely is a pretty name. I am Sharor and this is my cub's cub, Kerr."

Was she talking down to her? Maely almost preferred the she-bear's hostility to its patronization and was about to say so when Sharor began speaking to Kerr in their odd language of grunts and guttural moans. Kerr quickly moved to a shelf on the wall, and collected a pestle and mortar made of stone, two small bags, and a clay jar. He laid them all on the ground before Sharor, who sniffed at each. Then she huffed, and Kerr returned to the shelf one more time for a second, smaller clay jar.

Sharor eased herself to the floor beside Gryyth, and began adding measured amounts of the contents of the bags and jars to her stone bowl. She went to work mixing them and soon had a gray paste that she applied to Gryyth's burns. Contrary to what Maely expected, the paste actually smelled quite sweet, almost enticingly so. The burns were so extensive that Sharor had to stop and mix more of the paste halfway through her ministrations. Through it all Gryyth didn't so much as groan. That worried Maely.

After Gryyth's burns were covered in the gray paste, Sharor had Kerr fetch more clay jars from her shelf, what looked to be a wine skin, and an empty cup. The black she-bear mixed several liquids into the cup–but nothing from the wine skin Maely noted–and then forced the contents of it down Gryyth's throat. Then Sharor let out a long breath, and turned to look at Maely.

"I have done what I can for him. If he lives out the night, then he should make a full recovery."

Confused, Maely asked, "What's the wine skin for?"

Sharor's sharp teeth showed in a very disquieting bear-grin, and she took a long pull from the wine skin. She wiped her mouth with the back of her paw and said, "I gained a taste for Aiestali sweet wine when I was younger. Always try to keep a skin or two of it on hand for stressful days." She proffered the wine skin to Maely.

Maely laughed, bent down to accept the skin, and took a deep pull. It tasted good, like liquid candy but with the calming effect of alcohol. Not that she'd drank much in her young life–Ez hadn't believed in imbibing what he called strong drinks–usually only at Harvest Festival.

Maely handed the wine skin back to Sharor who took another long pull before stopping it. Kerr made a noise that sounded like a petulant child's whine.

"No!" Sharor snapped. "Last time you drank the whole damned thing, and then didn't wake up for weeks."

Kerr growled something.

"Hibernating my furry ass! I've seen human cubs who can hold their liquor better than you."

Maely couldn't help but laugh at the exchange, and Sharor shot her a quick smile.

"How come you can speak Aiestali so well, or know of sweet wine?" Maely asked.

Sharor's smile faded and she sighed. Coming from a bear, it was a deep, guttural thing that sounded almost like a growl. "I was captured by an Aiestali slaver when I was scarcely more than a cub and lived almost four decades as a servant to a master apothecary."

Maely looked at the pestle and mortar and the clay jars of ingredients. "So these aren't mystical Ursaj healing potions?"

Sharor bellowed a laugh. "Sheera root, aloe, poppy extract, and Darva powder."

Maely was a little disappointed. "And the draft you gave Gryyth?"

"Gawl herb tea to break his fever."

"Oh. So you learned herb craft from your master?"

"Yes."

"How did you get back here? How did you escape him?"

Sharor bowed her head. "My master often tested experimental concoctions on me to ensure their safety. One blinded me. After that, I wasn't much use to him, and so he set me free. I wandered helpless in these woods until I was nearly starved to death. That's when Kerr's grandfather, Garren, found me. He saved my life, nursed me back to health, and gave me five strong cubs before he died."

"I'm sorry," Maely was surprised that she meant it.

Sharor waved dismissively with one paw, while reaching for the wine skin with the other. "It was years ago."

She unstopped it again and took another long pull. When she finished, she was a little out of breath. "Besides, you sound too young to bear the sins of your people."

That irritated Maely. "I'm fifteen," she snapped, and then added sheepishly, "almost."

Sharor chuckled. "You have spunk, child. I like that. Can you tell me what happened to Gryyth? And how you came to be alone with him in these woods?"

That question chased away Maely's rising mirth and she sank to her knees. She didn't answer Sharor, but instead stared deeply into the fire pit at the center of the cave. Half a dozen white logs crackled and snapped as the flames devoured them. She let the dancing fire hypnotize her. It was almost as if she could see her entire journey appear before her in the fire; from Genra to Rasha, to the rock lands, the chaos in Imaris, and finally the total destruction of Aiested.

"You said an Allosian did this?" Sharor gently prodded.

Maely nodded, gaze still fixed on the fire. "His name is Jenoc. He's trying to destroy my people."

"Your tribe?"

Maely shook her head. "Humans. All of us."

"And you are sure it was a real Allosian? Not just some human with powerful talises?"

Maely looked up from the fire. She ground her teeth in irritation. She hated it when people didn't take her seriously.

"Pale skin, jewel-colored hair, and godlike powers? Yeah, I'm pretty sure." She immediately regretted using so much sarcasm and continued in a more amicable tone, "I fought him alongside his sister, Kairah. She was trying to stop him from starting a new talis war."

"And Gryyth fought with you?"

Maely nodded, suddenly feeling drained. "He's Prince Raelen Taris's bodyguard. The prince was also trying to stop Jenoc. He rode off to try and stop his army from attacking Haeshala and asked me to find Gryyth some help."

A lull in the conversation prevailed until broken by Kerr's guttural moaning. Even though Maely couldn't understand what the Ursaj was saying, the tone in his voice bespoke fear. Sharor made some quick replies in their language before again fixing her milky white eyes on Maely.

"Kerr says he saw something just before he found you. I am not quite sure I understand what he means. Something about the forest dying?"

Maely nodded, suddenly feeling sick. All those refugees she'd escaped Aiested with had died along with the forest, she was more and more certain of it.

"A green, see-through wave of magic came from the direction of the city. Everything it touched instantly withered and died. We barely outran it before it pulled back. I think it came from Aiested's broken..." Maely trailed off when she caught sight of Sharor's countenance. The she-bear's white eyes were wide, and her muzzle hung open. "What's wrong?"

Sharor cocked her head as if listening for something.

"What is it?"

Sharor raised a paw indicating she wanted Maely to stop talking. That nettled Maely and she was about to snap at the Ursaj when she heard a voice, not with her ears but inside her head. It reminded her of when Jenoc had brutally invaded her mind and sifted through her memories. *Was this what Jekaran experienced when the sword talked to him?*

The voice was very faint like an echoing whisper, and Maely had to concentrate to hear it. Even then she couldn't make out what it was saying. Then, as fast as it had come, the voice had gone.

"What was that?" she asked.

Sharor turned back to Maely. "The Mother calls."

CHAPTER 69

Mulladin decided that circumventing Aiested by a mile would be safer than cutting through the ruins of the city. Perhaps he was being paranoid, but he thought it better to stay as far away as he could from the broken Apeira well. He was becoming more and more certain that it was the source of the withering wind that had sucked the meat off the bones of corpses and destroyed the Rikujo's stolen ship.

It was night now, and though he was a mile south of the city, the unnatural cloud cover blocked out the moon making it nearly impossible to see. He ought to find a place to rest and sleep, but he doubted he could sleep. He was also haunted by the notion that the Rikujo wench he'd fought off might still be alive and following him. He had nothing to base this on, but when he tried to tell himself he was being foolish, instinct wouldn't let him completely snuff out the spark of his anxiety.

He looked at Jek's sword, now carried in his right hand. Why had it glowed when that withering wind assailed them? Why hadn't he and the Rikujo woman decayed like everything else? Did it have something to do with the sword? They were both holding onto it when the wind came. Did it protect them? How could it? The talis was drained of an Apeiron charge and had no magic.

A few times rustling in the bushes on the side of the road, or some other nightly noise startled him, but otherwise his trek through the night was uneventful. When dawn came, Mulladin's fatigue asserted itself, and he decided to find a safe place to rest. Another few miles of walking brought him into contact with a small band of Aiested refugees.

They were a motley assemblage of all classes, peasants, merchants, and even some nobleman, many of whom were still in their night clothes. It was almost comical to see lords and ladies in sleeping shirts and gowns acting haughtily and ordering about the others, or at least attempting to. The peasants outnumbered them, and they paid the aristocracy as little deference as they could get away with. The four hundred or so refugees mostly congregated by class, but the children appeared to have less inhibitions about mixing castes and ran between camps laughing and chasing each other.

It made Mulladin smile, and a sense of his former simplemindedness faintly brushed a cord of a memory.

He slid the sword back into his belt before approaching a group of men whom he guessed to be merchants as they were dressed better than the majority of the refugees, but not quite so fine as to be noblemen. He hoped they could spare him a bit of bread. They fell silent as he approached, all keeping wary eyes on him and the sword hung at his belt.

"You are on the road from Aiested?" Mulladin asked.

One of the merchants gave him a curt nod.

"As am I," Mulladin said. He stopped five paces away from the group.

"That a weapon talis?" a fat merchant asked.

Mulladin groaned within himself. *I should have wrapped the cross guard to cover the well shard.* "Yes, but completely drained, I assure you."

"You look too young to be one of the king's generals," a gray-haired woman said.

"I'm not," Mulladin replied.

"Then how'd ya get—"

"What is going on here?"

Mulladin glanced to his left to see a tall man with long black hair approaching. He was dressed in dark robes that looked to be covered with dried blood, but there was no sign of injury on his pale face.

The merchants all hastily bobbed bows.

"My lord Loeadon," the fat merchant stammered. "This traveler has a weapon talis."

Loeadon's gaze fell to the sword hanging at Mulladin's hip and his face immediately changed. "Arrest him!"

Mulladin turned to run, but was grabbed from behind by his collar. He gagged as the front of his shirt pulled tight against his throat. He pulled free with a rip and made to run, but something hit him in the back of the head. Mulladin stumbled forward, vision blurring. He crashed to his knees, and instinctively felt at the back of his head. It was warm and wet. He examined his fingers and found the tips covered in blood. Someone had hit him in the back of the head. *With what?* He didn't see the merchants carrying any weapons. As if in answer to his question, a missile flew past his right ear, missing him only by a few inches. It crashed to the ground, and Mulladin realized it was a large rock. They were throwing rocks at him!

He made to stand, but was tackled from behind. He found himself face down in the dirt, someone vigorously pressing on the back of his head where he'd been hit by the rock. He put his palms flat on the ground and roared as he launched himself backward. The man on his back yelped as he was thrown clear.

Mulladin staggered to his feet and spun, hand reaching for Jek's sword. Light flashed across his vision as something hit him square in the face. Another rock. Tears blinded him, and warm blood spilled out of his nose. Mulladin bellowed and charged forward, unable to see but confident he'd have no trouble finding a target. He hoped it would be the man called Loeadon. He crashed into someone, and the man screamed as they both were carried to the ground. Still tear-blind, Mulladin began pounding on his victim with his fists. He felt the satisfying crunch of cartilage that signaled he'd broken the man's nose.

Payback in kind. He grinned.

Something whipped through the air, then there was pain in his head, stars across Mulladin's vision, and finally, all went dark.

He woke to find himself leaning sideways against a tree, hands bound behind him. He pulled his legs back to get them under him, but found them bound as well. His frustrated growl drew the attention of the man called Loeadon, who was standing five paces off to Mulladin's right. The tall man with the long black hair turned, revealing that he held

Jekaran's sword – point skyward, examining the blade. He lowered it and walked over to Mulladin.

"Where did you get this?" he demanded.

"Your mother gave it to me as a present for bedding her."

Loeadon smirked. "That juvenile barb wounds me deeply."

The sarcasm in the man's voice enraged Mulladin. "Go to hell!"

"Probably," Loeadon said, "but not yet. Now, I am only going to ask you one more time. Where did you get this?"

"And if I don't tell you?"

"Then I have no further use for you." Loeadon raised the sword again, testing its weight in his hand. "I'm not a swordsman by any stretch of the imagination. So, I apologize in advance if my killing stroke isn't clean or," he laughed, "immediately effective."

Fear replaced Mulladin's rage and he strained against his bonds, but it was no good. Strong as he was, they were expertly tied. That's when he spotted a lone soldier amidst the watching crowd of refugees. The man was short and thin, his breastplate looking too big for him. He approached them, the crowd parting to let him through.

Loeadon raised the sword, his hesitation and expectant stare giving Mulladin one last chance to confess. He was about to do just that when shouting caught his attention. Loeadon looked over his shoulder, sword arm lowering a few inches. If Mulladin's legs hadn't been bound, he could've kicked or tripped the man. More shouting ended those thoughts, and Mulladin let himself fall sideways onto the ground to see past Loeadon. Smoke rose from behind the crowd, followed by flames licking skyward. Fire. Something was on fire. The mass of spectators scrambled, the men of the group running toward the flames, while the women shepherded the children away.

"Inbred peasants," Loeadon muttered. "Can't even handle fire safely."

He turned back to face Mulladin. "What would they do without one of their betters to watch over them?"

Loeadon chuckled. "And I will. The king is dead, and likely the prince too, along with the chief general. With this talis, I will rule the–"

The soldier in the too-big chest plate grabbed Loeadon's sword arm. In one expert motion, he bent it backward so far that Mulladin heard the cracking of bone. Loeadon cried out, dropped the sword, and fell to his knees. His face had turned pale, and he made to cradle his broken arm, but screamed upon touching it. The soldier scooped up Jekaran's sword and struck Loeadon in the face with its pommel. The tall, long-haired man dropped hard to the ground, his broken arm flopping next to him at an unnatural angle.

Mulladin looked up at the soldier. The man removed his helmet to reveal a very feminine face.

"You!"

The Rikujo wench smiled down at him. "I win."

She replaced the helmet and turned to hurry away.

"Wait!" Mulladin shouted, but the woman ignored him. He thought about calling out to the crowd, telling them that she had assaulted and robbed Loeadon, but that was stupid. This was his chance to get away.

He rolled to his knees. Then, moving like an inch worm, he slowly crawled away from the camp, in the direction the Rikujo wench had fled. She had disappeared into the woods, something Mulladin himself needed to do before someone spotted him. The trouble was, not only did he move like a worm, but he also moved at a worm's pace. No, not a worm, a slug.

The fire—set as a distraction by that Rikujo woman, he was sure of it—would soon be defeated. Mulladin elected to deviate from his pursuit and crawl into thick underbrush a dozen feet to his left. This would conceal him nicely while he figured out how to get free of his bonds. The bushes were effectively conciliatory, too effective as it turned out. For he didn't see the sharp decline in the ground until he was already rolling down it.

Thorns, and rocks cut his face and hands as he tumbled down the hill, and he hit his head on several embedded rocks which made him woozy. Finally, his side struck something that arrested his wild rolling. It was a large rock with sharp edges that tore his clothes and bit into his skin. Even thought it'd hurt, Mulladin was thankful for the rock. It had both stopped him and would give him something to saw off his bonds. Mulladin went to work cutting his bonds. It took forever to get his hands free, but once he did, he untied his legs.

He stood, looking back up the hill. The smoke from the fire was gone, and he couldn't see the camp. After ascertaining his location, and the direction in which his quarry had escaped, Mulladin broke into a run. He had to get Jek's sword back–again.

CHAPTER 70

Jenoc blinked open his one good eye. It was dark and he lay face down on cold stone. He pressed his palms against the ground and pushed himself up. By reflex, he attempted a spell-casting that would light up the room but immediately froze. He had no Apeiron. His core was completely devoid of the warm energy that should've swirled within. Jenoc's breathing quickened, and he reached for the nearest Apeira well. He could sense it, less than a mile away; could feel the currents of energy flowing all about him, but he couldn't draw the Apeiron. It radiated into him.

Panicked, Jenoc stood and looked about in the dark. His eye had adjusted so he could make out shapes, but little more.

"Where am I?!" he shouted at the ceiling.

He winced as he expected the noise to aggravate his constant migraine, but no spike of pain assailed him. In fact, the ever-throbbing pulsing was gone. What did that mean?

Sounds from above drew Jenoc's attention. Were those footsteps? Scraping followed, and then light blinded him. Jenoc turned away from the ceiling, and was grabbed by the arms before he could say anything. Two men lifted him out of his cell, and he was able to abide the light enough to see a flat piece of square metal being slid back into place over a dark opening.

A booted foot flashed before Jenoc's eye followed by a flash of light and sharp pain. He rolled onto his side. He sputtered and tried to speak, but the blood running over his lip and down the back of his mouth choked him.

"Get up," someone snarled. "The only thing stopping us from tearing your guts out is our orders."

"Prince Isara wants to do it himself," a second voice added.

Rough hands lifted Jenoc from the ground and shoved him forward into a walk. His eye had finally adjusted to the light, dim though it was, and he could see he was inside a corridor made of square black stone bricks. He was walking a paved path lined on both sides by floor cells like the one he'd been pulled from. He was in a dungeon. But where? Prince Isara, the guard had mentioned. Then this was likely the castle dungeons in Isadara. It all come back to Jenoc: the plague box, the guard he'd forced to witness his crime, and then the pain that had felled him and robbed him of consciousness.

They continued to call Jenoc every filthy name he'd ever heard in the human's tongue as they marched him up several flights of stone stairs, finding excuses along the way to shove or trip him. He instinctively tried to spell-cast each time he was assaulted, and each time nothing happened. It was maddening. He could feel the Apeiron coursing all around him, but he couldn't take it in. What'd happened to him? The constant headache was gone, but it seemed to have taken his spell-casting ability with it. This was no doubt the result of his tampering with Moriora.

They were in the upper halls of the castle now, crowds of soldiers and servants stopping to stare at him as he was paraded past them. The guards didn't stop a maid with red-rimmed eyes from blocking them so she could spit in Jenoc's face. In fact, that act only drew cheers from the watching crowd of soldiers and servants. The woman was pulled aside by one of her fellow servants, and Jenoc's forced march resumed.

They passed a large mirror with an ornate golden frame hanging on the black stone wall, and Jenoc froze at seeing his reflection. The man staring back at him was a stranger. His throat constricted and his chest tightened as he studied his features. Gone was his ice-blue, jewel-like hair, replaced with strands of blond. His skin was no longer pale white, but a peach color, and the amethyst iris of his remaining eye was green like those of the people around him. He was no longer an Allosian.

Jenoc looked like a human.

He barely registered the sharp blow that goaded him back into walking, and the rest of the trip to the throne room was surreal. This was a nightmare. What had happened to him? Was this the ironic joke of some cruel god? To turn him into the very thing he hated? The very thing he wanted to destroy? That was too much, and Jenoc collapsed to the shiny black floor. The guards had to carry him the rest of the way into the throne room where they unceremoniously dumped him on the floor. His vision swam as the back of his skull struck the stone floor. That was followed by a quick kick to the ribs forced him onto his side.

"So, this is the piece of shyte Taris sent to kill our little ones?" A baritone voice shouted.

Jenoc managed to look up and found a heavily muscled man in a red-lacquered breastplate staring down at him. As with all Haeshalan royalty, the man had emerald-green eyes that oddly contrasted with his ebony skin and long, braided beard.

"Prince Isara," Jenoc managed to breathe out between coughs.

"You Aiestali are cowards!" He leaned down and spit in Jenoc's face. "I'm going to personally march all my brave warriors on Aiested to butcher every single one of your people."

Jenoc started to laugh. It was a hysterical sound that appeared to disturb some of the prince's guards. He didn't know why he was laughing. He was as an angel cast out from heaven, cursed and doomed to die. But Jenoc had long ago dedicated himself to destroying the humans, and the rage of the prince only confirmed that his plan was working. There would be a new talis war. Perhaps that's why he was giddy to the point of laughter, either that or his metamorphoses had robbed him of his sanity.

"You think this is funny?" Isara grabbed a handful of Jenoc's newly blond hair and forced him to get up so he could meet his eyes standing.

"My son," the prince said through clenched teeth, tears streaming into his beard. "You took my son! He was scarcely two years of age!"

Isara backhanded Jenoc so hard that he spun completely around as he fell back to the floor.

"I am going to make you suffer. I will torture you myself and then have my monks heal you so we can do it all again tomorrow. And the next day and the next day until you beg for death!"

"H-how can you lead your armies if you are going to spend each day torturing me?" Jenoc said with a hysterical sob-laugh.

Isara knelt beside Jenoc and leaned down as if he were going to whisper in his ear. "I will start your hell, but others will continue my work while I'm gone. And I will make sure you do not die until I return from war to kill you myself!" He grabbed Jenoc by the back of the head and slammed his face into the stone.

Four of Jenoc's teeth broke, and he laughed harder. Isara slammed his face down a second time, and Jenoc's nose crunched. Still he laughed harder, though now it was mixed with gurgling as he choked on his own blood. An image flashed in Jenoc's mind. His father, a tall man with long sapphire-colored hair being set upon by a mob of angry villagers. He'd been trying to reason with their leader, but they were whipped up into a frenzy and would have none of it.

The laughter only enraged the Haeshalan prince, and he continued to slam Jenoc's face into a black stone tile that was now smeared with red. More memories surfaced unbidden: his mother, torn dress exposing her left breast as a group of five men pinned her to the ground. Yet, even with the horror replaying before him, the laughter came stronger.

Isara was in a frenzy now, repeatedly slamming Jenoc's head into the stone. Despite all his threats of endless torture, Jenoc knew he'd die this day. His laughter stopped when his mind showed him Kairah, as a young girl, weeping as the vile men approached her. Rage replaced his giddy insanity. He had saved his sister from a fate like that of his mother's by spell-casting a wave of force that tore Kairah's assailants to pieces. It'd drained him to near the point of death, but it succeeded in scaring away the mob so that he and Kairah could escape into the woods surrounding the village.

Jenoc was losing consciousness now, but his burning rage gave him something to hold onto. He tried with every last bit of will to draw from Haeshala's well, but the Apeiron refused to come. He was about to surrender to syncope when his senses registered something new. Energy, not from the Apeira well, but emanating from Isara himself. Jenoc instinctually drew on that energy. It poured into him, but not in the same way Apeiron did. This energy had to be pulled from Isara, ripped out of him. The beating abruptly stopped, and the pain in his face faded.

Jenoc blinked open his eyes–both eyes–and lifted his head. He found Isara's guards staring at him, mouths agape and faces pale. He rose to his knees and turned to look back for Isara, expecting the man to resume his assault at any moment, but Isara lay on the floor unmoving. More than that, the man's black skin was shriveled and white, his thick muscular arms now little more than sticks. Isara was dead, and by the state of his corpse, Jenoc would've thought for years if he hadn't been alive a moment ago.

Jenoc stood, and the Haeshalen guards raised their spears, though they looked loathe to fight. He smiled and then blasted the first guard with a jet of fire, which reduced the man to ashes. Jenoc could cast again. The energy he'd siphoned away from Isara could power his spells, though he immediately realized something was wrong. The power it took to spell-cast the fire was double the amount of Apeiron it should've taken him, and though a basic spell of the Second Discipline, it left him so weak he nearly collapsed.

The other five guards advanced on him and Jenoc could feel the pulsing energy in each of the armored men. He grabbed for it, and to his astonishment, five translucent tendrils of greenish energy exploded from his chest–one for each guard. Jenoc marveled as the men withered before his eyes, falling to the ground looking less like men and more like centuries-old skeletons.

Power coursed into Jenoc, and he gasped, his entire self feeling miraculously revitalized. He stood in the center of the throne room, now emptied as the remaining attendants and guards had fled.

This is the other magic, Moriora Kairah had named it. He marveled at how similar it was to drawing Apeiron.

And, I can use it to spell-cast! Although that had been disappointingly less effective than when powering his spells using Apeiron. Jenoc touched his newly restored eye. The day before it had been burned from its socket by Kairah's magic, but now it was whole and functional. His nose was no longer tender, nor his face where Isara had shoved it into the onyx floor. Syphoning power from his enemies apparently healed him.

Mirror! I need a mirror!

Jenoc found one on the wall between two sconces with guttering flames. To his disappointment, his hair was still blond, eyes green, and skin pink. The energy hadn't returned him to his Allosian form as he'd hoped. He'd have to accept what he was now–human. *No, not human. I'm something else. But what?*

The energy in his core wasn't the same as Apeiron. It was chaotic, unorganized, and less pure. He wasn't sure why that was, and the power was decreasing with each of his breaths. That too was very different. Apeiron remained with an Allosian's body, only ebbing away as it was used to spell-cast. Oh, it did slowly decrease as it substituted for sustenance and sleep, but the process was too gradual to be noticed–like a leak in Jenoc's soul.

I will need to draw energy on a more frequent basis.

He noticed a serving girl cowering behind a stone column. Apparently, she hadn't had the good sense to emulate her companions and flee the throne room. She sobbed as she met his eyes. Jenoc just smiled.

Chapter 71

Jove's consciousness—now nothing more than a black sphere surrounded by crackling green electricity—floated and bobbed through the ocean of purple. Upon first arriving here, wherever here was, he'd sensed a powerful concentration of Apeiron, more potent, and more powerful than any well, even vaster than the purple ocean that surrounded him. It was some sort of fountainhead, the source and supply of all Shaelar's Apeiron.

He'd lost track of time in this place, and couldn't say how long he'd been seeking out the fountainhead. Had it been hours or had it been weeks? He had no idea. Time was different here, flexible in a way it hadn't been in the corporeal world.

The Hunger was starting to reassert itself. Since coming here, it had grown more intense and demanding, as well as more difficult to satisfy. He stopped moving forward as he paused to draw in more Apeiron. His new electric tendrils crackled and snapped and the ocean around him shuddered as he sucked in the energy. It took vast quantities now to slake his appetite, more than a thousand Apeira wells—no, a thousand times a thousand! And his need only grew each time he ate more of that sweet, delectable life.

Somewhat satisfied, Jove moved on. He sucked in one of the many currents of power and it propelled him forward. He continued to do this, catching currents and pulling himself toward the fountainhead, ever more excited as his senses reported to him that he was getting closer.

The surrounding Apeiron became sweeter, more potent, more powerful, and eating it became as novel as the first time Jove fed on Apeiron; the day he'd drained the crystal man with the jewel eye. The idea of recapturing that original thrill energized Jove and he pulled harder on the lines of power emanating from the fountainhead.

Soon he came upon something he hadn't expected to see in this place, though upon reflection it made a kind of sense. The fountainhead was a gigantic sphere of transparent glass. Jove imagined himself laughing as he zipped toward the sphere. This was it! This was where all of Shaelar's Apeiron originated. This was the ultimate source of sustenance and satisfaction Jove had been longing for–aching for. He slammed into the smooth surface of the crystal sphere and was rebuffed by a flash of white light.

For the first time in weeks, pain shocked through Jove, and the substance that made up his black-orb self fuzzed and pulled apart. Panicked, Jove sucked in more Apeiron, and immediately solidified.

How had this thing hurt him? Hadn't he long since transcended physical pain?

Jove warily drew closer to the sphere again, floating well away from its smooth glossy surface, and scrutinizing it. That's when he saw her. A beautiful doll, more beautiful than any doll he'd ever seen, even more wonderfully perfect than that doll with the purple hair back in Aiested. She floated inside the center of the sphere, curled up like a child when sleeping or afraid.

The woman had hair longer than she was tall, silver with a shiny glow that made it look metallic. It billowed about her naked body as though she were submerged in water. This was the fountainhead, the source of all Apeiron? Hot lust exploded inside of Jove. It wasn't the same kind of arousal he'd felt while in the flesh, for he had no flesh, but that familiar feeling of thrilling anticipation was unmistakable.

He had to have that doll.

Jove cautiously floated up to the curvature of the glass barrier, moving into it more slowly. Again it burned and threatened to undo him. He sucked in more Apeiron and pulled his essence back together.

"No!" he projected with the intensity of a scream. Echoing like sound, the thought carried through the waves of purple energy that surrounded him, racing off to some distant place. He spared little notice for the oddity.

He wanted—no, he needed that doll. He'd been denied that purple-haired goddess, and so deserved to have this silver-haired one instead. That perfect, naked form floating inside the glass ball that was the source of all Apeiron, represented the ultimate in pleasure, the ultimate in thrill. She was the last and end of all his conquests. She was a mixture of both his worlds, the new one of consuming life, and the old of gratifying the flesh. But he couldn't get to her. She was protected from him by that glass barrier. Fate dangled this doll before him, but held her just out of reach. It was so unfair!

Again, Jove mentally screamed, sending his anguished cry rippling out from him in every direction. With that scream came bolts of emerald electricity, a shaft of it striking out at the glass wall before him. When the lightning made contact, the sphere trembled and fine cracks appeared on the outer skin of its surface.

Jove shot out another bolt of green lightning, and more fine cracks appeared. He struck again and then again and again, all in rapid succession, drawing in a continual flow of Apeiron to strengthen him in the effort. Soon the cracks started to widen. The glass shell looked to be hundreds of feet thick, but the more he attacked, the deeper the cracks crept.

Jove smiled. He'd found a way to get to that most perfect of all dolls. It would take some time, but being dead, he had all the time of an eternity.

MAELY LAY NEXT TO GRYYTH, watching him breathe. He seemed to be sleeping much more comfortably since Sharor had ministered to him. He was still grievously wounded, and Maely wouldn't know for certain if he would survive until he woke. She rolled onto her other side, so that her back was to the large Ursaj warrior.

Although she had covered herself in animal pelts, and she lay on a fur rug, she was having trouble keeping the northern midnight chill from breaking through. *Hadn't these people ever heard of a blanket?* She paused at how ridiculous that thought had been. Of course, they didn't need blankets, they were covered in fur. She laughed, but it quickly turned into a sob.

She was alone again. Sharor had left with Kerr hours ago for the sky temple, left after that voice inside Maely's head had called to her. Sharor wouldn't tell Maely where or what the sky temple was, or what the voice that had spoken inside her mind meant, claiming it all to be sacrosanct. Neither would the blind she-bear take Maely with her.

"Someone needs to stay to tend to Gryyth," Sharor had said.

It made sense, and Maely didn't argue. She'd surprised herself in this, for normally such a patronizing refusal would've sparked her temper and unleashed her poisonous tongue. Perhaps she was just too tired to argue. Not just physically, but inside her heart–her broken heart. A tear rolled down her cheek.

"Jek," she whispered.

The man she'd loved rejected her, and it hurt like a dagger twisting in her chest. Well, truth be told, she had no idea what it felt like to have a knife stab her, but she was sure it would hurt like this, just not as bad. Worse still, Maely wasn't even sure the fool boy was still alive. It was very possible that if the king's guard hadn't killed him, the collapsing palace had. And if not the palace, then that fell wind. No! The sword would've protected him. Of course, she wasn't sure of that either, but it staved off the frightening possibility.

He'd rejected her, but she still loved him. When he'd told her he didn't love her, she thought her world was ending and had been ready to hurl herself from the top of Aiested's tower. But what if he was truly gone from her life, forever? Dead?

The very possibility threatened to overwhelm what little hope she held onto, and so she closed her eyes, and sought sleep. It took a while, but eventually Maely put her terrors from her mind and drifted into slumber.

"Where are we, cub?"

Gryyth's voice was weak, and raspy, but still deeper than any human man's. She opened her eyes to find the white Ursaj trying to sit up. She quickly moved over to him and gently pushed on his shoulder until he lay back down.

"We're in Sharor's den," Maely said as she quickly glanced over Gryyth's burns. They were smeared with dried mud from Sharor's medicine, so she couldn't tell if they were healing, but Gryyth didn't act as pained as he did before.

"I am thirsty," the bear-man rumbled.

Maely nodded and stood. Sharor had shown her an opening in the back of the cave that led to another chamber, significantly colder than the front, and not adorned with any kind of animal pelt insulation. There she found cleaned and dressed animals hanging from the ceiling, their absence of skin and heads hiding their identities, but Maely guessed they were deer.

In the corner of the room was a large cask filled with rainwater, but Maely opted to grab another skin of Aiestali sweet wine. It looked to be Sharor's last, but Maely didn't care. The alcohol would help the bear-man with the pain. She rushed back into the den's main cave, knelt next to Gryyth, and unstopped the wine skin. He tried to grab it, but she insisted on being the one to give him drink. He lifted his head up and took a long pull from the wine skin.

When he was done, he sighed. "Aiestali sweet wine?"

Maely nodded, and then gave him a second drink. He drank longer this time, and Maely had to cut him off when he'd drained half the leather bag.

Gryyth laid his head back and asked, "Is this a mountaineer's hunting cave? Did you find someone to help us?"

Maely re-stoppered the horn of the wine skin, and set it down on the ground next to Gryyth. She'd been tempted to take a pull herself, but guilt over her indulgence the night before stopped her. What would Ez say if he caught her drinking? That made her think of Mulladin, and her guilt weighed heavier.

"Help sorta found us. But it wasn't a hunter."

"Ursaj?" Gryyth's eyes roamed the pelt lined walls.

Maely nodded. "Her name is Sharor. She speaks Aiestali, and knows medicine."

Gryyth touched the dried mud on his chest. "Then I have her to thank."

Maely glanced at the cave entrance. "She's gone."

"Hunting?" Gryyth asked.

Maely shook her head. "She said she was going to your sky temple."

Gryyth turned over, moaning as the motion was too quick to spare him any hurt. Maely made to force him back down again, but he forestalled her with a paw. She let him finish sitting up, moving in to help him when he struggled. He inhaled slow deliberate breaths for nearly a full minute before he spoke again. Clearly, though he was on the mend, Gryyth had a long recovery ahead of him.

"Why?"

"She said that 'the mother' called."

Gryyth nodded slowly. "Yes, I remember hearing her voice in my dreams."

When the Ursaj refused to explain what that meant, Maely's patience evaporated. "What's happening?!"

Gryyth closed his eyes. "We do not speak of it to humans."

Now Maely was really getting mad. Sharor had patronized her in much the same way. Ironically, it reminded her of the way Kairah used to speak to her. "Then at least tell me what this sky temple is!"

Gryyth opened his blue eyes and stared at her for a long moment before finally rumbling, "It is a place where my people meet together."

"So, what makes it so special?" Maely demanded.

"It is the place where the Mother speaks to us."

"And who's this mother?"

Gryyth squinted his eyes shut and his breathing quickened. "May I have more of that wine?"

The bear-man's pain cooled Maely's rising frustration, and she quickly fetched the wine skin. This time he drained the bag until it wrung in on itself. When he had coaxed every last drop from the skin, Gryyth dropped the leather bag, and began to stand.

"What the hell do you think you're doing?" Maely snapped.

"I must follow the others and go to the sky temple," Gryyth panted.

"You can't leave!" Maely stood. "You need to rest and heal!"

"This is important," Gryyth growled.

"Then let me come with you."

"I am sorry, cub. You cannot."

Gryyth took five steps, and then very nearly collapsed. He had to steady himself by reaching out to the cave wall. Unfortunately, his paw struck one of Sharor's wooden shelves filled with ingredients. It all came down in a crash, and Gryyth just barely avoided falling to the ground. When he glanced back at her, Maely made sure to smirk.

She folded her arms. "I'm guessing you're gonna need some help getting to your sky temple."

Gryyth's only response was a growl.

Maely took that for an assent, and quickly moved to help steady the bear-man by sidling up to him and placing an arm up around his waist. She wasn't sure exactly how much help she was, and if Gryyth were to put his full weight on her, it would surely crush her, but he didn't argue further.

It was late morning when they emerged from Sharor's den, but still chilly and Maely almost asked Gryyth to wait so she could duck back into the den and grab one of Sharor's animal pelts, but she didn't want to give him a chance to re-think needing her help.

"So how far away is it?" Maely asked.

It took Gryyth a moment to answer, and Maely suspected that he was considering just how much to confide in her.

"Two days," he rumbled. "Longer for us."

Days? Maely started to panic. "Shouldn't we take some food or supplies?"

"We have to go fasting," Gryyth said.

That may be well and good for a creature that was protected from the cold by fur and had fat stores to spare, but Maely wasn't sure she could do it. "But you're sick."

Gryyth nodded. "And so, I will allow myself to drink from streams."

"What about me?"

"You can drink from streams, too."

"No!" Maely snapped. "I'm not as big or hairy as you! I'm going to starve or freeze!"

Gryyth stared down at her with his ice-blue eyes. Finally, he rumbled, "Go fetch something warm to wear."

"And food?"

Gryyth shook his head. "If you are to come with me, you must fast."

It was a compromise. Maely hated compromise.

She made sure to stuff some dried meet into her mouth as she pillaged Sharor's den for a pelt large enough to double as a cloak. She also secreted some of the bear-woman's deer jerky into her dress pockets along with red berries, and a fist-sized purple fruit she didn't recognize. She'd be damned if she was going to go two days without food. She finally found a pelt she could wrap herself in like a blanket, and left the den. When she emerged, she found Gryyth leaning against a pine tree, shoulders slumping and head bowed.

"You really shouldn't be traveling," she said.

He raised his head and looked at her. "This is important."

"You keep saying that. But what about your health? This trip is just going to make you worse."

Maely ducked under his left arm–though she probably hadn't needed to as it cleared her head by a good foot–and grabbed the Ursaj by the waist again.

"That is not as important as this," Gryyth rumbled.

The two started walking again.

"Why?"

Gryyth growled in warning.

Maely persisted anyway. "I heard the voice in my head too! So, doesn't that mean I'm already in on this?"

"Are you going to nip at my heels like this the whole way?"

Maely ground her teeth. "I helped save your furry ass! The least you could do is tell me what's going on!"

Gryyth made one of those bear-moans, and Maely wondered if that was the Ursaj version of a sigh.

The ground suddenly heaved and Maely held tight to Gryyth as everything shook, but his size was such that it did nothing to stop the bear-man from falling to the ground. He groaned as he fell to his knees. Birds scattered into flight, trees swayed as though they were being assailed by wind that couldn't pick a direction, and rocks slid down a nearby mountain.

Maely shot a look back in the direction of Aiested. She had long since passed out of being able to see the city or its broken well, but she could still see the black clouds swirling above illuminated green by rapid flashes of emerald lightning.

After a very long moment, the quaking subsided, and Maely breathed out her pent-up breath. But, it was only a couple of heartbeats later that she sucked in another gasp, triggered by what she saw. A spear of blackness shot up from Aiested, widening and becoming a column that looked to connect sky to ground. It continually poured upward and soon the clouds above began to funnel down to meet it, as if the dark pillar were sucking them in.

"The world is ending, isn't it?" Maely whimpered.

After a pregnant pause, Gryyth answered, "Yes."

CHAPTER 72

Mulladin lost his balance and very nearly fell on his face as the ground beneath him suddenly tilted to one side, or at least that's how he thought of it. He steadied himself against a brick building, and cast a look over his shoulder–the direction of Aiested. A column of midnight blackness shot up from what was probably the broken Apeira well, and poured into the dark clouds swirling above it. Gasps all around him told Mulladin the villagers of Gnot hadn't missed the sight either, despite the violent ground quaking.

Mulladin stayed as still as he could until the ground stopped shaking, and then continued down Gnot's main thoroughfare nonchalantly as the people around him shouted and pointed at the sky. After seeing the well at Aiested break, the clouds hurl down green lightning, and a wind of death pull apart men and ships, this wasn't something so grand. He laughed aloud at the absurdity of his attitude. Here the world was ending, and he'd already grown accustomed to it. Besides, Mulladin had more important things to worry about.

He'd tracked the Rikujo wench to this village. Apparently, all the lessons from Ez on hunting and wilderness survival were now accessible to him. He thought that odd. He'd always had the memories of Ez's instruction, but since his change, he could now understand and make use of them. And a good thing, too; he'd needed to forage for food as much as follow the woman's trail.

The village of Gnot was large enough to be a town or small city, with its hundred or so buildings, fenced perimeter, and a population Mulladin guessed to be no fewer than two thousand. He idly wondered why the people hadn't appointed a mayor and asked their lord-regent to grant them an official town charter and require their inclusion on royal maps. Probably something to do with avoiding an increase of taxes or the like.

Mulladin paused. How had he known that? Perhaps he'd overheard others talking about such things when he was dim, and like Ez's instructions on hunting and survival, the information only now made sense to him.

Mulladin shoved the thoughts aside as he caught sight of the Tolean woman with Jek's sword. She'd shed her stolen armor, and was dressed in a gray cloak with the hood drawn up. There was no sign of the sword, but he was sure she held it concealed under her cloak. Mulladin smiled to himself. Like the rest of the villagers on the street, her gaze was fixed on the northern horizon, at the column of blackness ascending into the dark sky. She hadn't seen him yet.

Mulladin quickly ducked behind a dung cart parked on his side of the street. He watched her shake her head, and turn away from staring at the sky. She disengaged from a group of villagers that had amassed around her, and then furtively scanned her surroundings.

Rasheera smiles on me this day. Mulladin couldn't help but grin at the providence that let him spot the Rikujo wench before she'd spotted him.

He watched her slip into a two story, slate roofed building of what was clearly an inn, as announced by the etching of a bed in the sign above the door. Mulladin stepped out from behind the cart, and strode across the street, taking care not to look too eager. He had her now.

When he pushed through the inn's one swinging door, he was greeted by a rowdy crowd of rough-looking villagers who belonged more in a carousing den than an inn's common room. It made him chuckle. Yes, Gnot certainly was a village in name only, for villages didn't have establishments such as this. These places of avarice belonged only to the metropolitan life. He decided that the misapplication of the label was a deliberate attempt to avoid higher taxes, or perhaps the scrutiny of the crown.

Mulladin stiffened when the point of something sharp pressed against his lower back.

"Move and I will sever your spine," hissed an accented female voice in his ear.

Mulladin sighed. He'd underestimated this woman–again.

Despite her warning, Mulladin spun around and shoved her into an empty table. Tipping the table over, she fell backward, cloak fluttering open to reveal Jek's sword hidden beneath. He lunged for her, but she was on her feet in one acrobatic motion, and spun, kicking a leg out. It connected with Mulladin's stomach, and he groaned as he doubled over. That's when the knee to the face came.

There was a flash of light, a loud crack, and then Mulladin was on his back looking up at the ceiling. The Rikujo woman stared down at him, a triumphant smirk on her face. Mulladin pretended to be more dazed than he actually was and the wench leaned down, chuckling. She opened her mouth to gloat, but it became a yelp as Mulladin kicked out, the bottom of his boot connecting with her shin.

She fell forward and landed so that she was on top, straddling him. She opened her eyes, and the two stared at each other. *She's actually sort of pretty.* His body traitorously reacted to her lithe frame pressing down on him. The Rikujo wench smiled at him, as if she could read his thoughts. Their faces were so close that he could feel her breath on his lips. The moment stretched, Mulladin's pulse quickened, and a powerful inclination to kiss the woman fell on him.

He head-butted her instead.

She rolled off him, releasing a torrent of muffled curses as her hands snapped to her face in an effort to staunch the pouring blood. Mulladin quickly scrambled up, leaned down, and drew the sword from her belt. He stepped away from her, lest she try something similar to what he had done to bring her down.

"I win," Mulladin chuckled, his laugh becoming heartier as he met her smoldering gaze.

He turned around to leave, but froze upon seeing two armored guards blocking his way, their crossbows leveled at his face and chest.

MULLADIN DUCKED as the tomato struck the bars of his crow's cage. It didn't do any good. The bars shredded the overripe fruit spraying his bowed head with juice and sticky pulp. *Well, at least they weren't throwing eggs*, he thought. An egg struck him in the shoulder, exploding its rotten yoke all over his shirt. He ground his teeth, and shot an angry glare at the cage hanging next to his–its occupant the Rikujo wench. She, too, was being pelted by trash, but not to the extent he was.

"This is all your fa–" he cut off as another egg struck him in the face, this time spraying yoke into his eyes and open mouth. He sputtered, and his temper flared when he caught the woman smirking at him.

The village of Gnot had a creative system of jurisprudence. Unlike Genra, in which criminals were arrested, and held in a guarded cell inside an old stone watchtower until the traveling magistrate could pay them a visit, Gnot's constable passed judgment and pronounced sentence on the spot. Thirty days of hanging in the crow's nest in the center of town, and to be subject to the taunts and abuses of passersby. Upon the day of their release they were to be expelled from Gnot and expected never to return.

That had been until the constable had found Jek's sword and Mulladin's lightning ring. Now both he and the Rikujo wench were to be held for a week and then taken to the nearest city for official judgment and hanging, Jek's sword remitted to the hands of the nobles governing that city, which in this case was Erassa.

Mulladin's attempts to explain himself, and what had happened in Aiested, were met with skeptical scoffs, and disdainful dismissals. Even when the ground quaked during one of his insistences that something cataclysmic was happening, and he needed to get the sword to an Allosian, the constable refused to believe. But Mulladin had seen the doubt in the man's eyes. He didn't want to believe the world was ending, and only grew angrier when Mulladin tried to convince him.

Blind idiots!

The barrage of trash, produce, and rotten eggs subsided as the group of villagers left to return their daily routines. They would be back, they or more like them. He wiped the egg off his cheek with the sleeve of his shirt.

"Well, are you happy?" Mulladin said to the Rikujo woman.

"Don't blame me.!" She rubbed her swollen nose. "You're the one who drew the attention of the guards."

Mulladin scoffed. "Because you had a knife to my back!"

"Well, if you hadn't followed me—"

"You stole my friend's sword!"

The woman narrowed her eyes. "It is my inheritance!"

Mulladin was about to demand she explain what she meant by that when laughing from an approaching figure caught his attention. He turned, fully expecting another crowd of villagers, re-armed with withering lettuce and rotting apples. Instead, a tall man with long, black hair and one arm in a sling approached. It was the man called Loeadon, and he had Jek's sword.

He stopped a meter away from them and grinned. "Two naughty little birds sulking in their cages, never to be free to fly again."

Mulladin's only response was a roar as he shook the bars, making the crow's cage swing from side to side.

Loeadon laughed. "You are both idiots. Gnot is the only village for several miles. If you were trying to evade me and my soldiers, why come here?"

The Rikujo wench didn't say anything.

"That's Jekaran's sword!" Mulladin shouted.

"So, you do know that farm boy? Well, I suspected as much. Did you know he killed the king?"

Mulladin didn't say anything. He didn't know that.

"If you came to Aiested to try to help him, that makes you co-conspirators."

"I don't even know him!" the Rikujo woman said.

Loeadon glanced at her. "But you stole a weapon talis. Another capital offense."

"If you're going to kill us, then just kill us," Mulladin growled.

"Speak for yourself!" the Rikujo wench said.

"I really ought to thank you." Loeadon lifted the sword and stared into the well shard. "I was worried that if the prince survived the fall of the palace, I'd have no way of dealing with him. Now I do."

He looked up at Mulladin. "Oh, and a lightning ring, too."

"If you're feeling so grateful, why don't you let me go?"

Loeadon lowered the sword and rested the point on the ground. "Do you know who I am?"

"A bugger-loving piece of ghern shyte?" Mulladin snapped.

Loeadon chuckled. "I am the leader of the royal cadre of polymaths. I was one of the most powerful men in the kingdom, until I fell out of favor with the prince. I was severely wounded on my way to a dungeon cell to await my execution. A monk came to heal me. It was about that time that the palace started to shake, and I took the moment of distraction to break the monk's neck, take his healing ring, and then escape. I had only just healed myself when all of the talises went dark."

"I don't care who you are!" Mulladin spat at Loeadon, but the arc of his phlegm was too sharp, and it landed only a foot away from the crow's cage.

Loeadon looked down at the spittle in the dirt. "I favor you with this story because it was my scheming to get this very sword that brought me to what I thought was my end. But the miraculous circumstances that allowed me to escape and then put the very object of my designs into my hand can mean only one thing."

Loeadon met Mulladin's eyes.

"The goddess wants me to rule the kingdom. She has chosen me."

"You're no devotee of Rasheera," Mulladin said.

Loeadon grinned. "Perhaps not. But whatever controls the destinies of men and kingdoms has given this gift to me, and I intend to use it. Once my entourage reaches Erassa, the sword will recharge and I will bond it. Think about that while you rot in your filthy bird's cage. Which reminds me. I've ordered the constable here to cease providing you with food and water. He is to let you die and leave your corpses to rot in the sun—forever."

Mulladin released another roar of pure rage and shook the bars so hard that his cage swung into his neighbor's. The resultant clash made his teeth rattle and his stomach twist. Loeadon just shook his head, turned, and walked away with Jek's sword.

CHAPTER 73

J enoc strolled out of Prince Isara's black stone fortress feeling more energized than he ever had before. Humans ran from the very sight of him, making him feel like a lion pouncing into a herd of gnus. Prayers in the form of screams echoed all around him.

"Please, God, protect us!"

"Spare us, Almighty!"

These filthy humans had different superstitions than the rest of the humans in Shaelar. Whereas most worshipped the goddess, Rasheera, the Haeshalan scum seemed to importune a male deity. It was all very fascinating, and Jenoc was sure his old self would've spent months researching the concept. Now he didn't care about academics. All he cared about was killing every last one of the vermin.

Some guards escorting a group of frightened wash-women spotted him, and sent the women on ahead while they stood their ground and leveled spears at Jenoc.

"How very brave." Jenoc laughed.

Then he raised a hand and a bolt of green lightning arced from his palm to one of the guards. A flash of light washed over the surrounding training grounds, and when it subsided, only a smoldering pile of human bones remained. The energy coursed into Jenoc, paying for that spell and then some.

He'd devised this way of combining his Moriora tendrils with a spell-casting of lightning to strike faster at escaping prey. To his surprise, combining the two vastly reduced the energy cost of the spell, and greatly accelerated the feeding process. He struck the other guard with a bolt of green lightning, absorbing his life force in one quick action, or bite, as he was starting to call it in his mind.

Screams from the fleeing humans echoed from beyond the perimeter walls of the fortress grounds drawing another cruel smile from Jenoc. He didn't need a talis war to exterminate mankind, not anymore. His original plan to use Moriora to wipe out the humans had been the correct choice. However, there was one drawback to this plan. It was going to take a long time for him to crisscross Shaelar, devouring the life of his enemies–likely decades. It was too long. He needed to expedite the process somehow.

He looked to the city's Apeira well rising from only a few miles away, and called to mind his first attempt at wielding the mysterious other magic. He had meticulously followed her instructions, but assumed the inversion spell failed. He'd attempted it at an undiscovered well near a small human village between Haeshala and Aiestal. What had the human vermin called their village?

Oh yes, Almott.

He remembered, because he'd had to visit the place in disguise to ascertain the exact location of the buried well. Of course, none of the humans in Almott knew they were living near a well, but they could tell Jenoc the signs that would confirm his suspicion: A near-zero infant mortality rate, livestock that reproduced double the amount of other villages, and harvests that consisted only of unusually large, pristinely ripe fruits and vegetables. Those villagers had claimed it to be the favor and blessing of Rasheera. That just made him laugh.

After Jenoc had excavated the well, and woven the complicated inversion spell that would summon Moriora, the well had cracked and turned the color of an emerald. When nothing else followed, he assumed the spell had failed. Now he realized it hadn't failed. It merely needed time to attune him to its alien power, to change him into something that could channel and wield it.

That thought gave Jenoc pause. After considering the implications for a long moment, he quickly left the training grounds, and returned to the city streets. He struck again and again at humans fool enough to let him see them, devouring them with only half his concentration as a new theory unfolded before his mind.

He now had green eyes like many of the Haeshalan people. Eyes the same color as the corrupted Apeira well he'd experimented on near Almott. Could these people be the Moriora equivalent of Allosians? But if so, why did they not know the power he now used to destroy them? Perhaps their abilities and nature were dormant? Could there be a way to draw it out? Awaken their powers? Would the inversion spell do to them what it had done to him?

Jenoc strode toward the city's Apeira well. He would need many allies with this same ability if he was to devour the entire human race and cleanse Shaelar. No, not allies, soldiers. Jenoc needed an army. But would he be able to control them? What if they used their powers to fight him? He could spell-cast, and they couldn't. Or if they could, they were surely ignorant of spell-craft. That would give him an advantage. But then, did he need to control them so much as unleash them?

Back in Isara's palace, when he'd used the man's siphoned energy to spell-cast, his core had grown cold and empty, and he was overcome with a panicked urgency to fill it. He would've done anything to rid himself of that horrible, hollow feeling. It hadn't abated until he drained more energy from the throne room guards, and even at a standstill, the stolen power inside of him ebbed away like sands in an hourglass.

If this power required frequent transfer of energy to avoid that feeling, perhaps that would be motivation enough for others who wielded it to concentrate on finding human prey. But what would happen to them when they ran out of people to drain? What would happen to Jenoc? He suspected that the Moriora would turn on him, devour his body from the inside out, ultimately destroying him. If that is what it took to rid the world of those who oppressed his people, then so be it.

He'd never consciously decided to give his life for his quest, but he hadn't had to. He was dedicated to this course, and would pay whatever price. That decision had been made for him years ago when had he knelt weeping next to his father's headless corpse.

Eventually, Jenoc reached Isadara's Apeira well. It seemed like a lifetime ago when he'd come here and left the plague box, although it had only been a couple of days. He craned his neck, fixating on the tip of the amethyst obelisk thirty feet above him. He could feel the Apeiron radiating from the well and was suddenly assailed by an overpowering desire to drain it. Tendrils materialized reflexively, but Jenoc held them back. He intuitively knew that he if touched the well, the spell to summon Moriora would fail. It had to remain pristine, virginal. But every part of Jenoc's being screamed to feed upon the potent, powerful energy with a burning lust hotter than all his other desires.

He fell to his knees, clenching his teeth and pouring every bit of his will into the effort of restraining himself. He sought his buried rage, calling it up with memories of his parents' murder. Images of the villagers of Teratra mobbing his father, holding him down while the mayor used a scythe to remove his head. He remembered watching from a closet as those same men held his mother down so they each could take turns raping her. That ended in her being beaten to death while a large, hairy man had his way with her.

Why hadn't they spell-cast to protect themselves? His parents weren't strong in the disciplines, they having been dedicated scholars, but they knew enough that they could've fought back. It was that damned Allosian pacifism. Foolish tradition that because Allosians were mightier and more intelligent than the humans, it meant they should treat them like helpless children. It was how Kairah thought. It had been an odd dichotomy; their parents trained in logic and scholarly analysis believing in the foolish idea that Apeiron had a creative will, and it was the Allosian's sacred duty to preserve life. But even Allosians would kill to protect themselves, so why hadn't his parents done something? Perhaps it was because they were caught off guard–the whole thing had happened so quickly. Or perhaps they were trying to keep the villager's attention on them so they wouldn't find Jenoc and Kairah.

Well, they had found them.

Jenoc remembered being pulled roughly from the closet and thrown to the floor. One of the men calling him, "Filthy fey larva!"

He had been kicked in the ribs and knocked to the ground, momentarily forgotten when the men discovered his sister. She was very young by Allosian standards, but old enough to pass for a human girl of thirteen. Jenoc remembered the men hooting and laughing when they found Kairah–she had always been beautiful, even as a child. The man who had beaten Jenoc's mother to death proclaimed his hideous intent to deflower Jenoc's sister, reaching for the front of her dress. That's when Jenoc had first lost control.

He'd always been adept with spell-casting, and before leaving Allose to study the humans, he'd enjoyed a celebrated status as something of a prodigy in the junior college of disciplines. His parents had forbidden him to spell-cast while among the humans, but he'd practiced in secret. At least until he'd been spotted creating fire by one of the filthy human villagers. That was the spark that'd enflamed the angry mob, the seminal factor in the tragedy that claimed his parent's life.

It was his fault.

Jenoc remembered casting from The Second Discipline with such reckless ferocity that all the humans in their cottage had exploded, each in a maelstrom of fire, flesh, and blood. The smell was horrendous, but the display of spell-craft had the desired effect. The remaining villagers, watching through the windows, fled in fright.

The casting had left Jenoc dangerously weak, having used too much of his Apeiron store in the attack. Since Teratra was a day's travel from the nearest Aeose, he was in danger of death. He only remembered pieces of what happened next, but it had been Kairah who had carried him out of the village and to a yet undiscovered well secreted in the white forest. From there they made their way back to Allose. Jenoc's rage hadn't truly started to accumulate until the elders of the synod refused to take any action against the human villagers. *It was that damned Allosian pacifism!*

Jenoc clung to that rage and pushed back the intense desire to drain Isadara's Apeira well. His breath came in ragged gasps as he stood and dismissed his translucent green tendrils. He began the mental recitation of the spell for summoning Moriora. It was a strange spell that required tapping into all five of The Disciplines, and then somehow inverting them. He still didn't fully understand the inversion spell, but knew enough to make it work. The energy in his core ebbed away, and Jenoc had to manifest a tendril and drain a corralled horse standing outside a nearby building to keep going.

Black clouds appeared in the sky, swirling above the crystal monolith, churning and roiling as though they were threatening the world.

Then, just as the cold, desperately hollow feeling in his chest recurred, a bolt of green lightning struck the Aeose with a deafening crack! The crystal monolith changed color right before Jenoc's eyes, turning from amethyst purple to emerald green. Then, as it had when Jenoc first attempted the summoning, the Apeira well released an explosion of translucent green energy in a wave that exploded outward. It rippled through the air, eventually losing its coloring and looking like heat distortions on a hot summer's day before disappearing on the horizon.

The crystal well cracked, and its emerald glow faded. Jenoc fell to the ground, gasping. He manifested tendrils in all directions, throwing them out with wild abandon until they found something to drain. They didn't have to stretch far; a crowd of onlookers had been watching from inside the cover of a guard tower. There were eight of them, probably soldiers with orders to kill Jenoc, but were too afraid to approach him. He drained them all simultaneously, their energy coursing into him and warming his core.

Relief rushed through Jenoc and he stood, looking about for any sign that he'd created more of his kind. He didn't see anyone. The wise humans, if there were such a thing, had evacuated the city square upon his arrival. Oddly, the shouting and screaming of the evacuating masses abruptly fell silent, as though all Isadara were holding its breath.

Jenoc, too, held his breath, working hard to fend off the fear of failure that tried to take him. Then, the screaming began, and he exhaled with a smile.

CHAPTER 74

"…But in this paradise, man did not understand things like work, or sorrow, or evil." The human monk, Irvis, was again sermonizing.

Kairah had learned all too quickly that to interrupt and question the former monk's preaching was somehow understood among the others to be an impropriety. Though she'd studied all the faiths humans espoused, she never quite understood what would drive them to believe in stories and ideas they could not substantiate. In fact, to suggest that empirical evidence should be a prerequisite for belief in the divine offended the devout. As she had quickly rediscovered when Irvis began his nightly, mealtime sermons.

He did not do this when we first traveled together. *Perhaps the death of his friend is his motivation for his focus on the tenets of his faith.*

Kairah knew something of what Irvis must be feeling. The longing for answers, the desperation to assign meaning to loss. The anger when nothing made sense. She herself had first started believing Apeiron had a sentient will that guided the growth of the world–the closest thing Allosians had to a religion–when her parents were murdered.

Jenoc hadn't taken the same path. He dealt with their parents' deaths with an almost fanatical need to prove the world merely a collection of random responses to stimuli and reactions to forces by other counter forces. He often ridiculed Kairah for her belief that there was a guiding power operating in the universe. For him, existence was a cruel state in which only strength and superiority of intellect proved one's worth, the reward of which not being eternal bliss with one's departed kin, but simply another day of life. It was a depressive, almost nihilistic view of the world, which appealed to her intellect, but warred against an instinct she couldn't dismiss.

Irvis continued, "The Divine Mother, therefore, left mankind so that we could learn to live without her continual blessings, and the life of ease which her immediate presence provided. But one day, when we prove worthy, she will return to grant us peace and everlasting life. That time will be one of everlasting prosperity and joy–the Age of the Infinite, some call it."

The sound of leathery skin slapping against itself startled Kairah, and she turned to find Karak slapping his one good hand against his stump.

Irvis frowned. "That was a sermon Karak, not a bard's story."

"Daka, not story." Karak continued to grin. "Esk, good story!"

Irvis huffed. "So, what do the Vorakk worship, if not the Divine Mother?"

"Spirits, aka."

"It is the grossest heathenism to worship the dead!"

Their debate faded into background noise as Kairah stared into the dancing and crackling flames of their campfire. She sat on a rock trying to lose herself in thought to distract from the feeling of hunger that gnawed at her middle. She detested the sensation, not so much because she was unaccustomed to it, or that it was uncomfortable, but because the only way she could make it go away was to eat the meat that was now slow roasting on a spit over the cook fire.

It had been a deer before Karak skinned it and disemboweled it. With one hand, he'd needed Hort's help, but the big mercenary was only too glad to assist with his large hunting knife. Kairah knew she shouldn't resent the Vorakk for killing the animal. After all, it was Karak's superior hunting ability that had saved their lives. Fleeing from Taris, or Aiested as the humans called it, with no supplies or provisions would've meant a death sentence if it hadn't been for Karak. Perhaps they could've sought a small village, but that would've taken time, and right now they were pushing hard to reach Allose.

The scent of the meat both enticed and disgusted Kairah. Even when they'd been traveling to Aiested, she'd always been able to find fruit or roots to eat, but this terrain had been frustratingly sparse for fauna, and she had to preserve her Apeiron so tapping that to sustain her wasn't an option. The idea of devouring another living animal horrified her and it was only now that she'd ever had to resort to it. But perhaps the worst thing about eating meat was that Kairah had liked the taste.

It is not wrong to eat meat, Aeva said.

Kairah rolled her eyes. She would've told the flower that it was too much like what Moriora's vessel did, but she didn't want to expend any energy to communicate.

Thinking of the monster turned her thoughts to earlier in the day when the ground had trembled and something dark had shot into the sky over Aiested. Although she'd left the life sucking monster in the collapsing palace feeding on the city's Aeose, she doubted the creature was destroyed. Where was it now? Kairah had expended some of her stored Apeiron to scry Aiested when the quake happened, but wasn't able to see anything. She could view the surrounding landscapes, but where the city itself was, there was only an empty dark spot in her psychic vision. She considered scrutinizing it, but the last time she'd attempted to view Karak's "Eater" she'd been painfully rebuffed. Perhaps someone in Allose with more talent in the Fourth Discipline would be able to see something.

A sharp pain stabbed into Kairah's eye. It was so sudden and so severe it made her gasp. She sucked in several ragged breaths, and clenched the side of her head. The pain burned behind her right eye, throbbing and stinging all at once. Then it was gone, almost as quickly as it had come. Kairah exhaled slowly.

Kairah, can you hear me? Aeva's anxious voice abruptly flooded into her mind.

I hear you, Aeva, Kairah said, abandoning her Apeiron conservation effort.

You were in pain, Aeva observed.

Yes, Kairah projected. *Like the pain of a severe migraine.*

Like Jenoc, Aeva somberly observed.

Kairah's hand massaging her eye socket stilled and a chill thrilled through her veins. Jenoc's headaches began after he had tried to summon Moriora. They'd continued increasing in frequency and intensity since then, and diminished his ability to spell-cast. In her vision of the dead land, Kairah had touched the power that was Apeiron's opposite, and it had tried to force its way into her body. She succeeded in expelling it only by drawing desperately on Apeiron, but had assumed the whole experience to have been illusory. In her comatose state had she channeled Moriora? Had it damaged her as it had damaged Jenoc?

A startled cry drew her attention back to the others. At first she thought someone had seen her double over in pain, but quickly realized they were all looking at the human, Irvis.

"Divine Mother," he said. He was holding something in the upturned palm of one hand and an empty brown pouch in the other. It looked like the object was a ring.

"What is it?" Graelle asked.

Irvis made eye contact with Kairah. "It's charged."

"Does that mean we're close to Allose's well?" The little man called Gymal asked.

Kairah shook her head. "Not close enough to draw Apeiron."

She stood and walked over to where Irvis sat. How could that ring have retained a charge when all their other talises had been drained by Moriora's vessel?

"Use it to heal Jekaran!" Gymal ordered.

Kairah watched as Irvis put on the ring, and then moved to kneel next to Jekaran's prone form. The young man still stared straight ahead with glassy eyes, and that terrifyingly vacant expression.

It will not work, Aeva said.

It healed the mind of Maely's brother, Kairah responded.

After a tense moment, Irvis sighed. "Nothing's happening."

He sat back on his haunches, his brow glistening with sweat. The plump woman, Graelle, patted him on the arm consolingly.

Kairah sighed and looked down at Jekaran lying on Gymal's outspread cloak. After she'd learned the circumstances of Mulladin's healing, she had hoped the ring would work a similar miracle for Jekaran. The fact that it hadn't made her nauseating worry for the boy worse. Was his mind forever lost? The possible tragedy was affecting

Kairah more than it should. Jekaran was just a human boy, and while he'd proven to be a noble human, he was still one of the enemies of her people.

Aeva giggled.

This is funny to you? Kairah snapped.

Not his pain, but your view of the world.

Kairah's anger extinguished like flames doused with water, and she again was perplexed by the Spirit lily's cryptic remarks. She was about to ask Aeva what she meant, or how she'd known the ring wouldn't work when Karak interrupted.

"Reka fat monk fix Karak?"

Irvis sighed and nodded. Then he motioned for Karak to kneel next to him. The lizard man did so, and Irvis laid a hand on Karak's side where his scales had turned from a bronze color to a sickly grayish white–where Moriora's vessel had struck him.

The wound had proved resistant to healing earlier, and Kairah had to abandon her effort to do so when the process drew too much Apeiron from her core. Could this uniquely powerful talis do what she could not?

Graelle's hand shot to her mouth, and Gymal and Hort both gasped. The lizard man's missing hand was growing back right before their eyes. At the moment, it was a mass of undefined scaly flesh, but fingers were slowly taking shape.

Karak's side was a healthy bronze color once again, and the Vorakk shaman was staring at the upraised nub of flesh that now had basic digits. Less than a minute more passed before Karak had a perfect Vorakk hand, complete with the long sharp claws.

Irvis pulled his hand back from Karak and stared at the Vorakk with as much surprise on his face as the others. He opened his mouth to say something, but faltered and looked down at the healing ring he wore on his chubby finger. He looked up at Kairah and said, "Remarkable!"

"Yes," Kairah agreed. "Only the most talented of Allosian healers can restore severed limbs. I have never heard tell of a healing talis that could accomplish something so complex."

"Maybe it's because he's a lizard," Hort said. "I used to pull the tails off little lizards I found in the garden. I kept one once, and its tail actually grew back."

"Perhaps," Kairah said. "But this ring also repaired Mulladin's diminished capacity, which is something I know for a fact even the most skilled Allosian healers could not accomplish."

She extended her hand to Irvis. "May I examine that ring?"

Irvis nodded, still looking at a loss for words, and it took a moment for him to wrench it from his fat finger before he placed the ring in Kairah's open palm. She picked it up with her thumb and forefinger and held it up before her. Kairah gasped as the ring changed before her very eyes, morphing from a gold loop with an Apeira well shard into a silver band decorated with trailing designs of flowers–lilies if Kairah wasn't mistaken.

Gasps from the others and a shout of, "That's impossible!" from the short human called Gymal reported that the others had witnessed the oddity.

Kairah hadn't discerned an illusion spell-casting altering the ring's appearance; it was as if the very ring itself had changed shape. There were, of course, spells that could change the matter making up a thing, but they were generally difficult, ineffective, and temporary.

It was a gift, Aeva said.

"What?" Startled, Kairah had vocally responded to the Spirit lily.

"I said nothing, my lady," Irvis said. He shared a confused glance with Graelle before turning back to look at Kairah.

Curious though the ring was, it was little more than a distraction to Kairah. She straightened and extended her hand to return the ring to Irvis but froze halfway through the motion.

Her Apeiron store was refilling.

It was slight, very slight, but she could feel the warmth at her core growing stronger.

"This ring is radiating Apeiron," Kairah gasped.

"How is that possible?"

"It should not be," Kairah said.

CHAPTER 75

Raelen had never stolen a ghern before. He hadn't ever stolen anything, and wouldn't have needed to if the townsfolk would've believed he was their prince. He'd wandered into Ijell almost two days ago, having lost his ghern a day before to fatigue, and he himself suffering from the need for food and drink. Bread and water the townsfolk had been willing to give him, but when he'd proclaimed himself Raelen Lesta Taris, crown prince of Aiestal, and asked for a ghern, they had scorned him, and accused him of being a charlatan. Apparently, most of Raelen's subjects had little idea of what he looked like which for some reason was something he hadn't ever considered. He couldn't blame them though. Wandering into their town alone, filthy and travel-worn, wasn't exactly the traditional norm for a royal visitation.

The ghern bayed softly as he reached around the underside of its jaw and sawed at the rope that hitched it to the wooden post. The effort took far longer than it should've, and he anxiously glanced around the dark street as his hands trembled and heart pounded. Finally, the rope came free, and Raelen took the ghern by the bridle and began leading it away from the tavern.

He turned down a side street, keeping as best he could to the shadows. Fortunately, it was late, and the streets of Ijell were mostly empty. Several minutes later, Raelen had reached the opening in the palisade wall. There was one guard on duty, a fat man in old, dented armor, sitting on a wooden crate. His helmeted head kept drooping until he'd startle himself awake and the process would start all over again.

Raelen decided the best way through this would be to mount up, and just ride past the guard into the night. If the guard saw him, and if the man chose to report it, it would take a while to organize a pursuit, which would give Raelen plenty of time to get a safe distance away from Ijell. The road ahead wove through a small forest, which would give him plenty of cover should he need to hide.

He had put one foot in the ghern's saddle stirrup when something pointy pressed between his shoulder blades made him freeze.

"Put that royal foot of yours down, my prince," a man derided.

Raelen did as told, a cold nausea twisting his stomach as two other armed men stepped out of the shadows and converged on him. In the light of a nearby street lantern, he could see they wore the tabards of Ijell sheriff's deputies.

"You know what the king's punishment is for stealing a ghern? Oh wait, of course you do. You're the crown prince."

"No less than fifty lashings up to hanging, depending on the circumstances surrounding the theft," Raelen answered.

The deputy chuckled. "Well, you sure do talk like you could be a—"

The man didn't get to finish his taunt. Raelen spun on him, knocking the spear aside and slamming his open palm into the man's nose. His transference band was still drained so he didn't have Gryyth's borrowed strength, which probably saved the man's life, but his training in the Ursaj way of unarmed combat made him formidable enough on his own power.

The deputy stumbled backward, clutching a nose that fountained blood, and Raelen unleashed a flurry of sharp blows to his body ending with a backhand that spun the deputy around before he went down. By now, the ghern had trotted away and the two other deputies had converged on Raelen. Warily, they inched closer to him, spears held up so the points were aimed at his chest.

Raelen waited for one of the deputies to get brave and make a jab at him and he spun to the side of the man's spear thrust bringing down his arm to strike the deputies hands. The man cried out as he dropped his spear, and Raelen stepped behind him and slammed his open palm into the man's lower back. He fell forward, landing face-first onto the ground. Gryyth had taught Raelen exactly where to strike a man's spine to temporarily–or permanently if he wished–paralyze him. It worked, and the man's legs didn't so much as twitch as he writhed on the ground.

Finely honed instincts prompted Raelen to lean backward as a spear point blurred in front of his eyes. With lightning speed, he reached out and caught the haft of the spear just as the last deputy was retracting it. Raelen broke the spearhead off the shaft as he fiercely shoved the spear down, causing the deputy to lose his grip and the butt of the spear to fly up into the underside of the man's jaw. Raelen heard the loud crack of wood striking bone, and the man crumpled to the ground. Raelen stepped around the three fallen guards and casually tossed the broken piece of spear away. It clattered to the cobblestone street somewhere off in the dark.

Raelen's stolen ghern hadn't gone far, and he had little trouble coaxing it back to him. He mounted up quickly, glancing around for more of the Ijell law enforcement, but blessedly found none. He launched the ghern into a gallop toward the gap in the palisade wall, and fled without so much as a reaction from the sleeping soldier at the gate.

He didn't stop riding even once that night, not to stretch his legs, not take a meal, and not relieve himself. It wasn't the threat of Ijell lawmen pursuing Raelen that spurred him on, but his desperate need to reach Aiestal's army before they attacked Haeshala. The army's commanders had no idea that their orders hadn't come from the king, or even a human; but from an Allosian warmonger as part of his machinations to destroy the human race.

Morning found Raelen riding hard on a dirt road that snaked its way over a hilly plain. He was following the unmistakable tracks of the thousands of men, oxen, and wagons that were his army. He was tired, and falling asleep in the saddle, but his duty drove him on, and he used it to stave off collapse.

To his complete astonishment, another rider appeared and overtook him before matching his pace and riding alongside him. The rider was a young woman, a few years older than Raelen. She had a head of golden curls, beautiful blue eyes, and wore a fine riding dress, the sort the ladies of his father's court always wore on hunting days–dresses more fashionable than functional. The woman was his sister, Saranna–his dead sister. Dead after she'd hurled herself from one of Duke Eidol's castle towers.

"You are very brave, Rae," Saranna said.

Raelen smiled. Though he knew she was dead, the oddity quickly faded, and it felt completely normal that she would be riding alongside him. He tried to speak, but nothing would come out. It pained him as he wanted to tell her all that had happened since she'd died. He wanted to tell her of how he'd finally mastered the akami Gryyth had been trying to teach him for years. He wanted to tell her of his disastrous courtship of Lord Akell's niece. He wanted to tell her father was killed and Aiested destroyed. But no matter how hard he tried, he didn't have the power of speech.

Saranna flashed one of her familiar ruby-lipped smirks like she knew what he was thinking. "We haven't much time."

Raelen nodded, still disturbed he couldn't say anything; but it sounded like Saranna was in control. Perhaps she had bound his tongue?

"You ride into danger."

Raelen opened his mouth, but Saranna waived at him to be quiet. Not that he could've made a sound anyway.

"Just listen, Rae," she snapped. "You will face him again, but this time he fights with the power of death itself. You cannot fight him the way you did before. To touch him is death. His power cannot affect itself, so arm yourself with it, but don't partake of it."

Raelen didn't understand.

"I have to go now," Saranna said. "Know that I love you, and that I am at peace."

Raelen nearly fell out of the saddle as he startled, the sharp spasm snapping him out of sleep. His ghern was still trotting along, though it had strayed a little off the path he'd been following. Something on Raelen's periphery caught his attention and he turned his head just in time to see a small ball of white light streak away and disappear into the trees.

"A dream?" Raelen said aloud, relieved he could speak again.

It had to be a dream, yet it'd seemed so real. It wasn't like the other dreams–or sometimes nightmares–he'd had about Saranna since she died. Those always had a kind of cold, detached quality to them, though they too would sometimes feel real. This was warm, vivid, and Raelen could swear he smelled a trace of white thorn on the air–Saranna's favored perfume. Most of all, he had felt Saranna's personality. In his regular dreams, she always seemed to him an echo, or a distorted copy of his beloved sister. This Saranna had been crystal clear.

And what had she been talking about? *You will face him again, but this time he fights with the power of death itself. You cannot fight him the way you did before. To touch him is death. His power cannot affect itself, so arm yourself with it, but don't partake of it.*

Raelen reined in his ghern and stared after where he'd seen the ball of light disappear into the trees. He was tempted to ride in that direction, to chase after the light for it could be no coincidence that it had appeared when it did.

Seiro.

Raelen was king now. He had to sacrifice personal wants and wishes for the good of the kingdom. Is that what his father had done? Is that what he'd meant when he said, "If you want to someday wear this crown, then you need to grow up and learn what it really means to rule, what it means to make the hard decisions."

Could he have mistaken his father's shrewd and seemingly cold-hearted decisions for apathy and hardness when they had, in fact, been sacrifice? He'd always believed his father to be a tyrant, and perhaps the man died as such, but what if there was more to him? What if Raelen's father's actions had been sacrificial? What if the old king had acted against his feelings and conscience in trying to do what was best for the kingdom? What was best for his son?

Raelen shook his head as if to physically shake the thoughts from his mind. He couldn't get distracted by grief or questions, not now. Raelen had to stop a talis war. He snapped the reins of his ghern and trotted it back to follow the trail of the army.

It was dusk when he nearly rode down a black-robed man standing in the road. He was older, with long wisps of white hair falling from a balding head. Even so, he managed a very spry leap out of Raelen's way just in time to avoid being trampled. Raelen hadn't even had the chance to shout an apology before he was pulled from the saddle and slammed onto his back.

The hard landing expelled the air from his lungs, and he gasped as he looked up to find a slitted, silver helmet peering down at him. The armored knight quickly raised his visor to reveal two very wide eyes.

"My prince!" the knight blurted out. Then he fell to one knee at Raelen's side, not to help him up, but in panicked deference.

Raelen wanted to slug the man, first for pulling him down, and second for being so surprised by his identity that he wasn't helping him to get up.

No man should kneel at the feet of another man, Gryyth's voice echoed from memory.

Raelen rolled onto his side, coughing. "Help me up, soldier."

The knight snapped out of his stupor and helped Raelen to stand. "I beg your forgiveness, my prince. Had I known it was you, I—"

Raelen silenced him with a wave of his hand. "You were doing your duty"—he paused to scan the man's breastplate for a sign of rank—"captain."

The old man in the black robe hurried over, but froze when he saw Raelen. "My prince!"

"Don't you dare fall to prostrate yourself too, Paisen!" He'd recognized the old man as one of Aiested's polymaths. "Where is our army?"

"An hour's ride north," Paisen said.

"And so why are you out here?" The question escaped Raelen's mouth when he saw what Paisen was holding; an octagonal cut amulet atop which was a large Apeira shard–a dousing stone. They were well-finding.

It was standard practice for an Aiestali army, or any army really, to travel with a few well-finders. The discovery of a buried well could provide a basecamp and could mean the difference between victory and defeat, especially when a large contingent of your army bore weapon talises.

"We were—" Paisen began.

"Find anything?" Raelen interrupted.

Paisen nodded. "We didn't, but Lord Eskeba did. That's why the army turned north."

"Have we engaged Haeshala yet?"

"No, Your Highness." Paisen's answer evoked a sigh of relief from Raelen.

"Praise Rasheera!" He turned to the knight. "We've set up camp around a well, then?"

The knight nodded. "I shall lead you to it."

Raelen closed his eyes and sucked in a steadying breath. Divine Mother, but he was tired. And without Gryyth's transference of strength, his body wasn't as tough as it usually was. Raelen pressed a hand to his side, the answering pain suggesting at least one broken rib.

"You are a credit to your battle masters, captain."

Chapter 76

A half-buried Apeira well rose out of the side of a large hill surrounded by dozens of flags, hundreds of tents, and thousands of men. Raelen's transference band awoke, and he was relieved to find his connection to Gryyth strong. As long as Gryyth lived, he would have access to the Ursaj's phenomenal physical strength, so if the connection was present, it meant his mentor and friend yet lived.

He tapped the transference band to strengthen his body, and the pain from the broken rib faded. As it always did, white fur grew beneath his dirty tunic, not enough to cover his chest, but enough to be itchy and uncomfortable. He tried not to scratch at his chest as he was led on a winding path through the bustling camp. It wasn't all the way set up, so the soldiers he passed were mostly distracted by their work, though a few stopped to stare. He hadn't been sure they'd recognize him with several day's stubble and the road dust clinging to his hair and clothes. And if they were close enough, they'd be treated to the stink of ghern. Oh, what he wouldn't give for a bath, but there wasn't time.

It took half an hour to reach the command tent at the center of the camp. Here the soldiers guarding the entrance immediately recognized Raelen, wordlessly saluted, and then moved out of his way. He pushed through the split in the canvas and entered upon a scene of high-ranking soldiers surrounding a table with a map rolled out. Several argued as they leaned over the map, pointing to landmarks Raelen couldn't see from his current vantage. He folded his arms and just watched. Eventually one of the captains glanced at him, did a double take, and then bowed. The others looked around in confusion until they too saw Raelen and did as their companions.

"Prince Taris," said the full-bearded general at the head of the table. Oddly, the man didn't bow.

"General Vesarr Rahkanas." Raelen nodded.

Vesarr was the son of Aiestel's chief general, Osarr Rahkanas, a man now dead by the treachery of the polymath Loeadon. Raelen hadn't considered he'd have to be the one to inform Vesarr that his father had fallen. Then again, with the destruction of Aiested, he'd be surprised if the other commanders hadn't lost loved ones too.

"What are you doing here?" Vesarr asked, and Raelen thought he caught a note of irritation in the man's tone. That was odd.

"Aiested has fallen," Raelen said without preamble.

That evoked gasping and wide-eyed glances from the captains surrounding the table, some of whom froze in the middle of rising from their knees.

"Surely not," Vesarr said.

"I was there." Raelen unfolded his arms and walked up to the table. "Our Apeira well went dark and then shattered, destroying the palace. Further, some dark power rains emerald-colored lightning down on the rest of the city, destroying buildings and killing our people. We had no choice but to abandon the city."

Vesarr frowned, and if Raelen didn't know better, he would've thought the general looked skeptical. Well, it was a remarkable report with tragic implications. Perhaps he needed time to fully digest the information.

A dozen questions assailed Raelen, and Vesarr had to call his council of captains to order before there was quiet again. Raelen picked that moment to shake them further.

"My father is dead."

This time no questions came. Instead, all the captains stared at Raelen with eyes wide and mouths agape, and a few looked like they weren't sure if they should bow a second time.

"That makes me king, and as such, I am taking command of this army, and ordering an immediate return march to Aiested. We have thousands of refugees to look after." Raelen pointed to a thickly built captain standing at his left. "Captain, relay the order to strike camp. We're going to travel through the night."

He pointed at a taller man standing farther down the table. "Captain, you—"

"I am afraid I cannot allow that," Vesarr cut in.

The entire command tent fell quiet.

It took Raelen a moment to find his voice. "You cannot allow?"

Vesarr glanced around the tent. "Leave us," he ordered.

It took a moment for the command to sink in, and Raelen thought the general was going to have to repeat it, but the men saluted and obediently filed out of the tent leaving only two guards flanking the entrance.

"You too," Vesarr said as he waved the men away.

The guards saluted, disappeared through the slit in canvas and Raelen found himself alone with the general.

"You had better have a good explanation for this, Vesarr."

Vesarr sighed, straightened and stared Raelen directly in the eyes.

"Your father ordered that we not turn back for any reason."

"Not even if your prince commands it?" Raelen snapped.

Vesarr met his eyes. "The king's orders were explicit."

"I am your king, now." Raelen strode up to the table.

I am a clear brook flowing among the trees.
I am a meadow of clover in summer.
I am the moon silently watching the night.

"Are you?" Vesarr said. "I spoke to the king myself. He said that we had an Allosian adversary hiding in the court, one with the power to change his appearance. He said that I was not to trust anyone who might contact me with orders contrary to his, no matter who it was, even if it was you or the king himself."

"You think I'm the Allosian imposter?" Jenoc had used the fact that his efforts had been discovered to his advantage. It was a brilliant stroke.

Vesarr sighed again. "It fits."

Raelen couldn't argue that. Damn that fey wizard.

"Use your speaking stone to hail Aiested. You will see that no one is there to answer."

Vesarr shook his head. "I was commanded not to contact the king until after our assault."

Raelen pounded a fist on the table. "Don't you see? It's the perfect plan for ensuring we start a war!"

Vesarr slowly nodded. "Perhaps."

Raelen ground his teeth. "You know I could tear you to pieces Vesarr, should I wish."

Vesarr casually laid a hand on his sword. "It's possible."

A casual glance at the amethyst shard embedded in the clear spherical pommel told Raelen that the weapon was a talis. "But if you truly are my prince, then I know you to be a man of honor, a man who wouldn't murder an innocent soldier for simply doing his duty."

Raelen ground his teeth. He could do it. He was already drawing on the transference band. If he wished, he could smash through the table and tear Vesarr's heart out before the man could draw another breath.

...if you truly are my prince...

Raelen's reputation as an idealist was well known among the lords of the court. It was something that frustrated his father. Is this what he meant about learning to make the hard choices? The kingdom–no, the entire world was at stake–and one man stood in his way of saving it. Raelen had a duty to see that Jenoc's plan was thwarted, and he bore the lives of uncounted innocents on his shoulders.

He almost attacked, but an echo of Gryyth's voice stopped him. "*You will teach Seiro to your people, cub.*"

He knew what his father would do, what he would expect Raelen to do. King Raeleth Joran Taris the eighteenth would kill this dutiful, honorable man without a second thought, all in the name of the greater good.

I will not be like my father.

"I am your prince," Raelen said. "And you are right. I cannot kill you."

Vesarr's tight jaw line relaxed, and he drew in a deep breath.

"I will surrender myself to you, General Rahkanas." Raelen rolled his sleeve up to the shoulder, removed the transference band from his bicep, and laid it on the table. Immediately the pain of his broken ribs stabbed at him, and the white fur on his chest disappeared. It was all Raelen could do to not double over.

Vesarr leaned over the table and reached for the talis. Raelen put a hand on it just as Vesarr was reaching for it. He could feel the talis offering Gryyth's strength to him, but he resisted it.

"I have but one request," Raelen said.

"And that is?"

"Send scouts back to Aiested to confirm my story, and hold off your attack until they report back."

Vesarr took the transference band, and straightened. "That would take weeks. Delaying our attack is out of the question."

"General—"

"However," Vesarr cut him off. "I will send my fastest scouts to investigate your claims. They will report back via speaking stone, and if what you say is true about the destruction of our capital, I will halt the attack."

It was the best Raelen was going to get. "Thank you, Vesarr."

"Until then," Vesarr said, "I hope you will understand that I will need to keep you here under guard."

Raelen had been expecting that. He nodded, resigned to his fate but at peace within. He had made the correct choice by following Seiro, he could feel it. He just hoped his desire to keep a clear conscience and set the example didn't end with the destruction of his people or the world.

CHAPTER 77

"And then there's Leena. I got her two years ago from widow Daisys. She's the mildest of my cow– definitely the opposite of Bess. She'll bite and kick if you get too close. It makes milking her hard." Maely chuckled. "One time my brother, Mulladin, was trying to suck milk straight from her udder when..."

Gryyth released a gravelly sigh.

"Gryyth?" Maely made them stop. She had an arm hooked around the Ursaj's waist to help steady him as he walked. "What is it?"

"You talk a lot, cub."

Maely grit her teeth. She'd been worried the bear-man had been overwhelmed by another wave of pain caused by his blistered chest. The stubborn creature had refused to take anymore of Sharor's poppy extract because of his determination to fast, and so was experiencing the full pain of his burns.

"Well, what else are we supposed to do?" she snapped.

"The journey to the meeting place is meant to be a time of quiet introspection."

"That's boring," Maely said as she resumed walking. "If you're tired of me talking, then why don't you tell me something?"

Gryyth sighed again. "Like what?"

"I dunno," Maely said as nonchalantly as she could manage. "Why don't you tell me about the prince?"

She'd been intrigued by the tall, handsome older boy. Not just because of his physical appeal, but because of the strange way he'd treated her when he'd thought Maely a servant. And then there was his saving her on top of the palace tower when Jenoc tried to blast her over the battlements with a wind spell, which she had repaid by saving him from drowning in the courtyard canal.

"What do you want to know?"

Maely shrugged her shoulders, well at least the one that wasn't pressed against Gryyth's furry side. "He seems different. He's not like what I thought a prince would be like."

"And what did you think a prince would be like?" Gryyth rumbled.

Maely frowned. "All the nobility I've ever met are selfish bastards who treat peasants like ghern shyte—no, worse!"

Gryyth chuckled. "Yes, cub. Prince Raelen is different."

"Are you sure? I've met men who acted all proper when they were around people, but when they get someone alone they're just like all the others."

"I've looked after the prince since he was a cub. His Seiro is true."

Maely wrinkled her nose. "Seiro? What's a Seiro?"

"Seiro is a path my people follow. You would call it honor or morality."

"So, it's like what the monks of Rasheera teach?" Maely asked.

Gryyth shook his big head. "What they teach is only an echo of what The Mother taught us."

The mention of the Ursaj's esoteric religion reignited Maely's irritation. "You know sooner or later you're going to have to tell me something about where we're going and why."

Gryyth opened his muzzle then immediately froze as a wave of pain made him tremble. Maely swung around to face him, and helped him lower his furry body to the forest floor where he rested on his knees.

"Gryyth?" Maely asked. "Are you okay?"

Gryyth slowly nodded.

"I'll get some more poppy extract." Maely knelt in front of Gryyth and dug through her satchel.

"Cub, you know I—"

"Have to fast? Yeah, well, how are you going to make it to this sky temple of yours if the pain keeps slowing you down or making you stop to rest?"

The bear-man didn't respond and Maely smirked to herself at the victory.

"Here," she said as she produced a small leather bag, and then proceeded to pour some powder into her palm. "Open that muzzle of yours."

Gryyth didn't move.

Maely's temper flared. "You know, if I hold this stuff too long, I'm gonna get all silly, and then probably pass out. Then when I wake up, I'll have the craving and probably become a poppy-addict. Who knows, maybe I'll get so desperate, I'll become a poppy whore! What does your Seiro say about that?"

She met Gryyth's large, blue eyes, and the bear-man opened his mouth. She poured the powder onto his tongue, and then spit on her hand and wiped off the residual powder on the dirt.

"So bitter," Gryyth complained.

"Is that the real reason you didn't want to take it? Because the big, tough bear doesn't like his medicine?" she quipped.

Gryyth looked at her for a long moment and then rumbled a deep, rich laugh.

Maely couldn't help but laugh, too. She sat on the ground and said, "We should wait until it starts working before we keep going."

Gryyth nodded as he slowly rolled from his knees onto his bottom. They sat in companionable silence for several minutes. Maely was starting to like the white-furred bear-man and so decided to give him the quiet he'd pined for earlier. Consequently, she was surprised when Gryyth initiated a conversation.

"How did you get entangled in the plots of that Allosian warmonger?"

The peace Maely was feeling evaporated as Gryyth's question brought back all her worry, pain, and guilt. She drew her knees up to her chest and hugged them.

"A boy," she said in a soft exhale.

"Aww," Gryyth rumbled. "The farm boy with the sword."

"Jekaran."

"He is your friend?"

"Was." Maely stared at the grain of the pine tree directly in front of her, the lines making her think of the threads of a worn quilt.

"He is dead then?"

Maely looked from the grain of the tree to a half buried white rock in the ground. Was Jek dead? She'd agonized over that since fleeing Aiested, but deep down, beneath the storm of worry was a steady confidence that he'd survived the collapsing palace. "Probably not. The sword talis he has makes him almost invincible."

"So why do you say he was your friend?"

A warm tear rolled down Maely's cheek, the cold of the north forest instantly chilling it. "Because I did something terrible to him."

She was grateful when Gryyth didn't ask what, but a sudden need to confess overcame her, and she started to sob. "I love him, but he doesn't love me back, and I have a ring talis that can make people do what I want."

She sniffed and wiped her runny nose with the back of her hand. "I used it to make him kiss me and think he loved me. Worse, I helped Jenoc start the talis war."

Gryyth's only reply was a grunt of acknowledgement. For some reason that infuriated Maely.

"Is that it?" She snapped. "Don't you have something to say?"

"What am I supposed to say?"

"That I'm a selfish and immature lovestruck girl! That I'm as bad as a rapist!" She leaned her forehead on her knees. "That I'm a monster."

A heavy paw gently touched her shaking shoulders. It rested there, and Maely leaned into Gryyth's unburned side. He held her like that while she sobbed. "We were supposed to get married. Everybody knew it." She hiccupped a laugh. "Well, everyone except Jek. He didn't know I loved him until that day in the palace. Boys are slow."

She as much felt his words as heard them when he rumbled, "To be ashamed is to see the mud on your fur. To make amends is to wash it off in the river."

"Is that a proverb from your Seiro?" Maely's voice was muffled by the Ursaj's fur.

"No," Gryyth chuckled. "I heard it from a traveling minstrel who performed for the prince's thirteenth birthday. I just changed skin to fur."

Maely couldn't help but laugh. She pulled away from Gryyth and began wiping her cold wet cheeks. When the tears dried, she asked, "But how am I supposed to make amends?"

"Only you can know that, cub."

They sat in silence for the next few minutes, Gryyth's breathing growing less haggard; an indication that the poppy extract was starting to take effect. A moment later he announced, "I am ready to resume our journey."

Instead of standing, Maely reached into her dress pocket and produced her mother's ring. Gryyth stared at it intensely, but made no comment. "This is the compulsion talis," Maely softly said. "It belonged to my mother, but she didn't know what it was."

Maely scooted over to the half-buried white rock, and placed the ring on top of it. She then searched the ground until she found another rock, this one an ugly gray caked with dirt. She picked up the stone, raised it high above her head, and brought it down on the compulsion ring. The blow, fueled by her anger at what she'd done with the ring, came down so hard that it not only shattered the Apeira shard and jewel set, but chipped away a piece of the rock as well. She looked up at Gryyth.

He nodded and said, "You have just dipped yourself into the river. Next comes the washing."

Maely looked down at the broken compulsion talis and her guilt eased. Gryyth was right. This was only the beginning. She had to do more if she was to atone for her crimes.

Chapter 78

Mulladin started as a ball of mud slapped his cheek. No, not mud, he realized as the foul smell assailed his nostrils. Oxen dung–fresh and still warm. He turned in the direction of the throw only to be rewarded with another ball of warm excrement, this one striking him in the forehead. The laughter of two boys, probably no older than thirteen, rang out and he closed his eyes as he wiped the filth from his forehead.

He didn't get angry until the woman hanging in the neighboring crow's cage joined in on the laughter, to which he responded by hurling the remnants of dung at her, catching her in the eye and abruptly silencing her. He smirked as she unleashed a stream of cursing in Tolean and hurled pieces of rotting pulp at him from the morning's fruit and vegetable assault by the townspeople.

"You're going to want to save that for supper," Mulladin said as he shielded his face with an arm. "It's all you're going to get to eat."

The Rikujo wench spit at him, her wad of phlegm arcing too high and landing far short of his cage.

"You'll want to save your spit, too. I think the next drink we get will have to come from the clouds."

"This is your fault," the woman hissed.

Mulladin couldn't help but laugh. "You're the one who stole my friend's sword."

"It's my birthright!" she snapped.

Mulladin sighed, too thirsty and hungry to maintain his anger. They'd been hanging in the crow's cages for almost two days with only rotten produce to eat and a cup of pity water from the village monk to drink.

"Why do you keep saying that?"

The woman didn't respond, having shifted in her cage to put her back to Mulladin.

"Well, can you at least tell me your name? We are, after all, going to be dying together."

Still no response.

"Fine." Mulladin exhaled and leaned his head back onto the cold iron bars.

"Keesa," the woman said.

"That's not a Tolean name," Mulladin replied.

"I'm only half Tolean, you fly-ridden mound of shyte."

Mulladin was about to retort, but the smell of the oxen dung on his face stopped him. Then for some reason, he started to laugh.

"You mock me?"

Mulladin shook his head, unable to form words.

"Suffering has already made you mad," Keesa concluded aloud.

When Mulladin was able to speak again, he said, "I'm not mad."

Keesa didn't say anything, and a sidelong glance at the woman revealed her confused expression.

"I am a fly-ridden mound of shyte. Oxen shyte, to be exact." He motioned at the smears of dung on his face where he'd tried to wipe it off.

To his complete surprise, Keesa started to chuckle and then joined him in a fit of laughter that lasted a full five minutes. Villagers began to point and chatter with one another, and a few who'd been preparing to pelt them with more rotten vegetables dropped their produce and walked away. Apparently, their pathetic state mixed with hysterical laughter was enough to evoke some pity from the people. Either that, or it just wasn't as much fun to torment a crazy person.

Mulladin wiped away tears with a clean patch of his sleeve. "I'm Mulladin."

"You were with Argentus when he came to Lord Trous's manner."

"Yeah."

"You feigned being a simpleton and then interfered in the succession duel."

"And got a lightning bolt in the chest for my trouble." Mulladin rubbed his breast where a few days ago there had been charred flesh. He didn't bother with a reply to Keesa's "feigning being a simpleton" comment.

"You were Argentus's servant, then?"

Mulladin barked a laugh. "I knew him as Ezra, and he was my friend. Foster father, really." That invoked a feeling of hollowness in his chest, and he had to bite back an involuntary sob.

"Ezra?"

"Yeah." Mulladin coughed to cover the emotion in his voice. "He was a farmer. I didn't know he was the Invincible Shadow until a few weeks ago."

"A farmer?"

"He left the Rikujo years ago to raise his sister's son."

Keesa's jaw tightened. "The boy with the sword?"

An image of Jekaran's vacant eyes flashed across Mulladin's mind. "Jekaran."

"He killed Kaul?"

"I guess," Mulladin said. "I wasn't there. What's it to you, anyway?"

Keesa's eyes flashed, but the anger quickly faded and she shook her head. "I was supposed to kill Kaul."

"Why?"

"He killed my mother."

"I'm sorry." And Mulladin was surprised that he meant it. "In any case, he's dead. So you can take some satisfaction in that."

Keesa went on as though she hadn't heard him. "I spent years working my way up through the ranks of Rikujo enforcers just to get close to him. I did things that I'd never thought I'd do, things to gain favor or advantage."

A tear rolled down Keesa's cheek, leaving a trail through the drying oxen dung. "She never wanted me to become involved with the Rikujo, you know. She moved us away from the big cities when I was a little girl. She made me swear to stay away from anything that had to do with the underworld. But none of that mattered, not after he robbed, raped, and murdered her. Would've done the same to me if I hadn't hidden like a coward in the wardrobe closet."

Her tears flowed freely now. "I saw it all. Everything that bastard did to her."

Kaul's face with its hellish grin flashed in Mulladin's mind.

"I was only sixteen at the time, but I could've done something. Damn it, I should've done something! I was just so scared." She sobbed.

"He had a talis that did that," Mulladin offered. "I've felt its power."

Keesa shook her head. "It can be beaten."

"Only with practice."

"The monks of Rasheera teach that love can overcome fear. My love for my mother should've been strong enough, but in the end, I hid there, frozen, watching him humiliate and beat her." She sobbed. "I didn't even come out of hiding until two full days later–that's how scared I was that Kaul was still about. By then my mother's corpse had started to bloat and stink, and I couldn't stand the smell enough to get close and kiss her goodbye."

She leaned her head against the bars of her crow's cage, squinted her eyes shut, and sobbed. Mulladin watched Keesa, giving her the only thing he could– sympathetic silence. He shot a little girl carrying a basket of apples a dangerous look when she started to approach them. Apparently, his expression had been fierce enough to turn the child away. Why couldn't the ones who threw the dung at him be so easily intimidated? But those apples didn't look rotten. Maybe he should've let her chuck a few. If he could catch one...

When Keesa's sobbing subsided, she continued, "After burning down our house and setting fire to the farm, I swore to kill Kaul. That became my life. Everything I've done since that day was to fulfill that oath."

She wiped her eyes. "Then Rasheera decides to play me for a fool, and send another to take the kill that should've been mine."

Is that why she wanted Jek's sword? Was it some macabre trophy? The blade that killed the man she hated. But no, she'd said it was her birthright.

Keesa sniffed. "I was at Lord Trous's manner house during the guild lord's council. I'd planned to hang myself the very night Argentus reappeared. When I learned that he was going after his nephew and the sword, I set my sights on a new goal."

"You wanted the sword," Mulladin said.

Keesa narrowed her eyes at him. "No, I wanted to kill Argentus. It was his fault Kaul came after my mother."

What? Something started to bother Mulladin about the woman, a nagging sense that he was missing something important.

Keesa barked a harsh laugh. "But Rasheera took that away from me, too. That's when I decided to claim the sword. It was mine by right, after all, the only thing I had left."

Words echoed in Mulladin's mind, words from another life. Words he'd heard from a monster amidst a backdrop of flames. *Poor Arynda... I decided long ago, Argentus, that I would have everything you had and more. So, I started with her.* They were Kaul's words. Spoken as a taunt to Ezra just before he and Mulladin had made their escape.

"Divine Mother," Mulladin gasped. "You're Ez's daughter!"

"I'm the daughter of the Invincible Shadow!" she snapped. "Not the skinny old farmer you call Ezra."

"Arynda was your mother."

Keesa glowered at him. "He talked about her?"

"He loved her," Mulladin said.

"Then why did he abandon her?!" she shouted. "Why wasn't he there to protect her from Kaul?!" Tears were pouring down her cheeks again.

Anything Mulladin said would just upset Keesa more, and truth be told, he really didn't know much about Ez's relationship with the woman Arynda or why they'd parted. Was it when Ez left the Rikujo or before? He probably hadn't known about fathering a child, of that Mulladin was pretty sure. The man he knew as Ezra was too honorable to abandon his own daughter.

"Excuse me," a small voice said.

Mulladin started and instinctively covered his face, but no fruit or feces flew at him. He cautiously lowered his arms and found a little girl standing below his hanging cage. It was the same girl with the basket of apples. She was small, probably only seven or eight years old, but tall enough to extend an apple up to him.

"What are you doing?" Mulladin asked.

"It's for you."

Mulladin eyed it suspiciously.

"It's good." The little girl took a bite and chewed it. "See," she said, exposing chewed apple. Then she offered it again to him.

Mulladin shot a hand out and grabbed the apple, pulled it into his cage, and attacked it. The little girl giggled as she watched his desperate feasting.

"I have one for you, too," the little girl said to Keesa. Then walked over to her cage, and handed up another bright red apple.

Keesa actually said, "Thank you," before tearing into hers.

Mulladin ate the entire thing, core and all, not even stopping to pick out the seeds. "Can I have another?"

The little girl offered him another apple which he took, but didn't eat it quite so desperately. He glanced around the village to make sure no one was watching, for Loeadon had forbidden the townspeople from giving them real food, and he feared someone would chide the girl and take away the apples.

"She said you'd be hungry," the little girl said with another giggle.

Mulladin stopped chewing. "Who?"

"Aeva."

"Who's Aeva?" Keesa asked.

"My flower."

"You have a talking flower?" he scoffed.

The little girl's smile faded. "You don't believe me do you—no one does."

Not wanting to hurt the girl's feelings, and consequently lose access to her basket of apples, Mulladin quickly said, "I believe you. It's just, I've never heard of a talking flower before."

The girl's smile returned. "That's because she's special. I found her in the woods when Da sent me out to get firewood. She's really nice. I wanted to bring you to meet her, but she says there's not enough time."

Mulladin froze mid-bite. "Not enough time?" That was an odd thing to say.

"Yeah," the girl said. She fished in her pocket and produced a large iron key. "She told me to sneak this from my da and give it to you."

Mulladin glanced at Keesa. Her eyes were wide and she was trembling. "Is that the key to...?"

The little girl proudly nodded, and Mulladin snatched it from her hand.

"Aeva says to wait until night so you won't get caught."

Mulladin stared at the key, his hand trembling as he stuffed it into a pocket. "Thank you, uh..."

"My name is Jesh," the little girl said.

"Thank you, Jesh."

Mulladin glanced at Keesa. She had risen to her knees and was clutching the bars of her crow's cage with both hands. "Are you going to leave me here?"

Mulladin honestly didn't know how to answer. The woman had tried to kill him or at least put him in danger. She'd stolen Jek's sword, and was half-crazed with a lust for vengeance. But she was Ez's daughter...

"Aeva says you need her help to get the key back."

Mulladin hesitated. What was Jesh talking about? "You gave me the key," he said.

Jesh laughed. "Not that one, silly. The key you've been chasing. You know, the one the bad man with long hair took. Aeva says you have to work together if you want to get it back, and then you have to take it to the secret city. It's really important."

"Jesh!" a man shouted.

The little girl glanced over her shoulder, and when she looked back her eyes were wide. "I have to go, or Da's gonna spank me."

She hurried away before Mulladin could ask her what she meant.

A talking flower told her to free them? Could the little girl be playing pretend and they'd become a part of her game? Mulladin would've thought that if Jesh hadn't known they were chasing the sword. She called it the key. And what was this thing about the secret city? Was she talking about Allose? How the hell would she know about that? Mulladin only knew about it because of what Irvis had told Ez when they met up a few weeks ago.

"Well?" Keesa asked. Her voice was harsh, but her trembling hands and tight jaw belied her bravado. "Are you going to leave me here to die?"

Mulladin looked at her. He found that he was still angry with her, and the temptation to leave her to die was very real. But she was Ez's daughter. And she'd probably alert the guards if he tried to sneak away without her anyway.

"No," he sighed. "I can't leave you."

CHAPTER 79

The ring did not radiate Apeiron, as Kairah had first believed. The energy was very similar in tone, feel, and its ability to refill her internal Apeiron stores, but there was no mistaking that it was different. Not alien like Moriora, but truer. Where Apeiron felt warm, the ring felt hot. Where Apeiron felt clean, this felt absolutely pristine. Where Apeiron was potent, the richness of the power the ring radiated was nearly overwhelming. Kairah also sensed something inside of the ring, something that was active and intelligent; like an ego talis, yet without projecting any psychic voice–all things a human couldn't notice just by using the talis.

Another confusing oddity was that she'd seen the familiar ripple of fate around the ring when she took it from the human monk. Kairah had only ever seen the mark of the fated around people, never objects. But perhaps that was because the ring was alive. That was the only way she could describe the power pulsing inside it. It was like it had a soul.

Drawing on it took some adjustment at first. A little bit of the power had an effect exponentially greater than normal Apeiron. Spells she cast with the power were more powerful, and took less effort. With it, Kairah's skill was on par with other, more adept Allosian spell-casters. It was jarring, like when she'd made to lift an object, only to find that it wasn't as heavy as she anticipated. The power had also alleviated her throbbing headache. It was still there, but it was a quiet thing only causing mild discomfort.

But the most wondrous thing about the restoration ring was that, through her, it caused flora around her to grow. Grass became greener and grew taller in only a matter of minutes. Flowers appeared and bloomed, trees leafed, and even a dead gray maple revived to a healthy brown with green leaves. This was certainly no ordinary talis.

"I don't see a damn thing." Hort held Jekaran in his muscular arms like a mother would cradle a baby. "Just an empty valley surrounded by mountains."

Kairah looked up from the ring which she now wore on her hand. She hadn't asked the human monk for the official right of possession, but as an Allosian she wasn't required to. All talises rightly belonged to her people, and so she claimed it. He hadn't said anything in protest anyway, the man appearing to be unnaturally quiet and shockingly uninterested in studying her form.

He grieves for his friend, Aeva said. *Can you not speak comfort to him?*

That is not my concern. Kairah cast a glance to her side where Irvis stood, his chubby arm around Graelle. "Allose is cloaked in a spell that shrouds it from all eyes."

"Even yours?" asked the little lord, Gymal, in his nasally voice.

After all that's happened, you still don't think of them as people, do you? Aeva accused.

Aeva's uncharacteristically mature question surprised Kairah. *They are a lower form of life. You cannot expect me to consider them equals.*

She felt a sigh from the spirit lily. *Is that not what Jenoc thinks?*

Just because their life has value does not mean that they are my peers! For some reason Aeva's words angered Kairah—something that had never happened before.

And Jekaran? Is he also your lesser?

Kairah faltered. *He is different*, she finally sent. *He possesses a sense of morality that is sorely lacking in the rest of the human race.* Again, anger, and this time it came with flashes of memory; images of her dead mother lying naked on her back, blood dribbling from her nose. Kairah pushed the memory away. What was wrong with her?

You are tainted, Aeva said in answer to the thought.

Kairah's breath caught. Was Moriora corrupting her heart as it did Jenoc's? She'd thought since Jenoc had long suffered a vengeful fever that the Moriora only magnified his hatred. What if it had actually changed him? What if it was changing her?

"Lady Allosian?" Gymal repeated.

Kairah shoved her rising terror down and turned to face the others. "I cannot see it either, not with my regular sight. But I can see the Apeira aura of Allose's well and the thousands of my kin who occupy the city. I can take you there, and once we cross the boundary of the cloaking spell, you will behold the city."

"You never told us what your people will do to us," Hort said.

Kairah sighed. "Likely you will not be able to leave."

"They'll imprison us?" Graelle asked, her eyebrows raised.

Kairah nodded. "But it will not be like the practice of humans. It will not be in a dark dungeon in squalid conditions. You will be made comfortable, taken care of, and even free to wander most of Allose."

"So there's precedent. You've captured humans before?" Gymal asked.

"Yes," Kairah said. "From time to time some of your kind have discovered our city. They were not permitted to leave, but they did live out their lives in comfort and tranquility."

"You should've told us this!" Graelle snapped.

"Would it have changed your determination to accompany me? To see Jekaran brought here?"

Her question was met with silence.

"I will give you an opportunity to turn back now, even though you know where Allose is. I only ask that you tell no one of its location."

More silence, broken a minute later when Gymal finally said, "There are doubtless others who know or will figure out what happened to the king, or who was responsible for freeing Jekaran. That will put my neck in a noose, or my ass in a dungeon. I don't really have much to go back to."

"There's nothing left for us in the world of men either," Graelle said. She pulled Irvis close to her and the two locked stares. A heartbeat later Irvis nodded.

"Karak kill Eater. Then Karak die, aka."

So sure he will die? But then Kairah was becoming increasingly convinced that if they were to defeat the monster that was Moriora's vessel, it would cost her life as well. She wasn't being negative, just realistic. The creature had to be stopped, and like Karak, she would give her life to see it destroyed if that was what it cost. And if Moriora was corrupting her, she may have no other choice but death. She would not turn into a hateful monster like Jenoc.

"That leaves you, Mercenary," Kairah said to Hort. "There is no reason for you to accompany us any farther."

Hort glanced at the others and then looked down at Jekaran's face. He gently wiped the black strands of hair away from Jekaran's blank eyes. It was a surprisingly tender motion, like a loving father considering a terminally ill child.

Hort shook his head. "No, I have to see the boy healed."

Gymal's eyes snapped up to Hort's face. He opened his mouth to comment, but closed it again. Apparently, he had been as surprised as Kairah by the burly mercenary's answer.

Hort met her eyes and then grinned. "My latest wife was about to leave me anyway, after catching me in the bath with her mother. This way the magistrate can't force me to give her any of my money. It's all buried in a chest under the latrine." He laughed. "She'll never think to look there. And even if she did, there's no way in hell she'd fish it out."

"Your latest wife?" Graelle asked.

Hort nodded. "Number seven." His brow crinkled. "No, I'm sorry. I was thinking of her twin sister, Loria–she was number seven. Hedia is number eight."

TYRUS GYMAL HUFFED AS he worked to keep up with the long strides of the tall Allosian woman. It'd taken a few hours to descend into the valley, which had been an exhausting and perilous climb over rocks and horizontally growing trees. But now the terrain had blessedly leveled out, and they hiked over grassland toward the invisible city.

He glanced at Jekaran carried in Hort's arms. Taking him to Allose wasn't about avoiding implication in the king's assassination, though that definitely was part of why Tyrus hadn't turned back. It was about making certain Kybon's son got help from the fey people. They were his only hope of restoring the boy to his senses. He needed to see that done if possible, no matter the cost.

He didn't owe it to Kybon, not really. If anything, the lout had left life in Tyrus's debt–both figurative and financial. But he'd loved his cousin. The handsome, popular boy hadn't needed to be Tyrus's friend, despite their familial relationship. Kybon had wanted to be his friend, had chosen it, and for Tyrus that was a rarity. But it was more than that, Tyrus knew. Guilt played its part, guilt that he hadn't been able to see those responsible for Kybon's murder brought to justice. Guilt that he hadn't gone to his uncle and revealed that Kybon was dallying with a peasant girl. If he'd done that, maybe he'd still have his cousin.

He would never have forgiven me.

If it were any of the light-skirt baron's daughters or courtiers Kybon usually rolled around with, he would've eventually have pardoned any treachery on Tyrus's part. But this girl, Anarilee...Kybon was different about her. The idiot actually loved her.

Tyrus glanced again at Jekaran and then up at the man carrying him. Hort had surprised Tyrus, and he still didn't know what the mercenary's game was. Why did he care what happened to Jekaran? Was he trying to leverage the situation? Ingratiate himself to Tyrus in the hope of increasing his pay? It made sense, and it was in Hort's character as far Tyrus knew except for the fact that going to Allose meant they could never leave. Perhaps he was hoping for a cushy retirement and the chance of bedding one of the fey women?

But no, Tyrus had seen real concern in the man's eyes when he looked at Jekaran's blank face. Could he possibly like the child? Kybon had that effect on people too. Perhaps it was more that, in a world that seemed on the verge of falling apart, Allose offered safety. Tyrus didn't understand what this Eater was, but if anyone could deal with it, it would be those who wielded the power of Apeiron itself.

He threw a glance over his shoulder at the Vorakk shaman striding behind him. It made his skin prickle to have the lizard man at his back. While the Vorakk was technically their ally, Tyrus had no doubt the creature would eat him if the occasion arose. And it would be him first, he was certain; the blood of nobles was sweeter than that of the common folk. He nearly tripped and had to force himself to focus on the path ahead, but continued to steal glances at the lizard man as often as he could. It was during one of these backward checks that Tyrus caught the Vorakk speaking to no one.

Perfect. He's dangerous and insane.

But no. He wasn't talking to nothing. A glow fly hovered at eye level to the lizard man. It bobbed up and down, and was unusually bright. The Vorakk finished whatever it was saying, and the little ball of light zipped away. Tyrus started when the lizard man's slitted eyes focused on him. He looked away, but not in time to avoid stumbling over a fallen log. Tyrus crashed to the ground, evoking a spell of hissing laughter from the Vorakk as it stepped over him. He scrambled up, and continued on, curtly dismissing a concerned question from Hort.

The crossing of the boundary came without warning, or fanfare. One moment Tyrus was looking ahead at grassy hills with a meandering creek and thickets of trees, and then a white mountain suddenly loomed over them. Only it wasn't a mountain–it was a city made of stone so pristinely white it glowed with reflected sunlight. And rising even higher than the city's mammoth white towers and artfully sculpted turrets, was the biggest Apeira well Tyrus had ever seen. It was so tall that clouds–tinged with reflected purple light–concealed the top of the crystal monolith.

He'd stopped walking, but wasn't the only one. All the party save for Kairah stood still, overawed by the sight. The city was like Aiested, but in the same way that a sapling was like an ancient oak.

"Allose," Kairah announced, though to Tyrus it came too late and was ridiculously unnecessary.

Tyrus imagined that this was what dying and arriving at the gates to Heaven would be like. Did Rasheera live in a city like this? Surely if there were cities in the afterlife, they would be as grand as this. He couldn't imagine anything grander.

Flashes of purple light exploded all around them, and a heartbeat later, Tyrus found that they had been surrounded by Allosian men and women wearing glossy white, form-fitting armor. The most impressive part of the sentries, however, was their wings. Each looked like an avenging angel with a set of glowing silver wings sprouting from the back of their armor. They bore no weapons, but Tyrus was sure they were armed with innate magic or powerful talises.

"Lady Kairah?" a male sentry asked. Immediately, his helmet appeared to liquefy and melt off his face before being absorbed by the high collar of his chest plate. He had a perfectly sculpted face, and long cerulean hair that looked like it had been spun from glass.

"Peacekeeper," Kairah responded with a respectful nod.

"What are you doing out here?" The sentry glanced at Tyrus. "And who are these humans?"

The rest of the sentries raised their hands and pointed at Tyrus and his traveling companions. *They won't kill us*, he had to remind himself. The legends said Allosians wouldn't take a human life, but what then of Kairah's brother? The sentries started to advance on them, and Tyrus's bladder threatened involuntary evacuation.

Kairah raised her hand to halt the sentries. "They are my guests."

The sentries hesitated, all looking to their helmet-less captain for instruction. He nodded to them, and they ceased their attempt to close on the group, but kept their hands raised.

"You know the law, Lady Kairah."

"They are material witnesses," Kairah said. "I bring them here to testify before the synod."

The sentry captain furrowed his brow. "Testify of what?"

"The destruction of the Aeose at Taris, and the being who single-handedly destroyed it."

The sentries lowered their hands and looked to their captain. Although all Allosians were pale-faced by nature, the captain had actually turned a shade whiter. For some reason that made Tyrus feel like smirking at the Allosian, and so he did.

Tyrus wouldn't have thought it possible, but the magnificence of Allose's interior was even more awe-inspiring than when he first beheld the city appear in a seemingly empty valley. Even the smallest of Allose's structures were taller than the giant sequoias that grew north of Aiested, and every building was as much a work of art as the finest Aiestali sculptures.

Allose's towers, domes, and palaces all surrounded the base of the city's gargantuan Apeira well—its circumference having to be measured in the dozens of miles–and was the center from which a network of paved streets wove between smaller buildings in neat straight lines.

Beautiful arches with trailing floral designs, gazebos appearing to have been carved from single blocks of white marble, and multi-tiered fountains abounded within the secret city. But the thing that impressed Tyrus the most were the gardens.

Flowers and trees of all kinds grew everywhere, making the smooth, white thoroughfare they now traveled a road between floral walls splotched with a rainbow of colors. The flowers weren't wild or haphazard in their placement, but looked all to be carefully manicured, and deliberately placed. Even the smell of so many flowers, which Tyrus thought might be overwhelming, was perfectly balanced, and each whiff evoked thoughts of springtime and new life. The colors of the different plants and flowers were another wonder; reds, yellows, pinks, purples– and even some bizarre shades of blue, gold, and luminescent green– joined together as though arranged by the skill of a master painter.

Yes, this is what Heaven would look like.

The Allosians themselves weren't as varied in color or appearance as were their paradisiacal gardens. All were tall–Tyrus didn't think he'd seen any that were under six feet–with perfectly sculpted forms and pale youthful faces. Their jewel-like hair did differ in shades of purple, and even some blue, but other than that, it was difficult to tell one from another. Fortunately, they wore a variety of clothing, most loose-fitting robes, tunics, or dresses of white or purple. Aside from the sentries that now escorted them through the city, Tyrus didn't see any with shod feet.

Their little procession drew the attention of every passing Allosian, who stopped and gawked at them even long after they'd passed.

That's right, stare at the sideshow of ugly, dirty humans.

Would it be like this for the rest of his life? Would he be put on display for these fey people to study and stare at? Were he and his companions little more than new acquisitions for some Allosian zoo?

He wasn't sure why he was suddenly so bitter toward these people. Perhaps it was envy of their paradise and perfection. Why did they not share these things with the rest of the world? Why leave mankind to struggle in darkness, and poverty? But, then again, he knew the legends.

They had tried to help mankind once and were rewarded with being hunted to near extinction as reward for their charity.

They were led for nearly an hour through the white streets of the city but appeared no closer to its center, and their destination—a glass dome structure built around the base of the Apeira well. Tyrus was surprised when they veered off the main road, and were escorted to a gazebo set at the top of a long flight of marble stairs. The captain of the sentries motioned for Kairah to climb the stairs, but when Tyrus tried to follow, one of the sentries placed a hand firmly on his shoulder to stop him. He glanced at Kairah and then back at the sentry captain.

"I must insist that the council hall be off limits to your guests," the sentry said. "It would not do to bring humans into a place where even most Allosians are not allowed."

Kairah turned and took a step back down. "I told you, the synod needs to hear their testimonies."

"And they will," the sentry replied. "But by way of an echo stone. I will take them to a comfortable place to wait and interview them personally."

Kairah nodded and then turned to resume climbing the stairs. When she reached the top, she stepped into the gazebo and was surrounded by a flash of bright purple light. When the light faded, the Allosian woman was gone.

"Slipgate," the short, fat woman, Graelle, whispered from behind.

The example of unmatched talis-craft that the ancient Allosians, and humans, once used to instantaneously travel from city to city was a rarity in Shaelar. The king had one which Tyrus had used a few times, but only with great solemnity and under a contingent of guards. But in Allose they were used like simple garden gates. Ironically, it was the least impressive thing about the fey city.

He glanced at the sentry, and the man narrowed his eyes. *Rasheera send that the legends of Allosian pacifism are true.* Suddenly the urge to urinate renewed and pressed on his groin with terrible urgency.

"I need to piss," he blurted out.

CHAPTER 80

Kairah stepped down from the dais of the companion slipgate and shrugged off the brown robe the man Irvis had lent her. It was coarse, had a few holes in it, and it smelled offensive. Kairah would not address the wisest leaders of her people in such garb. She strode forward, clad only in her short, sleeveless shift, but the immodesty of the garment barely troubled her. She was with her people again, and they were not like the humans. Their passions would only be stirred if they deliberately stirred them. None would be aroused even if Kairah should walk into the synod completely naked.

That was a marked difference between her race and the other inhabitants of Shaelar. Allosian breeding was a careful, planned, and official process. Mates were chosen based on their strengths and traits, and then reported to the College of Disciplines for preparation, finally performing the act while being monitored to ensure conception. Even her parents, though mated for life, never undertook physical intimacy outside of the strict Allosian breeding protocol. No passion, no spontaneity, just cold, deliberate eugenics.

That's boring, Aeva said.

And you would have us pattern our procreation after the reckless violent practices of humans? They rape and kill because they cannot control their passions.

It isn't always like that, Aeva said.

Kairah scoffed. Most humans–primarily men–had significant trouble controlling their urges, particularly in the realm of sex. Kairah had faced such men when she first left Allose.

They would have done the same thing to me as they did to my mother.

An explosion of raw, hateful rage flared to life inside her chest. She clenched her jaw and for an infinitesimal moment, she wanted to lash out with her magic–kill the humans who wanted to rape her by immolating them with a column of fire as hot as her hate. *Another residual effect of my channeling Moriora.* She drew in several steadying breaths.

Jekaran isn't like that, Aeva said.

Kairah stopped walking. Aeva was right. Jekaran was an anomaly–a human who wasn't completely driven by lust or selfishness. He'd come to her rescue when those men tried to take her. She had been a stranger to him, but he risked his life to save her, even though she actually hadn't needed saving. And that hadn't been the only time. He'd fought to protect her in Imaris, and then slaughtered hundreds of human soldiers trying to bar his way to rescue her when she was an unconscious captive in Taris.

And yet, though tainted, he still chooses life, Aeva said. *He is still good.*

"What?" Kairah answered Aeva aloud.

He has Moriora in his blood.

"Aeva, how can you possibly know that?"

His eyes are green.

"Lady Kairah?"

Kairah glanced toward the voice and found a white-robed Allosian man approaching her. Behind him was a colossal domed building, at least a thousand feet tall, made entirely of colored glass. As large as the building was, it was nothing compared to the crystal obelisk that rose out of the dome's center–the Mother Shard. The glowing crystalline formation had a circumference measured in miles, and its distant peak disappeared in the clouds above.

Kairah nodded to the chamberlain. "The synod received my message?"

The man scrutinized her state of undress, but with a neutral look, not one of lust as she'd so often received from human males. "Yes," he finally said.

"And they will see me?"

The chamberlain flashed a smile. "You were successful in arresting their attention, my lady."

Kairah nodded, and strode toward the dome building and its open arched doorway. She stopped when the chamberlain said, "Might I fetch you a dress before we enter the council chamber, Lady Kairah?"

"This cannot wait," she said, and then continued forward.

Aeva giggled, but Kairah was too disturbed by what the Spirit lily had said about Jekaran to appreciate the flower's childish humor.

Jekaran has Moriora in his blood.

Something was different about Aeva. The Spirit lily had been acting strange ever since the day Kairah first left Allose. She had knowledge of things she shouldn't, and often spoke with wisdom that eclipsed that of any ancient sage. A quick sifting through Kairah's memories brought back more odd encounters with her sentient flower, though they'd been far less frequent over the last eight decades.

One particular memory stood out; the time Jenoc had brought her back to Allose from the village where her parents were murdered. After being healed and tended to, she found herself alone in her garden with Aeva. That's when she'd believed the flower was channeling the spirit of her dead mother, and so gave it her mother's name. Why had she thought the Spirit lily was her mother?

Because she had said it was, Kairah suddenly remembered.

She'd been sobbing and inconsolable when the gentle touch of the Spirit lily's mind reached out to her. Kairah remembered the warmth and comfort Aeva had radiated, and asked the flower what its name was.

No, she shook her head, *I asked, "Who are you?"*

The Spirit lily had responded, '*I am your mother*', after which Kairah began to call it Aeva–her mother's name.

Aeva! Kairah called. Aeva were you listening to my thoughts?

Silence.

Aeva! Why did you tell me you were my mother?

"Lady Kairah, student of the College of Disciplines, and descended daughter of the Oracle Jatyra," the chamberlain announced.

The next thing Kairah knew, she was standing in the center of a titanic coliseum-like amphitheater with hundreds of faces peering down at her from circular tiers of seating. Standing at an ivory podium twenty feet above the coliseum floor was the synod's Speaker.

Kannic was his name, and he was one of the oldest living Allosians in Shaelar–a man well into his fourth century by all accounts. Though, as was typical with Kairah's people, he looked to be a man in his late twenties, handsome, and in perfect physical condition.

"The synod recognizes Lady Kairah, and anxiously requests her to elaborate on her most unusual message."

Suddenly Kairah's state of undress began to bother her. *I have been spending too much time with humans*, she thought.

She slowly turned about, glancing around the massive coliseum at the hundreds of members of the Allosian synod. She opened her mouth but stalled when she caught sight of a woman standing at the very top of the tiered seating. Unlike the other Allosian women in the chamber, she had her head shaved and wore flowing robes of deep green. She wore rings on every one of her fingers, and multiple earrings running up the edge of her ears–all talises?

It was Allose's chief Oracle, Shivara.

Though descended from oracular heritage herself, Kairah had never met the mysterious woman. She, of course, had a permanent seat among the synod, but rarely attended. She was as old as Kannic, if not older, and was something of a recluse; preferring to stay in her tower dealing with the outside world through the handful of apprentice oracles who served her. Kairah herself planned one day to apprentice with the woman for a century or so to draw out her power. Now that wasn't necessary–not that Kairah had any idea how to invoke or direct her gift for seeing fate.

As she stared up at Shivara, their eyes met, and for a moment it was if the two of them were the only souls in the entire chamber.

What have you seen, child? An unfamiliar woman's voice asked her telepathically.

"Lady Kairah," Kannic prodded.

Kairah shook herself from the trance, and turned back to face Kannic: "Six days ago the Aeose at Taris, the place the humans now call Aiested, went dark and shattered into discolored shards."

A round of gasps, followed by a low murmur of comments bounced around the chamber. Kairah paused only a moment to relish the effect of her announcement before continuing, "Doubtless you perceived the psychic wave its destruction produced?"

"It was as loud as thunder," one of the council members said.

"And as bright as an exploding star," another added.

"You are witness to this?" Kannic asked.

Kairah nodded. "Myself, and thousands of humans, four of whom I have brought with me." She thought she caught some scandalized huffs from several members of the synod. "They, along with a Vorakk witness, are giving statements to the captain of the peacekeeper patrol that escorted us into the city; statements that will corroborate my claim."

"How did this happen?" a woman called out. "Nothing can destroy an Aeose."

"The other magic can." Instead of the cacophony of questions and challenges Kairah expected to erupt at her revelation, the entire synod fell silent. It was unnerving.

"The other magic is a myth," Kannic said. "There is no power but Apeiron."

"My brother believed in it. You are all aware of his views in regards to humanity and its right to exist in Shaelar. Well, Jenoc tried to summon the other magic to use as a weapon to purge humanity from our land. But something went wrong, and a monster was created; a human vessel that wields Moriora like we can wield Apeiron."

"Moriora?" one of the council members asked.

Kairah turned toward the voice. She wasn't sure who'd asked the question because the voice sounded like it could've belonged to either a male or female. "It is the name of the other magic."

"This is absurd!" another member of the synod shouted.

Kairah turned to face that voice, this time definitely a male. "I have seen it. I fought it in Taris, but it overcame me, and then destroyed the Apeira well."

"What do you mean you fought it?" Kannic demanded.

"I cast several spells from The Second Discipline at the creature, but it either absorbed them or stole the life-force of nearby humans to heal itself. I only escaped by the aid of a Vorakk shaman. For some reason, Moriora's vessel couldn't absorb the shaman's magic."

"Vorakk do not have magic," a woman from the third seating tier called out. She had amethyst hair so light that it looked almost pink. "They are little more than animals–barely even sentient."

Kairah ground her teeth. Had she ever been as deliberately ignorant as this woman? Hot anger blossomed in her chest, and she wrestled it back into submission before daring to answer the woman's challenge.

"I have also witnessed the use of the Vorakk power. As I said, it saved my life."

"How did this Moriora vessel destroy Taris's Aeose?" Kannic cut in, effectively preempting the brewing argument.

"It attached itself to the Apeira well and fed on the Apeiron inside. After that, the Aeose shattered, raining down enormous shards that had turned an emerald color onto the palace." Kairah continued to glare at the pink haired woman.

"The palace was destroyed?"

"Utterly."

"And did you see the vessel leave the palace?" Kannic asked.

Kairah shifted her gaze back to the Speaker. "I did not."

Kannic exhaled and nodded. "Such a thing would have killed an Allosian. If the legends and what you tell us is true, and if the other magic is the opposite of Apeiron as you claim, it would stand to reason that this creature would be of comparable durability to one of us. Therefore, would it not be safe to assume that it died in the destruction of the Taris palace?"

Kairah's heart started to race. "Speaker Kannic, I do not think it safe to assume anything about—"

"You said it could be hurt, did you not?"

"Well, yes, but—"

"If the palace collapsed on it, and you did not see it reemerge, then it must have been killed."

The synod's orderly quiet shattered into hundreds of overlapping comments and conversations, which for the most part, sounded as though they sustained Kannic's theory.

What! This hadn't been the reaction Kairah expected and she began to panic. "A darkness now covers Taris!"

Kannic touched a glass globe fixed to the top of his podium, and a deep gong echoed throughout the chamber signaling for the assembly to fall silent.

"What is this you say, Lady Kairah?"

"Clouds of impenetrable black rain down emerald-colored lightning onto the city and any who venture there. This lightning has the same life withering effect as the power wielded by Moriora's vessel. And when I attempted to scry the area, I saw only a void."

"Perhaps a residual effect?" a baritone voice put forth.

"Apeiron does not linger outside of an Aeose," someone else argued.

"Absolutely fascinating," another said.

How could her people not see the danger? How could they be so ready to dismiss this threat as though it were an academic experiment, the consequences of which were but subjects for study? She'd heard the creature when it crossed from the material world to the ethereal sphere, and it had been laughing, not dying.

They choose blindness, Aeva sent.

"There is no question..." Kannic said in a loud voice, and the synod fell quiet once more. "...that the matter requires further investigation." He looked down at Kairah. "We shall make it a priority to dispatch an expedition of scholars and peacekeepers to study this phenomenon."

Murmurs again cascaded throughout the assembly.

They covered their crime, Aeva said.

"But now, Lady Kairah, the council must ask you to divulge the whereabouts of your brother. He has missed several days of teaching at the College of Disciplines. If what you say is accurate about his experiments with the other magic, then he will need to be brought before this body for interrogation and judgment."

Jenoc's angry, burned face flashed before Kairah's mind. *You are as dead to me as father and mother*, his voice echoed in her memory. Thus far, she'd made a deliberate effort not to think about Jenoc, because the pain of his betrayal was almost more than she could bear.

It is I who betrayed him. Kairah had seen the incredulous hurt in her brother's remaining eye after she'd attacked him on top of the palace in Aiested.

"I do not know where he is." Kairah's voice caught and she swallowed. Tears wanted to come, but she held them back. "He goes about deceiving the human rulers in his efforts to ignite another talis war between their respective nations." That invoked gasps and scandalized remarks.

Kannic looked more disturbed at the revelation that Jenoc was trying to start a war than he did at hearing proof of the existence of Moriora and its incarnation in a human vessel. "That is a most grievous offense."

"That is why I left Allose in secret, to thwart his designs."

"And did you succeed?" the pink haired woman called.

You are as dead to me as father and mother.

A tear spilled down Kairah's white cheek. "No."

The chamber erupted again into a roar of overlapping talk and shouting, and Kannic had to sound his signal talis twice before the synod quieted again.

"Do you know the details of his plan?" Kannic asked.

"One of the humans I brought with me was a member of the Aiestal aristocracy. He claims that an army was dispatched to attack Haeshala, and that the final declaration of war was given just before Taris fell."

"Let the humans destroy themselves," a man shouted. "It is what they deserve!"

"Apeiron desires life," a woman called. "Should we not attempt to stop this war?"

"The humans are always at war," another shouted. "How is this any different?"

Kannic shook his head. "It is regrettable that one of our people started this human conflict, but the last time Allosians interfered in human wars, it very nearly destroyed us. Let them battle as they so often do unto whatever outcome. We shall remain safe here in Allose."

Kannic took a vote and nearly all the members of the synod voted to sustain his motion for nonintervention. Kairah wasn't surprised by this. Besides, there was a greater evil to contend with. Karak had confirmed by his Vorakk clairvoyance that the threat of the "Eater" still remained, though he didn't know any more than that. She explained this to the synod as they continued to interrogate her, but no one gave the Vorakk shaman's words much consideration.

She told them everything, even confessing it was she that stole the illusion pendant from the College of Discipline's treasury. She was about to tell them of the ring she wore, the talis that radiated Apeiron, when Aeva's words slammed into her mind.

No, Kairah!

More than the words, there was a tone of desperation in the Spirit lily's psychic impression.

Why?

Aeva's psychic presence abruptly vanished.

Aeva?

The Spirit lily didn't answer. Kairah would have to check on her sentient flower as soon as she could make it back to her tower apartment.

Finally, six hours after she'd entered the chamber, the synod was ready to dismiss.

"Lady Kairah, you were not authorized to leave Allose, and you admit to being the one who stole the illusion pendant," Kannic said. "However altruistic your motivations, these infractions will have to be considered, and I expect you to fully cooperate with the peacekeeper corps and the College Elders as they determine your punishment."

Punished for trying to save an entire race from extinction at our hands? Hot anger flared to life inside her chest.

"This concludes today's session of the—"

"I saw it!" Kairah shouted.

The coliseum fell deathly quiet.

Kannic glanced to his peers on his right and then on his left. "Saw what?"

Kairah slowly turned in a circle so that the entire assembly had a chance to see the fire in her eyes. "I saw what happened to the lands whence the humans came."

"What are you talking about, child?" the pink haired woman asked with a sneer.

"I beheld in vision a desolate land stripped of even the tiniest forms of life. The same black clouds that now circle Taris, with their shafts of emerald lightning, blotted out the sun. I saw bald black-rock mountains, and a ruined city full of bones. And in that city's center, a broken Aeose, discolored green. The same as the shards of the Apeira well in Aiested after it was touched by Moriora."

"Are you a seer now, child?" A man sitting in the second seating tier laughed.

"I am the descendant of an oracle!" Kairah snapped. "This you all should know."

"Lady Kairah." Kannic tried to cut her off but she wouldn't let him.

"Shaelar is infected by Moriora!" *As I am.*

"That will be quite enough, Kairah!" Kannic said.

"This corruption will spread from Taris, and Allose will be no shelter! We must do something or suffer the fate of our ancient human refugees!"

"Enough!" Kannic shouted.

Kairah opened her mouth to challenge the Speaker, but froze when words entered her mind.

Argue no more with these fools.

Kairah looked up to the top floor of the coliseum where she locked eyes with the bald oracle, Shivara.

Seek me out when this farce of a council ends.

You believe me? Kairah replied telepathically.

Shivara smiled down at Kairah and then disappeared in a flash of purple light.

Chapter 81

Apparently, the villagers of Gnot were quasi nocturnal, because it was nearly midnight before they'd finally all disappeared into their cottages. As soon as the last door slammed shut, Mulladin quickly reached for the key the constable's little girl, Jesh, had stolen for him. He'd hidden it under the left cheek of his buttocks which turned out to be a poor decision, as his immediate discomfort had quickly evolved into pain. He would've removed it, but of course, as soon as he'd put it away, there was a surge in interest among the villagers in pelting him with garbage. He hadn't had a private moment all day, and Mulladin was certain a duplicate key could be cast from the imprint in his ass.

Sweet relief made him smile as he slid the key out, and turned it in his hand. He rose to his knees and reached through the bars. He started when Keesa hissed, "Don't drop it!"

He shot her a scowl, though he doubted she could make it out in the dark of the overcast night. "If you don't want me to drop it, keep your mouth shut."

Keesa's only reply was an indignant huff, and Mulladin resumed his effort to insert the key into the lock. Several bawdy jokes flashed in his memory, jokes he'd not understood until this moment. They made him guffaw, and he had to bite his lip to keep from spoiling their opportune quiet any further.

"Shh!" Keesa hissed. "What's wrong with you?"

Mulladin had no idea how to explain that all his memories from a life as someone else were surfacing and eliciting new emotional reactions, so he didn't try. He just kept probing with the tip of the key until he succeeded in fitting it into the lock. He made sure it was all the way in—he laughed again—and then turned it. The lock popped open with a springy click, and it was the sweetest sound that'd ever touched Mulladin's ears.

Unfortunately, the lock had been the one thing holding the floor of the cage to its barred dome, as Mulladin learned from suddenly dropping four feet to the ground. His knee landed on a loose stone, and he had to bite back a stream of curses trying to erupt from his mouth. He stood, massaged his knee, and then limped over to Keesa's cage.

Do I really want to do this? Things had been different between them ever since she'd broken down and told him her story. Hearing how Kaul had destroyed her life made Mulladin feel a sense of kinship with her. Jesh had also told him that her "flower" said they needed to work together to get the "key" back to the secret city, and as unsure of what the little girl's instructions really meant, he felt compelled to follow them.

It didn't hurt that Keesa was pretty.

Mulladin shrugged off his hesitation and unlocked Keesa's crow's cage. She had the good sense to hold onto the bars when the floor dropped open and adroitly landed on her feet before ducking out from under the dome of iron bars.

"Come on." She darted for the nearest building.

She thinks she's in charge? Pretty or not, Ez's daughter possessed a natural talent for getting on Mulladin's nerves. He limped along after her as fast as the sting in his knee would allow. They stopped just outside the cottage belonging to the village constable—Jesh's father. He lived within site of the village's center where they'd hung in the crow's cages.

They hopped a low fence surrounding a well-manicured yard and skulked around to the back of the cottage where there was a small barn. Keesa slipped in through a side door, and Mulladin nearly knocked her over when he stepped into the total blackness of the stable.

"Hey!" Keesa snapped.

She shoved him away from her harder than Mulladin thought was necessary. He massaged his ribs where she'd pressed her hand. "That hurt!" he whispered.

"Good," Keesa said. He couldn't see anything but her silhouette as she carefully moved about the barn.

"You think anyone in this inbred village is going to have a ghern?"

"I can smell it."

Mulladin scoffed. "They don't smell all that different from bullocks, and those are too slow. We'd be better off running."

Keesa's silhouette stopped moving, bent over, and then a dim yellow light lit up the barn. She stood, triumphantly raising an oil lantern in her right hand. Mulladin glanced around the stables. Sure enough, a black-furred ghern bayed at them from a pen two stalls down a long aisle strewn with straw. The other occupants of the barn were a pair of goats, three sheep, a couple pigs, a cow, and an old gray bullock with red horns and a droopy middle.

"See?" Keesa smugly said.

"There's only one." Mulladin waved at the animal.

"We only need one." Keesa hung the lantern on a hook on the wall. "Go stand guard outside while I saddle it."

"Who said you were in charge?" Mulladin grumbled as he limped out of the barn.

He stood nervously glancing between the rear of the constable's cottage and a closed gate in the back of the fence. As Mulladin's eyes re-adjusted to the night, a rag doll in the center of the yard caught his atten-tion–Jesh's doll. It sat slumped against a stone watering trough, one of its button eyes hanging off its face by a few threads.

You have to get the key and take it to the secret city. It's important.

The secret city had to be Allose. But the key? Could that really be Jekaran's sword? And what was it a key to? And was he really taking seri-ously the message a little girl claimed came from a talking flower? He glanced around the yard looking for any unusual flowers, but it was too dark for him to see. *She said she found it in the woods, you dullard.*

The barn doors exploded open and Keesa rode out on the ghern at full speed. It leapt over the wooden fence and flew off down the road.

"Hey!" Mulladin yelled, and immediately regretted it. Where was she going? *We only need one*, Keesa had said about the ghern. The words sunk in. She had betrayed him.

"Dammit!" He limped back into the barn as fast as he could, and assessed the remaining animals. The closest thing to a suitable mount was the old, sagging bullock with red horns.

Mulladin swiped the lamp from the wall, and hobbled over to the bullock's pen. The animal stared at him with its black eyes while it placidly chewed some straw. It was not exactly an energetic creature. Mulladin unlatched the pen's gate and threw it wide. Holding the lantern in one hand, he climbed up the side of the pen, wincing as the effort flared his knee pain–he must've hit hard for it to be giving him so much trouble–and climbed onto the back of the bullock.

"Ya!" he shouted. The bullock didn't do anything. "Ya!" He slapped the animal's rump, but it only snorted.

"How did you get out of your cage?"

Mulladin whipped his head toward the voice. The constable was walking down the aisle, heavy crossbow leveled at him.

"It was the talking flower!" Mulladin blurted out.

"That's what Jesh says. I don't like that you've been talking to my little girl."

Mulladin inwardly groaned.

"Get off Old Genzin, you damned lunatic!" The constable raised the crossbow a little higher, taking aim at Mulladin's face.

Mulladin acted on the first idea that popped into his mind, and threw the lantern at the constable. It struck him, throwing off his aim just as he fired. The bolt slammed into Old Genzin's hindquarters, and the beast bellowed. It exploded into a run, and Mulladin had to grip its red horns to keep from being thrown. It bucked and kicked, breaking open the pig pen to the delight of a squealing piglet that raced down the aisle and out the side door.

The rampaging bullock knocked the constable against the door of the sheep pen, but not before it stepped on the lantern, which of course broke and spilled lamp oil across the straw covered floor. The dry straw went up instantly, flames spreading across the surface of the puddle of lamp oil, and before Mulladin knew it, the inner walls of the barn were on fire.

Mulladin used his grip on the bullock's horns to steer it toward the barn's open main doors. The enraged animal charged into the night, taking to the one road leading out of Gnot. When the animal began to slow, Mulladin reached back and ripped the crossbow bolt out of Old Genzin's rump. The bullock bellowed and Mulladin nearly fell from its back as it leapt forward into another wild charge.

Steering it was easier now that they'd reached the road, the bullock probably familiar with the way, but the creature wasn't as obedient as a ghern. It also wasn't as fast, but it was all Mulladin had. He prayed it'd be enough.

Chapter 82

Old Genzin lived up to his name. He tired easily, and Mulladin had to repeatedly jab the bullock's rump with the crossbow bolt to keep it running. Mulladin felt sorry for the poor beast, but he needed to catch up to Keesa. His pity for Old Genzin evaporated when the bullock bucked him off and into a roadside marsh.

Mulladin swallowed a mouthful of muddy, mosquito-infested water before he'd realized what'd happened. He erupted out of the shallow water in a spray, and wiped his eyes just in time to catch Old Genzin gallop off the road and disappear into the dark. Mulladin spouted a stream of the worst curses he knew as he slogged out of the marsh, and back onto the road. He found the crossbow bolt he'd been using as a spur and picked it up. He was going to need a weapon, and this was as close to a knife as he hoped to find.

Mulladin jogged along the road, following fresh ghern tracks he hoped belonged to Keesa's mount. As the night wore on a chill tinged the air. Mulladin's damp hair and clothes made his teeth chatter, and he was convinced running was the only thing staving off a hypothermic death.

A couple hours into his run, Mulladin stopped abruptly at the sight of lights a mile or so off the road. He hesitated only a heartbeat before leaving the road. Running cross country was more taxing, and by the time he was close enough to make out a caravan camped inside a thicket of trees, he was sucking air. He collapsed to the ground until he caught his breath and then crept through the trees, careful to keep as quiet as he could.

For a big man like Mulladin, that was difficult, and it was only by sheer luck that he'd not alerted an armored scout patrolling mere feet from his position when he'd broken a branch beneath his boot. Well, luck and the fact that the guard looked to be totally disinterested in his job. Mulladin froze as the guard yawned, cast a perfunctory look into the dark, and then turned to return to the circle of wagons enclosing the camp. Definitely not a man taking his duty very seriously.

While watching the guard return to camp, Mulladin recognized the two swords crossing over an Apeira well embroidered on the back of the man's tabard–Aiestali royal guards. This was Loeadon's caravan. The sword was certain to be in one of the large canvas tents. That meant Keesa would be skulking about the camp somewhere, if she hadn't already swiped the sword and escaped.

But Mulladin hadn't expected to catch up to Loeadon for miles yet–if at all. The rancid scents of refuse and used latrines indicated that the caravan had been parked here for a couple of days. *But why?* Mulladin shifted his position to get a better look at the wagons, thinking perhaps one of the vehicles had lost a wheel or broken down. That's when a new, more sickening smell slapped him in the face.

It was the tart stink of bile mixed with the foulest diarrheic stench he'd ever breathed in. He gagged and covered his mouth and nose with the back of his sleeve. It was the kind of sickly reek that only animals were capable of producing. Mulladin scanned the camp until he found a picket line of oxen–pitched an unusually long distance from the rest of the camp–lying on the ground. One of the beasts simultaneously produced vile liquids from both ends, making its neighbor snort. Though dark, the sick animals were accosted by a swarm of flies so numerous, Mulladin could hear their discordant buzzing even from a distance.

The ox who'd just produced a volcanic eruption from opposite orifices bellowed as it was doused with water from a camp worker with a kerchief tied so that it covered his mouth and nose. A second worker splashed the same ox, making it snort and lash its tail.

"I saw her!" the first camp worker argued. "She was feeding 'em apples!"

"Apples don't make oxen sick like this!" the second worker countered.

"They does if they's poisoned!"

The first camp worker laughed. "Why would a little girl poison apples?"

Mulladin smiled. *Rasheera bless you, Jesh. And your talking flower.*

The thought invoked a small pang of guilt for having caused a fire in her father's barn, one that was sure to cause a lot of damage if it didn't burn the whole thing down. Fortunately, he'd seen Jesh's father escape the inferno, running toward his cottage and screaming fire at the top of his lungs. It'd been that distraction that'd made Mulladin's escape possible.

Mulladin moved away from the picket line. The horrific stink coated the inside of his nose, and he didn't obtain any relief until he'd circled to the far side of the camp. There he was able to make out one tent bigger than all of the others. It didn't look as fancy as Gymal's tent, but he imagined that it was the largest Loeadon could get his hands on in his flight from Aiested. The presence of two armored soldiers guarding the tent flap was all the confirmation Mulladin needed.

The sword would be inside that tent, but how was he to get at it? Perhaps he could ambush one of the patrolling guards and take the man's uniform? It was a cliché that always found its way into every bard's tale, and Mulladin wasn't sure how effective it would be in reality. Especially with Aiestal helmets being opened face. But he couldn't...

A woman approached the two soldiers standing guard in front of Loeadon's tent. She had long dark hair and was wearing a peasant's shift that was unlaced on the top so that it kept falling down her right shoulder–and probably giving the guards a privileged view of her cleavage if not her entire chest. The middle of the shift was incongruously tight, unabashedly celebrating the woman's perfect hourglass shape, and didn't even fall far enough to fully cover her backside.

Mulladin shoved down his feelings of male appreciation by taking in a deep breath, and then gagging at the taste of oxen sick. It turned out to be a very effective turnoff. The woman–a camp whore by her choice of outfit–was speaking with the guards. They nodded and one held the tent flap open for her as she ducked in. In spite of the dim light of pole torches, Mulladin had recognized the woman. Keesa was making her move. The question on just how far Ez's daughter would go to get the sword from the renegade polymath both disturbed and intrigued Mulladin, and it took another deliberate whiff of oxen diarrhea to refocus him.

Mulladin crept around the outer perimeter of the camp, staying in the trees and trying to be stealthy. He might as well been an Ursaj in a glassblower's shop. Leaves crackled, twigs snapped, and he even startled a hare out of hiding, causing it to streak across the camp and attract the barking attention of two hounds. Fortunately, the guards weren't really on their guard, and no one came to investigate his blundering.

Loeadon's tent was closer to the wagons, which were parked only a stone's throw away from the tree line. This let Mulladin sneak into the camp, crawl under a wagon, and almost right up to the renegade poly-math's tent. He pocketed his one weapon, the crossbow bolt plucked from Old Genzin's rump, and scooted forward on his stomach. He found a cloth bundle lying in the grass underneath the wagon; rolled up clothes still caked with dried egg yolk and bits of tomato. These were Keesa's clothes. He'd found the wench's path of escape.

He looked up at the tent. Its interior light cast silhouettes of Loeadon and Keesa, and Mulladin was close enough to hear them softly talking.

"As soon as your friends get here, we can begin," Loeadon said, sounding as though he were talking about a meeting of the village council instead of rendezvous for sexual debauchery.

Mulladin was very relieved to hear that nothing had happened yet. For some reason the thought of Keesa debasing herself to get the sword stung him with a mixture of sadness and... jealousy?

"Stand over there, and strip." Loeadon's silhouette waved Keesa away.

Mulladin ground his teeth. He already hated Loeadon, and knew the man was a total bastard, but his ordering Keesa about like she was an animal invoked a hot rage like nothing he'd ever felt before. *Why was that? He hated Keesa, didn't he?*

Mulladin shook his head. Ever since he'd awoken with the mind of a man, his emotions were erratically shifting, and surging. One moment he'd be saddened to the point of tears, and the next he was murderously angry or laughing like a drunk. Perhaps eighteen years' worth of memories and experience seen all at once through new eyes was causing this "mood-storm?"

Keesa's silhouette moved away, but didn't start to disrobe as far as Mulladin could tell. He berated himself for feeling disappointed at that. Now really wasn't the time for such thoughts. Loeadon's tall silhouette turned his back on Keesa, and leaned down to open what looked like a trunk on the floor. He reached in with his one good arm and stood, holding the shadow of coiled rope, or was it a whip?

Sick bastard!

Loeadon began to turn around, but Keesa's silhouette surged forward, reaching up to the tall man's head. The shadows bled together, and Mulladin couldn't tell what was happening, but if he had to guess, it looked like Keesa covered the renegade polymath's mouth with something which quickly caused the man to collapse.

Keesa's silhouette bent down, and Mulladin heard her rifling through a trunk. He glanced down at the bundle of clothes and then crawled backward out from beneath the wagon. He crept around the wagon bed, and waited for Keesa to find Jekaran's sword, which only took her a few moments. She used it to slice a line in the back wall of the tent and emerged and went straight for where Mulladin had found her bundle.

He stepped out from his hiding place. "Looking for your clothes?"

Keesa jumped, raised the sword and gripped the handle with both of her hands. "How the hell?"

Mulladin grinned and then made a show of looking her up and down. "You know, I like you better with your hair down."

"Give me those!" she hissed.

"Give me the sword," Mulladin replied.

She scowled at him.

"Or not." Mulladin shrugged. "Personally, I like what you're wearing."

Keesa's jaw tightened.

"We can fight here and be captured... again. Or you can give me the sword, I can give you your clothes, and we can leave together."

Keesa sighed and then drove the sword point first into the ground. Mulladin chuckled and tossed her the bundle of clothing. She unrolled it, and held out her breeches. She lifted one leg, and then scowled and Mulladin.

"Turn around!" she hissed.

Mulladin chuckled again, and turned his back to give Keesa a bit of privacy. "You know, I really did mean it."

"Mean what?" The rustle of cloth and crinkle of leather conjured up all sorts of improper images that Mulladin had to strain to expel from his mind.

"I like your hair loose."

The air blasted out of Mulladin's lungs as something slammed into his back. He fell to his knees, eyes wide as he struggled to draw in a breath. Keesa sprinted past him, still wearing her loose shirt, but now clad in trousers and holding Jekaran's sword in her right hand. She paused to look down at Mulladin, flashed a grin, and then screamed at the top of her lungs.

"Shyte!" Mulladin wheezed.

Guards called to one another, and the sound of jingling mail grew louder. Mulladin scrambled up. The world swam as his sudden exertion in an oxygen deprived state made him dizzy, but his fear and anger were enough to compensate. Each successive step become steadier until he was sprinting through the trees.

"Lord Loeadon's been attacked!" A shout echoed behind Mulladin. He didn't turn to look, but kept his focused on Keesa's barely visible outline.

He gritted his teeth and channeled all of his rage into pumping his legs, but it wasn't enough. He caught up with Keesa just as she was mounting her ghern. She held the sword with her right hand, and snapped the beast's reins with her left. The ghern leapt into a sprint, dodging and weaving through the trees and disappearing from Mulladin's view.

How was he going to catch her now? He clenched his fists, and turned sharply to his right, running back toward the camp. There were gherns there. Not as many as oxen, but he'd seen a couple while he'd been scouting the perimeter. He just hoped Jesh hadn't fed any of her poisoned apples to them. As far as he could tell, only the oxen had been sick.

A torch came into view ahead of him, its flame illuminating a white tabard painted yellow by the flickering yellow light. Mulladin didn't stop his run, but instead lowered his shoulder and turned it into a charge. The guard's eyes widened and he opened his mouth to say something, but never got the chance. Mulladin crashed into him, knocking the man into a nearby tree. He slumped to the ground, unconscious.

Mulladin considered stealing the man's uniform and armor, just like in the bard's tales, but had no time. The sounds of soldiers crashing through the trees already echoed behind him. So, he picked up the man's torch and sword and sprinted back toward the camp. The light would make him a target, but he needed it for the diversion he was planning. That was another tactic he'd learned from storytellers; the hero always needed a diversion to escape. Well, fire worked for him before.

Two wash women dropped their baskets as Mulladin exploded out of the trees and back into camp. He ran past them, ready to toss the torch onto the nearest canvas tent, when a woman emerged hand in hand with a child that couldn't be older than two.

There were refugees from Aiested in this camp.

Ez's voice echoed from his memory—a moment when he was still dim, and the two were sitting in front of a hearth awaiting execution.

For while the fool always looks to his own regard, the hero for others is aware.

Mulladin ground his teeth, and held onto his torch. He couldn't set the camp on fire if there were women and children in it.

Two guards spotted him, and charged. Mulladin quickly located the picket lines and ran as fast as he could, dropping the torch on the ground where it harmlessly guttered. There were three gherns tied to a separate picket near a watering trough a furlong from the sick oxen. Mulladin pumped his legs like a madman and covered the distance in what had to be record time. He raised his sword, swinging it down and severing the rope tethering the nearest ghern. The animal snorted and bucked in protest as Mulladin climbed on.

The beast lacked reins and a saddle, so Mulladin wound his hand into the tuft of white hair on the top of the ghern's head and smacked its side with the flat of his stolen sword. The ghern leapt over the trough and ran into the trees. Mulladin had a difficult time steering it, but when the animal learned that a yank on its hair in one direction meant to turn that way, it became easier.

Guards called to one another, but their cries grew distant the farther away Mulladin fled into the trees. They weren't giving chase, probably on account that they'd been caught so unprepared. Sure, they were patrolling the camp, sort of. But it was clear by their bored yawns and their drinking and gambling, that they weren't expecting a raid.

Mulladin didn't know which direction Keesa had ridden off in, but it didn't matter. There was only one place Ez's daughter would go–Erassa, the closest Apeira well. She'd made a critical mistake sobbing out her story to him, for by it he knew how desperate she was to charge and bond Jekaran's sword.

He smacked the flat of the sword against the ghern's right flank and it had the desired effect of spurring the animal into a faster gallop. He had to catch up to Keesa before she reached Erassa. If he believed Jesh's story about the talking flower–and Rasheera help him, he was starting to–there was more at stake here than just recovering Jekaran's sword.

Mulladin ground his teeth to stave off a bout of cold nausea. Until now, fear had been the one emotion that hadn't surged or overwhelmed him. In fact, it'd actually diminished since his transformation. The fact it assailed him with a potency to rival the time Maely lost him in the woods was definitely not a good sign.

Jesh's words abruptly came to his mind. *...you have to take it to the secret city. It's really important.* He nodded to himself. He had no idea how, or why, but what the little girl had told him was true. He had to get Jek's sword back, and then he had to do the impossible–find the legendary city of the fey folk, a place hidden from humans for centuries by powerful magic.

"Shyte."

CHAPTER

83

Tyrus sat on the most comfortable chair he'd ever sat upon. It had no pillow or padding, but was made entirely of one piece of material he couldn't identify, like a statue sculpted from marble. The substance from which it was crafted was soft, and pliable, yet firm at the same time. This allowed for the seat, back, and arms of the chair to mold to fit Tyrus arms, back, and posterior. It was comfort like Tyrus had never known.

If there was a theme to Allose, Tyrus thought, *it would be that—comfort.* Or perhaps convenience would be a better word. Talises were everywhere, often built into the very architecture itself. Doors opened for him, the air always had a fresh floral perfume about it, and there were even small automatons in the likeness of humans to fetch food, drink, or whatever he desired.

The refreshment served to him, however, did leave something to be desired. The food the Allosians ate consisted primarily of fruits, sweet breads, nuts, and some kind of edible grass—no meat. Tyrus could get used to it, he knew, and in fact all their foods were likely healthier than his usual diet. It was sure to make him live longer. But Tyrus wasn't sure he'd want to live for very long without alcohol; not a drop of which could be found anywhere in their waiting lounge. Nor did any of the ivory-colored automatons know where to get some. He'd asked nine of them, and even a real, live, Allosian, but no one recognized Haeshalan brandy, or Tolean wine. Hell, he'd settled for the disgusting barley swill his peasants called ale. But not a drop of liquor was available.

Kybon always did accuse me of being dipsomaniacal. Perhaps his cousin had been right.

Tyrus glanced at Jekaran. The boy was lying on a very comfortable looking couch that was really more of a bed. He looked peaceful, with his hands folded over his stomach, and a silk pillow propping up his head so he didn't choke on his drool. If it hadn't been for his unfocused stare, and his shallow breathing, he could've been a corpse in repose.

Tyrus hated that arrogant child. Or, at least he had. He wasn't sure what he felt now. You couldn't really protect someone without coming to care for them a little bit. Or was that just him projecting his love for Kybon onto Jekaran? The two were so damned alike in their brashness, and cocky "spit in the eye of the gods" attitude, that he very well could be confusing his feelings.

Tyrus was surprised to find himself crying. The boy might be nearly intolerable, but he had something Kybon lacked–nobility. Oh, not the status granted to them by their family's house, but true nobility of character. Jekaran was selfless in his determination to protect the Allosian woman, Kairah. And he'd spared Hort instead of executing the man. Tyrus didn't think Kybon would've been so merciful. His cousin had always been a bit of a bully. Jekaran, on the other hand, stood up for the weak and vulnerable. Could Tyrus have been mistaken? Was what he named brash arrogance actually courage?

He found himself standing next to the ivory-framed bed upon which Jekaran lay, tears still pouring down his cheeks. He looked into the boy's vacant eyes. "You are an infuriating little snot. You've always caused me stomach pain, and driven me to drink on more than one occasion. I've aided your family and protected you the best I could for sixteen damn years, and all I ever got in return was ridicule and vitriol! At first I did it for him. But now..." Tyrus wiped his leaking nose on his forearm. "I'm not sure why I've given up everything for you. You fight me and hate me."

He started to sob. "Your father was my best friend. I loved him. We were as close as brothers. We spoke everyday no matter where in Shaelar we were. Well, he mostly did the talking, and I mostly listened." Tyrus hiccupped a laugh. "He was everything I wanted to be: Handsome, athletic, charming. And then one day he was gone, and I didn't even get to say goodbye!"

Tyrus was aware of Irvis, Graelle, Hort, and the Vorakk shaman watching him, but he didn't care. "Then I found out about you." He laughed again. "Did you know I actually considered coming for you when Anarilee died, and raising you as my own? I was even going to name you Kybon, after him. But your uncle beat me to you. Since then I just watched from afar, trying to help where I could, but not out of any kind of love."

Tyrus shook his head. "No, I hated you even when you were a bawling brat. And in time, you came to hate me back. I never really understood why. After all, you were my kin. I should've been an uncle to you. But now it's clear to me. I hated you because you remind me so much of him. Seeing your face, so much like his, always stabbed me in the heart."

Tyrus gave another hysterical laugh. "And when you started acting like him..."

He was sobbing now, right hand covering his eyes while he leaned on the left for support. "Damn you, boy! Losing you is like losing him all over again! Wake up! I can't relive that pain!"

Words failed him, and Tyrus just stood there, shoulders shaking as his whole body was wracked with the force of his weeping. He started when an arm gently pulled him into a half hug. It was the chubby man, Irvis. He didn't say anything, but just stood by Tyrus, letting him weep.

After a few minutes Tyrus dried his eyes, and Irvis let him go. A door opened and Kairah strode in trailing four Allosians dressed in long white robes. She herself was wearing a lavender dress, like the one she wore when he first found her half drowned and unconscious. Praise the goddess for that. Seeing her prance about in a shift that showed off her cleavage and didn't even fully reach below her thighs was a distraction Tyrus didn't need. He was disgusted with himself for those thoughts. The world was ending, and here he was failing to control urges invoked by a beautiful, half-naked woman. Well, she wasn't half naked anymore, but even now her dress accentuated her form, and made his cheeks feel warm. He had to look away.

"This is the human child?" A male Allosian with a square jaw and dark violet hair asked.

"His name is Jekaran," Kairah answered.

The Allosian man smirked and shared a glance with his three companions. "And when I was a child I had a very colorful parrot, but I did not name it."

"Why you sanctimonious son of a bitch!" Tyrus snapped.

The man's eyebrows raised and his mouth hung open. A beat later his infuriating smirk returned. "That same parrot also knew some words, and could even sing a song or two."

Tyrus's fists balled and he surprised himself by taking several steps toward the Allosian man before Kairah intercepted him.

She pressed her hand gently, but firmly on his chest to stop him. "They are here to help," she said quietly.

He looked up into her amethyst eyes. "They're going to heal him?"

"Yes," the Allosian man answered loudly.

Tyrus shot him a baleful glare.

The white-robed Allosian walked to the side of Jekaran's bed and peered down at him. "Normally healing a human would be a waste of our valuable time, but the malady Lady Kairah described intrigues us. And it afforded an opportunity for my students to receive an introductory lesson on healing the mind."

Hort growled.

"Students?" Tyrus glanced back at Kairah.

"Elder Sallynder is the master over healing at the College of Disciplines."

Tyrus resumed his scowling at the pompous purple-plumed peacock of a man. "He can fix Jekaran's mind?"

Sallynder leaned in close to Jekaran's face and scrutinized the boy's right eye. "I am the most accomplished Allosian healer in over a thousand years."

"You could've just said 'yeah,'" Hort scoffed.

Sallynder looked up with narrowed eyes. Then he turned to his three students. "Let us begin."

"Will you need my assistance, elder?" Kairah took a step toward Jekaran's bed.

Sallynder laughed. "No Lady Kairah. I think not. This is best accomplished only by a master and my advanced students."

Tyrus mouthed a silent mocking of Sallynder's words and Hort laughed. Then, remembering the ring Irvis gave to Kairah, he met her eyes and opened his mouth to ask if it should not be part of the process. Before the words could form, Kairah's eyes narrowed and she shook her head. *How had she known I was going to ask? Why didn't she want him to bring up the miraculous talis? Didn't Jekaran need every bit of healing magic they had?* He let it go, trusting in the Allosian woman's knowledge of magic over his own anxieties.

The four, white robed, Allosian healers surrounded Jekaran's bed. They each placed a single hand on his chest, Sallynder's first, topped by the right hands of each of his three students. They closed their eyes. Tyrus wasn't sure what he'd been expecting, but the ritual lacked any display of magical light, or arcane thunder. If not for what was at stake, Tyrus would've found the whole thing disappointing.

Five minutes into the silent ceremony, Sallynder's brow twitched and his jaw tightened.

"What's happening?" Tyrus whispered to Kairah. "Is it working?"

The woman's only response was a curt shushing.

Tyrus's worry turned into panic. He didn't know the first thing about Allosian magic, other than how to use talises, but his gut screamed at him that something was wrong. He looked at Irvis, probably the human who knew the most about magical healing among their group. The chubby former monk's eyes were wide, and he chewed his lower lip.

"Aek!" the Vorakk shaman standing behind Tyrus shrieked.

So, the others sense it, too. Just as Tyrus opened his mouth to demand an explanation, Sallynder sucked in a gasp, and staggered backward. One of his students caught him before he could fall to the ground. The Allosian master healer looked sick, strands of his jewel colored hair sticking to his sweaty brow, and dark circles now ringing his eyes.

"Master?" the Allosian student holding Sallynder up said. "Master, are you all right?"

Sallynder breathed in deep and then straightened. He gently pushed his student away and looked at Kairah. "I cannot put the shards of his mind back together," he admitted, all arrogance gone from his tone.

"Why?" Kairah's voice was taught and Tyrus thought she sounded on the edge of tears.

Sallynder stared down at Jekaran. "Because," he hesitated, "a piece of his consciousness is missing."

CHAPTER 84

Mulladin's ghern bellowed a trumpet-like cry as it precariously slid down the hill. It scrambled to regain its balance which nearly resulted in him being thrown from the beasts' back. When they reached the level ground of the road below, the ghern staggered drunkenly before righting itself. Unfortunately, the advantage he'd gained from charging down the hill was negated by his mount's loss of balance, allowing Keesa to pull ahead of him.

Mulladin had caught up to her just after sunrise, and this was his latest failed attempt to cut her off or overtake her. Erassa was visible down the road, and they would soon be in range of the city's Apeira well. Mulladin had to get the sword back before Keesa bonded it.

"Ya!" He slapped his ghern's flank with the flat of his stolen sword. The beast surged forward, but foam at its mouth and a shudder to its breathing told of exhaustion.

Keesa's mount looked to be in a similar condition, but the woman was significantly lighter than Mulladin, and so unlike his, it probably wasn't ready to drop dead just yet. If he didn't do something now, Keesa was going to win this race.

Mulladin tossed the camp soldier's sword away from him. It clanged to the road behind him in a puff of dirt. Then he drew out his memento charitably given to him by Gnot's constable. He jabbed the crossbow bolt into his ghern's thigh. The animal bellowed and leapt forward. Ez had taken him, Jekaran, and Maely to Jeryn once to watch a race. He'd seen the ghern riders lean forward and put their heads against their ghern's neck whenever they forced their mounts into a sprint, and so he did the same. He wasn't sure if this helped, but his ghern did run a little faster.

Keesa's wide-eyed glance was gratifying when he rode up beside her. He returned the crossbow bolt to his pocket, and then yanked right on his ghern's tuft of hair. The beast veered toward Keesa and crashed into the side of her ghern. She screamed, and both animals staggered to the edge of the road, but remained upright.

"You're insane!" Keesa shouted.

Mulladin flashed an impudent smile and then reached for her reins. Keesa kicked at him, her boot connecting just above his knee, the same knee that still throbbed from his clumsy crow's cage escape. He grunted, and had to pull his arm back to maintain his balance. Keesa took the opportunity to veer her ghern left, this time slamming her mount against his. Both animals staggered back to the middle of the road, and the maneuver succeeded in putting some distance between them.

As Erassa loomed closer other travelers appeared on the road ahead, the closest of which was a wagon en route to the city. They split up, Mulladin riding around the wagon's left side and Keesa on the wagon's right. The driver—a man wearing clothes spun of sack cloth that marked him as a farmer—lost his pipe when his mouth fell open at the sight of what he was sure to think were bandits ready to rob him. Consequently, he hollered at his team of oxen while snapping their reins and prompting them to run faster.

Keesa made sure to keep the wagon between them, and both ignored the farmer's pleas to leave him alone. Mulladin's ghern started to flag, each of its breaths sounding increasingly labored signaling the beast was about to drop. It started to slow, putting Mulladin just behind the wagon's left rear wheel and a metal peg on the wagon bed's railing that was likely meant for anchoring rope when the farmer needed to tie down a load.

Mulladin shot out his hand and gripped the small post. He leveraged his weight, pulled his left leg up onto the ghern's back, and pushed off. The poor animal fell and rolled backward as Mulladin left its back and landed hard on his knees in the empty wagon bed. He didn't look back to see if the animal had survived—he very much doubted it—but instead launched to his feet and stepped across the wagon bed so that he was within reach of Keesa and her mount.

She glanced up at him, mouth forming words that Mulladin didn't give her time to say. He thrust out both arms, enclosed her in a hug, lifted her off her ghern and fell backward into the wagon. The farmer was yelling at them now, in between his calling for help. Keesa threw her head back against Mulladin's chest. It was probably meant to crush his nose, but he was so much taller that the blow struck the top of his chest. It hurt, and Mulladin reflexively released Keesa. She rolled off him, landing on her stomach. They both scrambled to their feet, but the rocking of the wagon made it difficult. Keesa reached for Jek's sword, which was hanging at her hip in a sheath–where had she gotten that? Mulladin made to tackle her around the waist, but Keesa side stepped and elbowed him in the side of the head.

Mulladin grunted and spun, trying to get hold of the smaller woman a second time. He grabbed her around the chest, flushing when one of his hands gripped a breast. She growled and threw her weight back against him, shoving his back into the side rail of the wagon. The rail cracked, but didn't break–praise Rasheera for that.

Mulladin regained his footing and shoved Keesa forward toward the front of the wagon. The driver cried out when Keesa slammed into his back. He glanced over his shoulder, looked at the ground, and then leapt from the driver's seat. Mulladin followed the farmer with his eyes. The man's straw hat flew off his bald, liver-spotted head as he rolled off the road and into grass.

He realized his mistake a heartbeat too late. Keesa kicked out, catching him behind the left knee and sweeping him. He fell onto the wagon bed, back hitting the wood followed by his head. Keesa tried to step over him and make for the open back of the wagon, but Mulladin rolled to his right and hugged her legs. She went down, kicking back at him before she even hit the wood. Her heel connected with his shoulder. The lightning strike of pain made him let go but it also fueled his rage. Mulladin scrambled forward, took Keesa by the shoulders and slammed her down against the wagon bed–hard. Her eyes widened and she coughed, trying desperately to get a breath; his slam having expelled the air from her lungs.

"Stop it!" Mulladin shouted in her face. "We're supposed to be on the same side now!"

"I'm on my own side," Keesa wheezed.

Mulladin shook her. "No! We have to take the sword to Allose!"

Keesa coughed out a mocking laugh that was cut off when the wagon violently bounced, throwing Mulladin off her. He quickly climbed to his feet, but stayed crouched low, one hand on the top of the wood back of the driver's seat as he surveyed their surroundings.

They were no longer racing down a dirt road. Instead they were bouncing along a cobblestone street, oxen panicked and charging. People were shouting at them, some calling for the guards, and others jumping out of the way. That's when the steel point of a sword pressed against the side of his neck. He berated himself for having dropped his guard–again.

"Careful." He gulped. "We hit another bump and that could stick through my throat."

Keesa's eyes were narrowed, and she gripped the handle of Jek's sword with both hands. Mulladin flicked his eyes to the Apeira well rising from the center of the city. Any moment now the sword talis would recharge and then bond with whomever was holding it.

The reins of the oxen were sliding back and forth across the wooden plank that was the driver's seat. They were within his reach, if he dared to move. But would Keesa kill him?

"Fine," he said. "You win."

Keesa scowled. "You're giving up?"

"I know when I'm beaten."

Keesa didn't lower the sword, but she did let the point stray a little from his neck. That's all he needed. Mulladin shot his hand out, grabbed the oxen's reins, and pulled right as hard as he could. The beasts turned so sharply that the wagon tipped up onto its two right wheels. Keesa fell forward, the sword flying out of her hands and clanging to the cobblestones. One of the wagon's wheels buckled, then snapped, and the naked axel hit the street in an explosion of sparks. The wagon flipped.

Mullidin landed hard on his left shoulder, the sudden stab of pain signaling a break. He screamed as he rolled to a stop on the street. The wagon smashed into a shopfront in an explosion of wood and glass.

Another of the wagon's wheels broke loose and spun through the air, crashing into a passing carriage. Still in a frenzy, the oxen continued charging down the street dragging half of a wagon behind them in a flurry of sparks.

Mulladin forced himself to sit up. He frantically glanced around until he found Jekaran's sword. It was a dozen feet away, and the amethyst jewel embedded in the cross guard was glowing. That's when he spotted Keesa, about an equal distance from the sword. Her loose shirt was torn open exposing a scandalous amount of breast, and a large gash marred her forehead. Their eyes met, and for a heartbeat the entire world seemed to freeze.

The moment thawed and they both burst into a desperate charge for the sword. Pain stabbed Mulladin's broken shoulder with every fall of his foot. He grit his teeth, ignoring the agony and throwing all of his strength into the sprint. Keesa dove, and so Mulladin did the same. He reached his hand out as he flew toward the sword. If he could just brush it with the tip of even one of his fingers, he would bond it.

An explosion of light and sound stunned Mulladin at the same time something slammed into him. He crashed against a wall, a muffled thunk accompanying a new explosion of pain in the back of his skull.

When he opened his eyes, the world was white and silent. Then shapes formed, and his vision returned along with the sounds of the city. Where the sword had lain just a moment ago, there was now a shallow crater in the street. He desperately looked around, ignoring the warm wetness running down the back of his neck. Jekaran's sword lay nearby, and it was smoldering.

Laughing.

Mulladin looked up and found a tall figure robed in black standing a short distance away. His raven hair was windblown and several strands stuck to his pale face. Loeadon's sling was gone, and he moved his arm like it'd never been broken.

"I must thank you again for this lightning ring." He examined the talis that was fitted to his right ring finger. "A suitable compliment to my restoration ring." He wiggled the fingers of his other hand, one of which bore the healing talis. "But I'm afraid both of these are nowhere near as valuable as that sword talis."

Something moved on Mulladin's periphery and Keesa lunged for Jekaran's sword. Loeadon waved a hand at her and a bright blue bolt of lightning fell from the cloudless sky, striking down between her and the sword. She was thrown sideways into a fruit stand, knocking the flimsy wooden structure and its produce into a mess of splinters and juicy pulp.

Mulladin stood, but froze when Loeadon pointed at him.

"Don't," the renegade polymath commanded.

"The world is falling apart, or hadn't you noticed?" Mulladin retorted. "You saw what happened to Aiested. If I don't get that sword to Allose, then…" Then what? He didn't know. All he had was the word of a little girl quoting her "talking flower", and a nagging foreboding that grew by the hour.

"Allose?" Loeadon took four steps toward him. "You mean to say that you, a Rikujo thug, know where the legendary hidden city is?"

"Well, not really."

"I thought not." Loeadon pointed at him and a crackling bolt arced from the polymath's finger and struck Mulladin in the leg.

He cried out, falling to the street, the sharp sting of his broken shoulder suddenly shamed by the burning in his leg. He looked down to find a smoldering black spot on his pants.

Divine Mother, it hurts!

Mulladin rolled onto his side, cradling his wounded leg. He looked around, desperate for any kind of help, but the citizens of Erassa had fled at the first obvious use of weapon talis magic. A contingent of armored guards stood fifty feet away, but they didn't approach. Probably waiting for more of their fellows before attempting to take down a man who commanded lightning. Keesa was gone too. For some reason that comforted him. Ez's daughter would live.

Loeadon was already striding toward Jekaran's sword. He'd gotten to within five paces of the weapon talis when Keesa leapt from a nearby rooftop and crashed into him. Loeadon screamed—an entirely too feminine scream—as he went down. Keesa pummeled the renegade polymath repeatedly in the face, so hard that a stream of blood shot up and splashed her in the eye. She had to take one of her fists out of the fight to wipe the blood away, but before she could resume smashing in Loeadon's face, she was hurled off him in a burst of electricity.

Loeadon staggered to his feet, his nose and mouth covered in blood. But his nose was no longer bleeding, and a swollen eye suddenly opened as the inflamed skin reduced and smoothed. The restoration ring was making killing the man a near impossible task. When he was fully healed, he walked over to Keesa who lay writhing on the ground.

"You lying bitch!" He kicked her hard in the stomach. Keesa's cry of pain was cut off as Loeadon kicked her a second time. This time she vomited. He stepped back and pointed the finger adorned with the lightning ring down at her.

A thin stream of crackling electricity arced down and connected with Keesa's stomach. Unlike Loeadon's other attacks with the magic, he maintained this bolt in one continuous stream at a level that wouldn't kill Keesa outright.

In the short time Mulladin used the lightning talis, he learned he could control the intensity of his blasts. With a little concentration and practice, he could produce enough power to simply stun a foe, or enough to fry their internal organs with a single shaft of death. Loeadon obviously had experience with controlling electricity, because what he was doing now was sadistically impressive.

Keesa convulsed and tried to scream, but her jaw wouldn't unclench, muffling the sound. Her neck muscles bulged, she arched her back, and balled her fists in unnatural contortions like that of an arthritic crone. Loeadon's entire focus was on torturing the woman, giving Mulladin an opening. He glanced at Jekaran's sword. It lay maybe twenty paces away. If he could just touch it, he'd have the power to cut Loeadon down, lightning ring or not. But what would happen to Keesa?

Loeadon was increasing the power of his continuous stream of electricity, the man's face foreshadowing an ensuing homicidal climax. He met Keesa's wild eyes. If Mulladin went for the sword, Keesa would surely die. Something in her eyes told Mulladin that she knew it too.

He had to get the sword back, no matter what. His instincts had told him that long before Jesh delivered the message of her prophetic flower. Keesa was his enemy, there was no denying it. She'd tried to kill him. But she was also Ez's daughter, a cousin to Mulladin in a way.

Words from Ez forced their way into his mind, and it was less like the echo of memory from their time in Trous's manner and more like Ez was speaking into his ear.

But closely resemble they one another, both heroes and fools at first, and it's only at the fork of destiny's road that the truth will at last emerge. For while the fool always looks to his own regard, the hero for others is aware. And will suffer and die when called upon, even for strangers in his care. It was the final stanza of the Lure of Fools poem. The part he regretted withholding from Jek.

In that moment, Mulladin made his choice.

Mulladin reached into his pocket with his good arm and pulled out his crossbow bolt. He gripped it in his hand like a dagger, and then stood and threw himself at Loeadon. He brought the point down on the back of Loeadon's neck, stabbing through the man's long black hair. He felt the bolt puncture the man's skin, rupturing muscle and breaking bone as he pushed it in with all of his remaining strength.

Loeadon's attack on Keesa immediately ceased as he began coughing up blood, and scratching at his throat where the sharp point of the crossbow bolt protruded. Mulladin let go of the bolt and started wildly pummeling the renegade polymath with his fist. He heard a crack after landing a particularly fierce blow on the man's shoulder.

"That's for my shoulder!" he shouted, hoping the ironic injury would look intentional.

He lifted his arm for another strike but his muscles spasmed and he froze. Pain like fire shot through every limb and digit, as crackling electricity surrounded Loeadon like a shield. Mulladin shook, unable to move, breathe or even unclench his raised fist. Sparks exploded in front of him and he was thrown back a good twenty feet. He bounced off a wall, rolled on the cobbles. Loeadon turned around and pulled the crossbow bolt out of the back of his neck. His drooping shoulder shifted and realigned itself, and the gaping hole in his throat closed. The crossbow bolt clattered to the cobblestones. Mulladin sucked in deep ragged breaths. The pounding in his chest and ears came in irregular bursts, and blood poured from his mouth. He was dying. He knew it, and so did Loeadon.

The renegade polymath walked past Keesa who was lying curled up in a ball, her shoulders shaking as she alternately sobbed and gasped for air. Loeadon bent down and picked up Jekaran's sword. A wicked smile split his face, and he ejaculated a wild laugh. He turned to face the watching Erassa guards and thrust the blade into the air above his head.

"I, Ical Loeadon, leader of the Aiestali royal cadre of polymaths, am your new king!"

If he expected cheers from the on-looking soldiers, he didn't get them. The men in armor just glanced at each other in confusion. Loeadon frowned.

"Perhaps a convincing demonstration is in order." He lowered the sword and held it in front of him with both hands gripping the handle.

The Erassa city guard began to back away, but Mulladin knew they wouldn't get far. Loeadon's eyes blazed with sadistic eagerness. The demonstration wouldn't be for them, because Loeadon wasn't going to leave any of the soldiers alive.

The renegade polymath took two steps toward the contingent of guards and froze. The emeralds peppering the sword's blade were glowing.

"What is this?" Loeadon said, raising the sword to examine the shining bits of green. "Is this some—"

He didn't get to finish his question because he started screaming. Still gripping the sword's handle with both hands, Loeadon fell to his knees. His hands wrinkled, his hair fell out in clumps, his face thinned, and his eyes shriveled and fell from their sockets. Loeadon's scream cut off and he fell into a mass of bones and dust piled upon a discarded robe. The sword clanged to the ground, and the emeralds dimmed until they ceased to glow.

Blackness encroached on the edges of Mulladin's vision, but before the darkness of death took him, he saw Ez kneeling over Keesa. Perhaps he was hallucinating as it was said people close to death were wont to do, but he didn't think so. Ez looked up at Mulladin and smiled. Mulladin smiled back. Then the world went away.

Mulladin gasped and opened his eyes. Keesa's face stared down into his. He was surprised that it bore no cuts or bruises, and then he realized all of his pains were gone. He rolled his broken shoulder and it responded without any sharp sting. His heart was pounding strong and steady, and his burnt leg was whole. Keesa flashed him a smile and then wiggled her fingers in front of his face, showing off a silver and gold ring capped by a small diamond cut amethyst.

"Loeadon's restoration ring."

Keesa frowned. "My restoration ring. The lightning ring is mine now, too. I figure these are payment enough."

Mulladin sat up. "Payment for what?"

"That." Keesa waved at the sword lying on the ground in front of Loeadon's bones and robe.

"You're letting me take it?"

Keesa looked away. "You came to my rescue when you could've grabbed the sword. No one's ever done anything like that for me, not without an angle." She met his eyes. "Besides, the damn thing ate that guy alive, so I'm not gonna touch it."

Mulladin laughed and Keesa smiled. A small ball of light, like one of Karak's spirit orbs hovered where Mulladin had seen Ez. He opened his mouth to tell Keesa to look, but it zipped away and disappeared into the sky.

"What?" Keesa asked. "Did I forget to heal your brain?"

Mulladin laughed again, and Keesa helped him stand. He had to avert his eyes as her torn shirt offered a view that Irvis would appreciate. Thinking that Ez might actually be watching him made Mulladin shove away the ember of arousal. He walked over to Loeadon's remains. The Erassa guard were inching closer, obviously still hesitant but resolute. Mulladin glanced at Keesa and was surprised to find her wide-eyed with her mouth half open. Would the sword eat him too? Well, there was only one way to find out.

Mulladin bent down and grabbed the sword's wired handle. The advancing soldiers halted, raised their shields and leveled spears at him. Mulladin stared into the large round amethyst adorning the sword's cross guard.

Mull!

Mulladin started. He recognized the voice inside his head.

"Jek?"

The sword laughed, and Mulladin was sure. It was Jekaran.

CHAPTER
85

Kairah passed through the door-less archway that led into the cavernous first floor of Shivara's white tower. A tall woman with cheek-length light-purple hair stoically waited for her. She was dressed in a maid's sundress, fashioned to look like the one's worn by the children of human nobles. It left her shoulders bare, and the effect of the woman's abnormal height made it too short. The whole outfit, complete with red bow, appeared to be designed to make the woman look like a young girl only a year or two into puberty and was an odd choice for an Allosian ruler's servant. To add to the strangeness of the servant's outfit was the fact that she bore a weapon sheathed at her left hip–an elegant rapier with a well-shard embedded in the weapon's pommel.

"I am here to see the oracle," Kairah said.

The servant curtsied, and then wordlessly turned and began walking away.

Kairah followed the willowy young woman through the ivory halls of Shivara's tower. Apparently, she was mute, or at least she was acting that way. Kairah had tried to engage her a few times, but she only replied with nods and gestures. Kairah didn't know if the girl was being dutifully non-conversational by command of Shivara, or if she was just shy. Either way, it made for a long trip to the top of the tower.

Kairah brushed her ring finger with her thumb. The unique energy-producing talis was gone. She had given it to the human monk, Irvis, to keep hidden. After Aeva's warning not to reveal its existence to the synod, Kairah had been very careful not to call attention to it, and decided she best not wear it to her meeting with Allose's preeminent oracle.

Pain lanced through Kairah's head and she had to shut her eyes and lean against the wall. Removing the ring talis had invoked a worsening of her symptoms; the headaches becoming more frequent and severe. She sincerely hoped that one of her fits wouldn't strike while she met with Shivara. The woman was supposed to be quasi-omniscient and Kairah didn't need Shivara suspecting she'd been tainted by Moriora. That was the other thing she hadn't revealed to the synod. With her lonely mission to stop Moriora's vessel, trying to heal Jekaran's broken mind, grieving Jenoc's betrayal and disappearances, she had enough to worry about without becoming a subject for study, or worse—quarantine.

When the pain passed, she found the mute woman blankly staring at her. Annoyance heated Kairah's chest and she snapped, "No need to aid me. I am well. But thank you for asking."

The girl didn't react. That only made Kairah angry, and she had to exercise all her willpower to keep from unleashing a tirade on her. Kairah's ill temper was another symptom of her corruption, and removing the energy ring had only made it worse.

The biggest challenge her chronic anger presented was the temptation to defy the synod's commands and make what she knew about the destruction of Taris and Moriora public knowledge. Their refusal to resolve on more than a lackadaisical study of the destruction wrought by the being Karak called The Eater enraged her. How was it that a body of Allose's most sagacious minds did not grasp that all of Shaelar was in danger?

Well, perhaps one had.

Kairah's hopes for this meeting with Shivara were high. If anyone else could sense the danger it would be Allose's master seer.

"I am sorry," Kairah forced out.

The girl's only response was to turn and continue down the hall, which flared Kairah's anger, but she quickly calmed herself. She needed help, but had no one to confide in.

Aeva, Kairah called. *Aeva answer me!*

Aeva hadn't spoken to her since she appeared before the synod. After the attempt to heal Jekaran failed, she'd taken him, the other humans, and Karak to her apartment in one of the many white towers that made up Allose's residential districts. While there, she'd sought Aeva in her private atrium, but no matter how much Kairah pled, Aeva wouldn't answer. The Spirit lily was there physically, but not in any other meaningful way. She scrutinized the flower with all her meager Fourth Discipline skill, but all she could get was a sense that Aeva was distant or distracted. That made absolutely no sense at all since Kairah was standing directly in front of her. It only added to her frustration and sense of loneliness. Worse, she feared her inability to communicate with Aeva was another result of her worsening condition. Would she be able to stop Moriora's vessel before she succumbed to the power that even now poisoned her?

Oh, how she wished Jekaran were well, not just for his sake, but so she had someone to talk to. The boy was uneducated, unrefined, and in many ways represented all that she disliked about humans, but there was an earnest honesty to him. He was also very entertaining, and of all her human companions, Jekaran was the only one who could make her laugh.

> *Two worlds, but one heart,*
> *opposites that are one.*
> *Can fire love ice?*
> *Can the dark love the dawn?*

The memory of the poem she'd seen carved on Allosian ruins near the west sea came unbidden.

> *So were the two lovers,*
> *a prince and princess opposed.*
> *Yet in the secret midnight of a garden,*
> *their love could freely flow.*

"Aeva?" Kairah whispered, thinking that perhaps the Spirit lily had spoken to her, so sudden had the words popped into her head.

Yet the universe is balance,
and fate would have her due.
Their love would bring destruction,
and end the worlds each knew.

"Aeva?" She said it so loudly that the mute girl glanced at her. Kairah met her eyes and then looked away. *Aeva?* She repeated in her mind.

Aeva didn't respond.

Where had that come from? Two lovers? Jekaran was not her lover. He was just a boy, a human boy! Yet, as absurd and blasphemous as it was, Kairah couldn't deny a growing affection for Jekaran. She shoved the problem to the back of her mind. There were much more important issues she had to contend with, such as saving the world.

They reached the end of the corridor, and Kairah was introduced to a dome-shaped room reminiscent of the talis treasury in the College of Disciplines, albeit smaller. Wall to wall bookshelves, a trove of talises from every discipline, and a vast three-dimensional projection of constellations and planets near the ceiling awed her. She craned her neck to gaze into the swirling points of light dotting multicolored nebulae floating above her.

The girl tapped on Kairah's shoulder and motioned for her to keep following. Kairah nodded, still marveling at the chamber's abundance of wonders. Had she known Shivara possessed such a collection of books and artifacts, she would've petitioned to apprentice with her years ago. That was one thing she had in common with her brother. Both she and Jenoc loved knowledge, although they approached study with very different philosophies and motivations.

They left the planetarium and entered another hallway, and then a smaller square-shaped room tiled from floor to ceiling with multi-colored clay squares. The humidity and smell of perfumed water struck Kairah as soon as she stepped into the bath chamber, and she found Shivara floating face up and naked up on the steaming water. Her eyes were closed and she looked asleep. Kairah glanced at the servant girl, not knowing what she should do if anything. The mute girl stared at the floor, and so Kairah copied her.

Shivara kept her eyes closed, bald head bobbing upon the water. "Thank you, Etele. You may return to your work."

The mute girl dipped her head and departed.

"Mistress Shivara," Kairah began. "If you require me to return at a more convenient time, I can—"

"Nonsense, child."

Shivara opened her eyes and righted herself so she was standing in the bath, the steaming water rising to just above her waist. She walked toward three marble steps. "Fetch for me my robe." Shivara waved a hand toward a long, green garment hanging from a peg by the bath chamber's door.

Kairah walked over and took the robe. "Mistress, I—"

"I used to have hair as long as yours." Shivara emerged from the water and dried her entire body with a gentle current of warm air as she strode toward Kairah. "It was such a bother when bathing; always fanning out and tickling my ears." She stopped in front of Kairah, meeting her gaze and then turned and presented her bare back.

Kairah draped the robe over Shivara's shoulders and the oracle threaded her arms into the sleeves, before drawing the robe closed. She walked to the chamber door. "I find a warm soak helps to clear the mind."

Kairah followed her out of the bath chamber and back through the white corridor to the domed room full of wonders. The floating depiction of space fuzzed for just a moment upon their entering the room, but then continued as before. The distortion had been brief, but hadn't occurred the first time Kairah had seen it. She dismissed the oddity.

Shivara craned her bald head to look up into the swirling model galaxy. "Beautiful, is it not?"

"Breathtaking," Kairah whispered.

"It still causes me to marvel that each little point of light is a world, and the brighter ones, fiery orbs like our sun."

"I am afraid I have never studied more than the basics of astronomy." Kairah was transfixed on the image, walking slowly into the room with her head still tilted upward. "My studies were focused primarily on magic."

Shivara waved at the stars. "And is this not magic?"

Kairah lowered her head and looked at the oracle. "I apologize for not using the scientific term. I meant to say—"

Shivara laughed. "I believe the word magic is the best description for the marvelous forces that weave existence. It is infused with a sense of mystery, and I am not so arrogant as to think I have learned a fraction of the universe's secrets." She lowered her head and met Kairah's eyes. "You are descended from an oracle."

"Yes, mistress," Kairah said. "I am the third great-great-grand-daughter of the fifth great-granddaughter of..."

Shivara waved a dismissive hand. "I do not care about your genealogy, Kairah. None of that matters if you cannot manifest the gift. And from what you told the synod, it sounds as though you have seen a vision of the past."

Kairah nodded.

Shivara stepped toward a table upon which sat a long brass telescope suspended by a crescent-shaped, rocking base. "What else have you seen?"

"That is the only proper vision, mistress. Aside from that, I have only seen the rippling aura of fated souls." And one talis. She shoved down the thought, worried that Shivara might be trying to see her mind. Shivara was clearly accomplished in the Fourth Discipline, as she'd been able to telepathically speak to Kairah during her appearance before the synod, and so Kairah needed to be on her guard.

"I see." Shivara moved onto another instrument, this one silver and spiral shaped. "Did you know that the oracular power is not classified to any one Discipline?"

"Yes."

"Do you know why that is?"

"Because it touches all Five Disciplines," Kairah recited.

"Correct." Shivara idly spun the spiral shaped apparatus clockwise. "Life, the elements, space, perception, and time itself flow into one stream of power that when tapped into, can reveal all things–really a sixth discipline. Existence is nothing more than a set of forces," Shivara changed the spin of the silver spiral so that it spun counterclockwise, "and counter forces."

Kairah had heard those words before, from Jenoc. Perhaps both were quoting some text Kairah didn't know of, but it wasn't likely. Her training in Allosian philosophies and history was extensive. But if it were so common a phrase, why hadn't she heard it?

"Mistress Shivara, I believe Moriora's Vessel remains a threat. The synod may not take my words seriously enough to do something about it, but surely they would listen to their oracle."

Shivara craned her neck again toward the miniature galaxy hovering ten feet above them. "Did you know that some of the early Allosian theologians believed that the laws of magic could be different on other worlds? And that, although based upon the same core principles, they could be constructed in different ways to achieve different ends?"

Kairah should've been irritated that Shivara was not listening, but the oracle's words were hypnotic. "I had not heard that."

Shivara went on as though Kairah hadn't spoken. "And one world's power, if it interacted with the laws of a separate world, could bleed together to form unexpected results and new magic?"

Kairah's breath caught. "Are you saying that is what Moriora is? An alien magic?"

Shivara looked at her and smiled. "Or the child of the magics from two separate worlds."

"But where did it come from? How did it get here? How did Jenoc discover how to summon it?"

"So many questions that even I do not know the answers to. But together, perhaps we can solve this puzzle and discern what we are up against and how to stop it." Shivara reached out a hand. "Will you help me, Kairah? Will you join your power with mine to pierce this veil of mystery?"

Kairah reached out her hand to take Shivara's, but collapsed to her hands and knees when a wave of pain stronger than anything she'd felt before crashed down on her head. Her sight blurred and she vomited. Then she started to scream.

CHAPTER

86

Raelen sat in an area of the tent partitioned off from the center compartment, effectively making a room for him, or a cell. Although it had no bars, and he could cut the canvas and slip out if he wanted, Raelen was bound by something stronger than metal and stone– Seiro. He was bound by honor to remain in General Vesarr Rahkanas's custody by his own oath.

Raelen lay on his cot, arms folded behind his head, unable to sleep. Though bathing, shaving, and wearing a clean pair of trousers and tunic should've made him comfortable, he was anything but. Something was wrong, he could feel it.

At first, he thought the anxiety was over his failure to persuade Vesarr to abandon his father's orders, but the more he considered it, the more he realized that wasn't it. He was worried the scouting party wouldn't report back in time to stop Vesarr from launching his assault on Haeshala, but the general seemed to be dragging his feet, delaying over technicalities and minutia. It was obvious to Raelen that Vesarr was trying to give him the benefit of the doubt. That alone was its own victory. No, the foreboding was something else.

When Raelen was little, he used to wake up screaming from one recurring nightmare. It was a ridiculous thing to him now, but for a five-year-old boy, it'd been terrifying and only Gryyth's deep, gentle voice could soothe him back to sleep. The dream was of a giant, fire-breathing Vorakk coming to attack Aiested. It never actually arrived to wreak destruction on the city, but the dread was truly awful, the suspense of awaiting death the terror that made him cry out from sleep for his Ursaj protector.

Raelen remembered feeling the thunderous footfalls of the approaching Titan, hearing the primal roars from miles off, and seeing a fountain of fire erupting from a mountainous silhouette on the horizon. He hadn't felt such an urgent need to run and hide like that in years, not until now.

Raelen rolled onto his side and stared at the gray canvas wall. He'd been in Vesarr's custody for a few days now, waiting for the general's scout team to send word from Aiested and corroborate his claim that the city was indeed destroyed and the king dead. Had he wanted, Raelen could've killed Vesarr and taken command of the army, all in the name of the "greater good," as his father would've expected. But he'd chosen to trust the teachings of Seiro that if he did the honorable thing, his path would be lighted, and he would know what to do. No such enlightenment had come to Raelen yet, but that didn't make him doubt his choice.

He'd proven to himself that he would not rule like his father, and that gave him a quiet confidence he'd never possessed. Raelen finally felt like he knew who he was. Granted, his father had spoken truth; there were times when sacrifices indeed had to be made for the greater good, but Gryyth taught him never to act against his conscience. That was the very essence of the Ursaj philosophy of Seiro. Killing Vesarr had seemed wrong, even though legally Raelen had the right, and so he surrendered. In retrospect, it'd been a simple choice.

Humans always complicate things. That was something the Ursaj was fond of saying.

Raelen tried his other side, but sleep remained elusive. Thinking of dreams reminded him of the strange vision he'd had of Saranna.

Vision? What, am I a soothsayer now? He scoffed.

It was just a dream, he kept trying to persuade himself, but it wasn't working. Something about seeing Saranna haunted him. Oh, he'd dreamt of his dead sister before, sometimes to the warming of his heart, and at other times to his waking in bitter tears. But there was something singular about this dream, a unique feeling, like Saranna had, in fact, been there.

Her words wouldn't stop bouncing around inside his skull: *You will face him again...* Who was "him?" *...but this time he fights with the power of death itself.* What could that mean? Did it mean anything? *You cannot fight him the way you did before. To touch him is death. His power cannot affect itself, so arm yourself with it, but don't partake of it.*

Raelen sighed and reached to touch his bicep, but caught himself. His transference band was gone, probably locked away in a footlocker somewhere in Vesarr's sectioned off room. Its absence led Raelen to realize he had a habit of brushing the talis with his fingertips whenever he was worried or afraid. It made sense. It was a special connection to his mentor and closest friend, one that transcended distance.

He wished Gryyth were with him right now.

Shouting, followed by the distinct snapping of crossbow triggers.

Raelen sat up.

An unintelligible command evoked the metallic echo of hundreds of swords being drawn at once. But it was the choral battle cry of a hundred Aiestali soldiers that spurred Raelen off his cot and through the partition's curtain. A soldier shot a wide-eyed glance at Raelen, but didn't stop him as he left his private section.

"What's happening?" he demanded.

"We're under attack." Vesarr emerged from his sleeping quarters. A squire was frantically trying to keep stride with the general in an attempt to buckle on a breastplate.

"Haeshala?"

"Or raiders. But I don't know of any raider chiefs so brazen they'd attack an army, not since the advent of the Invincible Shadow." Vesarr walked up to stand over his table covered in maps. The squire looked relieved as the general's stopping made it easy for him to finish buckling on the man's armor. "It's hard to be certain. I've sent three scouting parties to the east, but none have reported back. We tried to reach them via speaking stone, but the talis behaves like its twin stone is dead."

Raelen walked up to the table. While technically a prisoner, Vesarr hadn't treated him like one. For the most part he was free to move about the main chamber of the tent, and could even walk about camp, though the general insisted he take along an escort. By Vesarr's hesitancy to attack Haeshala, and his continued show of respect toward Raelen, he suspected the man believed he was actually who he said he was. It was another evidence to Raelen that'd he had done the right thing in not challenging Vesarr for control of the army.

A young soldier, only two or three years Raelen's junior, rushed into the tent. His face was red, his eyes wild, and he was panting. "General... Rahkanas..." he gasped, so panicked that he didn't even remember to salute—a breach of protocol punishable by ten lashings.

"Who are you?" Vesarr demanded.

"It's Captain Nylar's Mora..." The young man paused to suck in several breaths.

"What about them?" Vesarr snapped.

"They're gone!"

Earlier, Raelen overheard Vesarr dispensing the nightly watch assignments; Nylar's six hundred soldiers had been the men charged with guarding the camp's perimeter.

"What? Where did they go?" Vesarr's face was turning red.

The young soldier shook his head. "They're dead."

A scream punctuated the young man's words, the cry multiplying into a chaotic chorus of hundreds.

Whatever Raelen dreaded was coming, had finally arrived.

JENOC SMILED as two score of his children surged forth, consuming the soldiers as they pushed past their lines. The fighting men of Aiestal hardly had time enough to scream before they withered into desiccated corpses. Jenoc was impressed with the soldier's discipline. Even in the face of certain death, they held their ground. Only a few ran, and those Jenoc struck down personally with bolts of green lightning. He found the skill to be unique to him among his army of Moriora wielders, a phenomenon he attributed to his centuries-long lifetime of channeling Apeiron and being trained in the Five Disciplines of Allosian spell-casting.

By way of the ritual he'd learned for calling Moriora, he'd succeeded in transforming a third of the population of Haeshala's capital city—all the humans with green eyes—into life-leeching demons. The green eyes connection was a fascinating academic mystery the old Jenoc would've thrilled to explore. But study and research no longer interested him. The passionate scholar was gone now, replaced by an avenging angel; a general at the head of an army of thousands all wielding a fire that would purge Shaelar of its human infestation. But as formidable as he was, and even with a host of acolytes at his command, it wasn't enough. Not if he were to truly exterminate the vermin that was humanity.

It'd taken less than twenty-four hours for Jenoc's children–some fifteen thousand vessels of Moriora–to completely strip the Haeshalan capital city of all life. Some resisted their new natures at first, even going so far as to try and fight off their fellow Moriorans. Interestingly enough, one Morioran could not drain another of its life force. They could wither flora, fauna, and people, but not each other. It was a curiosity the old Jenoc would've sought with a fevered obsession to understand; that man had been beaten to death on the floor of Prince Isara's throne room. But even those noble souls trying to protect their families and friends eventually succumbed to the hunger, devouring those very dear ones they'd fought to protect.

By the end, all of Isadara had descended into chaos, and it'd taken a combination of Jenoc's unique command of the green lightning along with a subtle broadcast of telepathy to convince them to accept him as their new god. For some reason, the ones who'd devoured their own kin were the easiest to dominate.

After destroying Isadara, Jenoc and his army swept across the countryside, leaving the grasslands rocky and desolate in their wake. How fortunate for him to have intercepted not one, but three scouting parties sent forth from the very army he'd schemed to launch from Aiested. He'd almost forgotten about them, and was even more delighted to learn they camped about an Apeira well. Fate truly had sanctioned his efforts and mission.

Forcing his children to abstain long enough for him to interrogate the soldiers had been difficult. Even with his promises of unlimited food, displays of power, and psychic manipulation, his hold over the Moriorans was tenuous at best, especially the hungrier they became. That was why Jenoc had only brought forty with him to attack the Aiestali army.

One of Jenoc's daughters snapped a translucent green tendril toward a soldier with green eyes, but Jenoc immolated her with a pillar of fire before she could feed on him. Killing a Morioran was extremely difficult, even for him, and used a disproportionate amount of power to accomplish. The trick was to exterminate the vessel by inflicting an overwhelming amount of damage all at once. The attack had to be quick, and leave nothing more than ashes behind. Anything less, and the Morioran could rebuild itself by siphoning energy from the life around it. Unfortunately, this kind of spell-casting cost Jenoc several times the effort and energy it used to, and so he only relied on it as a last resort.

"I said do not eat the ones with green eyes!" He shouted both with his voice and mind. The others flinched, but didn't do more than hesitate before they returned to their slaughter.

They will frenzy when they get close to the camp's Aeose, and I won't be able to stop them from destroying it. It'd been nearly impossible for Jenoc himself to resist feasting on the Apeira well back in Isadara even with all of his training and discipline. In the end, he'd only resisted the overwhelming pull by tapping into his hate.

He had to get to the camp's Apeira well before any of his children if he was going to succeed.

Jenoc rushed forward, using three successive bolts of emerald lightning to drain approaching soldiers. He broke the outer perimeter of the camp, ignoring any who ran from him, and only devouring those foolish enough to try and stop him.

RAELEN GRABBED Vesarr by his upper arm, stopping the general as he made for the open tent flap. "Let me fight!"

Vesarr stared at him, green eyes appraising.

"If I meant to kill you or anyone here, I would've already done it."

Vesarr gave Raelen a sharp nod. "Get the prince his talis," he commanded his squire.

The boy dashed into Vesarr's sectioned off room, emerging a moment later with Raelen's transference band. Raelen took the bracelet-like piece of jewelry and snapped it around his right bicep. Immediately he could feel his connection to Gryyth and his chest warmed and loosened with the relief of finding his Ursaj friend still alive.

Vesarr lifted his full-faced helmet from underneath his arm and fitted it over his head. He drew his sword, a wavy-shaped blade of red steel that began to glow as soon as it was out of its sheath.

"This is like no flame brand I've seen."

Vesarr shook his helmeted head. "It is a flare kris. Very dangerous and very rare. Be sure to stay a few extra paces away from me when the melee starts. It produces small explosions when I strike at my foes."

Raelen nodded and followed Vesarr out of the tent.

The camp was a maelstrom of confused shouting and frantic movement. Raelen scanned the scene, trying to locate the attackers. The purple glow of the Apeira well looming twenty-feet above him wasn't much for lighting more than a dozen or so feet out. Had it been bigger, perhaps it would've made seeing in the dark easier.

Raelen caught a flash of green on his right periphery. He turned just as screaming rang out from that quarter of the camp. "Vesarr!"

The general glanced to where Raelen was pointing just as two more flashes of green washed over the tents and massing soldiers. He nodded and broke into a jog. Raelen followed, transforming his limbs into perfect copies of Gryyth's white-furred forearms and claws. Less visible was the expanding of muscle beneath the skin of his arms and legs and across his chest, and even his teeth grew pointy and his hair changed from sunshine blonde to dirty-snow white.

He outran Vesarr, leaping over soldiers and pounding the ground with clawed feet that tore through his leather boots. He pushed a soldier out of his way a little too hard, sending the man crashing into a group of his fellows, all of whom fell sprawling.

"Sorry," Raelen caught himself shouting. Not very princely.

The screams grew louder in time with the increasing rapidity of emerald flashes. What was happening? Talis craft to be sure, but Raelen hadn't ever seen a talis that produced the color green in its effects. Soldiers fled, not away from him, but toward him, trying to outrun the danger ahead. When he drew close, Raelen bounded over a mass of fleeing soldiers. He landed right in front of a man he'd come to know and hate. His hair was blonde, and eyes green, but Raelen would know that face until his dying day.

"Pariel!" Raelen shouted.

Jenoc glanced at him and smirked. "My Prince. I am surprised to find you here." He sounded genuinely excited.

"Why are you attacking my army? I thought you wanted us to go to war."

"I am not here to attack your army." Jenoc laughed. "I am here to recruit them."

"You're madder than I thought if you think that any of these brave men would elect to follow you." Raelen tried to ignore the fact that all of his brave soldiers were currently fleeing the scene.

Jenoc's smile widened. It was an unnerving rictus that looked very out of place on the usually stoic man. At least, he'd never smiled much when Raelen had known him as his loyal Navarch, Pariel.

"They will not have a choice."

What did that mean?

Deciding that further parlay with the monster would be a waste of time, Raelen charged. Although he bore down on the Allosian with an open claw raised to strike, the man didn't move. Raelen brought his arm down, claws raking Jenoc's face, bear nails tearing four fleshy runnels down the Allosian's perfect cheek, but producing no blood.

Pain exploded in Raelen's fingers. He bellowed as he aborted his charge. The sudden reversal of momentum caused him to lose his footing, and he crashed to the ground. His four fingers, just a heartbeat ago thick and powerful, were withering right before his eyes into a substance that resembled a prune. Raelen screamed. His skin tightened and shrank, and his fingers crumbled to dust. All he had left were pieces of bone protruding from blackened nubs. The skin around the edge of the nubs had shrunken tightly across the breaks, reducing the flow of blood to a mere trickle.

Raelen cradled his hand, staring up Jenoc with wide eyes. The Allosian pointed at one of the fleeing soldiers and a bolt of green lightning arced across the distance separating the two. The soldier flashed with a halo of emerald light, and then was gone. The skin of Jenoc's cheek knit together and smoothed, leaving no evidence of the wound that marred him just seconds before.

Jenoc smirked. "I want you to see what I am going to do, My Prince." With that he strode away, wading back into the confused mob of soldiers and recommencing his magical attacks.

Raelen stared at his fingerless hand. It'd been his dominant hand. How would he write, play the harp, or steer a ghern? What an odd thing to think in the heat of a battle. He ground his teeth and tears threatened, not from pain but from the crushing pressure of defeat. Jenoc was going to do something horrible to his men, but he couldn't stop him. In fact, he literally could not touch the man.

Saranna's words come back like a lightning strike to his brain: *To touch him is death.*

"Saranna…"

She had spoken to him! Her spirit did come to him to prophesy of this very moment. It hadn't been a dream. Hope rekindled inside Raelen. Not only did the soul of his dear sister warn him of Jenoc's return, but she'd also given him a clue for how to stop the Allosian.

Raelen ignored his pain with one of Gryyth's mediation mantras;

> *The wind cannot silence me.*
> *The dirt cannot smother me.*
> *The rain cannot drown me.*
> *The cold cannot touch me.*
> *I am the ever- burning flame.*

What was it Saranna had said to him?

You will face him again, but this time he fights with the power of death itself. You cannot fight him the way you did before. To touch him is death. His power cannot affect itself, so arm yourself with it, but don't partake of it.

Raelen didn't understand, but the frightened shouts of his men made him growl a very Ursaj-like growl, and he stood. He had to do something. He had to stop Jenoc. He didn't have time to puzzle out Saranna's cryptic instructions. Perhaps if he struck hard and fast, he could kill the Allosian warmonger in a single blow. It would likely cost him his life, but he was ready to give it.

Seiro.

JENOC STOOD before the looming purple, crystalline obelisk at the center of the Aiestali camp. He craned his head back to take in the entirety of it. Twenty-feet tall was a small Aeose, especially when compared to the miles high Mother Shard at the center of Allose.

His screaming hunger begged him to reach out and drink from the Apeira well, but he fought it. He hadn't come this far, sacrificed this much just to give into appetite. He began the ritual, again casting from all Five Disciplines and then inverting them–just as she had shown him.

As before, the effort drained him, but fortunately sustenance was plentiful. Jenoc consumed the life energy of dozens of soldiers as he tapped into the very fabric of reality, the most basic building blocks of the universe. He found the rhythmic cadence of Apeiron, and interrupted it, replacing order with chaos. The rhythm changed from a steady pulse into a frantic, wild, cacophony of random beats.

Even with unlimited sources for his magic, the effort was taxing. Not just his physical body, he realized, but the ritual was doing something to his mind. Not corrupting him, or making of him something else, but taking something from him. It was like the spell demanded payment in more than just Apeiron. It required a piece of his very being–his soul.

Jenoc tensed with the effort. He balled his fists at his sides, and his hand brushed something sharp concealed inside the pocket of his cloak. Kairah's geode. Why had he brought that with him? Thinking of his sister's betrayal fueled Jenoc's rage, and he completed the spell with a hammer's blow of unnecessary force.

The Apeira well exploded.

RAELEN BOUNDED toward the center of camp, growling and shoving soldiers out of his way. He drew more deeply on his transference band, the strength of Gryyth reinforcing him and dulling his pain.

He could see the tall Allosian now. He was standing at the base of the camp's Apeira well, waves of translucent force pulsing from him. Raelen had no idea what the monster was doing, but it couldn't be good. Perhaps he was going to use the well to power a spell that would kill the entire army? Raelen growled and charged.

He'd closed to just ten paces when the Apeira well exploded. The blast hurled him backward so hard that even Gryyth's borrowed stamina couldn't keep him from blacking out when his head struck the ground.

When Raelen awoke, he hurt all over. But one sharp, cold stabbing in particular drew his attention. It was like being speared by Loeadon's lethal icicle all over again. His fingers found it before his eyes did. An emerald-colored shard of crystal, as long as a short sword, pierced his right shoulder and protruded from his back. He cried out, and every twitch of his muscles was agony. An image of the gigantic piece of Aiested's broken well flashed before him. It had been the same color.

Raelen forced himself to roll onto his side. He screamed, but his voice was drowned out by the roaring cries of his army. The well was gone. Not even its base remained. Jenoc was gone too. *Then why the screaming?*

That's when Raelen saw it: a bedraggled man in a wrinkled and torn diamond cut overcoat—the vogue fashion of the Haeshalen nobility. His skin was pale, and his eyes rimmed by dark circles. He was grinning as he walked through the mass of moving soldiers. One of Raelen's fighting men raised a sword to strike the Haeshalan wild man down but froze as a tendril of warped air, translucent green in color, speared him through the chest. The soldier convulsed, and then withered into a desiccated corpse.

More figures—men, women, and youths, not soldiers—strolled around the killing field striking out with tentacles of the same power at any who were foolish enough to come within ten feet. Their victims suffered the same fate of the withering soldier.

Raelen staggered to his feet. He called upon Gryyth's strength to aid him, but felt nothing. His transference band was empty, its Apeiron charge gone.

"My Prince."

Raelen turned, his shoulder both on fire and freezing at the same time. He found Vesarr standing a few paces away. His helmet was off, and he held his flare kris at a lazy angle. He was hunched over, one arm folded about his stomach like he was going to be sick.

"General?"

Vesarr looked up and Raelen gasped. The man's face was as pale as the flesh of a corpse, and he bared his teeth in a grimace of pain the likes of which must've far exceeded Raelen's own.

"You're wounded?" Raelen grunted.

Vesarr touched the side of his head and squinted his eyes closed. "It's so cold," he sobbed out. "It's eating my stomach." He screamed and fell to his knees.

Raelen instinctively backed away, the motion sending jolts of pain lightning throughout his arm and drawing involuntary tears from his eyes. Vesarr looked sick. Could Jenoc have set off a plague box? Loeadon spoke of crafting one. Perhaps Jenoc took it?

"So cold," Vesarr cried. He looked up and met Raelen's eyes. "I'm sorry."

A spread of tendrils made of the same warped, translucent green energy the Haeshalan wild man had wielded, sprang from Vesarr's chest. They struck like vipers at Raelen but just when they ought to have sank into his flesh, they evaporated.

Vesarr's eyes widened and he shook his head. He struck out with more of his magic vines, but the same thing happened. Vesarr struck his stomach with a gauntleted fist. "No!" he screamed, and then struck again, and again, and again.

"Vesarr stop!" Raelen barked.

Vesarr stopped, crawled backward until he could scramble up, and then broke into a run. Though every step was electric torture, Raelen followed. Two more of Jenoc's creations struck out at Raelen as he passed, but as with Vesarr, their tendrils of energy vanished upon contact.

Vesarr was screaming now, running hunched over with his free hand pressed against his middle. He ran back to the command tent and stopped to snatch a lantern hanging from a pole. He broke the lantern open, showering himself with oil, and repeated the action with a second lantern. He flipped his flame kris around so that the point rested against his stomach and glanced back to meet Raelen's eyes.

"Vesarr, no!" Raelen shouted.

Vesarr shook his head and then rammed the wavy-shaped blade into his gut. Nothing happened. No blood, no fire. The talis was drained of its Apeiron charge, just like Raelen's transference band. Of course, that didn't explain the lack of spilling gore or the absence of any pain expressed on the general's face. Vesarr yanked the wavy blade free and dropped it on the ground. He looked about wildly, and smiled upon seeing a quarter of the camp engulfed in flames–the flame caster's brigade.

Vesarr tore off in the direction of the flames, his mad laughter drowned out by the shouting and screams coming at Raelen from all sides. Raelen tried to pursue, but the pain of his wounds was too much. He impotently watched a tongue of flame lick up above the blaze raging in the flame caster's quarter as Vesarr dove into the inferno.

Raelen staggered forward and fell to his knees. The impact jerked the shard of green crystal impaling his shoulder and Raelen opened his mouth to scream, but vomit poured out instead. He choked and sputtered as blackness encroached on the edges of his vision. The world went silent as the black swelled and devoured his sight.

JENOC'S HARVEST was disappointingly meager. Out of the entire Aiestali army, he'd created less than a hundred new children. It had sated the hunger of the others who'd disobeyed him and mobbed the army–killing the soldiers to a man–which brought them back under his control. That was helpful, and the destruction they wrought was awe inspiring, but not enough. He'd need a bigger army to unleash on Shaelar if he was going to destroy all of humanity.

He needed more Moriorans.

Jenoc mentally listed the different Apeira wells in the vicinity. There were at least a dozen, both discovered and hidden, but none were large enough to effect a change larger than a few miles. He needed a big Apeira well like the one in Taris. But no, that was too far away. He'd lose control of his minions long before he reached Aiested.

A thought came to him, sudden and illuminating like a revelation from one of the human's fictitious gods. There was an Apeira well close by that was powerful enough to broadcast his Moriora spell across all of Shaelar. If he could do that, turn every green-eyed human in the land into a Moriora wielder, he wouldn't need to control his children. They would be everywhere, crisscrossing the land and devouring their fellows until all of Shaelar was a boneyard.

The Mother Shard in Allose was the key to completing his mission, to exacting his vengeance. But what of his people? Would they not die too? Jenoc laughed. They didn't matter anymore. Kairah didn't matter anymore. All he cared about was punishing the whole world for his suffering. And then he would die too, shining bright like a supernova before collapsing in on himself and becoming nothing.

He looked in the direction of his homeland, and telepathically relayed his command to the thousands of monsters making up his army. Now he was a monster too, but then perhaps he always had been one.

CHAPTER 87

"If you don't know who Jekaran is, then how do you know me?" Mulladin asked the sword.

You don't need to say the words out loud, Jekaran chided.

Mulladin glanced at Keesa who sat opposite him, cross legged, on the dusty wooden floor. They'd easily fled from the frightened city guard, and were holed up in the attic of the cooper's shop–unbeknownst to the cooper.

"I want Keesa to hear what I'm saying." Mulladin was kneeling over the sword, which was placed on the floor between them. "So, you know me? But no one else?"

There was that bastard with the long black hair. I knew him.

"Why did you kill him?"

He was going to kill a lot of people.

"Isn't that what a sword is for?"

I only kill evil people.

"Ask it if it remembers anything from when we were..." Keesa hesitated, "competing for it."

Mulladin arched an eyebrow.

Keesa rolled her eyes. "Fine. When we were trying to kill each other."

I can hear her, Jekaran said in a flat tone. *And there was nothing before the Apeira well woke me.*

"So, you don't know Maely, or Kairah?"

I know them.

"What about Ez?"

At the mention of Ez's name, the sword fell silent. Maybe "silent" was the wrong term, Mulladin decided. It was like the sword just disappeared from his mind.

"Jekaran?"

It was a full minute before the sword spoke again. *Mull!* It enthused, in the exact same excited tone he'd first heard it speak his name.

"Jekaran?"

The sword mentally laughed. *If that's what you want to call me.*

It'd said those same words the first time.

"What's wrong?" Keesa's thin eyebrows were drawn down.

Mulladin shook his head, but didn't respond to her question. "Do you remember what we were just talking about?"

The sword projected confusion. *I just awoke.*

Yes, something was definitely wrong.

"Could you give me a moment of privacy to talk to my friend?"

The pretty girl? The sword projected the image of a sly wink. *You sure you don't need more than a few minutes? Wait, what am I talking about, you're a virgin, aren't you? You'll probably only need—*

"I'm not a virgin!" Mulladin blurted out. Horrified he'd said that out loud, he looked up at Keesa with wide eyes.

She arched an eyebrow. "Are you?"

Mulladin didn't answer. Of course he was, but it wasn't his fault. Until just a short time ago, he'd possessed the mind of a six-year-old. He'd had those feelings, of course, but he didn't understand them, and no decent woman would take advantage of a simpleton that way. He remembered the girls from Graelle's brothel. They hadn't had any qualms about flirting with him. They probably would've... He flushed.

"You are!" Keesa laughed.

Mulladin rose so abruptly that he forgot to stoop, and struck his head on one of the attic's low wooden buttresses. "Dammit!" As he rubbed his scalp he bent down, grabbed Keesa by the forearm, and pulled her up.

"What're you doing?"

Mulladin towed her to the far corner of the attic.

"Whoa! I'm not gonna help you with that problem. If you think—"

"Shut up!" Mulladin hissed. "Something is wrong with him."

"Him?"

Mulladin rolled his eyes. "My friend–your cousin–is definitely in that sword."

"Like his mind or his soul?"

"Hell if I know." Mulladin glanced back at the sword lying on the dusty floorboards. "But it's definitely Jek. He knows who I am and remembers our life together…"

Keesa sniggered. "So, that's how he knows you're a virgin?"

Mulladin just narrowed his eyes. "He also knows my sister, and my other friends. But when I asked him if he knew your father, he shut down, and when he finally started talking again, it was like it was right after Loeadon died. Like he'd just woken up and the last few hours never happened."

Keesa's smile faded. "You said he killed my father."

Mulladin nodded.

"Perhaps that did something to his mind," Keesa said. "Maybe he's broken."

Mulladin rubbed some more at the goose egg rising on the top of his head. "Maybe the Allosians can do something to fix him. Kairah and the others are probably already there."

"You mean Allose?" Keesa sighed. "You still think what that little girl said about her talking flower is true; that you need to take the sword to the secret city?"

"The sword talks," Mulladin snapped. "Why not a flower?"

"A prophet-flower?"

Mulladin threw up his hands, and they struck the wooden beam above him. "Ow!" He pulled his hand down to examine a sliver that'd lodged itself in his finger. "At the very least," he said while sucking on his wound, "Jekaran's body should be there. If we bring the sword back to him, maybe it'll fix him somehow and he'll wake up."

"Okay." Keesa's tone was patronizingly patient. "Let's say you're right. Where is Allose? How do we find a city that polymaths and scholars have been searching out for centuries?"

I know where Allose is, Jek projected.

Mulladin realized they'd stopped whispering. He walked back and knelt over the sword. "How do you know where Allose is?"

"It knows?" Keesa asked.

Because that's where Kairah is.

Though Mulladin didn't know much about magic, the fact that the sword would know where Kairah was did make a kind of sense. Kairah had Jekaran's physical body, and if the sword was still connected to it...

"Can you tell me where Allose is?"

I can show you.

Mulladin cried out as images flooded into his mind. He was so startled, he fell backward and landed on his side with a loud thump! It didn't last long, but Mulladin now knew how to find the ancient Allosian city as though he'd made the journey a hundred times.

"Damn rats!" A muffled voice shouted from below. "Adna! Adna! Where's my hammer?"

"We need to get out of here." Keesa helped Mulladin up.

He bent down and took the sword. "I know where we need to go."

"Is it far?"

"Yeah. A hundred miles northeast of Rasha."

"Rasha's at least two hundred miles away from here!" Keesa walked to the window by which they'd gained entry to the cooper's shop attic. "It'll take us weeks to get there on ghern back, and we don't have any gherns. With the city guard on high alert, it's gonna be hard to steal any and we'll need at least four to cycle riding so we don't kill them." Keesa raised one leg and put it over the window sill. "Guess we can wait a few weeks until things settle down and then..."

"No!"

"Let me guess." Keesa rolled her eyes. "The talking flower spoke to you and said we had to hurry?"

"Haven't you seen what's happening?" Mulladin snapped. "The darkness over Aiested is spreading. The ground shakes, and there was that wave of force that disintegrated your boat."

Keesa didn't say anything.

"I don't think we have weeks!" Mulladin walked over to the window and stared Keesa in the eyes. They were quite pretty–like liquid pools of–shut up!

Muttering and movement came from beneath a trapdoor set in the floor. The cooper was coming to deal with the rats.

"So how are we going to get to Allose?"

"Trous's manor house is in this city." Mulladin smiled.

"You want to use the slipgate?" Keesa cast a worried glance at the trapdoor which was now shaking. "The manor house is still a Rikujo stronghold, and they're sure to have gotten a report about what happened in Aiested by now. Someone else will have already stepped forward to claim leadership, and I doubt they'll be friendly to us."

The trap door in the floor burst open and a bald, liver-spotted head crowned the square opening. Mulladin and Keesa quickly slipped out the open window and onto the shop's roof. They crawled up the tiled incline and crouched in the shadow of a chimney.

"We have the sword of the Invincible Shadow." Mulladin raised the sword for emphasis. "And I was with Ezr...." Mulladin glanced at the sword. He didn't want to say the name again in front of Jekaran. "... Argentus," he finished.

Keesa glanced at the sword and rolled her eyes. "That's why they'll be hostile! The new leader will see you as a threat."

"Then we fight our way in."

That's the spirit, Jekaran said.

Keesa frowned. "You can use that thing?"

That was a good question. If a piece of Jekaran's mind was trapped in the sword, would it work for him like it'd worked for Jekaran?

I'll help you fight.

That was good enough for him.

Mulladin nodded at Keesa. "And with your lightning ring, we shouldn't have any trouble forcing our way to the slipgate."

"They'll have weapon talises too, idiot."

"Then what do you suggest?" Mulladin snapped.

Keesa looked past him and Mulladin shifted to see what she was staring at. It was Erassa's Apeira well, thirty feet tall and glowing with a soft purple aura. "You really think the world is ending?" she asked.

"Don't you?"

"And you think we can actually do something to help stop it?"

"Honestly, I don't know," he said. "But my friend, your cousin, needs this sword. And I'm gonna get it to him."

Keesa met his eyes and quietly asked, "Why did you save me?"

That caught Mulladin off guard. "What?"

"Why did you save me? I'm your enemy. I stole that sword and tried to kill you!"

"You weren't trying that hard, were you?" Mulladin smirked, but Keesa didn't laugh at his jest.

"Was it because of what that little girl's flower said–that you need me? Or was there another reason?"

Mulladin shifted uncomfortably. "Look, I'm not sure now's the time for this."

"Every man I've ever known, starting with Kaul, has only hurt or used me. Are you using me too, Mulladin?"

He shook his head.

"Then why save me? Why do you care?"

Mulladin considered that.

Because you think she's gorgeous, Jekaran said.

"Shut it!"

"What?" Keesa scowled.

"I wasn't talking to you." Mulladin looked her in the eyes. She is pretty. "Your father took me and my sister in when our mother died. He fed us, watched over us, and pretty much raised us. He cared about us when no one else did. I think that's the reason I care. Because someone who didn't have to care cared about me first."

Keesa threw her arms around Mulladin and planted her lips on his. She kissed him long and deep. Mulladin was so surprised that the handle of Jek's sword slipped from his hand, and he had to lunge to catch it. The sharp move unbalanced him and he slipped taking Keesa with him as they rolled down the slope and off the tiled roof. They landed in a trough full of hay, much to the consternation of a feeding cow. It snorted and moved away.

Mulladin quickly located Jek's sword. It was lying on the ground a few paces away from the trough. He'd landed on top of Keesa and quickly rose to all fours, panicking at her tearstained red face.

"Are you okay? Keesa?"

Then he realized she was laughing. Her eyes were clenched shut, but tears squeezed out of them. She was laughing so hard she was turning purple, apparently not able to breathe. Mulladin started laughing too, mostly out of relief that he hadn't crushed the woman. When Keesa got a hold of herself, she shoved Mulladin so that he fell onto his side. Then she rolled on top of him, pressing him down and leaning in to kiss him. He kissed her back.

Jekaran wolf-whistled inside his mind, but Mulladin didn't care.

Chapter 88

Raelen woke to an agony that exceeded any physical pain he'd ever known. His shoulder was on fire and freezing at the same time, a contradiction that reminded him of being speared by Loeadon's magic icicle. He rolled onto his good side, but the movement jostled the shard of crystal embedded in his flesh and he screamed. His vision darkened, and he very nearly passed out again, but managed to cling to consciousness by mentally reciting one of Gryyth's Ursaj focus mantras.

> *The wind cannot silence me.*
> *The dirt cannot smother me.*

Raelen whimpered and shuddered as he gingerly worked to sit up.

> *The rain cannot drown me.*
> *The cold cannot touch me.*

"I am the ever-burning flame!" Raelen's strained voice echoed across the empty camp.

It was dawn, and though the shadows were long, the awful scope of the destruction surrounding him was clear. Tents were tipped or completely collapsed into heaps of poles and canvas. Swords, shields, and armor lay rusted and broken all around him, as though they'd belonged to a people hundreds of years removed. The ground was black and barren, not a single blade of grass anywhere to be seen. And there were bones, lots of bones, stripped entirely of flesh and so scattered that trying to reassemble any one corpse would be an exercise in futility. The sheer totality of the devastation was awesome, and nearly made Raelen forget his physical pain.

He moved to stand, but froze when the stabbing cold in his shoulder objected. He looked at the emerald colored shard sprouting from his flesh. The skin around the shard was blackened, not like it had been burned, but like dead flesh surrounding a festering wound. It couldn't have gone foul this soon, could it?

He debated about whether he should wrench the green crystal from his shoulder, and another failed attempt to stand convinced him of the necessity of doing so. He gently touched the shard with his opposite hand–the good hand, praise the goddess–and was surprised to find the crystal cold, almost to burning like cardice. He plucked a stray stick of firewood from the ground–he hoped it was a stick and not a bone–and put it in his mouth for something to bite down on. Then he took several deep breaths through his nose, closed his eyes, and gripped the protruding shard so tight that its edges sliced into his palm.

The cold cannot touch me.

He drew in one last deep breath, and then yanked as hard as he could. A muffled scream exploded from deep within him, and he bit down so hard on the stick in his mouth that it snapped in two.

Almost two feet of emerald crystal tore free of his flesh with surprisingly little blood. Raelen collapsed to his back, tears stinging his eyes as he hyperventilated. He vomited and nearly passed out, but clawed his way back to full consciousness just as the tunnel of blackness was about to swallow his sight. He gripped his wounded shoulder with a bloody palm, the pressure helping him to weather the shock.

He stayed like that for almost an hour, and by the time he had the strength to move, the sun was high in the sky. Raelen examined the tear in his deltoid. The jagged hole was surrounded by necrotized tissue, and a cold numbness inside his muscle restricted its movement. Raelen gripped his shoulder and carefully sat up. It hurt, but was a faint echo of the stabbing pain the embedded shard had produced. He glanced down at the crystal. It was smeared with blood from his sliced palm.

It's a piece of an Apeira well, or had been.

Why had Jenoc destroyed an Apeira well?

Raelen did another cursory sweep of his surroundings, but the only thing he found was Vesarr's charred corpse smoldering amidst piles of burned canvas. The general was one of those things; the monsters in human shape that fed on the living. *Was he always one? Was this some sort of elaborate betrayal engineered by the Allosian warmonger?* Raelen didn't think so. There was something in Vesarr's eyes when he'd attacked Raelen–horror. The general was appalled that he attacked his prince, even as he was doing it.

He'd seen that look before, on the face of a nobleman at court who attempted to beat his eight-year-old son to death when the boy testified of his father's deviancies. Raelen had broken protocol and seized upon the man himself, stopping the beating and nearly tearing the man's heart out.

Good thing Gryyth was there to stop me.

Raelen glanced at his transference band. It encircled the bicep of his unwounded shoulder. The Apeira shard embedded in the talis was dark. He really could've used the stamina it offered right now, not to mention the comfort of a connection to Gryyth. He found himself desperately wishing for his Ursaj protector.

Vesarr's wavy-shaped red-steel blade lay on the ground half a dozen paces away. His own general had tried to devour him–but it hadn't worked. Neither had any of the other of Jenoc's monsters been able to touch him. *Why?*

"His power cannot affect itself," he recited what Saranna had told him and then glanced at the blackened hole in his shoulder.

He'd been pierced by the green well shard when Vesarr attacked him. Before that, he'd been every bit as vulnerable as his soldiers. He raised his fingerless hand before his face and wiggled his blackened nubs. He examined the dead skin around his shoulder wound, prodding it and feeling nothing.

"Arm yourself with it, but don't partake of it."

Raelen choked out a laugh. "Arm yourself, Saranna?" It was a pun, something his sister had been fond of in life. A personal touch signing the experience and proving it authentic. "It was you!" Raelen laughed again. "Saranna?" Raelen called. "Saranna?"

His sister didn't answer.

He was disappointed and confused; he could've really used her counsel and company at the moment, but apparently communicating with the dead was said to be a miracle for a reason. Whatever laws or barriers that separated the world of the living from the dead must've been difficult to transcend, otherwise such a wonderful thing would be common place.

"She said her time was short." It was comforting to speak aloud to himself. What else had Saranna said? "Arm yourself with it, but don't partake of it."

Raelen looked at his blackened wound, and then at his transference band. The emerald shard killed the flesh around where it pierced him, and touching it was painful. It was similar when touching a normal well shard, except that only tingled the skin. With talises, the actual well shard didn't need to touch the bearer's flesh. It could grant power as long as there was a conductor of some kind bridging the skin and the shard. The green crystal was a shard of an Apeira well, so shouldn't it work the same as a talis?

Raelen found a one-inch piece of the green crystal lying on the ground. He sucked in a breath when he picked it up, and quickly wrapped it inside the bottom of his tunic. The pain ceased as soon as direct contact was broken. He tore off a piece of the cloth, wrapped the shard in it, and then shuffled back to the command tent where he found a leather thong in Vesarr's traveling trunk. It was wrapped around a ring, not a talis but obviously some sentimental memento.

"Sorry, Vesarr." He broke the leather cord with his teeth.

He tied the thong around the bundled shard and then, moving slowly so as to not aggravate his shoulder, looped the makeshift necklace over his head. He winced at the pain from his arm, and used his blackened nubs to slide the bundled shard under his shirt so that it touched his skin–like a talis. He wasn't at all sure this would work. Physically touching the green crystal was painful, and apparently too much contact would kill his flesh.

By the same token, too much cloth would act as a barrier to connecting with a talis. He was no polymath or talis hunter and so didn't know exactly how much material would inhibit a connection, but this was the best he could do. The cold radiating from the shard was still present, but no longer painful. That encouraged him, and he exited the command tent.

If what Saranna had said proved true, then wearing the crystal would protect him from Jenoc and his minions' life draining magic. Hopefully that would give him the opportunity he needed to strike a fatal blow. His transference band was drained again, but Gryyth's training had made him lethal enough on his own. If he could get his hands around Jenoc's neck... but no. He'd marred the Allosian's perfect face and watched it heal right before his eyes.

Fire.

Vesarr had become one of those life leeches, and fire ended up being what destroyed him. Raelen would need to somehow immolate Jenoc. His eyes rested on Vesarr's flame kris and he gingerly retrieved it from where it lay on the ground. The talis was dead, but if Raelen could recharge it, it'd be the very thing he needed to fight Jenoc. But what about the thousands of life leeches that followed him? Raelen would need help.

He prayed to Rasheera for exactly that, but if no help could be found, he would still follow, find, and kill the Allosian warmonger. That would probably cost Raelen his life, but with the severity of his wound, and his dead flesh, he likely didn't have more than a few days anyway before infection poisoned his blood—unless he could find a monk with a healing talis, which wasn't likely this far from a city.

Raelen ducked back inside the command tent and rifled through Vesarr's belongings until he found a thick leather satchel. He dumped out its contents, walked outside, and made his way to where the Apeira well had been and loaded the satchel with green crystal shards. If he found allies, they'd need the same protection. It was a desperate chore, one he guessed was probably wishful thinking, but it never hurt to be prepared.

"A cub that eats twice his weight before winter will be glad when he wakes twice as big as when he went to sleep." Raelen smiled, but the smile quickly faded. Oh, how he wished his Ursaj friend was here with him right now.

Once his satchel was as heavy as he had the strength to carry it cross country, Raelen left the camp with Vesarr's flame kris tucked into his belt and the bag full of crystal shards slung over his good shoulder. The weight of it was burdensome, and so he stopped and rid himself of half of what he'd originally gathered. Even with a lighter pack, his weakened physical state slowed him considerably.

Once out of the camp, pursuing Jenoc proved to be simply a matter of following the swath of withered plants, trees, and blackened ground–a road paved with death itself. Finding the monster wasn't Raelen's problem; catching up to Jenoc for even the chance to kill him was going to take a miracle.

Watching the bare ground stretch into the horizon did make it look like a black road. Where was the man going? Certainly to find more victims, perhaps a city? It didn't matter. Raelen was like the shot arrow, committed to the air, racing toward his target, and unable to turn back. Either he would hit his mark or he would die. Probably he would die either way, but the reality of an afterlife made sure to him by his sister's appearance brought him comfort.

"I'll see you again soon, Saranna," he whispered.

CHAPTER 89

Maely gaped at the white spire of the sky temple. It rose as tall as the ancient red-barked trees that surrounded it, reaching over a hundred feet into the sky. The building itself was just as impressive, the roof that served as the base of the spire over half as tall. It was clearly of Allosian design, made of a white substance that seemed to glow against the forest backdrop, and decorated with trailing designs, amethyst jewels, and glowing purple runes. Four smaller spires–though still some thirty feet tall–rose out of the ground, evenly spaced a hundred yards away from the main building.

A netting of vines and thin branches grew around the base of the four smaller spires, and had been pruned to extend horizontally until it joined with the vines of its neighboring spires, making a kind of natural fence. It was tall too and made it hard to see inside the temple grounds. The growling-moans of the Ursaj's native tongue emanated from inside the vine-fence–hundreds of the creatures if Maely guessed right.

The vine fence writhed and moved like a den of rattlesnakes, and the branches and leaves parted of their own accord to allow an Ursaj to exit the temple grounds. He wasn't as big as Gryyth, and his black fur was mottled with gray. The bear-man's left eye was permanently squinted shut and patches of missing fur revealed a diagonal scar crossing the closed lid from crown to cheek.

"Wait here, cub," Gryyth rumbled.

Maely ignored him and continued to help him walk as he

approached the other Ursaj. An exasperated growl was the only reproof Maely got, a reaction due in part to Gryyth's increasing pain and weakness. They'd run out of poppy, and Gryyth's fever had returned. Combined with the bear-man's stubborn commitment to fast, his condition had worsened over the last two days of travel.

Maely was supposed to fast too, but her self-denial was more a matter of imposed necessity than spiritual ritual. She'd run out of her secret store of jerky early on in their journey, and had resorted to eating wild berries and bamboo shoots to stave off hunger. The pains of her personal famine reasserted themselves with a vengeance upon smelling the unmistakable scent of cooking meat wafting from inside the temple grounds. They were feasting in there, and Maely wanted in more badly than she'd ever wanted anything in her life–at that moment anyway.

"Glynn," Gryyth rumbled.

The smaller Ursaj roared in delight and fell to all fours as he ran up to them. "You yet live, cub!"

Maely didn't know what else was said as the two broke into their guttural, moaning language. Clearly the older Ursaj knew Gryyth, and they were friends or family or something, because he attempted to embrace him. He stopped when he noticed Gryyth's wounds, and his jovial sounding moans, turned to clipped growls.

"Ahem," Maely fake coughed.

The Ursaj named Glynn looked down at her. Maely's chest tightened as he inspected her with his one good eye. He moaned-barked something to Gryyth who shook his head.

"She is a human cub, and is protected by Seiro."

Maely shot a look up at Gryyth. "Wait, what did he say?"

"He asked if I brought you for the feast."

Maely's mouth dried. "As a guest, right?"

Gryyth just grunted, and Maely decided she didn't really want to know.

"She fought against the one who burned me," Gryyth said to Glynn. "She helped to save my life and assisted me in my journey here."

Glynn squinted down at her. "That does not mean she can enter the holy grounds."

"She heard the call of the mother," Gryyth softly rumbled.

Glynn's one eye widened. "She lies."

Maely's anger ignited, burning away her fear, and clenched her teeth so hard that it hurt her jaw. She thumbed her bare ring finger, a part of her wishing she still had her compulsion talis.

"No human can hear the mother."

"I can confirm her story." Gryyth looked down at her, and his kindly azure gaze tamped down Maely's rising rage. "Time is short anyhow, so what does it really matter?"

Glynn fell silent. He glanced behind him at the wall made of fauna and then back to Maely. "She can enter."

As if the Ursaj's words had been a command, the vine fence writhed again and parted. Glynn took over helping Gryyth walk and Maely followed them through the opening. It closed behind them, and that's when Maely first noticed the thorns on the vine's branches. Whatever magic made the vine fence function wasn't just decorative. She cringed as the image of thorn-covered vines lashing out to take hold of her arms, legs, and neck played in her mind and she hurried away from the fence.

The sky temple was dome shaped but open on one side like an amphitheater. Ursaj of every size, sex, and color walked about or sat on the ground both within the temple and on the grounds around. There had to be a thousand of the bear-people, all eating, drinking, and laughing like they were at Harvest Festival instead of a council meeting to discuss the end of the world. Browning carcasses of deer, wild boar, and pheasant rotated on spits over a dozen cook-fires interspersed throughout the assembly. It smelled wonderful.

Maely's stomach growled so loud that Gryyth glanced back at her. He nodded at the nearest source of cooking meat, and Maely smiled. She would've ran to the food if she hadn't been so exhausted. The Ursaj tending the spit was white like Gryyth, but much smaller. It looked up at Maely with bright blue eyes and said something in the Ursaj's moaning-growling language.

"Can I have some?" Maely pointed at the browning carcass of a boar rotating over the fire.

The little bear responded with widening eyes accompanied by a high-pitched sound.

"Can I have some?" Maely mimed eating and then patted her

stomach.

The little bear glanced around as if looking for help.

A familiar Ursaj voice barked and huffed from behind. Maely whirled to find Sharor looming over her. She was holding onto Kerr's arm, milky white eyes fixed on Maely. The little white bear made a response and then carved a chunk of flesh from the boar with its claws and proffered it to Maely. She snatched it from the bear's claws and sank her teeth into the meat. It tasted sooo good!

"Thank you," Maely muttered around a mouth full of chewed pork.

"What are you doing here, cub?" Sharor asked.

Maely swallowed a piece of meat that was too big and had to work to gulp it down before answering. "I came with Gryyth."

"I guessed that. But no one save Ursaj are allowed to enter the sacred grounds around the temple of the mother." The she-bear's tone was mournful for some reason.

"Gryyth said I could come in because I heard the voice of the mother."

Sharor slowly nodded. "That was a remarkable occurrence."

"Why?" Maely took another bite of pork. Juice was running down her chin but she didn't care. She was so hungry and the meat was moist, tender, and most surprising of all, seasoned.

"Come with me, cub." Sharor pointed toward the temple, and Kerr escorted her through the crowd.

Maely followed, finishing her cut of meat far too quickly. She shot a longing glance back at the cooking boar and found the small white bear staring at her. He wasn't the only one. Every Ursaj she passed paused to take notice of her. It was both unnerving and irritating.

As Maely followed Sharor the crowd became thinner and she got a better look at the sky temple's interior. A small Apeira well rose from the ground there, maybe nine or ten feet tall at best, and at its base grew a single white lily.

Maely sucked some meat juice from her fingers. The saltiness of the pork had made her thirstier. She passed a barrel full of dark red liquid and veered toward it, assuming it to be wine. Kerr barked something at her.

"No, cub!" Sharor snapped.

Maely started. "I'm thirsty."

"That is for our sacred ritual."

Maely rolled her eyes. "Fine."

"Now come." Sharor waved for Maely to resume following.

They moved to within just a few feet of the Apeira well and the white flower. Sharor slowly lowered herself to the ground where she sat cross-logged. She barked-moaned something at Kerr who nodded and walked away. Maely sat on the ground next to the old she-bear.

"So what is all this about?" Maely waved at the crowd of Ursaj and then reddened. *Sharor is blind, you dullard. She can't see you wave.*

"Long ago, the mother chose a few from our ancestors, the bear, and gave them reason and speech. That is how the Ursaj race was born."

"Are you talking about, Rasheera?"

Sharor shook her shaggy head. "You're thinking of what your monks teach. Doubtless they originally worshipped the mother, but the dogma that has grown up around the truth is so convoluted that the divine of their religion is very different from the truth."

"But we are talking about Rasheera?"

Sharor sighed. "For the sake of simplicity, and time, yes."

That rankled, and she was about to protest the patronizing when the single lily growing at the base of the Apeira well drew her attention. In spite of being within the well's purple aura, it seemed to shine white with its own glow. And if Maely didn't know better, she thought she could feel a gentle heat emanating from the flower.

Sharor continued. "The mother also gave to the Ursaj a special gift. Although she was gone, we could still commune with her, and hear her call."

"The voice I heard in my head?"

Sharor nodded. "This gift came with a responsibility, however. We were to live strictly by her laws of honor."

Maely tore her gaze away from the flower and met Sharor's milky white eyes. "Seiro?"

"Yes."

"The Vorakk were created in a similar way, though they are jealous of us because we have direct communion with the mother."

"Didn't the mother give the Vorakk anything?"

Sharor nodded. "A lesser gift. They can communicate with the spirits of the dead, and even call upon them to aid them."

Maely thought of Karak's spirit orbs. *Were those actually the souls of dead people? Ghosts?* She shivered.

Kerr returned with a drumstick that he gently fitted into Sharor's hand, and a wooden bowl for Maely that was filled with clear water. She took the wooden bowl, and upended it with both hands, eagerly draining it so fast it spilled down her dress.

Sharor patted Kerr's paw with her free hand. "Thank you, cub."

Kerr made a clipped Ursaj reply and then walked away.

Maely lowered the bowl, gasped, and then called, "Thank you!"

Sharor took a bite of her drumstick–ironically in a much more civilized way than Maely had attacked her slice of pork–and chewed in silence.

Maely wiped her chin with the back of her arm. "So all Ursaj follow Seiro?"

Sharor swallowed. "No. But the few who break their covenant lose the mother's gift and slowly transform back into ordinary bears."

Maely surveyed the crowd of feasting bear-people. "Is this all the Ursaj?"

Sharor laughed. "How many do you count?"

Maely winced. "Sorry."

Sharor laughed a second time. "Think nothing of it, cub. From the sound of it, I'd wager close to a thousand have heeded the mother's call. Those who haven't come either can't, or are apostates slowly changing back into brutes. Our patriarch, Glynn, waits to allow those who may be late to arrive before starting the ceremony."

Maely eyed the barrel of wine set alluringly only ten paces away. She was still pretty thirsty and Sharor wouldn't know if she took a drink. She caught Kerr watching her from afar and gave up the idea.

"So what is this ceremony? What does it do? Is it a spell that'll drive back that evil energy coming from Aiested?"

"We do not spell-cast."

"Then why do you have an Apeira well?"

"There isn't time to explain it all." Sharor took another bite of her meaty drumstick–an entire boar's leg by the looks of it.

"If time is so short, then why are you having a feast?"

Sharor hesitated and then carefully said, "It is preparation for the ceremony."

Maely eyed her empty bowl and shot another glance at the wine barrel. Kerr was standing close to it. Dammit! "So, are we going to go inside that temple?"

"The mother names it Empyrean. It is a vessel to the heavens. She bade the Ursaj of old to dig it out of the ground, for it was buried."

"Neat..." Maely made sure the word dripped with sarcasm. "Do we get to go inside?"

Sharor shook her head again. "Ursaj are not allowed inside."

"Then, why have it?" The irrationality of the Ursaj's mysticism was really starting to get on her nerves.

"The mother said it was the chariot of one of her champions and would be used in the last of all battles."

Maely rolled her eyes and pulled some grass from the ground. "So, is this ceremony something that you do once a year? Like Harvest Festival?" She casually tossed the grass into the air.

Sharor had her drumstick raised for another bite, but stopped. She lowered the food and set it on her lap. "Any Ursaj can come here at any time to commune with the mother. We can even importune her to call the others. But, this ceremony has never before been performed. You see, Maely, the Ursaj are the mother's guardians."

Maely furrowed her brow. "Why would a goddess need bodyguards? And besides, I thought you said she was gone."

Sharor shook her head and quietly muttered, "Not enough time, cub."

"Fine!" Maely huffed and folded her arms. "So am I going to be a part of this ritual?" She glanced at the wine one more time, hoping that she could be. The wine looked delicious.

Sharor didn't answer right away.

"Well?"

Sharor closed her eyes. "I don't know, cub. I would hope not. But because you are here, I don't know. I also don't know how or why you heard the mother's call. That isn't supposed to happen."

More Ursaj began to gather near the Apeira well, seating themselves beside one another in a ring around the well. Once the first circle was closed, they formed another larger circle, and then another.

"Is it time?" Maely watched an Ursaj she-bear suckle a tiny doll-sized cub as she sat cross-legged on the ground.

"Almost."

Maely was irritated when Sharor offered nothing further. "So what happens now?"

"Now we wait until the mother speaks to us again. If she commands it, we will commence the Kasei."

Maely surveyed the concentric rings of sitting Ursaj. More were still forming at the edges of the circle. "I thought you said Glynn was just waiting for stragglers."

"It appears he is done waiting." She cast a sidelong glance at Maely with her milky eyes. "You and Gryyth were lucky to arrive when you did. More confirmation that the mother called you."

Maely looked about for Gryyth, but didn't see him until she leaned to her right to see around the Apeira well. He was sitting nearly opposite her in the first circle. His snout was tightly clamped shut, and his breathing was so shallow that Maely could tell from fifty paces away.

"Gryyth needs more medicine," she whispered to Sharor. "His fever has returned and I think he's getting worse."

Sharor's eyes were closed and her snout slightly raised as if basking in the heat of a campfire. "There is not time, cub."

"But..."

Sharor's blind eyes snapped open and she glared at Maely. "No more questions. You are here with us now and cannot leave, so you will respect our ways!"

Maely was speechless. The usually jovial she-bear had suddenly gone from sagacious good humor to steely sternness.

"What am I supposed to do?" Maely finally asked with an embarrass-ingly shaky voice.

Sharor closed her eyes again and returned to her meditative pose. "Listen for the mother's voice."

And so Maely settled back into a sitting position mirroring Sharor's, closed her eyes, and tried to hear the voice of a goddess she wasn't even sure she believed in.

CHAPTER 90

Kairah's eyes snapped open. Shivara's willowy girl-servant, Etele, leaned over her; large youthful eyes somewhat vacant even as they were fixed on Kairah. Etele straightened, and nodded at Shivara who stood watching Kairah from the foot of the bed upon which she lay.

Kairah sat up, both her fists suddenly full of the silk sheets beneath her as the world spun. Etele steadied her with a hand until the wave of dizziness subsided. Kairah's head throbbed like it never had before. She squinted her eyes closed, seeking darkness to help mitigate the pain caused even from the low light ambience of the bed chamber.

"You have touched the other magic, child. Haven't you?" Shivara said.

The woman spoke differently than she had before, less properly, less like an Allosian. If Kairah didn't know better, Shivara's informality of speech sounded like a human's. She also had the trace of an accent Kairah couldn't place.

Kairah nodded, and immediately regretted the action.

"You will continue to have increasingly worse headaches as your condition worsens."

Kairah cracked her eyelids.

Shivara walked over to a dresser set against the wall opposite the bed. She turned to examine herself in a large mirror set atop the vanity. She picked up a small teardrop-shaped vial of liquid from the vanity and raised it to her face, spilling two drops into her eye and then repeating the action for her other eye.

"Your ability to cast spells will also weaken until your skill is a shadow of its former glory."

Kairah fully opened her eyes and winced as the light from a dimmed glow orb made it seem like the sun itself was burning within the room. She closed her eyes again and massaged her right temple.

"The alien power is changing you at the most basic levels. It is rewriting your essence into something drastically disparate like a spurned lover's adoring sonnet converted into a lament of despair."

Kairah chanced opening her eyes again, and had to shield them with a hand. "How do you know all this?"

Shivara turned to face her and smiled. "Moriora, and other alien powers, have ever been my life's study."

"You knew of the danger, and you never told the synod?"

Shivara laughed. "Child, I am over a thousand years old. I have outlived six synods and I can tell you that each was just as unwilling to delve into such mysteries as our current leaders were unwilling to take your warning seriously." Shivara slowly rounded the foot of the bed. "Allosians are more like humans than they care to admit, especially when it comes to how they react to change. In fact, in some ways they're worse. Nothing can quite rile an Allosian like changing the rules of a world that they have come to rely on."

"A thousand years?" Allosians didn't live longer than four hundred so far as Kairah knew. There were now and again one of her people who might reach nearly five centuries of life, but those occasions were rare. "How have you achieved such longevity?"

Shivara sat on the bed and gently brushed a strand of amethyst hair from Kairah's forehead. The contact made her skin prickle with an electric sensation that was only a few shades shy of painful.

"What are you doing?"

Shivara ignored her question. "We are seers, Kairah. The mysteries of the universe are ours for the taking."

"And is it by your oracular gift that you know so much of Moriora?"

"That..." Shivara smoothed Kairah's hair, "and experimentation."

Something pulled on Kairah, not a physical motion, but something from the ethereal plane. The sensation was so light that she very nearly missed.

"What do you mean experimentation?"

Shivara didn't answer. Instead she just stared at Kairah with a coy smile on her face. Kairah started when Shivara abruptly stood. "Come with me, child. I wish to show you something."

Shivara turned and swept from the room in a flurry of green robes. Etele followed silently as she always did. Kairah threw off her covers, and placed her bare feet on the stone floor. She winced, but this time not from her headache–which still pounded behind her eyes–but from the cold of the stone floor beneath her.

Allosian talis craft had evolved over the centuries to such a sophisticated degree that it could provide every comfort imaginable. One of the common talises used in constructed Allosian dwellings was an ember–a spherical stone that warmed the walls and floors of a building. Every home Kairah had visited in Allose had one, and this was the first building she'd encountered where such a talis was not utilized. Why?

She started for the door, but veered to the vanity set against the wall. She examined the teardrop shaped vial of liquid Shivara had dripped into her eyes. It was the same amethyst color of Kairah's hair.

"Do not dawdle, child," Shivara called from the hallway.

Kairah put the vial down and left the bed chamber. Shivara stood in the hall waiting for her, arms crossed and a lacquered fingernail tapping her painted lips.

She wears face paint like a human noblewoman.

"Come," the oracle ordered.

They returned to Shivara's study, and she led Kairah to a chair inside a large alcove. The chair was silver, with ornate designs covering its armrests and legs. It was not plush as most Allosian furniture was wont to be, but smooth and metallic. Above the headrest rose a five-pointed star made of the same silver metal. In the center of the arcane symbol was a diamond-cut Apeira well shard.

"I have never seen a talis such as this." Kairah traced the faintly glowing lines trailing along the chair's silver armrests.

"That is because it's unique." Shivara pointed at the seat. "Sit, child."

Kairah eyed the chair.

"It is quite safe, I assure you."

"What does it do?"

"Opens one's eyes." Shivara caressed the silver star above the head-rest. She caught herself and glanced back at Kairah. "It will enhance your oracular senses; magnify your psychic sight in much the same way a looking stone enlarges a vista."

"Is this how you learned of Moriora?"

Shivara smirked, an expression that flashed her dimples. "I have used it to see farther than you can imagine, through time and space and beyond."

Kairah's chest tightened. "Beyond?"

"Sit, Kairah." Shivara motioned again at the chair.

Aeva? Kairah called. But the Spirit lily didn't respond.

"What about my condition? Will that not interfere with this talis's function?"

"It is powerful enough to compensate for your diminished abilities. Trust me. Now sit."

Kairah reluctantly obeyed.

Shivara traced fingers lightly down Kairah's forehead and across her eyelids, making them close. Again she felt the nearly painful prickle. She tried to open her eyes, but Shivara forced the lids down.

"Keep your eyes shut, for often we can better see the infinite when our eyes are closed to the world around us."

A long moment of silent blackness elapsed before the talis finally awoke to form a connection with Kairah's mind. *That was odd, it ought to have been charged and ready to function, but it was as if it had to draw on the Mother Shard to refill first.* Kairah was going to ask about that when another sensation hit her.

It was the same as what she'd experienced when having her vision of the human's desolate homeland, right before she woke in Aiested; when her mind was free but still tethered to her faraway body.

Shivara's voice sounded distant. "Don't try to force your expanding sight, just let it take you where it needs to go."

Shaelar appeared before Kairah's disembodied vision, as if she were looking down on the continent from far above, but it was different—bigger. Where the west coast ought to have been there was more land, much more. In fact, the continent extended west almost the entire length of Shaelar's original size.

Unless this is the original size and shape of the land.

Some among her people theorized that Shaelar was once part of a bigger continent, and that the two had split long ago because of some tectonic cataclysm. So it was the past Kairah was seeing, but how long ago? She fell, the land racing up to meet her and Kairah's faraway stomach flipped. Just before crashing into the ground, she stopped and her vision expanded. She could see in all directions at once. It was very much like scrying, just on a much larger scale.

The entire land was green, lush, and fertile. Before her rose a magnificent city, glowing white–Allose. But where was the Mother Shard? The towering crystal monolith, like a pillar of the sky itself, was missing. Kairah reached out across the continent with her uninhibited senses, looking for other Apeira wells, but found none. That didn't make sense. Where did the ancient Allosians get their Apeiron?

She willed herself into the city, and was immediately in the center where the synod's council dome should've been. Like the Mother Shard, it was gone. In its place was a mountainous staircase topped by a simple flat, circular platform. The platform was large enough to hold hundreds of people, and there were other staircases leading up on all sides to provide access.

A crowd formed on the platform; men and women dressed in simple robes of white and wearing sandals. But they were not Allosian. They were human, with eyes and hair as varied in color as the humans of today. Where were the Allosians?

A white light descended from the sky and the humans knelt to the ground as one. When the light reached the platform, it resolved into the most beautiful woman Kairah had ever seen. She had flowing metallic-silver hair that fell below her waist, and was dressed in a sleeveless white tunic similar in design to that worn by her human worshippers.

Light and power radiated from the woman, an aura of brilliant white outlining her features. One of the humans stood and approached the divine being. She had long blonde hair, and bright blue eyes. She knelt in front of the silver-haired woman, who extended a hand and gently caressed the kneeling woman's hair.

The scene shifted to six cloaked figures standing in a circle inside a familiar domed room with star charts and maps of the cosmos laid unrolled on tables. The six held hands and chanted with eyes closed. A column of white light appeared in the center of their circle, and Kairah expected to see the glorious woman reappear. But the figure that resolved from the light was male, and remained translucent as though he were not actually in the room. He had hair like the divine woman, save instead of shimmering silver, his shoulder length locks were glittering a metallic gold. He was the most impressive specimen of manliness Kairah had ever beheld with a chin that was square and cleft, a sharp nose, and eyes that glowed blue.

The cloaked chanters, save one, fell to their knees. The one still standing drew down her hood and Kairah recognized the same blonde woman from the previous scene. Kairah thought she recognized the face, but the woman fell back to her knees before she could identify her. The blonde woman reached up to the ethereal man with an open hand as if pleading for help. He smiled a wide smile full of perfect white teeth and opened his hand palm up. A small ball of pulsing emerald energy appeared in his hand.

Green lightning.

Kairah stood in a familiar location—a white city surrounding an emerald colored Apeira well broken in two. It was the city from her first vision, except instead of being full of bones, thousands of Allosians ran about, pushing past each other to get away from something Kairah couldn't see. Screams rang out from the direction her people were retreating, and Kairah had to push her way through the panicked mob like a fish swimming upstream.

Tentacles of green energy lashed up above the crowd, and Kairah knew the horror from which her people fled. It was a creature like the one she'd faced in Aiested. When she fought the Moriora vessel, she'd been able to protect herself by drawing on Aiested's Apeira well, but the well here was destroyed. The creature lashed out at a family scrambling to duck into an open building. A mother, the purple haired babe she held in her arms, and a man who'd tried to shield them withered and collapsed into dusty piles of bone.

Kairah took a step toward the monster, preparing to cast a spell, when she froze. Screaming from another direction drew her attention and she turned to find another Moriora vessel feasting on six Allosians all at once. This one was a woman, and she wasn't alone. Dozens more like her waded through the crowd killing indiscriminately, faces alight with malicious ecstasy.

The ground shook so violently that buildings fell, and hundreds were granted quick deaths by the crumbling debris–a fate preferable to having the life force sucked out of them. An explosion made Kairah spin about. On the horizon, where there should've been ocean, a fissure the size of a canyon formed. It snaked its way across the land, opening a breach hundreds of miles wide and thousands deep. Sea water fountained up into the air before crashing down again and filling the breach. Kairah covered her ears to the desperate shrieks that assaulted her from every direction. It became a physical thing, heavy and pressing down on her. She sunk to the ground, her own mouth open in a silent scream.

Kairah exploded out of the silver chair, took two steps, and collapsed to the ground. She was trembling so badly that she looked like the humans who suffered palsy. Tears flowed down her cheeks, and she shot Shivara a wide-eyed stare. The woman stood to the side of the chair, arms folded across her breasts as she stared down at Kairah. She showed no emotion, but just studied her with an arched painted eyebrow.

Experimentation?

"Tell me what you saw," Shivara finally said.

Kairah sat up and hugged her bare shoulders. She didn't know if the chill she felt was physical or imagined, but either way she was very cold.

"Kairah, what did you see?" Shivara asked a second time.

"A nightmare."

Chapter 91

The glass-like barrier continued to crack and shatter as Jove pounded against it with his bolts of green lightning. He'd bored into the translucent sphere so deeply, very little remained separating him from the stunning silver-haired doll. She continued to float in the center of the glass sphere like she was under water, legs drawn up to chest, her arms wrapping around her knees. Her metallic-silver hair billowed about her body, mostly covering her nude form, but occasionally giving Jove glimpses of her alabaster skin. Though disembodied, the fire of lust welled up inside him, demanding to be released in a torrent of passion no doll could survive.

But he needed his body if he was going to enjoy this; this business of being an amorphous greenish-black ball of energy wouldn't do. This place was neither death, nor life. The floating islands of rock were definitely physical, as was that doll. Perhaps it was somewhere in between?

Before Jove had died–no, changed–he'd been able to heal his physical body by using the energy he'd siphoned from other living things, and then from the Apeiron in talises and the Apeira well. Could he do the same thing to regain his physical form?

He ceased his barrage of emerald bolts and floated upward. Then, sucking in as much Apeiron as he could–and his capacity had grown great–he focused the way he did when he wanted a particular part of his body to heal quicker than the rest of him. Only, this time he focused on the memory of his body itself. The moment stretched, or was it hours?

Time was strange in this place. But be it short or long, nothing happened.

Jove roared with his mind, throwing every bit of rage and lust into a second attempt, drawing the Apeiron all around him to the limit of his capacity. He'd once drank straight from a tube attached to the bottom of a rain barrel his father had placed on the roof. There was so much water pouring into his mouth that he began to choke and sputter and it exploded out of his nose.

Jove felt like that now, save he could open his "mouth" wider, like a python unhinging its jaw. Jove opened himself more and more until a torrent of Apeiron flowed into him from all directions, making the purple cloud surrounding him shudder.

MULLADIN CREPT around a bush sculpted into the shape of a bear. The likeness was uncanny, and in the dark, its silhouette might've convinced him it was the real thing, until he realized it wasn't moving.

Keesa followed behind him, hood of her newly "acquired" cloak drawn up. After arguing about different approaches to infiltrating Trous's mansion–Mulladin wanted to fight his way in with Jekaran's sword, something Jekaran favored too–they'd finally agreed on stealth first, and force as their fallback option. Mulladin gritted his teeth. Skulking about the courtyard like this was a waste of time. Why had he given into Keesa's argument so quickly?

Because she promised to "fix" your virgin problem when you get to Allose. Jekaran laughed inside his head.

"That's not why!" Mulladin said a little too loudly.

"Quiet!" Keesa hissed. "Talk to that damned thing inside your head."

Keesa's allure may have had something to do with his unusually quick acquiescence. Even when he was dim, he'd been stubborn as Maely so often reminded him. A pang of grief slapped his chest. His sister was dead.

Don't be so sure about that.

Mulladin opened his mouth to answer, but clamped it shut and responded only with his mind. *Why do you say that?*

Maely is smart and tough. She would've gotten out of the palace before it collapsed.

Mulladin furrowed his brow. *I wish I had your optimism, Jek.*

A crossbow armed guard passed by on the opposite of the bush-bear without even stopping.

"Now," Keesa whispered.

The two of them ran in a half crouch, crossing open courtyard and ducking behind another bush, this one sculpted in the likeness of a gigantic fish. They were close to a door set into the far side of the east wing that served as one of the mansion's servant entrances. All they had to do was wait for one more patrolling guard to move far enough away and they could make a run for the door.

Keesa leaned in close so that their faces were nearly touching, and Mulladin couldn't help but think of her soft mouth pressed against his, the tip of her tongue gently parting his lips. He'd never kissed a woman before, not like that, but it came surprisingly easy. Or at least, if he'd showed any clumsiness, Keesa hadn't mentioned it. Her promise of fixing his problem came back to his mind, and he flushed.

His emotions were still potent as old memories took on new color and meaning. Each feeling came with a thousand mnemonic echoes, all compounding into a single emotional response. Fortunately, as a simpleton, he hadn't had experience with sex, so the feelings were mostly new to him, and not loaded with eighteen years' worth of memory. He was very glad for that. He wasn't sure what a surge of amorosity would've caused when Keesa had attacked him with passionate kisses.

A mess, Jekaran said.

"Stop listening to my thoughts!"

Keesa slapped his shoulder. "Be quiet!"

Mulladin glanced in the direction of the approaching guard. "Sorry."

Keesa rolled her eyes and then pointed at the single wooden door only ten yards away. "The servant's entrance usually isn't locked, but if it is, I want you to..."

Keesa cut off as the steady purple glow from Erassa's Apeira well suddenly flickered. "What was that?"

Again the purple reflecting off the mansion's white stone walls went dark before returning a heartbeat later.

It's coming, Jekaran said.

"What's coming?" Mulladin asked aloud, but this time Keesa didn't chide him.

"What did the sword say?"

The ground lurched and the two fell over. A deep rumbling accompanied the quake and the bush-bear behind them tilted over so far that its trunk snapped, and it fell onto its side in an explosion of leaves. Mulladin stared at the sky. The moon was gone, and he couldn't see any clouds or stars. The horizon was completely black.

"The hell?"

A bright bolt of green lightning split the northern sky followed a heartbeat later by a deafening clap of thunder.

"Shyte!" Mulladin stood, no longer caring if the guards saw him.

"What are you doing?" Keesa tried to whisper it but failed.

"No more time for stealth." Mulladin raised Jekaran's sword and used it to point at the servant's door. "We have to get to the slipgate, now!"

Keesa stood, glancing nervously in the direction of the guard. "Why?"

The sound of powerful wind picking up howled from the north.

Keesa's eyes opened even wider. "That sound—"

Run! Jekaran shouted.

The two exploded into a sprint.

"Hey!" the nearest guard shouted.

A twang rang out and Mulladin's arm whipped up of its own accord, Jek's sword striking a crossbow bolt from the air. Before the guard could fire off a second shot, Keesa cast a bolt of blue lightning that took him in the chest. He flew several feet and crashed into a bush shaped like a giant cat. The sudden explosion of light against the dark of the night left a green after image in Mulladin's vision which he furiously tried to blink away.

Keesa next turned her weapon talis on the servant's entrance, a bolt arcing into the center of the wooden door and exploding into splinters. Some of the wood debris caught fire and landed with their flames guttering on the ground. Another green phantom swam across Mulladin's vision, replacing the fading one. When he'd used the talis, he always shut his eyes when he cast, and not knowing when Keesa would cast made avoiding the blinding light difficult.

"Warn me before you fire off lightning like that."

"You can't be serious," Keesa snapped.

Mulladin huffed and ran into the mansion first, Jek's sword held ready. The power of it was intoxicating, and he started to think less harshly of Ezra's fall into crime so long ago. With a power like this, who wouldn't succumb to all its promises of fame, fortune, and taking whatever you wanted.

The sword suddenly shutdown, Jek's presence vanishing from Mulladin's mind. It became heavy in his grip and the blade tilted downward, unbalancing Mulladin. Of course, it was at this moment that two Rikujo enforcers rounded a bend further down the carpeted hallway. A boom followed by a rippling in the air followed and the wall on Mulladin's right exploded into dust and chunks of stone.

Keesa released a bolt of lightning, but her aim was off, and the arc of blue electricity obliterated a chandelier. They backed up, exchanging weapon talis blasts with the enforcers, the pandemonium of the battle and its destruction of the mansion's interior making it difficult for both parties to aim.

A trio of black-clad enforcers appeared behind them, and Mulladin swore. Blessedly, these bore more traditional melee weapons; a sword, a mace, and two long daggers. They began to charge.

"Take care of the ones behind us!" Keesa shouted.

"Um..." Mulladin worked to lift Jek's now heavy sword.

"What's wrong?" Keesa fired a bolt of lightning that forked into two smaller lines of crackling blue. A grunt confirmed that one of the lines had struck true.

Mull! Jekaran's friendly voice rang in Mulladin's head and the sword once again grew light in his grip.

"Jek, help!"

Mulladin's mind cleared, his fear muted, and he exploded into a run toward the thugs charging them from the rear. He met the one with the sword first, blades clashing in a shower of sparks. Mulladin's swing was so fierce that it knocked the Rikujo swordsman off balance giving Mulladin the chance to whirl past him and lop off the raised arm of the man with the mace. He danced back just in time to avoid a swiping knife, and spun to the side, swinging his sword out and parting the swordsman's head and shoulders from the rest of his body. Jek's blade cut smoothly, like it met no resistance at all–a hot knife through butter–allowing Mulladin to finish his motion without stopping.

He faced the Rikujo enforcer brandishing the two long daggers. The man was short with dark skin. His eyes widened, and he mouthed something that looked a lot like "That sword!" Mulladin didn't give the enforcer time to beg for his life. He swung high, the sword coming down in a diagonal cut. The enforcer raised his knives to block, but the sword of the Invincible Shadow sliced through both steel and skin.

Mulladin's mouth hung open. Had he really just slaughtered three trained fighting men? And in what couldn't have been more than six seconds? He shouldn't have been surprised, not after seeing Jekaran besting an entire army of royal guard on his own.

Good job, Mull, Jek said.

The hall fell quiet and Keesa ran up to him. Her black hair was covered in plaster dust, and a trickle of blood ran down the side of her head.

"You're hurt!"

"One of the bastards clipped me with a blast of their concussion rod and I hit my head on the wall. I gave it back to him with lightning to his face, though! His eyes actually exploded."

The glow orbs in the chandeliers flickered.

It's getting closer, Jek said.

"That death wave is coming!"

Keesa broke into a sprint, and Mulladin followed. They didn't encounter any more resistance until they had to cross the mansion's open foyer. A wailing alarm talis drew a dozen guards, but after dispatching two or three enforcers with Jek's sword, the remaining fighters fled in terror. One fell when he took a bolt of lightning in the back.

The mansion was shaking now, the glow orbs flickering constantly in their swaying chandeliers. Keesa hadn't ever used Trous's slipgate, but she'd used others, and she knew where the basement was. That combined with Mulladin's memory quickly saw them down several flights of stairs and into the long basement tunnel line with alcoves full of contraband. The door to the room where the slipgate was kept still hadn't been repaired from their assault the night they left to save Jek, and one lone guard peaked out to see who was approaching.

"Hey!"

Lightning flashed over the tunnel and the guard fell dead. Keesa and Mulladin stepped over his burnt body and hurried up to the white structure that resembled a garden gazebo. Mulladin jumped up onto the dais, transferred Jek's sword to his off hand, and examined the plinth upon which was set a glowing map of Shaelar.

Blessedly, the round stone that was the key was still in the talis. Mulladin was about to praise Ez for his foresight, but cut off the thought as quickly as it formed. Apparently thinking of the man was enough to trigger whatever it was that made Jek's mind lock up.

Keesa stepped up beside him and stared down at the glowing map of Shaelar. She pointed at several glowing dots. "So which one is it?"

Mulladin asked Jek where on the map Allose was, and then pointed at a mountain range. "It's here."

"There's no slipgate there!" Keesa waved at the other glowing dots on the map. She was right. There wasn't a glowing dot where Allose should be.

Mulladin asked Jek about it, but the sword just projected a mental shrug. The communication was so familiar in tone, that Mulladin actually pictured Jek shrugging his shoulders.

The room rocked, and the rumbling and the hissing of the death wave–the same one that'd destroyed Keesa's ship back in Aiested–grew louder.

"Coordinates!" Keesa tapped the map and lines suddenly crisscrossed the image.

"What the hell are coordinates?"

"You big dumb ox!" She shoved Mulladin aside. "Slipgates can find other slipgates if they know exactly where to look. Ask the sword if it knows Allose's longitude and latitude!"

I can hear her, Jek said, his tone full of annoyance. And then he relayed some numbers that Mulladin repeated.

Keesa touched the keystone and shut her eyes. A heartbeat later, another glowing dot appeared on the map of Shaelar, this one in the mountains.

"That's it!" Mulladin laughed. "Take us there!"

Keesa gave him a sharp nod.

Nothing happened.

"What's wrong?"

Keesa shook her head. "I don't know. I gave the command, but it's like Allose is closed."

"Closed to a slipgate?"

Keesa scowled at him. "Did it ever occur to you that the Allosians might know how to lock their slipgates?"

He hadn't considered that. "How do we unlock it?"

"How should I know?"

The shaking of the room intensified, and the pieces of the room's wooden door started to particularize and rise into the air. The death wave was here. The tiny emerald jewels on the flat of Jek's sword lit up. That had happened last time, and both he and Keesa had survived that wave by holding onto the sword. Could they do so a second time? It made sense that it should work, but Mulladin knew next to nothing about magic.

A wooden beam crashed through the plaster ceiling and smashed against the floor. It too started to unmake right before their eyes. More pieces of plaster broke free from the ceiling, and a support beam tore through the room's east wall. Even if they could survive the wave itself, this mansion was a modern construction, made of wood and plaster instead of stone. When the wave hit them in Aiested, it had destroyed wood, flesh, and cloth, but not stone. The sword could shield them from the magic, but Mulladin doubted it would protect them from being crushed by a collapsing building.

Mulladin looked at the glowing dots on the slipgate's map. None were more than four day's ride from Allose, but there was a slipgate in Rasha. He knew that city, had been there with... "Take us to Rasha!"

Keesa didn't respond. She was staring wide-eyed at the translucent, green wave that rolled steadily toward them.

"Keesa!"

She shook herself and shut her eyes in concentration.

The world around them flashed purple, but when the light faded, Mulladin found that they were thrust into near total darkness. The soft glow from the companion slipgate only revealed the area immediately around them–the stone floor of a castle? The air was musty and stale, and the sound of a slow drip echoed from somewhere to their right.

Mulladin stepped off the dais and when his foot hit the floor, a single glow orb awoke. It wasn't mounted on the ceiling or walls as was common, but was loose on the ground. Alone, it was little better than a torch, but it shed enough light to reveal a pile of rubble.

"It says we're in Rasha," Keesa said from behind him. She was still standing on the slipgate, looking over the plinth and its map of Shaelar.

Mulladin picked up the glow orb and lifted it above his head. His chest constricted at the sight of a mountain of stone debris piled to dozens of feet and reaching just below the top of an arch that marked a hallway. He turned slowly, surveying the room. A tiny forest of glowing mushrooms grew where the flagstones were broken up, and replaced with dirt.

"I think we're underground."

Twelve miles beneath Rasha, Jek supplied. How did he know that?

The darkness and dank air pressed in on Mulladin, and he desperately wanted to leave the subterranean ruins. "It doesn't look like there's a way out." He returned to the slipgate and stepped up onto the dais. "Take us to the next nearest slipgate."

Keesa looked up from the map, the talis's purple glow reflecting in her wide eyes.

"What's wrong?"

"Erassa's gate is gone, as is Aiested's and every other point on this map except for Allose." Keesa glanced back down at the plinth and its map of Shaelar. "And it's locked."

Mulladin forced a laugh. "What're you saying?"

"We have no way out," Keesa said. "We're trapped."

Apeiron swirled about Jove and disappeared into his black and green form. He sucked in more and more, oceans worth of the succulent purple energy. Patches of black begin to appear in the nebulae surrounding him. Had he eaten so much Apeiron that the supply was dwindling? What would happen when it was all gone? This place would darken for sure, but the doll was radiating Apeiron. He looked down to the glass sphere below him and the beautiful woman encased inside. He was devouring Apeiron faster than the white-haired doll could create it. What would happen when he ran out?

Jove needed to slow his consumption before he exhausted the supply, but he couldn't. The more Apeiron he ate, the more he needed, and Jove never had been any good at denying self-gratification. He shoved the concern aside and drew in still more Apeiron. His spherical body began to change shape, twisting and growing. Soon he was the shape of a man, but without any human features—like a living silhouette.

It's working!

Jove cackled with his mind, and it soon became a real sound as his mouth and ears formed. Next, eyes showed him the purple ocean surrounding him, something he'd already perceived with his mind, but now saw with both. He watched the rest of his naked body reform, a hideous grin splitting his face.

Gravity took hold on him again—albeit not as strongly as in Shaelar—and Jove alighted on the floating island of rock closest to the glass sphere. He landed as though kneeling in prayer, looking up at the jagged hole he'd dug into the translucent sphere.

Jove stood and fired another barrage of green lightning bolts from his newly restored hand. The crackling shaft of emerald power struck the remaining thin layer of the glass sphere and broke it open.

He barked out a triumphant laugh.

CHAPTER 92

Waiting for the mother to speak was terribly boring. Hours had passed, and Maely shifted uncomfortably on the ground. Sitting cross-legged was making her ankles hurt. At one point, she shifted and stretched her legs out, but a disapproving shake of Gryyth's furry head from across the circle made her reassume her original position.

Maely groaned softly. How do they do this? Most of the Ursaj had sat as still as statues with their eyes closed as they listened. The only ones who moved and made noise were the cubs, and their mothers when they needed something.

Maely sighed and resumed staring at the Apeira well. She never thought she'd get tired of looking at one of the glowing purple obelisks, but hours of sitting in silence had stolen away the mystical awe of the crystalline tower. She shifted her focus to the glowing flower growing at the base of the well. It was very beautiful, and looked every bit as magical as the Apeira well.

Thunder rumbled in the distance.

Almost hypnotized by the white lily, Maely's thoughts wandered and she found herself wondering about the fates of all her friends. Was Jek alive? Did he hate her? Where was Mulladin? Was he still with Ez? Had Irvis ever caught up to them? Where did Karak go? She was even a little worried about Kairah–but only just a little.

Where was the prince? Had he succeeded in reaching his army, and stopping the talis war? Gryyth had told her a lot about Raelen over the course of their journey. Apparently, the man was an adherent of the Ursaj's Seiro, and trained by Gryyth in the ways of the Ursaj's unarmed fighting. Of course, when you weighed hundreds of pounds, were nearly twice as tall as a regular man with fangs and claws, why would you need a weapon? But Raelen was human, and he trusted Gryyth enough to adopt the fighting style.

That wasn't the only odd thing about the prince. Gryyth had spoken proudly of Raelen's accomplishments, almost like the bear-man was the prince's father. But the deeds Gryyth listed weren't what Maely first expected. They weren't contests of physical prowess won, or scholarly attainments, or political or military victories. Neither were they the boorish bragging of a friend vicariously enjoying another's sexual conquests.

No, the virtues Gryyth touted about Raelen were simple things like the man's kind treatment of his servants, his interest in the welfare of his father's people, a love for a departed sister, and his near-obsession with changing the world into a better place. Had they come from a human, Maely would've immediately dismissed the claims, but there was a plain honesty to Gryyth–to all the Ursaj. They spoke confidently of the things they knew, without any signs of doubt. Could royalty like Raelen, someone even more powerful than the nobility, actually reach manhood without the taint of corruption Maely saw in all others of high station? The idea was as absurd to her as the world being round, but that'd turned out to be true. Probably.

Jek was good and kind, if not a little stupid, but he was a peasant. Not that all peasants were specimens of benevolent humility–all men could be bastards. Still, Maely found a disproportionate amount of kindness and decency in the poor people of the world, and she'd always believed poverty to be a kind of virtue in and of itself. But if a poor man could be as lecherous and cruel as a rich man, couldn't a prince be truly noble?

I need you.

The voice's sudden intrusion into Maely's thoughts made her jump. She looked at Sharor. "I heard that."

Sharor looked down at her, milky eyes focused as if the she-bear actually could see Maely. She nodded. "This part is not for you, cub. You may watch, but do not interfere. And no matter what, do not partake of the ceremonial wine."

Maely ground her teeth. Why exclude her now when she'd already seen so much, and heard the voice of the mother–whoever that was. It didn't sound like a divine being. The voice was small, and childlike.

Glynn stood with ten others and made his way to the barrel filled with the red wine. He took a wooden bowl from the top of a stack of bowls and dipped into the wine. He lifted the bowl, full and dripping, to his mouth and took a drink. The others followed and then they took the bowls to the sitting Ursaj who drank and passed the bowl to their neighbor at the right. Everyone drank, even the cubs, some so young that they had to be fed the red liquid by their mothers.

When the bowl came to Maely, she considered disobeying Sharor. Partly because of the injustice of her exclusion, and partly because she was thirsty, and the wine looked really good. She held the bowl for a moment before sighing and passing it on.

Upon drinking from the bowl each Ursaj would stand and walk to touch the Apeira well. It was only large enough to accommodate a circle of twelve, the first being Glynn and his followers. The Ursaj that followed touched the Ursaj in front of them so that eventually they formed columns of bear-people running single file out from the well and making it look like a star.

Being in the first circle, Sharor and Gryyth were right behind those actually touching the well. Maely didn't join in the file but did stay by Sharor's side as Kerr helped her stand and she walked to take her place behind Glynn. With one paw on Glynn's shoulder, Kerr's paw on hers, Sharor looked down at Maely.

"You are a good girl."

Maely furrowed her brow. "Thanks?"

Sharor chuckled. "I think we would have been good friends, once you grew up a little."

"Hey!" Maely snapped. Then Sharor's words registered. "What do you mean would have?"

Glynn fell to his knees first. He shivered and moaned and then slumped, paw still extended to touch the well. Others of the Ursaj touching the well did the same, all falling in a way that let them maintain contact with the amethyst obelisk.

Maely's heart pounded. What was happening? She moved up to touch Glynn on the shoulder. He didn't respond. She shook him, but again received no response. She whipped around to face Sharor.

"What's happening?"

"We are answering the mother's call." Sharor clenched her eyes shut, fell forward, and started convulsing. White foam dripped from her maw, but she diligently held onto Glynn's lifeless form as she too faded.

Maely glanced at a wooden bowl set on the ground behind her. It still had a bit of red wine pooling in its base.

Not wine. Poison.

Maely ran, ducking under three lines of Ursaj until she reached Gryyth. He was kneeling, the pain of the poison making him tremble, or was it his burns? Or both? Maely flung herself down and embraced the white bear-man.

Her tears dripped into his fur, and she sobbed, "Why?"

"The mother needs us," Gryyth rumbled.

Anger, horror, and grief warred inside Maely, and she opened her mouth to curse Rasheera, but only a desperate plea escaped her lips. "Don't leave me here alone!"

"The mother is still here." Gryyth patted her back with his free paw, the pressure frighteningly weak. "Remember, you still need to wash the mud from your fur, cub."

Those were the last words the blue-eyed Ursaj said to her.

JOVE STARED down through the bore he'd dug to the silver-haired doll. His floating rock island now hovered over the glass sphere, positioning him so he could drop down inside it. Jove wasn't certain if that'd been happenstance, or if he'd somehow moved the floating rock. Either way it was a long fall from his perch, through the orb's glass walls, and to the center where his doll awaited him. But gravity's hold here wasn't normal. Jove would fall, but he would do it slowly.

Jove sank into a launching crouch, and was about to jump when a distant sound gave him pause. That in and of itself was strange, as the only thing he'd heard in this place up until now was his own voice and the crackling of his lightning. He stood and turned in a circle, surveying every direction of the purple ocean and its floating islands of rock. The sound grew louder. It was bestial, like a lion or a bear. Yes, that definitely sounded like a bear, but not just one, dozens. Maybe hundreds?

Jove took a few steps toward the direction of the sound. Stars appeared amid the wash of purple atmosphere–that was new–and grew larger, and larger. Not stars, but balls of white light. They raced toward him, hundreds of them. He remembered seeing their like before, when he fought the Vorakk shaman back in Aiested. Then he'd only faced a few of the things, and they weren't as large as the ones that now flew directly at him.

I can't eat those!

Jove growled and turned to jump down the hole, but was struck mid-leap in the back and was flung into the purple sky. The dilution of gravity doubled his kinetic motion and he soared away from the glass orb until he managed to grab hold of another piece of floating rock. He landed, but before Jove could stand, another ball of white light crashed into him, followed by another, and then another. They assailed Jove like vengeful hail, each striking down with the force of a thick fist. Pummeled from every side, Jove covered his head and whimpered.

Blow after blow kept him kneeling, his tears dripping on the gray rock. He leaned halfway over the edge of the asteroid giving him a perfect view of the glass sphere through which he could see his perfect, silver-haired doll–his prize. He had to have her! His entire miserable life had led him to this moment. The thrill of all thrills awaited him, just barely out of his reach. Jove's sniveling turned into a howl of agony, but the hail of glowing balls didn't relent.

CHAPTER 93

Tyrus felt useless. Or perhaps it was helpless? No, it was definitely useless. Kybon's son lay in a coma, he was a lifelong prisoner now, and according to Kairah and the Vorakk shaman, the world was ending. It was all very, very aggravating.

And where was Kairah? It'd been days since the Allosian woman had brought them to her tower apartment, afterward excusing herself to go visit someone she said could convince her synod to act. It'd been amusing in a grim sort of way to find Allosian politicians not all that different from their human counterparts: resistant to change, and fully willing to risk the greater good just to preserve the status quo.

He'd thought Kairah would've come back by now to tell them what the next step in their plan to save Jekaran and the world was, but not even the Allosian guards tasked with keeping watch over them knew when she would return. Were they supposed to just wait and do nothing? It seemed wholly inappropriate to be lounging in a garden while the world fell apart. Tyrus had never been a man of action, not like Kybon, but he'd always found some way to solve problems. Right now he couldn't do anything but wait, and it was maddening.

Useless!

He sat in Kairah's atrium. Like everything else in Allose, it had a grandiose, almost dreamlike quality. It was so thick with greenery that one could forget they were inside a white tower, hundreds of feet above the ground.

Miraculously, the garden appealed to all five of Tyrus's senses; flowers painted in hues he'd never seen in nature before with some actually glowing, a symphony of smells that impossibly mixed honeysuckles, spice, and the smell of springtime, the relaxing trickle of a fountain gently pouring into a reflecting pool, sweet air like sugar that actually tickled his taste buds when he breathed it in, and a perfect temperature with a gentle, cool breeze.

Tyrus closed his eyes and drew in a deep breath through his nose. His usually congested nasal cavity was clear and open, like when he sailed the sea. It felt good, almost as if the air were healing his sinuses. He opened his eyes and shifted on the white stone bench set near the shimmering reflecting pool. A white lily, glowing against a backdrop of green, grew in the center of the garden next to the reflecting pool. For some reason Kairah had ordered Hort to lay Jekaran down on the soft grass in front of the flower.

Jekaran.

The boy's glassy stare was broken only by mechanical blinking. Tyrus slumped his shoulders. As much as he disliked the Allosian healer who'd attempted to restore Jekaran, he'd hoped and prayed for the man's success. Let the peacock claim all the credit for saving the boy; Tyrus just wanted him to wake from his state of living death.

The atrium was a popular retreat for the members of his party, and when he was not keeping vigil over Jekaran, someone else would. It wasn't necessary of course, save to force water and mush down the boy's throat, or change him when he messed himself–something that Hort claimed responsibility for doing for some reason.

The big mercenary lay on the ground next to Jekaran, snoring. He as much as Tyrus rarely left Jekaran's side. It was strange, and when Tyrus had asked for an explanation, Hort had muttered something about once being a healer or an herb master, or some kind of backwater peasant shaman.

Tyrus glanced around the garden and found the Vorakk talking to a tree with his weird hissing and sign language. No, not a tree. A glow fly? But Tyrus hadn't ever seen a glow fly that big. It was white and hovered at eyelevel to the lizard man. Then it zipped away and disappeared. No, that was not a glow fly. Tyrus had seen the Vorakk start campfires by summoning similar-sized balls of fire. Was this another display of his strange magic?

After the floating white orb disappeared, the Vorakk quickly slipped from Tyrus's view. *What's he up to?* He didn't trust the lizard people, and over the course of their trek to Allose had sleep-deprived Hort by making the mercenary stay awake while he slept in case the creature desired to taste noble blood.

In spite of his fear of being eaten, or his dedication to keeping watch over his cousin's son, Tyrus found himself following the Vorakk through the garden. The creature slipped out of the atrium and back into Kairah's apartment where he approached the chamber door. Tyrus followed, checking his robe pocket for his stun baton.

The Allosians confiscated their other talises, but left this one with Tyrus. Apparently, the stun baton was human crafted, something the Allosians looked down on. *They look down on a lot of things.* Tyrus was admonished that as long as he didn't use the weapon, he'd be allowed to keep it. The Allosian peacekeeper who'd said it made it sound like Tyrus was a child refusing to give up an old stuffed bear. He thought perhaps he was beginning to understand just how his peasants saw him.

Tyrus followed the Vorakk out of the apartment and into the hall that ran in a circle on their level of the tower. The lizard man disappeared around a bend in the corridor, and Tyrus broke into a jog to catch up. When he rounded the bend, he found the hall empty. Tyrus stopped. *Where had the scaly bugger gone?* He turned to retrace his steps when a rippling like heat lines in the space in front of him resolved into the Vorakk. Tyrus squeaked and raised his stun baton, but the lizard man slapped it out of his hand before he could discharge the talis. The Vorakk hissed as he loomed over Tyrus.

"Isk, why little rich human follow Karak?"

"I don't appreciate you calling me little." Tyrus tried to sound indignant, but really his biggest concern was that he didn't wet himself.

"Rok!" The Vorakk made a sharp gesture with his claw.

Tyrus summoned all his courage, such as it was, and straightened. "Where are you going?"

The Vorakk's slitted eyes narrowed as it looked down at Tyrus. Then it grinned, showing a maw filled with sharp teeth. "Esk!"

Tyrus gulped.

"Reka, little, rich human help Karak?"

"Help you do what?"

The Vorakk—Karak—pushed past him and resumed moving through the white hallway. "Save stupid human boy, aka."

"You can save Jekaran?" Tyrus bent down and grabbed his stun baton before hurrying up to Karak's side.

"Ssk."

Tyrus took that for a Vorakk yes. "But how? Even the Allosians couldn't heal him. Do you have some Vorakk magic that can do it?"

"Isk, Karak have spirits not magic."

"Whatever!" Tyrus took hold of Karak's forearm and made him stop. "How are you going to save him?"

The Vorakk looked down at Tyrus's hand and hissed, at which point Tyrus quickly drew it back. "Karak follow spirits, aek!"

As though that'd been a comprehensive explanation, Karak continued striding down the hall forcing Tyrus to jog just to keep up. They entered a box-like device that served as a carriage moving up and down the tower's numerous floors. Though it was less work than climbing stairs, the sudden vertical motion made Tyrus's stomach flip and bile rose in his throat.

They reached the ground floor, and Karak strode out of the tower's lift. A pair of Allosian peacekeepers in their strange winged armor stood stoically flanking each side of the arched entrance.

"Little, rich human help, reka?"

"That is why I'm accompanying you."

"Then talk to guards, rok," Karak hissed in a low tone.

"What?"

But before Tyrus could protest any further, one of the Allosian guards pointed at them. "Halt." The peacekeeper sighed. "What is it you need, now?"

Tyrus looked at Karak for instruction, but the lizard man just hissed. "We, um, were told that we were at liberty to explore your fair city."

"Where is Lady Kairah?" The second guard, a female with dazzlingly sapphire hair, asked.

Are you an Aiestali lord or a sniveling child? Tyrus drew in a deep breath and in his best tone of offended sarcasm said, "I was not aware that Lady Kairah was our wet-nurse. Are we also to suckle at her breasts when we are hungry?"

The woman guard blinked. "Well she is—"

"I was told that Allosians treated their captives like guests. I guess all those stories of Allosian enlightened civility were fancy."

The man's perfectly square jaw tightened. "You are free to go where you wish inside the city with the exception of the synod's coliseum and the College of Disciplines. Only Allosians are permitted there."

"That's better." Tyrus stepped past the pair of guards and motioned for Karak to follow. "Come, Karak."

Tyrus was twenty paces down the street before he exhaled his pent-up breath.

Karak hissed something that Tyrus thought must be Vorakk laughter. "Little, rich human good talker, esk."

"It comes with being noble born."

Karak's hissing laughter grew more intense and Tyrus suspected he was being mocked. "What do the spirits say we are to do now?"

"Isk, only one spirit. Skinny old human, aka."

Tyrus rolled his eyes. "Fine, what does that spirit say we should do?"

"Go there, aka." Karak pointed at a white cylindrical building rising several stories above the city skyline.

"Why? What's there?"

"Uska, fey door."

Fey door? What was the lizard man talking about?

They strode down several connecting streets–drawing the attention of every Allosian walking about the city–winding their way toward the cylindrical building. As they drew closer, he considered the writing scrawled in gigantic glowing letters above a massive arched double-door entrance. He knew all three languages spoken in Shaelar, and their differing dialects, but he could sooner count the stars than read what was written on the face of the building.

They traversed a wide causeway lined by statues spaced evenly on both sides of the white stone path. Some of the statues were broken, and there were gaps in the sequence.

What happened here?

More jewel-colored heads turned to appraise them and several Allosians muttered. That's when Tyrus spotted a symbol above the glowing letters. He knew that glyph. It was the ancient symbol of knowledge. Divine Mother!

"Karak!" He stopped the Vorakk by grabbing his scaly forearm. Karak hissed at him, but this time Tyrus left his hand in place. "I think that's the College of Disciplines."

Karak shrugged, the motion extricating him from Tyrus's grip. "Uska, spirit says fey door there."

"We're not allowed in there!"

Karak took a long look at the building before flashing a toothy grin. "Daka, we climb."

"This is madness!" Tyrus whispered.

Karak resumed walking, but changed directions and led them around the side of the massive structure that itself looked like it ought to have been a column in some giant god's colonnade. Karak walked up to the building's rounded base. They stood in the shadow of a large tree, one with a smooth white trunk and translucent golden leaves.

"Little rich human get on Karak's back, rok."

Tyrus craned his head. The building's wall was smooth, and the closest window was very, very far up–perhaps a hundred feet. "Can you climb that?"

"Isk." Karak hissed and motioned to his back.

"Someone will see us!"

Karak smiled and disappeared, leaving only a slight distortion in the air resembling heat lines.

"That's all well and good for you, but what about me? You don't think someone will find it odd to see a human slowly rising on the side of one of the largest buildings in the city?"

Karak's blurry outline stooped and picked up a golden leaf from the white tree. As soon as he touched it, the leaf disappeared. Apparently, the Vorakk could veil whatever they touched. It made sense. Otherwise Karak's loin cloth and medicine bag would remain visible when he was not.

Tyrus looked up again. He was out of excuses.

"Aek!" Karak hissed.

"Fine! Fine!" Tyrus approached Karak's blurred outline. "Well I can't very well climb onto your back if I can't see you."

Karak reappeared, crouched down, and motioned at his back with a claw. Tyrus took a deep breath, as if he were going to leap into deep water, and climbed on. Everything turned gray. And although Tyrus could see himself and Karak, the washed-out colors of the world around him signaled they were invisible.

Karak leapt ten feet straight up, jolting Tyrus and making him tighten his hold on the lizard man. Karak's claws dug into the stone, and though they didn't penetrate deep, it was enough to keep them on the wall.

Karak climbed quickly, scaling the curved surface of the college like a spider. Tyrus made the mistake of looking down as they were halfway up and thereafter had to clench his eyes shut until they were climbing through the open window.

Tyrus let go of Karak, and the color of the world returned to normal. The screams hit him a heartbeat before the humidity and smell of soap. He spun and nearly fell into one of the steaming bathtubs built into the tiled floor. A half-dozen jewel-haired, and very naked, Allosian women were pointing at him and shouting. One dove under the water of her bathtub while others scrambled out.

"Oh dear."

THE SEALED CHAMBER miles beneath Rasha was not a secret, as was evidenced by the dozens of chests and barrels stowed in the shadows on the far wall. Someone had used the place to hide their treasures. Mulladin nudged a human skeleton with the toe of his boot. It fell over from its sitting position and clattered to the floor. A metal collar around its neck and manacles on its wrist marked it as a captive or slave. Either he'd been trapped here like they were, by accident, or someone had sent him here to die a slow and painful death.

Mulladin's chest tightened and he closed his eyes. He had to get out of here! The darkness pressed in on him, and breathing became more difficult. He'd always been afraid of enclosed spaces, and a particular instance when he'd fallen down a dry well was coming back to him. Fortunately, the emotion didn't come with the surge that came when other old memories recurred. Perhaps his newly capable mind was settling? Well, that was all fine and good, but it would mean nothing if he died here.

Mulladin kicked the skull so hard that it split in two, both parts sailing through the air and smashing into the wall. There was that familiar explosion of extra emotion.

"Stop that," Keesa called from the dais of the slipgate. She sat on its one step, staring at the rubble that sealed off the room's only exit.

Mulladin had tried to cut through the rock with Jek's sword. While the magic of the blade let it slice through the chunks of stone as though they were made of wood, the effort was futile. There was just too much stone, and they didn't have the strength or means to clear away so much rubble. Slicing into the walls of the chamber had proved equally useless as there were no adjoining chambers. Just miles and miles of rock in all directions, at least, that's what the sword said.

"Come over here."

Mulladin obeyed, joining Keesa where she sat.

She leaned her head on his shoulder. The explosion of euphoria and mild arousal helped to mute Mulladin's rising anxiety and he hooked an arm around Keesa's waist and pulled her close.

"You're claustrophobic, aren't you?"

"I don't know what that means," Mulladin said. Although he was no longer dim, Keesa had a way of making him feel like he was still a simpleton.

"It means you're afraid of being trapped, especially in tight spaces."

"You're very educated for a Rikujo thief."

Keesa scoffed. "Mother was having me trained to impersonate a noblewoman."

"For a scheme?"

Keesa laughed. "You could call it that."

"What?"

"Mother planned for us to move to Maes Tol, her homeland, where we would start a new life as a widowed noblewoman and her very eligible daughter."

"She was going to marry you off?" Heat simmered beneath Mulladin's words, and he quickly stamped out the rising flame.

Jealous? Jekaran chuckled.

How can I be jealous? It was just a plan. There isn't even a person involved.

"She wanted me to have a good life, away from the Rikujo and away from Arge..."

Mulladin shot her a wide-eyed look.

Keesa rolled her eyes. "My father," she said, "should he ever return." She clearly didn't appreciate having to tiptoe around the subject of Ez just to placate the sword.

The conversation lulled, and the two of them sat in silence for several minutes. Under other circumstances, the alone time would've been romantic.

"I think you're brave," Keesa suddenly said. "And loyal. You're a good man, Mulladin."

Mulladin laughed.

"You disagree?"

"I've only been a man for a matter of days."

Keesa hesitated. "I know you're uneducated...but kissing while I lay on top of you with our clothes on isn't actually—"

"Not that." Mulladin drew in a deep breath. "You saw Trous electrocute me?"

Keesa nodded.

"Well, the healing that saved my life changed me."

Keesa pulled away and stared up at him. "What are you talking about?"

Mulladin ran his hands over his face. "I wasn't acting like a simpleton, I was a simpleton–a man with the mind of a child. The talis used to heal my wounds changed that. Gave me the capacity of an adult."

Keesa didn't say anything.

"Well?"

A smile slowly crept across her face. "That's why you're so ignorant, and a virgin!"

The remark actually smarted, and Mulladin ground his teeth.

"Don't be like that." Keesa started laughing. "I'd been wondering how someone so intelligent and handsome could've remained"—she hesitated—"inexperienced."

"Well, now you know." Mulladin turned away, frowning.

Keesa's soft hand touched his cheek and forced his head to turn back so that their eyes met. "It's a compliment, you big, dumb ox."

Staring into her large, brown eyes cooled Mulladin's irritation.

Keesa moved in so that her lips brushed his as she whispered. "I may not be able to help you with your ignorance. But I can fix that virgin thing."

Before Mulladin could respond, Keesa pressed her lips against his with a passion that nearly made him forget his own name.

You know I'm still here, right? Jek said.

TYRUS AND KARAK flew down the massive white hallway following a single, glowing spirit orb. Well, Karak flew; it was all Tyrus could do to keep up with the lizard man, not that he was actually keeping up.

"Aek!" he shouted back at him, which Tyrus had learned was Vorakk for "hurry your ass up!"

"I'm–trying–to!" he panted.

A group of five robed Allosians flashed into existence several feet in front of them. Karak made a motion with his hand and a dozen small glowing orbs appeared in the air around him. They swirled about like playful glow flies until Karak pointed at the Allosians. Then the glowing lights aligned horizontally, turned blue, and released a hurricanic gale. The blowback was so strong that Tyrus slowed, the wind assailing him and threatening to throw him backward. The blast hurled the Allosian standing in the center of their quinate blockade back fifty paces and blew his comrades on either side of him into the convex walls so hard that they left cracks in the white stone.

As they ran past, one of the Allosians stirred. Tyrus bent down and rammed the stun baton into his chest. The purple-haired man convulsed and fell still. There wasn't a lot Tyrus could do to help, and honestly, stunning the man likely made no difference. It was frustrating.

The glowing ball darted to a set of gold-leafed double doors where it hovered. Karak slid to a stop and Tyrus was grateful for the chance to catch his breath. The doors had well-shards in them, and Tyrus knew they concealed one of the vertical carriages that allowed people to ascend and descend the floors of Allosian buildings.

The doors parted of their own accord, and Karak stepped inside. Tyrus followed, and closed his eyes as the lift rocketed upward. The doors opened on a massive dome-shaped chamber that had to be the top floor of the cylindrical structure. More slipgates than Tyrus had ever seen filled the room. They lined the walls, satellites to one enormous slipgate at the room's center.

"Reka, little, rich human open fey door?"

Tyrus smiled. That, he could do. Perhaps he wasn't useless after all.

MULLADIN'S HEART pounded as hard as though he'd sprinted a mile. His cheeks were flushed, and his chest was warm. Keesa was lying on top of him, smothering him with wet kisses and nearly choking him with her tongue. She sat back on his stomach and grabbed the fringe of her shirt and started to lift it.

Ding.

Keesa froze, her shirt pulled up to just above her naval.

"Why are you stopping?" Mulladin panted.

Keesa looked toward the slipgate and let her shirt drop back down.

"What?" The warmth in Mulladin's chest had suddenly shifted to the heat of annoyance.

Keesa got off him and stood, slowly walking over to the slipgate.

Mulladin's anxious irritation and arousal both faded at the sight of a blinking light on the slipgate's console. He scrambled to his feet and watched Keesa step up onto the dais. She looked down at the map of Shaelar and gasped.

"Keesa?"

She met his eyes. "The Allosian slipgate is open."

Chapter 94

Blow after blow struck Jove's bare flesh, making it impossible for him to rise. He lashed out with his green lightning, but it didn't affect the white balls of light assailing him. He cried, as he was pummeled by the never-ending barrage.

Hanging over the edge of the floating rock island, he could see the doll through the glass sphere. Oh, how he wanted her! Oh, how he needed her! She was his ultimate conquest, and Jove was sure he'd finally found a thrill that would eclipse the pleasure of his first kill. He'd known pleasure, but never again did it rise to the ecstasy of breaking that first doll.

What was her name again?

He still couldn't remember. But he did remember her face. He'd never be able to forget that. Porcelain skin framed by shiny black hair, a lock of which he'd kept for years. The thing he loved the most about her though, were her eyes. They'd been a beautiful shade of blue, bright like the sky. And then glassy and lifeless. Still pretty, but dimmer in death; their whole affair tragically ending too soon.

Jove clenched his eyes shut, tried to ignore the attacks, and focused on drawing in as much Apeiron as he could. The purple ocean all around him shuddered, and the power flowed into him, first healing his wounds, and then rushing into his core. He drank more, and more, and didn't stop. He would have that doll!

———✦———

MAELY KNELT NEXT to Gryyth's corpse, sobbing. All around her lay dead Ursaj, old and young, even the tiniest cubs still held tight in the crooks of their mother's arms. It was all so senseless. Why would the Ursaj's mother do this to them? What was the point of wiping out an entire species? Wasn't that the same as what Jenoc wanted to do? It enraged her, and she screamed at whatever god or gods would allow life to be such an unfair nightmare. She screamed until she was hoarse, and then resumed her pathetic sobbing.

Maely had never felt so completely forsaken, not since the day her mother died. She was alone, hundreds of miles from civilization, her friends gone, her brother gone, and now Gryyth and Sharor were dead. She had food and water, the remnants of the Ursaj feast were plentiful, but that would not keep forever. It would spoil long before she could eat it all, and there was no way she could carry very much of it with her, not enough for a sojourn of hundreds of miles. Not that she even knew which direction she should go.

A distant rumbling drew her gaze to the sky. Rising above the trees to the south was a thunderhead emitting flashes of green lightning. Her chest tightened, and her stomach twisted. The withering translucent green wind was coming again. The dark clouds were rolling closer at an alarming rate, and she had maybe an hour before they converged on the sky temple. With those clouds would come a wave of unstoppable, all-consuming death. If the speed of the clouds' approach was any indication, she wouldn't be able to outrun it this time. Besides, even if she did, where would she go?

Maely looked down from the sky and her eyes locked onto a wooden bowl on the ground a few paces in front of her. It looked to still have some of the red liquid in it, enough for her to drink. She'd already faced this temptation once, but her renewed loneliness fell on her like a physical thing, and she decided she'd rather die by poison then be stripped apart piece by piece. So, she reached for it.

That's not good for you.

Maely started. "Who's there?" She stood and glanced around.

A little girl giggled, but the sound wasn't an exterior thing. It was inside her head, like when she heard the voice of the Ursaj's mother.

"It's you, isn't it?"

I'm Aeva.

"You made them kill themselves!" Maely screamed. "They're all dead because of you!" Her sobbing resumed.

They're warriors.

"What the hell is that supposed to mean?" She stumbled toward the Apeira well and sank back to her knees, hugging herself as she wept.

Don't cry, Maely.

"Why shouldn't I? I'm going to die, and I'm going to die alone." She leaned forward so far that her forehead touched the dirt.

I'm here.

Maely lifted her head, her eyes falling on the glowing white flower growing at the base of the Apeira well. Somehow Maely understood that the voice came from that flower. She twitched, suppressing an impulse to reach over and pull it out by the roots.

"What are you?"

I'm Aeva.

"The Ursaj called you their mother. The human monks call you the divine mother. You're the goddess Rasheera, aren't you?"

I'm only a dream.

"Don't talk riddles at me!" Maely tore grass from the ground and flung it at the flower. Was the voice really Rasheera? If so, she'd just exploded at her god.

Please don't be mad.

Maely pounded the grass with a fist. "And why not? It's over isn't it! It's all over!"

There's still hope.

She shook her head, her tears spraying the petals of the white lily. "Can't you see the sky? It's coming for me. It's coming for everyone!"

Perhaps this is what she deserved–death. After all, she had helped Jenoc start the talis war, abandoned her brother, and worst of all, she'd forced Jek to love her by the magic of her mother's ring. Sure, Maely may have dipped herself into the river, but there was just too much mud for her to wash off. Better that she drown.

You are not bad, Maely.

She wanted to scream at the voice to get out of her head, but loneliness and fear of her approaching death made her hold back.

You care about people. You want them to be happy. You want it so bad that it makes you mad when they do foolish things.

Maely hiccupped a bitter laugh. It was true. She'd never thought of it that way, but it was a perfect summary of who she was. Aeva seemed to understand her better than she understood herself.

"I tried to stop Jek from going with Kairah. I tried to save him from the king. I tried to make him love me..." She broke into another fit of shuddering sobs.

You can't force people to do things. It's wrong.

Maely laughed. "I could. I had a compulsion talis. But even that wasn't enough."

But you broke it.

Aeva must've been peering into her thoughts to know so much about Maely, and see what she'd done. Maely recognized the familiar feeling. It was like the time Jenoc had broken into her mind, though where that was brutal and violating, Aeva's touch on her psyche was gentle, warm—kind even.

"That's not the only thing I've broken." She scrubbed her eyes with her forearm. "I've done terrible things, Aeva. I helped to start a war that will kill everyone, all because I wanted Jek to love me. I deserve to die."

You can still help fix things.

"How?" Maely scoffed. "I can't get away from that death wind. And even if I could, I don't know where I am or where my friends are. For all I know, they're dead."

An image of Mulladin exploded into Maely's mind. He was running with Karak, Gymal, and a girl with tan skin and black hair pulled into a ponytail. And he was fighting with Jekaran's sword?

Jek's dead? It's the only way Mulladin could wield the sword.

As if in response to the thought, another image formed. This one was of Jekaran. He was lying in a garden, sleeping, and was that Gymal's mercenary sitting by him, feeding him from a bowl of mush? What happened to Jek? The image in her mind changed again, this time resolving into a dirty and badly wounded man dragging a satchel over blackened ground. He stumbled, and his face became visible. It was the prince. Raelen.

The vision ended, and Maely stared at the white lily.

You can help him.

"Show me more!"

You have to go now.

Maely was about to protest, but another thunderclap–this one much closer–stopped her. "Where am I supposed to go? How am I supposed to get there?"

Empyrean...

Maely glanced up at the massive white structure looming above her. She hadn't seen any doors or windows. "You want me to go inside the sky temple? Will it protect me? Is there a displacement talis inside?"

Aeva didn't respond. Was something wrong?

"Aeva?"

The ground shook. Maely stood and craned her neck. The sky above was dimming, and explosions of green flashed from within black clouds. The storm had arrived far faster than she'd expected.

Panic thrilled through her. It was too late for her to run. Maely looked around for a place to hide, and her eyes settled on the white arch overshadowing the Apeira well. Could the Ursaj sky temple protect her? When she'd first encountered the wind, it withered and pulled apart all that it touched. But she'd been out in the open then. Could a stone shelter protect her? She exploded into a run underneath the arch and toward the front of the temple. She looked frantically for a door, but only found the white wall. She extended a hand to touch it, looking for seams that might indicate some sort of entrance. The white material was not stone. It was smooth like glass, but hard like metal.

A bolt of green lightning struck the ground a hundred feet behind her. Maely began pounding on the wall, and screaming for someone to let her in. She doubted any of the Ursaj would be inside, but what else was she going to do? She glanced back at another lightning strike, and made to pound again on the wall. Her fist hit nothing. She looked back at the wall and found a black opening just her size. She stepped in and fell.

The hole above her closed like a mouth as she fell away from it. A moment ago, the hole had been in front of her. Now it was above her, and the direction in front of her had become down.

Maely closed her eyes expecting at any moment to smash against the floor, but instead she jerked to a stop. Had she landed? Maely opened her eyes and found herself suspended in the air. Gently, her feet moved downward, righting her so that she was standing, or would've been standing if she were floating. Once upright, she was lowered to a floor.

Abrupt illumination made her cover her eyes, but she hadn't needed to. The light was soft and comfortable. It came from all directions and revealed a large chamber. Maely looked up to where the door had been. That direction was now up for her and she couldn't begin to puzzle out how that'd happened. Taliscraft was the only possible explanation.

The sky temple's inner room was oval shaped, and in the center was a round platform rising half a foot from the floor. Shelves and doors lined the walls, and there were even beds inside molded alcoves. Was she safe inside here?

Maely carefully walked over to the platform and stepped up onto it. It turned purple and an audible male voice asked something in a language Maely had never heard.

"What?" She called.

After a beat of silence, the voice spoke again, this time in Aiestali. "I apologize for the delay. It took me a little longer to learn your language than I had anticipated."

Long? It'd only been seconds, and Maely had only said one word. "Who are you?"

"My name does not translate well into your language. But the closest thing would be Empyrean."

Maely scanned the chamber. "You're not a person, are you?"

"No, mistress. I am—"

"Don't call me mistress!" Maely balled her fists at her sides.

"Very well, then. What should I call you?"

"Maely."

"Well, Maely. To answer your question. I am what you would call an ego talis."

Like the sword? "Then how come you don't talk to me in my head?"

"I can if you wish me to. But this is easier should anyone join us."

"What?"

The temple rocked, and Maely stumbled off the platform, falling to the floor and landing on her stomach. Apparently, she wasn't safe here after all.

"May I suggest we leave this place?" Empyrean asked without even the slightest fear in his voice.

Maely scrambled up to her feet. "How?"

"Stand on the control dais."

Maely guessed Empyrean meant the raised platform. She leapt up onto it and stood in the middle of the circle. The disc turned purple again, and suddenly the chamber was gone. She looked around, finding herself back outside amidst the dead Ursaj. Darkness made it look like night, the only light coming from Aeva and the Apeira well. Green bolts of lightning rained down in rapid succession and one struck the Apeira well. It exploded into a storm of green shards, and Maely threw up her arm to shield herself, only she didn't have arms.

She looked down, but found that she had no body either. "Divine Mother!" She shrieked. "I'm a ghost!"

"No, Maely," Empyrean's soothing voice said from somewhere unseen. "You are perceiving what I perceive."

"What are you?"

"A vessel," Empyrean answered.

"Like a boat?"

"You could describe me that way. But the analogy breaks down because I am not a water craft."

A wave of translucent green energy tore through the trees. Just like before, the trees dropped their foliage, withered and broke apart. The wave of death was pushing forward, killing the grass and devouring the corpses of the Ursaj, and it didn't appear that it was going to slow and retreat anytime soon.

"Go!" Maely screamed.

The sky temple shook and the ground around it started to crack and separate. Fissures formed all around the temple's base, and entire swathes of ground collapsed inward falling into the unknown depths. The sky temple's shaking increased in violence as it started to rise out of the ground. Explosions of dirt and rock shot into the air as the temple pulled upward. That's when Maely understood what Empyrean was. She'd seen something like him before, on the roof of Aiested's palace. This wasn't an Ursaj temple; it was Allosian sky ship–a gigantic one.

The white spires acting as posts for the vine-fence pulled up from the ground, clods of dirt falling away and revealing that they were attached to massive white wings. They tore free of the vine-fence just as the wave of translucent green energy started to wither the greenery.

Maely was about to tell Empyrean to hurry when it jerked free of the ground and shot into the black sky. The darkness only lasted a few heartbeats and then Maely was soaring through blue. The sight and sensation of flying like a bird was enough to shove all other concerns to the back of her mind, and she almost forgot that she wasn't the one sailing through the clouds, which were once again soft puffs of white. Empyrean rose above the clouds and hung in the air.

Maely looked down, marveling at the sea of clouds beneath her. She stretched her arms out–or at least that's how she thought of it–and leaned forward. The wind picked up as she exploded back into an aerial climb, rising higher and higher until the blue sky began to turn purple. It was cold this far above the world, but Maely kept pushing, wanting to reach such a height that she could look down and see the entirety of Shaelar.

Maely twisted with the curving horizon and found herself hovering between a blue-brown globe below and an endless blackness above.

"Well, I'll be damned. Kairah was right. The world is round."

"This is as high as I am capable of flying," Empyrean said.

Maely didn't answer, but reveled in the unexpected serenity of space. She'd left all of her problems below on the planet, and the quiet of space lulled her into a trance. For a moment, she wanted to stay here forever–it was so incredibly peaceful.

That's when Maely noticed the western edge of Shaelar. Where she could see through cloud cover, the ground was not green or brown, but black. The wave of life-destroying magic had spread out from Aiested in all directions and appeared to have eaten up hundreds of miles of land. Almost the entire western coast was black.

No, she hadn't left her problems behind, and she couldn't stay up here forever.

Maely pictured herself diving off a cliff into a lake, and Empyrean suddenly dipped. Fire engulfed Maely, and while she could feel the heat, she knew it was just a semblance of the burning Empyrean was taking. But if it hurt the sentient airship, he didn't say so.

Clouds raced up to meet Maely as she plummeted back to Shaelar. Green and brown land filled her vision, and soon she could make out forests and rivers. Maely laughed at the fluttering in her stomach and pushed forward even faster.

"Shall I take over navigation, Maely?"

Maely poured her excitement, grief, and anger into the dive, and for some reason it made her feel better; like the relief a frustrated scream or a good cry could bring.

"Maely?"

A forest filled her view, details resolving quickly as she fell closer. She streaked down like a meteor, covered in fire and filled with fury.

"Maely?" Empyrean's usually calm voice actually held a note of concern.

Maely pulled out of the dive so late that she brushed the forest's canopy, sending up an explosion of frightened birds. She laughed and gave Empyrean back control of the airship. The change from soaring through the sky to simply standing on a purple circle was so jarring that she wobbled and stumbled off the dais and slid to her knees on the floor. She laughed a relieved laugh of pure joy. She'd needed this, it had helped drive away the gloom and grief.

"That... was... incredible!"

"Why thank you, Maely." Empyrean said, and he actually sounded flattered. "It is my pleasure to serve. But next time, please don't wait so long to pull up."

"We're really flying!" She laughed again.

"Indeed we are."

"And we can go anywhere in all of Shaelar?"

"So long as we are not too far from an Apeira well. My energy store is vast, but it powers hundreds of talises, and prolonged flight away from a well could result in a crash."

The blackened ground of Shaelar's west coast flashed before Maely, and her giddiness faded. She couldn't fly west now, and if the death wave was spreading, eventually there would be no more Apeira wells, and nowhere to run.

You can still help fix things, Aeva had told her.

"But you'll let me fly anywhere I want?"

"So long as we are within a healthy distance of an Apeira well. Do you have a destination in mind?"

Maely nodded. "East."

Empyrean hesitated and then carefully asked, "Could you be a little more precise?"

"I'm not sure where exactly." Maely stood. "I just know that he rode east, toward Haeshala."

"Who?"

"Prince Raelen. I need to find him."

CHAPTER 95

Mulladin batted a blast of purple energy out of the air mere inches before it would've struck him in the chest. Wind ruffled his shaggy black hair as Karak swept a horizontal tornado across the large chamber. It blew the Allosian spell-casters out of their path and deposited two in the basin of a tall fountain with a splash.

Red lights pulsed above and below them from within the very stone of the floor and ceiling, and an assertive chime repeatedly sounded around them. They'd been forced to abandon the slipgate room before Gymal could find any gates inside the city for them to retreat to. Spell-casters, usually marked by Allosian men and women dressed in white robes, appeared from thin air, and commenced trying to stop them. The strange magic closet that Gymal called a lift ceased to work, and they'd been forced to fly down several flights of stairs amidst a storm of magic attacks. Now they were on the ground floor, trying to find a way out of the enormous building that was the College of Disciplines.

"I don't understand," Keesa shouted. "I thought Allosians were a peaceful race."

"Why do you think we're still alive?" Gymal snapped in his nasally tone.

Mulladin ground his teeth. Even when the little lord was helping them, he still managed to come off condescending and insufferable.

"If they wanted us dead, they could've killed us already," Gymal finished.

Mulladin caught sight of a mammoth arch set into the curved wall of the chamber. It housed two double doors at least as tall as the fountain in the center of the chamber, and the grandeur of the portal marked it as the front entrance.

Mulladin pointed at the doors with Jek's sword and resumed sprinting, and the others followed. Screams erupted from a crowd of Allosian students congregating near the main doors, and they scattered to all directions when they saw him coming.

They're not scared of you, Jek laughed. *It's Karak.*

"You sound like you're having fun," Mulladin panted.

I am!

The large doors of the front entrance swung inward and a dozen Allosians wearing white, form-fitting armor with silver wings marched in.

"Oh dear," Gymal said. "Peacekeepers!"

That must've been the Allosian term for guards or soldiers, for the armored men and women walking in lockstep definitely had the air of seriousness about them that Mulladin had found common in military types.

Mulladin grinned. He was eager to test his power with the sword against a foe that posed a real threat, instead of poor unsuspecting Rikujo enforcers. And thus far, their tactic of hiding and running hadn't afforded him the opportunity to really engage any of the Allosian spellcasters.

"Are you ready to have some real fun, Jek?"

"Who's he talking to?" Gymal demanded, but no one answered him. This wasn't the first time he'd asked this question, and there simply wasn't enough time for an explanation.

Mulladin didn't really want to answer Gymal anyway. He could barely stand the short, nasally lord's existence, to say nothing of talking with him.

I can't fight them, Jek said, all mirth gone from his psychic voice.

"What? Why?" Mulladin slid to a stop, forcing the others to do the same.

Because they don't intend to kill us.

"How can you know that?"

I can feel it. Karak's tricks won't be enough. We'll have to wipe them out if we want to get past them, but all they want to do is disarm and capture us.

Mulladin growled. "Since when has that mattered?"

They aren't evil.

"What's wrong?" Keesa asked. She held her hand up, ready to start casting bolts of lightning.

"Jek says we can't fight them."

"Why?"

"Come on!" Mulladin grabbed Keesa by the arm with his free hand and towed her toward another connecting hall.

"Did you say Jekaran told you?" Gymal shouted.

"Uska, stupid human boy in sword."

A wide ring of purple light formed on the ground around them and Mulladin slammed into an invisible barrier. The force of his collision at top speed threw him backward, and he would've fallen had Keesa and Karak not caught him.

Mulladin shot a glance behind them. The peacekeepers steadily advanced. He growled, shrugged off Keesa and Karak, raised the sword high above his head, and then brought it down on the invisible wall. The tip of the sword met resistance for only a fraction of a second before continuing its downward arc. A dome of crackling purple energy flashed into existence around them before shattering like glass, and the ring of light surrounding them winked out.

They resumed their desperate retreat, the peacekeepers now running and closing the distance behind them. Keesa fired off two bolts of lightning behind them, one striking a female peacekeeper square in the chest. The blow didn't stop or even slow the Allosian sentry. Instead, the white, form fitting armor she wore flashed purple and simply absorbed the blast.

A second dome of invisible force formed around them, but this time Mulladin didn't even stop or slow. He just swung the sword in a horizontal cut and dispelled it. They continued to close ever faster, and it was only by the Vorakk shaman's intervention that they were able to maintain their lead. The lizard man summoned a dozen small orbs of fire and directed them at the peacekeepers. The marble-sized fireballs drew red lines on the polished floor that erupted into walls of fire separating them from their pursuers. Of course, the Allosian peacekeepers, in their white helmets and armor with silver wings, either leapt the dozens of feet over the flames, or barreled through them. Still, the surprise was enough to slow them, and Mulladin led the group into the connecting corridor.

Allosians in robes leapt out of their way as Mulladin lead the others through a hall that curved slightly on the right, stretching past doors set at regular intervals. He slid to a stop when he came to a part of the wall where a door should've been. Instead there was a gaping tear in the white stone that stretched from the floor dozens of feet up to a cracked arch. Mulladin didn't think, he just ran into the chamber beyond and found himself at the top of a flight of stairs leading down to the floor of an amphitheater.

Stone benches ran the circumference of the circular chamber, interrupted at regular intervals by stairs leading down to the floor. The chamber was a mess. Debris littered the ground and stairs, and benches in one entire section were nothing more than cracked chunks of marble.

"What happened here?" Keesa asked.

Mulladin shook his head and then flew down the steps two and three at a time, taking the last ten in a single leap.

Showing off for your girlfriend? Jek teased.

Mulladin didn't reply. Instead, he located a large open doorway leading to a hall behind a glass lectern. The others followed, and they exited the amphitheater just as the peacekeepers started hurling bolts of purple energy at them from the top of the stairs.

The corridor, like all the others in this building, was wide enough for ten wagons abreast with a ceiling so high it could accommodate a giant. Double doors, gold-leafed and decorated lavishly by runes and gemstones, awaited them in the corridor's terminal wall.

Mulladin slid to a stop in front of the doors, gripped a handle that was more art than utility, and pulled. Both doors swung open with an ease that belied their mammoth design. Mulladin shepherded the others inside before slipping in himself. He caught sight of the peacekeepers entering the hallway just before slamming the doors shut.

"Vorakk!"

His name is Kara, Jek corrected.

Mulladin rolled his eyes. "Karak, can you use your magic to seal that door?"

"Ssk!" The shaman motioned with a hand and more of his floating balls of light appeared.

These turned light blue and then zipped into the gilded surface of the doors and disappeared. A heartbeat later, frost crept out from the seam dividing the two doors and spread until it entombed them in a thick layer of ice.

Mulladin turned away from the doors grinning, expecting Keesa to mirror his pleasure. Instead, she, as well as Gymal, were staring with craned necks at walls rising hundreds of feet and lined with treasure-filled shelves.

"Talises!" Keesa gasped. "Those are all talises!"

Mulladin lowered Jek's sword and walked into the chamber. The sheer number of talises sitting in glass boxes was awe-inspiring–a fortune hundreds of times greater than that possessed by all the kings that ever ruled in Shaelar combined.

"I think we're in the center chamber of The College of Disciplines, and this is some kind of vault," Gymal said. "Like the one in Aiested, only much much bigger."

"Vault?" Mulladin's stomach soured. They might as well have run directly into a prison cell. "So, we're trapped?"

"We are in a chamber filled with talises, peasant!" Gymal snapped.

"Displacement talises!" Keesa glanced at Gymal.

"Yes," the weaselly little lord said with a weary sigh. "If we can find a shift bracelet, or blink ring, or any other kind of displacement talis..."

Mulladin started when something slammed into the frozen doors. He whipped back around as a second impact shook the doors. The ice cracked, but held.

"Karak, can you fix those cracks and keep the doors frozen?"

"Ssk!"

"The rest of us need to find displacement talises!" Mulladin broke for a spiral staircase rising from the center of the chamber's glossy floor.

Keesa followed, eventually overtaking him and bounding up the stairs to the second level. Mulladin glanced back down at Gymal. The little man was standing in front of a tall pedestal with a glass orb hovering above it.

Mulladin gritted his teeth. Was that arrogant ass just going admire the scenery while he and Keesa did all the work? "What are you doing?"

Gymal raised his hand and gently rested two fingers on the orb. It glowed in response.

"Hey," Mulladin repeated.

"Quiet!" Gymal snapped. "I need to concentrate."

A moment passed, and then Gymal opened his eyes. "Third level, in the eastern-most section."

Apparently, the orb was some kind of guide to the inventory of the vault. Mulladin felt stupid, but didn't apologize–he'd be damned thrice over before he ever apologized to Gymal. He resumed climbing the stairs, following Keesa onto the third level, which was really nothing more than a five-foot balcony running along the wall of the chamber.

He caught up to Keesa in what must've been the eastern-most section, and joined her in opening glass boxes and sifting through their contents.

Uh, Mull...

He overturned a glass box, dumping its contents onto the floor, and kneeling to sift through the talises looking for anything that could teleport them out of the vault.

Mull...

Mulladin lifted a thick silver necklace with a large diamond encasing a well-shard for a charm. "Keesa?"

She looked back at him and shook her head. "That looks like a shadow catcher."

"What's a shadow catch...?"

Gymal screamed.

Mulladin stood and ran to the balcony's thin rail. His first thought was that the peacekeepers had broken through the door, but Karak's balls of blue light continued to crisscross and disappear into the frozen doors, melding cracks together, and adding inches to the ice wall.

Mulladin looked from Karak back to Gymal. The little man was sprinting toward Karak, running so fast that he tripped on his robes twice before finally reaching the lizard man. Mulladin jogged around the circular balcony trying to get a view of what was scaring Gymal. He stopped when the hulking form of a gigantic crystal statue stepped from the shadows of an alcove on the chamber's far side.

"What the hell is that?"

Crystal golem, Jek said. *I was trying to warn you, but you were too busy gawking at your pretty necklace.*

"Keesa!"

She was already at his side staring down with wide eyes at the colossal glass form. It steadily clomped toward Gymal and Karak, and Mulladin was about to shout for Karak to use his magic to stop it when he noticed the streams of water pooling around the lizard man's ankles. The peacekeepers had apparently stopped trying to batter their way in and were now using magic to melt the ice.

Karak closed his eyes, and his balls of light redoubled their speed, darting in and out of the door in a pattern, trying to counteract the heat from the other side. No, Karak couldn't both fight that thing and keep the peacekeepers out.

You wanted a challenge, Jek said.

"Keep looking for something to get us all out of here." Mulladin climbed up onto the balcony railing.

"What are you doing?" Keesa shot a hand out, but Mulladin jumped before she could grab his tunic.

He fell toward the glass monster, sword pointed down. He'd seen Jek fight using the power of the sword, seen him jump impossibly high and land without so much as a spraining his ankle. He hoped, very sincerely, that the sword's power would do the same for him.

Strike at the well shard in its face. That's how I killed the one I fought.

Mulladin shifted the sword's point toward the crystal golem's head. He'd fallen to about five feet from the glass monster when it pivoted and flung up its huge arm. A glass hand crashed into Mulladin, swatting him out of the air and hurling him into the wall. He hit hard and fell another twelve feet to the floor.

Of course, it was frozen in ice and unable to move at the time.

"You could've mentioned that," Mulladin groaned as he worked to stand. Sharp pains from his ribs, shoulder, and leg made him fall back to the floor. He looked up to find the twenty-foot tall glass sentinel clomping toward him.

Something bounced on the floor off to his left, and Mulladin turned to see what it was. A ring clattered to a stop just outside his reach. Mulladin glanced up. Keesa was leaning over the rail, arm still extended. Mulladin lunged for the ring, ignoring the protests of his broken bones. When his hand clasped around it, warmth flowed into him. Pins and needles like when his foot would fall asleep washed over his whole body. He gritted his teeth, and when the uncomfortable sensation past, his pains were gone. He slipped the ring onto his finger, and rolled out of the way just in time to avoid being stomped by a giant crystal foot.

A bolt of lightning struck down from the third level and connected with the crystal golem's shoulder, spinning it to one side and forcing it off balance. Mulladin charged the glass automaton, sheering off its right leg as he passed beneath it. The titan fell forward, catching itself with an arm on the wall.

Mulladin spun and leapt for the crystal golem's back. He swung the sword in a diagonal arc, the tip of the blade sinking into the translucent surface as easily as though it were water. When he landed, the glass titan fell into two pieces.

"Ha!" Mulladin shouted, but his elation faded at the sight of the crystal golem's parts liquefying and flowing back together.

I said you had to strike at the well shard in its face!

"Yeah." Mulladin raised the sword, and charged.

The golem's hand hadn't even reformed when it swung at him. Mulladin leapt over the swing and brought the sword down on the golem's shoulder. He'd been aiming to decapitate it, but missed. His sword slid through the chest of the glass titan as he came down, but the blade hadn't gone all the way through, and the crystal golem healed itself before he could strike again.

A flash of purple at his side resolved into Keesa. She was wearing a diamond tiara with a well shard embedded in its center, and held a gold chain, a silver bracelet, and a medallion in her arms.

"Give me one of those and let's get the hell out of here!"

Keesa shot a lightning bolt at the golem, knocking it back and forcing it to pause and heal a hole left in its chest. "We have a problem."

"Just one?" Mulladin twirled the sword and brought it up to a guard position as he faced the congealing golem.

"Warding stone. We can travel inside this room, but not out of it."

"Golden womb of the goddess! What else could go wrong?"

As though fate were mocking him, the sound of cracking ice resounded through the chamber.

"Fey soldiers break through, aek!"

They were trapped between a contingent of trained spell-casting Allosian soldiers in magic armor and a giant living statue that was practically indestructible. Whole once more, the crystal golem stood, its well-shard placed so as to make it look like the creature's eye.

"The well-shard!" Mulladin shouted at Keesa.

She fired off another bolt of lightning, but the golem caught the blast by sacrificing its hand. She fired again, but it blocked the bolt with its other hand. Before Keesa could fire a third shot, the first hand had grown back, and the glass titan was charging them.

I have an idea, Jek said. *But you'll need to let me take control of your body.*

The scene of Jekaran impaling Ez suddenly replayed in Mulladin's mind. He shoved the memory down before it could travel across his mental bond to the sword. If he gave up control of his body could the same thing happen to Keesa?

Come on, Mull!

The crystal golem shook the ground as it strode toward them.

Trust me!

Memories of Mulladin's life with Jekaran streamed into his head; the time when he was sobbing over a dead dog and Jek was comforting him, another time when they were wrestling and Jek let him win, the time when Loemas and his brothers had him cornered and were pelting him with cow dung and Jekaran got between them. Did he trust Jekaran? Of course he did. But was the sword really Jek?

"Okay." Mulladin lowered his mental defenses and invited the sword to take control.

He charged the crystal golem. Keesa shouted after him, but Mulladin could no more reply than he could stop. He ducked a swing, whirled to the titan's side and sheared off its left leg. The golem crashed to one knee. Mulladin leapt up an inhuman ten feet toward the chamber wall, pushed off it, and sailed back toward the golem. He landed on the giant's back, ran up its spine, and sat around the back of its neck so that his legs dangled over its shoulders. Then he rammed the sword into its head.

To Mulladin's surprise, the sword stopped a half an inch short of the crystal golem's well shard. The sword made Mulladin carefully push the sword forward so that the tip touched the shard. Another consciousness crowded into Mulladin's mind, and he began to lose himself in three different streams of thought.

The connection formed by the sword touching the crystal golem's well shard let Mulladin see the creature's instructions: protect the treasury from thieves. A peacekeeper named Inarin had given the golem those orders using a command word. Mulladin–or was it Jek? He could no longer tell–pressed against the golem's mind, trying to change its orders. A barrier obstructed him–the command word. It pushed back, trying to drive Mulladin from its mind, but he pressed harder. The barrier shattered, and Mulladin suddenly knew the crystal golem's command word–Elayse. Using that knowledge, and directed by Jek's consciousness, Mulladin changed the golem's allegiance, and its instructions.

Mulladin slid off the golem's back and fell into a crouch in front of Keesa. When he stood, Jekaran released him, and his body was his own again. Keesa stared at him, her mouth hanging open and her eyes wide.

"What did you do?"

"Got us some help."

Mulladin commanded the golem using a mental connection facilitated by the sword, to break through the doors. Startled peacekeepers leapt back as the crystal golem hurled ice encased door debris at them. Two peacekeepers rocketed into the air and flew at the golem, but it just batted them out of the air as it had done Mulladin.

They ran down the corridor, letting the golem fight off any of the peacekeepers that tried to stop them. Keesa had given each of them a displacement talis, except for Karak. Apparently, the lizard man couldn't use talises, but he didn't act concerned. As soon as they'd climbed the stairs out of the amphitheater and were back in the hallway, the lizard man disappeared in a haze of blurry lines.

The building's warding stone still prevented them from traveling outside, and so they needed to get outside the building before they could disappear. They ran through the corridors and back toward the enormous room with the tall fountain. The crystal golem followed after them, fending off attacks from pursuing peacekeepers and drawing out a chorus of screams from crowds of unsuspecting Allosian students.

Because he was feeling particularly spiteful, Mulladin commanded the crystal golem to smash the tall fountain on their way out. He chuckled, but Keesa glowered at him.

"What?"

The destruction of the fountain did more to help them than Mulladin expected–not that that had been part of his motivation–causing a convenient dust screen that allowed them to slip out of the College's front entrance. As soon as they passed the threshold, something changed. It reminded Mulladin of carrying firewood on his back and the relief that followed his dumping the load into the box by the hearth.

"Where's Jek?"

I'm right here.

"Kairah's tower." Gymal placed a hand on Keesa's shoulder, and on Mulladin's back and the world disappeared in a flash of purple light.

CHAPTER
96

R aelen wept.

It wasn't because of the pains from his wounded shoulder, or his maddening thirst, or even his overwhelming desire to go to sleep and die. No, Raelen wept for the tiny skeleton still held tight in the arms of its skeletal mother. Its long pink sleeper marked it as a girl, and looked to have been lovingly made in anticipation of the birth as the cloth was noticeably better quality than the blankets, curtains, or any other cloth in the house. He found no other children in the one room cottage, which likely meant this couple was young and the baby girl was their first child.

The scattered bones of another adult–likely the father–lay strewn across the dirt floor. A rusted sword lay broken in two pieces in the dirt beside him. Had this man been a soldier? He clearly died trying to protect his wife and baby daughter. Did he even realize he'd never stood a chance?

Raelen ground his teeth in an effort to quiet his shuddering sobs. He'd been able to keep the sorrow distant, even after he found the skeleton of a small child hiding inside an outbuilding. But this, this was more than he could bear. The utter profaning of precious, new life, and the casual, brutal extinguishing of hope–how could such cruelty exist in the world? What creator would allow such horrors?

He stumbled out of the cottage, and into the village square. Blackened, dead, ground cluttered with bones extended in all directions. He shuffled over to a small brick well that marked the village's center. There wouldn't be any water, but spent half an hour winding the crank and retrieving the bucket on the off chance he could find a drink.

Nothing.

Raelen sniffed and scrubbed his grimy forearm over his eyes. If such wanton death and unmitigated suffering were making him question the existence of god, then the same darkness was absolutely validating his belief in a devil. And that devil's name was Jenoc.

He'd been following the trail of death for days now, his strength slowly ebbing with each passing hour. He knew now that he didn't have a chance at catching the monster, but his righteous indignation spurred him on all the same. Without food or water, or medicine, his anger was the only thing keeping him alive.

Raelen left the little village, a place so insignificant that it likely didn't appear on any of his father's maps. But people had lived here. Children had played here. Farmers had grown crops, and those innocents had had their destinies stolen from them.

It was noon now. The sun stood high in the sky, and without any trees to shade him, or any flora to retain moisture, Raelen was exposed to the full force of the sun's fury. He wasn't sweating anymore, and knew that was a bad sign. But that might've been the fever baking him from within and not the sun cooking him from above. His shoulder wound festered with infection and had started to stink. He was hallucinating, hearing voices and seeing phantoms. Though he couldn't be sure if the ghosts he saw were truly products of his mind, not after his encounter with Saranna. He wanted to believe them real, but he doubted very much that ghosts of his loved ones would be telling him to give up and die.

But then again, perhaps it was good advice. It was inevitable. Why was he even still continuing the chase? He would never catch Jenoc, much less have the strength to kill the Allosian monster.

Seiro.

That was why he kept going, not his anger or desire to see justice done. Seiro, honor, was why he couldn't just lay down and die. He had to keep fighting until the very end. He thought he heard Gryyth's voice.

"Do you remember the tale of Keth the courageous, cub?"

"Tell it to me," Raelen wheezed through parched lips.

Gryyth laughed. "Always wanting a story. Even when you already have heard it dozens of times."

Raelen stumbled and fell forward, landing on his knees. The bare rock tore his trousers and scraped his exposed knee.

"Keth had a she-bear and four cubs. He had built a comfortable den inside the lee of a large mountain. One day, while he was hunting, a mighty quake shook the land. Keth ran back to his cave and found the entrance collapsed. The rocks sealing the cave's one opening were large and made of heavy granite, and not even an Ursaj as mighty as Keth was could move or lift them alone. No other Ursaj lived close, and to go for help would surely mean the death of his mate and cubs.

"Keth prayed to The Mother for strength and went to work trying to move the boulders. He made little progress, and the task was weakening him, but Keth did not relent. Ten days he pushed, pulled, and strained, but was only able to open up a hole no bigger than a badger. The smell of death wafted out and was so strong that Keth's strength left him, and he fell to the ground. He roared a roar of such sorrow and anguish that it was said even the goddess wept. Just as he was about to give up and die, Keth heard something.

"A small paw reached out from within the darkness of the hole. Keth took hold of it and pulled his youngest cub from the rubble. His mate and three other cubs had died, but his littlest cub, Jaror, was alive. Keth lost much, but had he given up trying to free his family, he would've lost all."

It was a nice story. Raelen had heard it many times. But it did nothing to rouse his spirits. It was too late. He was dying. He had failed to bring justice when it was his express duty to do so. He'd failed to avenge his father, and his people.

Raelen fell onto his face.

A shadow fell over him, and something blocked out the sun. It felt good, like the cool shade of a large tree in summer. He remembered Saranna and his other siblings going for picnics with their mother when he was very young. He saw the memory as though it were before him; all of them eating, playing, and laughing beneath a large oak.

Raelen smiled and then the darkness swallowed him.

MAELY HELD Raelen under the arms, heaving and pouring all her strength, such as it was, into the effort of dragging the unconscious prince up a slope that fed into the large opening in Empyrean's belly. Like the door that admitted her, it had just opened out of the solid white material that the Allosian airship was made of. The new opening's displaced substance then liquefied and stretched eight feet to the ground where it had solidified into a ramp.

The floor congealed, and reformed the moment Maely pulled Raelen into the ship. She fell to the ground and rolled onto her side panting. "Tell me again why you couldn't just talis him aboard?"

"Because I was not crafted with any displacement talises. Those consume a lot of Apeiron, and being designed for spending time away from Apeira wells means that my creators wanted my energy use to be conservati—"

"Whatever!"

Empyrean actually sighed. "His condition is critical. You need to get him into one of the restoration chambers."

"Teleporting costs too much Apeiron, but healing doesn't?"

"One is more necessary than the other, Maely."

The south wall opened up revealing a chamber with horizontal glass tubes, the lid of one sliding open. Maely sighed, removed the strange wavy sword from his belt, and then resumed dragging Raelen into the room. It took everything she had to hoist him the four feet up and deposit him into the bed of the tube, and it hadn't been a gentle process. She winced each time his lulling head struck the edges of the restoration chamber's glass case.

He groaned when she accidentally gripped his wounded shoulder. "Sorry, your highness."

With one final shove that rolled Raelen onto his back, Maely collapsed to her bottom and rested her head on her knees. Sweat trickled down her back and forehead and it took her over a minute to catch her breath.

"All that rich food makes you nobles fat."

Though, in truth, Maely had only seen lean muscle on the prince's chest and arms–not that she was looking. Even filthy, feverish, unshaved, and stinky, the prince was handsome. It reminded her of Kairah's impossible beauty and constant perfection.

"Mistr–I mean, Maely."

Maely lay back onto the white floor. "What?"

"Something is wrong."

She sat up, her chest going cold. "Is he…?" She couldn't bring herself to say dead. What if her clumsy jostling of Raelen had killed him? She didn't think he'd hit his head that hard.

"Something is hindering the flow of Apeiron into his body. Consequently, I cannot heal his wounds."

Maely scrambled up and leaned over the open tube. "I don't understand."

"It is hard to explain to someone who does not have an advanced understanding of talis craft and spell-casting, and I…"

Maely growled.

Empyrean actually stuttered. "R-right. Let me explain it this way. Each time I try to transfer Apeiron from myself into him, I encounter something that accepts and expends the power, but produces no healing effect."

"Then use more Apeiron!"

"I see that my analogy was inadequate. Suffusing him with more Apeiron does not change the result."

Maely gritted her teeth, not out of anger, but in an attempt to stave off panic. Aeva had all but told her she needed to rescue Raelen. Was she too late? What would happen if he died? Was he supposed to help stop the withering wind spreading across the world? She wasn't sure about his fate or the reality of destiny, or even if that is why Aeva had pointed her in this direction. She was sure that she liked the prince. From everything Gryyth had told her, and the way he'd always treated her like a real person and not an inferior, she believed he was a good man. Something that, to her mind, was even more of a miracle than a giant flying airship the size of a castle.

She touched his forehead and the heat from his fever was nearly painful. Tears welled in her eyes, and she lowered her head to rest it on the side of the healing chamber when something arrested her attention.

Something green dimly glowed beneath his dirty tunic. Maely lifted the shirt up and found an emerald-colored shard of crystal resting on Raelen's chest–dimming until it no longer glowed. It'd come loose of some cloth wrapping and the top part of the jagged chunk was wrapped in a leather thong that looped around the back of Raelen's neck. The emerald shard reminded Maely of the destroyed Apeira well in Aiested, and was the same exact shade of green as the lightning that fell from the dark skies above the city.

She reached out to take the emerald, but hissed and snapped her hand back. It was cold. So cold that it burned her fingers.

"What is it Maely?"

"Try healing him again."

"But, if I—"

"Do it!" Maely snapped.

The emerald lit back up.

"Stop!"

The emerald's glow dimmed and faded away.

Maely grabbed the leather thong and snapped it off the back of Raelen's neck. Then she lifted the emerald shard off Raelen's chest. "Try it now."

"Remarkable," Empyrean exclaimed. "The flows are no longer inhibited."

Maely watched as Raelen's color changed from glossy pale white to the warm peach color that was his regular skin tone. His cuts faded, and the yellow pus around the hole in his shoulder evaporated as his flesh knitted back together.

Maely glanced down at Raelen's hand where he'd lost all of his fingers. They didn't grow back. "Why aren't his fingers growing back?"

"They are, it is just taking an inordinate amount of time and dispro-portionate level of power to restore them."

"Leave them," Raelen rasped.

Maely was so startled that she dropped the emerald to the floor.

The glow orbs of Empyrean's healing chamber flickered.

"Something is draining my Apeiron charge at an increasing rate."

Maely quickly picked up the emerald, forgetting to hold it by the leather cord, and yelping at the intense cold. She nearly dropped it a second time before she collected herself.

"It is an anti-Apeira shard. It devours Apeiron instead of producing it." Raelen sat up. "Jenoc made it. Like he made the one that destroyed Aiested."

Maely stared at Raelen and then, remembering herself, she tried to curtsy. "My prince."

Raelen scoffed. "Don't call me that." He lifted himself out of the restoration bed, and stood.

That's right. His father died.

"Sorry, I meant my king."

He stood and rolled his newly healed shoulder. "That's not what I meant."

"Then..."

He placed his fingerless hand on her shoulder and flashed a tired smile. "Raelen will do."

Maely bobbed her head.

"If the world doesn't come crashing down around us, then maybe I'll be king. But of what I'm not certain. The capital is in ruins and my largest army has been annihilated."

Maely felt sick. Raelen hadn't been able to stop the talis war after all– the war she helped Jenoc start. All those soldiers were dead because of her.

"Haeshala won the battle?" She choked back a sob.

Raelen shook his blonde head. "No. I'm fairly sure Jenoc wiped them out too. At least, the ones that didn't join him."

Now Maely was really confused. "I thought Jenoc wanted us to fight Haeshala and wipe each other out? Doesn't he hate humans? Why would he want them to join him?"

Raelen took the emerald shard from Maely by the leather band and bundled it back into the dirty piece of cloth that had fallen free. "It's a long story." He glanced around the white room. "But I can see I'm not the only one with tales to tell. What's happened since our parting?"

"It's a long story." Maely smirked.

Raelen grinned. "Thank you, Maely, for rescuing me and bringing me here. Wherever here is."

"You are onboard the Allosian airship Empyrean."

Raelen glanced around. "Who is that?"

"It's Empyrean," Maely answered. "He's kinda stupid, but he means well."

"I can hear you, Maely."

Raelen laughed. "The airship talks? The White Hawk couldn't do that."

Maely pictured the much smaller craft Jenoc had used to fly off the palace tower in Aiested. "Empyrean is a lot more," she hesitated. "What was the word you used?"

"Sophisticated."

"Yeah, that." Maely walked out of the healing chamber and back into Empyrean's circular command center. "More so than other Allosian airships. At least that's what he says."

"I did not spend eight hundred years half buried in the ground and rebuilding myself to be so ill-treated." Empyrean actually huffed.

"And he's really sensitive."

Raelen laughed again. It was good to hear him laugh. Maely thought it sounded brave for some reason.

The prince touched the metal band encircling his bicep. "Is Gryyth here? Without an Apeiron charge, I can't feel him through my transference band."

Maely's smile disappeared.

"What's wrong?"

She sniffed and focused on the wall, not able to meet Raelen's eyes. What was she supposed to tell Raelen? That his friend and protector, the one who'd practically raised him and instilled in him the Ursaj sense of morality, had drank poison and killed himself? All because a talking flower told him to?

"He didn't make it," she said.

Raelen unconsciously touched his transference band. "He succumbed to his burns?" His voice was thick and unsteady. It made Maely want to start sobbing again.

Strong and brave though he was, there was a peculiar, almost child-like vulnerability to the prince—an innocence. Not naiveté, or any lack of understanding, but a simple goodness. He comprehended the world, but at the same time hadn't partaken of the ubiquitous cynicism Maely had seen everywhere she went. She couldn't bring herself to hurt him.

"Yes," she lied.

Tears welled up in his eyes, but he blinked them away and tightened his jaw. His whole hand clenched tightly into a fist, and he emitted a very Ursaj-like growl. "The White Hawk had a built-in weapon talis–one that shot lightning. Do you have something like that, Empyrean?"

"I am afraid not."

"Sophisticated my ass," Maely said. And immediately her eyes grew wide and she shot a glance at Raelen. Had she really said that in front of the crown prince of Aiestal? Fortunately, he didn't seem to notice or care.

"I am not a warship, Maely. My primary purpose is to facilitate transit of Allosian dignitaries."

"You have no ability to fight?" Tendons in Raelen's neck were bulging and his fair complexion reddened.

He blames Jenoc for Gryyth's death.

"I can mimic and project a weapon talis's effect so that it manifests outside myself. This mechanism can also magnify the specific talis's function and power."

"Are you carrying any such talises?" Raelen glanced around the circular, white chamber.

"I am not. I apologize."

Maely glanced at the strange wavy sword with red metal blade. "What about that? What does it do?"

"It's a flare kris. It casts explosions of fire and burns when it cuts." Raelen stooped and took up the sword. "But it has no charge."

"That will not be a problem," Empyrean said.

Raelen met Maely's eyes. "You can charge talises?"

"Sadly, no. Talis to talis Apeiron transfers are not possible. However, a talis does not need an Apeiron charge for me to discern the spells woven into the weapon, and so I can still mimic its functions and magnify its effects."

"That's incredible," Raelen said.

"Don't do that," Maely said.

"Do what?"

"Feed his ego."

Empyrean sighed again.

Raelen lifted the red sword up to eye level and scrutinized its dark well shard. "You told me back in Aiested that you had a score to settle with Jenoc."

Heat ignited inside Maely's chest. Yes, she did want revenge on the man who had burned Gryyth, violated her mind, and used Maely to further his evil designs. More than the sword, he was at the center of all the misfortune that'd befallen her. Raelen said he'd also been the one to destroy the Apeira well in Aiested, causing all the suffering and death and that evil withering wind that devoured Aiested's refugees.

"Yes, I do."

Raelen met her eyes. "Well it's time to make him pay for all the sorrow he's wrought. I'm going to kill him, and you're going to help me."

Maely smiled.

Chapter 97

Graelle stared at the beautiful, white flower growing in the center of Lady Kairah's garden. She wasn't sure if it was a trick of the light, or if the flower was actually glowing. Either way it was one of the most beautiful specimens of decorative flora she'd ever seen. She had a garden too, back in Imaris. Nothing anywhere near as grand as this, but she took pride in it. She'd always had a garden.

Many people turned to family, friends, or Rasheera for comfort during hard times. Well, Graelle's one living sister had long ago shunned her, the few friends she had made over the years often lived very brief lives, and Rasheera... well, the goddess never had answered her prayers. Graelle always supposed that was because she was a whore–that's what the monks said anyway. She'd gone to a monk once, seeking absolution and a chance at a better life. It actually hadn't been all that long ago, maybe fifteen years. Upon finding out what her profession was, he'd wanted a sampling. No, the goddess was a lie. Just like every altruistic notion and silly promise of a life beyond without pain and sorrow. Reality was just a cruel accident.

At least that's what she'd believed until a few weeks ago. Now she wasn't so sure, and her confusion was all because of the chubby, white-haired man trundling his way over to her, holding a plate of fruit.

Irvis groaned as he sat down on the soft grass next to her. "I'm starting to think," he popped a grape into his mouth, "I might be getting old."

Despite her gloomy mood, Graelle couldn't resist a chuckle and suddenly life didn't feel quite so hopeless. That was the kind of effect Irvis had on her.

"You're what? Fifty?"

Irvis popped a second grape into his mouth and then proffered the tray to her. "Fifty-eight."

Graelle took a wedge of red fruit peppered with small white seeds. "Well, you have a young face."

Irvis set the tray on the ground between them. "That's why I was able to win the heart of a beautiful woman scarcely past her thirtieth year."

Graelle playfully swatted him on the shoulder. "If you're going to flatter a woman about her age, at least make your false compliment believable. Else it sounds like you're mocking."

Irvis's eyes widened. "I wasn't...I mean...I would never..."

Graelle rolled her eyes, but turned away so he couldn't see her smile. "You don't know much about women, do you?"

"I know a lot about women," he huffed, then added, "About their bodies anyway...guess I don't know so much about what goes on inside them."

"That sounded kinda dirty," Graelle said.

Irvis laughed. "It kind of does."

He pulled her close, and she snuggled up to him, and they sat in silence for several minutes enjoying the fruit and the ambience of Kairah's incredible garden.

Irvis continued to surprise her. She'd thought for sure that when Argentus died, he'd have drawn inward to grieve. While he had been subdued, and inclined to random bouts of crying, Irvis retained his native cheerfulness, often making jokes, mostly at the expense of himself. She'd asked him about it and was surprised at his answer.

"I know Argentus's soul lives on, and one day I'll see my friend again."

Despite his lascivious inclinations, Irvis was a true believer in the Divine Mother. A contradiction that Graelle found earnest instead of hypocritical. In a strange way, it was refreshing. He'd been completely forthcoming about his past indiscretions, but hadn't displayed any of the behavior he'd confessed to. He'd given up his monk's robe to Lady Kairah to afford her some modesty on their trek from Aiested. And though Graelle kept watching, she had yet to catch him staring at the perfect specimens of proudly displayed Allosian femininity that existed all about them. He didn't even look when one Allosian woman bent over right in front of him, unwittingly offering Irvis a pristine view of her perfectly sculpted backside.

He hadn't even made any attempts to take advantage of Graelle herself, which also was refreshing. He respected her in a way that no man ever had, even tried to be a better man to impress her. Impress her! A former whore and now a whoremonger. A woman who'd long ago given up on worshipping or even believing in the divine.

Her reflexive cynicism kept trying to assert itself and explain away his chivalrous behavior as a ploy to lull her into trusting him so he could use her body like so many others had. But each time she started believing that, one look into his chubby round face and his honest eyes quashed such suspicions. Irvis, for all his faults, was genuine.

She found herself lying in his lap letting him stroke her gray hair. "Why?" Her voice was quiet, but in the peacefulness of the garden, it still sounded loud.

"Why what?"

"Why do you love me?"

His gentle stroking lost its steady rhythm, and he froze.

"It's okay if you don't have an answer." She closed her eyes as he resumed stroking her hair.

"No, I do." He spoke with a confidence she'd only heard in his tone when he preached about the goddess.

She opened her eyes, surprised once more by this strangely incongruous man. Faithful but lustful, attractive though homely, and confident even in his self-effacing humility.

"What is it then?"

Irvis didn't respond for a long time, and Graelle was about to ask again when he said, "Do you see that white flower?"

Graelle glanced at the glowing lily. "It's beautiful–has magic for certain."

"It's called a Spirit lily," Irvis said. "They're extremely rare, and grow only near an Apeira well. You see, they drink in Apeiron instead of sunlight and water."

That explained the flower's other-worldly appearance.

"Some people believe that you can commune with the souls of your lost loved ones through a Spirit lily, but my brotherhood deems that heretical superstition. Yet, there are those even among the monks of Rasheera who claim to have heard a voice speaking to them through the flower."

Graelle turned her head to look up at Irvis. "They talk?"

He nodded. "I was intrigued by this, and so made a study of it under the guise of trying to understand doctrines that led the Divine Mother's children away from her. My research was well received, and I was charged with investigating such a case in a village north of Rasha. While I was expected to evaluate the supernatural claims being made by the villagers and even one acolyte, the brethren primarily wanted me to quash the stories, teach, and correct the people, and if necessary destroy the flower."

Graelle scoffed and turned her head back to let Irvis resume stroking her hair. "Intolerant zealots."

"Perhaps. But the monks mean well. And we..." he choked back a sob "...they do a lot of good, healing the sick and caring for the poor."

Graelle didn't comment any further. Before she met Irvis, she'd considered all ecclesiastical authorities dogmatic tyrants at worst, and manipulative hypocrites at best. But she knew how much Irvis loved his religion and also how it pained him to now be an outcast.

"When I got to the village, after meeting their elder who, though my age, had a young and extraordinarily attractive wife with perfect breasts and..."

Graelle pointed and cleared her throat.

Irvis chuckled. "Right. My apologies. Their elder took me to see the flower. It'd grown under a tree in the midst of a manicured garden the villagers said had appeared on its own. I didn't find an Apeira well, but guessed it was some hundreds of feet underground as my purification ring recharged.

"Next, I interviewed the villagers who claimed the Spirit lily had spoken to them. There were two dozen or so, but I was able to winnow that down to just a handful of people who weren't telling tales or seeking attention. One in particular, an old woman, impressed me the most. She said the flower had spoken to her as with the voice of a child, reassuring her that her recently departed husband's soul lived on. This is remarkable because the old woman had heard the Spirit lily call to her as she was shuffling out of the village at night on her way to leap off a nearby ravine, so lonely and grief-stricken she had become."

"But it wasn't her husband that spoke to her?" Graelle glanced to the far side of the glowing white flower where the boy, Jekaran, lay on the grass, the muscular mercenary sitting cross-legged next to him.

"No. And that's one of the reasons it caught my attention." His hand stopped stroking her hair, but he left it gently resting on her temple. "Most of the others reported dead children and wives and even the spirit of an old king speaking to them, telling them all sorts of nonsensical things like where to find buried treasure, or telling them they should lead the village, or leave their wife–all of it self-serving garbage talk. But this old woman's account rang true. It stood out much like this flower stands out against its backdrop of green."

"Poetic."

Irvis snorted in response, which somewhat ruined the effect. "I determined that the flower could not be anything evil, for it provided beauty, life, and peace. The three cardinal Rasheeran tenants that describe the Divine Mother.

"Now, I mentioned the elder's wife for a reason. While on this mission I was taken by one of my lustful moods. As always, I fought it for a time, but before I knew it, I was sneaking around the elder's home at night, trying to catch his beautiful wife... in an immodest moment."

Graelle smiled. Though Irvis was honest about his failings, he still couched them in tactful language in an attempt to minimize their seriousness.

"I wasn't caught, except by my own shame. I was overcome with remorse, and self-loathing, and retreated to the garden where the Spirit lily grew. There I knelt in prayer for hours, begging the Divine Mother for forgiveness, and pleading with her to cure my wicked inclination. A cure I repeated over and over again, all I desire is a cure, I sobbed.

"Finally, when the aching of my knees and the sheer emotional exhaustion became too much, I stood to leave. That's when I heard the voice."

"The Spirit lily?" Graelle scrutinized the white petals of the flower.

"It came to me in the voice of a little girl."

"What did she say?"

Irvis hesitated. "Now this is the part you are sure to find difficult to accept."

She scoffed. "We are sitting in a garden of a tower in the legendary lost city of the Allosians discussing a talking flower while the world outside is supposedly ending. I am very much beyond difficult to accept."

Irvis gently took her shoulders, sat her up, and turned her so that the two were facing each other. "The little girl voice said to me this is your cure, and then..."

Irvis glanced away, his chubby face flushing red.

Graelle furrowed her brow. "What?"

"The flower showed me a vision."

"What did you see?" She lovingly rubbed his arm. This was obviously difficult, and she was trying to be encouraging.

Irvis met her eyes. "I saw you."

Graelle hadn't expected him to say that.

She pulled her hand back. "What do you mean you saw me?"

"I saw you, but it was more than just seeing. I felt your soul, and knew you. I saw your life. I saw your struggles, I saw when your only remaining family, a sister, turned her back on you. I saw you degrading yourself to survive, I saw you kill—"

"Stop it!" Graelle shook her head. "That's impossible."

Irvis flashed a sad smile. "But most of all, I felt something I'd never felt before. It was strong, and invincible. It swept away my petty lusts and I knew what it was–love."

Tears rolled down Graelle's cheeks. She stared at the Spirit lily, ashamed that Irvis was seeing her cry. "H-how long ago was that?"

"Years ago."

Graelle sniffed. "Then why didn't you come to me sooner?"

"I didn't know who you were. I mean, I knew that you were a Rikujo guild boss, but I didn't know what you looked like and so I couldn't make the connection. Besides, I was supposed to be celibate. Finding you meant leaving the brotherhood, and I wasn't ready for that." He cupped her chin and gently turned her face back to look at him. "But when I saw you in Imaris, I remembered the vision."

Could it really be true? It wasn't the supernatural powers at play that warred with Graelle's acceptance of the story, but her own sense of self-loathing and worthlessness. Why would any god or goddess recommend her to a man like Irvis? Someone who, despite his flaws, was earnestly trying to follow a path to the divine?

"I..." Graelle began.

Shouting.

They both turned toward the direction of the garden's entrance–which was mostly concealed by greenery–and jumped when Lord Gymal rushed in. And he wasn't alone. A young woman with tan skin and black hair worn in a ponytail, ran in after him followed by...

"Mulladin!" Irvis shouted. He scrambled to his feet and then helped her to stand, keeping an arm around her waist. "Where have..."

Graelle felt Irvis stiffen. "Divine Mother!"

Graelle didn't know what had stunned Irvis, but her gaze settled on a finely crafted weapon Mulladin held in his hand. It had a large amethyst jewel in the center of its cross guard and a sleek blade peppered with tiny emeralds. Graelle knew that weapon. She'd seen it hanging at the waist of Argentus himself. It was the sword of the Invincible Shadow.

Chapter 98

Kairah's spell-casting was growing weaker. To her mounting horror, it'd become impossible for her to cast from the Third Discipline–Space, and the Fourth Discipline–the collection of spells that made up the Sensory discipline. That was likely the reason she could no longer communicate with Aeva when out of the Spirit lily's immediate presence. Of course, that didn't account for her not being able to speak with Aeva when she briefly visited her after taking Jekaran and the others to her apartments. Was that three days ago, or four? She was losing track of time. Another symptom of my deteriorating state? Or was it just that Shivara was working her relentlessly?

The eccentric Allosian oracle had Kairah sitting in the silver chair–a talis Shivara named the Zikkurat–for hours at a time, after which she would demand detailed accounts of what Kairah saw. Apparently, only one with the ability to see the weaves of fate could use this particular talis. Kairah didn't know why Shivara never sat in the chair herself, but assumed it to be part of the oracle's training.

While all of Kairah's other spell-casting powers were diminishing–even her prodigious talent in the First Discipline, Creation, was suffering–her sense of fate and ability to see into time remained strong. Perhaps that was the purpose of Shivara making her use the Zikkurat so much? Could constant use of Apeiron to cast certain spells slow Moriora's creeping corruption? Like a muscle being exercised to avoid atrophy?

Her latest excursion of seer-ship ended, and Kairah leaned forward in the chair. She was growing physically tired, something that shouldn't be happening in the presence of the Mother Shard. She wiped her forehead with the back of her hand.

Shivara immediately began her interrogation. "Did you see him?"

Why can she not give me a moment's rest?

Kairah shook her head. "I saw a swarm of locusts descending on a bountiful field of wheat. A white eagle followed, intent on devouring them. An army of little reptiles awaited the swarm, but the locusts had stingers with venom strong enough to kill both the lizards and the eagle, and..."

"No, child," Shivara snapped. "The future is protected by a strata of symbolism designed to veil its true meaning. An oracle has to push through that imagery to see the true vision. You have to cast your mind forth and not let distraction slow your momentum. Otherwise you will not punch through the stream of time."

"I apologize, mistress. I am fatigued. Perhaps that is making it difficult for me to reach the highest state of seeing."

Shivara stared at her for a long moment. "It's the corruption." She turned away and idly spun a metal spiral resting on one of the room's many tables. "It's making your body less able to absorb Apeiron, and so you will start wanting to sleep, and"—she hesitated—"eat. I will have Etele fetch you some fruit."

The willowy girl entered the room immediately as though she'd been waiting just outside the door for Shivara's telepathic call. But perhaps that wasn't the case. The woman stepped up to Shivara and stared her in the eyes. As always, Etele did not utter a single word and so their communication must've been psychic.

"At the College of Disciplines?" Shivara answered back aloud, like Kairah did with Aeva whenever possible. Contrary to what Kairah originally thought, it was as if Shivara was weak in the Fourth Discipline, like Kairah herself. For she always addressed Etele audibly.

I am entirely powerless in that Discipline now. The thought was bitter and stoked the quick fires of Kairah's increasingly chaotic anger. She reined it in.

Most Allosian spell-casters when in the presence of an Aeose would spell-cast for even the most trivial of reasons. In fact, they were encouraged by their teachers to do so whenever they could and for whatever reason. It helped train them, and develop their abilities. Shivara wasn't like that. She employed a lot of talises, none of which she used directly.

Well, she is almost a thousand years old. Perhaps her conservative nature is a holdover from a different time.

Shivara's age still astonished Kairah. She'd been told all her life that Allosians rarely reached more than four centuries in age. Yet this woman had existed for over twice that, still looking as young as Kairah herself.

"That doesn't concern me. Go." Shivara waved a hand at Etele. "Fetch Kairah some of those blue bulbs from the Levanta tree you've been cultivating."

Etele nodded obediently and then disappeared through the doorway.

"Thank you, mistress."

Shivara smiled. "Tell me again of the man you saw in your initial vision."

That irritated Kairah. Shivara was obsessed over the being with metallic-gold hair, the one who'd appeared to a clandestine circle of human worshippers and given them something. "He was tall, perfectly proportioned, had shoulder-length glowing hair the color of burnished gold. He wore a sleeveless robe of white that also appeared to glow, and—"

"And he said nothing to you?"

Kairah hesitated. The oracle hadn't asked that question before. "No, mistress. I was but an invisible observer of all the events in that vision–as always."

Shivara glared at Kairah. It was a look of such sharp anger and accusation that Kairah actually sat back in the chair, as though too close to a burning flame.

Why is she angry with me? If Kairah didn't know better, Shivara looked as though she were reacting to someone lying to her.

The expression passed as fast as it had come, and Shivara replaced it with another one of her smiles. "It will take Etele several minutes to return with the fruit. Why don't we invoke one more vision and then we can rest for a while."

That sounded very appealing. Kairah nodded, trying to ignore her increasingly demanding hunger pangs and sat back in the Zikkurat. She closed her eyes and let the talis's disconcerting sensation of detachment wash over her. It swept away her sense of physical self, which did make her hunger and fatigue fade into background noise.

"Try again to direct the vision," Shivara said from somewhere far away. "Channel them as they come, ignoring irrelevant details and focusing on what it is you need to see."

The prospect of controlling her oracular experiences was new to Kairah. It made sense though. An oracle wouldn't be as valuable if she couldn't find answers to specific questions. She regretted more and more procrastinating her training with Shivara.

"Think on the man with the gold hair." Shivara's voice was no more than an echo now.

Kairah tried to do as Shivara wanted, but each time she entered the Zikkurat's trance, the golden-haired man seemed unimportant. Other matters drew her clairvoyant attention. Clouds of thickening blackness unfurled up and down the continent's western coast, emerald lightning striking down upon the land accompanied by a translucent green wind that destroyed everything it touched.

Past or future?

She often grappled with the difficulty of placing the chronology of what she was seeing. Sometimes a vision would start in the past and then suddenly shift to the future. Kairah wasn't certain how she could tell, but found that scrutinizing the images eventually yielded the answer as to whether she was seeing history or prophecy.

A nagging fear rose in her mind. What she was seeing was neither past nor future, but the present. This was happening now. Moriora's vessel, Karak's Eater, was sucking the life from the world on a massive scale.

Karak was right; he did not die in Taris. He has become far more powerful, his reach exponentially wider. I have to stop this!

Kairah wrestled with the stream of information deluging her, focusing not on Shivara's question, but on her own need. *Where was the Eater? How was he doing this? How could she destroy him before he destroyed them all?*

Kairah felt the vision contorting, shifting, changing shape. It was as if she were bending a bar of metal, difficult but with the right amount of pressure... Again, ancient Allose appeared before her, but it was populated not by Allosians, but humans.

Thousands gathered around the base of three mountainous staircases leading up to a circular platform at the top. Kairah had seen this structure in her first vision, though now hundreds did gather on the platform, all bowing reverently. A column of white light descended from above, touching the center of the platform. When it faded, the silver-haired woman stood in the center of the kneeling humans. She smiled at them, as a parent smiles lovingly at their playing children.

The blonde woman with the familiar face Kairah had seen in her first vision, the one who secretly communed with the apparition of the golden-haired man, rose before the goddess. Her hands were locked together as if in pleading. The goddess smiled indulgently, glanced around the crowd, and then nodded. She raised an open hand and white light coalesced into a pulsating orb, like a miniature sun. The sphere of perfect white energy faded, leaving behind a small object in the goddess's hand–a ring.

Kairah scrutinized the ring and immediately could make out the etchings of lilies running along its silver band. She knew that talis. It was the ring the human Irvis had found, the talis that produced an energy stronger and purer than Apeiron.

The silver-haired goddess slumped her shoulders as if weary. The blonde woman nodded at a man to her right who reached out and collected the ring from the goddess. She gave the man a tired smile and then met the eyes of the blonde woman standing directly in front of her. Something seemed to pass between them, and then the blonde woman's blue eyes hardened. She whipped up her right hand and manifested a ball of emerald energy in the shape of a flickering flame. The goddess's eyes widened, and she leapt back, throwing both of her arms out in the process, palms turned out as if to push back an attacker.

A heartbeat later the green flame exploded into a beam of energy that struck for the silver-haired woman's heart. It smashed against an invisible wall just inches from the goddess's palms. The beam of emerald light split into five crackling bolts of electricity arcing wildly in the air. The five lines of green lightning encircled a translucent sphere that had formed around the goddess. The glass-like sphere expanded outward, and the green electricity wove together around it.

The blonde woman's eyes widened, and she retreated, pushing through the crowd of on-looking humans and flying down the stairs. A few others followed–members of the woman's cabal to be sure. Waves of power erupted from the cage of green lightning surrounding the goddess and her protective barrier, and the ground shook.

The crowd of humans standing on the platform fled, joining the throng of thousands watching from below into a wild mob of chaotic flight. The stairs supporting the platform swayed, shook, cracked, and then collapsed. The circular platform fell away, leaving the goddess, her barrier, and its cage of electricity hanging in the empty air.

Pulses of white light pushed through the green electricity, but dimmed upon contact, and changed to a purple Kairah knew all too well–Apeiron. The blasts of white, then purple energy increased until they shot out from the goddess in every direction. The cage of emerald lightning, however, did not dissipate. It expanded with each wave of the goddess's repelling spell, and amethyst crystal formed like frost and started encasing the green power that attempted to crush her.

The ball of warring colors fell from the air and smashed into the pavement below with an explosion that rocked the entire city. Fissures snaked out from the point of impact, breaking up manicured stone and causing buildings to sway and collapse. The light from the explosion faded, although Allose continued to shake with increasingly violent quakes. At the point of impact there was a hole in the ground opening into a bottomless shaft. Apeiron, like a geyser of purple lava, shot thousands of feet into the air. It slowly crystalized and hardened into a towering amethyst obelisk; the Mother Shard.

Smaller towers of purple crystal erupted from the ground all over Shaelar, many of them exploding up through cities in seismic catastrophes that killed thousands.

The vision shifted.

The blonde woman with her group of conspirators stood at the base of the Mother Shard. Their eyes were closed and they were chanting something Kairah couldn't hear. When they finished their spell, a blast of Apeiron exploded from the Mother Shard, expanding outward across the continent.

As the wave of power passed through the blonde woman, her hair and eyes changed. No longer did she have curly yellow tresses, but instead long, straight strands of jewel-colored hair fell to her shoulders. Her eyes changed to purple, and the peach color of her skin paled to an alabaster white. As the wave of power passed over the land, it wrought like changes in all the humans it touched. But the pulse of Apeiron weakened the farther from the Mother Shard it traveled only to dissipate entirely before it could reach all the cities in Shaelar.

The millions of humans that remained unchanged were located mostly on the western half of Shaelar's ancient super continent. Kairah saw them band together over the years, joining thousands of Allosians to oppose what had been done to their goddess. They made talises of all varieties for the humans, talises to aid in everyday life and travel. But mostly, they created weapons.

Kairah saw the humans, aided by their comparatively few Allosian allies, marching against others of their kind in battles and fighting with displays of incredible power. The war lasted for decades, with the human rebels gaining little ground. Emissaries from Allose were sent to the west to broker peace with the humans. Included among the envoy were some of the original conspirators who had aided the blonde woman in her treachery against the goddess. They lived among the humans, preaching to them in an effort to sway them to their side. More years passed, and while open war had ceased, the battle raged on in argument and politics.

The scene shifted again to the nightmare Kairah had already beheld. Moriora vessels attacking Allosians and humans, an emerald-colored Apeira well cracked and broken. A massive quake collapsing thousands of miles and replacing them with what was now the west sea. It continued longer than it had the first time, showing Kairah the humans, now separated by an ocean, hastily building a fleet of wooden ships. No more Allosians could be found among them, but Kairah did see that some of the humans now had green eyes. They abandoned their ruined cities and homes, launching into an unfamiliar sea under a sky churning with black clouds and illuminated by flashes of green lightning.

Kairah found herself vomiting on the polished marble floor of Shivara's study. Tears poured down her cheeks and blood ran from her nose. She looked up to find Shivara staring down at her. There was no empathy or even the slightest bit of concern in the oracle's face–just coldness.

"Did you see him, Kairah?"

An invisible dagger of ice stabbed Kairah square in the chest. She now knew why the face of the blonde woman from the vision looked so familiar; it was the very same face she was staring at.

Chapter 99

Mulladin stared down at Jekaran's catatonic face. His eyes blinked but were unfocused and empty. He breathed, but with it came drool bubbling out the side of his mouth. It made Mulladin want to weep. He'd always looked up to Jekaran, a man younger than he was, but someone who always treated him like a brother. Jekaran defended Mulladin when the other children in the village bullied him. He wrestled with Mulladin and helped him with his chores. He never showed irritation with Mulladin, though he knew that in his dim state he'd sometimes been overbearing and needy. Jekaran was a true friend, his best friend. It was heartbreaking to see the normally active, vibrant, and expressive young man lying in a state of living death.

That is one handsome guy, the sword said.

Mulladin would've laughed if he weren't fighting so hard to choke back tears.

"Mulladin, how did you find that?" Irvis motioned at the sword. "How did you find us? Where's Karak?"

Mulladin shook his head. "We don't have time for the story. We've got over a dozen Allosian soldiers hunting for us, and they are probably pretty angry. As soon as they figure out where we've gone they'll be here in a flash...literally."

Irvis's face paled. "What have you done?"

Mulladin flashed Irvis a wicked grin and then knelt next to Jekaran's body. Gymal's muscular mercenary put a non-threatening, but very firm hand on Mulladin's shoulder. "What're you about, boy?"

Boy?

Mulladin threw off the mercenary's hand and stared him down. "I'm trying to help him." He glanced about the garden. "Where's Kairah?"

"We haven't seen her in days," Graelle said.

"Damn it!" Mulladin shouted.

"Mulladin." Irvis knelt beside him. "We tried to have Jekaran healed, and Allose's most powerful healers couldn't restore him. They said there was a piece of his mind that was missing."

"I know!" Mulladin held up the sword. "It's in here!"

Irvis glanced at Graelle. "I don't understand."

"It's true," Keesa said. "My cousin's soul is trapped within the blade."

"Did she say cousin?" Irvis asked.

"And just who are you, anyway?" Gymal snapped.

"I'm the one who helped save your ass!" Keesa glanced down at the little lord, who was standing only a few paces away. The contrast was humorous, but again Mulladin didn't feel like laughing, not after seeing Jek like this.

To his credit, Gymal didn't back down. "And I'm the one who helped save yours!"

"We don't have time for this!" Mulladin shouted. His anger was rising quickly and frayed nerves, exhaustion, and eighteen years' worth of new emotions all at once was making it very difficult to control.

As if to punctuate his words, a talis mounted above the entrance to the atrium chimed and a disembodied voice asked, "Lady Kairah?"

"Divine Mother! They've found us!" He glanced down at the silver bracelet he wore on his skinny wrist–one of their stolen displacement talises. Gymal looked up with wide eyes and a paling face. "Someone's activated a warding stone. We're trapped!"

"We can't teleport out, but that also means they can't teleport in," Keesa said.

"Until they've assessed our situation and are ready to strike," Hort said.

"You, girl." Graelle pointed at Keesa. "Go answer that and pretend to be Kairah."

"What?" Keesa shot an incredulous look at Mulladin. "I don't even know the woman!"

"Just talk like a noble!" Graelle snapped. "And try to convince them we're not here. Stall them as long as possible."

Keesa's ponytail wagged as she nodded and hurried off.

"Lord Gymal." Graelle pointed at the weaselly little lord. "Go search this place for talises. Find something we can use to defend ourselves."

Hort met Mulladin's eyes. "He has the sword. Can't we use that?"

Mulladin shook his head. "We're going to need it to heal Jek."

Gymal scowled at Graelle but moved off to do as she'd ordered. "Come help me, mercenary," he called back.

"Find them your own damn self!"

Gymal stopped, turned, and shot a surprised look at Hort. It disappeared as the little lord's face reddened. "How dare you defy me? I hired you to—"

"I resign!" Hort shouted.

Gymal blinked stupidly. "You what?"

Hort turned around and took a threatening step toward Gymal. "I've had enough of you, you whiney little troll! I'm done!"

Gymal lingered, his expression vacillating between rage and shock.

"Now get your bugger-lovin' ass out there and find us talises!"

That made Gymal turn and hurry out of the atrium.

Oh, that was delicious! The sword chuckled. *I think I'm starting to like that big mercenary.*

Mulladin set the sword on Jekaran's chest and picked up his hand and placed it on the handle.

Nothing happened.

Mull? What're you doing?

"Come on!" He'd hoped simple contact in the presence of an Apeira well would re-bond Jekaran to the sword and fix his mind. "Come on, Jek! We need you!"

He grimaced. Was he bonded to the sword? Did they need to break the bond before Jekaran could reconnect with it? Linked to the sword he was, but it was a tenuous connection and Jek could withdraw his consciousness at any time, especially when... "Ez!" Mulladin blurted out.

As always, the psychic presence of the sword's consciousness winked out, and Mulladin was left alone with his thoughts. He waited patiently for the sword to reawaken, but when the round amethyst started to glow again, nothing changed. "Come on!"

"No, they doth not be with me here in my domicile," Keesa intoned from several feet away.

"By Rasheera's breasts!" Graelle swore. "She's as terrible as a first week girl feigning ecstasy. They'll know we're here for sure!"

Irvis placed a hand on Mulladin's shoulder. "I might be able to help."

Mulladin looked up at the chubby monk. "How?"

Irvis produced a small sliver ring from his trouser pocket. It was a unique design, with etched flowers on the band. Mulladin recognized it immediately. "That's the ring that healed me."

Irvis nodded. "It didn't work the first time we tried it on him, but maybe now that you've brought the sword back..."

Mulladin stood. "Do it!"

Irvis sucked in a deep breath and nodded. He twisted the ring onto a chubby finger and then knelt next to Jekaran and placed a hand on the boy's forehead. Irvis closed his eyes and furrowed his brow. Mulladin held his breath and watched as Irvis ministered for a full minute before the monk exhaled and sat back on his haunches. He shook his head.

"Dammit!" Mulladin tore a branch off a small tree and hurled it at a glass wall. The glass didn't shatter or even crack, which only aggravated his anger.

"I'm sorry." A tear rolled down Irvis's cheek. "I can sense that all the fragments of his mind are there, they just won't fuse back together. I don't understand why."

Mulladin fell to his knees. "All that for nothing!" He bent over and hugged his middle, trying to warm away the sudden onset of cold nausea.

What's wrong, Mull? The sword asked.

Why could he still hear it? Hadn't he broken their link? Mulladin's ignorance of talis-craft and the arcane in general had never been so humiliating.

"I need you to rejoin with your body."

My body is a sword.

Mulladin pointed at Jekaran's still form. "No, that's your body!"

You're talking crazy, Mull.

"Don't you remember being human? Don't you remember growing up with me and Maely in Genra? Have you forgotten our lives together? How can you not remember Harvest Festival three years ago when you had me help you pour a bucket of freezing water on Ez, and…"

The sword's presence again vanished from Mulladin's mind. He shot a look at Irvis.

"What?" the chubby monk asked.

"Every time I mention Ez to the sword, it retreats from my mind for a moment. When it returns, it's like it's forgotten recent events and everything except who I am."

"It's the trauma of causing Argentus's death." Irvis nodded to himself. "I've seen something like this before. A man brought his wife to the monastery. She was catatonic, and he explained she'd been that way since accidentally smothering her newborn child in her sleep."

"How'd you help her?"

"Well, a regular talis healing wouldn't work. They never do on ailments of the mind. So we summoned the handmaidens from the Rasha convent, and they took her in and cared for her until the brotherhood could requisition a soul speaker–a kind of talis that lets humans communicate psychically."

"Did that work?"

Irvis shook his head. "The monk who went inside her mind found that she did not want to come back from her broken state. To do so, she'd have to face the pain and guilt of what she'd done."

"What happened to her?"

"She eventually died while still young. The sorrow was just too much for her."

"Well, that's not very encouraging."

Irvis frowned at him. "Jekaran is made of stronger stuff. If we could communicate with his core consciousness, and convince him that Argentus's death wasn't his fault, he might come back to us."

Mulladin pounded the ground with a fist. "Only we don't have a soul speaker!"

Irvis stared at the sword resting on Jekaran's chest. "We may not need one."

Mulladin followed his gaze to the sword. "I just told you! Every time I bring up Ez, Jekaran hides and forgets."

Keesa ran over to them. "They saw through my rouse. Peacekeepers are already on their way."

"Well maybe if you would've left out the word domicile! I thought you were training to impersonate a noble?"

"My focus was on the education. I hadn't learned the acting part yet!"

Mull! The sword said as it reawakened.

Irvis grabbed Mulladin's hand and placed it on the amethyst jewel in the pommel of the sword. Then he brought Jekaran's hand up and similarly positioned it.

"What are you doing?"

Irvis laid his hand adorned with the silver ring on top of both Jek's and Mulladin's hands. "I'm going to start infusing the sword with energy."

"You can't do that with a talis," Keesa objected.

"I can with this one!" Irvis met Mulladin's eyes. "I'm going to try to heal the connection. If this works, you might be able to communicate with Jekaran. If so, then try to convince him to let me heal him. If he allows it, I think I can bring him back."

"That's a lot of ifs, Irvis."

Another chime from the speaking stone rang through the atrium.

Mulladin glanced at Keesa and then back at the round-faced monk. "Do it!"

The world went white.

Mulladin found himself walking into a forest clearing. Gone was Kairah's garden, Keesa, Irvis, and the others. He was alone. Mulladin glanced around and immediately recognized the place.

This is where Jek and I come to wrestle.

Movement from behind.

Mulladin whirled just in time to see Jekaran jog out of the trees. He smiled broadly at Mulladin. "You beat me here."

Mulladin just stared. "Jek..."

Jekaran hardily slapped him on the back. "You're different."

"Yeah. Irvis healed..." Disorientation faded and Mulladin remembered that he wasn't actually back in Genra, but inside Jek's mind. "It worked."

"I'll say it did! You sound like a regular man." Jekaran laughed. "Incredible!"

"Listen, Jek, I need you to come back."

Jekaran frowned. "But we just got here. We go back now and Maely will make you muck the cattle stalls."

"That's not what I mean." Mulladin gestured to the trees and sky. "This place isn't real. We're actually in Kairah's garden. Your mind broke apart and we're trying to put it back together."

Jekaran forced a laugh. "I have no idea what you're talking about."

"Right." Mulladin nodded to himself. "Tell me, what's the last thing you remember?"

Jekaran's smile disappeared. "Racing you here?"

"No, before that."

"You okay, Mull? You're not making any sense."

Mulladin kneaded his forehead with the heel of his hand. "Do you remember your trip to Aiested?"

"Yeah! That city is incredible!"

"Do you remember what happened there?"

Jek's eyes flicked to the ground. "Mull, why're you going on like this?"

"Do you remember fighting the king's guards?"

Jekaran stepped further into the clearing. "Come on, let's start. I learned a new hold from Hyric that I think you'll—"

"Do you remember killing Ez?"

Jekaran froze, his back still to Mulladin.

"You do, don't you?" Mulladin took a step toward him.

Jekaran shook his head. "Ez went into town to get a cut of—"

"Ez died!" Mulladin shouted. "You ran him through with the sword."

"Nice try, Mull." Jekaran spun around and forced a smile. "But you'll have to come up with something better if you're going to fool me. And next time don't be so morbid."

Mulladin stepped up to Jekaran and gently grabbed his shoulders. "It wasn't your fault."

Jekaran surprised him by shoving him away. "Stop trying to prank me."

"If this really is a joke, then why are you getting upset? I've never seen you get angry over a prank."

Jekaran didn't answer.

"It was the sword, Jek. It had you in a battle frenzy and Ez just got in the way."

Jekaran grabbed the sides of his head with his hands. "No!"

Mulladin stepped in again. "You need to face this and forgive yourself. If you don't, then you'll die. And we need your help right now! Kairah's missing, the world is falling apart, and we're about to be captured!"

"I don't think I'm in the mood to wrestle anymore." Jek turned to leave the clearing, but Mulladin grabbed his arm.

Jekaran scowled down at Mulladin's hand. "Let go of me, Mull!"

"Jek, please listen. Ez told me something before he died."

Jekaran yanked his arm free.

"He told me about the Lure of Fools poem. He told me he taught it to you to try to keep you from following in his footsteps."

"Adventure is the Lure of Fools..." Jekaran murmured.

Mulladin nodded. "That's the one. But what he didn't tell you is that there was another part of it;

But closely resemble they one another, both heroes and fools at first, and it's only at the fork of destiny's road that the truth will at last emerge. For while the fool always looks to his own regard, the hero for others is er' aware. And will suffer and die when called upon, even for strangers in his care.

"He said that he was proud of you for only using the sword to protect others. He said that you were not a fool, but a hero."

Jekaran shook his head. "I don't know what you're talking about. Ez is—"

"Dead Jekaran. Ez is dead!"

"Get out."

"Jek please. We need your—"

"I said get out!" Jekaran shoved him hard in the chest.

Mulladin found himself staring up at the atrium's glass dome. He was lying on the stone walkway of Kairah's garden, the back of his head throbbing. Keesa looked down at him, her eyes wide.

"Mull?" she asked, her voice on the edge of hysteria.

Irvis's round face appeared. "Are you okay, boy?"

Keesa helped Mulladin sit up. He was no longer near Jekaran's body, but on the ground, ten paces now separating them. "What happened?"

"The sword flashed and you were thrown back," Keesa said.

Mulladin touched the side of his head and nodded. "We were in Genra, and he acted like everything was normal until I brought up Ez. Then he got angry and told me to leave." Mulladin stood.

Irvis glanced back at Jekaran. "It sounds like he's lost inside his memories."

Mulladin shook his head. "Not lost. He's hiding."

He strode back and knelt again at Jekaran's side. He stretched out his hand and reached for the sword. As soon as his fingers touched the hilt, pain exploded in his mind. He snapped his hand back and the pain abruptly vanished.

"What's wrong?"

"He's shut me out."

Gymal burst into the atrium carrying two objects: a three-foot long rod of polished obsidian capped with an amethyst jewel, and a choker made of gold. "This is the best I could find." He tossed Hort the black rod, and the choker to Graelle.

Hort's eyes widened and he grinned. "A void scepter."

Gymal nodded and pointed at Graelle. "And that's a shield talis. I figured out how to lock the outside doors, but I don't think that'll keep the peacekeepers out." He looked down at Jekaran. "Can you help him?"

Mulladin shook his head. "He won't let us."

The speaking stone mounted above the atrium door chimed again and a disembodied voice announced, "Human vandals. We know Lady Kairah is absent, and that you are hiding in her chambers. Dispossess yourself of talises and open the doors or we will force our way in."

Mulladin shared a look with Keesa.

They were out of time.

CHAPTER 100

K airah put the Zikkurat between her and Shivara. "It was you!"

"Answer my question, child." Shivara took a step toward her.

Kairah trembled with a mixture of fear and rage. "You caused all of this!"

"Did you speak with him?" Shivara shouted, her usually calm demeanor giving way to a wide-eyed feral look. "I know Boulos reached out to you once. I can sense his imprint on your soul."

Boulos? "The being with golden hair?" Kairah hadn't ever spoken to such a being. Unless... "The voice I heard in my vision of the dead land. That was him?"

"Yes!" Shivara took a step toward her. "Did he give you a message? Is he pleased with the fire I've started? What am I supposed to do now?"

Fire?

Kairah stepped backward, colliding with a table and knocking several glass instruments onto the floor where they shattered. "I saw only the past. When you communed with him and he gave you the power to strike at the woman with silver hair."

Shivara's eyes narrowed. "You saw her, did you?"

Kairah took a slow step to her right. "She is real then? The goddess Rasheera?"

Shivara scoffed. "She always made us call her Mother. And yes, she is very real, but I wouldn't call her a goddess."

Kairah inched to her right, preparing to break for one of the chamber's doors. "Did she not create Shaelar? Did she not create us?"

Shivara took another step toward Kairah. "She is one of the ascended; a race of immortal beings who spell-cast on a level far beyond anything we can achieve. But a goddess?" Shivara shook her head. "What kind of goddess could be deceived and trapped by her own children?"

Aeva! Kairah strained her will, but the mental call never left her skull. She no longer had the ability to spell-cast from the Fourth Discipline.

"So that is what you did? You trapped her in the center of the planet? In a cage of crystal?"

"That was not our plan." Shivara stepped to the right, casually matching Kairah's slow movement toward the door. They stared at each other across the row of instrument filled tables, separated only by a few feet. "We were supposed to kill her."

Though weak, Kairah readied a spell from the Second Discipline–a simple ball of fire. She was too weak to fight Shivara, but if it gave her the distraction she needed to run...

"How do you kill an immortal being?"

Shivara flashed a toothy smile. "By exploiting her weakness."

"Gods do not have weaknesses."

Shivara laughed. "Compassion was her weakness. You see, Mother was going to leave us. She said we needed to prove to her and ourselves that we could hold to Seiro on our own..."

Seiro? Wasn't that the Ursaj code of honor?

"...show her that we could be obedient and benevolent without her here to guide us. If we could achieve this, she promised to share her immortality and power with us. She would ascend us to the plane of existence upon which she herself lived and teach us to spell-cast." Shivara's smile faded. "She was going to abandon us to a life of toil, disease, and death. No more would she provide us food, build us cities, or heal our injuries and sicknesses. We were going to have to learn how to survive on our own."

"Such is the way of all parent and child relationships."

"No!" Shivara swung an arm out and knocked a bronze cube supported by a metal rod onto the floor with a deep dong!

Kairah started and had to bite off a scream.

"What kind of mother abandons her children?" Shivara screamed. "Takes from them the comforts of home and exposes them to the dark?" Shivara calmed herself with a deliberately deep breath. "We had nowhere to turn. So we called out through the void of space, searching for someone to save us."

"Boulos?"

"Another ascended being." Shivara's smug smile returned. "He took pity on us, and promised to grant us immortality and the ability to spell-cast without our having to devolve into a helpless race of mortals first. He only required that we assassinate mother so he could take her place as our god.

"He changed my followers and I, gave us the power to spell-cast, taught us how to shield our minds, and instructed us to beg Mother to leave a portion of her power behind before she left us."

Kairah remembered the ring Rasheera had produced for Shivara in the vision, the same ring recovered by the human monk, Irvis. It radiated a power more potent than Apeiron, and had a healing power unmatched by any other talis.

Shivara glanced at the rings on her fingers. "This would weaken her, and make her vulnerable so I could strike at her."

The image of Shivara's blonde human self holding the green flame replayed before Kairah's mind. "With that Boulos's own power–Moriora?"

Shivara shook her head. "We created Moriora, not him."

Kairah remembered standing amid a city of bones staring up at black clouds lit by shafts of emerald lightning and asking an alien mind, "Who did this?" To which it responded, "You did."

Shivara's eyes unfocused as she stared at the past. "He showed us how to take the primal elements of existence and shape them into something that could physically manifest on our plane. He lent us a bit of his alien power to craft a magic out of the natural forces of decay and death. One touch from that corruption and Mother would wilt and die."

While Shivara wasn't looking, Kairah spell-cast a gentle gust of wind against the door and pushed it so it opened a few inches. She was relieved to find it unlocked, but even creating such a small blast of air was far more difficult than it ought to have been.

I do not have much time left.

"But you were not fast enough." Kairah's voice trembled.

Shivara's eyes refocused and she shot a glare at Kairah. "Mother was able to erect a shield in time to stop Moriora from touching her. But once the power was unleashed, it would not stop until it consumed her, and so it continued to press against her shield. She pushed back, but in her weakened state it took all of her power and concentration. The result was that all her other spells failed and she fell through the ground to the center of the planet. There she was able to create a pocket of reality where her plane and ours intersected, which somehow allowed her to halt my Moriora attack. The effort of maintaining the balance costs her dearly, though, and so she sleeps–paralyzed and vulnerable. And although Mother's power continues to radiate from her, it is corrupted and weakened when it passes through the Moriora web, crystalizing and eventually radiating Apeiron."

"And did you make the Apeira wells to feed on that power? To keep her weak?"

"You do me too much credit." Shivara laughed. "The Aeose are simply portions of Mother's crystal prison that she has pushed out from the center of the planet. After failing to kill Mother, our ascended patron ceased communing with us, although he did leave us with our gifts. So we used our ability to consume and manipulate energy to syphon the Apeiron. It extended our lives and changed our physical appearances to what the world commonly attributes to the racial features of an Allosian.

"Through experimentation we devised a means for sharing our gift with Mother's other children, though the process was imperfect, and left a great many without the blessings of longevity, eternal youth, and spell-casting enjoyed by those now called Allosians."

Kairah called to mind the vision of Shivara and her followers casting a spell at the base of the Mother shard, and the resultant wave of power that exploded across Shaelar.

"The humans. They are the original creation?"

Shivara smirked. "Most of them."

"What is that supposed to mean?"

"In its corrupted state, Mother's power did not grant us the immortality we sought. We could still succumb to injury and our bodies would simply cease to work after a few hundred years. We began to experiment with Moriora, and found that we could use it to draw in far more Apeiron than we otherwise could. We could also steal the life energy of other creations. This let us repair our bodies without healing spells, and stave off death indefinitely."

Horror stabbed Kairah in the heart. "You created the monsters I saw feeding on the humans."

Shivara nodded. "Those who experimented with Moriora found that the more life they consumed, the more they needed to sustain themselves. Those with weak wills quickly gave into their ever-growing appetites, and went insane. They would feed on anything they could.

"By this time, the humans and those Allosians ungrateful for what I'd given them, had gathered in the west and formed an army. Their intention was to march on Allose and free Mother from her prison. Those Allosians loyal to Mother devised a way to grant their human cousins access to spell-casting. That was the origin of talis craft. The traitors made weapon talises which they used against us. Unfortunately, those proved very effective, and so I was forced to call for a parlay."

"The ambassadors you sent to the opposition were infected with Moriora." Kairah shook her head. "You sent them to destroy the enemy army!"

"My original cadre of disciples. They had proven too weak willed to abstain from overindulging in the life force of other creatures." Shivara grinned. "So I sent them to our enemies and instructed them to use the same spell we'd used for turning humans into Allosians to spread their corruption and make more of what we called life-leeches. Though, that only worked on Allosians, and not in every case. Some were merely transformed back into humans, the only physical difference being that their eyes were green. Apparently, choice and one's disposition has something to do with that." Shivara waved a dismissive hand. "I never did puzzle that out."

Jekaran is descended from corrupted Allosians. That had apparently been what Aeva meant when she said Jekaran had Moriora in his blood.

"When my old friends had lost control and, with the new leeches they'd created, destroyed the opposition, we quarantined them by collapsing a large portion of the continent and raising the sea to bar their way. Though survivors showed up a few years later on the new western shore–a refugee army. They brought their talises with them, and with a fresh supply of Apeiron to charge them, they continued their war."

"The history we were taught...Humans were never the aggressors. They were the ones trying to save Rasheera and stop you." Kairah's fear was receding and quickly being replaced by a flame burning within her chest. "You made the creature that destroyed the well at Taris!"

Shivara belted out a loud laugh. "No, that was your brother. He came to me desperate for guidance on how to deal with his rage over the murder of your parents. I feigned a vision telling him that it was crucial for the survival of our species that he purge the land of humans, and that his tragedy was fate's way of choosing him to accomplish this. True, I taught him how to summon Moriora and cast the inversion spell, but the destruction he's wrought has all been of his own making."

Shivara was a monster with the blood of millions on her hands. She'd created Moriora and tried to slay her own creator. Worse, she had set Jenoc on the path of hate and revenge. Kairah flung out her hand and the fire of anger smoldering in her heart found expression in an eruption of very real flame. The stream of fire engulfed Shivara's bald head, and the woman stumbled backward with a scream.

Kairah broke right and ran for the door. She flung it the rest of the way open and exploded into a run. She'd only gone a few paces when something cold struck her in the back. She froze, unable to breath, speak or move as a familiar sensation thrilled through her. It felt like she was drawing on Apeiron, but instead of absorbing it, the energy flowed through and then out of her.

Shivara walked from behind Kairah and turned to look her directly in the eyes. The woman's head was a mass of smoldering black flesh, but didn't stay that way for long. The charred skin smoothed and pinked, her ears reformed, and eyes returned to their sockets–but they weren't eyes of purple as before. The color of Shivara's eyes were a bright emerald green. Hair sprouted from her bald head, but not the Allosian shade of amethyst. It was black, and lustrous, like Jekaran's.

Dozens of oddities suddenly made sense; the reason Shivara's talises drained when she touched them, why the oracle shaved her head, the purpose of the purple eye drops, and the uncomfortable tingle Kairah felt whenever the woman touched her.

Shivara was a Moriora vessel.

"You've seen much, Kairah. Far more than any of my other students. I was hoping your unusually strong oracular gifts would have allowed you to search out my ascended patron. Since I used up poor Etele, I haven't had anyone to sit in the Zikkurat, and I was hoping you would've remained ignorant long enough to make contact with Boulos. What a pity."

Shivara withdrew a small, thin tendril of translucent green energy from Kairah's back. She gasped and fell to the floor.

"Your sequestered apprentices," Kairah panted. "Just disposable tools to you, so you could continue using talises?"

Shivara examined a lock of her newly grown black hair. "Mainly so that I could use the Zikkurat, but also so I could be discreet in my feeding. Etele's predecessor, a girl whose name I forget–that does happen to one after she passes her first millennium of life–she was the only one of my students who managed to reach my former ascended patron, the first time I'd had contact with him in centuries. He promised me that if I started the fire for him, once the world burned down, he'd reward me with true immortality."

Shivara leaned down so that she was close enough to Kairah's face to kiss her. "I'm going to be a goddess, Kairah. And you're going to help me until you can no longer spell-cast. Then, once your transformation is complete, you will beg to join me just for the food I have to offer." Shivara stroked Kairah's cheek, the contact causing the same uncomfortable tingling sensation as before. "Immortality can be very lonesome. It will be nice to have a companion. You and I are going to be very close, Kairah." Shivara kissed her and Kairah seized, the contact pulling more Apeiron through her. It was just like when Moriora's vessel had kissed her back in Aiested–paralyzing.

Aeva! Kairah screamed inside her mind. *Rasheera! Mother!*

No one answered.

Visions of lustful men covered in blood and worse looming over her flooded back into her mind, and for a moment, Kairah was a young maid again on the floor of a human cottage; helpless and vulnerable. She put all her fear and desperation into one last mental scream and it actually broke free of her skull.

Jenoc! Help!

CHAPTER
101

The grass and trees withered as Jenoc passed, almost as if they were bowing to him. Their energy, paltry as it was, flowed into him, dulling his hunger pains and keeping him energized. He glanced at the thousands trundling along behind him–his children. They were his legacy, the tool by which he would end humanities dominance of Shaelar. They were the sword of his vengeance.

Jenoc was close now. He could feel the Apeiron radiating from the Mother Shard like a warm breeze. Even had he not known where his home was, he would've been able to find it by Apeiron's mouthwatering scent alone. Before his transformation, like all Allosians, he had been able to sense the Mother Shard from miles away, even take some of it into himself. But now his sense for the powerful energy had magnified a hundred-fold. He could taste the power like never before, but not partake of it. No, as he'd learned, he couldn't do that unless he was in direct contact with the Aeose–it was maddening.

They would cross the boundary soon, and then Allose would be visible. He had to make certain to reach the Mother Shard first, else one of his children were sure to feed on it and corrupt the Aeose before he could cast the spell that would transform all the green-eyed humans in Shaelar in to life-leeching creatures like himself. With his knowledge of the city he would have little problem beating the others to the Mother Shard. His children would also be distracted by the frenzy of feeding on new prey, Allosians filled with Apeiron. Each one like a miniature Aeose.

Yes, Jenoc would have little difficulty achieving his goal, realizing his revenge. His people would also die along with the humans. That was unfortunate, but Jenoc couldn't let sentiment get in the way of his destiny.

Kairah will die too.

Jenoc reached into his cloak pocket and fingered the jagged crystal edges of the geode he kept there. No. He couldn't let sentiment get in his way. It was his destiny to destroy the humans. The oracle had made that clear.

An explosion rocked the world.

Jenoc whirled to find a wide, deep crater where moments before had stood dozens of his children. A second blast of red fire erupted on his left flank. Cries of confusion and fright carried on the wind, and Jenoc spun about, searching his surroundings for the wielder of the flare talis. He could find no one. There were talises that allowed one to cast from a great distance, but those had passed into history during the war with the humans. So where could...

A shadow fell over his army, hundreds of feet long and nearly as wide. Jenoc looked up just in time to see something white block out the sun—an Allosian airship. A massive Allosian airship.

THE WIND WHIPPED Maely's hair and she trailed wisps of cloud as she dove toward Jenoc's army. At least that's how she imagined it. She actually couldn't see herself. All she saw was what Empyrean saw as it swooped like a hawk for a field mouse. Another red explosion bloomed from the ground, throwing up body parts and scattering Jenoc's soldiers.

"Bring us around for another pass," Raelen ordered.

He was standing beside her on a second smaller circular dais, though while piloting Empyrean, she couldn't see him. He had insisted she fly the ship so he could focus on attacking Jenoc's army of life-sucking monsters. She'd wanted to argue that she had as much right as Raelen did to see Jenoc dead, but the prince did have more experience using talises, specifically weapon talises. That, and well, he was the prince. You didn't argue with the prince.

Maely hadn't believed Raelen when he first told her about the creatures who fed on the essence of grass, trees, animals, and people. But following the trail of blackened, desolate ground had convinced her that the nightmare Raelen described was very real. It only made her more enraged at Kairah's brother. She may not be the one to cast the spell that would destroy Jenoc, but she was an integral part of the plan to bring about his demise. She wasn't sure if that would be enough to qualify as washing the mud off her fur, but it was going to have to be. Still, it felt a poor trade for the misery and death she'd helped to cause. Was there anything she could give to pay for her portion of what Jenoc had done?

Maely banked and turned so that she was flying at the mass of monsters instead of following them from behind. She swooped again, and Raelen cast two explosions simultaneously, leaving deep craters in the blackened ground. Empyrean had copied the spells laid on the wavy red sword called a flame kris, and at Raelen's direction, the ship was casting intense, scarlet explosions of fire he claimed were many times larger than the original talis could produce. It was impressive, but Maely wouldn't tell the sentient airship that. He was too uppity already, and didn't need a bigger head... well, if he had a head.

"Empyrean."

"Yes, Maely?"

"Can you make me see them up close, like through a looking glass?"

Maely flinched as the indecipherable mass suddenly leapt so close that she could see the haggard faces of each of the individual monsters in her view. She'd expected them to be snarling, fanged, creatures with red eyes and claws, but it disturbed her to see just how human they looked. They stared at the sky with wide eyes and gaping mouths. They were afraid, and Maely almost pitied them—almost.

She quickly scanned the mob for Jenoc, but found no heads of ice-blue hair in the crowd. "I don't see him!"

"He looks different now," Raelen answered. "Like one of us."

Maely looked from face to face, but didn't see Jenoc. Well, that just meant they'd have to burn them all.

JENOC WATCHED THE ENORMOUS, aerial construct–a craft that was more edifice than ship– bank and fly toward them. Two more explosions rocked the ground making him stumble. Who was this? Peacekeeper scouts? Certainly the ship had to have been sent by his people. Yet, Jenoc did not know Allose to be in possession of one of the ancient talises. All the Empyrean sky vessels were supposed to have been destroyed in the first talis war. Where had this come from? Why hadn't the masters of artifacts at the College of Disciplines known of it?

His admiration of the supernal specimen of ancient Allosian talis craft faded when one of his children fell to the ground a smoldering skeleton. Could whomever piloted the craft know how to kill Moriora vessels? But how?

Well, whatever the explanation, Jenoc was going to have to destroy the ship before it killed anymore of his children. His old self would've been saddened by the idea of destroying the artifact, and losing a chance to study it. He just laughed at that.

USING EMPYREAN'S MAGNIFICATION POWER, Maely scrutinized the faces of dozens of the life sucking monsters below. She kept her swooping and diving focused on the front of Jenoc's army, reasoning that would be the most likely place she'd find their leader. Explosion after explosion sent black rock and human debris into the air. They'd succeeded in scattering the mass of monsters, but there were thousands, and it was going to take time to kill them all.

Maely focused on one group running away from her. They fled in all directions save for one lone figure standing at the epicenter of their retreat. Maely made the image of the man's face larger and her breath caught. He had long blond hair and green eyes now, but there was no mistaking that perfect face, or that smug smile.

"I found him!"

"Where?" Raelen sounded as eager as she felt.

With both of them connected to Empyrean, they could communicate telepathically. It wasn't to the same degree that Maely had experience when Jenoc broke into her mind, but it was similar. They still needed to use words to convey specific ideas, but they could share emotional impressions or images of what they saw. Perhaps that's why both mirrored each other's anxious desire to destroy Jenoc. Or maybe it was just because he was a total bastard.

Maely sent the image to Raelen and she felt his anger flare.

"Get us closer!"

Maely pulled her view back and banked, coming around and then pitched Empyrean into a steep dive.

Jenoc manifested his Moriora so that it wrapped around and enveloped him. He turned and craned his neck at the fast-approaching airship. The pilot had spotted him, and was moving in for the kill–just as he'd hoped.

When the craft was almost on top of him, the air around Jenoc turned hot and heat lines shimmered in his vision. Then the world went red in an explosion of crimson fire.

"You got him!" Maely shouted, though she hadn't needed to. Raelen could see what she was seeing through their psychic link.

The prince didn't respond, but Maely felt a sense of grim satisfaction suffuse their bond. After a moment, he finally said, "Let's hit him one more time, just to be sure."

Maely banked and Empyrean veered back toward the smoldering crater. As they approached, the smoke cleared, and Maely gasped. Standing in the center of the crater, completely whole and unburned, was Jenoc. His curtain of blond locks hung over his face, but by the magnification of Empyrean's magic, she could see his perfect white teeth framed by a feral smile.

Jenoc threw up his hands, channeled the energy from the blast that had been meant to immolate him, and cast it back at the approaching airship in a stream of red fire. It engulfed the spire protruding from the nose of the craft, and then punched through the hull and exploded out the top.

The airship tilted hard to the left and swerved away from him, on fire and trailing smoke. It rose into the air, but quickly dropped again, repeating the cycle several times and each time falling lower and lower. The wind whistled as it streaked down toward the valley below.

THE WORLD LURCHED and Maely found herself no longer in the sky, but lying on Empyrean's smooth, white floor. The ship was shaking, and whatever magic kept everything inside the cabin in place was failing, for objects slid across the floor and she could feel every jolt and turn of the ship. Raelen's dirty brown satchel fell from where it hung on a hook protruding from the wall, scattering emerald colored shards across the floor and making the lights flicker as the anti-Apeiron well shards started to consume the airship's energy.

Maely glanced around and located Raelen. The prince was likewise thrown from the circular purple dais that allowed one to join with the airship. He scrambled up, and tripped as the ship lurched again.

"Empyrean!" Maely cried out.

"I am sorry, Maely," the polite voice replied. "I am unable to repair such severe damage while in flight. I am attempting to mitigate the impact of our forced descent and inevitable and sudden touchdown."

"You mean we're going to crash?"

"Yes. And as my ability to dampen the resultant kinetic forces is hampered, I would suggest finding an anchor for yourself."

The ship was just as pretentious and condescending as Kairah, something that would've irritated Maely if she wasn't about to die. She scrambled up and latched onto the now empty hook protruding from the wall. It was almost too small to hold onto, but it was the best she could do as Empyrean's walls were also smooth and the cabin devoid of furniture.

"Take my hand!" Maely called out to Raelen.

The prince stumbled over to her, joined his hand to hers, and the two pressed themselves against the wall.

JENOC WATCHED the massive white airship arc downward. It punched through an invisible barrier, causing translucent purple ripples in the air. Those waves, like heat lines, shimmered and the cloaking shield hiding Allose from view shattered like glass. The white city, Jenoc's home, and its massive Apeira well popped into existence before him. The airship descended into the city, clipping a tower that spun it as it went crashing down into the streets. When it crashed into the ground, it slid, rolled, and smashed through several buildings before finally coming to a stop.

Jenoc grinned. What a perfect distraction! He'd thought he was going to have to deal with the peacekeepers, but this would keep them busy and afford he and his children the chance to flood into the city unmolested. The sight of the Allose and the Mother Shard caused his army to frenzy, and they broke into a frantic dash toward the city–toward their feast.

IT WAS dark inside the ship's cabin, and save for a loose glow orb rolling slowly across the tilted floor, Maely would've been lost in blackness.

"Empyrean?" She sucked in a sharp breath upon trying to move her leg. Pain flared at touching it, and she guessed it to be broken. "Empyrean?"

The ship didn't answer.

"Raelen?" Maely called next.

She frantically surveyed the dim cabin until she found the prince lying at the bottom of a sloping incline beneath her. He wasn't moving. Maely carefully moved down the tilted floor. She yelped as she lost her grip and involuntarily began to roll. A scream ripped from her lips when she slammed into a wall that was more like a floor, and the pain in her leg was so intense that her vision swam and she started to faint. She clawed her way back from syncope by sheer strength of will, and breathed deeply until the fiery agony diminished to a lesser throbbing.

Maely located her glow orb, which had blessedly landed in such a way that it rolled to a stop against her head. She grabbed it and turned so she could see Raelen. She'd nearly landed on top of the prince, who lay crumpled just a few feet from her. His blond hair was mixed with red as blood from a gash in his scalp leaked down the side of his head. His head lulled to the side, but he was still breathing.

"Raelen!" Maely stretched out her hand and gently touched his shoulder. "My prince?"

He didn't respond.

"Empyrean?" Maely shouted.

This time the ship answered, albeit in a weak voice. "I apologize, Maely. That landing was a little rough."

Maely was so relieved that her crying changed to laughter, though tears continued to roll down her cheeks.

"Did you hit your head, Maely?" Empyrean sounded confused.

"No, but I think Raelen did." She wiped her eyes again. "Can you tell what's wrong with him?"

"He has a concussion and some broken ribs. I fear without a healing, he will not wake for some time, and there is a chance he could suffer further harm."

"Can you heal him?"

"I am sorry, Maely. Most of my talises are damaged or inaccessible."

Maely's stomach twisted. "Can you move at all?"

"It will be some time before I regain any mobility."

Maely clenched her teeth. "Well, what can you do?"

"I can open an exit."

The wall above her liquefied and flowed open.

Maely nearly wilted under the sense of crushing despair. How was she supposed to crawl back up the sloping floor with a broken leg while towing the injured prince? She rested her head on Raelen's leg and sobbed.

"Reka?" A voice echoed down.

Maely snapped her head back up to find a reptilian head poking in from the opening in the cabin wall. "Karak!"

She froze. The Vorakk looking down at her was a shade of green so dark that it nearly appeared black. It was also smaller than Karak, and had white bone protrusions rimming its brow. It was a different Vorakk.

"Shall I shut it out?" Empyrean asked.

She almost said yes, but right now the humanoid lizard was her only chance at escape.

"No."

As if that had been an invitation, the Vorakk climbed into the cabin and crawled on all fours along the wall and floor. Just where had they crashed? As far as she knew they were nowhere near the southern region of Shaelar and the Vorakk desert. She watched the lizard man descend, sudden trepidation seizing her breast. What if it wasn't here to help? What if it was here to eat her?

Maely glanced around for anything she could use as a weapon, and found the flame kris lying half beneath Raelen's side. It was a minor miracle the wavy red steel hadn't cut him. She reached up, took hold of the handle, and slid it out from beneath Raelen's ribs. She tried to be careful, but the fast approach of the Vorakk made her pull a little too quickly, and she cut Raelen's tunic. She winced, hoping she hadn't cut the flesh beneath, but the lack of blood quashed that worry.

She raised the small sword just as the dark little Vorakk reached her. It clung to the sloping floor three feet above her and stared at the red steel of the sword. Then it flashed a toothy grin.

"Uska!" It extended an opened-clawed hand to Maely.

Maely eyed the claw, and then hesitantly surrendered the flame kris. The Vorakk took it, slid it inside a belt at its waist, and then reached down again. Maely glanced at Raelen. If the lizard man had wanted to do them harm, it already would have. It'd come to rescue them, and right now it was their only way out. Maely took the Vorakk's hand and yelped when the Vorakk jerked her up. It twisted and raised Maely up so that she landed on its scaly back.

"Rok," it hissed.

Apparently this Vorakk didn't speak Aiestali like Karak did.

Maely wrapped her arms around its neck as it launched into a climb up the floor and wall. It climbed through Empyrean's open portal, and Maely gasped as the sight of an Apeira well so massive that it equaled the size of a small mountain. All around the well were beautiful white towers, and other ivory buildings that looked as much like works of art as they did pieces of a city.

Jewel-colored heads of hair were everywhere. Thousands of Allosians gathering to inspect Empyrean while others cleared away white chunks of rubble from collapsed buildings.

We crashed landed in Allose.

The Vorakk climbed down Empyrean's wing and gently deposited Maely on the ground.

Before she could ask it to go back for Raelen, the creature was already climbing back up the airship's side and disappearing back into the round opening in the hull. It took several minutes for the Vorakk to remerge, a fact that had Maely's stomach twisted in knots. She panicked when the Vorakk appeared from the door alone, but her fear dissipated when the creature reached an arm inside and pulled Raelen out. The prince climbed out of the ship with the help of their Vorakk benefactor, and descended the wing.

Raelen held a brown satchel in his other hand, a bag Maely knew held the green shards of the corrupt Apeira well. If they were in Allose, would they really need those shards? Couldn't the Allosians fight off Jenoc and his army of life sucking monsters?

It became clear as to where Jenoc's army had been marching. Maely had assumed they'd be en route to strike another human city, not Jenoc's homeland and his own people. Or maybe he was coming to convert them, as Raelen had described he'd done with the Aiestali army. Either way, their situation had just gone from hopeless to the best possible scenario.

Raelen landed next to her. Dried blood caked his blonde hair to his face. Even battered and bloody he managed to look handsome.

Golden womb of the goddess! Now is not the time for that!

The little dark Vorakk landed in front of them, and Maely got her first complete view of the creature. Like Karak, it wore a loin cloth, but also a piece of cloth wrapped around its chest covering two breasts. It was a female.

"What's your name?" Maely asked.

The female Vorakk just grinned at Maely, returned the wavy red sword to her, and then vanished. Maely examined the flare kris and was encouraged to find its well-shard glowing. The talis had recharged.

Raelen knelt at her side. "Are you hurt?"

She nodded. "I think my leg is broken."

"This must be Allose." Raelen fished in his bag and pulled out the amulet he'd made.

"What're you doing?"

Screams and shouting erupted all around them. Maely surveyed the crowd of on-looking Allosians who were pointing, shouting, and running away.

"I don't think this is over yet." Raelen slipped the leather band over Maely's head and slipped the cloth wrapped emerald shard underneath her neckline and between her breasts.

She blushed furiously and opened her mouth to reprimand him for his indecency, but stopped herself.

Don't be stupid! He's just offering me protection. And though she would never admit it, the contact had been a little thrilling.

Raelen quickly fashioned another amulet from an emerald colored shard he'd pulled from the bag. He winced as he held the jagged crystal with his naked skin, but didn't shirk at the pain.

"Aren't we safe here?"

"Perhaps." He looped the second amulet around his bloody head. "But I'm not done with Jenoc."

He stood. "Stay here. If an Allosian offers to heal you, take off the shard."

She knew that! She'd been the one to discover that the pieces of the corrupted Apeira well blocked healing.

"Try to explain to them what is happening." He took a step away from her, but stopped when she reached up and caught him by the hand.

Another thrill washed through her at the skin to skin contact. "Please don't leave me."

Raelen looked down at her and smiled. Then he bent over and kissed her on the forehead. "Don't worry. I'll be back." With that, he broke into a jog away from her.

Maely looked away from a group of approaching Allosians, afraid they'd see her blushing of all things.

I am a stupid, silly girl.

ALLOSIANS DIDN'T WITHER and die when Jenoc fed upon them. Instead, they instinctively pulled more Apeiron into them to counter his magic which in turn fed him more energy. This of course only fueled Jenoc's power, giving him back the ability of unlimited spell-casting, which he used to terrible effect.

Explosions of fire, bolts of lightning, and waves of raw force knocked dozens of swooping peacekeepers from the air. Jenoc thought it would be harder to attack and kill his own people, but his rage burned inside him like an ever-expanding forest fire. Allosians would, of course, wither like anything else if they were dealt fatal blows. But that was just their residual Apeiron being sucked from an already lifeless body.

He stepped over one such body, still clad in white, form, fitting armor. The talis's Apeira well-shard, mounted in the center of the breastplate, went dark when Jenoc brushed the armor with a foot. That was fascinating, but the question as to why he couldn't just keep pulling on the Mother Shard through a talis didn't entice him like it once would have. He was no longer a scholar, or a master of the College of Disciplines, or even an Allosian. Jenoc was something else. He was terrible. He was vengeance incarnate. He was death!

Thousands of his children flooded the streets of Allose, leaping onto jewel-haired victims. Slack smiles of ecstasy shone on his soldiers' faces as they fed. Of course, their feast would end when Jenoc cast the inversion spell and destroyed the Mother Shard. Fortunately, until then, his children would be preoccupied with their new source of food and would not seek his prize.

Hundreds of Allosian men, women, and children fled in a wild mob. It made Jenoc feel like a lion surprising a herd of wildebeests with nowhere to run. He smiled and shot a bolt of green lightning at the retreating Allosians.

But the bolt didn't connect. It struck something small and white floating in the air and then dissipated. *What was that? It looked like a glowing ball of light. More appeared like stars in the night sky.* One streaked for Jenoc and caught him in the chest. It slammed into him with tremendous force and hurled him backward. Jenoc found himself on the paved street, and quickly scrambled up to all fours. He looked up and through a curtain of blonde hair he saw them.

They appeared as if from the air itself. Wavy heat lines resolving into reptilian humanoid forms. Vorakk. Hundreds of Vorakk. They were spread out in front of Jenoc's army, forming a wall between them and the fleeing Allosians.

Jenoc growled and stood. *How had they found Allose? Why had they come? Could they have known about his coming? Impossible!*

Jenoc cast a whirling cyclone of pure force around himself, and lunged forward. The white balls of energy came at him, but he knocked them back with his tornado of force. They could block and resist Moriora, but apparently the Vorakk's magic could not do the same for a regular spell-casting. That would protect him, but he was the only spell-caster among his army.

Jenoc descended on a Vorakk shaman, batting away the lizard man's orbs of light. He dropped his shield and shot out a hand taking the Vorakk by its scaly neck. His touch grayed the lizard man's bronze scales, and it withered before him as its life energy suffused Jenoc's core.

The brittle leather skin of the beast fell before him like a dropped satchel, and Jenoc kicked it out of his path. This development was unfortunate, but ultimately didn't matter. His forces would surely overwhelm the comparatively small force of Vorakk. They just wouldn't be able to provide as much of a distraction for him as he'd hoped. It would take longer for Jenoc to reach the Mother Shard if he had to fight his way through the city.

Something crashed into him from behind.

Jenoc reflexively cast a bubble of force with him at the epicenter and threw his assailant off. He stood at the same time Prince Raelen rolled and sprung up into a ready crouch. *Why was the prince still whole?* That much contact with Jenoc should've withered him so severely that he would be incapacitated. Jenoc manifested a Moriora tendril and whipped it at the prince, but it evaporated the instant it touched him. He frowned.

The prince smirked. "What's the matter, Pariel?"

Jenoc tried again, but met only the same result. "You are not one of us—your eyes are blue."

Raelen charged, leapt, and spun in the air. Jenoc was so shocked that he didn't move fast enough to avoid Raelen's fist, and the prince landed a jaw-cracking blow that staggered him. Jenoc regained his focus in time to avoid the follow up attack–two clapping fists, each intended for a side of his head. Jenoc ducked the attack, and slammed his own open palm into Raelen's chest. His hand struck something hard. The prince grunted, and tried to step away from Jenoc, but not before he grabbed the prince's shirt and tore open the front. The sweat-stained cloth fell away to reveal a bundled object hanging on a leather band about the prince's neck. The wrapping was open just enough for Jenoc to catch the glint of an emerald green crystal beneath.

He grinned. "You have made a Moriora talis. Very clever."

Raelen roared and charged, but this time Jenoc was ready. He unleashed a bolt of emerald lightning, striking Raelen in the left shoulder. The prince cried out as he was hurled into the white wall of a building. He slumped, then crumpled to the ground.

Jenoc laughed. "Your protection might gain you advantage over one of my children, but they are not spell-casters, as am I."

Raelen lifted his head, blue eyes wide, his face red.

The idea of showing the prince just how outmatched he was enticed Jenoc as much as the Mother Shard tempted him to feed on it. But his discipline won out–something that was becoming increasingly rare and difficult–and he turned away. He had to get to the Mother Shard first, before any of his children corrupted it by leaching off its power. Plus, some of his growing sadistic need was satisfied by the thought of Raelen witnessing the inauguration of the catastrophe that would end mankind.

Jenoc spell-cast and launched himself into the air, smiling at Raelen's impotent howl of rage. He rocketed into the sky above Allose. With an inexhaustible source of food, he was free to spell-cast as he once had, without concerns for the extra Apeiron it cost him.

Two flying peacekeepers swerved to intercept him but he lashed out with tendrils of warped greenish force and used them as conduits to draw on the Mother Shard and fuel his flight spell. His robes fluttered as he soared toward his goal, the paralyzed peacekeepers in tow.

Jenoc! Help!

The psychic scream broke Jenoc's concentration and he fell from the sky, landing hard on his right leg and shattering it completely. It was a momentary inconvenience as the power he sucked through the two peacekeepers quickly restored him. They landed behind him a heartbeat later, their corpses withering when their heads struck the pavement.

"Kairah," Jenoc whispered. The scream had come from his sister.

Jenoc unconsciously felt in his pocket for the geode and was surprised when his fingers brushed its jagged edge. With all his fighting and flying it ought to have fallen out, but it was still there–like his concern for his sister was still there. He clenched his teeth. No! Kairah had betrayed him! She'd sided with the humans! She was dead to him!

He took several running steps in preparation for resuming flight but stumbled to a stop as the memory of lustful men surrounding his sister struck his mind like a physical blow. She'd cried out in exactly the same way then, and Jenoc had torn the would-be rapists to pieces with all the power he could then muster.

Other memories streamed in unbidden. He remembered Kairah helping his exhausted self walk as they stumbled back to Allose, orphaned and helpless. He remembered Kairah clinging to him, sobbing on their first night in the wild. He was so burnt out from spell-casting beyond his normal ability that he couldn't even light a fire to keep them warm. And Kairah had been so young that she hadn't learned any spells yet. He remembered Kairah's proud smile as she presented him with the overpriced geode. A worthless rock that had become his most valuable possession.

Jenoc looked in the direction from which the psychic call had emanated, and recognized the tower keep of Shivara the Allosian Oracle. He pulled the geode out and stared into its purple crystals.

"It looks like an Aeose," Kairah had said so many years ago when she gifted him the overpriced bauble.

She was in danger somewhere inside the Oracle's tower and needed his help. He had to go to her, to save her, didn't he?

No.

He deposited the geode back into his pocket and looked away from the tower, refocusing his attention on the Mother Shard. Kairah had made her choice. And he had made his.

She was on her own.

Chapter 102

Boom!

The doors to Lady Kairah's apartment shook as some kind of magic struck it. Or maybe it was just the peacekeepers themselves. Perhaps their white form-fitting talis armor gave them greater strength? Fine cracks spider-webbed across the door as another impact shook the whole tower.

Tyrus gripped his stun baton tightly, ridiculously pointing it at the doors as though it was a nova wand, or a concussion rod. The squat, fat whore mistress, Graelle, stood in the same position, but she actually had a concussion rod, apparently smuggled past the peacekeepers who'd searched them by hiding it in her ample cleavage. That mental image made Tyrus shudder.

This was a nightmare.

Jekaran was no better for their attempt to heal him, and now they'd lost the advantage of his powerful sword talis. The boy, Mulladin, who Tyrus had always known to be a dim simpleton, was no longer able to touch or wield the weapon. He glanced over his shoulder at the atrium. Through the glass doors he could see Mulladin kneeling next to Jekaran's body, the monk Irvis and woman Keesa standing vigil.

Could sure use her lightning ring right now. The urgency of their need had made him break decorum and ask to borrow it, to which the girl just laughed. Not that it was hers anyway, filthy Rikujo thief. And what was it she had said about being Jekaran's cousin?

Another boom refocused Tyrus's attention on the breaking doors. He glanced around at his comrades in arms. Hort stood in front of the atrium's glass door, spinning the black wood scepter in his hand as they anxiously awaited the inevitable peacekeeper intrusion.

"Stop spinning that about!" he snapped.

Hort stopped spinning the polished black shaft. "Why?"

"Don't you know what it does?"

Hort grinned. "Sure do."

"Just don't let any of the lines touch," Tyrus said. "You're likely to tear this whole room to pieces."

Hort laughed and resumed twirling the scepter. It was infuriating.

Tyrus refocused on the shaking doors, cracks now glowing with the light of the outer hall. They had only seconds left before the peacekeepers stormed the room, and–if they were lucky–captured them. Though, by now, Tyrus was certain the Allosian's tolerance of them had expired, and even the peaceable fey folk were angry enough to kill.

I'm sorry, Kybon. I tried to save your son. I tried to honor your memory.

Everything fell silent.

Tyrus exchanged looks with Graelle, and then Hort. The big mercenary stopped twirling the void scepter, and slowly stepped up to the set of cracked double doors. After listening for a long moment, he opened them.

"Are you mad?" Tyrus shouted.

"They're gone." Hort swung the door completely open to reveal an empty corridor.

Graelle lowered her concussion rod. "They had us cornered. Why would they just leave?"

"I'd praise the goddess, but my gut tells me something else drew their attention. Something more urgent." Hort walked back toward Kairah's atrium.

Tyrus couldn't help but agree with the brute. He'd been caught at sea in a storm once, dragged along with Kybon on one of his stupid adventures. The sea had been eerily calm just before the massive storm struck. They'd made it back to land, but three days late and as soaked as drowned corpses. Kybon laughed about the whole affair afterward, but

Tyrus remembered the horror in his cousin's eyes while the ship rocked, and waves pounded them.

The peacekeeper's sudden retreat felt like that calm before the storm descended upon them. But then, perhaps the storm was already here.

Tyrus followed the others back into the atrium where Hort gave Irvis, Mulladin, and Keesa a quick explanation of what just occurred–well, as far as they were able to explain it.

"It's probably a good time to get the hell out of here," Hort said.

Irvis shook his head. "We can't move Jekaran."

Hort frowned. "We did before. It ain't gonna hurt the boy."

Mulladin pounded the grass with a fist. "The sword won't move and we can't touch it!"

They stared at each other, and Tyrus felt the crushing defeat settle on all of them at once. "Let me try to reach him."

They turned as one to gape at him.

"You just have to touch the sword talis, right?" Tyrus shrugged.

"That sword sucked a man's life away because Jek didn't like him." Mulladin shook his head. "He hates you! What do you think will happen if you touch it?"

Tyrus looked at the ground, and then at Jekaran's empty face. "He's my cousin's son."

Mulladin threw up his hands. "What, is everyone here related?!"

Tyrus ignored the outburst and continued. "Lord Kybon El Toreevan III."

Keesa gasped. Apparently, the lass knew the name. Well, why not? Kybon was from one of the great houses. Everyone would know the family name.

"He was a philanderer and a reckless fool." A tear slipped down Tyrus's cheek.

"Jek's the bastard of a noble?" Mulladin's wide eyes made him resemble the dim simpleton from Tyrus's memories.

"Not a bastard. Kybon fell in love with and married Anarilee. I performed the ceremony. For obvious reasons, it was kept a secret. He planned to reveal the marriage. He just had to convince my uncle–Lord Toreevan II, to accept it. He was murdered before that could happen." Tyrus sniffed, his voice sounding more nasally than usual. "Since then,

I've tried to keep an eye on Jekaran, though he's gone out of his way to make that a very distasteful charge."

"Does he know?" Irvis asked.

"I tried to tell him after he was arrested in Aiested, but..." Tyrus met their stares in turn. "Kybon was like a brother to me. I owe it to his memory to try and wake Jekaran."

Mulladin shared a look with Keesa. "He might kill you."

"I know." Tyrus knelt next to Jekaran. "I just touch the sword?"

Irvis slowly nodded.

Tyrus wiped his eyes once more and then extended a trembling hand.

Suddenly he was standing in the village square of Genra. It took a moment for him to orient himself, not because he didn't recognize the location, but because a heartbeat earlier he'd been inside Kairah's atrium in Allose.

The scene was so real, complete with villagers milling about and children laughing as they chased each other around the well that Tyrus almost wondered if everything else had just been a dream–almost.

He found Jekaran surrounded by a group of smaller children. He was trying to vertically balance a wooden dowel on his nose. He succeeded for a few seconds, to which the children clapped and cheered. They let out a collectively jeer of disappointment when the dowel tipped to the right and fell. Jekaran snapped up his hand and caught it before it hit the ground. Then he made an extravagant bow, complete with flaring an imaginary cape. The children laughed, took the dowel, and ran as a mob to their next distraction. Jekaran laughed and smiled a grin that could've been taken straight from Kybon's own face.

When Jekaran noticed Tyrus approaching him, the smile faded. "What do you want?"

"I–I..." Tyrus didn't know what to say.

Jekaran cocked an eyebrow. "The great Lord Gymal at a loss for words?"

"Your father was my cousin," Tyrus blurted out.

Jekaran stiffened. "What did you say?"

"He was a lord who married your mother in secret."

"Have you been piping cannabis again?" Jekaran shook his head and turned away. "Wait until I tell Ez! He's gonna love this. Any chance you can wait here while I go fetch him? Maybe we can get Hyric to color trap your..."

"You're my kin, Jekaran. The son of a cousin who was as dear to me as any brother."

"Damn, you are fuddled!" He stepped away.

Tyrus shot out a hand and grabbed Jekaran's arm.

"Let go of me, my lord," the boy said through clenched teeth.

"Listen to me, Jekaran. You have to wake up. You have to come back to us."

Jekaran threw off Tyrus's hand. "You should go to Hyric's and buy some bread. I'd wager you're gonna be hungry enough to eat today's entire batch."

"I'm not fuddled!"

Jekaran spun to face him. "Okay, so if this lord is my father, then where is he? You said he married my mother, so that implies she was more than just a tryst. Why did he leave?"

"He was murdered by a jealous ex-lover."

Jekaran's anger appeared to ebb. "You're serious, aren't you?"

"Yes."

"You're saying we are family?"

Tyrus smiled. "Yes, yes! That's right."

Jekaran burst out laughing. "Does that mean I'm a lord?" He turned and walked away. "That was rich. Too bad you're not going to remember this when your brain fog lifts."

"Jekaran, please. The peacekeepers could be back at any moment. We have to escape."

Jekaran just kept laughing as he walked away.

Tyrus waved at the village around him. "This isn't real. You're in Allose. Your mind is broken because you accidentally slew your uncle."

Jekaran stopped. "Get out."

Tyrus walked toward him. "You have to accept it. Forgive yourself, or whatever it is you need to do so Irvis can heal you."

Jekaran whirled. "Get out!"

"Jekaran you need to—"

Pain struck Tyrus's head like a physical blow and the world washed out.

He woke to Hort patting him–none too gently–on the cheek. Tyrus waved away the mercenary and sat up. All eyes were on him. He glanced at Jekaran, now several feet away from him.

"He won't listen."

Mulladin nodded. "I wouldn't try that again if I were you."

Sharp pains from his lower back, ribs, and elbow assailed Tyrus as he stood. "I am inclined to agree."

"What do we do now?" Graelle glanced nervously at the atrium door. "Can you try to reach him, love?"

Irvis shook his head. "I don't think anyone can."

"Then we leave him," Keesa said.

"No." Hort stepped away and knelt next to Jekaran's body and extended a hand toward the sword.

"Are you serious?" Irvis caught Hort's wrist. "The boy hates Lord Gymal, but you've actually fought him. He's going to see you as a threat."

Hort easily pulled his wrist out of Irvis's grip. "If I die, I die. It isn't like I don't deserve such an end."

He touched the large amethyst jewel on the sword's cross guard.

JEKARAN NEARLY TRIPPED on the too-long hem of Irvis's robe. He had to hike the garment up like a dress to keep up with the big mercenary escorting him to Gymal's camp. It being night didn't help any, and he fell after tripping on a lose stone the long robe had hidden from his view. Hort helped him stand, and Jekaran nodded his thanks.

"I have a confession I want to make to you, Brother Ulan."

Jekaran's chest tightened. Hort said the name in a deliberate way that made it sound like he knew it wasn't really Jekaran's name. Could the big mercenary know what he was up to?

"Speak, my child. For the Divine Mother is always ready to forgive the truly penitent."

"It's not the Divine Mother's forgiveness I need."

Jekaran didn't know how to respond to that. "Then why—"

"I told you how I was an apothecary once."

Jekaran nodded. He did know that. But how? Hadn't he only just met this man? For that matter how did he know Hort's name?

"You said that venture failed when you were unable to heal your dying son."

"Yeah. That's what I need to confess."

"But you already told me that... um... my child." Jekaran had to hastily add that last part. He was breaking character, but for some reason that didn't feel like it mattered.

Hort choked out a bitter laugh. "I lied to you. In part, anyway. Nemel was four days away from his seventeenth birthday." Hort smiled and shook his head. "He was so excited to finally become a man. I tried to tell him that it wasn't just a boy's years that made him a man, but his walk and way of living. Said to him that there were wrinkled geezers that were less a man than he was for how they lived. He wouldn't have any of it. He was stubborn like that." Hort glanced down at Jekaran. "He was stubborn like you."

Jekaran wrinkled his brow. "Why are you telling me this?"

"Because I have to confess."

"Confess what?"

Hort's nostalgic smile faded and he refocused on the distant lights of Gymal's camp. "Nemel got sick. It wasn't anything serious. Just a sniffle. Well, we had this big feast planned for his birthday, and Nemel didn't want to spend the whole affair hocking and spitting wads into a spittoon. And I think he had plans to get a kiss from the mayor's daughter. So, he asked me for some Aetar seed oil. Doesn't cure the sniffles, but it helps ya breathe. Dries up the snot, ya see."

"You told me he'd taken sick with a fever and died."

Hort's eyes lost their focus. "I never was good at keeping my stories in order." He chuckled nervously. "Always chaffed at my first wife's temper, that. See, the bottles looked the same, and I didn't bother checking the label."

Jekaran reached out and took hold of the mercenary's corded bicep, halting both of their walks. "What are you saying?"

Hort stared at him for a long moment before quietly answering, "I mistakenly gave Nemel Jeder powder I'd been keeping in an oil-like suspension. Do you know what Jeder is?"

"It takes away pain, like poppy."

Hort nodded. "And like poppy, it can make you sleep. It's excellent in small doses. But you take too much and you'll stop breathing and never wake up. The dose for Aeter is five times the size of a single dose of Jeder."

Jekaran sickened as he realized what Hort was telling him.

"Shoulda known when Nemel started yawning and asked if he could skip his chores to lay down for a nap. I let him, on account of his being sick and it being his birthday. When it came time for the party, I tried to wake him, but my boy had stopped breathing in his sleep."

"Divine Mother," Jekaran breathed out.

Hort turned and resumed walking. "My wife was the one who figured it out. She was so angry she told the whole town, tried to convince the magistrate I'd done it on purpose. I think that was just the grief. She didn't really believe it, and neither did the magistrate. But that didn't stop the constable from keeping me locked up during Nemel's burial. Eventually they let me out, but after that, the wife took my other little ones to live on her father's farm, and no one would have me tend their sick. Can't say that I blame 'em. That's when I packed up, and went back to the other thing I'd been good at–killin'. But this time I did it for money and not for the king."

Jekaran didn't know what to say. "You—"

"Killed my own son," Hort finished. "Yeah. Tried to get past it at first by seeking comfort from the goddess, but women, liquor, and fighting is quicker medicine."

"And did they help?"

"Yeah, but just to keep me from feeling the guilt and pain. Problem is though, none of that ever lasts, and it always takes more to numb yourself the next time."

Hort stopped walking, slumped his shoulders, and turned to face him. "That's what you're doin' right now."

Jekaran shook his head. "I don't know what you mean."

"Yes, you do."

Something pounded on the door of Jekaran's memory. He shook his head, as if that would drive it away. "No. I really don't know what you're talking about."

The two of them were suddenly in front of a free-standing door on a glass plain surrounded by whiteness above and below. Jekaran was wearing his normal clothing again, not Irvis's brown monk robes, and Hort's clothing bore tears and stains it hadn't a moment before.

Jekaran stared at the lonely door. "There's nothing on the other side."

"Yes, there is," Hort said.

"What?"

A tear rolled down Hort's hairy cheek. "Pain."

Another heavy knock shook the door and Jekaran slowly backed away. "Then why would anyone want to open it?"

"Because something else lies beyond."

Jekaran stopped. "What else?"

"Healing." He wiped his eye with the back of his harry forearm. "See, I always knew that, but never had the courage to face my pain. I just kept numbing myself with vice. That was until I got tangled up with you. You reminded me so much of Nemel that I haven't been able to think of much else. It's forced me to confront what I did and what I lost."

"But that hurts."

Hort chuckled. "Like flames eatin' your flesh."

Jekaran wanted to turn and run from the door, but the glass plain infinitely expanded in all directions making retreat pointless.

"How did do you do it? How do you survive the flames?" He could actually feel heat radiating from the free-standing wooden door.

"By holding onto the good times, remembering the love you shared, and finding a new purpose." Hort met his eyes. "I've found a new purpose."

"No." Jekaran shook his head with increasing ferocity. "No, I can't do this!" He turned and ran toward the infinite white of the horizon.

"Jenoc, help!" a woman screamed.

The familiarity of the voice arrested Jekaran's flight. He turned back toward Hort. "What was that?"

"Your new purpose." The eerie quiet of the place carried the normal volume of Hort's voice to Jekaran as though he were standing directly in front of him.

"Kairah…"

But closely resemble they one another, both heroes and fools at first,

She screamed again.

Jekaran walked back to stand in front of the door. "And the only way to help her is through there?"

Hort nodded.

…and it's only at the fork of destiny's road that the truth will at last emerge.

Jekaran slowly reached for the doorknob. The metal burned and he drew his hand back. *How could he survive the flames beyond the door? Surely, they would kill him.*

Kairah screamed again.

For while the fool always looks to his own regard, the hero for others is er' aware. And will suffer and die when called upon, even for strangers in his care

Jekaran drew in a deep breath, reached out, and took hold of the scorching knob. His palm sizzled and the pain nearly overwhelmed him, but Jekaran grit his teeth and turned it. The door flew open, revealing not a fiery inferno as he'd expected, but showing him a scene of chaos and death; Jekaran himself slaughtering the king's soldiers with wild abandon. He was fully enthralled in the sword's battle frenzy, and though the sword wasn't controlling him as before because of their fusing, Jekaran had partaken of its violent spirit.

Ez ran up and call out to him, and though he paused in his work of death, he didn't stop. Something in Ez's hand caught Jekaran's attention— a stun baton not unlike Gymal's. Ez waited until Jekaran's back was to him, and then ran up, baton aimed at Jekaran's back. The scene slowed down as if to torture Jekaran with every detail as he watched himself whirl, and slam the sword through Ez's chest.

Ez smiled and then collapsed, sliding off the sword as he fell to the floor.

Jekaran had done it! He'd killed his uncle! Killed the man who raised him, who taught him to read, and to farm. The man who'd loved him like a son; the only father Jekaran ever knew. He wished he could blame the sword, but it hadn't been possessing him like before. Their minds were joined, and Jekaran's movements were his own.

But he hadn't meant to do it. Divine Mother, but he hadn't!

After pausing to talk to Ez, he'd shoved his joy at his uncle's sudden appearance to the back of his mind, and returned to letting the music of the sword's magic guide his dance of death. The sword gave him a psychic awareness of his surroundings, but that sense was different than sight. He could perceive objects, and people, but only in an odd, detached sort of way. The people were nothing more than heartbeats, breathing, and motion. And the speed at which Jekaran fought demanded immediate, almost prescient reaction to maintain his martial dominance.

Fused as he was with the sword's mind, Jekaran was moving and reacting with a rapid superiority he'd never before attained. In fact, he was moving and striking so quickly, that physical sight was distracting and slowing him down. Thus, Jekaran kept his eyes shut, depending exclusively on the sword's psychic perception as he fought. That was why he hadn't registered it was Ez sneaking up on him until the sword was already plunging through his uncle's chest. Like with Hort's son, it had been an accident. A horrible, tragic, life-shattering accident.

Jekaran fell to his knees and sobbed. Hort disappeared and the world around him resolved into a storm of red fire that threatened to consume him. It burned, oh how it burned! And Jekaran was tempted to surrender to the flames and the cessation of life they offered, but a woman's face appeared before him. A woman with flawless white skin, amethyst hair, and deep purple eyes. He knew and loved that face. Loved the woman behind the eyes. He'd touched her mind and soul, breathed her scent, and heard her laugh. He loved her, and in that love he found strength.

Though he couldn't extinguish the fire, his determination to rescue Kairah gave him the strength to stave off immolation. He pushed back the flames until they parted and opened a way before him. Jekaran sprinted down the aisle of fire toward a point of light that grew brighter as he ran toward it until it consumed him. Jekaran lost all sense of his physical form, and floated disembodied in a cloud of white.

You've done what no other has ever done, the sword said to him. *You've come farther than any have ever come. All that I have, all that I am, my knowledge and the power, is yours now. Truly you have mastered Azrin.*

He didn't know what that meant, but before he could call out to the sword, a rush of energy suffused him. It was cool and refreshing, while at the same time warm and comforting. Was it Apeiron? Was he channeling the energy through his body? It was impossible for Jekaran to know as he had no frame of reference, but the power soothed, comforted, and most importantly, it healed.

"Kairah!" Jekaran shouted.

His eyes snapped open and he sat up. Gone was the world of white, replaced by a beautiful garden full of plants and flowers the likes and colors of which he'd never seen. Irvis drew back a trembling hand, eyes wide and mouth hanging open as he stared at a glowing ring on his finger.

Hort sat beside the chubby monk, tears pooling in his eyes. The big mercenary smiled at Jekaran, and Jekaran smiled back; not an arrogant or cheeky smirk as he was wont to do, but a smile that he hoped showed Hort his understanding and gratitude.

"Jek!" Mulladin shouted. Then he hugged him around the neck, squeezing so hard that Jekaran had to struggle for breath.

"Mull!" Jekaran wheezed, and the big man let go.

Tears ran freely down his cheeks making him look again like the boy-man he'd once been.

"Boy," Irvis said.

Jekaran looked at him and smiled. "Uncle Irvis."

The chubby monk lunged forward and embraced him in a hug almost as fierce as Mulladin's. "I thought we'd lost you."

Then tears were pouring down Jekaran's face. "I killed him, Irvis... I killed Ez..."

"Hush." Irvis shook his head, his white hair tickling Jekaran's cheek. "It was an accident."

Jekaran gripped Irvis tighter and sobbed into his shoulder. After a moment of this, Irvis pulled back, wiped his face with the back of a meaty forearm and met Jekaran's eyes.

"It wasn't your fault. It was the will of Rasheera."

Jekaran bowed his head and shook it. "How can you say that?"

"Because," his voice caught, "he offered his life to the Divine Mother in a covenant. He offered it up in exchange for her interceding to save you from the sword."

Jekaran glanced at the blade that rested on the ground next to him and growled. "But I'm still connected to it, I can feel the bond."

Irvis looked ashamed. "It was necessary to re-bond you so I could put your mind back together. I'm sorry."

"Then Ez's sacrifice meant nothing." Jekaran reached out, took hold of its handle and lifted it so he was staring directly into the round amethyst embedded in the cross guard. "I hate you!" He shouted. "Do you hear me? I hate you!"

The sword made no response.

Jekaran's anger muted and he shot a glance at Irvis.

"What's wrong?"

"It's not answering me."

"It spoke to me in your voice when I used it," Mulladin said. "It held a piece of your mind."

"The fusing," Jekaran muttered.

"The what?" Gymal demanded in his nasally tone.

"Back in Aiested, when I was fighting the king's soldiers, the sword suggested we join our minds to access its full power." Jekaran looked up at Gymal and then set the sword down on the ground. He gasped.

"What is it?" Irvis touched his shoulder.

"Usually when I let go of the sword, all my fighting knowledge and skill diminishes or disappears." He met Irvis's eyes. "I still have it all."

You have mastered Azrin. What did that mean? He'd have to ask Kairah. The memory of Kairah's desperate scream struck him like a physical force, replaying with such clarity that it was like hearing it a second time.

"Kairah!" He grabbed the sword and stood. "She's in danger!"

Maely limped along as quickly as she could, frequently having to lean against an Allosian statue, or the white wall of a building to rest or avoid falling. She dragged her ruined leg behind her, gritting her teeth and spouting a stream of profanity so foul it shocked even her.

The pain was sharp and made her nauseous, but that's not what evoked her unusually creative and exhaustive litany of curses. The Allosians who originally had come to her aid after Empyrean crashed had abandoned her. They literally dropped her and ran when Jenoc's army swarmed into the city streets.

"Gutless, jewel-haired, milkmaids," she growled.

The monsters with the ghostly green tentacles mostly ignored Maely–though now and again one would lash out at her. They all did the same thing when their magic tendrils disappeared; gasped in surprise and made two or three subsequent attempts before moving on to easier prey. Maely touched the chunk of green crystal beneath her shirt. It was doing its job in protecting her, but that didn't erase all her fear, especially for Raelen.

He'd run off, presumably after Jenoc himself, leaving her to the care of the Allosian onlookers. Since being left for dead, Maely had steadily moved in the direction she'd last seen the prince go.

"That's her!"

Maely snapped her head to the left where she found three of Jenoc's monsters; a woman and two men all leering at her. Their skin was pale, and they had dark circles below their green eyes, making them look sickly. But their wide grins belied their weak appearance.

"She's got some kind of talis protecting her." The woman pointed.

"I don't see any talis." One of the men scoffed.

"See that bulge under her shirt?"

Maely reacted by looking down at her chest. It was stupid and only served to confirm the woman's accusation.

The second man, a tall figure clad in the armor of the Aiestali army, laughed. "I see it!"

The three advanced, and Maely pressed her back against the wall of the building she'd been leaning on.

"Stay back!"

She tried to draw the flare kris from where it hung at her belt–which was useless as the talis drained the moment Raelen put the green shard around her neck–to defend herself, but the two men surged forward, pinning Maely by her upraised arms against the wall. She cried out as the woman moved in and tore down the bust line of her top. Hanging in her cleavage was the bundled shard of green crystal.

"This is it, isn't it?" The woman smiled and took hold of the shard.

Maely hoped it would burn the woman, or repel her or something, but she was completely unaffected. "If I snap this off, you'll wither like all the others, won't you?"

Maely was so terrified that she couldn't have answered if she wanted to.

The woman leaned in at the same time she drew the leather band taut around the back of Maely's neck.

"Wait," the soldier said.

The woman stopped pulling and glanced at her companion.

"Let me have some fun with her first."

The woman rolled her eyes and let go of the shard. She opened her mouth to say something when an explosion of wind threw her to the side. The two men released Maely and ran to their leader. When they knelt to help her stand, three balls of red light appeared and began circling them. A heartbeat later, a column of fire ten feet tall erupted into existence. It completely engulfed the three, and was so hot that Maely's skin burned from her proximity to the pyre. It quickly burnt out, leaving behind three charred skeletons where the men and woman had been.

"Reka, silly human girl hurt?"

Maely turned to find a Vorakk she knew very well standing a dozen paces away.

"Karak!"

Maely made to run to him, intent on giving the lizard man a hug, but fell to the ground. Karak was there in half a breath, lifting her from the ground to carry her over one scaly shoulder.

Normally, Maely would've been irritated at being hauled about like a sack of potatoes, but she was so grateful to see the Vorakk shaman, and to be safe, that she kissed the back of his scaly neck to which he responded with a gentle pat on her back.

"What are you doing here?"

"Karak find fey girl, aek."

Karak leapt into an impressively fast sprint.

"Kairah? Is Jek here too?"

"Ssk!"

Hope like a warm summer's breeze engulfed Maely. "He's alive?"

"Ssk! But sick, aka."

"Sick?" Maely's warmth gave way to a wave of cold. "How? Is he okay?"

"No time for to talk, aek!"

Karak bounded over a fallen statue of an Allosian woman holding a shield, and Maely held onto his neck and shoulders as they drove further into the white city.

THE WORLD of purple clouds surrounding Jove in this strange place was now pockmarked by dozens of black patches. The energy that was Apeiron was not infinite after all. No, like all things, it could have an end.

"I am the end," Jove growled. "I am death!"

He released the pent-up power he'd ingested in a concussive explosion that shook reality and repelled the white orbs of light attacking him. Free of their incessant assault, he scrambled up and fixed his gaze on the silver-haired doll inside the glass sphere below him. He licked his lips, and the familiar lustful thrill of anticipated violence energized him. Jove glanced up at the balls of light. They rode out the wave of power, and then rallied. They streaked back toward him like angry falling stars. Jove grinned and leapt over the edge of the floating rock, diving for the hole he'd bored into the silver-haired doll's protective shield.

Falling took too long, and so Jove sucked in more Apeiron and propelled himself forward. It reminded him of swimming, which reminded him of hiding in bushes and watching for bathing beauties. They often came alone to the lake outside his village, and those were the ones that never left.

He rocketed through the hole in the glass sphere, but slowed to hover upon reaching the center of its interior where his prize floated. She was absolutely, without a doubt, the most beautiful doll Jove had ever laid eyes on. He giggled as her long, silver hair fluttered about them. It was so shiny–like metal. Jove tried to touch it, but the hair sharply jetted away from his hand, as though it were itself alive, aware, and afraid.

The rejection enraged Jove, and he shot out a hand and snatched a fist full of her hair. It burned his hand, but the fire of his anger was hotter. Jove roughly jerked the doll's head toward him. She glowed with a really quite beautiful soft white aura. Jove's rage gave way to cruel lust, and he roughly pressed his lips against hers, forcing her mouth open to slip in his tongue.

The doll screamed. Not with her mouth for she couldn't talk, but with her mind. It exploded out from her in all directions, rippling the air and echoing into infinity.

The glass sphere surrounding them shattered.

RAELEN GROANED and rolled onto his right side, the one that wasn't burned from Jenoc's bolt of green lightning. He was mostly certain it hadn't done more than blacken the flesh around his ribs, but he couldn't be sure without a healing talis. But, Divine Mother, did it hurt!

All around him Jenoc's army savaged the Vorakk. In stark contrast to the fleeing Allosians, the lizard people fought bravely, not giving any ground even when it meant their death. They had shamans among them, but many attacked with clubs and claws instead of the balls of energy that was Vorakk magic. The shamans lasted longer than their comrades, but the futility of their resistance was quickly becoming apparent. They were being overwhelmed.

"Raelen!"

He looked up to find Maely held in the arms of a Vorakk shaman. The lizard man bounded over to him.

"Reka?" it hissed.

"He's the prince of Aiested," Maely said.

The Vorakk glanced to the side, shifted Maely to one shoulder and extended an open claw palm up. A red ball of light coalesced floating above the Vorakk's hand and then streaked away. Raelen followed its trajectory as it slammed into one of Jenoc's charging monsters. Upon impact, the life leech exploded into flames and changed course to run away screaming.

"No can stay here, aek."

Raelen stood. "I need to find Jenoc." He turned in the direction he'd seen the Allosian monster fly away.

"Need to find fey girl, stop Eater, aek!"

"Jenoc's the Eater!" Maely said, her tone sounding both surprised and excited.

Raelen turned back to face the two. "You speak of the Allosian woman, Kairah?"

"Ssk."

Raelen guessed that for an affirmation. "She can help us stop her brother?"

"Uska, help stop Eater."

"Here," Raelen reached for the leather band around Maely's neck. He carefully lifted it up and over the girl's head.

"What're you doing?"

"I fear I am unable to destroy him on my own, even with the shard protecting me. I'm going to need help." He motioned at the flare kris banded to Maely's tiny waist by a crude leather cord. "It's useless while wearing the shard."

Maely glanced down at the flare kris, then met his eyes and nodded.

Raelen offered Karak the emerald shard he'd taken back from the girl.

"Reka?"

"It'll protect you from the touch of the Eaters."

The shaman took the bundled shard with his free hand, examined it and hissed. He glanced at Maely and then looped the leather band over his head. Next, he reached out a hand and conjured another ball of light.

"Tak!"

"What is it?" Raelen asked.

The Vorakk, apparently named Karak, flashed a smile that revealed an unnerving number of sharp teeth. "Daka, spirits still come."

Raelen didn't know what that meant. Perhaps Karak had been concerned the emerald shard would interfere with his strange Vorakk magic the way it interfered with talises? Raelen was about to ask him when the whole world shuddered.

The very air all around them rippled with translucent waves of force. Raelen's skin tingled, and something inside of him shook. It was as if the solidness of his very core quivered, and the world both without and within loosened.

Then the scream came. It was so loud, shrill, and desperate it seemed to silence all other sound. Raelen shared a look with Maely and Karak.

When the tremble in reality ceased and normal sound returned, Raelen asked, "What in the name of the goddess was that?"

THE SCREAM WAS SO loud Jekaran dropped the sword and covered his ears. But that didn't help; the scream was more than sound. It resonated with all his senses at once: hearing it with his ears, feeling it shake the inside of his body, and sensing it drill into his mind.

Most of all though, the scream brought a profound, gut twisting sensation of dread. His heart beat faster, and the thrill of crisis washed over him. Jekaran looked at the others. They too were futility covering their ears.

The shuddering wave of dissonance subsided.

Was that Kairah? What was happening to her? He'd never experienced such a terrible expression of suffering before. It lit the fire of his anger, and Jekaran leaned down to grab his sword but froze when he saw the white flower in the center of the garden. A moment before, it had been straight and glowing white. Now it drooped, and its aura was gone. A petal fell loose and rocked on the air until it alighted on the lawn where it curled.

"I have to find Kairah!"

"She left nigh unto four days ago," Irvis said.

"Where did she go?"

"She said something about seeing an Allosian oracle," Graelle supplied.

"That doesn't help me."

Jekaran held up the sword and examined the round well shard set in its silver cross guard. Before, the sword had exhibited a supernatural ability to perceive its surroundings, and could even sense things that were hundreds of miles off. Now that Jekaran had absorbed the sword's consciousness and power, could he do the same?

He closed his eyes and concentrated, and a secondary awareness blossomed in his mind. It was just like the time the sword had let him see in the total dark of Gymal's tent when he'd first tried to steal it back from the weaselly little lord.

He's my kin. And more noble than I'd given him credit for.

His psychic sense expanded out from him in all directions, and showed him the garden in which they all stood, then the apartment, then the entire tower and all its halls and rooms. The sense raced out from him, covering the streets of Allose, and rolling on until he found her. She was imprisoned in a nearby tower, in pain and fading? And there was something else...

Jekaran opened his eyes and fixed them on Hort. "Something's out there, in the streets–an army."

"Aiestal?" Gymal asked.

"No, they're not human." Jekaran shook his head. "I don't know what they are, but they're destroying everything in their path."

"Now we know why the peacekeepers left," a young woman who was holding onto Mulladin said.

Keesa, her name was Keesa. Jekaran had a faint memory of watching her nearly seduce the big man, but it was fuzzy and dreamlike. There was also something more mundanely familiar about her face.

"Stay here and hide. I have to go to Kairah. I'll be back as soon as I can."

"We can escape! We have displacement talises"—Gymal began—"they just don't work in here."

Hort scoffed.

Gymal shot the big mercenary a scowl. "I meant we can leave this tower and get out of Allose."

"I don't care how you do it, just stay safe." Jekaran took a step toward the exit, but Irvis caught his arm. He looked back at the chubby monk and found him proffering a silver ring to him.

"What's this?"

"Take it to Kairah." Irvis glanced at the wilting flower. "I fear she is going to need it."

Jekaran nodded, and pocketed the ring.

"I'm going with you, brother Ulan!" Hort stepped up beside him.

"So am I!" Mulladin stepped up on Jekaran's other side.

"Is that a weapon talis?" Jekaran pointed at the slender black scepter gripped tight in Hort's fist.

The big mercenary grinned. "A void scepter."

Jekaran didn't know what that meant. "Whatever's out there will be coming. I need you two to protect the others."

The young woman at Mulladin's side snorted, an expression that reminded Jekaran of Ez for some reason.

"Jek," Mulladin pled, and for a moment he sounded like the boy-man he once had been.

Jekaran smiled. "Thank you, my friend, for finding my lost soul."

Mulladin threw his big arms around Jekaran and whispered in his ear. "I saw him, Jek. I saw Ez's spirit. He helped me during my fight with Loeadon."

Tears spilled down Jekaran's cheeks, and he pulled away from Mullidan. He couldn't find his voice, so he just smiled his thanks. Then he whirled, and charged out of the atrium, sword held low at his side.

Not a sword; a key.

The sudden impression made Jekaran falter and he slowed to a stop in the corridor outside Kairah's apartment.

Where had that come from?

If the thought hadn't come in the tone of his own voice, he would've thought it a comment from the sword. He looked at the weapon. *How was it a key?* He shrugged off the oddity and leapt back into a run. Mysteries and magic could wait. Kairah needed him.

⁂

THE TASTE of the doll's power was infinitely more delicious than even pure Apeiron. Jove shuddered with pleasure as the hot energy streamed into him, painful at first but warming his core, tingling his skin, and sating his hunger. He was paralyzed in an orgasmic-like seizure. This is what he'd been seeking his entire miserable life. The sheer pleasure transcended all other sensations, and Jove reveled in the same ecstasy he'd felt the first time he'd killed in the heat of passion.

What was that girl's name? A part of him continued to wonder.

A set of large paws gripped Jove by the shoulders and tore him away from his doll. He screamed. It was like being tossed from a warm spot in front of the hearth into a frozen river at midnight. In the weightlessness of this strange realm, he twirled head over heels until he could draw in enough Apeiron to slow and right himself. The purple energy he once thought so succulent was nothing now that he'd tasted the fiery essence of the silver-haired doll. It was a cold three-day-old stew whereas the doll's power was an entire feast of piping hot venison!

Jove growled and faced his opponent; a white bear with bright blue eyes. It was translucent in an ethereal way, as though it were a ghost. Other balls of white light surrounded him, each resolving into bear-like humanoids with fur that was an assortment of blacks, browns, and grays.

Something was different about his assailants. Jove could sense a change. Not just in them, but in everything around and inside them. He was different too. Drinking in the silver-haired doll's power had changed him somehow. He threw out a hand, a bolt of green lightning arcing at the white bear in front of him. It dodged, and the other bear creatures flew at him. He targeted an even larger, brown bear-man closing on his right and released another emerald bolt that struck the creature square in the chest. The brown bear-man roared in pain and its appearance fuzzed. It faltered for a heartbeat but then resumed its aerial charge. Jove struck at it again and this time when the green spear of electricity connected, the bear glowed white, and then exploded into millions of tiny pieces. That halted the advance of the other bear spirits and they all floated in place, watching their comrade disintegrate into star-like particles.

Jove drew his hand back, staring at it in wide-eyed wonder. He'd changed again–evolved. He could kill not only the bodies of living things, but their souls as well. He could devour all things! He could wipe the smallest particles of life from existence itself–send them to a soulless grave. Now he absolutely and truly had become death!

Jove cackled and began striking out at the bear-spirits. Each time one of his bolts of emerald lightning hit its mark, the target would glow white like a super nova and explode into tiny stars. This didn't make the others retreat however, for they came at him from all angles. These bear-spirits were determined to bar his way to the silver-haired doll, but they couldn't stop him. Not anymore. He would have his doll–both body and soul.

CHAPTER
104

The scream belonged to the goddess Rasheera. Of that Kairah was certain. She hugged herself and curled up on the finely woven rug at the center of the chamber. The room had been some sort of receiving hall, but since had become the luxurious prison of Shivara's victims. Kairah was not alone here, at least not physically.

The chamber was a twisted museum of sorts, the art on display being Allosian women with overpainted faces, brightly colored bows and other trinkets woven into intricate hair fashions, and wearing fine ball gowns or other themed fashions. They were alive, if one could call their catatonic state life, standing or sitting in different places, never moving; their blank faces and empty eyes staring unceasingly at nothing.

What had Shivara done to them? They were little more than empty shells, dressed and decorated by Shivara herself as though they were a collection of life-sized dolls. The woman Kairah had thought was an oracle had recruited these women because of their oracular gifts, under the pretense of training them. Her lifelong requirement of no contact with family and friends, sold as a means for facilitating intense training, had been a way for Shivara to avoid suspicion and cover her crimes. She'd employed each of the dead-eyed women in turn to use the Zikkurat in her attempt to commune with the being who'd tasked Shivara with slaying Rasheera. Boulos, she called him.

But that was not the extent of Shivara's monstrous crimes. She kept these women to use as conduits for absorbing Apeiron, a buffer between herself and the Mother Shard. Direct contact with an Aeose by a Moriora vessel corrupted and destroyed the Apeira well, but pulling the power through an intermediary let Shivara continue to spell-cast, and hide for a thousand years in Allose itself. The woman bragged of her unsurpassed discipline in pacing her feeding. Apparently drawing on too much life essence too quickly exponentially increased the appetite resulting in corruption and madness–the fate that had befallen Shivara's co-conspirators in the plot to assonate the goddess.

Looking at the statue-like, mindless dolls of the women made Kairah think Shivara wasn't as adept at avoiding the corruption and madness as the woman claimed. Kairah's morbid find of a withered corpse lying in a corner near the far end of the room was evidence enough of that.

Kairah closed her eyes. She had to escape and free Rasheera, but she could no longer spell-cast, something Shivara claimed was the immediate precursor to the full and final metamorphosis of an Allosian into a Moriora vessel. Strangely, the speed of the transformation process was affected by an individual's predisposition to anger and violence–something to do with attunement to the essence of death and destruction. According to Shivara, Kairah's fierce discipline in resisting the urge to kill and destroy had significantly slowed her corruption.

That and the silver ring. But Shivara didn't know Kairah had found Rasheera's talis–the first talis.

"Aeva," Kairah whispered. "Mother."

But the spirit lily–an aspect of the goddess's sleeping consciousness–didn't answer. Kairah was alone. But even a sleeping deity could touch and influence the world. Kairah had had hours to contemplate recent events and had concluded Rasheera had been active in subtly arranging events to favor her release.

Aeva's gentle insistence that Kairah steal the illusion pendant and leave Allose to warn the humans of Jenoc's plot. The ripples of light around Jekaran that had marked him to Kairah's eyes as a fated soul, and someone she should follow. The silver ring coming into the possession of the chubby monk, Irvis. Vorakk clairvoyance warning Karak of the creature who destroyed Taris, the Eater.

"It was all you, wasn't it?" Kairah whispered to Aeva, hoping against the impossible that the goddess could somehow still hear her. "You were guiding me, trying to lead me to the truth."

But why hadn't Aeva just told Kairah everything?

She had a theory.

Aeva both was and wasn't the goddess Rasheera. According to what Kairah had seen while using the Zikkurat, Rasheera was in a kind of coma, the power she was expelling to resist the crushing force of Moriora taxing all of her strength. In this unconscious state, her mind continued to function similarly to the way a person dreamed while they were sleeping. The will and desire to escape was still present and manifest in the world through Apeiron in subtle, and indirect ways. Although it was difficult to control a dream, one's own desires still found expression in the imagery and feelings. Perhaps Aeva was the equivalent of that. But who really knew the extent and power of the subconscious of a god?

Still, all her fate weaving had not been enough.

Even if Kairah was to escape, she didn't know how to free Rasheera. The ancients knew how. They marched against Shivara and her armies to get to Allose so they could. If there hadn't been the real possibility of the humans and their Allosian allies being able to free Rasheera, then Shivara wouldn't have needed to decimate and isolate them. And whatever ritual was involved had to be performed here, in Allose. Perhaps on the Mother Shard?

Kairah grit her teeth. She didn't have enough information, and she couldn't escape the sense that time was quickly running out. Something was terribly wrong with the goddess. The multi-dimensional scream Kairah had heard confirmed that. Something was attacking the goddess. Was it the creature who destroyed Taris? Karak said the Eater was still a threat. Could he have meant Shivara? Or could the man she fought have survived the destruction of the Apeira well and somehow gone to the same realm as the goddess? What would happen if he fed on her, corrupted Rasheera like Moriora's touch corrupted an Apeira well?

Kairah had a pretty good guess.

The goddess would die, and with her, all of her creations. She doubted that Shivara realized she too would cease to exist. She was nothing more than a pawn in a rival god's intricate plan. That too disturbed Kairah–the existence of such powerful beings and the fact some of them possessed the capacity for evil.

Kairah sat up, trying to avoid looking at the other women in the room. They were fortunate compared to what Shivara had planned for her. She was to become Shivara's eternal slave. Something like an acolyte, co-conspirator, and captive lover all in one. Kairah wanted none of it, but Shivara hinted that when she completed her transformation, she'd have no choice but to obey if she wanted a food supply. Did Shivara know what she'd done in spreading Moriora? She called it setting the fire. Did it even enter her mind that she herself would not escape when the world burned down?

As if thinking the woman's name had called her, Shivara strode into the room, her head once again shaved, and burnt clothes replaced by an elegant red gown from some human kingdom lost to history.

The mindless Etele trailed her, holding a pair of hair shears. *Did she mean to cut my hair so as to also hide my Moriora nature?* Kairah had to fight back the rage that threatened to consume her. *I give into that and I will finish my transformation.*

Shivara had said that Kairah's enraged outburst earlier, in which she attempted to incinerate the woman's head, had been the catalyst in accelerating her metamorphosis which finished stripping away Kairah's already diminishing spell-casting ability. That had disappointed Shivara as Kairah's ability to use the Zikkurat died with her spell-casting.

"You're still resisting your fate."

Kairah sat up. "I would sooner choose death than become like you!"

Shivara chuckled. "That's not an option for you, child." She waved at Etele and the woman obediently stepped back behind her. Shivara took several steps into the room. "You are destined for immortality."

"By stealing the life from others?"

Shivara bent to examine the face of one of her mindless dolls. "My patron promised to change me so that I will no longer have to feed on others. Once I ascend, I can offer the same to you."

"Do you not realize that your god has abandoned you? He ignores you because you are no longer of any use to him."

Shivara's eyes flashed, but she quickly regained her self-possession. "He is a god. Gods cannot lie."

Kairah was becoming more and more certain Shivara was completely mad, and this expression of irrational faith in a deceitful and murderous being's honesty was just one more indication that her assessment was correct. Kairah was getting angry, something she couldn't afford as that would serve to accelerate her transformation and bring it to completion. So, she decided to change the subject.

"What is wrong with them?"

Shivara gently caressed the pale face of the dead-eyed woman, this one dressed disturbingly like a young human girl complete with sundress and oversized bow. The outfit reminded Kairah of the outfit Maely purchased in Imaris. The memory seemed like it'd come from a thousand years ago, instead of the matter of weeks it actually had been.

"A long-term side effect of continually using someone as a conduit to feed off the Mother Shard is significant mental trauma, another effect of being touched by Moriora. It usually takes years, but eventually the proxy loses their mind. After that, their ability to draw in Apeiron slowly diminishes until they lose it altogether."

Kairah glanced at the corner where the desiccated skeleton dressed in a purple gown sat staring at her. She had to fight back another surge of anger. This woman was demented, sick, and absolutely in love with death.

Kairah stood. "Etele seems different."

Shivara's painted lips turned up in a smile. "Observant of you, child." She straightened and waved at Etele. "She is different. Over the long years, I've had many proxies, and the isolated life I've been forced to live has given me plenty of opportunity for experimentation."

Kairah shivered at the way the witch emphasized the word.

"When Etele broke, I bonded her to an ego talis to see what the mind of the talis would do with an empty shell. Imagine my delight when it took complete control of the girl."

Etele was nothing more than an ego talis bonded to a blank mind? She thought of Jekaran when the sword talis took control of him. Etele's stare wasn't quite as dead as the stares of the other women in the room. There was intelligence behind those eyes, non-Allosian intelligence.

"And it serves you?"

Shivara stepped behind Etele, and slowly caressed the willowy girl's bare shoulders. "The ego talis was confused and still sought a master. Therefore, it latched onto me, though no actual bond exists between us. As you no doubt have puzzled out, wielders of Moriora can't use talises. But Etele's loyalty is no less solid." Shivara stepped around the girl and traced her lacquered fingernails across Etele's cheek.

Kairah ground her teeth. This was worse than compulsion. At least compulsion left the victim's mind intact. Her anger waxed hotter, and Kairah's emotional control started slipping.

"She obeys me in all things." Shivara gave a throaty chuckle.

Kairah's rage exploded. "Monster!" She lunged at Shivara, but before she could touch the woman, pain like nothing Kairah had ever experienced erupted behind her eyes.

It was exquisite agony. In comparison, her previous headaches had been comical parodies. She fell to her knees, burning bile spewing out of her mouth and nose. Her sight became a kaleidoscopic swirl of different colored lights, and sounds rang in her ears with offpitch, oscillating volume. She'd lost control and was finally completing her transformation into a Moriora vessel, a life leech.

No! I will not become what she is!

A psychic awareness blossomed out from her mind, and she could feel the life energy in each of the mindless women Shivara kept in the room, though not in Shivara herself. The cores of energy pulsated like a heartbeat, each rhythmic thrum an invitation enticing Kairah to take it for herself. If she took that power, she could spell-cast again. She could fight Shivara. She could free Rasheera.

Kairah very nearly succumbed, but the memory of Moriora suffocating her, trying to drive out all her Apeiron, strengthened her resolve. It was augmented further by the memory of the first time she sensed Moriora in the creature Karak called the Eater. The sensation had been one of cold rot and darkness. A morbid song of loneliness, grief, and despair: the song of death. The power being offered to her disgusted her. She would rather die herself than partake of it willingly.

I am sorry, Mother.

The heartbeats faded and Kairah's sight returned. She found herself on the floor, hair mashed to her temple as she lay in a puddle of bile and blonde hair. Kairah sat up and took hold of her new golden locks.

"Strange." Shivara loomed over Kairah. "You've changed, your hair is different, and your eyes are green, but I can still sense life in you."

Kairah stood and wiped the putrid smelling bile from her cheek and temple. "I have rejected Moriora, and I have rejected you!"

Shivara frowned. "Like those ancient Allosians who fell and joined the humans."

Purple dye spilled down the woman's cheek revealing the green color of her right eye. It might've been a tear, but Kairah guessed that tears had long since ceased to roll down the witch's cheeks.

"Unless you want me to reveal your secrets to the synod, you are going to have to kill me." Kairah didn't want to die, but she didn't see any other way out of this. Her new human form was significantly weaker than her Allosian body. She was tired and hungry to a degree she'd never known.

Shivara lowered her eyes and nodded. "I truly wanted you for an equal, Kairah." She sighed. "But it appears I am destined to ascend alone."

"You are not going to be exalted. Your god has abandoned you."

Shivara grinned maliciously and looked up to meet Kairah's eyes. The hellish look on the woman's face was so disturbing that Kairah took an involuntary step backward.

"It's been a long time since I fed on a human." Shivara took a step toward her. "They don't taste as delicious as drawing Apeiron through one of my slaves, but I have to confess..."

Shivara took another step toward her, and Kairah took another step backward. She glanced around, but there was nowhere to run.

"...I've come to relish watching the flesh of my prey wrinkle and dry." She closed her eyes and drew in a shuddering breath. "To feel their life ebb away and flow into me. It's a pleasure unmatched by the most delicious of foods, or the most sensual of touches." Shivara's eyes snapped open. "I'm going to take my time devouring you, Kairah." Shivara shook her head and took another step forward. "No, your end won't be quick." She licked her ruby lips. "I'm going to drain you and then have Etele heal you, and we'll repeat the process over and over until your mind breaks. Only then will I kill you."

Kairah stepped back again but collided with a stone pillar. Shivara smiled and slowly reached for her.

Bang!

The doors to the receiving chamber slammed open startling a scream out of Kairah. Both Shivara and Etele whirled. Standing in the doorway with his left arm thrust forward, hair hanging down to curtain his eyes, was Jenoc.

Chapter 105

Though he now had green eyes and long hair that was blonde instead of ice blue, Kairah never would have mistaken that proud face for one of a human.

"Jenoc!" Kairah darted to the side and put as much distance between herself and Shivara as she could.

"You dare to harm my sister, Oracle?" Jenoc straightened and strode into the chamber.

Shivara smirked. "It's the angry little boy." Her smirk turned down into a frown. "You dare intrude upon my inner sanctum?"

"You are a life leech." Jenoc stopped a mere five paces in front of Shivara. "I ought to have known. It is how you knew so much of the other magic."

"You should be on your knees offering me worshipful praises in gratitude! Without me, you would still just be a powerless, angry, hurt little nothing! I gave you the sword you needed for your vengeance! And this insolence is how you repay my generosity?"

Kairah sprinted along the far wall of the chamber until she was able to round a corner and place herself behind Jenoc. She stepped up to him, but he waved her back.

"See that you keep away, sister. My touch is death."

He was a life leech, now; an arcane leper, destined to suffer a similar fate.

"Jenoc, she is working at the behest of a powerful ascended being to destroy our world and kill the goddess Rasheera."

If Kairah's revelations surprised Jenoc, he didn't show it.

"Run away, Kairah." Jenoc ordered. "And do not stop running until you are far from Allose."

"But Jenoc, I—"

"Go, Kairah!"

Kairah glanced at Shivara who was matching Jenoc's intense glare without blinking. "Take care, brother. She is a powerful spell-caster."

"So am I."

"Brother..." Kairah searched for profound words to convey her love and gratitude, but nothing she could conjure even approached adequate.

"Take this." Jenoc reached into his cloak and produced a small geode.

Kairah recognized the trinket as a gift she'd given her brother when they were children. She reached out her hand and Jenoc dropped it into her open palm. She closed her fingers about it and hugged the worthless rock to her breast. "I love you."

Jenoc met her eyes and flashed a small, sad, smile. "Goodbye, sister."

Kairah lingered a moment, wanting to embrace her brother; once lost but now returned to her in her hour of need, but she couldn't. In her brief time living among the humans, she'd seen mothers agonized over plague-stricken children, unable to hold and kiss them as they died for fear of contracting and perpetuating the spread of the disease. She thought she understood what that felt like now.

"Run!"

Unable to cast, and therefore powerless to fight Shivara or help Jenoc, Kairah did the only thing she could do, and ran.

JENOC'S HEART broke as he listened to the rapid slapping of Kairah's bare feet fade. He'd been denying it, but he could sooner stop loving Kairah as he could surrender his hatred of the humans. After all the horrors Jenoc had wrought, he was surprised he could feel love anymore.

"What is your actual design, Shivara?"

The woman just smirked.

"I do not believe what you told my sister is the whole of it, nor even true."

Shivara chuckled. "She summarized it very well."

"There is no goddess."

"I would not call her that myself." Shivara turned to the side and took a step toward one of the room's couches as though she were intent on sitting. "But Rasheera is an immortal being with a transcendent ability to spell-cast."

Jenoc scrutinized the Allosian oracle, ready for even the slightest indication she was going to spell-cast. "And you seek to slay her?"

"I tried once already, but only managed to imprison her." Shivara reached the couch and sat next to an Allosian woman that held so perfectly still, Jenoc had first thought her a mannequin. "My god gave me a chance to redeem myself by spreading Moriora across all of Shaelar. That's why I taught you the inversion spell."

Jenoc clenched his teeth. "You used me!"

"Nonsense." Shivara examined the blank face of the woman she sat next to, even going so far as to buff out a smear of rouge with the sleeve of her red dress. "You wanted to annihilate the human race. I simply gave you what you asked for."

"I did not ask to be changed into a monster!"

Shivara cocked a painted eyebrow. "You were already a monster, boy. It's why I chose you to start the blaze that would burn this world down."

"That is not what I wanted!"

"But it's what you want now, isn't it?" Shivara stood, keeping one hand on the dead-eyed girl's face for some reason.

Jenoc glanced at the floor. "I do not know what I want. Coming here to stop you from harming my sister has given me a clarity I have not had for months, clear thinking I did not even know I needed."

"That's the corrupting influence of Moriora, the price we pay. Feelings of anger, and actions of violence attune your soul to its power giving it greater hold upon you. Unfortunately, this also twists the mind, the end result being insatiable hunger and total madness."

Jenoc scowled. "If madness is to be my end, then death is to be yours!"

Jenoc's psychic senses reported an influx of Apeiron transferring from the dead-eyed girl into Shivara herself. He manifested his Moriora and wrapped it into a shield around him just in time to absorb a wave of force stronger than anything he'd ever experienced. It was so powerful that it even managed to shove him backward through his shield.

"Go after her, Etele!" Shivara shouted.

Jenoc made to strike at Shivara's servant, but was forced to parry another casting, this one a net consisting of lines of light. He'd never seen a spell like that and could only guess at its function.

Jenoc could not afford to divide his attention between two targets, so the slave girl was able escape and chase after Kairah. Shivara was fast and strong, and he'd already discerned her to be the most adept spell-caster he'd ever encountered. But Jenoc himself was no mean student of the Five Disciplines. He met Shivara's stare for stare and attacked.

TEARS STREAMED DOWN Kairah's face and every step away from Jenoc came with a stab to her heart. Although he'd disowned her for siding with the humans that he reviled, in the end, her older brother hadn't abandoned her. He'd come to her rescue just as he'd done on that awful day so long ago.

Explosions and the other sounds of a caster's duel echoed from behind her, and it took all of her willpower to not turn back. But she couldn't help him fight Shivara, both because she no longer could spell-cast, and also because she had to warn the synod and find some way to free Rasheera.

Kairah sprinted through the white hallways, lungs burning in a way she'd never known before. Her body no longer absorbed any kind of energy, and so she was entirely dependent on its natural functions to supply her strength. She was shocked at just how weak and fragile she felt.

Is this how humans always feel?

Footfalls from behind.

She glanced over her shoulder and found Etelegiving chase. She apparently retained all of her Apeiron-augmented physique as evidenced in the alarming rate at which she was closing the distance between them.

Kairah reflexively tried to cast a ball of fire behind her, but nothing happened; no warm swell within her chest, no wave of electric force flooding her extremities, no gratifying explosion of power as the spell took shape. She was human now, unable to absorb Apeiron and unable to cast spells.

Kairah broke left down a connecting corridor and burst through two doors into Shivara's planetarium. She locked the doors a heartbeat before Etele smashed into them. They held, but white dust rained down from the doors' arched frame signaling they wouldn't keep Etele out forever. Kairah could keeping running, but the woman; faster, stronger, and probably able to spell-cast, would inevitable overtake her.

Kairah ran to the center of the room beneath the massive projection of stars and planets that swirled near the ceiling. There were talises in this room, out of Shivara's presence long enough to have re-charged. Kairah frantically began searching the tables and the various oddities they displayed. She found several talises, but the only one that proved of any use was a silver wand that could repair and build stonework. With it, she could further seal the entrance to the room and buy her some time to escape. It would work, unless Etele could spell-cast.

Bang!

Kairah started and whirled toward the doors. She expected to see Etele stepping in the room, but to her surprise, she found them still closed.

"Kairah?"

Kairah turned toward another set of doors leading into the chamber from the opposite wall. They were open, one of the two slowly swinging back after having clattering against the wall astride the archway. Standing in the open doorway was a young man with messy black hair, green eyes, and a silver sword with a large round amethyst embedded in the cross guard and tiny emeralds peppering the tapered blade.

"Jekaran!"

He laughed, and Kairah was surprised at how much she'd missed that laugh. She ran to him and threw her arms around his neck. "You are alive."

Jekaran stammered a moment before pulling away and looking at her. "And you're blonde!"

Something was different about Jekaran. He appeared more confident and moved with an Allosian-like grace. She couldn't spell-cast, but Kairah still retained her arcane expertise. "You have mastered your link to the sword!"

An explosion of wood and stone announced Etele had broken through, and one look at the splintered remnants of the doors scattered across the floor confirmed Kairah's fear that the slave could spell-cast. Kairah let go of Jekaran and turned to face the mindless woman. She kept herself protectively in front of him, aimed the mason wand at Etele, and cast. Four walls of white stone materialized around the slave girl, boxing her in and forming a ceiling to trap her.

"Neat tri—"

Kairah grabbed his arm. "Run!"

But it was too late. A thin blade sharply protruded from the front wall of Etele's stone box. It sliced to the side and then down, then to the side and then up. A square of white stone fell forward and landed on the ground, followed by Etele ducking through the opening.

Maybe it hadn't been spell-casting the mindless slave girl used to break open the planetarium doors. Kairah's eyes fell to Etele's rapier. No normal blade could cut like that through stone. Kairah groaned upon seeing the circular amethyst jewel embedded in the rapier's handguard. She'd seen it upon first arriving in Shivara's tower, and assumed it was a talis, but now she understood the horrifying truth. Shivara had said she'd bonded the mindless Etele to an ego talis as part of her abominable experimentations.

The rapier was that ego talis.

Jekaran pulled away from Kairah and launched into a run toward Etele. "Jekaran, wait!"

Etele surged forward in a blur of motion, crossing the dozens of paces in a heartbeat, and struck. Even with the supernatural speed the sword lent him, Jekaran nearly parried the thrust too late. He knocked aside Etele's thin blade, and whirled; horizontal cut aimed for Etele's neck. The slave girl blurred again, rapier snapping up and stopping Jekaran's sword mid swing.

Jekaran's mouth hung open and he was about to say something, but Etele fell into splits, rapier following her as she dropped low and slashed. Blood sprayed and Jekaran stumbled backward, a large tear in his trousers exposing a diagonal red line across his thigh.

Kairah threw up another stone box around Etele and ran to catch Jekaran before he could fall down. "Her rapier is like your sword."

"Yeah," Jekaran said through clenched teeth. "I guessed that."

The top of Etele's stone prison fell in, and the woman rocketed into the air, skirts of her dress fluttering. She flipped and landed in front of the box, blank eyes staring at Jekaran as she whipped her rapier out to the side and held it horizontal.

Jekaran straightened, favoring his injured leg as he brought the sword up into a two-handed guard position. "There's a healing ring in my pocket. Irvis gave it to me."

Kairah gasped. "I could kiss that human!" She shoved her hand into Jekaran's pocket and pulled out Rasheera's ring.

"You'd better not do that," Jekaran said.

"True," Kairah agreed. "I do not wish to encourage his lustful feelings for me." She examined the engraved images of lilies that ran across the silver band.

"It's not that. He has a girlfriend. She strikes me as the jealous type."

Though it was completely inappropriate for their circumstances, Kairah found herself laughing. She threaded a slender finger through the ring, but before she could begin a healing, Jekaran shoved her to the side. She crashed into a table, knocking a dozen metal instruments to the floor.

Etele swung her rapier down before she even touched the floor, and Jekaran blocked the attack. The clashing of the two weapon talises sounding forth a resonant clang accompanied by an explosion of crackling purple sparks. Kairah searched for the mason wand, but found it lying on the floor a dozen paces away next to Jekaran's leather boot.

Etele landed, leapt back, bent low, and lunged. Jekaran side-stepped, whirled, and brought his sword down in a diagonal slice, but Etele blurred away and the sword whistled through empty air. The two ego talis bearers commenced a blinding dance of swings and parries, and Kairah didn't dare get close enough to grab the mason wand.

Kairah scrambled to another nearby table, sifting through its oddities for another talis she could use to help Jekaran. She reached for a star-shaped amulet but froze just before her fingers touched its silver chain. The goddess ring was glowing, the lines on the band that made up the semblance of lilies shining white. A hot energy suffused Kairah's skin, not painful like heat from a flame, but electric like... like when her body absorbed Apeiron.

JENOC DEFTLY WOVE several Disciplines together and conjured a disabling attack on Shivara's mind while at the same time increasing the gravity around her in an invisible vice. She deflected the psychic assault at the same time she pushed back against his sphere of force. Jenoc strained to maintain the casting, but his stolen Apeiron store was decreasing at twice the rate it did when he was Allosian. He ceased his attack, and struck out with something more basic; a whip made of fire. Shivara sliced the whip from the air with a beam of white light and it evaporated.

She laughed. "I am over a thousand years old, boy. I was the first human among our race to acquire spell-casting. I know secrets you could never dream of!!"

"Human?"

"That's right! You don't know!" A cruel smile touched Shivara's ruby lips. "Allosians are actually human, albeit changed at the cellular level so as to be able to absorb and redirect energy."

The revelation struck Jenoc like a physical blow. "No..."

Shivara eagerly nodded. "That's right, boy. You are the very thing you hate!"

"But they are so depraved and violent..."

Shivara pouted and said in a tone of mock sorrow, "They can't help it, I'm afraid. Partly because of interbreeding with those who have dormant Moriora in their blood, and partly because of the absence of Mother's presence and light. Not to mention that I have actively suppressed tenets of Seiro."

Seiro? Wasn't that the Ursaj code of honor? The thought was one of thousands of questions swirling in Jenoc's mind as it made dozens of connections. Puzzle pieces from history he'd never been able to fit into the official Allosian narrative started to fall into place. Rage ignited inside him, and he scowled at Shivara.

She grinned in response. "For centuries, I have controlled the appointees to the synod through my feigned divinations. I've led them by my authority as oracle the same as a bullock is led by its iron nose ring. I used them just as I used you."

Jenoc growled.

"That's it," Shivara purred. "Lose yourself in the anger. Revel in the urge to consume and destroy. Wild, mindless, insanity is near for you, I think."

Jenoc threw his hands forward as a desperate ragged scream tore from his lungs. At the same time, he telekinetically took hold of two massive pillars behind Shivara and yanked them from their footings. The columns tore free from the high ceiling and fell, tree-like, toward the bald woman, but Shivara and her dead-eyed slave disappeared in a flash of purple. The other slaves, sitting stoic on couches in the square between the stone columns, weren't so lucky. The marble pillars crushed and rolled over them in explosions of stone, dust, and blood. Shivara reappeared at the far end of the long, narrow chamber with an arm hooked around the waist of her slave.

Why had she taken that girl with her while letting the others die?

Rage and a lust to destroy were clouding his mind once again. He shoved back the question and spun out another spell that tore a hole in the air. A portal to an abyss of absolute blackness yawned wider and wider as it sucked in chunks of stone debris and broken furniture.

Shivara cocked an eyebrow. "Who taught you how to make a singularity?" Her robes fluttered toward the growing mass of blackness, as though she were caught in a high wind. "That was one spell I've intentionally withheld from the College."

Jenoc didn't answer. He just poured as much Apeiron into the spell as he could. He would have to feed soon if this didn't succeed in engulfing the oracle. He'd had the spell in mind for a while–a spell he'd puzzled out from studying a void scepter in his personal collection–it being his contingency plan in case he needed to destroy any appreciable number of his Morioran army.

The secret wasn't the fire, as he'd originally thought, but striking in one swift, decisive, blow. You had to decimate a Moriora wielder in one attack so they couldn't regenerate. Sucking the bald witch into nothingness would work.

Shivara's slave stumbled forward, the vacuum of the black hole sliding her four paces before Shivara reached out and grabbed the girl. When she made contact, the girl's purple aura flared and a wave of Apeiron poured into Shivara–but to Jenoc's surprise the slave didn't wither.

Shivara waved her off hand and Jenoc's all-consuming void collapsed in on itself and vanished. He was low on Apeiron now, so low that his skin was beginning to flake and a chunk of his hair sloughed off and fell to the floor.

"I have to admit, I am impressed. You really do live up to your reputation as a master of the College of Disciplines, or at least what passes for a master these days." Shivara let go of her slave and took half a dozen steps toward him. "I was going to take your sister as my lover, make her my ascended consort." She tapped one finger against her cheek and looked Jenoc up and down. "Perhaps you would be a superior choice."

Jenoc stumbled to one knee. "Go to hell, witch!" He had Apeiron enough for one last powerful demonstration of his acclaimed reputation, and then he would die. It was better than he deserved.

"I do think I will need to teach you how to control that temper of yours, if you are to remain coherent long enough for Boulos to raise us."

Jenoc looked past Shivara to her blank-eyed slave. The Allosian woman, dressed like a little girl's doll, continued to draw Apeiron. This close to the Mother Shard, it was an autonomic thing for an Allosian to absorb energy, much like breathing. What would happen if he fed on an Allosian, one who could channel Apeiron? He'd been so focused on being the first of his kind to reach the Mother Shard and cast the inversion spell that he hadn't stopped to try it.

She's a conduit! Shivara was using the slave to draw Apeiron through her and fuel her spell-casting. He knew he ought to have made the connection much earlier than this moment, but his rational mind was fading, lost in a storm of hatred and all-consuming lust for destruction.

Jenoc lashed out with a tentacle of Moriora and speared the slave through the chest. Her aura flared as he pulled Apeiron through her and into himself, healing his physical wounds and replenishing his core.

Jenoc had nearly died of exposure when he was a boy after spell-casting to save Kairah from the humans that murdered their parents left him weak. He remembered the dry pain of thirst, and the sweet relief when Kairah had found a stream from which they could drink. Drawing in potent Apeiron instead of its lesser forms from the bodies of men and animals was like that, only a hundred-fold. The pristine energy coursing into him was delicious and sating in a way he'd never known. It made it difficult for him to focus on Shivara.

The false oracle's smug smile was gone, replaced by a contortion so fearsome it actually frightened Jenoc. She had manifested a tendril and was also feeding off the slave while screaming something at him. Jenoc pulled more and more Apeiron through the mindless girl, surprised that he had long ago exceeded the amount he'd always believed to be his limit.

Moriora is the erasure of limitations and boundaries, Jenoc the scholar said from far away. That voice was faint, and growing fainter. He was losing himself. Somehow the more Apeiron he drank in, the slippier his rational thoughts became. It was intriguing, but unimportant. All that mattered now was destroying this monster.

But he was a monster too. Had been one ever since the day he'd lashed out and obliterated the men who'd killed his family, but that wasn't what changed him. He'd gone further than justice could sanction and destroyed the entire village of Taratra. Every man, woman, child, and animal had died that day. That's really when Jenoc had become a monster, not when he first cast the inversion spell. Well, if it took a monster to slay a monster, then perhaps in his death he could find some redemption.

The slave girl's aura shined brighter and brighter as both he and Shivara glutted themselves. The girl began to convulse, and a red trickle ran from her nose. They were killing her, but Jenoc couldn't stop drinking in the energy even if he wanted to. It was more delicious than anything he'd ever tasted before.

The slave girl's mouth opened in a silent scream and then the flow of power abruptly stopped. Her eyes dried and disappeared from their sockets as her skin stretched and shrank tight against her skeleton. She exploded into little more than bits of bone and dust.

"You insolent fool!" Shivara's screaming had at last become audible.

Jenoc burned with the vast amount of Apeiron he held. He rose and met Shivara's wild-eyed stare with a smirk. "Now let us truly see who the master spell-caster is."

THE COMFORTABLE WARMTH suffusing Kairah's skin had quickly heated to a painful fire, and as much as she tried, she couldn't remove the silver ring. Something new was happening to her, changing her at the very basic levels.

Why hadn't the ring had this effect on me before?

It had powered her spell-casting and slowed the progression of Moriora's corruption. The power that was decay and death had left Kairah when she refused its proffered metamorphosis, but could it have left Aeose in her blood? She was like Jekaran now, human with the potential to absorb energy. Perhaps with the obstruction of Moriora's power gone, the goddess ring could... what? What was it doing to her?

Jekaran leapt off a wall, sailed through the apparition of a planet, and clashed with Etele. They hung in the air as if frozen, purple electricity arcing from the steel of their kissing blades. An explosion rippled from them, distorting the holographic display of the cosmos as they broke apart, each falling into a ready crouch. Bloody boot prints covered the planetarium's glossy floor, and Jekaran's right pant leg was soaked through. The sword allowed Jekaran to ignore his physical wounds, and Kairah had seen him fight through a concussion, internal bleeding and broken limbs, but eventually the damage would take its toll. To make matters worse, Jekaran had suffered several additional serious wounds since the commencement of the duel.

If I could only get close enough to heal him.

All restoration talises required skin to skin contact with the intended recipient of the healing, but getting close to the two combatants' dance of death was suicide.

Kairah gasped. The electric burning inside her core flared and a halo of white light rippled away from her and coalesced around Jekaran as he flipped headfirst over Etele. He landed, spun, and parried three thrusts from Etele before knocking her back with a kick to the stomach. Light fused into Jekaran in a rush making him gasp and shudder. When it faded, the oozing gash in Jekaran's thigh was gone. Kairah had healed him without even touching him!

Jekaran glanced at her, but before he could say anything, he was on the defensive of a barrage of rapier jabs and quickly sucked back into the duel.

Kairah examined the glowing ring. The healing had felt less like using a talis and more like spell-casting. Was the ring restoring her ability to channel energy? The heat in her chest had slightly faded when she healed Jekaran, but immediately resumed building hotter as it spread along her entire body. She was glowing now, a nimbus of white light outlining her form.

Kairah grit her teeth and stumbled forward, landing against a silver chair with a pentagram holding an amethyst jewel for a head rest–the Zikkurat. The talis Shivara had forced her acolytes to use to maintain her deception, and try to contact her god.

The Zikkurat responded to her touch.

Shivara had said that only Allosians with the oracular talent could use this talis. Kairah had never heard of a talis that would only function for an Allosian, but perhaps only oracles could use it because they already knew how to sift through the complex communion with fate.

I need answers. I need to find and free Rasheera. But would the Zikkurat work for her while she was wearing the goddess ring? Talises often conflicted with one another, and Kairah had no idea what the ring was doing to her. The interactions could also sometimes be lethal, especially when trying to combine the use of two powerful artifacts.

More is at stake than just my life.

After a glance at Jekaran–who was bearing down on Etele with a blinding whirlwind of sword swings–Kairah pulled herself up and sat in the silver chair. The planetarium faded to a vision of absolute white.

CHAPTER 106

Tyrus's idea had turned out to be a monumentally stupid one. Yes, they were out of the tower, and therefore outside the influence of the warding stone that held them there, but no, they definitely were not safe.

The sky above Allose had grown black with roiling clouds within which flashes of green lightning came in regular intervals. But the real danger wasn't coming from above. No, it was right there with Tyrus on the streets of the magical city.

Feral men and women with tentacles of translucent, green energy growing from their backs and chests, roamed the streets of Allose. They used their otherworldly tendrils to paralyze and kill any who strayed too close to them.

Their little group had encountered two of the monsters upon exiting Kairah's tower and had only managed to escape because Irvis had dropped one of the displacement talises. The monster was distracted by it, feeding on it like a guard dog tossed a piece of freshly cut meat. That left them with not enough talises to escape the city, not that the others really wanted to.

Hort and Mulladin both seemed determined to find and help Jekaran, now that their opportunity for escape had evaporated. Even Irvis and his whore-mistress lover refused to take the remaining shift bracelet and escape. Tyrus had been tempted to volunteer under the guise of going for help, but he didn't want to look like a coward. Truth be told, Tyrus hadn't liked the idea of leaving Jekaran either, and although they were caught in a maelstrom of death and chaos, it felt right to remain in the city.

"Oh, we're going to die, aren't we?" Tyrus whined.

"Probably." Hort laughed, actually laughed!

"You're insane! All of you people are insane!"

"Yup," Hort cheerfully agreed.

Tyrus let out a very unmanly scream as one of the monsters with the magic tentacles charged them from an alley. Hort shoved him out of the way, spun the black scepter, and swung it in front of the charging monster, drawing a horizontal line of absolute black that hung in the air. When the monster collided with the line it tore through its neck, decapitating it. But that wasn't all the black line did. Before the creature's head could fall, it compressed in a nauseating mess of broken bone, fluid, and pink sinew and was sucked into the black line. Like a beast sated by eating its fill, the line faded.

Tyrus covered his mouth but vomit still spilled through his fingers.

Hort eyed the headless corpse sprawled on the ground and then twirled the scepter. "Handy! It almost looks like this was created for fighting these creatures."

A bolt of lightning erupted from behind Tyrus, and he clapped his hands over his ears a moment too late. Keesa was casting blue shafts at another approaching monster; this one a woman wearing a tattered dress that looked to have once been of fine and expensive make. The style was not Aiestali, Tyrus noted, but Haeshalen, as evidenced by the sharp diagonal cut of the cuffs, and the neckline high enough to show the chest but hide cleavage. In fact, many of the monsters wore Haeshalen-noble clothing, tattered and dirty though it was.

Not many people had the kind of eye for fashion that Tyrus did. Not many unwed noble men collected fine dresses. Truthfully, not many unwed noble men liked to wear fine dresses. It was a guilty pleasure he kept to himself for obvious reasons.

They turned a corner onto one of Allose's arterial streets where they found a mob of panicked Allosians fleeing toward the center of the city. Peacekeepers herded the crowd, occasionally breaking away to battle one of the life-sucking monsters. At best, they could repel or delay them, most often they were paralyzed and set upon by packs of the creatures and devoured.

Tyrus broke into a run toward the Allosian mob and was surprised when the others followed him. He guessed they'd come to the same conclusion as he had–there was safety in numbers. And, of course, their best chance for reuniting with Jekaran was to be at the center of the action. It was like following smoke to find the fire that produced it. Perhaps the old saying, "where there is smoke there is fire," ought to be replaced with, "where there is chaos, there is Jekaran."

Tyrus found himself laughing. "Divine Mother, I'm just as insane as the rest of them!"

A SINGLE, glowing white flower rose from the ground at the edge of an endless abyss. A wind from within the void pulled at the petals of the spirit lily, and one actually broke free and was sucked into the darkness. The flower's aura dimmed and it sagged as it began to wilt.

"Aeva!" Kairah screamed. "Mother!"

Kairah... Aeva's voice was frighteningly weak.

The void pulled at the flower with increasing vigor.

"Tell me what I must do!" Kairah shouted, and even her voice seemed to get sucked into the infinite darkness.

The Eater has come...

"How do I find you? How do I stop him?"

The spirit lily's glow winked out, it wilted, and then was pulled into the darkness.

"No!' Kairah screamed.

Aeva was gone, but something on the ground remained, uprooted when the spirit lily had been pulled into the void. Kairah focused her disembodied gaze on the object. It was silver, and glowed with a faint white light. What was it?

Plant it, a voice very much like Aeva's, only more mature, whispered.

Kairah looked closer. The object was a tear-drop shaped bulb, the kind used to plant flowers, though this one appeared to be made of molten quicksilver. Kairah reached for it.

I have to plant this? But where? Where can I plant it that the void cannot just pull it in?

Guided by an intuition she couldn't account for, Kairah lifted the liquid metal bulb and pressed it to her chest. The bulb flashed white and then melted into her heart.

Kairah's eyes snapped open. She was back in Shivara's planetarium, sitting in the silver chair that was the Zikkurat. The sounds of Jekaran's duel with Etele returned, as did the fever that scorched Kairah's skin from the inside out. She glanced at the goddess ring glowing white on her finger.

What did the vision mean? She'd sat in the Zikkurat for answers but was now more confused than ever. She sat back and closed her eyes. The future. Instead of reaching out to Rasheera, she would concentrate only on the future. Perhaps the answers lay ahead.

She saw nothing.

Kairah pushed again, and the Zikkurat activated, but it showed her only blackness. Icy horror impaled her chest. The Zikkurat could show her nothing if there was no future to show. She stood from the silver chair, wobbled, and collapsed to her knees. The searing heat from the energy coursing through her was agony.

She ignored the pain as best she could, slowed her breathing to calm herself, and sifted through memories of the vision she'd seen of Shivara imprisoning the goddess. There had to be a clue for how to free Rasheera from her crystalline prison.

The Eater has come, Aeva had said.

Somehow, the creature Kairah had fought in Taris had broken into Rasheera's prison. She remembered hearing the monster's laughter echo across two planes of existence just before Taris fell. It was there, in the center of the planet, it had to be. It was with Rasheera who was unconscious and defenseless.

Although the spirit lily in her vision had already been consumed by the void, Kairah didn't think it meant Rasheera was dead. If spell-casting worked the same way for the goddess that it did for Allosians–albeit on a cosmic scale–then that meant her spells would fail with her death. In the case of a deity, that likely meant all creation would unravel.

The pain flared hotter, making Kairah wince and grit her teeth. What was happening to her? She'd been certain the Moriora had left her body when she refused to become a life leech. Could she have been wrong? Was she so corrupted that the energy from Rasheera's ring was destroying her? If that were true, then it was more reason for her to be quick in discovering the secret to releasing the goddess.

She focused on her memories of what the Zikkurat had shown her of the past. What was it that Shivara had done? She blasted Rasheera with Moriora. What had Rasheera done? She manifested a shield to block the cage of energy trying to crush her. The shield had pushed out, mixing with the Moriora which diluted the energy until it crystalized as an Apeira well. The Mother Shard now stood where the attempted deicide had taken place, rising from within the planet.

That is the door to her prison. All Apeira wells were doors to her prison. Kairah remembered the Eater in Taris touching the well. He'd done more than just feed upon it. He'd used it to enter Rasheera's dual realm.

Kairah stood and found Jekaran. Etele was standing on a table parrying his blows. She performed a flawless backward, single-handed handspring, flipping off the table just as Jekaran cleaved it neatly in two.

We need to get to the Mother Shard!

Kairah took a step toward Jekaran but faltered and crashed into a bronze tesseract sat atop a metal pole. The instrument crashed to the ground, Kairah going with it. She screamed as the heat consuming her burned even hotter.

Kairah's scream distracted Jekaran and he nearly took the point of the blank-eyed girl's rapier through his throat. He folded backward, and then spun to the side, landing a staggering kick in the woman's stomach. Jekaran straightened, and raised his sword, but she was already recovered and again on the offensive forcing him to desperately deflect five lightning-strike thrusts.

Divine Mother, but she's fast!

Jekaran knocked her thin blade aside and punched her in the face. At first, he'd tried to avoid dirty tactics like that, on account of his foe being a woman, but any quarter he showed her resulted in injury or loss of advantage to himself. He could almost hear Maely saying, "*Idiot! Girls can fight just as well as boys.*"

The girl's blank stare didn't falter as her head rocked back from the force of his blow. Jekaran took the opportunity to break away and scan the chamber for Kairah. He found her slumped over a bronze cube, grimacing in pain and trying to stand–and was she glowing?

"The hell?"

Pain and cold metal dug into his side and he jerked back just in time to deny the girl's rapier further penetration. He turned his dodge into a diagonal cut, but the woman moved away just in time.

He was about to ask the sword for advice but caught himself. They were no longer two separate minds yoked together, but one being. Jekaran's consciousness had swallowed up the sword's sentience and absorbed its knowledge and power–*You have mastered Azrin.* That actually caused a pang of sadness. He'd been getting used to the psychic company.

He parried, dodged, ducked, and swung, but couldn't ever inflict any significant wounds on his opponent. They were too evenly matched, a fact Jekaran had not faced since bonding the sword talis. And she too fought as though there were no disparity between her mind and that of her ego talis. The woman's sword, despite being forged in a different style, was identical to his.

No, a thought came to him. *Not identical.*

Jekaran glanced at the steel that made up her rapier's thin blade. It bore no emerald shards.

The scene of those green specks shining like stars when he killed Kaul flashed in his mind. *I drained his life and used it to refill the sword's Apeiron and heal myself.* Then, another scene replayed before him. Ez staring into his eyes, blood trickling from his mouth. The emerald stars lit up then, too.

"No," he choked out and unbidden tears blinded him.

He'd drained Ez's life force, too. Did that mean his uncle's soul was gone?

I'm the Eater.

He faltered and the blank-eyed woman rammed her rapier through his shoulder and then quickly pulled it out. Jekaran choked out a bellow of pain, and barely managed to bring the sword up to parry her follow-up thrust, a strike meant for his heart.

I'm the Eater. The sword had told him as much when it confirmed he had evil in his blood.

The slave girl sliced his thigh, and he stumbled. She kicked up, the heel of her bare foot connecting with Jekaran's jaw. She held her foot above her head with the flexibility of a dancer and then brought the heel down on the back of Jekaran's head. He went down, his sword clanging as it struck the floor beside him. His heart stung as though it were being squeezed by two strong hands, and a crushing nausea filled his stomach. He resisted his supernatural instincts to roll to the side and snatch the sword. He didn't want to keep fighting.

You were right, Ez. I should've listened to you. I should've resisted the lure of fools. He wasn't sure exactly what he could've done different other than not going after the sword when it called to him. In retrospect, that had been the linchpin decision that tied him to this fate, and he hated himself for having made it. *You'd still be alive if I had simply left it alone.*

The woman's rapier pierced his back, driving through one of his lungs, forcing Jekaran to cough a smattering of crimson on the marble floor. He knew his end had come, and even thoughts of saving Kairah didn't rouse him to defend himself. It wasn't cowardice or even surrender to grief that kept him down, but his love for the woman. She wasn't safe with him, not if he was Karak's Eater. Not if he was capable of killing the man he loved like a father. Eventually he'd kill her, too.

I am a mad dog that needs to be put down.

The woman leveled her rapier at his right eye and then drew back in preparation to ram it through his socket. A ball of light, like one of Karak's spirit orbs, appeared behind the slave girl and Jekaran used it as a focal point to steel himself against the coming deathblow.

Fool, boy! A familiar gravelly voice said.

Ez?

And then his uncle appeared behind the slave girl who stood frozen with her arm cocked back. His uncle stepped forward, passing through the slave girl like smoke, and knelt in front of Jekaran. He could actually smell the tobacco on Ez's breath. He was really here.

Ez smiled. "You aren't the Eater, boy."

"But the sword said—"

"Just that you have the potential in your blood. It's why you can use the sword to drain Apeiron. I could never do that because I don't have your gift."

"A gift?" Jekaran sobbed. "This thing that I am is not a gift!"

Ez shook his head. "If only you could see you the way I see you." He put a very physical feeling hand on Jekaran's shoulder. "Mull told you the end of the Lure of Fools poem?"

"Ez..."

"But closely resemble they one another, both heroes and fools at first..." he began.

"Ez, please... I'm not—"

"Quiet boy!" he snapped, and the familiar expression, though rebuke, actually comforted Jekaran. "I don't have much time, so dammit, you're going to listen!"

Jekaran nodded.

"Closely resemble they one another; both heroes and fools at first, but it's only at the fork of destiny's road that the truth will at last emerge. For while the fool always looks to his own regard, the hero for others is aware. And will suffer and die when called upon, even for strangers in his care."

Ez flashed a tender smile and stroked Jekaran's hair. "I didn't tell you that at first, because I wanted you to only have the warning. See, I was afraid you'd turn out like me-a fool. But like the poem says, I just couldn't tell the difference, not until you actually faced the world.

"You risked your life time and again for your friends without letting concern for your own safety hold you back. Even now, right here, you're ready to give your life to protect those you love. You're not selfish like I was. Don't you understand? You are not a fool, Jekaran. You're a hero."

Jekaran broke into tears. "But I killed you, Ez."

Ezra shook his head of unruly gray hair. "I gave my life to free you from the sword. And even in that I was a fool. For I thought you couldn't handle its power, but I was wrong. You're perhaps the only one in all of Shaelar who can."

"Ez..."

"Now stop belly aching and get up! Use your gift to save yourself and the rest of us!"

Ez disappeared, as did the ball of light hovering above the slave girl. Time unfroze, and the point of the woman's rapier shot toward Jekaran's face. But, instead of dodging to the side, Jekaran shot his arm out, grabbed his sword and leapt up and toward the slave girl. Her rapier took him in the chest, just as he ran his sword through her heart.

They stared at each other, both mortally impaled, both silent. Jekaran willed the emerald shards on his blade to life and they exploded into a shine. A rush of energy flowed from the dying woman into the sword, and then into Jekaran himself.

The woman's eyes focused, the blank look of one controlled by an ego talis disappeared, and a tear spilled down her left cheek. "Thank you," she whispered.

Jekaran's healing flesh pushed her rapier out of his chest and it clattered to the ground. The woman closed her eyes, a relieved look on her face as she withered to little more than a skeleton in a dress. The bones fell apart, and Jekaran wrenched his blade out of her ribcage.

He glanced around the room looking for the mysterious ball of light that had heralded the appearance of his dead uncle, but found Kairah instead. She was kneeling on the floor next to the bronze cube, eyes clenched shut and mouth twisted in a grimace of pain.

He ran to her. "Kairah!" When he touched her shoulder, he yelped and snapped his hand back. "You're burning!"

Kairah nodded, keeping her eyes closed. "It is the ring."

Jekaran glanced at her hand and found a band of hot white light where the silver ring had been. "What's happening?"

Kairah shook her head. "We need to get to the Mother Shard."

SHIVARA HUNG in the air raining spears of white light down like judgments from heaven. Jenoc moved quickly, dodging and weaving between the room's massive marble columns. He flung twin lines of black at Shivara–slices that in reality opened into the abyss of space beyond Shaelar–

but she dismissed them with a casual wave of her hand before they could reach her.

She retaliated with a spear of white light that tore through the top of the pillar Jenoc had used for cover. Chunks of marble the size of a man crashed to the floor around him, and the remnants of the pillar wobbled. Jenoc telekinetically picked up the falling column and hurled it into the air to intercept more spears of light. The airborne pillar exploded and Jenoc used the screen of dust and debris to veil his teleport. He appeared in the air just above and behind Shivara and let himself fall, grabbing the oracle and taking her down with him.

Before they struck the ground, a wave of pure force exploded from Shivara, tearing free one of Jenoc's arms and hurling him back dozens of feet. Jenoc slammed into the chamber wall, and then fell twenty feet to the ground. His bones were knitting back together and his arm reforming before he even stood.

Such a dramatic healing cost him dearly, and once again, his Apeiron store was diminishing at an alarming rate. Even so, Jenoc held so much energy that even half was far more than he'd ever held as an Allosian.

A cage of red lines sprung up around him, but Jenoc countered with a sphere of force that bubbled out from him and dispelled the thin lines of crimson fire. A pulsing ball of black energy flew at him, and Jenoc threw up a translucent purple wall. He gasped when the black sphere passed through his shield without stopping, and he had to teleport out of the way. He reappeared behind Shivara, but she whirled before he could cast and blasted him at near point-blank range.

Jenoc flew backward, but this time slowed himself before impacting a marble column by molding gravity below and behind him. He landed on the floor, threw his hands forward, and twin spears of light, identical to Shivara's favored attack, exploded toward the oracle. Her eyes widened and she quickly wrapped herself in translucent green energy that absorbed the spell.

"You learned that spell just from watching me cast it?"

Jenoc kept his hands up, readying several more spells. "I am a quick study."

"You are indeed the prodigy everyone claims you to be."

"This cannot go on indefinitely, Shivara. One of us will eventually run out of Apeiron. Skill with spell-casting will not decide this fight."

"I agree. But you will not outlast me. I have an Apeira well's worth of stored energy. Surrender now, and I will let you join with me, Jenoc." Shivara reached out a hand. "Be my consort and I will teach you wonderful secrets, and not just spell-casting techniques." She smirked.

Rage within begged Jenoc to strike out, but he struggled through the impulse, and clung to reason. Attacking Shivara outright wasn't working. She was far more skilled in spell-casting as well as using Moriora for him to hope to best her.

Kairah.

He focused on his sister, picturing her smile as she proudly gifted him the worthless geode, a treasure that became the most valuable of all his worldly possessions. Jenoc's thoughts began to clear, and he was able to analyze the situation in his familiar logical way.

He cast a spell of his own design, one that he'd often used on fellow Allosians in the synod to gauge their receptivity to his proposals. It was a minor mind probe, one Jenoc had crafted to be nearly undetectable. It wouldn't penetrate the target's mind, but would get close enough to perceive feelings, attitudes, and intentions. He'd compared it to listening at a door when trying to teach it to Kairah.

Shivara narrowed her eyes, and Jenoc tensed. Only if a spell-caster knew what to look for would they be able to detect Jenoc's light psychic touch. A breathless eternity passed, and when Shivara didn't react, Jenoc exhaled softly.

A stream of impressions floated into Jenoc's mind. Shivara was obsessed with the ascended being Kairah had mentioned. The image of the man with metallic gold hair was ever in the forefront of her thoughts, and she was increasingly worried that he would abandon her.

Beyond that was a surprising amount of mental and emotional discipline, so much so that Jenoc couldn't see past her psychic barriers, at least not without pushing harder which would alert Shivara. But those walls of discipline were weakening and bulging like a failing dam holding back a flood.

Jenoc moved away from Shivara's psychic wall, and gently sifted through more of Shivara's unguarded thoughts. She was sincere in her offer to accept him, but they would not be equals. He would be her servant. After outliving all her loved ones, Shivara was lonely and wanted a companion. That need had become twisted and was the impetus behind her keeping mindless slaves about her. But she wanted more than just playthings. A thousand years of life and secrecy had made Shivara desperate for an intelligent companion.

Shivara was vain and prized her survival above all else. She wanted power, and despite her claims to the contrary, the intensity of her despair, and her weakening barrier of mental discipline convinced Jenoc that she was already quite mad. A desperate idea began to take the shape of a plan.

Kairah.

Jenoc retreated from Shivara's mind, lowered his hands and straightened. "I know when I am beaten."

A satisfied, and triumphant ruby-lipped smile spread across her face.

"You are impressive and beautiful, Lady Shivara. I do not wish to die, and so I will accept your offer upon one condition."

Shivara's smile disappeared. "You dare dictate conditions to me?"

Jenoc bowed his head. "Perhaps I should have phrased it as a request."

Shivara lifted her chin, suspicious eyes studying Jenoc. A spell similar to his light mind probe fluttered against his consciousness, and he quickly sealed up his true intentions behind an iron façade of resignation and selfish intrigue. Apparently, it fooled the false oracle, for she retreated from his mind and smiled again.

Shivara walked toward him. "Very well, Jenoc. What is this condition?" She stopped three paces in front of him.

"That you spare my sister." Jenoc's jaw tightened as he detected another subtle scan of his thoughts. "Instruct your servant to allow Kairah to leave in peace."

"And if she goes to the synod?"

"They are no threat to you, no threat to us. Can we not come out of the shadows to openly rule Allose?"

Shivara took another step closer. "Why the sudden change of heart?"

"Because I am beaten." Jenoc made sure to decorate that thought as a deception Shivara could easily detect.

"You're lying."

Jenoc released another carefully manicured thought as though he'd been trying to hide it. "You are now my only hope for wiping out the humans. If the only way I can have my vengeance is by joining you, then so be it."

Jenoc stared unflinching into Shivara's green eyes, and it took all his effort, skill, and subtlety to remain confident and mask his true intentions.

"My, my. You are single minded, aren't you?" She gave a throaty chuckle. "I could find other applications for that."

Shivara's mind probe retreated and she slinked forward and put her arms over Jenoc's shoulders and clasped her hands behind his neck. She looked at him for a beat, and then passionately kissed him. Jenoc kissed her back with twice as much ferocity, pulling her into him so their bodies pressed together.

One of the many ways Jenoc excelled in spell-casting was his natural talent and command of the Second Discipline–elemental. He could cast faster than anyone in the history of the College of Disciplines, and early on in his arcane career had broken dozens of records. It was almost an automatic thing for him, the time between his aura flaring and the manifestation of the spell nearly instantaneous. It made him difficult to defeat in caster duels, as his opponents were always caught off guard when he wove the elements.

His solution was basic, and underwhelming, and truth be told he had gleaned the idea from prince Raelen's aerial attack on his army hours earlier. But Shivara wouldn't be expecting something simple from Jenoc, not after he'd impressed her so. His only reservation was that he wasn't certain if Kairah had gotten away. His concentration wouldn't let him cast his mind out to find her. She'd had a strong head start and was cunning. *She would have gotten out*, he told himself, though it brought little comfort. Now was his chance, and if he didn't take it, Shivara was certain to murder both he and his sister. Jenoc didn't have a choice.

They broke their kiss and Shivara licked her lips. Jenoc smiled and let his psychic guard down. Shivara's eyes widened, but it was too late. A supernova of red fire engulfed them both as it exploded outward.

Jenoc's final thought was of a beaming young girl proffering a geode to him.

Kairah registered the explosion just as the red inferno erupted through the walls. Instinct took over and she grabbed Jekaran by the hand causing him to hiss in pain at her burning touch. With her other hand, she touched Jekaran's sword on the ground beside them and cast. A transparent, glass-like sphere encased them, shielding them from the firestorm roaring all about. Then in a flash of white light, they vanished.

CHAPTER 107

R aelen raised his forearm to shield himself from the heat. An explosion of red flames, not unlike the fire produced by the flare kris now borne by Maely, ripped out of the top of the tower.

"Kairah!" Maely screamed and clenched tighter to Raelen's forearm.

The tower crashed down in a storm of white dust and flying pieces of stone. A globe of light produced by Karak shot into the air above, pulsed, and a bubble of blue energy engulfed them. It deflected several large chunks of debris and remained until the demolition was complete and the dust settled.

The globe of light that had protected them floated down and hovered in front of Karak's reptilian face. "Fey girl gone, aka."

Raelen gently disengaged himself from Maely and made sure she was balanced on her good leg before he took a step toward the mountain of rubble. "Jenoc, too, is dead then?"

It wasn't the end he'd hoped to have administered to the warmonger himself, but Raelen supposed this was justice enough for the horrors Jenoc had wrought. Seiro dictated that vengeance was acceptable only as it also served justice. Anger at wrongs was the sign of a noble soul, but to lose one's self to hate was destructive. Though disappointed, Raelen found that he was also relieved. He'd been skirting that line. It was probably for the best that Jenoc had not died by his own hand.

Gryyth. Tenets of Seiro were so completely enmeshed in his relationship with the Ursaj that thinking of them dredged up his yet unexplored grief. He wished his friend were with him. Raelen hadn't realized how much he relied on the Ursaj for comfort and confidence. It was like losing Saranna all over again.

"Uska, not dead. Fey girl gone, aka."

"She got away?" Maely asked.

"Ssk. Have to find, aka. Stop Eater, aek."

Maely frowned. "Wait, I thought Jenoc was the Eater."

An explosion erupted from within the mountain of rubble, and Raelen had to duck to escape a chunk of white rock crushing his head. The dust settled around a solitary figure; blackened so severely that he looked like a three-dimensional shadow. Although his back was to them, Raelen could see that a quarter of the top of his head was missing. Smoke billowed from his burnt skin as he surveyed his surroundings.

He turned his head in their direction and stopped. A single dot of green glowed where his one eye should've been. Then an aura of the same-colored energy outlined the figure, and a spread of tendrils launched at them.

Raelen leapt in front of Maely and deflected three of the ghostly tentacles. The others struck at Karak like vipers, but vanished upon contact with his scaly bronze skin. White teeth appeared on the creature's burnt face in a parody of a smile.

"My Prince," it rasped.

Divine Mother, it's Jenoc! Burnt beyond recognition, but there was no mistaking that condescending voice even through its hoarse tone.

"Jenoc," Maely gasped.

Jenoc began to trundle down the mountain of debris, green tentacles reforming and floating all about him.

"Maely!" Raelen shouted.

The girl raised the flare kris and pointed the blade at Jenoc, and an explosion of red flame engulfed him. They were so close to the blast the intense heat scalded Raelen's skin. The fire faded but Jenoc remained, outlined in that same green energy, it swirled about him like a shield. His blackened skin began to crack, and then smooth, color returning to parts of his face.

Maely raised the red steel sword again, but Raelen grabbed her wrist.

She looked up at him, eyes wide. Raelen shook his head. "He's somehow absorbing the talis's magic and using it to heal himself."

Jenoc resumed shuffling toward them. "You have proved a clever adversary, My Prince. I admit, I underestimated your tenacity and resourcefulness."

There was something wrong in Jenoc's voice. It was not the rasp that had disappeared when he healed himself, but the way he said his words. His self-possession and aura of purpose were gone, and although he'd always been an enemy, now he seemed a dangerous predator. He was injured, feral, and insane.

Raelen charged, batting away two striking tendrils and leaping at Jenoc. He spun in the air and cracked the monster across the face with a hand–the one missing fingers. Flakes of the man's charred skin sloughed off his face, and Jenoc staggered backward. Raelen followed up with a knee to the stomach, and then threw both hands forward with open palms and struck Jenoc in the chest. Raelen heard ribs crack, and the monster flew into the mountain of rubble. He watched the pathetic creature writhing, and realized that his rage and hate for the man were gone. All he felt was a sick pity for Jenoc, and an obligation to put him down like a rabid dog.

Jenoc laughed as he rose and threw a burnt hand out with a bolt of green lightning that arced into Raelen. The blast burned through his thigh, and he went down. Maely screamed, and Raelen rolled onto his side to see her. Jenoc was shambling toward Maely who was tripping and trying to run.

She blasted Jenoc with another red flare, and Raelen couldn't blame her, but like before Jenoc shielded himself with his green magic and further healed himself; though he was still horribly burnt and disfigured. Raelen struggled to stand, but his upper leg spasmed and he collapsed.

Pain is as the wind and I am the ancient tree.

It can blow and blow against my bark, but I do not bend.

It took all his physical strength and power of will, but he managed to rise. He longed for the transference band and the Ursaj level of stamina it provided, but even if Gryyth were still alive, it would be useless while he wore the emerald shard that protected him.

Jenoc closed on Maely, green tendrils reforming and snaking toward her. "We're not finished, Pariel!" Raelen shouted in hopes that he could divert the monster. But Jenoc ignored him. He was intent on killing Maely, probably so he could drain her life and use it to fully repair his body.

Raelen hobbled forward as fast as he could, but he wouldn't reach Maely in time.

SHARP PAIN SHOCKED Maely's broken leg as she tried to run. She tripped, and the impact from her fall drew a scream from her lips. Jenoc loomed over her, tentacles of translucent green energy spreading out from his chest and back, making him look like he had the wings of a twisted angel.

He laughed. "Little, lovesick Maely. I see you traded your compulsion ring for that flare talis. I fear it was a poor trade."

Three balls of light crashed into Jenoc's chest, lifting him into the air and hurling him back. Karak appeared in midair, raising a claw as he arced down toward Jenoc's fallen form. The Vorakk shaman crashed down on him and swiped at Jenoc's face. An explosion of force rippled the air and launched Karak backward. He flipped and landed in a ready crouch, forked tongue darting in and out as he hissed.

Jenoc's burnt skin cracked as he rose. "Vorakk! And how, pray tell, did you filthy lizards find Allose?"

Karak flashed a toothy grin. "Daka, spirits know. Spirits tell Vorakk to come to fey city, aka. Uska, fight Eaters."

Three more orbs appeared around Karak, turned into orange fireballs, and streaked toward Jenoc. The Allosian wizard reacted with three bolts of green lightning which collided with the balls of fire. To Maely's horror, the orbs exploded, not into flames, but into a thousand tiny specks of light.

"Tak!" Karak hissed. The usually unflappable lizard man sounded as horrified as Maely felt.

None of the other life sucking monsters had been able to absorb or counter Vorakk magic. Could Jenoc truly be that much more powerful?

"Rasheera save us," Maely whimpered.

JOVE SENT bolt after bolt of green lightning at the Ursaj ghosts. They had to be the legendary bear people, for they were larger than any bear Jove had ever seen, and they stood like men. *Where had they come from? Why were they trying to stop him?* It didn't matter. After tasting the pure ecstasy that was the silver-haired doll's essence, he'd gained the power to destroy them. The Ursaj spirits fought ferociously, but they were no match for him. He was a god! He had to be. For only a god could annihilate the otherwise immortal souls of men and beasts.

He stood on one of the many floating islands of rock that made up this strange place. A large black bear-man landed behind him and gripped him in large furry arms. It lifted him up, squeezing, and although the creature was a ghost, its crushing embrace was plenty real. Jove manifested his power as a green aura-like shield, and the Ursaj bellowed and dropped him. He whirled and finished it off with a shaft of lightning to its head, the spirit flashing white and then exploding into millions of tiny white stars.

Claws raked his back, and although they didn't draw blood or cause pain as they might have when he was alive, they were effective in severing his spine. Jove's body might have been bloodless, but he sustained injuries like any other man, damage that could incapacitate him. He dropped to the ground, snarling, sputtering and desperately trying to rise, but his legs wouldn't work.

A white-furred tree trunk of a leg entered his field of vision, and he craned his head up to find the white bear-man who'd originally interrupted his special moment with the silver-haired doll. Its blue eyes narrowed, and it growled as it lifted its foot and positioned it above Jove's head. The massive leg pounded down like a mechanical piston, and Jove's head split open. He lost his ability to see and hear with his body but could still perceive his surroundings with his spirit.

Jove sucked in a torrent of Apeiron, healing his crushed skull. His sight and hearing returned, and his spine aligned and knitted back together. When the white bear's foot came down for another killing stomp, Jove manifested his green shield, and the foot tore apart like glass upon impact. The white bear turned back into a ball of light and zipped away, but Jove lashed out with more lightning. The white orb deftly dodged the first two emerald bolts but the third struck true. The sphere of white light pulsed and then exploded into a galaxy of tiny star-like embers.

Jove rose and was pleased to find he had annihilated every single one of the Ursaj ghosts. He looked up to the silver-haired doll hanging in the cloud of Apeiron above him and frowned. Hadn't she been glowing brighter? Anxiety constricted his chest. No, no. She couldn't die. Not yet! Not before he'd had his special time with her.

Jove launched himself upward and stopped to hover just above the floating woman. He studied her chest and found that she was still breathing. Relief washed over Jove, and he wiped tears from his eyes. He hadn't lost his chance.

He drew close and gently caressed her cheek. "Shh, it's all right. I'm back. It's just you and me now. There isn't anyone left to disturb us."

Tyrus pushed his way through the crowd making a path for Hort, Mulladin, Keesa, Irvis, and Graelle to follow.

Why are they following me of all people?

He'd been worried there would be peacekeepers here in the... what had they called it again? Oh, yes, the Tameion Nomoi; the building where the Allosian's ruling council conducted its business. But all the peacekeepers were engaged trying to turn back the life-sucking invaders, so no one took any real note of the six humans, even though they were armed with talises.

Tyrus pushed through a crowd huddled in a large archway and entered a massive coliseum. Its domed ceiling was made entirely of glass but had no segmentation or metal frames keeping it together. It was if the entire dome was one convex piece. The white stone of the coliseum was tinted purple by the light of Allose's massive Apeira well visible through the glass ceiling.

The concentric rings of seats starting from the speaking floor were filled with frightened Allosians. A small, purple-haired girl eyed Tyrus from the lap of her mother, and he gaped. She was the first Allosian child he'd seen since arriving in the city. There were more, of course, but they were a minority among the thousands of adults.

A tall Allosian dressed in white robes embroidered with glowing purple runes stood on the speaking floor addressing the crowd. His voice boomed and echoed throughout the chamber, and Tyrus guessed he had some kind of voice amplifying talis or was spellcasting to achieve the effect.

"The peacekeepers will hold. There is no need to evacuate Allose," the man called.

"What are they?" one woman yelled. "Their touch kills, and spellcraft does not stop them!"

Her question sparked an overlapping din of shouts, and indecipherable chatter. The speaker raised his hands to call for silence but went unheeded until his third admonition. But even then, the crowd was restless, and a low murmur permeated the coliseum.

"Please, there is no need for disorder. Their numbers are comparatively few, and although they have abilities we cannot explain, they can die. We have already destroyed a third of their numbers."

"That was not us!" a man from the lower bowl shouted. "It was Vorakk magic that turned back those monsters long enough for us to escape!"

The crowd erupted into another deafening roar of confusion.

"Please," the speaker patiently begged. "All the details are not yet—"

"This catastrophe only came upon us after the arrival of those humans!" someone screamed.

"They led these creatures here!" a woman added.

Uh oh... Tyrus glanced around wildly. Heads were already turning and a few Allosians pointed at them. Perhaps coming here hadn't been such a good idea.

Dozens of Allosians seated in the upper rows stood and shouted at Tyrus and his group, and before they knew it, they were divested of their talises and being shoved toward the floor of the coliseum. Hort had tried to fight back, but didn't have room enough to swing his void scepter and Keesa had cast one bolt of lightning, but she'd intentionally shot it over the crowd, an act Tyrus suspected had been to intimidate them, and force the mob back. It didn't work, and they were overpowered.

Tyrus stumbled and rolled the last six steps to the coliseum floor. Fortunately, he hadn't fallen hard, and after shaking off a brief wave of vertigo, he climbed to his feet. The Allosians who had apprehended them appeared to wear the same uniform robes as the guards they'd fought in the College of Disciplines. They now held their talises, and one was gaping openly at the black rod she'd taken from Hort.

"That's mine!" Hort moved toward the woman but froze in an unnatural half-stepping pose.

The speaker in white robes waved a hand and Hort fell to the floor. "We shall have no violence in this place!"

The thousands of spectators apparently disagreed. They shouted and called for punishment.

"Peace-loving fey people, my ass," Mulladin growled.

The speaker raised his hand, but the crowd did not fall silent. Instead they grew more agitated, and someone even spell-cast a ball of fire at them. It dissipated with a wave of the speaker's hand, but more attacks came.

Tyrus had seen a minor lord of the eastern province deposed by his peasants once. The vile bugger deserved it as he had preyed on their young sons for decades. His serfs had surrounded his carriage, and hurled fruit, bottles, and eventually rocks until his guards were overwhelmed. Then they tore open the cab of the carriage and he suffered amateur testicular removal surgery before being stoned to death.

The same wild anger Tyrus had seen in the faces of the mob that killed Lord Hafston was rife on the faces of the thousands of Allosians surrounding them. But, instead of rotten cabbage, or rocks, they were throwing lightning, and fire.

"Stop!" the speaker called, his magic making his voice boom through the room.

But it did no good. The crowd was in a frenzy, frightened and channeling that fear into aggression.

That's it, we're going to die.

Just as angry Allosians began to descend en masse to the coliseum floor, a blinding flash of white light exploded from the center of the speaking floor. Everyone froze, and the roaring coliseum fell silent.

The light emanated from a sphere that gradually resolved into two humans; a blonde woman in a sleeveless purple dress, and a young man with messy black hair holding a silver sword.

KAIRAH STOOD. She could spell-cast again, a fact that was as glorious as it was confusing. Casting the shield spell and transporting them away from Shivara's tower had diminished the burning within her veins, making the pain manageable. Though, like before, Kairah could feel the heat inside her steadily rising again.

She glanced at the silver ring on her finger and found it a burning ring of white light. Not only could she spell-cast, but Kairah sensed she had full access to all Five Disciplines, something not even Jenoc could boast. And, not only could she cast from all the Disciplines, Kairah's psychic senses discerned that she was more powerful than she'd ever been even in the First Discipline, Creation, for which she was celebrated as unusually gifted.

Kairah scanned the thousands of Allosian faces staring down at her with wide eyes. They were motionless, many with mouths agape. What were they so enthralled by? Surely her sudden appearance wouldn't be surprise enough to silence a crowd of thousands.

"Lady Kairah?" Kannic eyed her blonde hair.

Kairah turned to face the white-robed speaker. "Speaker Kannic, assemble the synod. We need to—"

"You shine like the sun..."

Kairah looked down at herself. A shining nimbus of light outlined her form. It was like a flare of her Apeiron aura when she cast except white, much brighter, and constant, whereas Apeiron auras only flared when casting. *What was the ring doing to her?*

Kairah shoved the question to the back of her mind. "Speaker Kannic, are the members of the synod here?"

Kannic appeared not to hear her.

"Lord Kannic!" Kairah snapped. Did she just actually show temperament with the head of the synod?

The tall man shook himself. "Yes, Lady Kairah. Most of us. Allose is under assault by an army of creatures like unto the description of the one you claimed destroyed Taris."

Claimed? Were her people really so willfully blind? Was she ever so foolish? No wonder Shivara had been able to deceive them for centuries. Not only did they not know the truth, they did not want to know it. Her people were zealous about maintaining their complacency even when the end of all things stared them in the face.

"Oracle Shivara is responsible for the spread of Moriora. She herself is a Moriora vessel."

"The oracle brought this calamity down upon us? Those monsters swarming the city are her creation?"

"Through my brother Jenoc. Shivara is ancient and working at the behest of an alien power to kill the goddess Rasheera."

"Goddess?" Kannic put a hand to his head and looked down. The man looked as if he were going to vomit.

I am not going to be able to rely on him or any of the synod. They are too confused and afraid. Kairah herself would have to act.

"Kannic, you need to get everyone out of the city now!"

"We cannot leave Allose! Where will we go?"

"There are plenty of slipgates to facilitate an evacuation." Kairah glanced at the transfixed spectators.

"Lady, Kairah. This is a fantastic claim indeed."

Kairah wanted to slap the speaker, and not because of any residual Moriora in her blood, but because he was a fool. All of them were fools. Everything she'd learned about Allosian nobility and superiority to the other forms of life in Shaelar had been folly, perpetuated by a mad deicidal witch.

Another psychic scream thrilled through Kairah accompanied by the same wave of instability she'd sensed the first time Rasheera screamed, though this time it was underscored by a physical quake that rocked the coliseum. The glass dome filtering in the purple glow of the Mother Shard shattered and rained shards of glass. Screams rang out, followed by shouting and crying.

Kairah looked up as a particularly large shard of glass fell toward the coliseum floor. But before it could crash down on them, a wave of white fire pulsed from Kairah's shinning aura and incinerated the falling glass. It hadn't been a spell, or at least it wasn't something that Kairah had willed to happen. It was almost like an arcane reflex.

The broken dome gave Kairah a view of thick, black clouds interspersed with green flashes swirling above the top of the Mother Shard and obscuring it. The darkness was the same as what she'd seen around Aiested, and in her vision of the dead land. The end had come.

Kairah met Kannic's eyes. "Go!" Her words rang with the familiar undercurrent of a compulsion spell, though that, too, had been unconscious.

Kannic bobbed his head and issued orders to other members of the synod.

Had she just used compulsion on the Speaker? The very idea made her sick. But perhaps if there was ever a time to subvert another's will, it would be to save their life, and the lives of thousands.

"Lady Kairah!"

The scrawny, little balding man named Gymal rushed up to her; Mulladin, Irvis, Graelle, and a young woman with tan skin following.

"What's happening?"

Kairah ignored Gymal's question. "Where is Karak?"

"The last I saw him was when we were escaping the College of Disciplines," Mulladin said.

That wasn't good. Kairah needed the Vorakk shaman, and his clairvoyance if she were to have any chance at learning the secret of how to free Rasheera and stop the Eater. That desperate, harrowing scream could only mean that they were out of time. Kairah craned her neck to stare through the broken skylight at the Mother Shard.

"What is it?" Irvis asked. "What's wrong?"

"What's wrong?" Gymal scoffed. "Are you really asking that?"

"The Mother Shard is the door to Rasheera's prison. I need to open it, but do not know how."

"The Divine Mother? Imprisoned?" The chubby monk shook his head. "That's impossible!"

Kairah didn't bother arguing with Irvis. *Aeva... Mother... Tell me how to free you!* She sent the communication out without any of her usual difficulty. The transmission was so clear and powerful that Kairah was surprised it didn't audibly manifest.

She waited for several heartbeats but received no response. What was happening to Rasheera? What was Kairah supposed to do now? The Spirit lily, or the subconscious will of the goddess, had set her on this quest, had guided her every step. Now Kairah was left to herself; alone with the fate of all creation resting on her shoulders. The sheer magnitude of what she faced overwhelmed her.

"Here!" The muscled mercenary, Hort, trotted up. He was carrying a black rod, and several smaller talises which he proffered to the others. "I made that snooty Allosian bitch give 'em back to me." He laughed. "Guess she was too frightened to think straight. Else she'd've just blasted me with that lightning ring. She was a beauty though. Love that purple hair."

Kairah drew in a steadying breath, and met Jekaran's eyes. He stared back and flashed a small smile. To Kairah's surprise, that simple but familiar expression calmed and reassured her, and her fear receded. She could do this. Rasheera had manipulated fate itself to bring her to this point.

Another quake rocked the room, and cracks appeared in the glossy marble floor.

"Come," she said. "We must access the Mother Shard."

Jekaran nodded, and followed Kairah as she jogged to an arched doorway leading off the coliseum floor. Gymal, Hort, Irvis, Graelle, Mulladin, and the tan skin girl followed. For some reason that too, the willingness of these humans to follow, strengthened her. *You are human now,* she reminded herself. No, that wasn't true. She'd always been human. Her supposed superiority was a lie. She cringed at the thought that she had been deceived into thinking herself better than the other intelligent beings in Shaelar. *How could she have been so foolish?*

They'd just passed into the hall branching off the coliseum when new screams erupted from behind. At first Kairah thought it the response to another tremor as they were coming frequently now, but the screams had a more desperate tone to them.

"The hell?" Mulladin said.

Kairah ran back to the doorway and scanned the thousands of Allosians lining the coliseum's upper tiers. More shouting and screaming drew Kairah's attention to an entrance at the top of one of the coliseum's mountainous staircase. A mob of Allosians scrambled away from the arched opening, the thinning mass revealing a dark figure standing just inside the doorway. Kairah's eyes automatically adjusted so that she could see the figure up close as they did when using a looking stone. Again, she had spell-cast without any conscious thought.

The entrance to the coliseum leapt closer to her view and she gasped. A blackened skeleton in tattered rags that mostly had melted to its bones shambled forward. In its skull's eye sockets burned two glowing emerald dots. A web of translucent, green tentacles spread from the skeleton's chest and back striking like vipers at the fleeing Allosians, syphoning Apeiron and causing pale flesh to regrow over the creature's charred bones.

"Kairah!" It shrieked in a rasping voice afire with hate.

Jekaran stepped up to her side. "Divine Mother, what is that?"

"Shivara!"

The heat inside Kairah's body flared hotter. She slumped, and Jekaran steadied her with an arm around the shoulders. Despite the burning she was no doubt inflicting upon him, Jekaran didn't let go until Kairah straightened. The contact left blisters on Jekaran's skin and Kairah healed him with a half a thought, something that drew a gasp from Irvis.

"Kairah!" Shivara began descending the stairs. Her skin was nearly all restored, and long black hair grew from her bald head. The burnt strips of robe did little to obscure her nudity, but the witch appeared not to care.

She dragged half a dozen Allosian bystanders with her, tethered by tendrils of Moriora and looking like the morbid train of a ceremonial gown. With that many conduits for Shivara to syphon Apeiron, she would have endless energy to fuel her spells. And if Jenoc hadn't been able to defeat her, what chance did Kairah stand?

I am more powerful now. But Kairah couldn't be diverted. Rasheera needed her, and all of Shaelar needed Rasheera.

"Kairah! I know you're here! Come and face me, girl! See how you fare when your brother is no longer alive to protect you!"

Jenoc...

"That sounds like my third wife." Hort chuckled.

Kairah glanced down the corridor, toward the chamber of the Mother Shard and then back at Shivara descending the coliseum steps.

"Go, Kairah," Jekaran said. "I'll deal with that thing."

Kairah looked into Jekaran's green eyes. A tear ran down her cheek and sizzled into a puff of steam. "She is like nothing you have ever fought. She will kill you!"

Jekaran glanced at Shivara and chuckled. "She doesn't look so tough."

It pained Kairah to allow him to fight Shivara alone, but she knew where her duty lay. She had to free the goddess, or everything would unravel; Allose, Shaelar, the entire planet!

"I wish I could express my gratitude for you philematologically, but my lips would burn yours."

"You mean kiss me?"

Kairah nodded. "But I fear the heat I am producing—"

Jekaran cut her off. Her feverish lips scorched his, and when he pulled back his mouth was blistered.

"Ow..." He half groaned; half laughed.

Kairah smiled and healed him. How could she have believed Jekaran was her inferior? The young man was brave and selfless in a way that miraculously ran counter to his Moriora nature.

Hort stepped up to the entrance, black scepter twirling in his hand. "Looks like it's just you and me, Brother Ulan."

"And me." Mulladin stepped up and flashed the lightning ring that he now wore on his finger, and Kairah caught a scowl from the tan-skinned woman.

"I can help." Gymal stepped up holding a stun baton of all things.

"You damn idiot!" the fat woman, Graelle, said. "Here!" She tore Gymal's stun baton out of his hand and replaced it with her concussion rod.

More tears sprang to Kairah's eyes. It wasn't just Jekaran. How could she have ever thought these humans anything but noble and brave?

"Thank you," she said.

"I will accompany you, Lady Kairah," Irvis said. "If the Divine Mother is indeed in peril, then it is my duty to aid her in any way I can."

"And I'm comin' to make sure he doesn't try staring down your dress!" Graelle folded her arms.

Irvis kissed Graelle on the cheek. "Yours is the only cleavage for me, love."

Keesa stepped up to Gymal and wrenched the concussion rod from his grip. "You go with them." She nodded at Irvis and Graelle.

"Keesa, no!" Mulladin said.

"Shut it, you big dumb ox!" she snapped back.

"I can fight!" Gymal protested.

Jekaran turned toward the short, balding lord and placed a hand on his shoulder. "No, you can't."

Gymal scowled.

"Go with Kairah. She will need help." Jekaran smiled. "And just so you know, you were right. I did hire that man whore to call on you in front of last year's well-finding camp. Cost me a whole silver Aies, money I was originally planning to use for some new festival clothes"

Gymal's scowl faded and he started laughing. Jekaran joined in, and Kairah was at a loss for understanding.

Even after spending months among them, Kairah still couldn't quite understand the unpredictable behavior of these humans.

No, I should no longer think of them that way. They are my friends.

"You see those Allosians Shivara is dragging behind her?"

"The dead ones?"

"They are not deceased. Shivara is using them as conduits to draw Apeiron from the Mother Shard. While she is connected to them, she will be all but invincible, and her fuel for spell-casting inexhaustible. Cutting her off from them is your only hope of defeating her."

"Go, Kairah." Jekaran nodded down the hallway. "Go save the world."

Kairah shared one last look with Jekaran, then left him and the others to fight Shivara–fight and almost certainly die. She told herself that the only way to help them now was for her to finish her mission and free Rasheera. That didn't make leaving Jekaran and the others to face the most powerful spell-caster in Shaelar, without her help, any easier. More tears sizzled off her cheeks into puffs of steam.

Chapter 108

"We're going to die, aren't we, Ulan?" Hort asked.

"Probably," Jekaran answered.

Hort grinned.

Jekaran eyed him. "What?"

Hort shook his head. "Getting killed by a gorgeous, naked woman has always been a fantasy of mine. Except in my fantasy I died from my heart giving out because of the intensity of the—"

"You're as depraved as Irvis!"

Hort shrugged and leaned his head to the right and popped his neck. "What can I say? Since my first wife left me, I've become a dedicated student of hedonism." He leaned his neck to the left and popped it.

"Thank you," Jekaran said softly.

Hort looked at him. "For what?"

"For looking after me. Helping me find my way back when I was lost."

Hort's smile waned. "You remind me so much of Nemel, it was like... like Rasheera gave me a chance to, I dunno..." He shrugged, looking decidedly uncomfortable. "Make things right."

Jekaran smiled.

"What's the plan?" Mulladin asked.

Jekaran glanced at Mulladin and Keesa who, despite her earlier display of bravado, was clinging tightly to Mulladin's big arm. Jekaran grinned, faintly remembering a scandalous scene of the two kissing in a feeding trough after falling off a roof. The memory was like something from a half-remembered dream.

"What?" Mulladin's eyes darted to Keesa and back.

Jekaran shook his head. "I'm just glad you're with me, Mull."

"Well?" Keesa asked, trying to sound impatient, but her quivering voice betrayed her terror. "What do we do?"

Jekaran looked through the arched doorway and into the coliseum. The witch, Shivara Kairah had called her, was standing in the center of the floor, green tendrils still attached to five bodies lying frozen on the floor. They weren't dead, but their eyes were just as unblinking.

Shivara's tattered rags fluttered about her naked body as she turned, scanning the thousands of Allosians frantically running out of the coliseum. She destroyed swaths of the retreating crowd with spears of white of light.

"I'll kill them all, Kairah!" she shrieked. "Unless you come out of hiding!"

Jekaran inhaled. "I'll keep her distracted. The rest of you go after those Allosians she's feeding on. Save them if you can."

"And if we can't?" Hort asked.

Jekaran didn't answer. He'd known as soon as Kairah had explained they were sources of power for the witch that they might need to be put down. It made him sick.

"Just try to get them away from her," he said. Jekaran looked at each of them in turn. "Ready?"

Mulladin and Keesa shared a look and nodded. Hort twirled his black scepter and grinned. Jekaran twirled his sword up and gripped the handle with both hands before launching into a charge back onto the coliseum floor. Upon nearing Shivara, he held the sword out to his right and down at an angle and then leapt ten feet into the air. As he came down, he raised the sword for a vertical slice, behind which he'd put all his momentum.

Without even turning to look at him, Shivara motioned, and a wave of force slammed into him. A beat later he found himself lying on the coliseum's floor. His sword clanged down in front of him. He shot out a hand and snatched the handle, rolled, and sprung up.

Now Shivara was looking at him. Her long black hair hung down over her face, glowing emerald eyes narrowing as she considered him. "You are, Jekaran. The one who rescued Kairah in Imaris." She glanced at the sword. "How, pray tell, did you get your hands on Azrin?"

You have mastered Azrin.

"That's what this weapon talis is called?"

Shivara took a step toward him. "It's the sword's name."

Jekaran wanted to glance around for the others but resisted the impulse. That would only give away their tactic. "Like its personal name?"

"Yes." Shivara took another step. "It is one of three crafted by artificer Meloldrin–the filthy traitor!"

Jekaran didn't know what the mad witch was going on about but decided conversation might be a better distraction than attacking her again. That, and his side smarted from being swatted from ten feet in the air.

"There are more like this?"

"Three. I have one called Irkalla, and Thanatos was destroyed hundreds of years ago."

Irkalla? That must've been the name of the rapier with which the slave girl had run him through, nearly killing him.

Shivara frowned. "But I can't sense Azrin's intelligence. What have you done to him?" she screamed.

Jekaran startled at the shout and worked to steady his shaking hands. Since bonding with the sword, he'd never really been afraid of an opponent. Even the slave girl hadn't frightened him; he'd just looked on her as a difficult challenge. This creature, though, she evoked terror in Jekaran. It wasn't her powers, godlike though they were, but the unpredictable, feral hate in her eyes. She was insane, cruel, and truly evil.

"I absorbed Azrin's knowledge and power."

"How?" Shivara cocked her head, the expression disturbingly child-like. "Such a thing shouldn't be possible." She met his eyes and a hellish smile spread across her face. "You are like me, though not yet awakened."

Jekaran caught movement on his periphery. Hort was behind Shivara now and positioning himself for an attack. Jekaran needed to keep her attention on him, so he kept talking, although all his enhanced senses screamed at him to attack before the witch drew any closer.

"I'm nothing like you."

Shivara appeared not to hear him, her eyes entirely fixed on the sword. "Moriora truly is the unbinding of all laws, and all order, just as Boulos said it would be." She met his eyes again and took another step. "Perhaps you are the one destined to be my consort."

"What the hell are you talking about?"

"You are quite young and not educated, but it should only take a century or so for us to remedy that. And with me as your teacher, you'll learn many things." She chuckled in a way Jekaran thought was meant to be seductive but came out making her sound that much madder. "I will need to awaken your Moriora first." Shivara closed her eyes and began casting.

"Now!"

Hort leapt forward, slashing the scepter and drawing a black line in the air across the green tendrils tethering the five helpless Allosians to Shivara. The tentacles evaporated, and Mulladin and Keesa moved in to grab the witch's hostages.

A concussive blast with Shivara at its center exploded outward. It struck Hort, Mulladin, and Keesa, throwing them away from the hostages. It struck Jekaran too, but this time he was ready. He held the sword in front of him in a guard position, willing the emerald shards to life. They shined up and down the blade, and Jekaran cut through the telekinetic blast like a tree standing against the wind.

Her eyes still closed, Shivara formed new green energy tendrils and recaptured her five Allosian conduits. Then a red line appeared in a circle around Jekaran, the witch, and her hostages. A wall of flames leapt up and burned along the red line until they were surrounded in a circle of fire.

Shivara opened her eyes and something else struck Jekaran. Waves of vibration thrummed through every part of him, making him tremble and want to collapse. He gritted his teeth and held tightly to the sword. Its emerald shards shined brighter but didn't have the same absorbing effect on this attack as it had before.

Ice filled Jekaran's limbs and his chest grew empty and cold. A pain churned inside him, a sensation not unlike being desperately hungry. He was shaking so hard that he was having trouble holding onto the sword.

"Azrin is interfering with the inversion spell!" Shivara snarled. "How?" The witch's eyes focused on the shining green dots peppering the sword's tapered blade and she gasped. "Melodrin, you cunning bastard! You crafted a key!"

Not a sword, but a key. The impression he'd received earlier repeated from his memory.

Shivara raised another hand so that she looked as if she were reaching for Jekaran. The wave of force smashed into him with renewed vigor, ripping at every fiber of his body and soul. It was as if something were trying to tear him apart from the inside out. He screamed, dropped the sword, and fell to his knees. It was all he could do to hold his essence together as Shivara's spell thrummed louder and louder in his ears. He knew that he shouldn't have let go of the sword, that now he was vulnerable. And though it lay but a few paces off to his right, he couldn't get to it for the pain. It was as if knives were stabbing every inch of his flesh and scraping his bones.

Then the offer was before him; a promise of relief from the pain and hunger if Jekaran would only surrender to it. He wanted to. Oh, how he wanted to! The unnerving feeling of every particle of his self being pulled upon was more than he could handle. But Jekaran knew that to accept the proffered relief meant destruction. He wasn't certain how he knew it; he just did.

Just at the point when Jekaran was about to surrender, he heard something over the thrumming in his mind–a voice; Ez's voice. It wasn't an actual vision like when he fought Etele, but a memory, dredged up from his subconscious and displayed to him as if by the will of another.

He'd been seven or eight, bent over a bucket and sobbing in between violent retching. Ez's hand slowly rubbed his back and he whispered, *"It will pass, Jek. It will pass."*

Jekaran screamed and rejected the offer of relief so strongly that his will actually rippled the air and struck Shivara. The assault on his essence abruptly ended as did the wall of flames that ringed them.

Jekaran heaved, wanting nothing more than to collapse and sleep, but instead he reached for his sword–Azrin–and stood. Again, he brought his blade up to a blocking position. Ready for a follow-up attack, he was surprised to find tears rolling down Shivara's cheeks. She wore a look so utterly hurt, that Jekaran couldn't help but to pity her.

"You too?" She sucked in a ragged breath. "You also reject me?" The pathetic, childlike pouting disappeared, replaced by lips twisted down, narrow eyes, and a tightened jaw. "Heartless bastard!" Shivara roared and a horizontal column of white light blinded Jekaran.

He clenched his eyes shut, and gripped Azrin's handle, holding the blade as if to parry a blow. The emerald chips on his sword shined, and energy flowed through Azrin and poured into him. It healed and reinvigorated him, and he took a step forward, pushing against the blast of power meant to incinerate him.

The light abruptly vanished, and Jekaran opened his eyes in time to see Shivara stagger forward. Another bolt of blue lightning struck her in the face, but her charred features quickly reformed.

Something else hit her from behind, and the witch whirled and cast another spear of light, this time at Keesa. Jekaran was in between them in a blur, sword swinging and absorbing the spell. Hort lunged at Shivara, his scepter splitting the air and revealing blackness beneath the skin of their reality.

Shivara disappeared a heartbeat before Hort landed and trailed a black line through where she had just stood. The witch reappeared a few feet away and launched a bolt of lightning that took Hort in the shoulder. He spun but hadn't quite hit the ground when Jekaran leapt over him, charging Shivara with Azrin poised to decapitate.

KAIRAH PUSHED OPEN TWO TALL, stained-glass doors. Beyond was a cylindrical chamber, miles in circumference and rising thousands of feet to an open sky. The massive Apeira well known as the Mother Shard was like a small mountain in size. Ringing its base was a pit that appeared to descend into the depths of Shaelar. A smooth walkway growing out of the chambers interior wall allowed for viewing the crystal monstrosity, but only a staircase in front of them rising to a circular platform allowed someone to get close enough to touch the Mother Shard.

"That platform has no rail." Gymal's voice trembled. "What if someone were to fall?"

"A brave lord like you is afraid of heights?" Graelle smirked.

"No," Gymal snapped. "I'm afraid of falling from heights."

Kairah crossed the floor, ascended the stairs to the platform, and stood within reaching distance of the amethyst wall. The others–even Gymal–followed, albeit with more measured steps.

"The Divine Mother is imprisoned in an Apeira well?" Irvis asked.

"No. Rasheera is encased in the center of the planet." Kairah extended a glowing hand. Her first theory was to simply touch the Mother Shard and use her new power to burn it away. She pressed her glowing fingers to the crystal.

Nothing happened.

She held the touch and willed energy into the Mother Shard. The well's soft purple aura flared, and electric lines of green appeared deep within the Apeira well, spider-webbing up and down the Mother Shard.

It was the cage of Moriora the Zikkurat had shown her; Shivara's spell designed to crush the goddess. The arcing lines of green slowly crept toward her, and intuitively Kairah knew she must not have even the slightest contact with the emerald energy, and so removed her hand. The glowing lines faded.

Aeva, I need you!

The Spirit lily didn't respond.

The heat inside Kairah flared, and she hunched over, gripping her stomach and clenching her jaw. Irvis moved toward her and she threw out a hand, motioning for him to stay back. "You saw what my touch can do."

Irvis slowly nodded and stepped back.

Ignoring the questioning looks from Irvis, Graelle, and Gymal, Kairah cast a spell producing a harmless explosion of colored sparks above them, and the burning pain diminished.

"Those green lines," Gymal said. "They make the Apeira well look infected, or diseased."

"More like poisoned," Kairah said. A thought struck her. Could it be so simple? Did all she need to do was cast a healing? She glanced down at the shining white band on her finger. The goddess ring contained a portion of Rasheera's untainted essence. Could she somehow use it to purge the Mother Shard?

The Apeira well–all Apeira wells–were a diffusion of Rasheera's power, caused by mixing it with Moriora. That's why the wells turned green and shattered when touched by someone wielding Moriora. The additional infusion of the other magic unbalanced the mixture in Moriora's favor. Could she somehow purge the lines of green from the Mother Shard? No, not just the Mother Shard. Kairah would have to somehow pull the arcane venom out of all Shaelar's wells simultaneously. Then the crystal prison holding their creator should return to a state of pure energy.

Kairah's mind was working faster than it ever had before, and it wasn't just from crisis-induced adrenaline, or desperate innovation. She was making connections in arcane theory that were well beyond her natural abilities. The ring was not only suffusing her with a burning power, but it was granting her greater intelligence. Not that Kairah hadn't been intelligent before–all her academic assessments declared her above average–but she hadn't ever had instincts this sharp. Nor had she ever been able to wrap her mind around Jenoc's more complex theories of spellcasting or understand how he reverse-engineered talises.

"Poison," Kairah whispered. She reached out both her hands and cast a far greater healing than she'd ever attempted, or even thought possible.

The spell she blanketed the Mother Shard with was enough to heal thousands of people of any injury or ailment save death, and Kairah was starting to think she could even undo that. The power resonated throughout the Mother Shard, making the lines of Moriora deep within reappear.

"What is she doing?" Gymal asked.

"It's a healing," Irvis said in astonishment.

Kairah closed her eyes and willed the spell's influence to expand further and further. She beheld each mile it encompassed as it raced across the surface of the planet, and then pushed below ground. She could see the entirety of the amethyst sphere at the core of the planet. It was misshapen with many points pushed so far outward that they rose through the planet's crust–Apeira wells.

Lines of crackling green light exploded to life inside the crystal as they snaked through the planet's core and its protruding nodes. Kairah pushed harder, attacking the Moriora and attempting to burn it away. But the Moriora fed on her power, and Kairah only succeeded in growing more purple crystal.

Kairah's arcane fever broke, and she collapsed to her knees. The goddess ring was silver again, only emanating the faintest white glow as was she. Though she had spent nearly all the power in the ring, it wasn't entirely exhausted and already producing more energy. No, she hadn't lost Rasheera's gift, but she had failed to purge Moriora from existence.

"Lady Kairah?" Irvis knelt next to her, his eyes wide.

"I am fine." She waved him away and stood.

"What happened?' Gymal asked.

Kairah could still see glowing emerald lines within the amethyst crystal, albeit they were fading. "I failed."

THE GROUND SHOOK, making Maely's already difficult balancing act even harder. She braced herself against a white statue until the rumbling subsided. She felt like a useless coward taking cover behind the fifty-foot visage of a nude Allosian man.

She'd retreated here on orders of the prince, who now fought alongside Karak against the charred form of Jenoc. Fought was probably the wrong word. Karak sprang about, fast and agile as ever, but each time he conjured a ball of light to attack Jenoc, the fallen Allosian obliterated it with a bolt of his green lightning.

Raelen moved much more slowly, his many apparent injuries–and likely some not so apparent–rendering him virtually stationary. Conveniently, Jenoc would usually come to him, and Raelen would employ his Ursaj martial arts against the monster with little effect.

Maely had wanted to try casting more flare bombs, but Raelen had told her such only fed Jenoc's power and made him stronger. That, and with them fighting in such close quarters, she was just as likely to incinerate Karak and Raelen as she was to hit Jenoc. So all Maely could do was hide and watch. It frustrated her to tears.

If only I hadn't smashed my mother's ring!

She had no idea if it would work on Jenoc now—it had barely worked before—but at least then she could do something.

"No," she whispered. The compulsion talis had made her into a creature every bit of a monster as Jenoc. With it, she'd done awful things.

Smashing the compulsion ring had been the start of her redemption; getting into the river to bathe. But Maely still felt dirty. In Gryyth's metaphor, the next step was scrubbing off her dirt. She'd thought she found a way to do that in saving Raelen and trying to kill Jenoc, but that part was turning out to be an impossible task.

The ground tilted and Maely's hand slipped from its place on the marble Allosian's foot. She pitched forward, crying out as a jolt to her broken leg sent a shock of pain up her thigh. A long fissure opened in the ground, snaking its way across the pavement. It ran right by Maely, causing the giant statue to break loose from its base.

Maely screamed, and moved away from the statue, but it turned out to be unnecessary as the giant likeness of the muscular man tipped away from her and fell into the yawning chasm only ten paces away. A geyser of lava shot out of the chasm as if it were licking its lips after swallowing the statue. The intense heat drew a whimper from Maely as she scooted away on her behind, broken leg stretched out before her.

A hiss drew her attention back to the fight, and she turned just in time to see Karak speared through the stomach by a sharp piece of debris from the remnants of the demolished tower.

"Karak!" Maely screamed.

That drew Jenoc's attention and he shambled toward her.

Maely frantically scooted away on the ground, but her only other option was to move closer to the ten-foot wide chasm boiling with a rising river of lava. Jenoc's face had healed to the point that Maely could recognize his features, but a good portion of the top of his skull was still missing. He had only one eye, and it was an otherworldly glowing point of green.

He grinned at her and manifested a spread of translucent green tentacles. Maely had but one recourse. She raised the flare kris and pointed the wavy red blade at Jenoc. One of his energy tendrils was already snapping toward her, on a path that would plunge it directly into her face. At the last moment, it suddenly changed course and sank into the well shard of her sword. It seemed a magnetic thing, as if the tendril was automatically drawn first to the purest source of Apeiron.

Maely's spell failed, and the well shard on her talis exploded into small, emerald shards. Jenoc sucked in a shuddering breath, and more of his blackened skin healed. He refocused on Maely and drew back his tendril of energy in preparation to lash out again.

Arms grabbed Jenoc from behind, and the monster's tentacles vanished. He roared, and struck at Raelen with his hands, but the prince's grip was sure. Raelen began dragging Jenoc toward the fissure in the ground and its burning red river.

Maely understood what the prince was doing. "No!"

She clenched her jaw as she stood. The pain was so intense that her vision began to darken, but she willed herself to remain conscious. She took a step toward the struggle and reached out a hand. Raelen was dragging Jenoc backward, on a path that would put them both over the edge of the chasm.

"Raelen!"

Something crunched beneath Maely's step. She glanced down and found green shards, the remnants of the jewel that powered her now useless talis. She snatched three and closed her fist around them. This would at least protect her should Jenoc lash out at her again.

Jenoc, too, apparently realized what Raelen was trying to do, as was evidenced in his desperate struggling. Just as they neared the chasm's edge, an aura of red light surrounded Jenoc tearing a scream from Raelen. The prince released Jenoc and collapsed to the ground, smoldering burns covering his chest and arms. The flash of fire had burned away the front of Raelen's tunic along with the leather band that held his green well shard. It rolled off Raelen's chest, and Jenoc kicked it away.

The monster grinned and manifested a single green tentacle to feed on the prince. In a suspended moment of time, Maely eyed the chasm, then Raelen, then Jenoc, and she knew what she had to do. Scrubbing dirt off in the bath sometimes hurt, and this would definitely hurt.

Maely clenched her fist tight around the sharp bits of emerald in her hand and lunged at Jenoc, giving vent to her leg pain in a ragged scream. He turned just as she crashed into him, her momentum carrying them both over the chasm's jagged edge.

Chapter 109

The concentric tiers of the coliseum were empty now, save for the charred remains of those not quick enough to escape Shivara's mad tantrum. That would deny the witch any additional conduits for drawing Apeiron, which meant Jekaran could kill her if he could cut her off from the five hostages she still held.

Shivara's tendrils evaporated each time she tried to sink one into Jekaran. He batted away a bolt of green lightning as he ran, trying to circle around the witch to get to the five paralyzed Allosians who were the source of her power. Shivara all but ignored Hort, Mulladin, and Keesa, deciding instead to focus her wroth on Jekaran. That was both good and bad. Good because it kept the others from getting killed, and bad because the reason she ignored them was that they poised no real threat to her. That put the onus of the battle entirely on Jekaran.

A bolt of lightning arced into Shivara's back, followed immediately by a blast from Keesa's concussion rod. It made the witch turn and gave Jekaran his opening. He smiled, rushed in, and sliced through the tethers linking Shivara to the paralyzed Allosians. Shivara growled and blasted Jekaran with a funnel of air. It struck him on the side before he could bring Azrin up to block and absorb it. He spun backward and slammed into the front of the speaking dais.

He'd managed to hold onto the sword this time–*Not a sword, but a key. A key to what?*

His eyes watered, and pops of light exploded across his vision.

Jekaran shook his head to clear it. When his eyesight wasn't dark or blurry, he stood. Hort was attacking Shivara now. The big man impressively dodged balls of fire, and parried Shivara's attempts to syphon his life away with that black scepter. It appeared to open tiny lines into a vast, sucking, emptiness. Hort even managed to get close enough to draw a black line in the path of one of Shivara's swings and the void ate her hand. She, of course, immediately grew a new one at the same time she struck Hort with a spear of light. It grazed the big man's abdomen, burning away flesh and sinew and leaving an open wound. Hort howled but managed to stay on his feet.

Jekaran blurred toward Shivara forcing her to turn her spellcasting on him. He raised Azrin and this time successfully blocked and then absorbed a shaft of searing light. His vision cleared further, and the pain in his back and head vanished.

Hort took the opportunity to flank Shivara, and Jekaran expected him to draw a line that would collide with her back when he instead swung at the Allosian hostages.

"Hort, no!" Jekaran shouted, but it was too late.

The big man had traced a line right through the necks of all five Allosians. The blackness sucked in their heads, leaving decapitated corpses that quickly withered, and shriveled to little more than skeletons.

Shivara shrieked and released a blast of power so fierce it demolished the speaking dais in the middle of the coliseum floor and cracked the walls beneath the first tier of seating. It also struck Mulladin, Keesa, and Hort. Jekaran watched in horror as the three were flung into the air like debris. Mulladin crashed into the wall beneath the first tier of seating and slumped to the ground, a line of blood trailing out of his ear. Keesa met a similar fate but arced up and came down so hard she crashed through a bench on the first seating tier. Hort was lucky, he lost his footing, fell to the floor and slid and rolled until he was stopped by a chunk of debris.

Jekaran absorbed the blast, but it was so strong that it still shoved him back. He stumbled, fell, and rolled. When he sprung back up, Shivara was passing through the archway leading out of the coliseum and toward Allose's giant Apeira well.

Jekaran glanced where his friends had fallen and ground his teeth when Mulladin and Keesa did not stir. Though burnt, bruised, and bleeding from an opening in his side, Hort rose, retrieved his scepter and began a stumbling run after Shivara.

Jekaran forced his concern for his friends to the back of his mind and leapt into a run. He streaked past Hort to the far side of the coliseum floor, toward the arched exit. Kairah was directly in Shivara's path to the Apeira well, and he had no illusions as to what the witch would do to Kairah when she caught her. What would happen if Shivara fed directly on the Apeira well itself? Nothing good, Jekaran knew that much.

RAELEN LURCHED to the edge of the chasm just in time to see Jenoc disappear beneath the flow of molten, red death. A few feet below him was an outcropping of rock to which hung a wild-eyed Maely. She held to the sharp edge of the outcropping with scraped, bloody fingers that left runnels in the soot as she slowly slid off the edge. Raelen shot a burned arm down and grabbed Maely by the wrist a heartbeat before she would've fallen. She shrieked, but quickly looked up and met Raelen's eyes.

"It's okay, Maely. I have you."

Without Gryyth's borrowed strength, and wounded and exhausted as he was, Raelen had to reach down with his other hand and strain to lift Maely up to where she could grab onto the chasm's jagged edge. He didn't let go of her until she pulled herself up and rolled onto the ledge, but the latter part of the extrication was mostly by the girl's strength. She surprised Raelen by throwing her arms around his neck and clinging to him. She trembled so badly that Raelen found himself smoothing her hair and whispering comfort.

It was an odd thing to do sitting on a quaking ground while an army of monsters attacked the city, but the fighting wasn't close. The other life-sucking monsters deliberately avoided Jenoc, and the few that had stumbled upon their battle had quickly gone on to seek other prey. Still, they were in no way safe.

Raelen stood, albeit slowly, and then helped Maely to stand. "That was a courageous thing you did."

Maely looked away from him and mumbled something that sounded like, "I had to scrub off the dirt."

What did that mean? "Well, you saved my life. I owe you my thanks." Although it hurt tremendously, Raelen bent down and kissed the girl on the forehead.

She started and looked up at him. She held his eyes for several heartbeats. Then, appearing to remember something, Maely frantically glanced around the tower ruins. "Karak!"

The two of them stumbled away from the chasm and toward a pool of glowing green blood. The Vorakk shaman was gone, but luminescent footprints tracked through the blood and led away.

"He's gone to find Kairah. We need to follow him!"

The ground lurched and the two only kept from falling by Raelen steadying them against a smoldering chunk of white stone.

"I fear this place is—"

"Going to hell?" Maely supplied.

Raelen wouldn't have put it in such a crude manner, but the description was accurate. "Yes. We need to get out of here."

"And go where?" Maely snapped.

The girl actually snapped at him! That wasn't something Raelen was used to. So far Maely had been clumsily deferential in her conversation with him, but he wasn't offended. Her blunt honesty was actually refreshing. Had their circumstances not been so dire, Raelen would've laughed.

"We are too injured to render any assistance to your friends."

"Tell that to Karak! Last time I saw him, he had five feet of white stone spearing him through his gut."

Good point.

Raelen wearily nodded, retrieved his emerald shard from the ground, and the two began to follow Karak's luminescent blood trail.

THE TALL, stained glass doors exploded. Kairah whirled, Graelle screamed, Irvis stepped in front of Graelle, and Gymal backed up to the platform's rail. Shivara stumbled into the room. She looked haggard, long, black hair disheveled and hanging in front of her face, and wrinkles creased the corners of her eyes and mouth.

"You!"

The goddess ring had only just begun to singe Kairah's veins again, and although she could spell-cast, Kairah was nowhere near the level of power she had been before trying to purge the Mother Shard. But she launched a fire ball at Shivara anyway.

The witch manifested her Moriora aura and absorbed the blast. Her wrinkles smoothed, and her face regained some color as she broke into wild laughter.

"If your brother couldn't kill me with all of his supposed expertise, what makes you think a flame talis would be of any use?"

Flame talis? She does not know I regained my spellcasting.

Shivara stepped into the chamber, still hunched like she carried a great weight, but her movements were less rigid than they had been a moment before. Kairah couldn't risk casting any other spells at the woman while she was wrapped in Moriora, lest Kairah end up healing her. She'd have to wait for Shivara to attack.

"I bet you stole that talis from my collection. Didn't you? Didn't you?"

The woman was full and truly insane now, that much was obvious by her hysterical tone and visible trembling.

"What was it? I see you holding nothing, wearing no jewelry on your—" Shivara froze, her glowing green eyes narrowing. She hissed. "Where did you get that?"

Kairah put her hand behind her back, but it was too late. Shivara had seen the goddess ring.

"It was lost when Mother fell. It's supposed to be deep within the planet! How did you get it?"

Kairah pushed back her fear and set her jaw. She had to force herself not to consider the fact that if Shivara was here, then Jekaran and the others were likely dead.

"It would seem that, in spite of being imprisoned, Rasheera has been successfully working against you, Shivara." Kairah's only hope now was to stall while the hot energy built up inside her, making her strong enough to kill Shivara with one overpowering spell. "I have seen the ripples of fate guiding me. Rasheera herself has been communing with me in the guise of a Spirit lily. And I suspect she brought others together to stop the threat of Moriora, and to stop you!"

"Mother always was stubborn," Shivara said. "But it's too late! She's failed! I have set the blaze that now burns across Shaelar! Soon this land will be desolate, and my master will have what he wants!"

"And what is that?" Kairah tried to will the fire inside to burn hotter, but it was more a fancy than an actual attempt. She could sooner will the sun to shine brighter.

Shivara wagged a finger at Kairah and laughed. "Clever girl. You are trying to stall me. Why?"

A wave of invisible discord thrummed through Kairah. It shook her, making her core feel fragile, as if it were ready to fly apart. Irvis groaned, and Graelle whimpered. Even Gymal apparently felt it, as was evidenced by his hiding his bald head in the crook of his arm. The wave was punctuated by a seismic jolt that produced fine cracks in the massive chamber's walls.

Shivara stared up at the Mother Shard, a delighted smile on her face. "You feel that, Kairah? The fire has burned its way into Mother's prison. It won't be long now before she succumbs to the poison."

Kairah gauged her reserve of energy. Although it was building faster, it was not yet two-thirds of what it had been. *I do not have a choice. I must kill her now.* Though she couldn't afford an extended duel for two reasons: The goddess was dying, and Kairah couldn't risk Shivara touching her with Moriora. Her quickening mind had deduced that to do so would infect her again, and perhaps even the goddess ring itself would be corrupted.

Shivara met Kairah's eyes. "I will ensure that this door is permanently closed so that Mother won't be able to escape the Eater. Then Boulos will speak to me again and reward me. I know it!" A dozen translucent green tentacles sprang into existence and struck at the Mother Shard.

Kairah gasped, and cast, but her shield materialized a breath too late, and the Moriora tendril shattered it before it even formed. Just as the snakelike undulating cords of warped air were about to sink into the crystalline surface of the Mother Shard, they evaporated.

Shivara suddenly arched her back as a blade punched out of from between her breasts. She stumbled forward, and Kairah saw... "Jekaran!"

He bore a look of concentration on his face, and the emeralds peppering the blade lit up.

Shivara shrieked. "That's not possible!"

Was Jekaran draining her Apeiron?

The witch's features aged, and she was clearly weakening. Still, she managed to cast a pulse of force that repelled Jekaran and separated him from the sword. Shivara straightened, reached to her back and yanked the blade out. She brought it around and held it up before her, examining it. Jekaran was poised to charge, but hesitated.

He is just as vulnerable to Moriora without direct contact with the sword!

Shivara flashed a grin full of decaying teeth, and then hurled the sword so that if flew from where they stood on the chamber's balcony and dropped out of sight. Jekaran exploded into a blur of motion, streaking toward the falling weapon.

Shivara spun and snapped out a green tendril, spearing Jekaran in the side. He tripped, rolled, and fell to the ground paralyzed. A resounding clang announced the sword meeting the depths at the base of the Mother Shard.

"Jekaran!" Kairah screamed.

He convulsed like he was having a fit, but his eyes moved to meet hers. They did not dry and fall from his sockets, neither did his skin prune and wither. Though he was frozen, Jekaran was not wasting away as he ought to have. It was like he was an Allosian...

"Conduit!" Shivara gasped. The witch's chest wound had closed, and she appeared young again. "He's a conduit!" Shivara closed her eyes, smiled, and shuddered with pleasure. Then she snapped them open and launched a spread of green tendrils at the Mother Shard.

Kairah's quickened mind, growing ever faster with the rising flame inside her, registered the attack almost before it came. She didn't have the strength to encase the entire Mother Shard in a protective barrier, so she created small discs of translucent power. She made certain to solidify them before pulling her reach back, so that the Moriora would have no chance of connecting with her aura.

A dozen tiny discs blocked the tendrils just inches before they sank into the Mother Shard. Each one exploded into tiny fragments that faded from existence before they could fall to the ground, and the tentacles of green energy evaporated.

Shivara growled and launched more tentacles, all the while holding onto Jekaran and using him as a proxy to draw Apeiron. Kairah met each tendril with a tiny glass disc, again repelling the mad woman's attempt to corrupt the Mother Shard. Didn't she realize that by destroying the Mother Shard, she would lose the very thing she depended on for sustenance and spellcasting? But then, Kairah surmised that logic had long ago abandoned Shivara, perhaps even before she'd become a Moriora vessel. How else could one be persuaded to slay their own god if she was not mad?

Shivara screamed, and manifested hundreds of Moriora tendrils, and Kairah stopped them all with her transparent shield discs. Another volley, and another successful intervention. Then another and another. Though powerful as she now was, that power diminished each time Kairah cast, and the gradual replenishment from the goddess ring wasn't fast enough to keep up. She couldn't do this forever. Eventually Shivara would wear her down.

JEKARAN HAD ONCE MADE the mistake of hiding near a tree during a thunderstorm. Lightning struck that tree, and though it didn't strike him directly, Jekaran remembered a paralyzing jolt flash from his hand touching the trunk, through his shoulders and chest, and then out his opposite hand. It'd been over in the blink of an eye, and while sore, he hadn't suffered any lasting injuries. This felt like that jolt, except it didn't end.

Jekaran couldn't move, save for involuntary trembling. He watched helpless as Shivara dueled with Kairah and longed to come to her aid. The feeling was all too similar to when the sword used to commandeer his body, shoving his consciousness aside so that all he could do was watch. How could he have been so stupid as to lose the sword? Since absorbing its knowledge and power, he'd hoped he hadn't needed to maintain physical contact to access his powers. That was partially true, but he couldn't shield himself from Shivara's spell-casting or green magic without using the sword in a physical blocking motion.

Movement at the door of the chamber caught Jekaran's attention. Hort shambled in, hand covering a bleeding gash in his side, and the other tightly gripping the polished black scepter. He steadily approached Shivara's back, stopping when he was four paces away from her. The mad witch didn't notice him, or else she didn't care. She was engrossed in trying to sink one of her hundreds of ghostly green tendrils into the Apeira well. They snapped out like vipers, but Kairah was just as quick with her spellcasting and was deftly deflecting Shivara's barrage, a fact that enraged the woman.

Hort lowered the black scepter so that its point touched the floor, and then began tracing a circle in lines of black so dark that they dimmed the light around them, as if sucking it in. Hort stopped an inch short of completing the circle and straightened. He glanced at Jekaran, met his eyes, and then winked. Then he turned to face Shivara's naked back.

"Hey, you needy bitch!"

Shivara started to turn.

"I'll be your consort!" Hort leapt forward, caught Shivara around the neck while at the same time touching his scepter to the gap in the floor between the black lines, thereby completing his circle.

As he launched himself backward, the floor inside the circle fell away into absolute blackness. Hort's skin withered, wrinkled, and dried, and Shivara shrieked as the two of them fell backward into the hole and were swallowed up in the void.

CHAPTER
110

The singularity in the floor disappeared and Kairah relaxed. Though the fire inside her had dimmed considerably, it was already intensifying again at an ever-faster rate. She lifted the hem of her dress and ran down the steps to kneel next to Jekaran. The boy had collapsed the moment Shivara disappeared and was lying on his side.

"Jekaran!" Kairah turned him over.

He looked up at her, wiped away tears, and smiled. It was infectious and Kairah couldn't help but smile back. "How are you still alive?"

"I dunno." Jekaran sat up, and then stood. Kairah rose with him, steadying him when he finally came to his feet, her touch blackening the sleeves of his tunic. Jekaran broke into a jog to the edge of the rail-less balcony that ran the circular interior of the chamber and looked down.

Kairah joined him, her eyes automatically magnifying the base of the Mother Shard to find the sword. It was lying with its point touching the crystalline surface of the Apeira well. The tiny emeralds on the blade shone like stars, and the amethyst jewel in the cross guard glowed. Then Kairah noticed something else. The crackling lines of Moriora deep within the Mother Shard had become visible again and were slowly creeping toward the point of the sword.

"Think you can translocate that back up here for me?"

When she didn't answer, Jekaran looked at her. "Kairah?"

"You can pull energy through the sword and into yourself?"

"Yeah. I did it first to Kaul. It recharges the sword and heals my wounds." Jekaran scratched his head. "Is that what saved me from shriveling like a raisin?"

Kairah kept her magnified sight on the sword and nodded. "I have never seen anything like it."

"Shivara said the sword's name was Azrin. She said it was a key."

Realization slammed into Kairah. "Two worlds, but one heart, opposites that are one," She blurted out. "Can fire love ice? Can the dark love the dawn?"

An Apeira well shard and Moriora well shards set together in a talis.

"That's from that depressing poem you read me, on our way to Imaris."

Was it really so simple? Kairah's vision returned to normal and she looked at Jekaran. "It is more than just a poem." Likely scrawled by an Allosian ally of the first humans, one who had the oracular gift. "It is a riddle, and I think I know the answer!"

"What answer?"

Kairah didn't respond but teleported the sword up from the base of the Mother Shard. She didn't dare touch it for the Moriora shards embedded in the blade, and so let it clang down at Jekaran's feet.

"So were the two lovers, a prince and princess opposed." She eyed the emerald shards and the round amethyst. "Yet in the secret midnight of a garden, their love could freely flow."

The two work together to drain energy from a target and capture that energy first for the sword, and then for the bearer.

"Kairah?" He bent down and picked it up.

Kairah strode back up the stairs to the circular platform bridging the balcony and the Mother Shard. "Yet the universe is balance, and fate would have her due." She reached out and touched the crystal wall.

Apeiron is a product of Rasheera's pure essence diluted by Moriora. Separating the two would be to destroy her crystal prison, and all the Apeira wells in Shaelar.

"Their love would bring destruction and end the worlds each knew."

Jekaran jogged up behind her. "Kairah, what's going on?"

Kairah turned her head to meet his anxious stare. "This is the door to Rasheera's prison. And you hold the only key that can open it." Kairah stared at the emeralds peppering the blade of Jekaran's sword. "It is the only talis I have ever seen that has both Apeiron and Moriora shards crafted into it. That, combined with your corrupt Allosian heritage is what allows you to pull energy through it and into yourself."

"He's descended from Allosians?" Irvis asked.

"All humans with green eyes carry tiny Moriora shards in their blood. That is how Jenoc was able to transform so many humans into life leeches. His inversion spell would not affect a regular human."

"Divine Mother!" Gymal swore. "The genealogy of our house claims to have an Allosian progenitor. It's always been considered fanciful, but if what you say is true—"

"Likely a corruption of the truth that your ancestors were once Allosian."

Jekaran raised the sword to study the glowing green shards. "How is this a key?"

Kairah glanced at the lines of luminescent green fading back beneath thick amethyst crystal. "Apeira wells are the product of Moriora tainting Rasheera's power." As if in response, the heat inside her flared, making her grimace. "It is like a snake's venom in the blood of someone who has suffered a bite."

Jekaran's eyes widened. "And you save that person by sucking out the venom." He looked at the sword again. "This sucks Apeiron."

"And the well shard provides a counterbalance and buffer so that the Moriora will not corrupt the Apeira well it syphons from." Kairah grimaced again but hid the expression from the others by facing the Mother Shard.

"So we just need to suck out the Moriora?" Irvis asked.

"Moriora cannot affect itself."

"But you just said..."

The awful truth settled on Kairah with a sinking sickness in her stomach. "All of the Apeiron will need to be drawn out. The Moriora will come with it." A tear ran down her feverish cheek, puffing to steam before it ever fell from her face. She looked at Jekaran. "I cannot use the sword."

Jekaran shrugged. "Okay. I'll do it. Just tell me what to—"

"You ignorant, peasant!" Gymal snapped. "She means all Apeiron."

"In the entire world?"

"Yes." Kairah said. "Unlike Allosians, who have physical limits to how much energy their bodies can receive to protect them from ever oversaturating themselves, those with Moriora in their blood do not have this limitation and so can take in as much energy as they desire. It would be very dangerous for anyone to channel that much Apeiron, let alone someone who does not have the cellular elasticity of a full-fledged life leech. The process could easily—"

"Kill me."

"Or turn you into a creature like Shivara." Kairah's tears flowed freely. "I am so sorry, Jekaran."

"What happens if we don't free the Divine Mother?" Jekaran asked.

"I am afraid she will die. And with her all of Shaelar, and whatever else she has created. Even the souls of her creatures will be unmade."

"Use your gift to save us all," Jekaran muttered. It sounded like he was quoting someone.

"What was that?" Gymal asked.

Jekaran nodded to himself. "How do I do this?"

"You will need to touch the point of your sword to the Mother Shard and draw in Apeiron as you have before."

"No, boy." Irvis reached out a hand and took Jekaran's arm. "There has to be another way."

"There is not," Kairah said, hating the words as they left her lips. She had just pronounced a death sentence on someone she loved.

"Is there a chance he can survive this?" Gymal pled.

"I do not know," Kairah lied.

"Don't worry, I've already cheated death a dozen times in just the last couple of months. My luck hasn't run out yet." Jekaran smiled at Irvis, but Kairah could hear Jekaran's thoughts. He was being brave for his friends. His smile slipped. "Just in case, if you see Maely again, tell her I love her."

Irvis nodded and let go.

"If I turn into one of those things, be sure to put me down before I can hurt anyone, okay?"

Kairah nodded, tears streaming down her cheeks. The flow was so heavy that her fever couldn't evaporate them all. How had she ever thought Jekaran primitive or inferior? It didn't take him even a full minute to agree to sacrifice himself. There was nobility in his soul greater than anything she'd ever witnessed in her people. *He is my people,* she reminded herself. *We are all the same.*

Jekaran walked up to the edge of the circular platform. He lifted the sword, studied it, and then laughed. "You were right, Ez. Adventure is the lure of fools," he said. "And I'm a fool." Jekaran sucked in a deep breath and plunged the sword into the Apeira well so deep that the blade sank to the hilt.

WHEN HE WAS SEVEN, Jekaran had once tried, against Ez's warning, to drink straight from Genra's well pump. Immediately the water had filled his mouth and started to choke him, leaving him sitting in the mud sputtering and gasping, and everyone in the village square laughed at him. Pulling Apeiron from the largest Apeira well in Shaelar was like that, except this time Jekaran couldn't pull back when the torrent began to choke him.

The emeralds on Azrin's blade shone brighter than Jekaran had ever seen them shine, as did the well shard embedded in the sword's cross guard. Jekaran's whole body vibrated and he had to clasp the handle of the sword with all his supernatural strength to keep from losing his grip.

The crackling green lines inside the Apeira well reached for him like ghostly hands. When they touched Azrin, they coiled around the blade and slowly wound up it until the lines of green energy began feeding into the well shard. The pain Jekaran had faced when Shivara had tried to turn him recurred a hundred-fold. He tried to scream at a head pounding so fierce that it caused an explosion of stars across his vision. A mixture of fire and ice poured into him, churned within his chest as though both powers were wrestling. An overwhelming hunger settled in his gut. It wasn't for food, but for energy. Strange though it was, the more power he drank in, the more he wanted.

You can have that power, something whispered. He could have all that and more if he would succumb and accept his true nature. Jekaran fought off the temptation. He would not become like Shivara! The darkness amidst the power coursing into him tried a different tactic, whispering that he was dying and the only way to survive this was to embrace Moriora.

You don't want to die, it soothed. *Accept my offer and live forever with your beloved Kairah.*

Kairah.

Jekaran was paralyzed by the ocean of energy flowing through him, and so couldn't look at the woman, although she stood just behind him. So, he summoned all of his memories of her in one mental collage.

Kairah smiling at him and calling him her courageous protector.

Kairah catching him staring at her across a campfire.

Kairah laughing at one of his fool jokes.

Kairah meeting his eyes as she pled with him to journey with her to Aiested.

Kairah kissing him.

Jekaran roared in defiance of the thing that was trying to corrupt him, and it retreated, though he could feel it hovering near–its very presence a continued temptation. But each time he considered surrendering, he thought of Kairah and held on.

Oceans upon oceans of Apeiron flowed into him now, and Azrin had grown hot in his hands. It didn't burn him, but he imagined that was only because the sword was part of him. Either that, or it was a trifling thing compared to the power coursing through every particle of his being. Purple light washed out the world around him, and ambient sound became far away and jumbled. It was as if the entire world had muted, leaving only the Apeira well, the sword, and himself.

Images sprang up all around Jekaran. Moving scenes that projected from Azrin; an Allosian man holding up the sword and examining its steaming blade. A web of spells overlaying the blade and settling into its metal. He saw a marching army of humans interspersed with Allosians. He saw the sea explode over hundreds of miles of ground. He saw a ship sailing across the sea. He saw that same ship sink to a watery grave. He saw robed men opening a chest and finding Azrin. He saw it wrapped in silk and taken to a vault. He saw a man looking down at the sword.

That man Jekaran knew. His face was smoother, and he had a full head of thick hair without the slightest touch of gray. His limbs weren't spindly, but lean and muscled, and he was dressed in black, but there was no mistaking the face, one that Jekaran had seen almost every day of his life.

Ez.

Ez took the sword but didn't use it. He ran from guards inside an expensive house that wasn't quite a castle, but far more than a mansion. He fought with a dark-skinned man whose knives could pass through solid matter, and was nearly overwhelmed. But then Ez bonded the sword and used its supreme power to defeat his enemy.

The vision changed to Ez leading a group of black clad thieves as they attacked a convoy so large that its armed escort was like a small army. Of course, nothing the guards could muster was any real threat to Ez, who slaughtered them with supernatural abandon.

Jekaran saw Ez dueling different swordsmen, one by one in an arena. When he had bested all his challengers, he lost control of Azrin and slaughtered the crowd. Jekaran gasped when Ez's fury failed to spare even a small boy. There was so much death, blood, chaos... and then bitter tears.

He saw Ez visiting Genra, knocking on their door which was answered by a young woman with lustrous black hair–Anarilee, his mother. She was pregnant, something Ez was not happy about. The two argued, and Jekaran saw Ez angrier than he'd ever seen him before; even when his uncle had been slaughtering innocent spectators, he hadn't looked so fierce. He actually slapped Jekaran's mother, who–to Jekaran's pride–didn't shrink from her brother. Instead she pointed at the door and shouted for him to get out.

The scene changed, though the setting didn't. This time Anarilee was lying on a bed, sweat running down her red face as she struggled to give birth. A woman clad in black leather with hair tied back into a pony tail acted the part of midwife while Ez looked on. A thin young man with a round face, and long golden locks stood in the doorway wringing his hands. Irvis? Had the scene playing out before Jekaran not been so serious, he would've laughed at just how surprisingly handsome the chubby monk had once been.

A baby's startled wail rang out, and the woman lifted the newborn child up so Anarilee could see it. She smiled, reached out to take the infant, but her arms fell limp. Ez started shouting, and then he ran to his sister and shook her. She didn't respond.

The next series of images came in rapid succession with blackness in between; Ez digging a grave.

Black.

Ez erecting a marker with Irvis looking on.

Black.

Ez inside their house holding Jekaran.

Black.

Ez in the cellar closing the lid on a long, bundled object wrapped in cloth.

Black.

Tears spilled down Jekaran's cheeks. Ez really had given up his glory and power as Argentus, and he had done it for him.

"Not just you, but for your mother too." Ez strode out from the purple light.

"Ez," Jekaran sobbed.

Ez smiled, and Jekaran's heart ached at the oh-so-familiar expression. "You're almost there, son. Just hold on a little longer."

"Will you stay with me?" Jekaran asked. "I don't want to die alone."

"You will never be alone again, Jek."

His resolve renewed, Jekaran nodded and gripped Azrin's handle tighter.

Jekaran shone like the sun. Kairah glanced at Irvis, Gymal, and Graelle. They had retreated, at her suggestion, from the platform and back onto the railless circular balcony that ran the interior of the cylindrical chamber. Their eyes were wide and Gymal shielded his with a hand. Even they could see Jekaran's blinding aura. Kairah herself had stayed as close to Jekaran as she dared. Not being able to wrap an arm around the boy to steady him while he suffered and sacrificed twisted her heart strings, but Kairah couldn't touch him. Her fever had reached a painful pitch again, and if it burned her, it would burn him. And there was the Moriora streaming into Jekaran along with the flood of Apeiron. To touch that now when they were so close would ruin everything.

The Mother Shard had liquefied, retaining its towering shape, but undulating and churning with the consistency of quicksilver. Electric green lines converged around the blade of Jekaran's sword as it sucked them into the glowing emerald shards. The ground shook, and chunks of white stone intermittently fell from the chamber's high walls.

A roar like wind through a canyon nearly deafened Kairah, but she didn't cover her ears. It seemed important to witness in full this moment. She owed Jekaran at least that much. In spite of the din and chaos surrounding her, and her anxious grief within, a soothing peace steadied Kairah It was a familiar feeling, one that often came when she was communing with Aeva.

My mother. That's who Aeva had told her she was when Kairah first asked as a young, grief-stricken girl. Of course, Kairah assumed Aeva to be the spirit of her murdered mother–

Aeva. The Spirit lily hadn't corrected her, but whether that was to hide her identity or comfort Kairah, she couldn't know. Either way it hadn't been a lie. Aeva was Kairah's mother. She was Shaelar's mother. She was their god, and she was dying. The unstable tremble in Kairah's bones told her that as well as the fact that all creation was unraveling at its most basic levels. The constant quaking beneath and the roiling black clouds above testified of the end of all things. Worse, her arcane senses reported all the elements, be they solid, liquid, or gas, had become unstable. The laws that bound matter together were dissolving and giving way to aberration and destruction.

Jekaran sagged, but held onto his sword. The light outlining him was now so bright that Kairah, even with her enhanced senses, could barely make out his profile. The blade of his sword glowed a cherry red, and thin cracks spider-webbed down the blade.

"Hold on, Jek," she whispered. Perhaps she ought to have shouted the encouragement, but she doubted Jekaran would've heard her.

The light, sound, and shaking all reached a crescendo, and the sword exploded in a blast of light so brilliant that it blinded all Kairah's senses; both mundane and arcane. For a long moment, all was absolute white. It was a frightening depravation that nearly made Kairah panic, but the world gradually returned.

Kairah gasped. She was steadying herself on the circular platform's rail. The Mother Shard was gone. In its place was empty air and a long, dark, shaft descending to depths unknown. She walked to the gap in the rail and peered over the edge. Where was Rasheera?

"Jek!" Irvis shouted.

Kairah turned to find the chubby monk climbing back up the stairs to throw himself to his knees at Jekaran's fallen form. She stepped over to them and examined Jekaran's mind, but there was nothing there. She spell-cast to scry the interior of his body and found stagnant blood, deflated lungs, and a motionless heart.

Jekaran was dead.

Kairah knelt opposite Irvis, Jekaran's lifeless body lying in between them. She reached out a hand to caress his face but stopped just before her fingers touched his cheek. Her fever had increased so much that the air around her was bent with heat lines. Her touch would blister the skin if not set the corpse on fire, and she didn't want to mar Jekaran's peaceful visage.

Irvis stared at the boy, tears streaming down his cheeks. "I'm so sorry, Argentus. I'm sorry I wasn't there when the boy first came looking for me. If I had been, none of this would've happened."

Graelle climbed the steps and knelt next to Irvis, who buried his face in her chest and sobbed. Gymal didn't approach, but remained at the bottom of the stairs, his face ashen.

The cruelty of it all stung her. It was so completely unfair. All Jekaran had done was come to her aid and she had led him to this.

"My courageous protector," she whispered, and a tear sizzled on her cheek.

Perhaps Rasheera can restore his life.

Kairah raised her head and glanced around. Shouldn't the goddess have emerged from her prison in power and glory? Another wave of instability rippled through all creation, making Kairah gasp and the others shiver.

Something was very wrong.

Kairah stood and returned to the edge of the platform. She stared down into the mammoth hole in the ground where the Mother Shard had just stood moments before. What was it Shivara had said? *The fire has burned its way into Mother's prison...*

Pain racked Kairah's entire body as the heat from within flared to a previously unreached level of intensity. She doubled over, grabbed her stomach and sucked in sharp breaths until she could regain her composure.

"Lady Kairah?" Graelle asked.

Kairah didn't answer. Instead she continued to stare into the open abyss that led to the center of the planet. The memory of her last vision from the Zikkurat flashed before her; a white lily withering before being sucked into infinite darkness.

Kairah spared one last long look at Jekaran's pale face, and then stepped off the platform and fell.

CHAPTER
111

J ove pulled back from the silver-haired doll and licked his lips. The kiss felt as though it lasted hours, and yet it hadn't. Time was odd in this place–this heaven. And surely it was Jove's heaven as he was a god left alone with a supremely beautiful, naked, and utterly helpless goddess.

He giggled, the thrill of lustful anticipation making him giddy as his eyes hungrily roved over the doll, taking in her perfect form. His hands could go wherever he wished, to every intimate place, and there was nothing she could do to stop him. That being so, there was only one place he wanted to touch this doll.

Jove lovingly traced his fingertips over the woman's collar bone, and then to the side of her neck. He extended the fingers of his other hand to run them through the doll's silver hair, metallic hair. That still awed him. He rubbed the soft spot of her throat with a thumb while bringing his other hand down to caress her shoulder and slowly moved it inward. Then all semblance of tenderness left Jove's caresses, and he clamped his hands around the woman's throat.

She started to gasp and then cough. Jove applied more pressure, and physical pleasure as he remembered it made him start to breathe faster. The doll's eyes fluttered open and he met them. Let her see the hateful lust in his eyes. Let her see the face of death itself!

The silver-haired doll started to thrash, but that only made Jove squeeze tighter. They all did that. Silly doll. Didn't she know that fighting him would only make it worse? He squeezed harder, his hot excitement building.

A lance of light slammed into Jove, forcing him to release the silver-haired doll as he was thrown clear. He spun head over heels and tried to suck in Apeiron to steady himself, but it was gone. Jove's eyes went to the blackness that now surrounded him. The purple cloud of infinite energy had vanished. Had he eaten it all?

He tumbled over one of the many islands of rock that floated in this place, reached out and stopped himself. He came down slowly and righted his body just as his bare feet touched down. Though blackness extended in every direction, Jove could still see. Another oddity about his new heaven.

His silver-haired doll had fallen, floated down, and was lying on another of the floating rock islands. Standing over her was a being outlined in brilliant white. He knew that woman. Though names frequently escaped him, Jove never forgot a face. That served him well on nights when the urge would strike but he could not find a doll to play with. He knew this doll. She'd been the one who'd tried to fight him back in Aiested. But she had purple hair then. Now her hair was blonde, the same colored hair as the first doll he'd broken.

What was her name again?

Jove licked his lips and smiled. Now he had two dolls to play with.

KAIRAH KNELT NEXT to the goddess. Her silver hair fanned out to the side and was so long that it stretched the length of her body.

"Aeva. Mother..."

"Do not touch me, Kairah." Rasheera's voice was familiar and strange all at once. It brought with it memories of joy and comfort, and Kairah realized she had known this being her entire life. "I am tainted."

"Mother, I brought your ring." Kairah held up the hand adorned with the band made of pure light. "Take it."

Something hit the ground behind Kairah. She rose and spun to find the naked man who was Moriora's vessel leering at her from only twenty paces away.

"You are also a pretty one." The creature ran a gray tongue over his lips. "Two dolls, all for me," he said in a sing-song voice.

Kairah was so disgusted that she didn't even deign to speak to the monster. Instead she raised a hand and blasted him with a beam of white energy. The light slammed into the Moriora vessel and forced him backward. But instead of disintegrating as Kairah had expected, he dug his toes into the ground and arrested his slide. Then he began to push back.

Kairah gasped as the creature sucked in her power and took a labored step forward into the stream of white energy. She poured more power into it, and for a few heartbeats it stopped the monster, but he adapted and resumed struggling toward her.

Upon seeing her shocked expression, the Moriora vessel cackled. "Silly, stupid little doll! You can't hurt me! I have tasted of that one's essence!" He motioned at Rasheera lying on her side, curled up into a ball. "It's changed me! Made me stronger! There isn't anything I can't eat! Not even your soul is safe from me!"

Partaking of Rasheera's essence had somehow attuned the Moriora vessel to her power, giving him the ability to absorb even the goddess's pristine energy. Not knowing what else to do, Kairah poured more energy into maintaining the beam of light, but the creature continued to shamble forward. The heat within her rapidly diminished, and a horrific realization stabbed Kairah in the heart; she was now the only thing standing between the goddess and the end of all things, and her power was running out.

TYRUS STARED at Jekaran's lifeless body as Irvis wept over it, and Graelle patted the monk's back. Tyrus couldn't walk. He couldn't weep. He couldn't stand. So he just sank to his knees and stared at his reflection in the glossy white floor.

I'm so sorry, Kybon. I tried to save him, but your son is dead. I've failed you.

Tyrus felt just as he had on that day so many years ago when he first received word of Kybon's death. The paralyzing numbness, the crushing sense of stopped time, the nausea of realization; it was all coming back to him in horrible vividness.

Jekaran was dead.

For some reason that robbed Kybon's death of any sense and meaning. Everything Tyrus had done to watch over and aid the boy, all the sacrifice and secrecy, all the patient enduring of his hate and ridicule. It had all been for nothing!

A wind rushed past Tyrus, making him jump. He looked up to see a ball of light streak by followed by a moving distortion in the air, one that dripped luminescent liquid. Karak materialized just before flying up the stairs to the circular platform. He didn't even spare a look for Jekaran or the others as he blurred past them and dove into the mammoth hole below.

THE MORIORA VESSEL had already closed half the distance between them and Kairah was beginning to falter. She closed her eyes and grit her teeth. She was throwing everything she had at the creature, but it only fed his strength. Kairah began to tremble as the reality of her failure and its epic consequences stared her in the face.

"I am sorry, Mother," she whispered.

She would hold off the monster as long as she could, and then Kairah would die. Everything would die.

"Help is coming," a familiar voice whispered into her ear.

"Jekaran?"

Karak, like a meteor, crashed down onto the Moriora vessel. Kairah released her spell just as her energy ran out. She stumbled backward and collapsed next to Rasheera. To her surprise, Karak did not wither away upon contact with the life leech, and the two wrestled, and traded blows. Kairah caught sight of something hanging around the lizard man's neck–an emerald shard of crystal.

The Moriora vessel cried out when Karak bit into his neck. The pathetic wail was less a shriek of physical pain and more the angry cry of a child throwing a tantrum. Karak ceased biting the monster, gripped him around the back of his neck, and then rolled off the edge of the floating rock island.

Kairah scrambled up and ran to the island's edge where she watched Karak hold the life leech fast as the two plummeted through empty space. The Moriora vessel gnashed his teeth, struggled, and managed to snap the band holding the emerald shard around Karak's neck. It glinted as it floated away, and then the Vorakk shaman started to wither. But even in death Karak didn't let go. When his dried husk of a body exploded into ashes, his spirit body appeared in its place and continued to hold the Moriora vessel around the neck.

The Moriora vessel bellowed as the two disappeared into blackness.

"Kairah," Rasheera's weak voice called from behind.

Kairah turned and rushed to the goddess's side. Her energy store was already refilling at an even faster rate than before, the heat of it already painful. Without touching Rasheera, Kairah cast a healing spell.

Nothing changed.

She cast again.

Still nothing.

"Mother, why does this not work?"

Rasheera's aura of silvery white winked out, and the metallic sheen of her hair had vanished so that it appeared a normal human gray.

The goddess flashed a wan smile. "You are such a dutiful daughter, Kairah. Filled with so much compassion, with so much hope for the future. But, I am afraid it is too late for me. I will soon pass into the void."

Kairah shook her head, panic rising inside her in time with the heat from the ring. "Mother, you cannot die!"

Ironically, Kairah felt the threat of loss more keenly than she'd expected. It wasn't just the terror of the world unraveling if its creator died, but a personal pain in Kairah's heart that was like... like... like when she'd lost her actual mother. Tears puffed to steam as they rolled down Kairah's feverish cheeks and she bowed her head, sobbing.

"You did not fail in this, Kairah. You were faithful in heeding all my admonitions and fulfilling the mission I gave you. This battle was a close thing, my omniscience pitted against that of another like me. And he only succeeded because he took advantage of the love I have for my children."

Kairah felt reality start to bend and pull apart as every particle of her being trembled.

"Even so, I had to acknowledge the possibility of my demise, and prepare for it."

"I do not understand," Kairah sobbed.

"I am afraid I must reward your loyalty and love not with peace, but with a greater burden."

As if in response to those words, the fire blazing inside Kairah intensified, making her wince. It was burning ever hotter and building at a greatly accelerated rate, the pain fast surpassing intolerable and approaching all-consuming.

Kairah worked through the agony and asked, "What is it, Mother? What can I do?"

Rasheera's stare bored into Kairah's very soul, and she whispered with both her mouth and mind, "Plant it."

Then the goddess closed her eyes and her body exploded into millions of tiny specks of light. The miniature stars faded, and Rasheera was gone. A scream tore from Kairah's lips, not a howl of grief, but of physical pain. The instant Rasheera died, the fire coursing through her had exploded and was so intense that the rock upon which she knelt glowed red.

Kairah fell forward onto all fours. Her breathing was ragged and irregular, her skin burned, and her shining aura became a nimbus of white fire. The power inside her was literally burning her away. She could relieve it by casting it out of her in a spell, but Rasheera's dying words gave her pause.

Plant it.

Kairah thought back to her last oracular vision. In it, she had taken the silvery lily bulb left behind when Aeva was sucked into the void, and had planted it in her own chest, replacing her heart. But what did the imagery mean? What was the lily bulb? How was she to plant it? Was she to cast a specific spell? She hadn't reached the highest and most literal level of the vision and so was stuck trying to interpret the dream-like symbolism.

Plant it.

The raging fire was consuming Kairah both body and soul, and would burn her out of existence if she didn't do something. But did that matter now? Existence itself was at an end. Perhaps she should just surrender to the inevitable.

"Aeva..." Kairah pictured the Spirit lily growing in splendor against a backdrop of green in her atrium garden. It was a reflex she adopted long ago to help calm her in moments of great stress.

I am your mother. Aeva had told Kairah when she was a new orphan all those decades ago.

My mother?

Suddenly all creation was before her. Kairah didn't see it with her eyes, but she could feel it all. It was like casting her mind out to scry places and people, except this perception had no limit. It cast beyond the boundaries of Shaelar and well into the blackness of surrounding space. And unlike a typical scrying, Kairah not only saw everything but she could also feel everything. It was as if she were suddenly connected to the world around her: people, trees, rock, and sky.

The white fire intensified, and understanding bloomed in Kairah's expanding mind. She had only been drawing on the goddess's ring to fuel her spellcasting, taking only the necessary amount of energy into her body and expending it immediately. What if she drew in all of it without casting any spells? What if she embraced it? What if she kept it?

She looked down at the goddess ring, now only a circle of white light.

Plant it!

An apt metaphor divinely tailored to fit Kairah's love of growing things. Seeds grew into plants, acorns into trees, and bulbs grew into flowers. The ring was a portion of Rasheera's essence–a seed, like a lily bulb.

Kairah raised her hand and pressed the ring against her breast. The ring disappeared in an explosion of silvery-white light that rushed into her and everything stilled. It was in this moment of frozen time that Kairah finally understood. Aeva's declaration that she was Kairah's mother hadn't been a lie to comfort a grieving child, or even a generic truth.

It had been a prophecy.

MULLADIN OPENED HIS EYES. A familiar face stared down at him.

"Maely!"

He reached up and grabbed his sister, pulling her down into a tight embrace. She struggled only a second before giving in and hugging him back.

"Mull. I'm so sorry I left you!" Maely sobbed into his chest.

Mulladin couldn't respond for the relief and tears that overwhelmed him. His sister was here. His sister was holding him. His sister was alive!

"This woman is hurt but breathing," a man's voice called.

Mulladin let go of his sister and sat up, pain from a dozen different places trying to pull him back down. It all became insignificant when his eyes fell on Keesa. The olive-skinned woman's face was smeared with dried blood, and she lay atop the wall above him. A blond man leaned over her; two fingers pressed to the side of her neck.

"Keesa!" Mulladin gingerly stood and made his way to the nearest staircase as quickly as his pain would allow. He climbed to the first seating tier, shoved the blond man aside and knelt over Keesa.

"Keesa, wake up!" He patted her cheek.

Maely limped over to the staircase but didn't ascend.

"Keesa, please wake up."

"Mulladin?" Maely called from below. "You sound different."

Mulladin ignored his sister and shook Keesa by the shoulders. Her eyes fluttered open and she flashed him a weak smile.

"Stop shaking me, you big, dumb ox, or you'll give me another concussion."

Mulladin bellowed a laugh and leaned down to embrace Keesa. She groaned in pain, but then hugged him back. Then he kissed her and kept kissing her. At first, she resisted but then melted into his kiss.

Maely gasped. "Mulladin! What do you think you're doing? Let her go this instant!"

Mulladin broke their kiss and smiled down at Maely. She had that familiar disapproving glower on her face that Mulladin knew so well.

"Kissing the woman I love."

Maely's frown disappeared, and her mouth hung open.

Mulladin laughed.

"How are you?" Maely faltered. "You're not—"

"Not dim? It's a long story."

"My restoration ring isn't working," Keesa said.

Mulladin nodded and helped her stand. "Neither is the lightning ring." He waved up to the broken skylight beyond which was an unobstructed view of the dark sky. "And Allose's Apeira well is gone."

"What does that mean?"

Mulladin shook his shaggy head. "I don't know."

The two joined the blond man and descended to the coliseum floor. Maely continued to stare at him, eyes wide and mouth open.

Mulladin drew her into another hug. "It's okay now, Mae. I'm okay now. I'll explain everything later. Right now, we need to find the others."

Maely pulled away from him. "Mulladin? Where's Jek?"

⁂

TYRUS TREMBLED as he peered down over the edge of the circular platform. The sight made him dizzy and he gripped a nearby rail all the while trying not to vomit. Why had both Lady Kairah and Karak leapt to their deaths? Was their cause so hopeless? The continued quaking and thunder from emerald lightning seemed to answer with a resounding, yes! Tyrus considered following suit and diving off the platform to end life on his own terms, but he was too much of a coward for suicide. The vertigo grew too much for him and he stepped as far away from the ledge as he could.

Irvis continued to weep over Jekaran's body, and Graelle soothed him with gentle whispers and a hand rubbing his back. Tyrus descended the stairs from the observation platform and crashed to his knees on the cylindrical chamber's interior balcony. He was so weary but doubted he could sleep even if he were surrounded in blankets and lying on a feathered mattress after having drained a bottle of Haeshalan brandy. *How could one sleep when the world was ending?* Another quake shook the room as if in agreement.

Voices echoed from the connecting hallway, and a moment later Mulladin shuffled in, arm hooked around Keesa's waist, each helping the other to walk. Well, at least those two survived, not that it mattered. Following Mulladin and Keesa was a young woman with short black hair, cheeks smudged with soot, and a dress torn so badly that it left much of her chest exposed. It was the girl from Genra, Maely, and she was with a tall, blond man with muscular arms and...

Tyrus threw himself forward so that he was prostrate on the glossy floor. "My Prince!"

Prince Raelen opened his mouth to say something, but was cut off by Maely's startled cry. "Jek? Jek?"

She hobbled past Tyrus and up the stairs and a shriek followed. "Jekaran!"

Tyrus couldn't bear to look. The sound of Maely's pathetic sobbing was too much. He caught a glimpse of Mulladin's ashen face, and for some reason that was what finally drew out Tyrus's own tears. He kept his forehead touching the floor and wept.

"You fool boy!" Maely's eyes burned both from her hot tears and from the fierceness with which she clenched them shut.

"You stupid, fool, idiot boy!" She laid her head on his chest. "Why did you have to leave Genra? Why couldn't you have been happy being a farmer? Why couldn't you have just been happy with me?"

Irvis touched her shoulder. "He sacrificed himself for us."

Maely threw off Irvis's hand. "Of course, he did!" She opened her eyes and stared at Jek's pallid face. "It's what he does!"

Maely sat up and held her stomach. She rocked back and forth, her hyperventilating preventing her from expelling any more words. Her worst nightmare had come true; a reality more terrible than even Jekaran rejecting her. Dead. Jek was dead. That cold, horrible fact made Maely want to lay down beside him and join him in death.

The quaking ground shook with intensified vigor.

"What's that?" Graelle cried.

"I fear it is the end, my love," Irvis said. "Hold onto me and we shall pass from this life together."

Good. Let it all end. Let this cruel, hateful world die.

The shaking grew so severe Maely's vision blurred from the sharpness of the constant motion. As the pieces of the chamber's wall and open ceiling started to rain debris, and large cracks snaked up the walls, a column of blinding white light exploded from the shaft below.

Maely shielded her eyes, and they watered as she refused to look away. If this light was the signal that the end had finally come, then dammit, she was going to watch. The thick, white pillar shot skyward, puncturing the roiling sea of black clouds and driving them back. Maely gaped as the darkness retreated, as if the light were washing filth from the heavens themselves. The white column continued to pour into the sky until azure firmament once again smiled down upon them. Then it faded, leaving behind a figure floating in the air.

It was a woman in a sleeveless, billowing white dress with long hair that fluttered about her–hair that was silver in color and glittered with a metallic sheen. A white aura surrounded the figure, so it took Maely a moment to make out the face.

Kairah's face.

CHAPTER 112

"Kairah?" Maely gasped.

Kairah smiled at her and the pain in Maely's leg vanished. Wide-eyed, she put some weight on it and found it capable of supporting her. Gasps from the others signaled they, too, had received healings for their injuries.

"The Divine Mother!" Irvis choked out. "Lady Kairah is the Divine Mother!"

Kairah glanced at the former monk, and when she spoke, her voice carried a musical, otherworldly echo that not only touched Maely's ears, but thrilled through her mind and heart.

"I am not Rasheera."

"Then..."

"I am her daughter."

Kairah was Rasheera's daughter? Kairah was a goddess? Though it definitely was Kairah, the woman had a new confidence about her. She'd always been frustratingly sure of herself, but this was much different. She was... was... well, divine. She was both foreign and familiar at the same time and radiated a peaceful calm.

Maely became very conscious of all the criticisms and meanness she'd directed at Kairah, and hoped the woman wasn't about to visit some form of smiting upon her. Did Kairah's new divinity let her know her thoughts and—

"Do not fear, Maely. All is forgiven."

Maely sighed. Apparently Kairah could read her mind.

Kairah laughed. "Yes, your minds and memories are open to me, and I see the whole of our story now." She smiled a genuinely kind smile at Maely, one that warmed her heart and drew out tears.

"You are a noble soul, Maely. Your willingness to sacrifice your life was a testament to this. Be comforted concerning your past mistakes, for you have indeed washed yourself clean."

She knew about Gryyth's story? Well, of course she did, Maely chided herself. *Kairah was God now, and God knew everything.*

"Your suffering has humbled you and taught you valuable lessons that will serve you well in your future years as queen."

Queen? Maely glanced at Raelen who stood beside her. He smiled at her and she blushed and had to look away.

"I have inherited some of Mother's memories, and I can assure you that none of you stand here by accident. She chose you, and worked through you, and others among your immediate connections. You are her champions."

Kairah motioned to Raelen. "Come forward."

Raelen stepped past Maely and bowed to one knee before Kairah. "Divine Mother."

Kairah laughed. "Rise, Raelen."

Raelen glanced at Maely, an uncertain frown on his face. It made Maely want to laugh. She'd never seen the prince looks so unsure. He'd always struck Maely as being like Kairah in that he was manifestly self-assured.

"I wish you to know that your training in the Ursaj way of Seiro did not come by accident. It was a preparation."

"Preparation for what, Divine Mother?"

"To teach it to your people, and by it make your laws."

Raelen bowed his head and struck his chest with a fist. "As king, I will make certain Aiestal follows Seiro, Divine Mother, I swear it!"

"Oh you are not to be king just of Aiestal, but of all of Shaelar."

Raelen's face paled.

"And this not by the might of armies, but the power of compassion and example. There are difficult days ahead, for talises have become no more than useless trinkets. The desperate will be looking for a true leader, and you will fill that role and return honor to the human race."

"We are to lose magic?" Gymal asked.

"Mankind has thoroughly proven that it is not ready for such power. Someday, perhaps, when men are wiser and more inclined to peace, I will teach you to spell-cast, but not for many years yet. It was this subject that led to Shivara's downfall. She was greedy, and impatient, and had she been wiser, she may have discerned that Rasheera had already given her the very thing she sought, but her selfishness blinded her and brought centuries of darkness."

"Your return was foretold, Divine Mother," Irvis suddenly cut in. "Will you not remain with us to usher in the age of the infinite?"

Kairah's smile widened as she looked upon the chubby, round faced man. "Gentle Irvis, that time will come, when humankind proves itself worthy. Until then, I must leave Shaelar."

"Why?" Irvis sounded on the edge of panic.

"For the same reason Rasheera planned to leave. So mankind can learn to live on his own. Is it not so with every child when they come of age?"

"I suppose." Irvis nodded to himself.

Kairah's eyes unfocused and she looked to the side, staring at empty air. "Also, there is a nefarious force hiding among the ascended beings of the cosmos. I must find him, and stop him from ruining other worlds as he tried to ruin Shaelar. For I fear his designs are far direr than simply slaying other gods. He is working toward something; a goal I do not know."

How could a divinity not know something? For some reason Maely felt a smug satisfaction at the idea that Kairah, although now a goddess, still wasn't perfect. It was petty, but, well Maely was still a little petty. Kairah glanced at her with a knowing look in her eyes.

Dammit! Reading someone's thoughts just wasn't fair.

"But you will return?" Irvis pled.

Kairah nodded. "But it may not be for centuries. Time for you operates differently than time for me now, I am afraid. However, regardless of whether you live to see it, we will one day be reunited. In death, man can come to possess the very powers Shivara and her disciples coveted, if you prove worthy of them. You have seen it in the intervention of spirits called by the gift of the Vorakk shaman."

Irvis nodded. "I will devote my life to spreading your word, Divine Mother!"

Kairah laughed and, despite Maely's determination to cling to her childish jealousy, the sound melted away the remaining bitterness she'd harbored toward Kairah. Was that some kind of good compulsion? If so, it was poetic irony that Kairah had used it on Maely.

"Gentle Irvis, you have something different to devote your life to now. Cherish this woman, and together build a life. Alone each of you are broken, but together you are made whole. That is what Mother intended for you when she answered your prayer."

Irvis smiled at Graelle and pulled her close to him. "Yes, Divine Mother."

"Tyrus Gymal," Kairah said. And the weaselly little lord bowed himself so low that his forehead touched the floor. "Rise, Tyrus."

Gymal lifted his head and waited expectantly.

"Your beloved cousin, Kybon, bade me give you a message."

Was Gymal crying? Maely didn't think the loathsome little man had a heart.

"Kybon wishes you to know that he is grateful for what you have done to honor his life. But he wants you to stop living in the shadow of his death. He said he desires you to move and become the great scholar he always knew you could be."

Gymal bobbed his head and choked out, "Thank you."

"Kairah." Maely was not about to start fawning and groveling before the woman, no matter how much power she held. She glanced at Jek's lifeless body. "Can you bring him back to me?" Her voice caught.

Kairah's smile faded. "What you ask is not an easy thing."

"You're the goddess now." Tears streamed down Maely's cheeks. "You healed us. Can't you heal him?"

"It is within my power, but..." Kairah shook her head, and her shining silver hair fluttered as though it were under water. "He does not wish to return to mortality."

"Why?" Maely bit her lip to stave off a sob. It didn't work.

Kairah floated down and landed in front of Maely. She smiled and drew Maely into a hug. Maely gasped as warmth suffused her entire being, both calming and comforting her.

"Because he desires to come with me. To help me find and stop the one who threatens the entirety of the cosmos."

"Idiot boy," Maely sobbed.

"Jekaran is a hero. Does he not deserve a hero's reward? To return him to his old life would diminish his sacrifice."

"What does that matter?" Maely leaned her head into Kairah's chest and wept.

"You cannot see it now, Maely, but our deeds have great effect. The very fabric of fate is built upon the choices people make. The selfish harm the cosmos, while people like Jekaran heal it. Our actions shape the nature of reality itself."

"That's stupid."

Kairah laughed and released Maely. "Someday you will understand."

Maely scrubbed her eyes with the back of her wrist.

"Jekaran does wish me to tell you that you are, and always will be, his friends." Kairah smiled and looked down at Gymal. "He says, even you, Gymal."

Gymal wiped his nose on his sleeve and laughed.

"I have purged Allose of Moriora. Those that wielded it have been returned to their natural state, as have all Allosians. Now you are one people." Kairah rose into the air. "Shaelar belongs to you now. Go, and do not just rebuild this world, but make of it a better one."

The white light outlining Kairah flared. A similar aura appeared around Jekaran's body, and both continued to grow brighter in tandem with one another. The light shone until it was too bright for Maely to stand and she had to cover her eyes.

Be happy, Maely. You deserve it, Kairah whispered to her mind.

And then the light and Kairah were gone, as was Jekaran's body.

Jekaran sucked in a breath. He hadn't really missed breathing in his brief time being dead, but doing it again felt good. He looked over himself. His wounds were gone, and his body was in better condition than it ever had been. Lean, corded muscle wrapped his arms, and his chest was defined like that of a veteran soldier.

He was also naked.

But as soon as the desire for clothes entered his mind, a white light appeared to obscure his nudity and then resolved into a white robe fitted perfectly to his new frame.

Jekaran took in his surroundings. He stood high above a gigantic, mostly blue sphere set against a backdrop of black speckled with stars. "I'll be damned. The world is round."

"Golden hair suits you, my courageous protector."

Jekaran looked to his right where Kairah flashed into existence. He ran a hand through hair that was no longer black, but the color of burnished gold. Kairah smiled and floated over to him. He reached out a hand and gently touched her silver hair.

"And silver hair suits you, my lady."

Kairah laughed and kissed him.

"It's nicer when that doesn't blister my lips." Jekaran looked down at the world below them, and a pang of sorrow stung his chest. "How did they take it?"

"As well as could be expected. Are you sure you do not want to say your farewells in person?"

Jekaran shook his golden head. "I'll come to each of them in their dreams. It'll make it easier for them... and for me."

Kairah took his hand, and they turned together to gaze upon the ocean of stars. "Boulos, Shivara called him."

"Do you think that's his real name?"

"Doubtful. But it is all we have to go on."

Jekaran squeezed Kairah's hand. "Are you sure you're ready? Do you need more time to recover from making me... um..."

Kairah shot him a sidelong glance. "A god?"

Jekaran chuckled nervously. *Were gods supposed to chuckle nervously?* "Yeah. I guess."

"I have already recovered, and my power will only continue to grow. You on the other hand, will be weak for a time. So you will need to stay near me."

"Have I ever been able to stay away?"

Kairah favored him with one of her thoughtful smiles, and although Jekaran felt better than he'd ever felt before, that smile made him positively euphoric.

"You will also need to learn spell-casting."

That wilted him a little. It wasn't fair that perfect omniscience hadn't come with his godhood. "Shouldn't we wait to go after this Boulos until I am able to protect you?"

Kairah squeezed his hand again. "I do not know that we can spare any time."

"Aren't we eternal now? Doesn't that mean we have all the time, well, ever?"

Kairah laughed and the musical sound was like a kiss to Jekaran's ears. "How about you let me do the protecting for once?"

The two stared into the endless expanse of stars.

"Shall we go, then?"

Jekaran glanced down at Shaelar. He would miss his friends, but now he could commune with them whenever he wished without even having to be on the same planet. He looked into their minds and sent them all a farewell. Except for Maely. To Maely he sent his love, and a promise that he would one day return to visit her.

Kairah smiled knowingly at him.

Jekaran grinned back. "Now I think I'm ready for another adventure."

Balls of light appeared around them and resolved into familiar shapes: Karak, Hort, a beaming Ez, and dozens of others including a woman who could've been Kairah's twin sister. And there was Jekaran's mother and father, floating close together and smiling.

Jekaran met Kairah's eyes, and they launched into infinity.

RAELEN STOOD WATCHING Maely as the others passed them. She'd stopped walking and was now staring at empty air, as though pondering some deep mystery. It lasted so long that Raelen worried something was wrong.

"Maely?"

She didn't hear him. When tears started pouring down her face,

Raelen reached out a hand and gently touched her shoulder. She jumped and looked at him.

"Are you well?"

Maely wiped the tears from her cheeks and nodded with a smile. "I am now."

They continued following the others, walking the floor of the coliseum and then commencing their climb of one the chamber's mountainous staircases. He should've been wounded and tired, but the goddess's healing had left Raelen feeling better than he had in months. He raised his hand, flexing new fingers. Kairah had given them back to him, but it seemed a small thing compared to the burden she'd laid upon his shoulders.

King of all Shaelar.

He was named, but not crowned. That would apparently take some time, probably years, and the collapse of a world's economy and social structure. What was happening in Haeshala and Maes Tol now that Apeira wells were gone, and talises ceased to function? Panic and chaos to be sure. What about his own kingdom? Where were his people? No, the goddess hadn't bestowed an honor upon him, but a sentence of life-long servitude. He wished Gryyth were still with him.

He started as a familiar voice broke into his thoughts. *I am proud of you, cub. You have become the king I always knew you could be.*

Raelen quickly glanced around the coliseum, nearly missing the sight of a small white ball disappearing through one of the chamber's windows.

"Thank you," he whispered.

"Who're you talking to?" Maely asked.

Raelen looked down at the young woman climbing stairs at his side. *She is to be my queen.*

Maely raised an arm and sniffed herself. "I need a bath!"

Someday. Raelen chuckled.

He liked Maely and her blunt honesty. He even thought her pretty. But she would need a couple more years to mature into a woman before she was ready for marriage. That was fine. Raelen could wait for her. His heart hinted that theirs could be more than just a proscribed union, but a true love affair. He could fall in love with this girl.

She caught him smiling at her and blushed. Then she glanced down at her ripped dress and the scandalous view of her chest it offered and crossed her arms over her breasts. Now it was Raelen's turn to blush.

"I wasn't looking, I mean I-I..." he stammered.

To his surprise, Maely started laughing. This girl was brash, blunt, and unpredictable, and Raelen liked that. He started laughing, too. Then he lifted off his dirty, torn tunic, and placed it over Maely's head. It was too big, and drowned her in fabric, but it restored her modesty.

Maely nodded. "You are the real thing, Raelen."

"What do you mean?"

"You're a true good man." Her eyes fell and lingered on Raelen's naked torso. She caught herself staring and blushed again, this time so furiously that her cheeks were nearly the color of a fresh cherry.

"I had a good teacher. And you know the funny thing?"

Maely shook her head.

"He wasn't even a man."

They finished climbing the stairs in silence, and when they reached the top, Maely slipped her hand into Raelen's. He looked down at her, squeezed her hand, and smiled. She smiled back and they jogged to catch up to the others.

Mulladin held Keesa's hand as they left the coliseum. Allose was dimmer than he remembered it, its white stone construction no longer reflecting a purple glow. Pieces of stone and other debris lay scattered everywhere, and large fissures in the ground opened on rivers of molten rock. Allose, the city that was supposed to be paradise, now looked like a ruined hell.

The most glaring difference, however, wasn't the ubiquitous destruction, but the absolute lack of jewel-colored hair among the crowds of people standing in the streets. There were hundreds of Haeshalans mixed into the crowd, but Mulladin could pick out the former Allosians by their loose white clothing, and their confused faces. It made him want to laugh.

"Serves those uppity creampuffs right," Keesa muttered, almost as if she had read his thoughts.

"They're going to have a lot to get used to. They'll have to relearn how to eat, sleep, work, and shi..." He glanced at Maely, whose fierce stare all but dared him to finish the curse. "Um... use the privy."

Maely's face relaxed.

Mulladin looked down at his sweaty and torn tunic. "I need a bath."

"I saw a large fountain not too far from here." Keesa pulled close to him. "I could join you. After all, I did promise to help you become a man."

"Absolutely not!" Maely snapped. "You're not going to be bathing or doing anything else together until you're properly married!"

"You can't tell him what to do anymore!" Keesa retorted. "He's a man now!"

"The hell I can't!"

Keesa looked to Mulladin for support, but he just sighed. "Yeah, she still can."

Before he knew it, Maely was forcing the prince–against his protests that the time for such was utterly inappropriate–to perform a hasty marriage ceremony. And though Keesa made several resentful comments about Maely's self-righteous bullying, the light in her eyes, and irrepressible smile said she welcomed the impromptu wedding.

The prince finished the ceremony with a weary sigh, pronouncing them officially wed by the crown, and Mulladin smiled down at Keesa, took her in his arms, and kissed her. However, before they could steal away to find a private place to consummate their marriage, another spontaneous wedding commenced.

Irvis and Graelle stared dreamily into one another's eyes as Raelen repeated the words that would also make them husband and wife. The idea of the chubby monk and the fat woman consummating their marriage helped to cool Mulladin's eager anticipation.

It was truly a new day, complete with new beginnings. Even the sun seemed to shine brighter. Something had lifted from Shaelar, a dimness that Mulladin hadn't ever realized was there until it was gone. He could relate.

Chapter 113

Jove climbed out from beneath a slab of stone and tumbled down the side of a mountain of debris. He crashed to the ground, landing on his right leg at an unnatural angle causing the bone to snap. Jove immediately manifested a spread of green tendrils and cast them out to syphon whatever life they could find, but there was nothing.

Jove leveraged himself against a boulder-sized chunk of stone and pulled himself to his feet. As always, his injuries caused him no pain, and he didn't bleed. He surveyed his surroundings and found that he was in the center of hundreds of ruined buildings. Though the skyline was missing several towers, Jove recognized this city. He was back in Aiested. But what had happened to the city? It looked as though a quake had shaken it into an empty ruin.

And empty it was.

Jove's tendrils anxiously waved about him looking for people, animals, or even plants, but found nothing, not even the tiniest of insects. Something had wiped out all life here. Had it been him? No, he'd only come to feed on the Apeira well and any unfortunate people who crossed his path. The memories seemed fresh as though they were from the day before, yet the crumbling stone and absence of people bespoke much longer.

The hunger began churning inside him, a cold emptiness at his core that made his entire body tremble. He needed to eat, he needed food! He hobbled about the street in a panic, looking for anything he might consume, but the very streets of Aiested had been scrubbed of life.

His eyes found the docks and the west sea. If there was water there, then there had to be life. All he had to do was reach the ocean. He staggered forward as fast as he could while the hunger grew more intense with every step. Hair fell from his head, and he had to spit out teeth with every breath. The ocean was too far away. He'd never make it in time.

Something moved on Jove's right periphery. He spun to find a young woman standing a dozen paces away, staring at him. He grinned and snapped out a translucent green tentacle. It was a pity he had to devour her without taking any time to enjoy her, after all she was a very pretty doll. Jove's tendril evaporated when it touched the woman's chest. He gaped, and then struck again and again, but his power failed to connect. A ball of light appeared in the air above Jove, floating down and resolving into another lovely doll. She was joined by more women, and then more, and then dozens. They surrounded Jove, all glaring at him with unblinking stares.

"Ghosts!" Jove growled. Souls of the departed. Why couldn't he devour them like he had before?

Something inside him had changed; no, not just inside him, but in the entire world. At the height of his power everything felt loose, pliable, unstable. Now everything felt solid again, everything but him. His essence quivered and threatened to fly apart, but Jove held on, keeping it together by sheer force of will.

The Hunger twisted inside him, its demand for food growing louder and more desperate. Jove staggered forward, but the women didn't move, and there were so many that Jove couldn't push through them. When he tried, he was rebuffed by a flash of searing light.

"Get out of my way!" he screamed.

The women didn't say anything to him, they just continued to stare. A chill washed over Jove—not the cold hunger churning the emptiness at his core, but actual fear. He recognized these faces, for he never forgot a face.

These women were his dolls. His broken dolls.

There were dozens of them; all young, a few even small girls, all accusing him with unblinking glares. As one they stepped forward, closing in a circle about him. Jove tried again to push through them, but this time the dolls in his path reached out and shoved him back. Though spirits, to Jove they were as solid as any wall.

"Let me through!" he snarled.

Not one of the dolls replied.

Despite his broken leg, Jove charged with the intent to break out of their circle, but he was shoved back a second time so hard that he crashed to the ground.

Jove examined an arm. His skin was starting to shrivel and slough off as clumps of hair littered the ground around him. He needed food, or the Hunger would devour him! Another ghost appeared, a girl scarcely into the first years of womanhood. She stared down at Jove and he knew her face. He'd never forgotten that face. It'd haunted his nightmares for years.

It belonged to Jove's very first victim.

As he stared into her blue eyes, the name he'd so long forgotten snapped back from the depths of his memory. "Elaynia!"

She had been his neighbor and childhood friend. But as Jove had started coming into manhood, and Elaynia flowered into a woman, she'd become the focus of his lusts and often the object of his violent fantasies.

Using his best trouper's skills, Jove had wooed the young woman with promises of future marriage, and they started to steal away to secret places so Jove could indulge his adolescent urges. Then one day, while they were cavorting in the woods, Jove lost control. She'd begged him to stop, but the thrill of squeezing the life from her while his passions escalated was intoxicating, and when it was over, poor Elaynia was dead.

Guilt crashed down on Jove like a physical thing. He'd panicked and disposed of her body with his tinder box. He'd so thoroughly immolated the girl that no one ever found even her ashes. Agonizing guilt gnawed at Jove for weeks, and he found relief would only come by repeating his dark deed with other victims. In time, he'd been able to bury much of the memory of killing his childhood friend, even achieving a voluntary amnesia of sorts, but Jove had never been able to forget the pleading in Elaynia's eyes as he throttled the life from her.

That look stung him even to this day, and he'd all but succeeded in forgetting the girl, to the point that a nameless face was his only recollection. But now Jove remembered, and the pain of his guilt rivaled the internal scouring of the Hunger.

The girl slowly raised an arm and pointed at Jove.

"I'm sorry, Elaynia!" he shrieked. "I didn't mean for it to go so far!"

All the broken dolls took another unified step toward him, closing the circle so tight that Jove could barely move. He cowered beneath their glares, mind afire with perfect recollection of all the pain he'd caused them. And there was more. Somehow they wordlessly transmitted to Jove a sense of what it had been like to suffer his tortures and die at his hands. This was compounded by the vicarious grief of their loved ones, the panic and the pain of searching parents, the anger of brothers, husbands, and the loneliness of children left behind.

Jove howled.

The deluge of memory and projected suffering overwhelmed him and he collapsed on his face. He whimpered as the Hunger turned on him. If he could not feed it, then it was going to feed on him.

A protracted, echoing scream tore from Jove's lips as his skin shrunk around his bones, and his eyes shriveled in their sockets. His body finally crumbled to ash and bone, but Jove's terror didn't end with death. Although the world around him was solid and stable once more, Jove's soul felt loose and vulnerable.

His broken dolls swarmed him and tore at the very fibers of his being. Piece by piece, Jove's soul was torn apart by the women whose lives he'd snuffed out. The world around him started to blur, and the last thing he saw was Elaynia's face. Then darkness swallowed Jove and obliterated his soul.

ABOUT THE AUTHOR

Jason King is a veteran of both Canadian-American wars, a cosmonaut by proxy, and has managed to achieve immortality...until he dies.

Born in Salt Lake City Utah, Jason grew up on a steady diet of anime, science fiction, Dungeons and Dragons, JRPG's, and chocolate cake donuts, which makes it all the more miraculous that he managed to marry a beautiful (and despite what his friends and family believe) very real girl. He is the proud father of four brilliant and wonderful children, and the hostage of two cats, a dog, four parakeets, two rabbits, and is haunted by the spirit of a Navajo shaman.

Jason is the CEO of Immortal Works press, and the author of the Valcoria series, and Thomas Destiny. He is also a grateful member of The Church of Jesus Christ of Latter-day Saints, and a proud "anonymous" member of the Space Balrogs comedy troupe.

For more about Jason's novels and short stories, please visit his website: www.authorjasonking.com.

Jason also blogs about his faith at https://authorjasonking.blogspot.com/.

This has been an
Immortal Production